The Fabulous Trashwagon

The Fabulous Trashwagon

by "BS" Levy

**art direction by
Art Eastman**

editing & research assistance from:
John Gardner
Bill Siegfriedt
Woody Woodhouse
Adam & Carol Levy
Karen Miller   Bob Finer
Janos Wimpffen   Henry Adamson   Tara Treacy

website at www.lastopenroad.com
thanks to Dick Carlson

Think Fast Ink L.L.C. - Oak Park, Illinois
2002

PUBLISHED BY:
THINK FAST INK L.L.C.
1010 LAKE STREET
OAK PARK, ILLINOIS
60301
WWW.LASTOPENROAD.COM
E-MAIL: THINKFAST@MINDSPRING.COM

WRITTEN AND MANUFACTURED IN THE UNITED STATES OF AMERICA

FIRST EDITION
OCTOBER 31, 2002

OTHER TITLES BY "BS"LEVY:
THE LAST OPEN ROAD 1994
MONTEZUMA'S FERRARI 1999
A POTSIDE COMPANION 2001

LIBRARY OF CONGRESS CATALOGING IN PUBLICATION DATA:
LEVY, BURT S., 1945-
THE FABULOUS TRASHWAGON
1. SPORTSCAR RACING IN THE 1950'S 2. AUTOMOBILE MECHANICS
LIBRARY OF CONGRESS CATALOG CARD NUMBER:
2002104535

ISBN: 0-9642107-5-4

DEDICATED TO MY MOM AND DAD
*AROUND OUR HOUSE, IT WAS ALWAYS
OKAY TO BELIEVE IN YOUR DREAMS....*

1: The Morning After

It was three ayem at Le Mans, and the rain had been pelting down pretty steadily for over five hours. But I wasn't worried. After all, I had Cal Carrington out in the car and Sammy Speed waiting on deck, calm and dry as a Sphinx in the Sahara thanks to the fancy black-and-silver canvas awning I'd erected over our pits to keep everybody out of the weather. Why, it almost looked like the entrance to the blessed Stork Club in Manhattan, only without the friendly doorman in brass buttons and patent leather shoes and our illuminated "Palumbo Panther" lettering out front where the famous, pink-neon stork might have been. I checked the stopwatch around my neck and, right on schedule, Cal and the Panther came streaming past in a teeming swirl of spray, doing well over 150 with the perfectly-meshed howl of that amazingly handsome, neat, clever, lightweight, all-alloy, roller bearing, double-overhead-camshaft, twin-plug, dual distributor, multi-stage supercharged, fuel-injected, three-liter V-16 turning ear wax into clover honey all up and down pit lane.

I built it myself, you know.

With a little help, moral support, business guidance and financial backing from our longtime Team Passaic patron Big Ed Baumstein, of course. Who is naturally just a few yards behind me in the pit stall, perched up under a multicolored Cinzano umbrella (just in case the roof leaks, right?) on an elevated director's chair with his name stenciled across the back. He's dressed up in this perfect white suit and wide-brimmed white hat outfit like Sydney Greenstreet wore in _Casablanca_, and he's got the usual butt end of a dollar Cuban stogie rolling from one side of his mouth to the other while our beautiful, long-legged, deep-voiced, dark-eyed and high-cheekboned Parisian masseuse/interpreter Monique is giving him a neck massage with strong, experienced fingers. She's really a knockout in this sort of short terrycloth robe outfit with white satin trim and gold "Palumbo Panther" lettering across the back, and she wears her long, silky hair cascading across her face like Veronica Lake so that only a single, mysterious, long-lashed brown eyeball is showing....

"Looks like another lap record," I tell Sammy. "Even at night in the rain."

"We'll see about that," he grins right back at me. But I'm not worried. I know my boys have a friendly little rivalry going—hey, that's always the name of the game between two great racing teammates!—but I know I can trust them both to think of the team first and take care of the car. After all, they can't help it if they're both quick as the dickens. And they know they can count on me to take care of everything else. Like the two extra pairs of goggles I make them wear around their necks in case the first set gets misted up or smeared with oil or cracked by a flying stone or something. Or the fat rubber bands I cut out of inner tubes and make them put around their wrists where their rain jackets overlap their gloves so the water won't run up their sleeves. Or the beautiful Monique with the high cheekbones, long legs, terrycloth robe and silky hair swept across her face so only one eyeball is showing waiting to give them a cup of steaming broth and a rubdown with heated oils just as soon as they get out of the car. Or having a tough, steady, quick, smart and experienced hand like Tommy Edwards on tap as a possible relief driver ever since his factory Aston Martin ride flipped into the sandbank at the hairpin (with his co-driver aboard, natch) during the heaviest of the downpour just after midnight. We were way out front, of course (and pulling away all the time), so there wasn't much to keep the boys amused except trading fastest laps in the wet and darkness. So I was glad we had Tommy there as a backup, waiting quietly and patiently under the Cinzano umbrella with Big Ed, just to keep Cal and Sammy from getting too rambunctious. After all, Tommy's the one who taught me those two great, Cardinal Rules of endurance racing: DON'T HURT THE CAR! and DON'T HURT THE CAR!

By God, when you're a team manager at Le Mans, you have to do a whole heck of a lot more than just design the blessed car, build it from scratch with your own two hands, test it, develop it, prep it for racing, assemble three or four truck-loads of cars and tools and spares and equipment and ship the whole shootin' match overseas to France where they eat snails and crepes and wear berets and all the pretty young women look at you like you're a tasty appetizer.

In fact, that's the easy part!

The HARD part is putting together a team of talented, dedicated, incredibly quick and yet disciplined drivers who understand that to finish first, you first must finish. Not to mention the legion of wrench twisters, jack pumpers, gas fillers, parts packers, timekeepers, scorers, transport drivers, English/French transla-tor/masseuses, gourmet training chefs poached (poached, indeed!) from the U.S. Olympic decathlon team, clerical staff, number crunchers, gofers and coffee warmers who all get along famously with one another and never—ever!—stay out beyond curfew or do any sneak-away partying or imbibing of spirits while the game is afoot.

There'll be plenty of time for that afterwards.

Plenty of time....

But then, suddenly, Cal and the Panther are late coming around. Sammy and I look at each other anxiously. And then here they come, slithering in out of the rain and darkness. Only we don't see them coming because the damn headlights are out! And then—my God!—we see little bluish-white sparks and flames lick-ing out through the side vent louvers and a wispy curtain of smoke pouring out from under the hood! Electrical fire! No question about it! The lads have it open in a heartbeat and sure enough it's the wiring from the fuse box to the voltage reg-ulator—DAMN that Lucas stuff!—but of course they have it out instantly with a quick blast from the fire extinguisher, and now all I have to do is survey the dam-age and figure out just what the hell we can do about it. I can feel every eye on me as I look at all the burned wiring and charred insulation. Including none other than Briggs himself from the Cunningham pits next door and team manager Ugolini from the Ferrari pits on the other side and Lofty England from the Jaguar *pits down the way and even "Death Ray" John Wyer from the Aston Martin pits on the end. "I'm sure I can make something up," I advise the crew grimly, "but I'm afraid I'm going to need a little time...."*

"Give me a flashlight!" I hear Sammy holler from the pit wall behind me. Before I can say a word, he's yanking Cal out of the car and climbing behind the wheel. "You may think you're a tick quicker than me in these sportycars," he says to Cal through a Charge-of-the-Light-Brigade smile, "but I bet you can't do THIS!" Then he turns and looks me straight in the eye. "You sure as hell better have something ready when I get back!" And with that he fires her up, jams the flashlight in his mouth, and wails off into the rain and darkness with his head craned way back so that feeble little flashlight beam is aimed in the general direction of the road ahead. I can't help wondering how much help it will be at a tad shy of three miles a minute down the long, undulating straightaway towards Mulsanne.

He's a brave one, all right.

But I've got other things to worry about. Like how I can jury-rig some sort of emergency lighting to get us through the rest of the night. And fortunately I've got some experience when it comes to that sort of thing thanks to the night I wired Old Man Finzio's tow truck spotlight on Cal's ratty old stripped-to-nothing TC for our drive through the mountains in that terrible rainstorm on our way to the Giant's Despair hillclimb in Wilkes-Barre, Pennsylvania, back in July of 1952. So I run out behind the pits and swipe one of the big Marchal driving lights off our transporter (which, by the way, wears crossed American and Italian flags over the sharp "Team Passaic" emblem on the door and huge "Palumbo Panther" lettering down the side in brilliant, P.T. Barnum-style gold-leaf) and rig it up with some long wires that'll stretch all the way to the battery—complete with an in-line fuse, of course—plus a couple loose pieces of angle iron and plumbers' strap and a fistful of assorted nuts, bolts, pop rivets, baling wire and sheet metal screws to hold everything in place.

Naturally I have it all ready by the time Sammy comes in at the end of one lap, flashlight still crammed in his face and eyes big as goose eggs from breathing through his nose and trying not to gag. He lets Cal help him out while I set up the light—Cyclops fashion, of course, just like the TC!—and it isn't ninety seconds before Cal is wailing off into the darkness again with the piercing, icy-white beam from that single Marchal lamp aimed dead-center down the middle of the roadway. We're home free....

"That was a pretty close one," Sammy allows, rubbing his jaw. He looks eastward, to where we can see the first dim, purplish-gray shadows of dawn starting to show behind the grandstands. "See that?" he asks, still massaging his jaw.

I see it, all right "Have Monique take a look at that," I tell him.

Sammy shrugs and shoots me a sly grin. "Not a bad idea."

As he turns to go, I reach out for his shoulder and stop him. "That was a pretty swell thing you did."

"Hey," he shrugs. "You would've done the same. So would Cal. I just thought of it first."

It was a nice thing to say, you know?

So the night and rain fade down but then there's fog and mist like you can't believe and even some of those seasoned European Grand Prix stars come in and say they can't go on just because they're going 150-plus through what looks and feels like cold, wet cotton and they can't see their blessed nose in front of their face. But of course Cal and Sammy aren't bothered by it at all, and I even send Tommy Edwards out for a stint after the fog burns off because I want him to be in on it and we're so far out in front that I want my guys to shower and shave and put on some clean, fresh, Palumbo Panther coveralls so they look their very best on the victory stand.

And then of course Cal wins the three-way coin match to see who gets the last lap and he naturally showboats a little by knocking another couple seconds off the lap record—hey, as long as he brings it home in one piece, you know?—and then we're all up on the victory podium and flashbulbs are flashing and corks are popping off bottles of the finest French champagne and all the European radio and TV and newspaper people are crowding around and jabbering at us through our interpreter (it's Monique again, only now in a daring, black-sequin cocktail gown that's cut so blessed low front and back that she's got cleavages pointing in both directions!) about the magnificent job our drivers did and of course Cal and Sammy and Tommy are telling her to tell all the European press guys that it was really me who did everything and about how I designed the car and built the car and organized everything and came through in the clutch when we needed a Cyclops-eye headlight in a hurry there in the middle of the night and rain. And then of course they all want to talk to me, but I just kind of shrug and allow as how I didn't really do much of anything. Hey, when you win the Twenty-Four Hours of Le Mans, you really don't need to gloat.

Later, after the hubbub has died down a little and we're leaving the podium with a nice, warm glow of exhaustion inside and a nice, heady buzz from all the champagne toasts swirling around in our heads, the long-legged, silky-haired Monique with only one eye showing sidles up next to me. "Aah wahnnt too bee weez yoouu, Buddeee."

"But what about the drivers?" I ask her.

"Non! Non! Not thee dryvairs. Eet ees yoouu 'oo made eet all 'appen, mon cher!" And with that she presses in real close so's I can feel all that fancy French topography up against me. But I start feeling guilty about Julie right away, and so I look over to Cal for a little support. And of course he sizes up the situation instantly and comes back with a perfectly typical Cal Carrington response: "Hey, this is France, Buddy," he grins. "Who's gonna ever know...."

As we head towards the garage area on a long, red carpet runner trimmed in gold—me and Monique, Cal, Sammy, Tommy and Big Ed all arm-in-arm—there are these pretty little French schoolgirls scattering handfuls of red, white and blue rose petals in front of us. And, no, I have no idea where the heck they got the blue roses. But they're throwing them in the air like fat confetti and several of them glance gently off my forehead. Only I notice they land a little harder than something like rose petals ought to. More like a shoe, actually...

"GET UP, PALUMBO! WE'RE GONNA MISS THE FRICKIN' BOAT!"

Well, that's Julie's voice. No question about it. And it's Julie's shoe as well. In fact, it's her dainty little white satin wedding slipper. And that's when I open my eyes to discover that my head hurts like hell and that I've spent our entire wedding night passed out in my tux in an overstuffed chair over by the window of the fancy penthouse honeymoon suite Big Ed booked Julie and me into on the top floor of maybe the forty-seventh or forty-eighth nicest hotel in New Jersey, with a big picture window overlooking the scenic rail yard and cement plant that overlook the Hudson River in that particular part of town.

Not that it's entirely my fault, you understand, on account of I'm sure I was suffering a few shuddering, nervous aftershocks from the wedding—hey, what guy wouldn't?—and maybe had one or six too many at that reception party we had in the private room on the second floor of Pete and Pasquale's Palermo Room Pizzeria and Pasta Palace in Passaic after the ceremony. But I felt like I needed it, you know? First off, I was worried plenty about my sister Mary Frances, who I found crying her eyes out on the back steps of the church just before the ceremony on account of that pompous, egghead/egomaniac live-in boyfriend of hers over in Greenwich Village—that Oliver Cromwell guy—had somehow managed, in spite of all of his degrees and academic honors and I.Q. points and novels in Esperanto, to do the same dimbulb thing that minimum-wage high school dropout types from our side of the Hudson do and knocked her up. It made me want to leave my own wedding, drive that rented limo directly across the bridge to Manhattan, pull up in front of that Greenwich Village apartment building they lived in that we went to on New Year's Eve, and leave the motor running while I skipped up the steps three at a time, knocked politely on his door, and, when he finally laid down whatever scholarly tome he was perusing and answered, demonstrate my displeasure by re-arranging his face for him. And maybe kick in a few ribs while I was at it.

Not that I'm a violent type of guy under normal circumstances. Fact is, I don't much like fighting. And that's probably because I've never been especially good at it. The few black eyes, chipped teeth and lumpy noses I've been involved with in my lifetime have generally wound up staring back at me out of my bathroom mirror the following morning. And so you learn to avoid such things. But this was a special sort of situation, and it never once occurred to me that I might not be able to rise to the occasion.

Only I had the wedding going on and so all I could do was get really steamed and disgusted about it. And worried for my sister, too. The only good news was that, through the anguish and anger, she'd finally come to realize what a pompous egghead/egomaniac asshole this Oliver Cromwell character really was. Although a fat lot of good it did her now. Anyhow, she faked "a headache" (all the female types in the wedding party much over the age of 14 nodded at each other knowingly) and begged off on the reception so's she could go home and have herself a real Niagara Falls of a cry. And I couldn't say anything to anybody about it—not a word, I promised her!—on account of I was the only one in the know. It's a sad fact of life that other people's troubles can hang over you like a wet cement cloud that nobody else can see. Especially if you happen to love and be close to those people, and it's even worse when you can't say anything to distribute the weight of that cement around a little bit.

So I was not in entirely the best frame of mind. And then I'd glance over and get a good, sobering look at Julie's mother, what with her loopy, highly-arched pencil-line eyebrows over those beady, twitching, bird-of-prey eyes and that painted-on, Homicidal Maniac-issue smile that she'd put on with her usual four or five pounds of makeup that morning. She had her hair all piled up on top of her head like some kind of spray-painted, barbed-wire gumdrop—done up in shiny gloss black—and she'd even gone out and bought herself a genuine imitation onyx-finish cigarette holder with diamond-crusted trim from Woolworth's, special for the occasion. She waved that damn thing around like an orchestra conductor's baton, and used it to smoke one after another of those hideous turquoise, pink, mauve, lime green and violet Vogue cigarettes of hers with the golden filter tips, giving off a smell I feared was destined to become all too familiar in my life in the days, weeks, months and years to come.

I figured I owed myself a little drink, you know? Or maybe even two.

And of course all my sportycar racing buddies like Cal Carrington and Carson Flegley and Tommy Edwards and Butch Bohunk and Barry Spline and especially Big Ed Baumstein were only too eager to oblige. Especially since my old Ferrari-over-the-cliff chum from Mexico, Javier Premal, had sent up two very nice cases of liquor to take his place at the reception seeing as how he had a previous engagement entertaining a pair of very attractive and professional 17-year-old twin sisters (who were probably not a day over 30, either one of them) on his yacht in Havana harbor. So attending a grunt-level, blue-collar Italian wedding in Passaic, New Jersey, really didn't take precedence. But, like I said, he did send the two cases of booze, and that was nice of him. One was filled with this fancy French champagne that made your nose tickle when you drank it and got all Julie's girlfriends from the Doggie Shake to giggling behind their hands and telling off-color Wedding Night jokes in the ladies' room. But it was the other case that captured the guys' imagination. Javier had sent us 12 fresh bottles of that same dangerous, high-octane, syrup-colored Mescal with the dead worm in the bottom that he'd introduced me to when we were on *La Carrera Panamericana* together. And I'd have to say this was some real Grade-A, Premium Quality stuff as far as Mescal is concerned. Why, by the third or fourth shot, you could toss it off without hardly gagging at all. And also by the third or fourth shot, I was showing all my racing buddies and even my old man's union shop guys from the chemical plant (and, by the latter part of the evening, anyone who happened by) how the person who took the last drink had to eat the worm. And also how, if you really wanted to showboat, you had to show its head (or tail, it was hard to tell which) out between your teeth and bite it clear in two before you swallowed it. Or that was the really *macho* way to do it, anyway....

Now you may be wondering just exactly what I was doing over at the bar with Javier Premal's Mescal instead of attending to my lovely new wife. And, lest you think I'm a complete jerk, let me explain that I was indeed taking care of all the usual wedding-type stuff like fawning over her and smiling at her and chewing off her garter at the appropriate time and kissing her right smack on the lips every time all my old man's union crew started banging their spoons against the glassware. But it was almost like I wasn't there, you know. Or, more precisely, like I was just one more stage prop. Like the table centerpieces or the bridal bouquet or the hired tux I was wearing or our five-piece dance band, The Monotones, that only had four pieces this particular evening because the piano player's father needed somebody to deliver pizzas and meatball sandwiches on account of his regular guy didn't show up. Hey, it could have been the accordionist. Nope, if you looked into Julie's eyes (which, by the way, I could seldom catch) you could see that this whole wedding business was really all about *her*, not us or me, and how blessed radiant she looked—which was plenty—and all the beaming, envy-inducing smiles she was busy exchanging with all of her unmarried girlfriends from the Doggie Shake. Plus I didn't much like the special, insider glances she kept sharing now and again with her mother (who, as the evening wore on, started looking more and more like one of those hideous, grinning skeleton haunts that pop out of the shadows at you on the spook train ride at Palisades Park). As you can imagine, this was making me feel somewhat lonely and left out. Not to mention a little nervous about the future. Especially since I caught myself remembering over and over again what Barry Spline had told me. You know, about how if you wanted to see what your wife was going to be like a few years down the road, just take a good, solid look at the mother. And that was a very scary notion indeed.

So I'd excuse myself every now and then and head off to the can or outside to bum a smoke or maybe take a breath of air—it didn't much matter which—and, if by some strange coincidence it passed me by the bar where Javier Premal's slowly-dwindling supply of high-octane Mexican hooch was being sampled, that was okay with me. Taken in sufficient quantity, that stuff could be amazingly reassuring. Not to mention relaxing. And the truth is most guys don't really need a reason or excuse to get stiff at a party. It's just something that happens. Although maybe you ought to think twice about it if it's your own blessed wedding. But, hey, toss off enough shots of Mescal and it's nothing to worry about.

Or at least not until the next morning, anyway....

So I admit I was maybe a little unsteady when I took Julie out for our first-ever dance together as man and wife (although I thought it was genuinely lovely—honest I did!—what with her skin all warm and glowing against mine and the gentle flutter of her eyelash against my cheek and the dimmed colored lights in the ceiling fixtures kind of swirling and rotating above us like tinsel and stars and quicksilver and reflecting back all gold and rose and silver off the chrome trim on the accordion and drum set....)

"Jesus, Palumbo, yer falling all over me!" Julie snarled in my ear.

"I lub you, Julie," I gurgled into the back of her neck.

"You sure as hell better straighten up before you dance with my mother!"

That sobered me right up. Honest it did.

So, the next time a nice, moderate-tempo number came up—I mean, I sure as hell couldn't see doing the jitterbug with her mom, and a cheek-to-cheek slow dance against that heavily powdered and grease-painted mummy skin was even more out of the question—I dutifully extended my arm and asked Julie's mother to dance. *"You just watch your step,"* she warned through a smile that reminded me of that "Joker" character in the Batman comic books you see on the drugstore news stand. *"I know what boys like you are after!"*

"I already had it!" I wanted to boast—just to see the look on her face, you know?—but I decided to keep my mouth shut instead. And, to be honest about it, that was the only smart thing I did all evening. I remember the song was the Patti Page hit *With My Eyes Wide Open* (which can sound pretty strange played by an accordion, a bass fiddle, a French horn and a set of brushes on a snare drum), and I sort of held Julie's mom at arms' length so's she wouldn't put my eye out with that damn Woolworth's five-and-dime cigarette holder of hers. I couldn't help noticing that it had already lost a few of its little chiseled-glass fragments that were supposed to look like diamonds on account of the glue apparently wasn't up to snuff. Her hands were cold as ice and she didn't take her glaring, frozen, dis-approving, bird-of-prey eyes off me once the whole time we were dancing together. Not once. In fact, I don't believe she even blinked....

The thing I was beginning to understand was that Julie's mom would never, *ever* forgive me for taking her away. Even if it was just to the apartment down-stairs, which, against not just my *better* judgment, but every sort of judgment of any type, size, kind, weight, height, length, width, breadth, manner or description I might have had, we were apparently planning to do. But even just the thickness of the floorboards between the first and second stories of that worn-down old frame duplex over on Fourteenth Street was enough—I was taking Julie away from her. And even if she was just a grim, angry, sneering, complaining, sour-faced, dried-up, mean-spirited old war widow who thought life was a dirty trick and was out to prove it to everybody, she didn't much fancy being alone. Even people who claim to hate everybody don't like being alone. I mean, who are you going to spew all your bile at if you're all by yourself? If there's nobody around to hear your moans and complaints and curses and grievances, is there really even a sound? Who knows? Not to mention that it had dawned on Julie's mom that she was maybe going to have to do her own dishes and wash her own clothes and scrub her own floors and clean her own windows for a change. And I don't think she relished that prospect one bit.

But I thanked her politely when the song was done and she gave me a stiff lit-tle quarter-inch curtsey in return and right about then the band swung into a real-ly upbeat rendition of Rosemary Clooney's *Come On A-My House,* which caused us to separate instantly by mutual instinct. Julie's mom headed back towards the head table (where Julie and her girlfriends from the Doggie Shake were whisper-ing what certainly would be labeled Locker Room Jokes if they ever heard guys telling them) and I headed back outside for another gulp of fresh air. Along with another gulp of Javier Premal's high-octane Mescal while I was at it....

Naturally Big Ed was there, leaning his bulk against the bar for support and with quite an array of empty glasses spread out in front of him. It was almost like he had taken root there, you know? *"How y'doin', Shport?"* he slurred at me, put-ting a meaty arm around my shoulders and regarding me in a proud, fatherly way out of eyes pointing in two different directions. He was on maybe his fourth or fifth Martini only by now without the bothersome necessity of either Vermouth or a stuffed olive—and he'd already been through several rounds of the Mescal wars and had personally eaten at least two of the worms. So you could say Big Ed was feeling pretty expansive and philosophical. *"Y'look a li'l shad,"* he observed, his head gently oscillating like it was trying to find the center balance-point of his neck. *"Wash wrong, Buddy?"*

"Aah," I told him, "I gotta lot on my mind, that's all."

"But thish ish your big night," he gushed, and then added a sloppy, drunken whooshing noise that followed his fist up towards the ceiling and then burst open like a skyrocket as his fingers scattered in the general direction of the ceiling tiles and fluttered gently down again.

"I dunno. I'm just a little edgy, you know? Like it's a dream or a movie or something and I wonder what the heck I'm doing here."

Big Ed's lips spread out into an enormous grin, but the eyes above it were very sad indeed. *"Welcome t'the Big Leaguesh, kid. You're in the shit with the resht of ush, now."* He got us a couple shots of Javier Premal's Mescal and then fumbled around inside his jacket, looking for something. *"Here,"* he said, handing me one of his prize Cuban stogies, *" have a shegar."*

For the first time in my life, I took one of Big Ed's dollar cigars and followed the wavering tip of his gold-plated Zippo to light it up. To be really honest, Big Ed's fancy dollar cigar tasted an awful lot like a burning cow flop. Not that I'd ever actually tasted a burning cow flop, mind you. But I couldn't really imagine it's much different. "This tastes like a burning cow flop," I told Big Ed.

"Yeah," he grinned wistfully. *"But itsch a really GOOD cow flop, Buddy."* He took a deep draw off his stogie and puffed out a lovely oval smoke ring. *"You'll shee. Y'get ushed to it after awhile."* He looked at me again and shook his head knowingly. *"Y'get ushed to a'lotta thingsh after awhile. You'll shee..."* We leaned back against the bar together, Big Ed and me, kind of making room for our elbows among the empty bottles and shot glasses while we watched our pungent wisps of dollar Cuban cigar smoke filtering up into the light fixtures.

"Y'know whatsh you got?" Big Ed asked dreamily—the way drunks always do when they're about to unlock the Mysteries of the Universe for you.

I shrugged.

He pulled in close, like it was a secret. *"Buyer'sh remorshe,"* he whispered in my ear.

"What?"

He said it again, slower and louder, taking care to enunciate every sloppy syllable. *"BUYER'SH REMORSHE!"* he repeated, like it was obvious.

"What's that?"

"It'sh when you think you want something, shee?" He held one knockwurst-sized finger up like an exclamation point. *"Only then, onesh you get it, you're not sho damn sshure you really wanted it in the firscht plasche."* Big Ed gave me a helpless shrug. *"It happensh all the time, shee."*

"Really?"

"Absholutely!" Big Ed nodded, ordering us another round of Mescal. *"In fact, I'm pretty sshure it wash one of the Twelve Plaguesh in Egypt."*

"The what?"

He waved me off. *"Doeshen't matter. Doeshen't matter."* And then he looked me right in the eye. Or as close to right in the eye as he could under the circumstances. *"The thing ish thish, Buddy,"* he poked his finger into my chest. *"It'sch an ADULT dishease. Shee? You're up in the Big Leaguesh with the resht of ush, now."* And with that, he rotated unsteadily on his heels and wobbled off in the general direction of the can.

I don't really remember much of the rest of it, except for my mom gurgling and blubbering all over me like one of those green ceramic carp in the fountain in Big Ed's driveway when we slow-danced together to *The Tennessee Waltz*. And of course old Carson Flegley oh-so-understandingly taking both my hands in his (funeral director fashion, you know?) and offering me his most heartfelt congratulations and buying me a drink and Tommy Edwards clicking our glasses together after buying me a drink and Butch Bohunk wiping a smear of *cannoli* off his chin with his bad hand and buying me a drink—hey, you can't refuse a drink from a guy in a wheelchair, now can you?—and Cal Carrington just grinning that sly, semi-evil cobra grin of his and getting me to buy him a drink.

Only it turned out they were all free anyway, you know?

In any case, I understand it took Julie and two or three other able-bodied souls to get me down the street to the hotel Big Ed had booked us into as sort of a little extra wedding present, and somewhere along the way I am told I fell victim to a wee twinge in the digestive tract and puked all over the tux rental company's best black patent leather shoes. Up in the room, I furthermore understand that I reached out for something to steady myself on my way to the john to maybe be sick again and it turned out to be the well-filled neckline of Julie's beautiful, off-white wedding dress. I more or less ripped the front right off of it. But I told her not to worry about it, on account of she most likely wouldn't be needing it again anyway. Not that sound, rational logic like that ever cuts much ice with women. After that, I'm told I spent the balance of our first night together as man and wife passed out in that overstuffed chair over by the window, blissfully comatose and snoring deeply enough to suck the paint off the walls....

As you can imagine, I awoke to one of the ugliest mornings in recorded human history. Naturally it was gray and rainy outside—what else?—and I could feel right through the roots of my hair and teeth that there was lots of rust and not a single finger-swab of grease on the wheels of those heavy, groaning freight cars rolling around in the rail yard down below us. And that's not even mentioning the union guys who were putting in a little time-and-a-half (or maybe even double-time) grinding up a few truckloads of slag and meteorite fragments at the cement plant next door. I remember kind of lolling my head over the other way and there was Julie, sitting bolt upright against the headboard of the bed with her knees drawn up under her chin and a pink terrycloth robe wrapped around the shoulders of the shredded remains of her wedding dress. She looked awful, what with dried tear tracks all up and down her cheeks and two cold, angry, bloodshot eyes staring holes right through me. On pure animal reflex, I opened my mouth to speak.

"Don't talk to me," Julie advised.

It sounded like good advice.

Well, I really don't want to bore you or agonize myself by recalling the next few hours of our marriage, but let me just briefly relate that I was subjected—and rightly so—to alternating blasts of icy silence and searing, flame-edged rants, raves, and recriminations. The phrase *"how COULD you??!!"* was kind of a recurring refrain—a chorus, almost—and all I could do was sit there and take it, all the while feeling about a sick, forlorn and miserable as a human being without a venomous snake bite or a sucking chest wound could possibly feel, nodding and mumbling every now and then in abject agreement with every blessed thing she was saying.

Only I was maybe still a little drunk, and so I was thinking to myself, as guys often do in the privacy of their own heads, *"Hey, what's the big deal, anyway? This, too, shall pass."* I mean, it's not like I'd killed anybody or fooled around with another girl or took her mom's imitation diamond-crusted onyx cigarette holder and chased her around the dance floor with it like I was going to stick it up her behind. I had to bite my lip to keep from snickering when I thought of that one. But the point is that a guy would most likely understand the way I acted. I was just a little nervous, that's all. And I couldn't very well refuse to share a few once-in-a-lifetime wedding reception toasts with my friends and racing buddies, now could I? Hell, all I did was act a little goofy and throw up on a pair of rented shoes—like that's the first time *that* ever happened, right?—and then maybe tear the front clear off some stupid dress that Julie was never going to wear again anyway. Why, as far as your average guy friends are concerned, that's just another funny story you can tell and toast and laugh over a hundred-dozen times down the road.

But I was coming to realize that women take stuff like that a little more seriously. Especially wives. Oh, sure, you eventually get to the point where you can laugh and joke about it. Like maybe after your first couple grandkids. But, up until then, it is something that will hang over your head like a full truckload of ripe, stinking manure, ready to topple down all over you the next time you step one tiny fraction of an inch out of line. And the time after that, too. And I guess that was my first real lesson in the facts of practical matrimony:

Men screw up. And women, God bless 'em, never, *ever* let them forget it.

It's just the way things are....

Big Ed had kindly borrowed Julie and me his black Sixty Special Caddy sedan for our honeymoon (you remember, the one with the suspiciously dark, thick glass in all the windows and air conditioning?) and we spent most of that warm, damp, dull and rainy late Sunday morning and early afternoon driving through a vacant-looking Manhattan and across Long Island to catch the car ferry to Cape Cod at the far end. It was the same exact route Big Ed and me took to our first-ever sports car race at Bridgehampton just thirteen months before, and also the same one Julie and me drove a year later in Big Ed's Jaguar, out to Cal Carrington's folks' shore cottage and that very special night we spent together out on the beach, just beyond the echo of the big racing party where Eddie Dearborn sat at the old player piano in his brand new, metallic-red crash helmet and led all the drunks in a raucous sing-along the night before he lost control of his matching new metallic-red Allard on the bridge over Sag Pond and got himself killed. Right in front of us. So there was a lot of stuff running around in my head, memories

I wanted to maybe share with Julie to sort of bring us back together a little and things I didn't dare mention on account of I knew it would do exactly the opposite. But I didn't say much of anything, really. So, in spite of 85-degree heat and jungle-issue humidity, we rode across Long Island in perhaps the dead coldest silence since the ice age. I didn't even have to turn on the air conditioning.

Things didn't get any better on the boat, which didn't quite turn out to be the romantic, Caribbean-style cruise ship that we'd envisioned but actually more your Staten Island Ferry type of watercraft, what with ugly scrapes in the hull paint from nudging up against dock pilings and long, unromantic rust stains down the anchor paths and a particularly heavy encrustment of seagull droppings all over the rear deck railings where we stood and watched Long Island slip slowly away into the gloom. "I guess that's why they call it a 'poop' deck?" I offered half-heartedly, but Julie didn't say anything. In fact, she didn't even bother to glare.

There wasn't a particularly heavy swell on the Atlantic that evening, but it was enough to remind my stomach of the night before, and I remember grabbing a neatly folded copy of the Sunday *New York Times* off one of the deck chairs as we headed through the metal door that led into the dark, narrow corridor to our stateroom. Not so much that I wanted to read, you understand, but I figured I might want something large, absorbent and disposable close by. Just in case. But not more than 10 paces into that tight, close, locker-room atmosphere inside the ship convinced me I was better off in the fresh air up on deck. No matter how cold or damp or windy it might be or how little sleep I got. At first Julie was going to stay downstairs by herself, but then she gave me one of those angry, disgusted grimaces women give you when they catch themselves letting you off the hook even a little and agreed to come back on deck with me. To tell the truth, I don't think she much cared for being inside the ship, either. Not that she would ever admit it.

Back on deck it was dark and wet and cold and windy—even under the awnings—and so we sat next to each other in a couple deck chairs with a plaid wool deck blanket over us. At first she made sure to stay a foot or so away from me—so our bodies wouldn't actually touch, you know?—but then, as the flapping wind and wet and cold bit in a little deeper, she blew out an exasperated sigh, jerked her chair over closer to mine, and burrowed her head into my shoulder. I couldn't believe how great that felt! But then she flashed her eyes up at me like two searchlight beacons at Sing Sing and growled: "Don't think I'm doing this 'cause I like you, Palumbo. I'm just cold." And was she ever!

Things didn't get much better when we got to Cape Cod. Julie'd booked us into this divine little place called "The Cod Boxes" that she'd seen in some travel brochure, and the picture on the pamphlet showed this absolutely adorable little white-clapboard shore cottage with handsome green storm shutters, bright red geraniums sprouting out of the window boxes, a serene view of pure, white sand and endless, vacant blue ocean in the background, and a perfectly trimmed green privet hedge out front. And, indeed, that's exactly where the owner and his wife lived. The rest of the cottages, just as the name implied, looked like a bunch of cod boxes. You know, the little wooden boxes with the sliding tops that your mom maybe buys when your dad is in the mood for a little *baccala*. They were square

and plain and flat-topped and featureless, and I guess they were originally var-
nished instead of painted so they did indeed look like a matched set of salt-cod
boxes scattered in the rye grass about 200 yards beyond the tide line, overlooking
the beach. Or at least that's what they looked like in the picture on the wall of the
lovely, cozy and entirely perfect little cottage/office where the owners lived. Only
what with the wind and sea spray and the salt air and all, the varnish didn't hold
up real good. So, in typical New England Yankee fashion, the owner drove his
pickup down the cape to a hardware store in New Bedford that was going out of
business and got himself one heck of a bargain Bulk Deal on 36 gallons of brand
new, top-quality, all-weather house paint. So long as he wasn't too choosy about
the color, anyway. Which is why The Cod Boxes now looked sort of like a bunch
of worn and weathered kids' building blocks scattered in the rye grass about 200
yards beyond the tide line, overlooking the beach. Our particular unit was painted
kind of a dingy off-yellow on three sides—imagine the yolk of a very old hard-
boiled egg—and a sort of dull, firebrick orange on the fourth. And I mean doorjambs, window trim, storm shutters, *everything*. I happened to notice that the first
two sides of the cabin next door were painted that same dull orange, and then it
switched to a sort of queasy grayish blue for the other two, which continued on to
the first side of the next cottage. It didn't take much imagination to see that this
guy simply used up each can of paint—right down to the very last drop, most
likely—and then switched to another. Like I said, a real New England Yankee.

The Cod Box cottages were really pretty plain, with just a screen door covering a windowless wooden door behind it and a couple long, narrow windows with
storm shutters propped out over them high up on the walls. Just under the eaves,
in fact, so they admitted hardly anything in the way of sunlight and even less in
the way of ventilation. It made me think of some sort of quaint, oddly-painted
clapboard mausoleum. Not that sunlight was a particular problem while we were
on Cape Cod, since it continued windy, dull, humid and rainy for our entire stay.
And it was even gloomier in our cabin, since Julie adamantly refused to let us
keep the front door open so some light and breeze might come in through the
screen. In fact, she made me keep it locked, too, on account of she was afraid that
there might be somebody, you know, *out there*. Even though we were the only
registered guests at The Cod Boxes that particular week. "Jeez, Julie," I'd tell her,
"it's really kind of dark and stuffy in here."

"I don't want anybody looking in here…" she'd glower at me, as if there was
an entire, leering bleacher section of peeping toms and Bowery rummies just outside our door, "…and finding out all about our business…."

Not that there was much of any real business—funny or otherwise—going on
during our stay on Cape Cod. Mostly, it just felt odd. For both of us. Oh, I hate to
be the one to break it to all you romantic, matrimonially-oriented types out there,
but honeymoons can be pretty strained and strange experiences. I mean, there you
are, committed right up to the earlobes in the sight of God, your family, the church
of your choice and just about everybody you know, and all of a sudden you find
yourself out in some highly foreign and unfamiliar place with some semi-familiar
stranger who is dealing with the exact same problems and questions that you are.
Not to mention that you are of the male persuasion and that she is decidedly

female (or vice-versa) and that there are certain basic differences of wants, needs, priorities, desires and temperament that you are both about to one-by-one discover about each other. And that can be highly unnerving.

Of course you think you *know* this person—hopefully very well, in fact—only up until now you've always pretty much just kissed them longingly goodnight and gone back to your miserable, aching, geez-whiz-I-wish-I-was-still-with-her (or him) solitude all by your lonesome. Only the *privacy* of that miserable, longing, aching solitude never bothered to occur to you.

And now that person you so ached and yearned and pined for is right there in front of you. All the blessed time, in fact. Inescapable. Aware of (if not actually watching, observing and evaluating) your every move. And so you've got to think twice before you pick your nose or check out what's growing between your toes or relieve yourself with a nice, hefty fart or belch or scratch yourself in certain private, primitive areas. Sure, all that stuff will come later. In fact, it may even become fun. But not on your honeymoon. No, sir. And so there you are, crammed together with this scary, strange and peculiar other person (who can't possibly be all that sharp or special, since, after all, they settled for *you!*) and you both find yourselves moving around quietly and cautiously on tightly-arched tippytoes—like blessed store-window mannequins on stilts!—and it all feels so weird and unnatural that both of you can't help wondering if you've not only made *a* mistake, but if maybe you've made the biggest single mistake in the entire history of mankind. I kept remembering what Big Ed told me while we shared cigars and way too many shots of Javier Premal's Mescal leaned up against the bar at my wedding reception. Buyer's Remorse. Yeah, maybe *that's* what it was. Plain and simple. No question it had been one of those twelve plagues in Egypt, just like Big Ed said....

And it didn't help that Julie was still so pissed off about me getting drunk and ripping her dress and then passing out on our wedding night that she couldn't stand the way I brushed my teeth. Or tied my shoes. Or even tried to act nice to her. Let me tell you a little something about anger, disgust and disappointment as it applies to men and women living in close quarters together for the very first time. Now, as far as the male of the species is concerned—that would be me—he's kind of a big, dumb, direct and well-meaning sort of slob who pretty much tries to steer a steady course (even when he has absolutely no idea where he's going), keeps an even keel, takes things as they come, forgives and forgets, and really only reacts to things when they're shaken or dangled unavoidably right in front of his face. Live and let live, you know? And we guys generally figure that, although there are surely people and situations that get us mad—in fact, mad enough to put our fists through things—there is no percentage in hanging onto anger or grudges or disgust or disappointment once the storm has passed and the hole's been patched up in the drywall. Hey, we build up to it, have our explosions—*BOOM!*—and that pretty much does the trick. Relieves the pressure. And then things go back to normal, right?

But, as I was just beginning to comprehend from firsthand personal observation, women go about things quite a bit differently. And I think it's one of those primeval, cave-man things that can be traced back to when they found themselves cooking saber-tooth tiger stew back in the old Neanderthal days. A woman's anger is like a fire, see. You supply enough fuel (which, by the way, is exceedingly easy for your average male person to do) and the fire flares up. But there's no big explosion, see? No real release of pressure. So, instead of blowing up and being done with, that anger just goes down into a sort of low, hissing ember. During which it is guaranteed to glow or flicker from time to time just to let you know that, whatever it was you did or said or didn't do or didn't say, it has definitely *not* been forgotten. And that goes on for quite a while. But nobody—not even a wife or steady girlfriend—can sustain that kind of energy forever. And so, eventually, that glowing ember fades into a sort of gray-ash smolder that looks like maybe the fire is out. Only if you stupidly stick your nose in too close to check on it (or, heaven help you, manage to accidentally dump a load of fresh fuel on those seemingly dead ashes) the whole thing blows up in your face, singes your eyebrows off, scorches the hair right out of your nostrils and the whole blessed process starts all over again.

I was slowly coming to understand that women don't forgive *or* forget. They just tolerate....

But, as any fool can plainly see, I had it coming. After all, I'd done my clumsy, drunken best to ruin that one moment in the entire, vast and endless flow of the universe when Julie had the chance to be the center of it all, and that was apparently right up there with the serpent tempting Eve on the all-time Great Unforgivable Sin list. So I spent most of the next three long, dreary days on Cape Cod being as polite as a hired butler and pulling out chairs for her and turning down the bed for her and going out in the pelting rain to see if I could find a few scraggly wildflowers to bring her in a bouquet. But it was like trying to thaw a glacier with a handful of stick matches, and I wasn't making a whole lot of headway.

"You wanna go anywhere today?" I'd ask her.

"Like where?" she'd answer like she was in another room.

"Oh, I dunno. Maybe up to Provincetown. We got Big Ed's car."

She'd look me up and down. "With *you?*"

I'd look over my shoulder both ways to see if there wasn't maybe somebody else in the room behind me. "They got all kinds of shops and antiques and stuff up there."

"It's raining," she'd say, and take out an emery board to go over her fingernails for maybe the 96th or 97th time.

Like I said, I wasn't making a whole lot of headway.

So I read that copy of the Sunday *New York Times* that I'd picked up on the ferryboat. Front page to back. A dozen times over. And I can tell you with absolute clarity that President Eisenhower and his guys were negotiating a prisoner-of-war deal that looked like the last big hurdle to finally arriving at a truce in the Korean War (which, it turned out, wasn't really a war at all on account of nobody declared war on anybody else and nobody won and nobody lost and it didn't solve or decide anything, even though plenty of American soldiers—including a bunch of my old high school buddies—got shot up or killed in the process). Oh, and they were having another big election in Italy. Again. Which of course made me wonder how the Italians could build magnificent and sweet-running things such as Ferraris and OSCAs and Alfa Romeos and Maseratis but couldn't keep their blessed government from throwing a rod and seizing up solid every time you turned around. Then again, an organized, purposeful, functional and thoroughly reliable government like we had was maybe what got you into wars that weren't really wars and never really solved anything like Korea. I remembered hearing in school one time that some famous patriot or other once said, *"the government that governs best, governs least,"* and it had never really occurred to me that you could accomplish that as easily with chaos, divisiveness and ineptitude as you could by policy, proclamations or design.

Speaking of the government, the paper said they were grinding through the final appeals in the Rosenberg spy case and that colored congressman Adam Clayton Powell from New York had grabbed himself another fistful of headlines by complaining that the House Un-American Activities Committee was going to investigate Dr. Ralph Bunche. Heck, they were investigating everybody, you know? But of course the communist threat was everywhere—in fact, almost the entire Sunday *Times Magazine* was devoted to the threat of something called "pink" communism in the middle east—and I guess that's why the mayor of San Antonio wanted to identify and brand all the subversive books in the local San Antonio library so's people would know not to read them.

Sounded reasonable to me.

Closer to home, there was almost a gang rumble in Red Hook, Brooklyn, between the Kane Street Midgets and the Gowanus Dukes that only got dramatically avoided at the very last moment on account of somebody squealed to the cops ahead of time and maybe they didn't really want to fight each other after all. I mean, talking tough and mixing up a few Molotov cocktails is a lot more fun than actually getting your nose broken or your head bashed in.

Oh, and Edmund Hillary—make that *Sir* Edmund Hillary—got himself knighted for being the first person to the top of a mountain his faithful Sherpa guide (who, by the way, didn't get anything) showed him the way to. Oh, and a British Canberra jet set a new record crossing the Atlantic in four hours and 26 minutes and a little boy was nipped by an alligator while swimming in a water hole marked "No Swimming" near Miami, Florida. The Dodgers, Yanks and Giants all won, a Dachshund of all things won some big, important dog show, and Roland Young—you remember, the guy who played "Topper?"—dropped dead. Plus Ethel Merman got herself married to some big-time airline mogul. The rest of it was mostly ads, and most of them were for women's clothing and home appliances. Which was a pretty good tipoff as to who they *really* write newspapers for. Although I admit I was real pleased to see an MGTD playing a major part in the full-page ad for Franklin Simon Men's Shop on page 4. And there was also a mention of the 162nd anniversary of the birth of John Howard Wayne. In case you didn't know (which I most certainly didn't), he's the guy who wrote *"be it ever so humble, there's no place like home."*

All of which got me to thinking again about what was going to happen with Julie and me.

Fact is, I had this nagging sensation eating away at me like *"I don't belong here,"* you know? And I could feel in the muggy, damp, dreary and entirely foreign gloom of Cape Cod that Julie didn't feel like she belonged there, either. I mean, when you got right down to it, we'd both grown up as regular old blue-col-lar, nose-to-the-grindstone, shot-and-a-beer working stiff types, and it felt really strange—eerie, even—to find ourselves sitting around all day in this faded yellow and orange clapboard mausoleum of a summer cottage on Cape Cod, listening to the low, faint surf rolling in and the echo of the bells on the fog buoys out by the boat channel. It was almost like we were playing hooky from real life. Maybe it sounds nuts—especially the way everybody always moons and swoons and car-ries on about honeymoons—but I think both of us couldn't wait to get away from all that salt air and rolling surf and back to Jersey where, even if it wasn't espe-cially scenic or romantic, at least you had a regular routine of stuff you knew you had to do and you never really had to think too much about what needed to be done next. Most usually, it was right there in front of you, screaming for attention.

And that's pretty much what I was thinking about when I opened my eyes from what hadn't been much of a night's sleep early Wednesday morning and looked over to see Julie all curled up in a fierce little ball on the other side of the bed, facing the wall. So I decided to go for a little walk along the shoreline to maybe mull things over. All by my lonesome, you know? I got up real quietly and slipped on my sneakers with no socks and this battered N.Y.U. sweatshirt that my sister Mary Frances must've got from that rat-bastard egghead Ollie Cromwell over in Greenwich Village who got her pregnant. That was another thing I was going to have to deal with—or at least help *her* deal with, anyway—when I got back home where I belonged in Passaic and the world started making sense again. Like I said before, I'm generally not a violent or vindictive kind of guy. But when-ever I thought about that highbrow, know-it-all, writing-novels-in-Esperanto-for-the-benefit-of-unborn-generations jerkoff and what he'd done to my sister, I start-ed getting these wild, torture-chamber daydreams—real Ripley's Believe-It-Or-Not stuff—about all the hideous things I'd like to see done to him and that he so richly deserved. Then again, with a guy like Ollie Cromwell, the worst thing you could probably do was to cut his tongue out. Or maybe stick an ice pick through both his eardrums so's he couldn't hear himself pontificate and make sage judg-ments about the condition of mankind any more....

I hadn't really said anything about Mary Frances to Julie. I mean, the right time just never came up. I only heard about it just before our blessed wedding ceremony, for gosh sakes, and I wasn't about to interrupt all the organ music, *"Do you take this?"* and *"I now pronounce you"* stuff to whisper, *"By the way, my sister Mary Frances is knocked up,"* in Julie's ear. About the only time we were alone was the short ride in Big Ed's black Caddy over to Pete and Pasquale's Pasta Palace, and that didn't exactly feel like the right time to say anything, either. I mean, that was before I got shit-faced at the reception, and so we were even kind of kissing. Not that it's any of your business. And of course after that little episode things were rather strained—not to mention strange—between Julie and me and so I never mentioned it. Plus I'd absolutely *promised* Mary Frances I wouldn't breathe a word of it to anybody. And so now I was wondering if wives or husbands counted when you promised somebody something like that. I was frankly amazed at what a huge, open-ended, Bottomless Pit of a question that was. Sure, I'd prom-ised to love, honor, and obey. And by God I was planning on it. But, far as I could recall, there was no little clause in there about sharing secrets or telling the truth. Or telling the whole truth, anyway. Or telling it all the time, either. Especially when you don't absolutely have to, you know? Or, worse yet, when it may cause some sort of irreparable grief, sadness, hurt or embarrassment to either your beloved spouse or some other unfortunate party.

Like yourself, for instance.

As you can see, I had an awful lot of stuff to think over. So I tiptoed across the floor, gently closed the door to our cozy little Cod Box mausoleum behind me, and headed silently as I could across the damp grass to the worn, narrow little pathway leading down to the beach. It was sometime before dawn—not that you could much tell, what with the usual Cape Cod fog settled over everything like a deceased cloud bank—and the tide was low and soft so's you could barely hear the ripple of the waves until you got right down by the water's edge. I headed generally northeast while the dark gray around me faded ever-so-slightly lighter, and I couldn't help remembering that night we'd had together on the beach at Bridgehampton—jeez, it seemed like a million years ago!—when Julie and I walked along so cozy arm-in-arm together and then laid down on that old, green Army blanket and did so sweetly and softly and perfectly-meshed and beautifully-the-very-first-time what we had never, come to think of it, done again since.

I counted the days back in my head and was astounded to realize that it had only been three weeks ago. Why, it seemed like another lifetime! And that's when I stopped very quietly so as not to disturb the memory and closed my eyes ever so gently and listened to the soft swish of the waves sliding in over the sand and tried to remember exactly what it felt like that night on the beach at Bridgehampton. That night when Julie and I were wrapped up so far into each other that you couldn't tell where one of us ended and the other one began. I even puckered up a little with my mouth slightly open, as if I could almost feel her lips against mine....

"Jesus, Buddy, what the hell are you doing?"

Julie's voice shot through me like a shotgun blast, even though she was talking in a whisper. I hadn't heard her coming up behind me.

"W-well, I, u-umm," I stammered, blushing into the fog.

"You're not *praying* or anything, are you?"

My mind was already racing through all sorts of stupid, lame excuses, but then I looked into her eyes—the eyes in which I so much wanted to belong again—and it all came pouring out of me. "If you gotta know," I admitted miserably, "I was thinking about us."

And then it all came out. All of it. How sorry I was about our wedding night (not to mention our wedding) but there was just nothing I could ever do to change it or fix it or make it better and so that's just the way it was always going to be. Forever. And also how I was so worried about my sister on account of that rat-bastard, celestial genius, novels-in-Esperanto egghead/asshole boyfriend of hers had managed to get her pregnant. I saw Julie's eyes get ever-so-slightly bigger when I told her that part. And also how desperately strange and gloomy and most of all *lonely* it felt out here in all this damned peace and tranquility on Cape Cod. How I felt so far away from her—so *very* far away from her!—and I just wanted to get back home to Jersey and have things back the way they were again between us. Or the way I hoped they would be, anyway. And, most especially of all right then, how much I loved and craved and desired and remembered and couldn't wait to get back to—if, indeed, there was a way back to—the way things were between us that special night we'd shared on the beach together at Bridgehampton. In the end there just weren't any more words. So I just stood there with my mouth kind of hanging open. Like guys do.

Julie looked up at me. For the first time since I could hardly remember when, that special heat and flash was back in her eyes. And I mean the sly, mischievous, fun one, not the *"I'd like to crush your balls in a bench vise"* one that I'd been seeing pretty much nonstop since the wedding. At least when she'd look at me.

"Lissen, Julie," I told her, "we just don't belong here, you know? We don't belong lazing around in this damn fog and quiet with nothing to do or cruising around on some damn ferryboat with nothing to do or…"

"Or?" There was just the faintest tickle of a smile at the corners of her mouth.

"Lissen," I continued, "what we oughta do is pack up our stuff right now. We still got a few days left. Let's just take us a little drive out to Provincetown—just to say we saw it, you know?—and then, hey, screw that damn ferryboat. We'll drive back to Jersey any way we want and stop wherever we want and do whatever the hell we want from now all the way through Monday morning. Whaddaya say?"

The tickle blossomed out into a wide, wicked smile. "You know, Palumbo, I may even be starting to like you again."

"You mean you forgive me?"

Her smile broke up into an even wickeder laugh. "Not in a million years, Palumbo. Not in a million years…."

So I took her hand and we walked back down the shoreline together, and by now a tarnished pewter dish of a sun was making itself visible through the gloom—it looked more like a full moon, if you want the truth of it—and I could feel the warmth and weight of Julie's body against mine as we made our way along the separate pairs of footsteps we'd left on our way out from the cabin. Once we got there, we packed our stuff and loaded it into the back of Big Ed's black Sixty Special and drove away. But not until after we laid down together on the bed for just a minute.

Just to get sort of reacquainted, you know?

And that's why it was almost noon when we finally settled the bill in that quaint little cottage with the green storm shutters and geraniums in the window boxes that was featured on the travel brochure and headed off for Provincetown. Or anyplace else interesting we might find along the way. While we'd been in the cabin, the sun had come out and burned off the mist and turned it into the first fine, clear day we'd seen since the wedding, what with a robin's-egg blue sky overhead and the soft roll of the surf coming in and the salt-air smell of vast distances and faraway, romantic places drifting in off the Atlantic.

Like I said, that's the way it is with women. They don't generally forget and they won't generally forgive, but they're the best there is when it comes to tolerating intolerable behavior. At least if it only happens once in a while and you're genuinely sorry about it afterwards. Of course, they have to make you walk over hot coals and freeze your balls in the icebox for a little while first. Maybe even a long while. But, if you've lucked into a good one, eventually it passes. And that's when you get to make up. Which, if the two of you are wise and lucky enough to take advantage of it, is really like falling in love for the very first time all over again.

2: The Home Front

I'm not so sure you need to know about that last couple days Julie and me spent driving out to the tip of Cape Cod and back in Big Ed's black Cadillac just so's we could spend maybe three or four hours meandering through more quaint little antique, junk and seashore curio shops than you have ever seen together in one place in your life. It was almost like Times Square, only with little bronze and ceramic lighthouses and whaling boats and pneumonia-candidate cod fishermen in windblown rain slickers instead of the Empire State Buildings and the Statues of Liberty that you typically find them hawking in Times Square. And, just like Times Square, I bet a lot of that stuff comes over on a boat from Japan. Just for the tourists, you know?

But it was fun watching all the city-type vacationers from New York and New Jersey and even Pennsylvania, Ohio, West Virginia and Minnesota gawking and haggling over all that stuff. And I knew where those folks came from, too, on account of I'm a genuine grad student, Ph.D. expert when it comes to license plates. Why, I even saw one from Washington. And not D.C., either. Which made me wonder why the heck you'd drive your family all the way across the whole blessed country just to look at another ocean? And a smaller one, at that. But I guess the answer is the drive itself. That must be the magic. I'm not much for sitting in a strange room in some strange (no matter how dear, quaint and scenic) town a few hundred or even thousand miles from home in order to try and relax. I feel out of place, you know? But to be in a *car* covering those hundreds or thousands of miles and feeling the tires rolling across the whole blessed length and breadth of this country and seeing all the little nooks and crannies and people and houses and landscapes and tiny, ongoing human dramas along the way, well, that's a whole 'nother thing entirely. In fact, traveling by car is one of the very best places I know. It's like being in your own living room—or even your own bedroom—watching the whole blessed world parade by for your own personal amusement. Plus you don't have to worry about one single thing—not one!—until you get to wherever the heck it is you're going and have to climb back out into the real world again. It's like, so long as you keep moving, nothing can catch you....

Not that Provincetown was a total bust. It was sunny and bright for the first time on our honeymoon and Julie bought her mom and Old Man Finzio each a nice Cape Cod souvenir bronze ashtray—a lighthouse for her mom and a cod fisherman in a rain slicker for the Old Man—along with three sets of little ceramic lighthouse salt-and-pepper shakers. One for my folks ("We can't come back from our honeymoon and not bring them *anything!*" was the way Julie put it, shaking her head that I could be so boorish and insensitive), a slightly smaller set for my Aunt Rosamarina (ditto) plus another large one that she planned to put away all wrapped in tissue paper until we had our own little house with its own little kitchen and breakfast nook with a sturdy maple Early American table that they would look simply perfect on. So long as the place mats and curtains matched, anyway.

We also had a cod fisherman-style street artist with an enormous beer gut and a bushy gray beard do a caricature of Julie and me on a thin sheet of polished copper using a kind of wooden stylus thing for a pencil. It only took him a couple strokes and it cost us a half a buck, but it was a really good job—he caught the look in our eyes, you know?—and I went along with it all on account of we were having fun and liking each other and even holding hands a little when we walked down the street. Fact is, it was one of our best days ever. Not that Julie was completely over being mad at me. That would happen at my funeral.

And then we took off in the general direction of Passaic, following U.S. Route 6 down the whole crooked, witch's-finger hook of Cape Cod and on across Massachusetts and Rhode Island, where we split off on some smaller roads just to try and stay a little closer to the seashore. It took us through some plain but interesting little non-touristy New England towns like Central Village, Adamsville, Little Compton and Four Corners, but eventually we had no choice but to head north towards Providence to get around the Sakonnet River and Narragansett Bay. But that was okay, because it was past eight-thirty and getting on towards dark and you can't do much in the way of sightseeing at night. At least not outside of New York City, anyways. And as we were driving through the darkness, it occurred to me in a flash that, right that very moment, it was coming on 2 ayem at the Twenty-Four Hours of Le Mans and some of my actual friends were over there racing. Or at least some people I knew, anyway. Tommy Edwards had left the day after the wedding—and in probably about the same shape I was—because he'd been signed on to drive for Sydney Allard again in one of their new, envelope-bodied J2R models. It was going to be a two-car team that year, and Tommy was flying over with this wiry little Russian immigrant named Zora Arkus-Duntov, who was also slated to share one of the cars. I found out later he was the same guy who designed and built those swell overhead-valve head conversions for Ford Flatheads (which is why they were called "Ardun" heads, natch), and Tommy said that Sydney Allard rated him pretty highly as both a driver and an engineer. That's quite a deal when you find a guy who not only knows how to turn a wheel, stir a gearbox and dance on the pedals, but also understands and sympathizes with all the little whirling, meshing, pumping and oscillating things those controls are connected to.

And damn if Creighton Pendleton wasn't over there, too. The stuck-up prick. But no question he could drive, and no less than Briggs Cunningham had invited him—for this one race only—on account of Briggs had this brand new C-5R race-car they'd built specially for Le Mans plus two of the C-4Rs we'd seen before (including the roadster Fitch and Walters used to win at Sebring in March and that wicked C-4RK coupe), and since he was moving his top two guys into the new car, he needed a couple extra hands for the "old" C-4R. And, based on his record, you had to agree that Creighton Pendleton the Third was a pretty solid choice. Even if he did win a lot of those races on account of he had the fastest car in that 4.1-liter Ferrari of his. Besides, he was right at home with all the yacht-harbor and summer-home types, and he'd of course been to France before and even knew enough of the lingo to order in a restaurant or chat up a likely young lady. To tell the truth, it was eating poor Cal Carrington alive that Creighton was going over to Le Mans with the Cunningham team while he sat home at Castle Carrington with his thumb up his behind, reading and re-reading that *Road and Track* article about the new Cunningham C-5R Le Mans challenger until he damn near wore out the pages.

"You know," I told Julie, "it's the middle of the night over at the Twenty-Four Hours of Le Mans."

"It's the middle of the night here," she yawned, and kind of snuggled in next to me on the front seat of Big Ed's Caddy.

Well, no question we were getting a little tired. But it's hard, once you've been rolling for a long time, to make that oh-so-final decision to halt the motion, pick a spot, and take a room for the night. And especially when you've never exactly done it before. I mean, Julie and me had been booked ahead into our hotel overlooking the rail yard and cement plant overlooking the shoreline in New Jersey and onto the ferryboat to Cape Cod and into the oh-so-appropriately-named Cod Box cottages on the ocean, but we'd never exactly checked in anyplace as husband and wife before. Just on the spur of the moment, you know? And so I found myself kind of hemming and hawing and shuffling around and looking guilty as hell as I stood across the desk from a flinty old guy in a plaid flannel bathrobe at this worn-down little tourist court we found just outside of Seekonk. The guy had thick glasses that made his eyes look like raw oysters on the half shell and hair frizzed out in every direction as if he'd stuck his finger in a wall socket.

"So yew lookin' for a room, eh?" he asked in a craggy, suspicious tone.

"Yeah," I admitted, trying to keep the color from rising up my face.

He looked over at Julie. "And this would be the little missus, eh?" he continued, sounding sarcastic as all hell.

"W-well, yes..." I started in.

But Julie was tired and sorely in need of a hot shower after our long summer day on the road, and she was not about to be messed with. *"Look, Buster,"* she snapped at him, *"we're married and on our frickin' honeymoon, okay?"*

That straightened him right up.

"And if you really need to see it," she continued, damn near baring her teeth, *"I can dig into our stuff and get our frickin' license out for you."* She held out her ring. In fact, she just about shoved it up his left nostril. *"Not that it's any of your business anyway, is it?"*

The guy backed up a baby step or two.

"Now if you'd be so kind as to give us our key. Or do we have to go find us another place down the road where the people aren't so damn nosy?"

Thoroughly convinced that, no matter what, he probably didn't have to worry about any hanky-panky going on that night, the guy in the plaid bathrobe took my five bucks and meekly handed over the key. To tell the truth, Julie could be downright frightening when she got like that—hell, I'd been on the receiving end enough times to know!—but it was pretty neat to be on her side for a change when she let loose with the old artillery. Whatever else you could say about Julie, she was not about to get pushed around or taken advantage of. Not by anybody. And, although I knew that could turn out to be a double-edged sword, it sure felt fine when it was cleaving things my way....

We slept really well together that night, and it's really none of your business what went on in the morning before we got going again. I mean, some things are better off left private. But Julie and me were feeling mighty chummy and cozy as we headed off on our all-day trek across the rest of Rhode Island and Connecticut to New York City and that final ride over the George Washington Bridge towards Passaic. We stopped for a major-league whopper of a breakfast at this diner in Cranston and lingered over coffee and the morning paper together—I was surprised to discover it was Friday, since I'd kind of lost track—and, for maybe the first time since we were married, I got a quick whiff of that nice, relaxed, satisfied, you-belong-here sort of feeling that keeps an awful lot of married couples together. Especially through the rough spots.

It's just nice to know you *belong* someplace, you know?

That afternoon we found ourselves kind of hustling for home in Big Ed's Caddy. Lord only knows why, since I had nothing but moving my stuff into the apartment below Julie's mom and listening to reams of sage advice from my old man and all sorts of car work backed up at the Sinclair to look forward to. But, just like old Butch told me after the accident that took most of his hand off and left him laid up in a damn wheelchair: *"A man's gotta work, Buddy."* And, if you're genetically predisposed to be a blue-collar, grunt-level working stiff like Butch and me, there's not much of anything you can do about it.

Besides, I had cars to fix. In fact, I had some of my best customers' cars to get ready for the races, and that meant each one was a fresh adventure in the making. Not to mention a nice chunk of change for Julie and me. My old undertaker buddy Carson Flegley had bought himself a trick new camshaft and valve spring set that he'd heard some of the really *fast* MG guys whispering about, and although it was all wrong for him—it was all fluff and feathers at anything much under 3000 rpm and would surely turn his TD into a temperamental, ill-willed beast that wouldn't idle in traffic and spit back through the carburetors and didn't have enough low-end torque to peel the damn icing off a birthday cake—he just *had* to have it. And I was only too happy to oblige (at least after I'd explained all of the above to him and watched the facts pour over his ears like pancake syrup without a single drop penetrating to his brain), seeing as how it was good work and Carson always paid on the dot. Cash money, too. Plus if I didn't do it, that second Hugo guy who got fired from Westbridge and then opened up his own foreign sports car shop on the Jersey side no more than 20 minutes away would be only too willing to handle it for him. Hey, the customer is always right, right? Even when they're wrong.

And it was a sort of rush job, too, on account of Carson was all revved-up about running the SCMA's Mount Equinox Hillclimb up in Manchester, Vermont, on June 20th and 21st, and naturally my incredibly wealthy but perpetually broke friend Cal Carrington was already sniffing around about maybe tagging along and cadging a few runs up the hill himself. Big Ed was up for it, too, assuming the Greek over at the body shop could get the leftover dents pounded out from Big Ed's minor-league skirmish with Skippy Welcher's Jag at Thompson in time for me to replace the second-gear synchro ring for maybe the third or fourth time before we left. Like I've said before, Big Ed used a shift lever kind of like a mean cop wields a nightstick. And with much the same results, too. Oh, I could let it go if I had to, but then I'd just have to be back thrashing on it the following week, seeing as how there was a road race scheduled the very next weekend way out in the boondocks of Sullivan County, near a town called Callicoon on the Delaware River.

And of course we all just had to be there.

Which was probably going to cause a wee bit of friction between Julie and me, seeing as how we were living kind of halfway between my creaky old pup tent of an apartment over my Aunt Rosamarina's garage (which Julie had oh-so-playfully christened "the shithole") and the back bedroom of her mom's place—Julie's old room—while we finished cleaning out and painting and more or less fixing up and redecorating our new home-to-be duplex apartment downstairs. As you can imagine, that's something Julie wanted to make happen sooner rather than later. On the other hand, I was in no particular rush about it, seeing as how the closer I got to Julie's mother, the further away I wanted to be. She made me nervous, you know? Plus there was no end to the stuff Julie and her mom wanted done before they approved the duplex apartment downstairs as fit for a good, upright, churchgoing Italian Catholic couple to live in. Even if neither of us were particularly regular about going to church. But it seems the people who lived there before us got divorced (or at least separated) and so every recognizable trace of them had to be removed, remodeled, or, at the very least, painted over with two coats of paint. After all, it might be catching. So good, bad, or indifferent, absolutely everything about that apartment had to be changed completely before we'd be allowed to move in.

The problem was that you have to actually be there—and preferably on the muscle end of a broom, hammer, saw, screwdriver, pliers, dustbin or paintbrush—in order to get that sort of thing accomplished. Which is kind of hard to do if you're already pulling overtime at the Sinclair every day and moreover planning to be away with your, umm, "customers" every weekend at the damn sporty-car races. Only Julie didn't put it quite so delicately.

"You think I'm a frickin' idiot??!!" she spit at me through clenched teeth as we laid in bed together in the back bedroom of her mom's apartment. She was trying to keep her voice down to an angry whisper so's her mom couldn't hear, but of course that was utterly useless on account of her mom was surely listening in through a water glass pressed up against the flowered wallpaper on the other side of the wall. Not to mention that the walls were already so blessed thin that I could hear it when her mom squeaked her cigarettes out in that bronze lighthouse ashtray we brought back for her from Provincetown. And about that "being in bed together," it's not what you might imagine. Especially for a young, healthy, state-certified signed, sealed, and delivered married couple. Because we were in no way touching each other in any way, shape or form from our uppermost hair follicles down to the calluses on the bottoms of our feet. Not with her mom just a few scant inches away on the other side of the wall. Listening....

"Jeez, Julie...." I whispered gently in the general direction of her ear.

"Keep your voice down!" she snarled back at me.

"But I am keeping my voice down," I whispered even softer.

"You want everybody to know our business?" she whispered so loud they could hear it over by the Williamsburg Bridge in Brooklyn.

So I moved my lips like I was talking but without actually saying anything. Just to see if it got a rise out of her. But it was like pissing gas on a bonfire.

"Look, we're married now. You got responsibilities, see."

I nodded.

"You gotta help me clean out that place downstairs and paint it up nice and tear up that awful old carpet and refinish the floor and hang the curtains and..."

I kept on nodding.

"...and fix the sink and that toilet that's always running—it'll cost us a fortune on our frickin' water bill—and pick up that set of table and chairs your Aunt Rosamarina said we could have out of her garage. I'm not really in love with them, but it was nice of her to offer and it'll do until we can afford to pick out a dining room set of our own. And I was thinking about maybe painting the doorjambs and moldings in this lovely shade of lilac that I saw in a fabric catalog. You know, just for a little contrast. And..."

By that time, I'd come to the conclusion that you can often get away with nodding and saying "uh-huh" and "yes, dear" and "oh, absolutely" every now and then once a female of the species starts going on like that. Only I *hadn't* learned that you can't always count on them rolling merrily along and not paying any attention to you when you're not paying any attention to them. And that, whatever you do, you definitely DO NOT say, *"Oh, whatever you say, dear."* Or words to that general effect. Because, if you do, you will find that their ears are not always filled to overflowing with the stuff frothing out of their own mouths, and that you've committed yet one more unforgivable and even more unforgettable matrimonial sin. Just listen:

"...and then I was thinking we'd paint the tile in the bathroom a nice sunflower yellow."

"Uh-huh."

"...and we could pick up some nice guest towels and maybe a little plush throw rug for the floor to match..."

"Yes, dear."

"...and we could even get a little pale yellow vase with some real sunflowers in it. Or maybe some of the fake cloth ones."

"Oh, absolutely."

"The girls at work say if you shop around, you can find cloth ones that look even better than the real thing..."

"Uh-huh."

"...but they last forever."

"Whatever you say, dear."

And then the temperature in the room drops a sudden 60 or 70 degrees and she freezes you in an icy, withering stare. *"Don't you even CARE, Buddy?"*

"Huh?"

"Don't you even CARE about how we live?"

"Well, uhh, *sure* I do."

"Hmpf," she snorts. And then she maybe even starts to sniffle a little over it. Or reams you a brand new asshole. It's hard to predict which. But you can rest assured it will surely be one or the other.

To tell the truth, I wasn't real thrilled with the prospect of living just a few inches of lath and plaster from Julie's mom. In fact, I much preferred the nights we spent over at my old apartment "packing up my stuff." Not that I had all that much stuff to pack—hell, you could fit everything I owned into one steamer trunk and have room left over for a fireplug and a stray mongrel dog to piss on it—but you can always find ways to stretch things out if you really want to. Like my Aunt Rosamarina said we could pretty much have anything we wanted out of the garage underneath my apartment that Cal Carrington and me damn near sent up in multi-colored skyrocket flames on the Fourth of July a year before. And going through old attics, basements and garages is one of those open-ended kind of jobs whose length is directly proportional to how much neat, strange, curious and unusual old stuff you stumble over and how much you really *don't* want to get around to some far-more-distasteful task on the old job horizon somewhere else. Like working on the downstairs apartment under Julie's mom's place, for example. Especially since I knew that getting that apartment done was going to have to take a back seat to the sportycar work I had backed up at the shop and the upcoming hillclimb and race weekends all my best customers were planning to attend. With me right there to take care of them and their cars, of course. I mean, I couldn't help it any if it just happened to be fun, too.

Besides, the way I figured it, a bathroom doesn't much care if it gets painted tomorrow afternoon or a week from next Tuesday, while the green flag drops on a sports car race at a very specific sort of time, and you are either there with the engine fired up, carbs tuned razor-sharp, ignition timing spot-on, tire pressures set, oil in the engine and Ethyl in the fuel tank or you have missed it for absolute ever. But that's not the sort of thing you want to be explaining to your new young wife—and especially if she happens to be of the short-fused Italian firecracker persuasion like my Julie—when you finally convince her to "lay down and rest for just a moment" on the cot-like bed that, besides the sink, shower stall, and commode, is the only remaining piece of furniture in the dark and strangely empty apartment over my Aunt Rosamarina's garage. Not hardly. Or when you're lying next to her (although not actually touching!) in the back bedroom of her mother's apartment just a few nights after you get back from your honeymoon. At least not if you plan on sleeping sometime before the following evening. If then. So you learn to just keep your mouth shut and do what you have to do instead of wasting both your time trying to explain things or attempting to reason with her. It was like Big Ed advised me over about our fourth or fifth shot of Mescal at my bachelor party: *"Lisshen, Buddy,"* he slurred in my ear while clapping a huge, sweaty armpit around my earlobes, *"...ash far ash marriage ish concerned, alwaysh remember that forgivenessh ish ushually a lot eashier to come by than permisshion."* He looked up through the haze of cigar smoke into the little 40-watt pink light bulb in the ceiling socket above us as if it was the blessed North Star. *"Yep,"* he agreed with himself, *"I'm absholutely sshure thash the mosht important thing to know when it comesh to marriage."*

I was beginning to appreciate the wisdom and symmetry of that notion.

But you do catch yourself feeling a little guilty. More than a little, in fact. So you maybe start getting up while it's still dark outside and tiptoeing downstairs with your shoes in your hand so's you can do a little more cleaning and scraping and painting here and there before you head off for work. Just to keep the peace, you know? But that only half works on account of fixing up your first apartment is something you're supposed to do *together,* right? And by "together," I am naturally referring to myself, Julie, and Julie's mom. The old battleaxe. Otherwise you will find come dinnertime (which, unless it was raining, we ate together on the rickety card table on her mom's two-by-four back porch overlooking the scenic rain gutters, garage doors, power lines and trash cans in the alley) that 95 percent of everything you have done is dead-nuts 180 degrees out-of-phase wrong. Like fr'instance:

"Say, whosa bright idea wazzit t'paint alla the doorjambs purple?"

"Oh, mom, they were *supposed* to be lilac."

"Looksa like a-purple t'me."

"Of course it looks like purple. Buddy didn't put enough white in the paint."

Mrs. Finzio looked at me like something she'd just stepped in. "Say, you a-color blind?"

"Uh, no. I..."

"You wanna 'nother pork a-chop?" she interrupted and shoved the serving platter under my nose. On it were two more remnants of what had obviously been a very small and sickly pig. And I felt genuinely sorry for that pig, seeing as how his earthly remains had been lovingly oven-roasted until they had roughly the same color, density and moisture content as petrified wood. Julie's mom smiled grandly as she dropped one onto my plate with a hollow *'clink!'*

Julie's mom was not exactly what you would call a great cook. She was more or less out of that old stew-meat school of culinary art that believes the longer you cook something, the tenderer and tastier and freer of harmful germs and bacteria it is likely to become. As a result, most of the meat served on the back porch of mom Finzio's apartment tasted like it had died of old age and then been left out in the desert for maybe a month or two to properly dehydrate before being cooked, plated up and served. And don't even get me started on the fish she served on Friday nights. She had a way of cooking *calamari* so it'd wear the edges off your teeth just trying to chew it. Although I'm sure it did wonders for your jaw muscles. And every once in a while—only on very special occasions, mind you—she'd buy a whole fresh flounder or halibut from the fishmonger over on Maple Avenue and proudly cook it up *"the way my momma useta do inna the old country."* Which, I can only assume, involved about six cloves of garlic and a blowtorch. But other nights we had some pretty decent pasta and gravy and meatballs or sausage and peppers to go with it. Those would be the nights my mom sent some over in a bowl covered with tinfoil.

To tell the truth, it was a little difficult getting used to living in the same few rooms with Julie's mom. She had a way of looking at me like you might look at a child molester or maybe the last surviving member of the Donner party. And I was *always* in the way. *"Hey! You with the feet! I gotta vacuum there!"* she'd screech, aiming her absolute favorite home appliance directly under wherever I might happen to be sitting or standing. But the worst of it was in bed at night with Julie. I mean, there she'd be. Right next to me. So close I could feel her breath on my neck and the warmth of her body all up and down beside me. And I knew she could feel *me* there, too. But of course as soon as she felt it, she'd kind of pull away and whisper: *"Ssshh. She'll hear us."*

Well, personally, I didn't think that would be such a bad thing. In fact, the louder and more athletic, the better. With maybe even some jungle grunts and a Tarzan yell or two thrown in right there at the end. But of course Julie wouldn't have any part of it. Not with her mom right there in the next room, most likely with her ear jammed into a water glass right up against the wall.

Things were going somewhat better over at the Sinclair. Of course Old Man Finzio had fired Butch while I was gone. More than once, in fact. But I got that all patched back together pretty easily (in fact, what with his doctor's appointments and all, I got the feeling Old Man Finzio really didn't care too much about the station anymore except as a place where he could go be mean and ornery in familiar surroundings), and I really counted on Butch to order parts and handle the phones and keep a close eye on my honest, hardworking, but generally inept and ignorant hayseed mechanic from Dubuque, Iowa, Raymond Tuttle. Not to mention his sawed-off parts runner brother, Tater Tuttle, who generally showed up around noon most days in his clattering, oil-devouring Crosley station wagon with his howling, oversexed hound-dog Barney in the back seat, a big, toothy grin on his face, pool cue calluses on his fingers, and a leaden beer hangover simmering under that enormous red pompadour hairdo of his. I swear, it looked like a chestnut-colored duck making a nest over his forehead.

But we all did our jobs and got along fairly well (at least if you discounted the occasional harsh words and threats of bodily harm that pretty much come with the territory whenever you've got mechanics working around each other in a car shop) so long as Old Man Finzio kept his cursing and muttering over in his usual position behind the cash register in the office. But I was glad to have him around in the late afternoon and early evening when people came to pick their cars up. If you run an automobile repair business, you are destined to have upset and dissatisfied customers just as surely as the Statue of Liberty shows her backside to Manhattan. It's part of the game. And Old Man Finzio was genuine World Class when it came to dealing with those kinds of people. And I was just the opposite.

So I'd generally stand there hemming and hawing and feeling guilty as hell when one of our fine, upstanding customers with a clapped-out, six-year-old Nash and nothing but lint in his pockets wanted to know exactly *why* his blessed carburetor needed rebuilding *just one week* after we'd got done relining his brakes (and which, by the way, his brother-in-law and the guy who picks up garbage on his block both assured him he got charged double for), and I'd now and then even catch myself cutting the guy a bit of a deal. But not Old Man Finzio. He was a block of solid granite. "Lissen here, Bub," he'd sneer, "I don't need yer damn bidness and I'm not so damn sure I even *want* yer damn bidness, but you asked us t'fix that damn car of yers an' that's exactly what we did. Now yew can cough up the cash now an' drive it home or yew can come back tomorrow and pay a storage fee on top of the repair bill. Fitty cents a day. It says so right there." And then he'd jerk his thumb back towards the faded cardboard sign above the girlie calendar that said as much. If things were going really right, Tater's old hound dog Barney would be right there at the Old Man's knee, growling and baring his teeth and looking menacing as hell. "Hey," he'd add with a sarcastic grin, "this is a free country. Yew can pick and choose never t'come back here again iff'n y'like. That suits us jest fine. But that's *after* y'pay us for what we already done." And then he'd pretend to have something better to do—like pick his nails, for example—and just let the guy stand there and stew there in his own juices for a while.

He always got the money. 100 cents on the dollar. Every single time.

And Old Man Finzio was just the ticket when it came to dealing with Skippy Welcher, whose doubly-dented, ex-everything XK 120M was still sitting there where he left it the night of my wedding rehearsal dinner, when I got a black eye on account of the handle came off the damn door we were tugging on and it hit me square in the kisser while depositing The Skipper ass-first in the ancient puddle of grease, Oil-Dri and antifreeze underneath the lift. He'd insisted that Big Ed was going to have to pay for fixing the pushed-in dents on both front fenders that made his Jag look like it was puckering up for a kiss, on account of they happened when he and Big Ed went into turn two at Thompson Raceway side-by-side and way too fast on account of they were both too damn stubborn to back off. So Skippy's Jag kind of slid up into the haybales the armband people had wisely put along the guardrail and Big Ed's Jag kind of slid up into Skippy's car in a kind of motorized pincer movement. In any case, I had Raymond drive it over to the Greek's body shop with Tater trailing along behind in his mosquito-abatement Crosley to bring him back and I guessed we'd worry about who was going to pay for it after it was done.

We had it back on Wednesday morning and it looked pretty decent—the Greek did really nice work, even if it was mostly putty and filler—and sure enough, as if by mental telepathy, The Skipper dropped by that very afternoon to pick it up. I'd kind of explained the situation to Old Man Finzio, and I could see a glint of sadistic pleasure flicker up in his grim old eyes as he mulled it over. "Yew go hide in the damn bathroom," he advised me as The Skipper clambered out of the Mk. V Jaguar sedan Milton Fitting was chauffeuring him around in and headed for the office door. *"And don't come out, see?"* he called after me.

So I watched the whole scene unfold through the crack in the bathroom door. And naturally it started with The Skipper pulling himself up in that aggressive little banty-rooster posture of his—shoulders cocked, eyes narrowed, lower jaw jutted out like the hood ornament on a Pontiac—and demanded his keys.

"Why, sure thing," Old Man Finzio agreed through a jagged smile. "But that'll be a hunnert and seventy-five dollars first."

The Greek had only charged us a hundred and ten.

Right away The Skipper's face started twitching and popping like pea soup coming to a boil. *"What??!!"* he screamed. *"It's Baumstein's fault! HE'S paying for it!"*

"Don't much care who pays for it," Old Man Finzio explained like he was hardly even paying attention. "All I know is that *somebody* better cough up a hunnert and seventy-five dollars or that fancy English sports car of yers sits right where it is."

"Where's that Palumbo kid?" Skippy wailed, his face turning a glorious beet-red. *"He'll tell you how it is!"*

Old Man Finzio kind of leaned across the counter so they were nose-to-nose and eyeball-to-eyeball. "I don't think yew unnerstand how things are around here, Mister Skippidee," the Old Man said slowly and evenly. "This here is *MY* gas station, see? Not nobody else's. And of all the things we do and don't do around here, the one thing we don't *never* do is give work away free for nothing...."

The Skipper was about deep purple by now.

"....and we don't take no checks and we don't extend no credik and no car *ever* leaves the proppity until the bill is paid, see? In full."

"BUT I TELL YOU BAUMSTEIN'S PAYING FOR IT!" Skippy shrieked, his usual-issue splatter of saliva flying off in all directions.

Old Man Finzio drew back just far enough to wipe off the end of his nose with a shop rag. It left an enormous grease smear right above his nostril. "Like I said," he repeated, "I don't much care who pays for it."

"I'll get my lawyer!" The Skipper screamed, shaking his fist in the air.

"Hey, he can pay for it too, if he likes. Don't make no difference t'me."

Skippy clenched up his fists and for a moment I thought he was going to hit Old Man Finzio, but right on cue, old Barney came up off the floor like he was shot from a cannon and took up his usual position right next to Old Man Finzio's thigh, growling ominously with his teeth bared and the hackles raised all up and down his back.

"Y'oughta know we charge storage for cars left on the proppity after we finish with 'em," the Old Man added calmly. "Fitty cents a day until it gets picked up."

Barney growled a little louder. Just for emphasis, you know?

The Skipper couldn't do much but just stand there, fists still clenched, looking back and forth furtively between Old Man Finzio and the dog. *"W-we'll just see about this!"* he sputtered, then spun on his heels and stalked out.

After the door of the Jag sedan closed behind him, I came out of the john and congratulated Old Man Finzio. "That was fabulous," I told him with genuine admiration.

"Hah! You jest let me deal with that jerk," the Old Man chuckled as Skippy's Mk. V disappeared down Pine Street.

"But what if you're off, uhh, you know, getting one of your treatments?" I asked.

"I ain't goin' nowhere till this mess is done with. It's the best God Damn medicine there is!"

Later on that afternoon, who should walk into the office but my sister Mary Frances. I hadn't seen her since the wedding party when I found her crying out on the curb because she'd gotten herself knocked up by that jerkoff/egghead N.Y.U. professor Oliver Cromwell creep with the enormous brainpan and condescending attitude and novels written in Esperanto for the benefit of generations yet unborn. In one way, it was nice to see that she finally saw through the layers of brilliance and accumulated knowledge to the vain, posturing, arrogant, bullshitting two-bit asshole of a human being at their core, but the bad part was that the news had come along a tad late and now she had one hell of a problem on her hands. You could see she'd been crying again—or maybe "still" would be more like it—but she'd hit that kind of lull in the storm women get to when they're all cried out and a sullen state of low-voltage anguish takes over.

"What am I going to do, Buddy?" she said like she was ordering dry toast.

"It'll work out," I told her half-heartedly. I mean, I really wanted to *help* her, you know? But I couldn't see an easy way out any more than she could. "What does old Oliver have to say?" It made me wince to say his name.

She sputtered a little first, like she was maybe going to start blubbering again. *"Don't you even mention him again!"* she finally spit out, leveling her eyes at me like a pair of howitzers. But I knew she was really just furious at him and I happened to be in the line of fire. And I figured it was stuff that had to be said, you know? I mean, being pregnant is really a two-person sort of a problem. Or at least it ought to be. And that's when I saw my sister look down and kind of wrap her fingers across her middle and realized that it's really a *three*-person sort of a problem. That hadn't really occurred to me before.

So I took a deep breath and tried again. "Look, Mary Frances, you're gonna have to figure out what you want to do here. You can't just sit here like a chicken nesting on the railroad tracks and wait for the damn train to run over you. You gotta *do* something."

I could see the tears welling up in her eyes again. *"Oh, I know...."* She said miserably.

"Do mom and dad know?"

She shook her head.

"Anybody else?"

She swallowed hard and choked back the tears. "Just one of the other girls at the apartment, I think. I didn't actually tell her. Not in so many words. But I think she knows."

"And what about Ollie? Even though we agree he's a full-fledged, card-carrying creep, you gotta decide what you want to do about him. You sure he's the father?"

She fixed me with a withering stare.

"Well, OK then. If he's the father, he ought to have some sort of responsibility here. I think it's even the law or something."

She set her jaw. "I never want to see that rat-bastard again. Not as long as I live."

"Yeah, I know. But I think you still gotta consider what *he* wants to do."

"Oh, *he* wants me to have it," she wailed, sparks showering out of her eyes.

"You mean he wants to get married?"

"Oh, no. Not old Ollie. He just wants me to have it."

"Just like that? Just *have* it?" Boy, I wanted to catch that guy in a dark alley someplace. In fact, maybe even not so dark. So he could see what he had coming, you know?

"Oh, sure. All his big political heroes have illegitimate babies running around all over the place. And all of his famous damn writers and artists and poets and philosophers do, too. He said even Ben Franklin."

"Ben Franklin? You mean *the* Ben Franklin? Are you *sure?"* It sounded somehow, I don't know, *sacrilegious* or something.

"Um-hum," Mary Frances nodded. "That's what Ollie says, anyway. He says a woman should feel *honored* to carry and care for one of his children. To—how did the rat-bastard put it?—*'to help perpetuate an exceptional gene pool.'* He says it's his duty to have children with as many different—oh, what did he call them?—*'suitable partners'* as he can."

It occurred to me that broad daylight would do just fine. I could see poor Mary Frances was getting herself ready to cry again, but there just wasn't anything left.

"So," I asked finally, "what're you gonna do?"

Mary Frances looked me right in the eyes, and it was like seeing a terrible storm brewing on the horizon that you know is heading your way. "God in heaven, I swear I don't have any idea," she moaned softly. "I really don't want a baby now. Not any baby. I mean, how the heck would I take care of it? Where would I live? At home? Oh, that would really be a bed of roses, wouldn't it? And especially not *his* baby. The world sure doesn't need any more arrogant, half-assed, rat-bastard jerks that think they're smarter than everybody else."

"Yeah," I said without thinking, "but it's yours, too…."

"Oh, I know," she wailed, her fingers tightening around her middle. And then she started to cry again. *"That's the awful part,"* she sobbed. *"The awful, awful, awful part."* I put my arm around her shoulders and I could feel the ache and pain and anguish shuddering right through her and seeping into me. No matter what happened, it was going to be awful and terrible and there was just no getting around it. I remember feeling terribly old and sad and clumsy and stupid. And I knew I had to say something to her—had to *do* something for her!— and yet I had no idea what.

"Don't worry," I said lamely, "I'll help you…."

She looked up at me again, a faint wisp of hope passing across her eyes even as the tears streamed down her cheeks. "Help me what?" she asked.

"Well, you know," I kind of mumbled, not meeting her eyes, "help you with, you know, whatever you decide to do."

Neither of us were going to say it out loud, you know?

3: Getting Back up to Speed

Needless to say, Julie wasn't real thrilled with the notion of me taking off with my racing buddies—er, *business customers*—for the SCMA's Mount Equinox Hillclimb just a week after we got back from our honeymoon. In fact, you could say she was just a wee bit annoyed. At least if the stomping, screaming, sparks showering out of her eyeballs and flying crockery were anything to go by. I mean, it's not like she didn't understand that I had to take care of our best customers. Lord knows if I didn't, old Hugo Two just 20 minutes down the road would be only too happy to. And I told her as much.

"Hmpf," she snorted. *"You're just running off to have a good time."*

So I tried to explain to her as how slaving away in the dirt and grease underneath assorted broken Jaguars and MGs was hard work. And long hours, too. And could I help it if there might be just a little fun and excitement and eating and drinking and partying and silly paddock pranks and telling of great, inflated-until-the-seams-leaked racing stories thrown in? It just wasn't my fault that race weekends were fun. I mean, *I* couldn't help it.

"You must figure you married the dumbest frickin' girl in New Jersey," was Julie's general response. *"And if you think I'm gonna sit here at home every frickin' weekend while you go run around with all your supposedly high-class racing pals..."*

"But Julie," I said in a tone so soothing it could have been an Arthur Godfrey laxative commercial, "I want you to start coming with me, Honey. These aren't just *my* customers, they're *our* customers. They're our *future,* see?"

"Yeah, I see. I see me sitting on my ass all by myself all day while you talk carburetor parts and a bunch of fancy European sports cars run around in circles. It sounds just dreamy."

"But we'll be *together,* see?"

To be honest, I couldn't see it either. I mean, Julie was dead right that sporty-car racing was mostly a guy-type thing. Oh, a few of the drivers brought their wives along. Or, more likely, their girlfriends. Or maybe their wives one weekend and their girlfriends the next. But the point is that there really isn't all that much to do or be involved in at a racetrack unless you're actually participating—either as a driver or, like me, as one of the support people who do all the grunt work while the drivers talk about that new, fuel-injected 300SL sports car from Mercedes-Benz with the outer-space gullwing doors or discuss tire pressures and lines through the corners or just stand around admiring themselves. Oh, the girl-friends try to make a good show of being interested and hanging on every word—hey, these racer guys are generally stinking rich and those girlfriends have their future alimony checks to think about—but if you take the time to make a serious inventory of the wives, most of them are bored stiff. Hey, if you're not bitten by the bug, a race weekend can seem pretty damn dull and pointless. In fact, racing is probably about as interesting and attractive to those bored-looking wives as interior decorating is to their husbands. Speaking of which:

"And what about *this* place?" Julie wailed, sweeping her hand around the still-unfinished downstairs apartment with the purple doorjambs and window trim and the un-sanded Spackle patches on the bathroom walls and the incredibly-oversized chandelier we got out of my Aunt Rosamarina's garage that she wanted to hang over the dining room table that we still had to get out of my Aunt Rosamarina's garage but couldn't until after I rented a sander and refinished the wood floor she'd decided she had her heart set on refinishing—Lord only knows why—before she put new carpet down. But I knew better than to argue with Julie when it came to fixing up our new apartment. Or almost any other subject, come to that. Plus there was a method to my madness, since I knew the longer I strung things out the new apartment project, the longer we could still find ourselves every so often over at my old, empty pup-tent of an apartment over my Aunt Rosamarina's garage. Like I said, there was nothing but the bed, sink, commode and shower stall in there any more. Oh, and no one listening on the other side of the wall through a water glass, either.

"Look, Honey," I told her in the most reasonable voice since Satan offered Eve that apple, "I just gotta take care of my guys at the races if we're ever going to make a success out of this business. And if we do, we'll be making the kind of money where we can have our very own house one day. Not some downstairs apartment in a duplex. And we'll be able to fix it up any blessed way you want." I was starting to discover that this was a *very* powerful line of reasoning as far as the female of the species was concerned.

"Any way I want?" she kind of sniffed.

"Absolutely," I assured her.

"Even if I want purple doorjambs?"

"Even if you want purple doorjambs."

"Oh, Buddy," she smiled and buried her head against my shoulder, "It's just I want to be settled in, you know? Not scattered all over the place like we are now. And I hate the idea of you being gone all the time."

"It's not all the time," I whispered into her hair. "It's just this weekend at Mount Equinox and next weekend at Callicoon…."

Julie froze rigid in my arms. *"You mean you're gone fricking NEXT weekend, too??!!"*

Big Ed picked me up well before dawn Saturday morning for the drive up to Vermont, and it felt really good to be on the road again and on our way to another race weekend. In fact, I think that's a lot of the magic, right up there with the speed and noise and parties and exotic cars and succulent-looking girlfriends. Race weekends are like an escape hatch from real life. No matter what's been gnawing at you or who's been screaming at you or how many things you've got to do that are still undone, from the moment you hit the road, it's like you're prisoner of this brand new adventure and, best of all, helpless to do anything about it. Worried about living just the thickness of the floorboards beneath your she-devil witch of a mother-in-law? Worried about your knocked-up sister and her egghead, know-it-all, worthless jerk of an ex-boyfriend? Worried about all those damn cars you gotta fix and doorjambs you gotta repaint? Hey, might as well not worry about it, chum. There's not a thing you can do about any of it until you get back on the treadmill of Real Life come Monday morning. So you might as well enjoy your freedom while you've got it, 'cause it ain't gonna last very long. And it's amazing how quickly all those "Real Life" problems and people and commitments get left behind in the growling, slightly-rich exhaust wake of a sweet-running XK 120 with a fresh, sharp tune job and brand new synchros in the tranny.

"So, how's married life, kid?" Big Ed asked over the engine noise and gear whine and the wind whipping in over the windshield.

"Oh, it's okay," I told him. "It just takes a little getting used to."

He laughed. "Well, you let me know if you ever do get used to it, Buddy. I never did."

"Not ever?" I mean, Big Ed had gone through quite a collection of wives.

"Nah. I don't think so. Not even the first time. It's like women and men are made out of different kinds of material."

For sure that was something I was beginning to see and understand myself. "You can say that again," I told him.

"See, women got this screwy nesting instinct. They want to make up a nice home and have it sink its roots right down deep into the ground so's it's anchored solid in one place."

I could see that already.

"But men like t'_run_, see?"

"Like run away?"

"Nah. It doesn't have to be 'away.' Doesn't have to be particularly 'to' anything, either. It's just enough to keep moving. To have some horizon t'chase or some direction you think you need to travel."

"So what happens?"

"In my case," Big Ed grinned, unwrapping his first fat Cuban stogie of the day, "divorce and alimony payments." He leaned isortclose behind the steering wheel to light it out of the wind. It took several tries, and we damn near collected an early morning egg-delivery truck in the process. _"STUPID SONO-FABITCH!"_ Big Ed hollered around his cigar while shaking his fist at the poor truck driver, who was all flailing arms and elbows just trying to keep his load of eggs out of the ditch. That was always the scary thing about riding with Big Ed. He drove like the highways of this country were his own private driveway, and everybody else on them were merely uninvited guests. "Anyhow," he continued without skipping a beat, "maybe you'll do better at it than I did."

I sure hoped so.

We stopped for gas and breakfast at a nice little roadside place just outside of Hartford, and I worried over a big plate of bacon and eggs and hash browns with pancakes and maple syrup on the side as to whether I should bring up the subject of my knocked-up sister Mary Frances? Of course I'd promised I wouldn't say anything to anybody under pain of instant death, but the truth is I'd already made a few inquiries around the shop and around town. Just to see if I could come up with anything in case Mary Frances decided to pull the ripcord and get rid of it. And—God strike me square in the forehead with one of those heavy, smelly incense things the priests sling around during Mass—I kind of hoped she would. I mean, I'd had visions of what it would be like for her if she just had the baby, and it was a genuine Life Sentence with no hope of pardon or parole for either her _or_ the baby. At least not in our neighborhood, anyway. And the only other thing she could do was maybe go away someplace and have it and then either give it up—and, if I knew Mary Frances, she could never do that once she had it all tiny and squealing and needy in her hands—or keep it and maybe come back in a few years like the imaginary husband she'd eloped with had been run over by a beer truck or died of a hernia or ran off with a hat-check girl or something.

It was a delicate sort of problem. And of course everybody you asked wanted to know right away who the leading man and leading lady of the soap opera drama might be, and, what with me being just married to Julie and all, a lot of them assumed I'd had some little side deal going on that decided to bear fruit at a most inopportune time. But I let them. Hey, it was better than letting on about Mary Frances. Because once something like that gets out, it's all over the fences and back porches and driveways and breezeways and fire escapes of our neighborhood in a matter of days. If not hours.

The other problem was strictly a medical one. Or medical and financial, anyway. When you ask around about something as hush-hush and delicate as this, you want to make it clear that you'd just as soon not have the girl in question laid out on the bloody, back-room chopping block of an off-duty meat butcher known for his ragged pork chops or visiting some scary-looking old gypsy fortune-teller lady with long fingernails and a straightened piece of coat hanger wire. But, at the same time, you want to intimate that price is indeed a consideration and that, hey, you're probably the guy who's gonna wind up paying for it and it's sure to be a long, long time—maybe never—before you'll ever see any of it back.

As you can imagine, old Sylvester came through with the name of some genuine medical doctor (no matter what the state of New York said about his license) who might be able to help out at a reasonable price. But he was a black guy up in Harlem and I wasn't real comfortable with that. I knew Mary Frances wouldn't be, either, in spite of all that "fellow traveler" stuff those pinko eggheads she hung around with in Greenwich Village talked such a great fight about. And of course Tater knew a topnotch veterinarian who moonlighted out of the back tournament room of a pool hall and bar over in Bayonne—hey, there was plenty of room and the lighting was good—but it kind of put me off that he occasionally charged admission for the gallery seats as a way to drum up a little extra cash.

So, after breakfast, riding along on a full tank and full bellies and with a nice, clear sky and warm summer sun over our heads, I finally got around to asking Big Ed if he knew anyplace where a girl who'd gotten herself in trouble could go to get things, you know, "taken care of?"

He looked at me kind of sideways. "This anybody I know?"

I shrugged half-heartedly.

He kept looking at me, waiting for an answer. But I didn't say anything. Like I said, I'd kind of promised Mary Frances I wouldn't say anything to anyone. "Sure I do," Big Ed finally told me around the butt-end of his cigar. "But you better make damn sure it's what you want to do."

"Oh, it's not for *me.*"

"I didn't think it was. But, whoever it is, you'd better make damn sure it's what whoever it is wants to do. It's a pretty big deal you're talkin' about." I knew Big Ed was dying to know who it was, but he was a good enough kind of pal not to ask.

"It's my sister," I blurted out.

"Sarah Jean?" Big Ed knew all about her deal with that flashy, wiseass kid whose family ran that trucking company in Jersey City.

"No, the other one. Mary Frances."

"With that phony college-professor type you were telling me about?"

I nodded.

Big Ed let out a low whistle. "You sure don't want him for an in-law, do you."

I shook my head. "He doesn't want to do the right thing by her anyway. And she doesn't want anything to do with him anymore, either."

"Well, I suppose that's a good thing," Big Ed allowed. "And you really don't want to see a young girl screw up her whole damn life over one mistake."

"No, you don't," I agreed.

"But it's a big thing, Buddy. Getting rid of it is no problem...."

"It isn't?"

Big Ed shook his head. "Nah. I can set you up to have it done in a regular doctor's office on Park Avenue if you want. First class all the way."

"You *can?*"

"Sure I can. Piece of cake...."

Boy, that was a relief.

"...but there's usually a lot more involved than you see on the surface."

"There is?"

Big Ed nodded. "Stuff like that runs deep and lasts forever, Buddy. You gotta be careful when you start messing around with life and death and female hormones and mothering instincts and all that sort of shit. It's unbelievably complicated. And it generally doesn't make any sense, either. And the worst of it is—whatever you do—it lasts for fucking *ever!*"

It sounded like Big Ed had some past experience where this sort of thing was concerned.

"But how much does it *cost?*" I asked, finally getting down to the real brass tacks of it.

"Don't worry about it," Big Ed told me. "I got a lotta favors I can call in. A lotta favors. You won't have t'worry about the money part. I can see to it for you. No problem." And that was the kind of guy Big Ed was. Oh, he could be loud and pushy and most times things were either gonna be *his* way or no way at all, but he truly enjoyed using his clout and dollars to help people out here and there. At least if he liked them. In fact, it was almost like you were doing *him* a favor just letting him do something nice for you. Sure, he maybe did it because it made him feel like a big shot, but I think you should judge people more by what they actually *do* than by what made them want to do it. Hell, the world's chock-full of people with all these grand ideas and noble intentions who don't do shit. Like that Oliver Cromwell character, for starters. He was a First Prize shithead if there ever was one. In fact, I was tempted to ask Big Ed about what other kinds of far-side-of-the-law friends he might have and what other sort of favors he could call in. I mean, it's not unheard of in even respectable Italian social circles for a gentleman who has taken unlicensed liberties with a young daughter to be found in an alley one morning with a few extra ventilation holes in his head and the rats dining on his private parts in a nearby trashcan.

Mount Equinox sits on the outskirts of Manchester, Vermont, in some of the prettiest New England countryside you'd ever want to see. It's a full 3,848 feet to the top—a genuine mountain—and I read someplace that it's actually the tallest one in the whole Taconic range. But the most amazing thing is that one single human being owned it. Owned the whole blessed mountain, can you believe it? His name was Joseph George Davidson, and he was a real, live Ph.D. chemistry wizard who came out of college just before World War One and got drafted by the government to help develop the mustard gas they'd let drift over the enemy's trenches to scorch their eyes and burn their lungs out. Only trouble was the wind would change every now and then and blow the stuff back over our trenches and scorch our own guys' eyes and burn our own guys' lungs out. So it wasn't the most loyal sort of weapon you could imagine. Later on, this Joseph George Davidson character spent some time down in Oak Ridge, Tennessee, helping develop the enriched plutonium they needed to make the atom bombs we dropped on Hiroshima and Nagasaki at the end of World War Two. And, while all this was going on, he found time to patent (or at least get hold of the patents) for a whole bunch of chemical formulas and go to work for Union Carbide, where he proved a tough and shrewd and ambitious enough egg to rise up through the ranks and become a vice-president and then Chairman of the Board. Plus, like most of your major industrial bigwigs, he was involved in a whole other bunch of other companies and committees and boards of directors and whatnot. So this Joseph George Davidson was one rich, powerful guy.

He was also something of a recluse, I guess, because he bought himself this whole blessed mountain in Vermont and built himself a few secluded houses on it where he and his wife and his dog could go to get away from it all. And of course he had to build himself a road to get up to those houses of his, and the one he built was a real lulu. In fact, it was so scenic and well-built and handsome that he put a damn tollbooth at the bottom of it and charged admission just to drive up to the summit. And the rubbernecking tourists lined up in droves. Like I said, this Davidson guy was a pretty sharp cookie. The road ran a full 5.2 miles from the tollbooth to the summit, and it was nothing but curves and switchbacks and hairpin bends the entire way—climbing steeply uphill all the time—and it was all green forest and smooth, perfectly laid blacktop and breathtaking overlooks and running along ridges where you could see four whole states and, if you squinted hard enough, damn near all the way to the Atlantic Ocean.

So it was one pretty impressive stretch of road. Not to mention that there were some fine and fancy old hotels down around the bottom where generations of snooty, upper-crust rich folks came to sip tea and the occasional nip of Scotch after a day of hiking or golfing or fishing or horseback riding or fooling around with somebody else's wife or daughter in the cool, clean mountain air. And so it was just the sort of place for the snooty, upper-crust young regulars of the SCMA to host a hillclimb. And so they did.

Now I'd been to the Giant's Despair hillclimb in Wilkes-Barre, PeeAy, the year before with my perpetually-broke rich buddy Cal Carrington (after an all-night drive through the Pocono Mountains in a torrential rainstorm with me sitting right square on the soggy floorboards of Cal's raggedy, stripped-down-to-nothing '47 MG TC with no top or windshield!), and so I figured I knew a thing or two about hillclimbing. Especially since, thanks to Cal, I'd even gotten a run up that hill at Giant's Despair myself. Nevermind that I blew the engine sky-high just getting ready to launch it from the starting line for my second try. Hey, stuff like that happens in the world of competitive motorsports. And the oil pressure hadn't been anything special all weekend, either. But I felt bad about it, because I was in the car when it happened (which made it somehow my fault, even if I didn't do anything wrong), plus I really thought Cal was some kind of Super Talent when it came to wheeling sports cars around—and he was—and I hated the idea that I'd somehow cost him his ride. Even if it was about the saddest, sorriest, strung-together-with-baling-wire-and-spittest MG TC racecar in all of North America. And maybe the world.

So I'd done my best to talk Cal up around the rest of the sportycar crowd and tried to help land him a few rides here and there to kind of nudge his career along. Although it took an awful lot of imagination to think you could have any kind of "career" in sports car racing. Especially here in the States, where it was all so devoutly amateur and really more a place for preening, silver-spoon-up-the-ass idiots like Skippy Welcher and Charlie Priddle to while away their time pretending to be heroes than a major professional blood sport. Oh, if you had a ton of talent and got some lucky breaks, you could maybe get expenses and a little extra on the side (or under the table) driving for guys like Ernesto Julio, the rich winery owner from Sonoma, California, who absolutely loved sports car racing, always got his hands on the very latest and fastest new Ferrari racing cars and, unlike Big Ed, never once visualized himself as the best guy to put behind the wheel. Or even next-best. And if you got *really* lucky and all the stars and planets lined up just so, you could maybe get a ride with Briggs Cunningham (or maybe even one of the legit factory teams from England or Italy or Germany) and go racing over in Europe, where they don't look down their noses at money—not hardly!—and, instead of demanding club memberships and entry fees, the promoters even pay "starting money" to the featured entrants just for showing up.

And that's what my buddy Cal wanted. More than anything else in the world, in fact. I remember the night we were sitting on the front porch together at some cabin out in the woods someplace on a race weekend—I think it might have been at Giant's Despair—and he told me as much. *"This is what I've gotta do with my life, Buddy,"* he said in the most desperate and serious voice I'd ever heard out of him. *"It's the only thing I've ever been any good at...."*

And he *was* good at it. Which is why I helped him con Carson Flegley into offering him a run up Giant's Despair in Carson's brand new, shiny-black TD (he took fastest time in the stock MG class, natch), and also arranged him that ride in a Ford Flathead-powered MG up at Elkhart Lake that damn near killed him and a newspaper photographer both when it ran flush out of brakes. What I really hoped was that somehow, someday, I could talk Big Ed into kind of stepping gracefully aside and letting Cal have a run in his Jaguar. Or, better yet, that year-old Ferrari Javier Premal drove over the cliff in Mexico (just as I was in the process of bailing out of it, in fact!) and that was now, according to perpetually-smiling North American Ferrari importer Carlo Sebastian, back home in Italy being *"fully rebuilt, better than new"* by *"genuine factory technicians."*

Only I got the feeling we wouldn't be seeing that car anytime soon, on account of there was some gentlemanly difference of opinion about who actually owned the car and was therefore responsible for repair costs at the precise moment it went off that cliff in Mexico (or, more precisely, when it came to rest upside-down with a crushing, metal-rending, glass-shattering *THH-WUNCK!!!* only a few moments later), and it has been my experience that rebuilding jobs of this nature tend to fall to the bottom of the pile, priority-wise, at repair shops from Memphis to Montauk to Maranello. Hey, it's just smart business, you know? So every time Big Ed got hold of Carlo Sebastian's ear and asked him what was going on with "his" Ferrari, he got more long-playing operatic bullshit, complete with sweeping finger-pictures in the air, about what a careful and conscientious job those highly-skilled and experienced craftsmen over in Italy were doing trying to re-inflate Big Ed's wonderful, thoroughbred Ferrari coupe—the teammate and exact twin of the car that had won *La Carrera* in 1951!—which had so unfortunately been flattened like a dropped eggplant against the bottom of that canyon in Mexico.

Oh, I figured it would all work out eventually. Carlo was as shrewd, sly, shifty, slick and slippery as they come, but he was no way an out-and-out thief. He was way too suave and continental for that kind of thing. So, sooner or later, he'd either have to cough up the car—hey, *nobody* wants to total out a Ferrari that costs more than most people's houses!—or explain as how those ace factory technicians over in Maranello had come across some previously undiagnosed misalignment of the frame members or destabilization of the drive train that made the car unrepairable and give Big Ed his deposit money back. Less maybe a small holdback fee for the transatlantic shipping and a little overpriced shop-floor rental over in Italy. But the key word here was "eventually," and the longer Carlo Sebastian could string it out with fluff and fairy stories, the longer it would be before either he or his best south-of-the-border customer, *"Poco Loco"* Premal, would have to put pen to paper and sign a check with a lot of zeroes to the left of the decimal point. It was a check neither of them really wanted to write....

But, either way—Jag *or* Ferrari—I wanted to see Cal Carrington get a shot one time in a really decent car. And Big Ed looked like a likely sucker for the job. If I could only talk him into it. Problem was, in spite of all the evidence to the contrary (and there was by now a whole, heaping pile of it), Big Ed still had this notion that he could be a racing driver—hey, he had the helmet, goggles and imported, string-backed driving gloves to prove it!—and the last thing anybody in that frame of mind wants to do is step aside and let somebody quicker get behind the wheel and show him up. It was bad enough when he co-drove his Jag at Sebring with Sammy Speed—Sammy ran rings around him—but at least Sammy was a legit professional with an established reputation on the AAA oval tracks for being skillful, seasoned, tough and fearless. To let some inexperienced, smooth-cheeked rich kid behind the wheel to do the exact same thing would be pretty tough on Big Ed's ego. And, like most racers, Big Ed had one of your giant, economy-sized egos. Also like most racers, it bruised easily and didn't heal up real quick at all.

Anyhow, we ran into Carson Flegley at the fancy old hotel Big Ed had booked us into, and, as usual, I flinched a little bit when we shook hands on account of Carson's family ran a funeral home and I was always a little nervous about where his hands might have been. But I was glad to see him, since he was a decent sort of guy in a somber, Hovering Vulture Funeral Director kind of way, not to mention a topnotch sportycar service customer who always wanted the latest, trickest, most ridiculously radical and impractical racing stuff available on his car and always paid cash on the barrelhead to boot. Plus he'd let Cal drive his car every now and then, even though Cal was a whole bunch quicker than Carson ever was. You had to be impressed with how it didn't seem to bother him. He'd just sort of stand there, looking at the time sheets or the stopwatch in his hand, and have this expression come over his face like he'd just ever-so-slightly been struck by lightning. "So, you drive up here with Cal?" I asked while we waited in line for registration under the shadow of the big, fluted columns that stood guard over the front porch of The Equinox, which was the name of that snooty and elegant old hotel on the edge of town that pretty much served as Event Headquarters for the SCMA.

"Nope, I came up alone," Carson explained. "But I've seen Cal around. He's been here a couple days already. Looking for rides as usual, I think."

"No surprise there."

"Uh-uh."

Sure enough, Cal showed up just about the time we got to the head of the line and, without even being asked in so many words, Carson put him down as a second driver. "Gee, thanks," Cal allowed while Carson forked over the second entry fee. "So," he added after Carson got his change back, "who's buying lunch?"

Well, you had to hand it to Cal. He'd overheard enough loose talk about the hillclimb at Mount Equinox and its five-point-two miles of twists and bends and hairpin switchbacks to know that it was going to take more that a check-it-out run up the course to get a handle on the place. Going fast was going to take skill and guts, of course, but going *really* fast was going to take something else. Familiarity. So he'd come up early—hitchhiked, can you believe it?—without much more than his helmet, a toothbrush, a few changes of socks and underwear, and a grand total of two dollars and forty-two cents in his pocket. Typical Cal. Even more typical, he'd made the rounds of all the fancy, old-money resort hotels and latched onto enough nose-in-the-air bluebloods who either knew him or knew his family that he ate well, drank well, slept well (albeit out on the porch one night) and still had the far side of a buck eighty in his pants pocket when we showed up just before noon on Saturday. He'd also gotten who knows how many rides up to the summit with assorted toll-paying tourists that he approached with a big, friendly grin on his face as they were waiting in line for the toll booth.

"My folks took the car this morning to go visit some friends," he'd explain through that confident, gleaming, rich-kid smile of his, "and I'd sure like to get a peek at the top of this mountain while the weather's so clear. Why, I'd even help out with the toll if I had to…."

But of course he never had to, because nobody ever asks a really wealthy person to pay for anything. Like it's some kind of blessed privilege paying for stuff for rich people, you know? And Cal had this way about him that you just *knew* he had money. Or came from money, anyway. It was *old* money, too. The kind that doesn't even crinkle when you run it over the edge of an Early American, antique maple dining-room table. From the casual, brushed-across blond flop of his hair to those faraway, icy blue eyes to the crease of his slacks to those oxblood Bass Weejun loafers that he wore with no socks and dull Lincoln pennies wedged into the slots on top, you could tell that Cal was worth millions. Even if he never quite seemed to have any of it on him....

So Cal had sneaked up for a little pre-event reconnoitering in order to give himself a bit of an edge on the off chance that he got a drive in something. Not that he let on about it to anyone but me and Carson. And we weren't supposed to tell anybody. See, the whole idea was for him to maybe score a guest run up the hill in somebody else's car and then knock everybody's socks off with how blessed fast he went. *"First time up the hill, too,"* they'd all marvel, and wonder exactly what planet he came from or what he'd eaten for breakfast that morning.

Mind you, he wasn't doing it just to con people and rub their noses in it. Okay, maybe just a little. But the important thing was to attract a little attention and maybe get some of those rich car owners to think about offering him a drive. Just to see what he could do. Only it didn't work out too well for Cal at Mount Equinox, even though he loved every inch of that serpentine, 5.2-mile charge up into the clouds and knew it better than anybody.

He just didn't have any luck.

Oh, I kept pestering Big Ed about giving him a shot in the Jag, and Big Ed kept saying *"we'll see, we'll see."* But he was saying *"we'll see"* the same way parents of young children say *"we'll see,"* which roughly translates into an equal-parts combination of "not a chance in hell" and "stop bothering me."

Cal did get in a few tries in Carson Flegley's TD and, based on the "unofficial" times for the "Practice and Familiarization" runs just after lunch on Saturday, he looked like a shoo-in for not only top MG, but top 10 overall as well. Up against the Jaguars and Allards and *everything!* But then everything went to shit. Oh, the car ran fine for Carson (once he got it up on the cam, anyway, which was probably a good 500 rpm past where he already should have shifted if he wanted the bottom end to stay together) but every single time Cal got in the car, something goofy happened. He'd take off from the start perfectly with just a polite little squeal from the right rear tire, and you could hear by the sound of the engine that he was going like blazes and carrying more speed and rpm up the hill than anybody else in an MG. Only then he had a plug wire come loose. And the next run it started overheating on account of the water pump wasn't spinning up to speed because the blessed fan belt had worked loose. All by itself, can you believe it? Turns out the adjustor nut for the generator pulley was mysteriously stripped. And then we found out Carson had tried to make himself useful by "adjusting" the belt tension when nobody was looking and maybe got a little over-zealous about tightening the nut because I'd warned him what might happen if it's not tight. The fan belt goes loose and the generator stops charging and the water pump stops pumping and the damn engine starts cooking in its own juices. Good thing Cal kept an eye on the gauges, and he pulled right over and switched it off as soon as he saw the needle climb. Just like you should. Even though he was only about three-quarters of a mile from the finish line and a likely new class record.

And what did he get for being such a gold-star Boy Scout?

A flat tire! Seems the right-rear picked up a tack or a nail or something during Carson's last run up the hill and it wasn't maybe wedged in deep enough to put a hole in the tube until Cal got behind the wheel and really started wailing on it. And then it went *BANG!* Or, more accurately, *POP-hisssssssssssssss*. And that was the end of it for Cal Carrington's final run at Mount Equinox. Not even a half-mile up the hill. Damn!

And meanwhile Big Ed and The Skipper had renewed their XK 120 rivalry somewhere around two-thirds to three-quarters of the way down the time sheets. Yep, Skippy had his car back. Had to pay cash for it, too, just like Old Man Finzio warned him he would. Only first he showed up with this supposed cop and raised all kinds of hell about how he was suing and how he was going to have the blessed building inspectors come by and close the place down for code violations (and believe me, there's no business owner in *any* decent-sized city, town or munici-pality who doesn't shiver in his socks when you say the words "building inspec-tor" or "code violations," on account of they usually run about fifty to a hundred bucks per syllable by the time it's all over). But Old Man Finzio was not about to be budged or intimidated. Especially when he noticed that The Skipper's "police-man" was actually wearing a bus driver's hat with some kind of cockamamie tin Town Sheriff badge pinned on it. Didn't even say what town, like it maybe came out of some kid's cap-pistol set like you'd find in the toy section at Woolworth's Five-and-Dime. So once he figured out that Skippy's cop was really just an off-duty security guard trying to pick up a few extra bucks, Old Man Finzio took out that sawed-off, lead-filled baseball bat with the friction tape wrapped around the handle (which was always sitting at-the-ready underneath the cash register in case he needed it), whistled for Barney, and ran them both off the property. The effort put him on a laughing-and-coughing jag that damn near killed him on the spot, but you could tell by the look in his eyes that it made him as happy as a mean, sick old fart like Old Man Finzio could ever get. He even fired up one of the bent-up Camels his doctor had forbidden him to smoke any more to celebrate. Got at least two or three good puffs out of it, too, before it started him hacking and coughing so bad that he couldn't even hang onto it and had to snuff it out.

But the point is that Skippy had his XK 120 back and he was angrier than ever at Big Ed. Which was just fine with me because, if you're going to have an enemy, a rich, nutty, never-did-a-day's-work-in-his-life asshole like The Skipper made for a really good prospect. It was just so *easy* to dislike him. And the more you got to know him, the more things about him you found to dislike. It was like strik-ing a really rich vein of gold.

And, for a variety of reasons that weren't very flattering to either one of them, Big Ed and The Skipper seemed destined to run in close company with each other damn near everywhere they went. Which is just another way of saying that neither one of them could pee a hole in the snow when it came to driving a racecar. Hell, you could see it in their eyes and the jerky, flinching, uncoordinated reflexes of their hands on the wheel. Few people on the outside really know it but, just like Tommy Edwards said when we were sitting around that deathly-quiet dinner table at the beach house near Bridgehampton the night after Eddie Dearborn got killed, racing is all about grace under pressure. That was the real heart of it. And you could see it plain as day when you watched a truly great driver like Tommy or Cal or even that stuck-up, nose-in-the-air asshole Creighton Pendleton the Third. And you could also see plain as day when it was missing. Like whenever you saw Big Ed or Skippy Welcher drive. It was like watching girls punch, you know?

Still, one of the neat things about racing is that there's always competition. Even buried way down towards the bottom of the field. Hell, if there wasn't, then you'd only have two or three Genuine Fast Guys in every race and the rest of them would sell their Jaguars, Porsches and MGs, buy a fishing rod or set of golf clubs, and find some other way to frustrate themselves over the weekends. And that's how Big Ed and The Skipper found themselves—squared off nose-to-nose (or, to be a little more accurate, nose-to-chest-hairs)—against each other damn near every place they went. Mount Equinox was no exception. On a climb that took well over six minutes for both of them, they wound up only seconds apart. And their private, blood-serious Quick Time slice of honor kept flip-flopping back and forth between them. First it was The Skipper by two seconds after their first runs. After their second runs it was Big Ed by a second. They both lowered their times again on their third runs (although, to put it in perspective, they were still mired down around the quickest TCs and TDs) with The Skipper back in front by an eyelash. And then, running true to form, they tried even harder on their final runs. The Skipper went first, and you could see by the set of his jaw and the crazed look in his eye that he was out for blood. The question, as always, was whether it would turn out to be his own blood or that of some poor, innocent bystander. Of course, being wound that tight works at pretty much cross purposes to that old "grace under pressure" thing we were talking about, and so it should come as no surprise that The Skipper got only about as far as the first hairpin switchback—a little ways out of sight up the hill, but not out of earshot—and we could all hear the screech of tortured rubber as he tried to take it in way too deep, locked up the brakes (so now he couldn't steer, either) and kind of nosed straight across into the pretty wooden guardrail Joseph George Davidson's construction crew put there to protect his mountain from idiot drivers like Skippy Welcher. It wasn't much of a wreck, really. Just some busted-up white two-by-fours and yet another XK 120 grille and bumper set for Milton Fitting to put on order and pay a left nut for when it finally arrived at Westbridge via air freight from England a couple days later. The funny part was that the Greek had just got done fixing it, and you should have seen all the damn filler, putty and chicken wire that shattered out all over the place. There must've been thirty pounds of it! Made you wonder if the Greek even owned a dolly and a body hammer.

Well, this turn of events left the door wide open for Big Ed to have a go at beating The Skipper's time and really rub it in. I mean, it was just *too* delicious! Only this gets us back to that old "grace under pressure" notion again, and no question Big Ed didn't have any, either. Oh, he didn't crash it like The Skipper did. Perish forbid. No, all Big Ed did was to hold it in first gear—hey, it accelerated better in first, right?—until the tach needle was pointing to something like 7 PM in the little electric clock Jaguar puts at the bottom of the rev counter. At which point the motor screamed *"ENOUGH!"* as one of the exhaust valves took a self-sacrificing suicide plunge into the top of one of the pistons.

So Skippy's time held up and edged out Big Ed—just barely, dammit!—and I had to once again scrounge around and beg favors and make promises of moderately-sized wads of Big Ed's cash to get his very silent Jaguar hauled back to Passaic and our own butts back as well. I wound up riding with the tow truck guy, who was some grizzled old Yankee coot with a Gabby Hayes beard that worked at a streetcorner gas station in Manchester and was only too happy to pick up such an unexpected windfall on a late Sunday afternoon. Especially since his sister's six-year-old daughter that he couldn't stand and that couldn't stand him either was having a birthday party, and this represented a great reason not to show up or buy a present. "Oh, they'll be mad and they won't invite me over for dinner for awhile," he chuckled. "But that's just fine with me, boy. I don't like them and they don't like me, and they only do it because I'm family and they figger they have to, see?"

Families. Oh, yeah, I'd almost forgot.

Like I said, that's the *real* magic of a race weekend....

Naturally it was a major thrash to get Big Ed's engine repaired in time for the Callicoon race out in Sullivan County the following weekend, but it was being put on by the New Jersey Sports Car Club, who hadn't been nearly as rude to him as the SCMA regulars over across the bridge in Manhattan (they'd even let him come to meetings, so long as he told entertaining lies about his adventures at *La Carrera* and the Twelve Hours of Sebring and bought lots of drinks), and so he figured he had to go. Besides, he'd heard there was going to be an all-Jaguar race, which meant he at least wouldn't be embarrassed by the quicker MGs for a change.

Personally, I didn't see where I could find the time to get everything done. I mean, what with Big Ed's engine and the painting and refinishing work that never seemed to get painted or finished at the new apartment and showing up for dinner with Julie's mother damn near every night so's she wouldn't feel slighted (even if I was gonna just turn around and head back to the shop to work on Big Ed's cylinder head or downstairs to put on or strip off another coat of paint or varnish) plus all my regular car-mechanic work, I felt like I was spinning around in circles with one foot nailed to the floor. It's a pretty desperate sort of sensation, believe me. And the worst of it is that you're so damn tired and your circuits are so damn overloaded that you can't sleep even when you get the chance. You lay down in bed and close your eyes and all you can see on the inside of your eyelids is all the stuff you gotta do as soon as you get up again. It's like a head-on view of a screaming Stuka dive bomber aimed straight at the back of your skull!

The beauty part, even though you never see it at the time, is that this strange sort of zombie-like autopilot kicks in, and if you just keep shuffling along and putting one foot in front of the other, somehow, some way, everything gets done. Or maybe it doesn't. The important thing is that you really don't give a good God damn anymore.

But sometimes things come up that snap you right out of it. Like when my sister Mary Frances called me at the Sinclair and said she wanted to see me. I remember her voice sounded like it was a million miles away. "You wanna come over and maybe have lunch?" I asked. "We could go right across to the sandwich shop."

"No," she said like she was staring off into space, "I just need to see you. It'll only take a minute."

"When d'you wanna come?"

"I can be there in a couple minutes if it's okay?"

"Where are you? Home?"

"No. I haven't been home. I'm at the pay phone at the grocery store around the corner." She sounded like maybe she was gonna start crying again.

"C'mon over," I told her, but she'd already hung up.

I noticed right away that Mary Frances was wearing one of Sarah Jean's dresses—one of those shapeless, unflattering, dark blue numbers that remind you of orthopedic shoes and Catholic girls' school—and she'd cut her hair, too. A lot like my mom's, in fact. "So?" I asked, trying my best to sound casual, "what's up?"

"Do we have to talk *here?*" Mary Frances rasped in a desperate whisper.

"Uh, no. A'course not. Uhh..." I looked every which way around the shop, "...why don't you step into my private office?"

I took her into the alley out back. Behind the sad, broken cars waiting for service. "So, what's on your mind?"

She looked down at the purse in her hand. It was also Sarah Jean's—a plain dark blue one with a matching strap and just a little flash of a golden clasp on top. It didn't look like something Mary Frances would carry at all. "I've decided I want to get rid of it," she told me in a quavering, uncertain voice. She was staring hard at that little golden clasp on Sarah Jean's purse.

"Are you *sure?*"

She choked back a swallow and nodded.

"Absolutely, positively sure?"

She nodded again. And then we just kind of stood there, a foot apart, like two dumb statues that didn't know how to move. I wanted to reach out and put my arms around her, you know? But it was like she was made out of ice. And hollow, too, so that if I reached out and touched her, she might shatter into a million tiny fragments and there'd be nothing left except a large, empty cold spot in the air.

"So," she said finally, still staring a hole through the clasp on her purse, "is there any way you can help me?"

So I told her about Big Ed and his fancy doctor on Park Avenue and how she wouldn't even have to worry about the money part, either. I could feel this big sensation welling up inside her while I spoke. It almost felt like relief but it wasn't, because it didn't well up and boil over the top like relief does. It just kind of built up pressure and held it and held it and held it and never let go. "So what do I have to do?" she wanted to know.

"I guess I gotta call Big Ed," I told her, and started back into the shop.

"You're not going to call from in THERE??!!" she gasped.

I turned around and I swear the look on her face was enough to tear your heart out. I mean, here was the sharpest, cleverest, prettiest, snottiest, most understanding, least forgiving and most hilariously sarcastic and independent older sister a blue-collar jerk from Passaic could ever hope to have. And she was just gutted, like a fish on the Jersey pier. It made you want to turn your insides out and cry, I swear it did.

So we went around the corner to the grocery store and I rang up Big Ed and explained the situation and he allowed as how he had to make a few calls and that he'd get back to me. Mary Frances didn't like that he'd have to call me back at the shop—I mean, I had work to do, and especially on his cylinder head if I wanted a favor like this one—but I assured Mary Frances that we could talk around it so's nobody would be the wiser. And I didn't have to worry about Big Ed mouthing off or saying the wrong thing if the Old Man answered on account of, even though he was kind of a loudmouth, Big Ed understood the Code of the Street and that there are some things that just need to be kept private. At least if you don't want to be found with your head bashed in.

"He wants to know when you want to do it?" I asked with my palm over the receiver.

"The sooner the better," she whispered, biting her lip.

So I told Big Ed and he promised to get back to me and I hung up the phone and we just kind of stood there by the bread rack, looking at each other. *"Oh, Buddy,"* she finally gushed, kind of lunging for me and burying her head in my chest.

I put my arms around her shoulders. Jeez, she was shaking like a rabbit, the poor thing. "It's gonna be okay," I whispered into her hair. "It's gonna be okay. You'll see."

I only wished I sounded more convincing.

So we went back to the Sinclair and I gave Mary Frances a dollar so she could go across the street to the sandwich shop and order a bowl of nice, homemade chicken dumpling soup and watch it grow cold in front of her while I worked on lapping in the new valves on Big Ed's cylinder head. It was actually the perfect kind of thing to do while you're waiting for an important phone call that's about to change the life of somebody you're close to forever. It's like something that keeps you occupied but allows your mind to wander, too. Oh, you've got to wipe the grinding paste off and peek in every now and then to make sure you're getting a nice, clean, narrow seat that's the same thickness all the way around and doesn't have any pits or burrs in it. But, other than that, I think it's a lot like running a pottery wheel. Not that I've ever actually run a pottery wheel, of course. But I'd seen them run on those 16mm films about the Famous American Indian Tribes of the Great Southwest that they used to show us in high school. You remember. Those 16mm "educational" movies with the gurgly sound and wooden acting and a big, jumpy hair-spider in the corner of the frame? And then the film would snap in two or hop a sprocket or freeze solid and burn clear through right in front of your eyes, and every wiseass in class would start making shadow puppets on the blank screen—little Vinny Angelo could make some really dirty ones (I always envied him for that)—and then the lights would blast on and the teacher would have turned a kind of deep, steamy shade of maroon and want to know just who, precisely, was making those locker-room humor shapes on the screen and did we all think that the human reproductive process was really so funny and....

"PALUMBO! Y'GOTTA CALL OUT HERE!"

See what I mean about letting your mind wander?

Well, of course it was Big Ed, and he'd come through as usual. "He'll take her right after his last patient today."

I didn't say anything. I was looking across the street at Mary Frances through the window of the sandwich shop. She was just staring straight ahead, not seeing anything.

"Is that okay? After work today?" Big Ed repeated.

"Yeah. Sure." I told him. "That'll be great."

So he gave me the address and I wrote it down—it was right smack dab in the middle of Park Avenue, just like he promised—and then he told me I ought to drive around back to the alley and that she should go in through the service door around 5:45 or so and take the freight elevator up to the seventh floor and it was the fourth door on the right. There wouldn't be any name on the door, just one of those thick, frosted glass panels, on account of it was the back door into the doctors' suite. But there'd be a nurse to help out and everything. And she didn't really need to know the doctor's name, anyway. But he was OK, Big Ed assured me. Did this kind of work all the time for a lot of the uptown families you read about in the papers. And I mean in the society pages, too, not just the front-page headlines.

"You got all that?" Big Ed asked me.

"Sure," I told him, although my voice sounded kind of strange and disconnected, even to me.

"You okay?"

I shrugged. Like he could see it, right?

"Lissen, Buddy. This is one of those shitty things you just gotta do. Like I told
you before, you're in the big leagues now."

"Yeah. I guess," I said half-heartedly.

There really wasn't all that much more to say.

"Oh, and Ed?" I remembered to say just before he hung up.

"Wha?"

"Thanks. Thanks a bunch."

"Hey, it's nuthin.' Askin' a friend to do something that's easy for him is
almost like askin' no favor a'tall."

It's funny, but I couldn't help thinking of the way Big Ed looked on the grid
at Watkins Glen for his very first sportycar race what seemed like a whole lifetime ago—even though it was still just short of a year—and how puffed-up and
beaming like an idiot he was in his freshly painted new crash helmet and split-lens
fighter pilot goggles and string-back driving gloves and the stub end of a dead stogie
sticking out of his smile. That was before any of us knew what a really hopeless
driver he was—himself included—and it was hard to imagine that the oversized,
funny-looking, overblown doofus in the crash hat and the loud, pushy guy Big Ed
could be when he wanted something done his way or the know-it-all, wise-in-the-
ways-of-the-world philosopher he could become when he had a couple stiff snorts
in him could also be this really kind, understanding, go-way-out-of-his-way-for-
you friend when the chips were down and you really needed somebody you could
count on.

Like I said before, I think you're better off judging people by what they *do*
rather than what they say or what they think. Or think they think, anyway....

So I told Mary Frances and she didn't say much of anything—just sort of nodded—and then, while Mary Frances waited out by the pump island, I asked Old
Man Finzio if I could maybe borrow the tow truck for a little trip across the George
Washington Bridge into the city. "During rush hour?" he asked incredulously. "Are
you *nuts?*" He was already plenty suspicious, and so I told him Mary Frances had
this terribly impacted wisdom tooth and so she had to go over for some emergency
oral surgery in Manhattan. Old Man Finzio didn't look like he was buying any of
it. "It don't look t'me like her jaw is swollen none," he observed. Then this ugly
little smile—like a snake smile almost—curled up around the corners of his mouth.
"You sure she ain't got some swelling someplace else?"

Jeezus! How the hell did *he* know?

"Look," I growled at him, "I work hard here fr'you. I bring in work and fix
the damn cars so they stay fixed and keep the customers happy and do everything
the hell else that has to be done. And if I need to borrow your stinking tow truck
so's I can help out my sister who's in so much pain she can hardly even talk..."

"From the wisdom tooth, right?" The snake smile curled up a little further.

"God Dammit!" I hollered at him.

"Hey, calm yourself down, sonnyboy. Ain't no call t'curse at me. Here," he said, faking like his feelings were hurt but still grinning like a water moccasin, "take the damn keys." He handed over the keys to the tow truck. "You're welcome to 'em. Anytime you want. Hell, this is your damn gas station as much as it is mine anymore."

"Thanks," I grumbled at him.

"And one more thing," Old Man Finzio called over my shoulder as I was walking out the door. "Make sure it's got a full tank of gas when you bring it back."

No question that meant it was on dead empty.

"And no stealing it out of my pumps, Palumbo. You fill up here, you pay for it. I'll be checkin' the register in the morning."

"Why would I do that?" I muttered so he couldn't hear me. "I can buy it four cents a gallon cheaper at the Mobil over on Franklin Street."

So I drove Mary Frances across the bridge into Manhattan in the Old Man's truck, and it actually wasn't too bad seeing as how most all the traffic was going the other way. But it wasn't what you could call a pleasant trip, on account of Mary Frances just sat there like somebody being wheeled to the electric chair and the stink of what we were about to do was hanging in the air like the smell of day-old cabbage soup. I mean, there were certainly two ways to look at it. On the one hand, it was like no more than pulling a sore tooth or clipping off a bothersome hangnail. No big deal, you know? And, on the other, it was something so big and awful and unthinkable that it echoed like a banging trash-can lid from one end of the universe to the other. It's not so much like we were *killing* someone as we were *preventing them from being.* Somewhere in the world that never was and never would be there was this person—a living, breathing, blessed, cursed, complicated, lost and confused individual just like you or me or Mary Frances or anybody else—who would never get the chance to be. They would never be able to stand there in front of a bathroom mirror and look at their reflection in the glass and wonder, like the rest of us do, just how the hell we got here and where the hell we're supposed to be going and just what the hell we're supposed to be doing with our lives. Only they wouldn't be asking those questions on account of they wouldn't be there. And that hole—that sad, empty space that never was—*that* was the thing making that hollow, banging-garbage-can echo that seemed to be everywhere and just wouldn't go away. But the most confusing part was that it wasn't simply one way or the other. Nope, it was both at the same time....

Anyhow, we got to the alley behind Park Avenue right on schedule around 5:30, and, even though we were on a block featuring some of the classiest and most expensive real estate in Manhattan, it was still your typical city back alley, lined with loading docks and windowless steel service doors and all the other gritty, practical stuff you never see or even think about when you hop out of a taxicab, tip your hat to the uniformed doorman and head in through the polished glass and brass revolving doors on the front entrances of those buildings. Being in an alley is like looking up a city's backside. It's also not a very good place to park, since there are "No Parking" and "Delivery Vehicles Only" and "No Stopping or Standing" signs put up or painted right on the fire-brick walls absolutely everywhere.

"You want me to go up with you?"

Mary Frances shook her head.

"You sure?"

She kind of half shrugged. "Maybe just up the elevator." We both knew Big Ed said only she should go into the office, but I figured it'd be okay if I went up the elevator with her. So I left the Old Man's tow truck parked in what appeared to be the least conspicuous No Parking zone—I mean, at least it wasn't in front of a doorway or anything—and we found the black steel fire door with the address he'd given me on it and, just like he said, it wasn't locked. There was nobody around inside, and we were in a dark, gloomy corridor with an uneven wooden floor that had seen a lot of two-wheeled hand trucks and heavily-laden movers' dollies over the years. A little ways down we found the freight elevator with its corrugated-metal clamshell doors and a hefty, worn canvas strap you had to pull on to open them up. It made a hell of a *clang!* when I did it. Then there was an accordion-style metal gate you had to open and just a little, low-wattage, naked light bulb dangling from the open iron framework that carried the freight elevator like some kind of huge, railroad bridge-scale lunch basket. I pulled the clamshell doors shut and punched the button for 7, and there was this big scraping, lurching kind of noise and the elevator started shuddering and creaking its way upward in the shaft. It was pretty creepy, if you want the truth of it.

When we'd finally shuddered and creaked our way up to the seventh floor, I opened the gate and the clamshell doors and we were in a darkened little service area with gray concrete flooring and a wooden door you could see light coming under from the other side. I opened it, and all of a sudden we were back in a fancy professional office building on Park Avenue again, what with thick, rich, sound-absorbing carpeting down the hallways and expensive, sculptured-metal wall fixtures giving off a gentle, reassuring golden light and a perfectly matched set of faceless oak doors with frosted glass inserts and polished brass doorknobs lining either side of the corridor. *"Fourth door on the right,"* I whispered.

"I know," she whispered back.

It was the kind of place that makes you feel like you need to whisper.

"I'm not supposed to go in with you," I whispered even softer.

"I know."

"Do you want me to wait out here?"

"No, that's okay."

"You sure?"

Mary Frances nodded and started for the door. But then she stopped and turned around, and I could see the tears welling up in her eyes again. *"And thanks for everything, Buddy."*

And then she was gone and the door closed behind her.

There wasn't much of anything to do but go back down to the tow truck in the alley, and, wouldn't you know it, damn if there wasn't one of New York's finest looking it over and checking out the Jersey plates and getting ready to write me up a ticket. *"HEY! WAIT A MINUTE!"* I hollered as I hustled over to stop him. Or at least try to. Stopping a cop from writing a ticket once he's already got his pen and ticket book out is a difficult thing to accomplish. "Jeez, officer," I said in the most humble, friendly, reasonable and subservient voice you have ever heard in your life, "I was only gone for a *minute....*"

He looked at me and then back at the tow truck and then back at me again. He was one of those burly, dumb, middle-aged cop-on-a-beat types who never had the brains or ambition or connections to get himself promoted up the ladder to where he could steal some *real* money instead of just nickels and dimes. Or maybe he was just one of those tin-badge boy scout types, which is another way to go absolutely no place in your average police department. "You see that sign?" he said, pointing to just one of three or four dozen "No Parking" signs lining that particular section of the alley. Cops love to ask you questions like that. And then wait for you to answer.

"Well, yeah, of course I did," I told him, doing my best to look real sad, ashamed and embarrassed about it.

"But you parked here anyway, didn't you?"

I couldn't believe he was waiting for a damn answer again. I mean, what the hell was I supposed to say? I've always hated it when cops and coaches and teachers and nuns and parents and uncles and, in fact, everybody in creation who thinks they have some God-given authority over you talks to you that way. And, what with Mary Frances upstairs going through Lord Only Knows What, I wasn't in much of a mood to take it. Only then some new and thoroughly enormous terror seized me. What we were doing was illegal. And not just a little illegal, either. And the last thing I needed was some cop to come nosing around and asking a bunch of questions and me winding up in Abortion Accomplice prison with a bunch of rapists and murderers and tax evaders and child molesters.

"W-well, I wasn't exactly intending to be *p-parking* here..." I kind of stammered, sounding guilty as hell of every unsolved rape, murder, tax evasion or child molestation that had taken place in the five boroughs of New York over the past 50 years, "I just kind of left it here for a minute while I went inside the building."

I instantly froze up solid. Why the hell did I say I went inside the building? Now he was gonna for sure ask me what I was doing in there.

"Oh? And just what was so important inside the building that you had leave your truck here in the alley in a No Parking zone?"

I felt my brain scrambling for a plausible lie. "Ahh, I'm sorry." I answered sheepishly, "but I hadda drop something off and I figured it'd be okay for just a minute...."

The cop just stared at me, like he was waiting for the rest of the story.

"...I work at a gas station over in Passaic, see..." my mind was racing, "...and we do a lot of work on these European sports cars, see, and..." this had better be good, "...and one of our customers left his, uh, briefcase behind when he dropped his car off, see..." it was all coming to me now, "...and it was all full of his medical records and stuff..." yeah, that made sense! I mean, it was a doctors' building and all! "...and he needed it back right away so Old M—I mean, my, uhh, boss asked me to run it over."

The cop looked at me kind of sideways. "He works here in Manhattan, but he takes his car all the way over to Passaic to get it fixed?"

"Well, see..." at least I was on home ground now, "...we don't just *fix* cars there. We also prepare them for racing...."

"Racing?"

"Sure," I nodded. "Sports car races like they have out at Bridgehampton on Long Island and up at Watkins Glen, too."

"Didn't somebody get killed there last year?"

"Yeah. A little boy. Bunch of other people got hurt, too. It was a real shame. You probably saw it in *Life* magazine."

"Yeah. That's it. I remember reading about it." The cop mulled it over in his mind. "Exactly what kind of cars do they run in these races?"

"Oh, MGs and Jaguars and stuff you never heard of like OSCAs and Aston Martins..." I was home free now. I could see it in his eyes. "And of course Ferraris. They're really something. A guy named Carlo Sebastian sells them out of a shop right here in Manhattan."

"I know the place!" He cracked the first smile I'd seen out of him. "I been by there once or twice." He looked at me sideways again. "You actually *know* Carlo Sebastian?"

"Sure I do," I said like it was no big thing. "I know his top driver, too. Creighton Pendleton. The third, I think."

"You know him, too?"

"Yeah," I admitted. "We've shared some stuff at the races."

The cop let out a sigh and folded up his ticket book. "Okay," he said like he was pardoning me for treason, "go on. Get lost."

Well, obviously there was nothing to do then but fire up the tow truck and drive off down the alley. *Damn!* I could have told him that other lie about dropping my sister off for some emergency oral surgery. Only what if there weren't any dentists—or at least no oral surgeons—in that building. Only how would the cop know? Or would he? And what would happen if Mary Frances came out and I wasn't there? Or, worse yet, what if something awful was happening in that doctor's office behind the frosted glass door—right that very instant!—and here I was driving off to who-knows-where in the Old Man's tow truck. So I pulled into the very next alley and kind of tried to hide it behind a garbage dumper surrounded by another dozen or two "No Parking" signs and ran all the way back to the alley behind the building where Mary Frances was getting her problem taken care of. And naturally she wasn't there. So I wondered if I maybe ought to go up and wait in the hall or maybe wait just inside the door (I mean, what if that same cop came up again? What would I say?) and so that's what I did. I kind of curled up against the wall by the silent old freight elevator and waited. Only then I started worrying about what if she went down the front way and then walked around back and I was gone? And I hadn't called Julie, either. Why, she and her mom would be sitting down to dinner and I wouldn't be there. I was for sure going to catch a steaming load of shit for that. And what about the Old Man's truck? Maybe it wasn't such a great idea to just leave it there...

"Buddy?"

I wheeled around.

It was Mary Frances. The nurse in the doctor's office had told her to take the front elevators down and walk through to the service entrance. I noticed she looked a little pale and unsteady, but you could see some of the weight was off of her. Although certainly not all of it. Not by a long shot. "You okay?" I asked.

Mary Frances nodded.

"How was it?"

She shrugged. "It was okay."

"You sure?"

She nodded again. "They were really nice. The doctor and the nurse, I mean. They made me feel a little better about it."

I gave her a hug and led her out into the alley. "I kind of had to move the truck," I explained. "Had a little cop trouble about where it was parked."

So we walked the two blocks over to where'd I left it and, wouldn't you know it, the Old Man's tow truck was in the process of being hitched up to another, somewhat larger tow truck with "City of New York" lettering across the door. *"WAITAMINUTE!"* I hollered for the second time in less than an hour. Well, I won't go into the gory details of trying to get the New York tow truck guy to cease and desist from hauling the Old Man's truck away, but the end result was it cost me everything I had in my pocket except toll bridge money and I had a 20 dollar ticket on top of it—20 dollars, can you believe it?—that I would have to pay in the next two weeks or the Old Man would get a damn summons in the mail. But at least we got everything taken care of before they hauled it away, since it would've taken maybe all night to track it down through the various nooks, crannies, curbsides, way stations, holding pens, and thoroughly disinterested and equally disgruntled desk sergeants of the New York Parking Police.

Still, it was almost dark by the time we were on our way back to Jersey.

"You okay?" I asked Mary Frances again as we headed onto the humming, expanded metal roadbed of the George Washington Bridge.

"Yeah," she said, sounding very tired indeed, "I think I am."

You could see just the faintest rosy tinge of the last bit of sunset over the hills far off in the distance in front of us.

"He showed it to me," Mary Frances said, looking out over the Hudson.

"He showed it to you?"

She nodded. "It didn't look like anything. Just a little piece of mess."

And then she started to cry again. Only it was a different kind of cry. Quiet, you know? She wasn't sobbing or shaking or anything like that at all. It was just this one fat, silent tear kind of rolling its way down her cheek while she looked out through the dirty side window at the boats and barges making their way down the Hudson. I got the feeling that faraway look in her eyes was one she'd have to live with for a long, long time. Maybe even the rest of her life. But at least she wasn't scared anymore.

As you can well imagine, Julie was none too pleased when I showed up at the duplex some three-and-a-half hours after suppertime. In fact, "none too pleased" is putting it kind of mildly. The only good news was that Julie was downstairs in what would someday—maybe even before Christmas—become our new apartment, painting the woodwork lilac while her mom was off playing Bingo like she did every Wednesday night. So at least we were alone. At least if you don't count all the people within earshot of Julie's voice, which probably accounted for all of New Jersey and New York State and maybe even a little bit of Canada, too.

"WHERE THE HELL WERE YOU??!!" Julie boomed in a voice that could be heard, not only at, but surely *over* the fabled roar of the Niagara Falls.

"Well, see, I, umm…" I started in with my usual resourcefulness and precision.

"You missed dinner," she snarled, her eyes narrowed like a leopard's.

"Well, I, err, uhh…" Jeez, this was worse than talking to that damn cop in the alley, "…I, er, ahh, I hadda work late on Big Ed's engine. It was all apart and a real mess and…."

She shot me a look that cut me off at the knees. *"I went over to the shop,"* she said like it was a death sentence.

Oh, Jesus!

So I came unraveled right in front of her and told her all about what Mary Frances had done about the mess that rat-bastard Ollie Cromwell left her in and how I'd helped out by asking around and arranging one of Big Ed's huge favors and then borrowed the Old Man's tow truck to take her into Manhattan and then I got to the part that was gnawing at me about the little niece or nephew of mine that was never, ever going to be anything more than a bloody stain on a napkin in some fancy doctor's office on Park Avenue. When I was finished with it, there wasn't much of anything to do but stand there like some idiot who just found himself on a rush-hour commuter train with all of his clothes missing. "And that's the truth," I added lamely, feeling weak and sad and miserable and like everything I had ever done in my life was probably dead wrong.

"You're not making this up, are you?" Julie observed, her leopard eyes kind of working their way up, down and around me like I was something that might or might not be good to eat.

I shook my head. "I wish I was," I told her. And I meant it, too.

"I can't believe this," she finally wailed in a strangely exasperated tone.

"Can't believe what?" I asked. I mean, her reaction didn't make any sense to me. Oh, I expected her to be upset. Upset about what I'd done and upset about not talking it over with her first—or at least telling her, for gosh sakes—and upset about not even calling to let her know where I was and why I was missing dinner and then lying to her about where I was and what I was doing on top of it. Why, she had a whole blessed selection of things she could be pissed off at me about. And I probably had it coming, too. But she wasn't screaming or yelling or shaking her fist at me. In fact, it was deadly calm all around her. *"You're telling the truth, aren't you,"* she said again. It wasn't a question.

"Sure I am," I assured her.

And then she looked at me so very strangely. Like she'd never looked at me before, in fact. "I'm late," she told me.

"Late?"

She rolled her eyes towards the ceiling. "Do I have to draw you a damn picture?"

Then it was quiet for a minute or two while the meaning of what she'd said advanced across my brain like a battalion of Sherman Tanks. "Y-you mean you're…."

The answer in her eyes was unmistakable.

"B-but *how?"* I wanted to know. I mean, we'd only been married for three weeks, and we hadn't really, you know, *done* anything until the third day of our honeymoon….

"You remember that night on the beach at Bridgehampton?" she asked.

Boy! Did I ever!

"Well…" and she let her voice trail off into that strange nether world where mysteries become certainties, certainties become mysteries, and little boys grow into men.

Finding out that Julie was pregnant and that I was about to become a father at the ripe old, freshly-married age of not quite 21 was news so big and a notion so enormous that I couldn't get my mind around it. Not hardly. On the one hand there was this overwhelming sense of being run over by a steamroller. Absolutely flattened. But then you blink and shrug and shake yourself to see if anything is broken or if maybe your intestines are squirting out your ears, and that's when you discover that everything is still right where it was and the world is rotating on its axis just precisely the same as it was before you got the news. The only thing that's changed, like I said, is that strange new feeling of having been flattened by a steamroller. And that kind of stays with you.

The rest of it comes in bits and pieces that make you feel all sorts of different ways and don't seem to fit together in the slightest. Like part of me was already drowning in a swelling sea of *ohmygodwhatthehellamIgonnadoNOW!* worries about money and living space and hospital bills and baby stuff—babies needed an incredible amount of stuff, I knew that!—and how I was ever going to finesse all this crushing new responsibility into all the other things I had going on in my life. And then there was this part of me that was just kind of amazed. Shell-shocked, in fact. But it was a surprisingly agreeable kind of shell-shocked. And then there was this other little banty-rooster side of me that was all proud and strutting and cocky and self-satisfied about it. Why, I could almost hear the guys in the locker-room shower at the end of my old man's shift at the chemical plant:

"Yeah, he's been puttin' it to her, all right."

"First shot outta the box, too."

"You mean first shot INTA th'box!"

haw-haw-haw

"Well, at least he ain't shootin' blanks."

"Sure ain't, isse?"

"Nope. Sure ain't."

haw

"Well, now the little prick's gonna find out what married life is REALLY all about."

"Sure is."

"Yep. Sure is."

"Poor bastard."

Like I said, I felt a lot of different ways about it.

Sometimes one at a time.

Sometimes one after the other.

And sometimes all at once….

But the saving grace of being a blue-collar grunt of a gas station working stiff is that the sun comes up tomorrow and you gotta go to work and, if you're nice to people and treat them right and are any good at all with their cars, you wind up with a plate so full of stuff to do that all those things in life that are simply too awesome and monumental and overpowering to deal with kind of get misplaced in the background while you go about your day-to-day business. Not that they're forgotten. Oh, no. You'll be adjusting the mixture on an S.U. carburetor or biting into a sausage sandwich with sweet peppers and onions on it at lunchtime or just staring at the blessed sports section in the morning paper while you drink your first cup of coffee and all of a sudden, right out of nowhere, it'll wash over you again like a wave of ice water:

OHMYGODWHATTHEHELLAMIGONNADO<u>NOW</u>???!!!

The only good news is that, eventually, it passes.

And then you get to forget about it again. At least for a while....

5: The Call of Callicoon

The proposed road race around the little resort town of Callicoon on the Delaware River out in Sullivan County, New York, had been a kind of hot potato for all the sportycar clubs in the area. Seems a bunch of the local innkeepers, restaurateurs and barkeeps had seen—or at least heard about—how the sports car crowd had filled the beds, drained the beer tappers, cleaned out the food larders and spread large, deep pocketfuls of folding money around the landscape and all up and down the main drags of towns like Bridgehampton, Watkins Glen and Elkhart Lake, and they decided that, seeing as how their country roads were already in place and probably as good as anybody's, they'd really like in on the action.

Only problem was, they weren't.

I guess the race got pitched first to the generally snooty, stuffy and suspicious-of-anything-much-west-of-the-Hudson New York Region of the SCMA—and you already know how I feel about that bunch!—and they were actually pretty excited when they heard that somebody actually *wanted* them to stage a race somewhere. Especially since this proposed race was out on some lovely, winding, scenic and swoopy country sports car roads and moreover handy to exactly the kinds of restaurants and bars and sleeping rooms (or sleeping-it-off rooms!) that the SCMA required to stage a proper race weekend. And it didn't hurt that the good folks and Chamber of Commerce types from the Callicoon area sent a delegation to a New York Region SCMA general business and bullshit meeting in Manhattan and bought plenty of drinks for everybody.

So the New York SCMA Region formed an ad hoc committee to study the situation, and, sure enough, the chairman of that committee was our old buddy Charlie Priddle. Not that it came as any surprise, since Charlie wound up chairing just about every damn committee the New York Region ever had. But he was happy to do it, since it was important work and good for the club and moreover allowed him a vast selection of opportunities to throw his weight around, make other people uncomfortable, nurture cherished personal vendettas, and, most important of all, lord it over all the real drivers who had the skill, guts, talent and grace under pressure that he never did. And there, in a nutshell, you have the ugly, two-sided truth of any volunteer organization.

At any rate, the committee had a meeting to decide what they wanted to do about this proposed road race out in Sullivan County, and they came to the conclusion that they really needed to send somebody—or, better yet, a whole delegation—out to check it out and get the lay of the land. So the committee reported back to the New York Region at their next business and bullshit meeting that they had a solid plan with a definite direction and so the matter was turned back over to the ad hoc committee to select a delegation and they had another meeting to review the possible candidates and reported back at the next general meeting that they had indeed come up with a roster of delegates. Who, to the surprise of absolutely no one, turned out to be the committee members themselves. So the head of the steering committee (who, strangely enough, also happened to be Charlie Priddle) directed the head of the ad hoc committee (it was amazing he could do all this stuff without mirrors, you know?) to present a budget for approval. So the ad hoc committee had yet another meeting wherein they decided that they could probably get away with seventy-five bucks a head (which, to be fair, included all the dinners and drinks already consumed at the ad hoc committee meetings thus far, all of which were held at a very nice second-floor steak and seafood restaurant with a balcony overlooking Sixth Avenue) and duly presented it to the board at the next general meeting. Whereupon it was approved unanimously and the treasurer (yep, one of Charlie Priddle's cronies again) wrote out a check. And then signed it. On behalf of the club, of course.

Now I have to tell you that I didn't envy those Chamber-of-Commerce types out in Sullivan County, on account of they had inadvertently handed Mister Charles Winthrop Priddle, Esquire, an opportunity to be displeased. And, if there's one thing in this world that Charlie Priddle knew how to do, it was be displeased. In fact, he was kind of an Olympic Champ when it came to being displeased and I was always amazed that he didn't go pro as a fruit inspector or a tax auditor or something. In any case, Charlie and his committee (which was only three people, to be honest about it) went out to Sullivan County to get wined and dined and have a looksee at the proposed 8.5-mile track layout, and Charlie was particularly impressed by the fine hospitality and the fact that the local Chamber-of-Commerce types were willing to shell out several thousand greenbacks for the necessary haybales and such and were quick to point out the lovely hillsides where spectators could stand and watch the cars go by and still be a safe distance from the roadway. Not to mention the stellar selection of steaks, chops, cocktails and after-dinner drinks they provided to ensure a positive response. It was one of the other committee members—an elderly gentleman of impeccable Scottish-American ancestry who'd actually done a bit of racing himself before the war but more or less gave it up when it became apparent he couldn't see much further than the end of his nose—who noticed that the road was terribly narrow and bumpy and the pavement was generally awful (two whole miles of it weren't even paved!) and that there were trees right up to the edge in many areas and gravel all over several of the most crucial turns. And he said as much. After dessert. Over coffee.

Well, Charlie hemmed and hawed and harrumphed a bit and even admitted that he hated to be wrong. But he relished turning on people even more, and so he suddenly and vehemently advised the good people and city fathers of Sullivan County, "this will never, *ever* do!" dabbed at the butterscotch pudding on his chin with the fine linen napkin that they had so graciously provided, and headed back to the next general club meeting to make his report.

Well, this threw the SCMA membership into something of a tizzy. Or at least those members who actually attended the monthly general bullshit and business meetings, which was really only about two dozen or so diehards—none of whom you could call star racecar drivers, and most of them much less than that—with the good of the club uppermost in their minds and nothing better to do on the third Tuesday evening of each month. To be honest, they had never before been approached by any city, county, hamlet, municipality, village, parish or township that actually *wanted* them to stage a race in their area. And Callicoon was moreover so keen on the idea that they were willing to foot the bill for most of the haybales and snow fencing and public address speakers and running of wire and whatnot it took to pull such a thing off. So the club wasn't real happy with the idea of blowing them off. Not hardly. And even Charlie Priddle, acting in his capacity as Chairman of the Ruddering Committee (which functioned at the other end of the decision-making process from the Steering Committee) was quick to point that out. But he was equally quick (now acting in his capacity as the lead SCMA delegate/evaluator assigned to the Callicoon project at seventy-five bucks per evaluation) to insist that certain members of the evaluation committee (and he was not about to name names, but it certainly wasn't *him!*) were of the opinion that the roadway was not suitable for their purposes. Not that Charlie Priddle would know a good road to race on from a bad one, since he couldn't drive a lick and everybody and his brother knew it.

So the club members found themselves at loggerheads over the Sullivan County road race deal, and, just like the participating, committee-oriented, show-up-and-get-plastered-on-the-third-Tuesday-evening-of-each-month membership of volunteer clubs everywhere, they fought and scrapped and yelled and threatened and questioned each others' I.Q. and ancestry long into the night. And the final upshot of it all was that they decided, in a *very* close vote, to send yet another delegation to Sullivan County to re-evaluate the evaluation evaluated by the first evaluation team and see just where they were.

Strangely enough, Tommy Edwards happened to be at the meeting that night—not exactly by choice—and that's how he got suckered into going along. It was all part of the leftovers from that awful, terrible accident that Skippy Welcher actually caused but Tommy got blamed for at Watkins Glen. You know, where Tommy swerved to avoid The Skipper's C-Type and sideswiped the crowd on Franklin Street and that poor little seven-year-old boy got killed? Well, the aftermath residue of that wreck was still following Tommy around like the stench off the back of a garbage truck. First he got his racing license suspended and he couldn't race at all. Or at least not with the SCMA, anyway. I mean, it was unmistakably *his* rolled-over, crumpled-up Allard fetched up against the curbing on Franklin Street and *his* face in the squad car getting questioned by the state troopers afterwards in the grisly two-page photo spread that appeared in *Life* magazine the following week. Against rock-solid evidence like that, what could expert, eye-witness accounts from people who were actually there and saw it and moreover knew what they were looking at possibly be worth? So, like I said, Tommy lost his license. And, to be honest, he really didn't have much stomach for fighting it at the time. He felt terrible about the little boy who got killed and all the people who got injured, his marriage to Ronnie was on the rocks, and he was drinking kind of a lot on top of it. Or at least he was showing the effects of drinking quite a lot, which he never used to.

But time has a way of passing and people have a way of going to bed every night and waking up again every morning even when they've kind of lost interest in life and haven't a clue why they're even occupying space on the planet. And, if they have good friends and are very, very lucky, they eventually discover that there's maybe something they actually want to do again. And that's what happened to Tommy. He realized that he really wanted to get back into a racing car. Like he'd said many months later when the whole bunch of us were sitting around that dinner table at the beach cottage near Bridgehampton the night after Eddie Dearborn got killed, *"inside a racecar is the only time in my life when I feel like*

I bloody well know what I'm doing...." And he wanted that feeling back. So he decided he'd see if he could do anything about his license suspension. And of course, like any volunteer club that delights in controversies, power struggles, the taking of sides and sleazy back-room deals, the SCMA had a thoroughly humiliating and complicated appeal process already in place that mostly amounted to composing a very formal, groveling and apologetic written request begging to be allowed the marvelous opportunity to appear before a special meeting of the three-member Drivers' Committee tribunal (Charles Winthrop Priddle Acting Chief Justice, of course) so that they could listen disbelievingly to your side of the story, exchange knowing looks and talk behind their hands, and then prod and pick and poke at you like you're some sad-eyed, helpless and unfortunate guinea pig in a third-grade classroom.

Tommy hated every snide, uncivilized minute of it. But, true to his British upbringing, he was a past master at remaining pleasant and courteous, maintaining a respectful tone, and suffering fools gladly, and so, after they'd thoroughly boiled him in oil, skewered him on a spit, and slow roasted him for a few hours, the Drivers' Committee went behind closed doors to decide just how badly they wanted to jerk him around. Charlie of course wanted to see him drawn and quartered. Or at the very least hung by his privates in a public place. But one of the other committee guys actually liked Tommy a little and knew rightly enough that the accident at Watkins Glen wasn't really his fault, while the third judge didn't care much one way or the other, but his law firm was trying to put over some real estate deal in midtown that included a small parcel of land belonging to a cousin or uncle or something of the second judge, and so the upshot of the whole thing was that they filed back into the main room, had Tommy rise and stand before them, and then Charlie cleared his throat and declared in a voice so grave and reluctant that it wavered ominously: "We have looked at all the facts and considered them carefully," he intoned, "and, against the better judgment of, ahem, certain members of this panel, we have decided to transmute your suspension. Henceforth, and for the next 12 months, you will be on strictest probation. Your driving and conduct will be under the closest scrutiny at all times. And you are instructed to report back to this committee for review every three months until your period of probation has passed." Charlie set his paper down on the table and extended his scrawny little neck so his beady little eyes were staring right into Tommy's: "You screw up or get out of line just *once,* Mr. Edwards..." you could see Charlie kind of gathering himself up for the last part, "...and it will be my personal pleasure to come down on you so hard and fast you won't know what hit you." It was true, too. For a guy like Charlie Priddle, making a real racer squirm was the best part of volunteering for all those committees. Hell, it made up for everything!

So the deal was that Tommy was at the general business and bullshit meeting to have his probation "reviewed" (or, as he referred to it, "seeing my bloody parole officer") the night the membership decided to agree that they couldn't agree what to decide about the proposed Sullivan County race and that they really needed to send another evaluation team out there to re-evaluate the evaluation of the first evaluation team. And, since Tommy was the only *bona fide* racecar driver in the whole damn room, somebody suggested they send him along, too.

Just to get his opinion, you know? But not as an actual delegate, seeing as how he wasn't on any of the club boards or committees or anything and his racing license was under strict probation anyway. But he could go as a "drivers' representative outside observer." Or, to put it in clearer language, on his own two bits.

To be honest about it, Tommy wasn't real keen on spending a day traveling out into the boondocks with the likes of Charlie Priddle. And Charlie was going again, too. After an incredibly long and needlessly parliamentary discussion, the club meeting regulars decided in a very narrow vote that, although Charlie really couldn't serve as a delegate on both the evaluation teams, he could go along in an advisory capacity to represent the interests and conclusions of the first evaluation team. And, naturally enough, receive the going rate of seventy-five bucks for his trouble. So, even though it shaped up to be a pretty awful experience, Tommy agreed to go because he knew it was important to suck up to these jerks with his racing license still dangling in the balance. He even did his best to appear eager about the trip, and I thought he should've been put up for an Oscar or something for that performance.

I always figured Tommy Edwards for about as brave, skillful and experienced a racing driver as you were likely to find anywhere—he'd raced here and there in England and even in Europe a little besides here in the old U.S. of A.—and he'd always said that the *risk* part of racing was a large portion of what made it so worthwhile. Which is why he pooh-poohed all those flat, dull, wide-open-spaces airport circuits on General Curtis Le May's Strategic Air Command bases. "Where's the bloody *penalty?*" he'd say, shaking his head in disgust. So when he came back from the evaluation trip with a whole bunch of second thoughts about racing at Callicoon, I knew there must be something to it. "Oh, I reckon I could drive it if I had to," he told me over coffee and a sweet roll one morning when I'd gone in to Westbridge early to pick up parts for Big Ed's car, "but it's a bloody awful circuit. It's narrow and dangerous and bumpy as hell, and I'm afraid we'll be picking people out of trees and ditches before it's all over."

I couldn't believe what I was hearing. "You mean you're *scared* of it?" I asked incredulously.

"Hey," he shrugged right back at me, "it's a scary place."

So, after a lot more arguing and in-fighting and questioning of I.Q.s and ancestry, the New York Region respectfully and regretfully took a pass on staging a race through countryside of Sullivan County in and around the town of Callicoon, New York, on the banks of the Delaware River. Only it didn't end there, because by now there was a big faction who'd lined up on the side of running the damn race, and they were not about to back down from their position on account of, well, they were just not about to back down from their position. If you've ever hung around volunteer clubs at all, you'll understand that perfectly. So they (meaning the "we want to run the race" faction along with the Chamber-of-Commerce types from Sullivan County) took the same proposal to the Westchester Sports Car Club. And they listened attentively to the pros and cons and sent their own team of crack evaluators (crack meaning "expert" in this case) and finally, after much more arguing and haranguing, came to the conclusion that, yep, it was just too blessed narrow and bumpy and dangerous. Whereupon the same folks took the same idea up north to the Connecticut Sports Car Club, who came back with the exact same response, only with a few "oh, my's" and "goodness gracious me's" thrown in for good measure.

Finally, with no place else to turn, those same folks took the same idea west across the Hudson and presented it to the New Jersey Sports Car Club. And they said: "OK, why the hell not?" Which really says a little something about the way things are over here in Jersey. I mean compared to New York and Connecticut. See, here in Jersey, we understand that *everybody* is gonna die of something some day. You included. *Capiche?*

So the New Jersey Sports Car Club agreed to run the race and the Chamber-of-Commerce types came up with the haybales and P.A. speakers just like they promised and a lot of the New York and Connecticut types made discreet rude noises and boycotted the event like it was the return of bubonic plague. Including Creighton Pendleton the Third and Charlie Priddle. But a bunch of us—Big Ed, Cal, Carson and me included—in solid defense of "our" club (even though not one of us had attended a single meeting) and moreover out to show those guys on the over-fed, over-bred and over-educated Mayflower side of the George Washington bridge that they were a sorry bunch of pansies indeed, headed northeast out of Passaic on Route 23 towards Sullivan County to put on a sports car race and have ourselves one hell of a good time. And hopefully not kill anyone in the process.

I've got to say that the drive up was about the best part of the whole weekend. We did the dull stuff out of Passaic while it was still dark, and I need to mention here that Julie was still rock-solid asleep when I tiptoed out to meet Big Ed and his Jag on the corner. So I had this delicious feeling of kind of sneaking out the back way with nobody noticing, you know? And that's a harder and harder feeling to come by once you're much past high school. Under a moonless sky and with the sun just threatening to lighten up the horizon off to the right and behind us, me and Big Ed scooted northwest on Route 23 on the buttery, six-cylinder growl of that Jaguar like we were staking claim to the entire rest of the country (west of the Hudson, of course) in the name of free men everywhere. Or at least in the name of men who had more sense than to work the same blessed job in the same blessed building eight hours a day, five days a week plus a little overtime at negotiated union wages.

The sunrise found us heading into the handsome pine forests of the Hamburg Mountains (which, to the best of my knowledge, have nothing whatever to do with the popular meat sandwich of the same name) and it was real pretty country. Neat road, too, and Big Ed was even nice enough to let me get behind the wheel for a spell after we stopped for a load of coffee, fried eggs, hash browns, pancakes, toast, bacon and sausages at a little roadside joint in Beaver Lake. I think the real reason he handed the Jag over was on account of he wanted to catch a little shuteye, and it wasn't long before getting up so blessed early and shoveling down all that great breakfast food had Big Ed snoring away with his head lolled over on his shoulder and a nice little pool of drool collecting in his shirt pocket. Which meant, so long as I didn't wake him up, it was just me and the Jag and the road. Boy, there's no sensation on earth like driving a strong, sleek, sweet-running sports car like Big Ed's Jaguar up a swoopy mountain road—especially when a nice, warm summer sun is just coming up behind you and the air spilling over the top of the windshield smells of lakes and trees and the smooth ribbon of asphalt rolling out in front of you cuts through lush valleys and climbs steep hills and curves around mountainsides and runs along the spine of ridges where all this fabulous landscape pours out around you on both sides for half-a-hundred miles in every direction. Or at least that's what it looks like, anyway. And it's even better if your belly's freshly full of breakfast and it's still early enough that the road is pretty much empty so you can maybe stretch the big cat's legs a little when you get the chance. And I got the chance. In fact, Big Ed was sleeping so soundly and the lullaby music purring out of the Jag's tailpipes was so sweet and soothing that I had her up to over ninety a couple times. Even brushed the magic ton one time on a downhill! And I kept her so liquid-smooth and fluid through the gears and corners that he never even stirred. Not once. Hey, I never pretended to be a great all-fired sports car driver like Tommy Edwards or Cal Carrington (or even that nose-in-the-air, Bermuda-tan Creighton Pendleton the Third), but I sure as heck know what to do with a steering wheel and a shift lever when I get the chance. Or at least I think I do, anyway....

Our route took us through the towns of Sussex and Colesville and right by High Point (which, as you may have already figured, is the highest place in all of New Jersey at 1,803 feet, but really not much more than a bump in the carpet compared to the Rocky Mountains out west, which Big Ed told me went up to around 15,000 feet, give or take a few) just before we crossed over into New York State and picked up Route 97 running along the limestone cliff edges of the Delaware River on a 30-mile stretch from Port Jervis up through the little two-by-four whistle stops of Sparrow Bush, Mongaup, Pond Eddy, Barryville, Tusten and Hunts Corners, and then another 13 miles on to Callicoon. It was one swell road, no lie. By this time Big Ed was awake again, and I could tell by the way his teeth gritted and his fingers dug into the dash cowling and he braced his legs against the transmission tunnel every now and then that he was genuinely impressed with my driving. And I was sensitive enough to his comfort and peace of mind that I'd slow down the pace a little whenever he shook his fist under my nose and called me a suicidal lunatic who was going to get us both killed....

Callicoon turned out to be a quaint and cozy little community that pretty much put its roots down when the Erie Railroad decided to stick a station there while it was laying tracks along the Delaware River to link the Great Lakes and the Eastern Seaboard. Before that it was just a convenient place where lumbermen could take the trees they'd cut down out of the forests and float them down the river to wherever folks needed them to build houses and saloons and schoolhouses and such in New York, New Jersey and Pennsylvania. I wondered about the name, and found out it came from some Dutch hunters and trappers way back when who found a lot of wild turkeys around those parts. Translated from the Dutch, "Callicoon" meant something like "Wild Turkey Creek." And that's just the kind of fascinating and thoroughly useless information that will be of absolutely no use for the rest of your natural life that you can pick up on your average racing weekend.

Like most rural getaway towns, there was lots of boring tourist stuff to do in and around the town of Callicoon. Why, you could look at the pretty scenery or put your boat in the Delaware River (if you had a boat, anyway) or you could fish if you had a fishing rod and license, or you could stroll up past the little antique, souvenir and curio shops. Although I noticed they were an awful lot like all the antique, souvenir and curio shops in Provincetown and Watkins Glen and Mexico and probably every other tourist spot in creation. It's just a question of whether your mantelpiece requires little carved wood, antiqued bronze or fired ceramic statuettes of lighthouses and cod fishermen in rain slickers, Mexican peasants in *serapes* taking a snooze against a cactus with a big straw *sombrero* pulled down over their eyes, or wigwam teepees and Indian braves in birchbark canoes. It's all a matter of taste....

But at least they had a movie theatre in Callicoon where, if you hung around until the Wednesday after the race, you could see Dean Martin and Jerry Lewis in *Scared Stiff* (which turned out to be nothing more than a hammy remake of the old Bob Hope movie *Ghost Breakers* and not nearly half as good—a fact that a lot of people missed just on account of it was in color). Anyhow, the "race circuit" was actually a little ways north of town and a kid at the local filling station told us we could get there by "just following Hankins Road." What he didn't tell us was that Hankins Road kind of went this way and that and split in two and doubled back on itself if you weren't careful and we apparently turned right on the paved part where we maybe should've turned left onto the gravel and found ourselves in Hortonville and well on our way to heading back into Callicoon again. "Nah, they got you all turned around the wrong way," a scrawny old geezer with most of his teeth missing told us. "All's y'gotta do is head up this way a piece on North Branch Road and take the left fork on Obenburg. It'll take y'right to it."

"Thanks," I told him.

"Say, that's one swell-lookin' car y'got there."

"Thanks," I told him again.

"We don't get many cars like that out in these parts." He rubbed the stubble on his chin. "Wot'll she do?"

"Two miles a minute," Big Ed beamed. "Maybe more."

"You fellas're plannin' t'go two miles a minute on the Obenburg Road?" He shook his head. "I sure hope y'got good insurance."

We ran into Cal and Carson and Carson's MG in the registration and tech inspection line in front of a farmhouse on yet another section of Hankins Road, and you could see that Carson's complexion was almost nonexistent on account of he and Cal had already taken a little spin around the circuit. With Cal at the wheel, natch. And even old fearless, devil-may-care Cal Carrington was of the opinion that this was maybe not the best place in the world to hold a motor race. "Oh, it's awful," he laughed. "I've driven up driveways that are wider and cow trails that are better paved." But I was sharp enough to see the angle he was shooting. If he got Carson nervous enough, just maybe he'd step aside and let Cal run the race. Just maybe.

Especially since they'd bumped Carson's TD up into the faster "modified" group on account of he was too stupid not to lie about all the stuff he'd had me do to his engine. I mean, hey, it's not like a bunch of the other supposedly "stock" TCs and TDs weren't running hot cams or richer jets or pop-up pistons or lightened flywheels or…well, you get the idea. Hell, you could hear the corduroy rumble in the idle of a lot of those cars. But Carson was doomed by nature to be an honest kind of guy, which is great when it comes to character but not really all that much use in a predominantly dishonest world. Or, as Big Ed put it: "Sure, there's a big difference between telling the truth and not telling the truth. And I'm not saying that you gotta lie or anything, see? But neither do you gotta tell everything to everybody just because you know it. Let there be a few gray areas, y'know? A few mysteries…." You got the feeling that Big Ed was something of a master when it came to gray areas and mysteries.

Not to mention that Carson's car was even worse off the pace as a "modified" MG than it had ever been as a stock one, and that's because he hadn't made the really *big* commitment of rendering his car totally useless as daily transportation by fitting a straight pipe, pulling off the air cleaners and yanking everything that would come loose with a screwdriver, wrench set, Vise-Grips, hacksaw, tin snips or cutting torch off the car to make it lighter. I've said it before and I'll say it again: horsepower helps on acceleration and even more on sheer top end, but light weight helps *everywhere.* And so a lot of the other guys with "modified" MGs were running with no lights or windshields or windshield wipers or windshield wiper motors or horns or seat cushions or running boards or carpets or sometimes even fenders. Or they'd use these cheesy aluminum cycle fenders off a motorcycle or something that were so damn light they'd flutter in the wind. All of which meant that Carson's TD was carrying a couple hundred extra pounds and poking a larger and uglier-shaped hole in the air than the fastest "modified" MGs he was now supposed to be running against.

Cal and Carson took another couple practice laps after registration—the first one with Carson at the wheel, the next with Cal—and you could see by the look in his eyes that Carson was weakening. Not only couldn't he do what Cal was doing with the car, but Cal could give him a damn off-the-cuff lecture about where and how you placed the car under braking to avoid the worst of the pavement divots and what you aimed for heading into the blind corners or over the blind crests and what you needed to be doing and thinking about even while he was hung out to dry in a full lock, tire-shredding powerslide and steering away like crazy on a road he'd never seen until that very morning. Only a certified ace talent like Cal Carrington could get away with something like that! Plus he was peppering it all with a kind of reverse sales pitch that he yelled at Carson oh-so-calmly over the wind noise and engine noise and the mournful squalling of the tires: *"Of course, if you misjudge this one,"* he'd say matter-of-factly while coming the thickness of a feeler gauge from sideswiping a tree, *"you're going to damage the car…"* he shot a quick sideways glance at Carson's expression, *"…and maybe do yourself a little damage, too…."*

Carson's eyes were the size of tea saucers.

"...and you've gotta line this one up just right..." he'd continue like he was folding eggs into a pancake batter while he snapped two perfect downshifts and Carson's MG slewed all over the road under desperate late braking for the north hairpin, *"...because it's blind and the pavement is iffy over there and it goes from blacktop to gravel right in the middle of the corner...."*

In fact, his eyes must've been stinging something awful on account of it'd been three or four minutes since the last time he blinked.

"...and if you go off here," he'd explain while the tires showered up dirt and stones at the outside edge of the roadway, *"...everything'll be fine because you'll probably drown..."*

Carson looked over his shoulder and saw those same stones and bits of dirt landing in the creek that ran alongside the road right there. He thought he could even hear them splattering into the water. Over the engine noise and everything....

Meanwhile Big Ed and me had gotten through registration and tech and took our own little tour around the course. It ran a full eight and a half miles from the farmhouse that served as official registration and start/finish line up to a tight hairpin that put you onto the unpaved, gravel section heading towards the teeming metropolis of Obenburg, which was actually considering the purchase of a stop sign. But at least the road turned back to blacktop and wound its way along and occasionally across the southern fork of Hankins Creek into the sleepy little crossroads of Fremont Center, where it made another sharp right and headed up across and along the northern fork of Hankins Creek and back to the start-finish line again. To be honest, it had a lot of nifty twists and dips and serpentine swoops and switchbacks and all the locals were really excited and enthusiastic, but, just like Cal and Tommy and the old guy of Scottish descent from the original SCMA evaluation delegation said, it was narrow and bumpy and lined with trees right by the roadbed here and there and, well, *dangerous.* I mean, I'd ridden on *La Carrera* in a Ferrari with Javier "Poco Loco" Premal (although not by choice, when you get right down to it), and that experience never gave me the itchy, claustrophobic, hemmed-in-on-all-sides feeling that parts of the Callicoon layout did. And the bumpy gravel section was downright spooky, seeing as how the tires don't steer or slow the car down very well when they're not touching the ground. At the drivers' meeting, in the interests of safety, it was decreed and agreed that everyone would hold their speed down to 60 miles an hour on the unpaved section. Right.

The local firemen from the surrounding towns were helping out the armband types with the haybales and roadblocks and running the field telephone wires from one corner to the next and then back to race control, but you could see that, like any group of mixed volunteers who had never done this sort of thing before, there was an awful lot of shrugging and head-scratching and wasted motion and just plain standing around going on, and so the schedule looked to be way behind even hours before the races were due to start.

But things got together eventually and the five-lap Fremont Trophy Race for stock MGs was flagged off at around 11:30 and there was a pretty decent crowd of mostly rubbernecking locals scattered around the hillsides to watch it. And they were stuck there for the duration, too, since the only way in or out was on the very roads the races were running on. To tell the truth, Carson should have been in that race. What with that rorty motor and all, I think he maybe could have done fairly well—maybe even cracked well into the top 20 or so of the 26 cars that started!—if he'd just been sly enough to keep his damn mouth shut. Maybe even better than that, since the race got red-flagged after two of the MGs running a good half-mile apart from each other left the road at the exact same place on the unpaved section from Obenburg to Fremont Center. The first car wasn't too badly damaged after sliding sideways through a ditch, launching itself airborne in a cloud of dust, and clouting a very stout tree stump that inexplicably got sawed off some two-and-a-half feet off the ground. But the driver had no more than shaken the cobwebs out of his ears when the second car came along and did an exact repeat performance. It was a lucky thing that neither of them got much more than a few bumps and bruises, and I must admit the cars looked pretty awful when they stopped the race to tow them in. Carson in particular didn't look so well when he saw those bent-up MGs coming in on two separate tow trucks.

After the volunteer fireman and armband types got the MG mess cleaned up, they restarted the race and some ringer in a Singer roadster who'd flown himself and his racecar all the way in from California—can you believe it?—simply ran away from all the MGs. It wasn't really a fair fight as far as I could see, seeing as how the Singer (which looked kind of like the ugly big brother of an MG TD) had a larger engine with an overhead camshaft and considerably more grunt. Plus it turned out later that the driver had done quite a bit of speedway racing and was maybe even a professional, hired-gun type that somebody was paying under the table to make the Singer look good. Especially to all the guys who owned MGs. In any case, he'd sweet-talked the officials into letting him start at the back so long as he didn't run for a trophy (he made it sound like he didn't have a chance anyway and simply *had* to be in the first race so's he could catch his plane back to California) and then of course he just blew by everybody and took off for the horizon. I guess the trophy didn't really mean anything to him—after all, it didn't come with any cash money attached—and besides, he'd brought this highly-pneumatic young Hollywood Starlet type with fluttering eyelashes and perfectly capped teeth that clattered now and then over multi-syllable words all the way from the west coast with him and, seeing as how she didn't know the first thing about sportycar racing or the difference between a 1250cc pushrod engine in an MG and a 1497cc overhead-cam engine in a Singer, all she knew is that he came from all the way in the back to beat all those other chumps no matter how hard they tried. And if that was enough to get his horn honked and chrome trim polished all the way back to Los Angeles, hey, a lousy tin cup started to look an awful lot like a lousy tin cup by comparison....

Meanwhile, this guy named George Rabe was leading the "real" race for stock MGs handily. And he was doing a really good job of it, too. Even Cal said so. As for me, I was just listening to the exhaust note of all those supposedly "stock" TCs and TDs and thinking that Carson's car wouldn't have stood out among that bunch at all. Not hardly.

What with the red flag and all, the schedule was now seriously behind (which is kind of the way things generally go at race meetings, and even moreso first-time events) and so it was decided to combine the rather meager entry in the

Callicoon Trophy Race for under-two-liter sports cars with the Delaware Valley Trophy Race for small-displacement racing cars and modified MGs. It looked to be a pretty tough field, what with some guy named A. A. Garthwaite from Bryn Mawr, PeeAy, running an OSCA against a handful of hopped-up and stripped-to-nothing MGs, a few more Singers (running where they belonged for a change), a Morgan, a Jowett Jupiter like Cal drove at Bridgehampton (he was gratified to see they'd actually sold one to a paying customer and took a lot of the credit for it to anybody who'd listen), an out-of-place Austin A40 sedan and a couple of those pesky Porsches that looked and sounded like a pile of tin poop but went like the dickens anyway. I personally expected Carson to punk out and offer Cal the drive before the race even started, but I've got to give him credit. With his hands shaking like he had palsy and face the same general color as the surrounding limestone cliffs, he did indeed strap on his helmet, set himself down behind the wheel, pulled up to his spot towards the rear of the field and pull his goggles down over his eyes. I swear, he looked like an inmate on his way to the gas chamber. If it made you feel like that, why on earth would you want to do it, you know?

Maybe just to prove you can?

At any rate, they flagged Carson and the rest of them off in a screeching cloud of dust and rubbersmoke and burning Castrol upperlube, and one of those Porsches rocketed off so quickly it made you wonder if he maybe hadn't been just a wee bit premature about popping the clutch and putting his foot down. Not that you could call it a particularly bad strategy, seeing as how the road was so narrow and difficult to pass on and the schedule was already so far behind and they weren't real likely to stop and restart the race just so's they could give him a wrist slap and send him to bed without supper. But the nimble little red-over-blue Italian OSCA (which was actually built by the Maserati brothers after they told Omer Orsi *ba fangu* and went back to Bologna to go broke on their own again) was clearly the class of the field on the tight and narrow Callicoon circuit, and it had already taken the lead by the time the race was red-flagged on the second lap on account of some bozo in a Singer decided to re-arrange the haybales. Not to mention the grille and fenders of his car. The interesting thing was that this happened right in front of Carson and damn near collected him in the melee and, by the time he pulled to a stop in the line of cars formed up single-file for the restart, Carson had decided that he felt a bit unwell and handed the car over to Cal. Just like that, can you believe it?

Well, you could see a good yard of daylight under his legs as Cal leaped into the black TD and strapped on Carson's helmet (I mean, what they were doing wasn't strictly legal unless you cleared it with the stewards beforehand), and you could see the steely look in Cal's eyes as he pulled the goggles down and waited for them to wave the green flag again. When it did, Garthwaite's OSCA made a real jet-propulsion getaway and stormed off with the lead. But some joker in one of the Porsches stalled it trying to get a big launch (and just so's you don't think I'm picking on the Porsche guys, it was the kind of thing that Big Ed or The Skipper would have done on a regular basis except for the hefty torque curve on those big Jag sixes) but the upshot of the whole deal was that he was right in the middle of this narrow road with barely a half-lane available on either side and a fence on the left and the sloping wall of the ditch down to the creek on the right and so everybody behind him had to kind of sit there and fume while he ground away at the starter and tried to get it running again. Everybody but Cal Carrington, that is, who sized the situation up in an instant and made one of those hair-trigger decisions that prove you're either a star-in-the-making or an idiot that's fully made. He jerked Carson's TD out of the queue on the creek side and charged past everybody with the car doing a kind of Carnival Side Show Wall-of-Death act on the grassy slope down to the creek, what with the car cocked all catty-wumpus and crab-walking while Cal steered like mad and the rear wheels churned up roostertails of mud. I glanced over at Carson and he looked about ready for his knees to buckle. Couldn't say as I blamed him, either. To tell the truth, I couldn't believe that Cal actually pulled it off.

But he did.

Still, the first four cars ahead of the stalled Porsche had quite a jump, and I wondered if Cal would be able to catch any of them. Two guys named Lake Underwood and Bill Wonder were having a swell battle for second in the quickest of the modified MGs, and I was pretty sure Cal couldn't touch them in Carson's overweight TD. But he was definitely reeling in the fourth-place MG, and by the third lap he was right on the guy's tail and looking for a way by. And naturally me and Carson were jumping up and down and hollering like maniacs and going generally berserk on the sidelines. Wotta race! And then Carson's MG didn't come around anymore.

There is no more hollow or helpless feeling than standing there on the start/finish straightaway and staring at the empty hole in the atmosphere where your car should have been. The rest of the racers were on their last lap (and it wasn't much of a race at the front on account of that OSCA pretty much had the legs on everybody, but the battle for second between Underwood and Wonder looked like it was going right down to the wire) and so I moseyed over to the timing and scoring table by the starter's stand and asked if anybody had seen the black MG with the number 19 on the side in white shoe polish.

"Somebody said it's in the crik on the other side of the course," a guy with one of the field telephones told me.

"Upside down, I think," a guy next to him added.

A cold rush went through my guts.

"And the driver? I mean, is he okay?"

The two guys looked at each other. "The station said he was out of the car, but I don't know if that means he got out or was thrown out."

I instantly remembered seeing Eddie Dearborn coming out of his tumbling Allard at Bridgehampton and getting his skull crushed against a marker stone. *"Jesus! Is there any way I can get over there?"*

They looked at each other again. "Well, I think the course vehicle will be going out there after the race is over." Before the answer was all the way out, I was running over to the nice new Ford convertible the local Ford dealership had offered up as a pace car (in return for a little cheap publicity, of course) and half-begging, half-demanding that they take me over to where the crash was. "You his family?" one of them wanted to know.

"Yeah," I said without thinking, "I'm his brother."

Well, the checker waved and the race was over and then the course car took me around to where they were winching Carson's MG up out of the creek. What a mess! Apparently Cal had gone to pass that fourth-place MG on the dirt section (you remember, the part where all the drivers agreed they wouldn't go over 60 miles an hour?) and the guy moved right over on him and forced him off the road. Or, to be fair, maybe he didn't even realize that Cal was there, since it was hardly the sort of place where you'd expect somebody to try and make a pass. At least not anybody sane, anyway. And so Cal got squeezed off the road and went for a wild ride through the ditch, launched airborne, cleared a fence, and then got himself pitched clear out of the car when the TD hooked a wheel on some low shrubbery and went tumbling down into the creek. Cal landed in the creek, too, and that's probably what saved him from breaking every blessed bone in his body. In fact, he got out without a scratch on account of the creek was kind of soft and muddy right there. But he was absolutely covered with this greenish-brown creek glop from top to bottom. It was actually kind of funny. All you could see were his eyes, and I have to admit they looked kind of bewildered. "What happened?" I asked him.

"I can't believe it," he grumbled disbelievingly. "The guy just moved right over on me. I had no place to go...."

And of course that's the dirty little secret that no driver wants to admit. No matter how blessed good you are, sooner or later—and often through no fault of your own—you're gonna wind up behind the eight ball. It's just part of the deal. Not to mention that wrecking Carson's MG was surely going to play hell with Cal's wheeling and dealing and bank-shot angle-shooting to line up rides for himself. Wrecking other people's cars, whether it's your fault or not, is most definitely frowned upon in racing circles. Bad form, don't you know? And the inescapable, cold, hard, iron-and-steel truth of it was that Carson's MG was fairly well mangled. Plus covered in a thick, dark, gooey, foul-smelling layer of creek bottom absolutely everywhere. *"My God!"* I said, shaking my head while I stared at the bent-up TD that Cal didn't own and surely couldn't pay for that was oozing muck and dropping pools of greenish-brown creek glop all around it. *"What the hell are you going to do NOW?"*

Cal shrugged and flashed me one of his famous, don't-worry-about-it Rich Kid smiles. Right through the mud and everything, you know? "Don't worry about it," he assured me, albeit a little uncertainly. "I'll figure something out."

No question it was going to take quite a bit of figuring.

Things got even worse for Team Passaic in the last race of the day, which was for Jaguars only seeing as how they were the only big cars to show up. None of the Allard guys even bothered once word got around that a certified and respected Allard 'shoe like Tommy Edwards thought it was a bad idea. Anyhow, following all the red flags and bent metal in the earlier races, the armband types came up with the bright idea of starting cars one at a time at 15-second intervals and keeping track of who was leading and where everybody was at the timing and scoring table. I figured it would be a real disaster, but they had this pretty girl named Joni Phillips running the watches, and she was quick and sharp and handled it perfectly.

Although it didn't hurt that she only had seven cars to worry about, seeing as how all the other Jaguar owners chickened out. I mean, "elected not to compete." Not to mention that there was this Charles Schott guy there with a highly-modified Jaguar "special" that looked more like an Indianapolis track car or one of those Formula One Grand Prix things I'd seen in *Road & Track* magazine. Only maybe a little cruder here and there, on account of he built it himself and started out with a wreck to begin with. But it was light and powerful and fast as stink, and no question he was gonna rub everybody's nose in it if the car managed to make it to the end of the race. Everybody else would be scrapping for leftovers.

I have to tell you, that Jag special really got the old wheels twirling in my head. Like about what a clever guy who knew his way around a set of tools could do with some decent parts and a little imagination. I mean, it's one thing to tune and set up somebody's MG or Jaguar and have it go out and win a damn race (not that we'd really been doing an awful lot of that with hotshoes like Big Ed and Carson Flegley behind the wheel) but it's something else entirely to build your own car from the ground up out of junkyard parts—like how they assembled the Frankenstein monster, you know?—and then put some ace race pilot like Tommy Edwards or, better yet, Cal Carrington behind the wheel and show all the Creighton Pendletons and Charlie Priddles and Colin St. Johns and Skippy Welchers and Carlo Sebastians of this world just exactly how clever and imaginative and sharp and shrewd and sly about everything you really are. I guess it happens to everybody who spins wrenches for racers eventually. You start getting this itch to build your own car. It's kind of an occupational hazard. But it's a fun thing to do so long as it stays in the daydream stage....

At any rate, I wasn't too keen on Big Ed running in the Jaguar race at Callicoon, but Skippy was there with his XK 120—excuse me, XK 120*M*—and he was too stupid not to race, and so Big Ed decided that he had to race, too. And, wouldn't you know it, he wound up right behind The Skipper when they lined the cars up at the start-finish line for their one-at-a-time, 15-second-interval, green-flag waveoffs. Far as I could see, Skippy got himself a little bit of an early jump on the flag (like somewhere between "three" and "two" on the starter's countdown) but Big Ed did him one better by revving her up and popping the clutch at something around "eight." Even so, The Skipper was long gone by the time Big Ed got rolling. Only Skippy got a little over-exuberant at that first hairpin where the road went from blacktop to gravel and spun right around. But it was a harmless spin for a change and he gathered it up, grabbed first with a mighty grind, and took off again. Only now he'd lost enough time that Big Ed could see him up ahead. And that's when I learned something really interesting about Big Ed's driving. If you hung a carrot out in front of him, he went faster. Not fast like Cal or Tommy or anything, but a lot faster than he could go trying to figure everything out for himself. And there was no tastier or more alluring carrot in the world than Skippy Welcher. Not to mention that when you're following somebody, you can copy what the guy up ahead is doing. And maybe even do it a little better. Of course, the problem with all that monkey-see, monkey-do crap is that the guy you're chasing down may be an even bigger idiot than you are. Otherwise why would you be catching him? Plus the really big question is what do you do once you've caught up to him? And the answer was that Big Ed didn't have a clue. Which is why Big Ed followed The Skipper straight into the haybales—right in his wheeltracks!—when Skippy misjudged that hairpin again, left his braking way too late, and went straight on across the gravel. So Skippy's Jag plowed head-on into the hay (using up another grille, two headlights and a set of bumperettes in the process) and before you could even blink, Big Ed's Jag skated right into the back of him with the brakes locked up solid and smoke pouring off the tires. It wasn't a really hard hit, but it was enough to mash the bumpers, shatter the tail-light lenses and put a dent in the trunk of The Skipper's car and ring Colin St. John's cash register for yet another Jaguar grille, set of headlights and bumperettes for Big Ed's. I figured the Greek at the body shop would be driving around in a brand new Lincoln if Skippy and Big Ed kept racing each other.

Naturally there was a lot of hooting and hollering and who-shot-John with the armband people about exactly who did what to whom, and of course The Skipper maintained that Big Ed had run right into him. Which was true enough as far as it went. The fact that he was already parked nose-first into the hay when it happened didn't seem of any consequence to Skippy. Or at least he never mentioned it. But eyewitness accounts from the corner workers set the facts straight. They were both idiots and neither one of them could drive a lick.

"You just wait, Baumstein," The Skipper warned, wagging a bony finger under Big Ed's nose and giving him a nice little spit shower in the process. *"I'm getting my C-Type back in a couple weeks..."* That would be the same C-Type I last saw on the business end of an ancient Mexican tow truck after The Skipper and faithful squire Milton Fitting went over a cliff with it on *La Carrera*—thanks in great measure to my good friend *'Poco Loco'* Premal. *"...We'll see who blows whom in the weeds then!"*

There were real teeth in that threat, too. I mean, a guy who couldn't drive a lick in a C-Type was surely going to run away and hide from a guy who couldn't drive a lick in a regular-issue XK 120. No question about it. And you could see that got the old gears spinning behind Big Ed's eyes. He wanted to beat Skippy Welcher in the very worst way. In fact, the worse a way it was, the better he liked it!

But I had more immediate problems to deal with. Like fr'instance how was I gonna get all this bent and broken metal back home? Fortunately Big Ed's car was still more-or-less drivable, but the headlights were smashed and the buckets were bad enough that you couldn't just pop new ones in. Even if you had them. And no question it would be dark well before we got back home. As for Carson's car, it was going to be a tow job for sure. And not a very easy one at that, what with one front wheel dangling and the frame bent and Lord only knows what else gone wrong underneath. Fact is, I was kind of worried about just how the heck Cal was going to make this right. I mean, the car was a mess and I was surely the guy who'd be asked to fix it, and no question I didn't want to be looking to Cal to pay for it. But then I saw Cal and Carson over by themselves in a very deep conversation—complete with some finger pointing and heavy gesturing and waving of hands in the air—and then Cal came over and told me what we were going to do.

Which is how Cal and me wound up hitching a ride back to Jersey with one of the corner workers (with Big Ed and Carson right behind us the whole way in the Jag with no headlights) just so's we could pick up the tow truck at the Sinclair and drive all the way back to Callicoon, where we hitched up Carson's MG, towed it most of the way back to Port Jervis, stopped at a convenient scenic lookout over the Delaware River, unhitched it, pushed it off the cliff, and called Carson Flegley's insurance agent. Only first we hosed it off a little. Especially those "19s" on the sides in white shoe polish.

"Y'know," I mentioned to Cal as we drove off in the Old Man's tow truck, "if I keep hanging around with you, I think we're gonna wind up sharing a cell together in the penitentiary."

"Nah," Cal assured me. "Not with my family background. My folks donate money to political campaigns and get drunk with senators and stuff. No way I go to jail." He shot me his very best Rich Kid grin. "But I'll come visit you in there," he promised. "Every other Thursday." I watched the ends of that cobra smile of his turn up even higher.

As you can imagine, Julie was none too happy that I stayed out all night running back and forth to Callicoon with the tow truck (not to mention getting myself involved in a minor little case of grand larceny...or maybe it was just insurance fraud?), and the fact is she had to get in line to yell at me on account of it was already coming on dawn when Cal and me pushed Carson's TD over the cliff near Port Jervis and so I was over two hours late getting to work at the Sinclair. And wouldn't you know it, Old Man Finzio needed the truck first thing that morning to pick up some meat cutter's Studebaker that wouldn't start. And of course I'd been up all night on top of it and so I was generally about as useless as a pile of pig shit around the station all day. Thank goodness Butch was there to cover for me. He'd pretty much given up on the crutches and the therapy sessions over at the V.A. hospital, and I guess things were going even worse than usual with Mean Marlene—some nights she wouldn't even drop him off at the bar!—and Butch really seemed to enjoy it when I'd have him roll his wheelchair out into the shop and give him some bench work to do. Not that he'd actually smile or say anything nice about it. That just wouldn't be his style. But he'd gotten pretty decent at using his left hand and that ham-shaped stump of a right to do stuff, and he could rebuild a carburetor or fuel pump or distributor just as good as the next guy. Better, even. But it didn't help his disposition any. And he was kind of letting himself go, too. You could see it. But it wasn't the kind of thing you could say anything about, you know? I mean, how would you feel if you'd made one stupid little slipup after your wife ran off to Tennessee and so you went out and tied one on and maybe weren't paying real good attention to your driving and all of a sudden—*bam!*—you're in a damn wheelchair for the rest of your life. Hell, something like that would turn anybody sour. And Butch was never really one of your sweetness-and-light types beforehand. Although he did get a kick out of the story about Carson's TD and the cliff overlooking the Delaware River and Carson's insurance agent, who we woke up out of bed when we called to tell him the sad story. Which, by extensive prior arrangement, went something like this:

"Hello?" He sounded kind of bleary, but that's probably because it was just a wee bit shy of four in the morning.

"Hello? Mr. Bender?"

"Yes?"

"This is Cal Carrington calling. I'm a friend of Carson Flegley's."

There was nothing but silence on the other end.

"Anyhow, Carson gave me your number. I just got off the phone with him."

Still nothing.

"I'm afraid there's been a kind of an accident."

"Oh?" You could tell he was beginning to get the drift of things that, somewhere, somehow, the shit had hit the fan and somebody was going to want him to write a big check. Or at least authorize the company he represented to write a big check, anyway. You could almost feel him perking up on the other end.

"Yeah. See, we were all out boating on the Delaware River today up past Port Jervis and there was some problem with his car and it wouldn't start."

"You're calling me at this hour because his car wouldn't start?"

"Well, see, there's a little more to it than that, Mr. Bender. Carson had to get back for a big wake or something Sunday evening, and so he rode back with another friend of ours, Ed Baumstein..."

"You mean Big Ed Baumstein?"

"The very same. Anyhow, as a favor I went back with our friend Buddy here who works at the Sinclair station over in Passaic to either see if we could fix it or tow it back. So Buddy fiddled with it for awhile and put something or other in the thingamajig on the engine..."

"I put a new rotor in the distributor," I chimed in from a few feet away. Just for a little added realism, right?

"...and so we headed on back. But then it started missing and sputtering again while we were going down Route 97 and so we stopped at this scenic overlook place just a little ways shy of Port Jervis to check it out." Cal gave it a dramatic little pause.

"And?" You could tell the guy was dying to know what happened.

"Well, I got out to go talk to Buddy in the tow truck and I guess the handbrake didn't set properly. Carson said he'd been having trouble with it..." That was important. You had to blame the car. "...and all of a sudden we looked around and the car was kind of rolling off backwards..." he let his voice trail off so the image of Carson's MG rolling backwards just kind of hung there in mid-air.

"And what happened then?" Mr. Bender wanted to know.

"Well, we ran after it of course..." Cal let his voice get real choked-up and emotional right there. Almost like he was gonna cry "...but it was just too late...."

Boy, was he ever full of it when he needed to be.

"But what *happened?*"

Cal swallowed hard and blurted it out. "His car went over the cliff."

"Over the cliff?"

"Yessir. Over the cliff."

"And was this a *high* cliff?"

"High enough."

"And where is the car now?"

"I think most of it's in the Delaware River."

"Most of it?"

"Well, it was dark, but we could sorta hear stuff smashing off it on the rocks on the way down." You had to admit, Cal had a real flair for detail.

The upshot of the whole deal was that the insurance guy told us we had to make out a police report, so we went to the cop shop in Port Jervis and got this extremely bored-looking desk sergeant to shuffle through the paperwork. And then we had to go back out to the scenic overlook with another officer just as it was coming up dawn to survey the remains. I must admit, we had done an exceedingly thorough job of totaling out Carson's TD. Just like Cal said, most of it was indeed in the river, with just the odd wheel, door, headlamp bucket and fender mirror scattered down the limestone cliffside behind it. Yep, it was a total, all right.

And that's exactly what Cal had in mind when he went to work on Carson about what they needed to do with that wrecked and thoroughly mud-baptized TD of his. Because what Carson *really* wanted was one of those brand-spanking-new

Austin-Healey 100 models that we'd seen for the first time at Sebring in March and that Carson left a continuous trail of drool around at the International Motor Sports Show at Grand Central Palace in Manhattan on Easter Sunday (and where, incidentally, it won the award for Best In Show, even though it was priced not too much more than an MG and a whole heaping pile of greenbacks less than a Jaguar). But the only problem was that he had this MG TD, see (or, rather, he and his father and the First National Bank had this MG TD), and his father and uncles and all the other assorted Flegleys involved in the family funeral parlor business in East Orange were none too thrilled with the notion of one of their own zipping around town in a blessed sports car. Didn't send the right sort of message, you know? Even if it was painted black. And the notion of trading up his less-than-a-year-old MG TD that they didn't like anyway for an even sleeker, swoopier, faster and flashier new model would sit even worse. Especially considering that those first few months of new car ownership are by far the most expensive when it comes to depreciation, and that was something the famously frugal fathers and forefathers of the Flegley funeral home family understood very well.

"What would happen if we went out and bought a whole showroom full of new caskets every time some hot new model hit the market?" his father asked sternly.

"We'd sell them I guess," Carson answered, already sounding pretty lame.

"Oh, sure we would," his father snorted. "Why, all the bereaved families would want the fancy new wood hues and narrow pinstripe satin linings and triple plated brass trim."

"So what's wrong with that?"

"Nobody would want our old models anymore. *That's* what's wrong with it." He shook his head and sighed disgustedly. "Why, we'd obsolete our own inventory and be forced to give ruinous discounts."

"It works for the car business," Carson muttered under his breath.

But Carson was a hard worker and excellent at giving comfort and support to the bereaved. Even while he was trying to gently encourage them into a "more distinguished" casket or a "more impressive" floral display or a "more fitting" marker stone or a flower car or an extra limo to carry the not-quite-so-closely-bereaved of the family that most-closely-bereaved of the family weren't speaking to anymore on account of the rumored provisions of the will. But the point is that Carson had a natural knack for looking sad as a Bassett Hound and sounding like he had incurable stomach distress, and those are two things you really want on tap in that line of work, seeing as how it allows the paying customers to feel more comfortable about feeling miserable. And that's real important in the high-end stiff disposal business.

Because of those skills, Carson was finally—albeit reluctantly—allowed to get the MG he wanted so badly. But only so long as it was black and kept hidden out of sight next to the flower dump on the far end of the lot behind the hearse and limo garages. Plus he was sternly admonished by his father and all of his uncles that he must always enter from the alley in back and *never* be observed snapping off a crisp downshift or executing a tire-squealing, four-wheel drift into the front driveway where the cars lined up for processions to the cemetery. Especially if there was a lineup in progress.

So Carson's MG had come fresh from the factory in Abingdon-on-Thames with a lot of family rules and provisions and conditions on it, and that's why he was all ears when Cal slyly observed after the accident at Callicoon that the only way he was ever going to finesse his way into a brand new Healey Hundred was if that MG just suddenly ceased to be. And Carson was something of a professional expert in the "ceased to be" business. In fact, Cal was quick to explain how he'd done Carson a great service by wrecking that MG for him and then coming up with a highly risky, illegal and underhanded scheme whereby he wouldn't have to pay dime number one to fix the damage. Like I said, Cal was really good at scheming out and selling that sort of stuff. Especially when he needed to be.

As to Mr. Bender and the insurance company he represented, things went off without a hitch. Having no one in the car when the wreck happened (at least according to Cal's version, anyway) was a real masterstroke. I mean, who could you blame? Not to mention that the family funeral home gave Mr. Bender's insurance agency a lot of very nice business—a brand new Cadillac hearse and flower car every other year plus a couple limos on the off year when they didn't get a new hearse and flower car—and then there was the fire and theft insurance on the funeral home itself and the auto and home policies on all the Flegley family personal cars and houses and Lord Only Knows how much life insurance. There's probably nothing like working in the mortuary business to make you sensitive about life insurance. And so it turned out that Mr. Bender was only too happy to sign off on this fishy-sounding MG story without so much as a raised eyebrow. Hey, what did he care? It wasn't his money. And he got his commissions whether the blessed company had to pay off or not. And that's not even considering that he would get to write a policy on Carson's new and more expensive Austin-Healey at an inflated rate on account of he was now a questionable risk. And maybe he could even pick up a little chunk of Big Ed Baumstein's rather substantial insurance load on referral.

That was something to look forward to, indeed.

So the insurance company settled and that very day (between funeral services, anyway) Carson hustled across the bridge into Manhattan to put a deposit down at Westbridge for the very next new Austin-Healey 100 to come in. Or at least the next black one, anyway....

"A black one is going to be a rather dodgy proposition," Colin St. John opined casually while he tamped a fresh wad of Cavendish into that curlycue Swiss pipe of his with the plated dangle chains and perforated-tin breeze lids. "Don't know if the lads at the factory are making very many like that." He looked up at Carson with vaguely uncaring eyes. "Oh, don't get me wrong. I personally think black is a stunning color. Very smart. But it's a dismal chore trying to sell one to the Great Unwashed, don't you know?"

The fact was that Colin already had a black one stashed away in the windowless meat truck garage on the other side of town where he kept all but a very few samples of his new car inventory in order to make them seem in short supply. And therefore ever so much more dear. Unlike many American car dealers, he believed that the car your customer *couldn't* buy was the one he'd more likely pay through the nose for. And the longer you strung him along, the more you could jack the price. Better yet, there weren't very many of the new Healey Hundreds in the states yet, so Carson couldn't really shop for one or compare prices. It was a seller's market for those first few months, and Colin St. John didn't need anybody to explain it to him. "It's not how many deals you make," Colin told me once over a couple Niagara Falls shot glasses full of questionable single-malt Scotch, "it's how much you make on the deals." And that, in a nutshell, was Colin St. John's philosophy of quality over quantity as it applied to the retail sports car business. "There's a rather nice black one up in Canada," he told Carson on the phone a few days later. About the same time he sent Sylvester over to the meat truck garage to start cleaning off the cosmoline and putting the bumpers and windshield on the black one he already had. "But there's a chap up there who's quite keen on it. I might be able to swing him around to trade for the new silver-blue one I've got in stock if a few American dollars change hands in the bargain." He could hear Carson breathing heavier at the other end of the line. "But we're committed to supplying the silver-blue one as a pace car for Alec Ulmann's race at Bennett Field at the end of the month..." he could almost hear Carson's heart pounding, right through the phone line, "...and then of course I'd have to pay someone to go up there to swap the cars for me and there'd be the usual nuisance of customs paperwork to muddle through at the border...."

Meanwhile things had thankfully settled down a little at the Sinclair and me and Julie and her mom even had a kind of uneasy truce going over at the duplex. What with Big Ed's Jag back over at the Greek's body shop but sound for a change mechanically and Carson's TD relegated to boat anchor duty in the Delaware River, I was actually catching up a little and closing the shop while it was still light out. Although it stays light pretty late right there at the end of June. And that was giving me time to finish up some of the unending list of stuff Julie and her mom kept adding to that Absolutely Had To Be Done to the new apartment before we could move in. So it was kind of a break that the only race coming up on the SCMA schedule was way the hell out at Offutt Air Force Base near Omaha, Nebraska, on July 4th weekend. And who the heck wanted to drive cross-country for two and a half days each way just to wind up in Omaha?

Especially when we didn't have any cars to run.

Not to mention that my newly pregnant wife had gotten it into her head that what we really needed was to invite the entire family over to our new downstairs apartment to celebrate the Fourth of July. You know, to kind of christen and consecrate the place for us. Even though it was already Tuesday, the 30th of June, and there was still a two-page shit list of stuff she and her mom insisted needed to be done and not a single throw rug or scrap of furniture on those freshly refinished floors of hers. But it was beginning to dawn on me that newly-pregnant young wives have a lot of newly-pregnant moods and opinions to take care of, and I was starting to see that growing up and getting married and accepting adult responsibilities is kind of a balancing act. Like those native guys you see wearing boar-tooth necklaces and not much else in the pages of *National Geographic* magazine, walking barefoot up a narrow, rocky path along the spine of a mountain ridge in some scenic, godforsaken country where they don't even have toilet paper (let alone flush toilets) with two huge water buckets or two hefty sacks of corn meal or two enormous bales of llama hides or whatever slung from this yoke-like wood balance beam laid across their shoulders. But the tricky part is that the loads keep getting heavier and the path keeps getting steeper and narrower and rockier the further along you go. But you gotta keep after it, you know? Just keep putting one foot in front of the other. Even when you have no idea what you're carrying or why you're carrying it or where the heck you're going.

I was also discovering that dealing with a woman wrapped up in all the magic, mysteries, physical changes, hungers, moods and discomforts of pregnancy was a touchy deal indeed. Why, one moment she'd be all "sweetie pie" and lovey dovey—in fact, sometimes she'd be downright, certifiably *hot* (not that it's any of your damn business)—and the next morning or next hour or even five seconds later it'd be: *"Don't TOUCH me! I look horrible. I'm big as a house. How could you DO this to me? I gotta go puke."* And then she would.

Plus she'd start crying like it was the end of the blessed universe over the least little thing. In fact, it was genuinely astounding what sorts of things could set her off. Jeez, she'd start whimpering and blubbering and gushing out salt water if the damn border stitching on the window curtains we'd picked out didn't *exactly* match all that damn lilac trim I'd repainted maybe five or six times by now—why, there were so many layers of paint on those window frames and the door jambs that they'd barely open and close any more—or she'd start bawling because the downstairs apartment *still* wasn't done and we were gonna wind up stuck between my old apartment and the back bedroom of her mother's place until two weeks after the earth plummeted into the sun. If not longer. And then she'd turn right around and get all angry and red-eyed at me because I wasn't getting along with her mother (and that would be the same exact mother she was complaining about living with until two weeks after the earth plummeted into the sun only moments before) and I didn't think that was fair at all on account of I never failed to get along with her mother one bit. Mostly, I just tried to avoid her. Or, if that didn't work, I'd simply nod my head and say "yes" to whatever the heck she was saying and try my best not to look her in the eyes. I gotta tell you, those bird-of-prey eyes of hers gave me the willies, no lie. They were so full of anger and disgust and disapproval and this ominous, looming thundercloud of a threat that, by God, one day she was gonna *do* something about it.

If there was one thing I was learning from all of this, it was that females and males are hewn out of distinctly different materials—or at least those materials are assembled quite differently—and that the impregnated female of the species, in particular, is a complex, delicate, short-fused and emotional creature with the vulnerability to make you want to take her in your arms and love and comfort and protect her until the end of time and yet the sudden, unexpected turn of temperament to claw your eyes out and feed your spleen to sewer rats if you give her a reason to want to. And, on certain days of the week, it doesn't even have to be a very reasonable sort of reason at all. But it's all just nature at work and, like all such things, it's immense and unfathomable and overpowering and far beyond the understanding of an ordinary, blue-collar, shot-and-a-beer working stiff grease monkey kid from Passaic, New Jersey. Or anybody else of the male persuasion, for that matter. And so you come to realize that the best course of action is just to do what they tell you to and try to stay out of the way.

Not that you can.

Which is exactly how you wind up getting sucked into "family things" like this Fourth of July fest that didn't even seem to exist just a few short months ago. Like before you got married or became an expectant father. Now these "family things" are probably very good for you, because they take up a lot of time and effort that might otherwise be squandered on such things as making a living or fixing up the place that your wife has been ranting and sobbing and bleating about not being able to move into or maybe even sneaking off on a race weekend someplace with your buddies. But you can't do any of that stuff, because your very own mother (who, it turns out, has been in amazingly regular—even daily!—contact with your new wife ever since the start of wedding plans) has planted the seed that it would be really *perfect* if the whole family got together to celebrate the Fourth of July. Including my sisters and their husbands and kids and Julie's mom of course and even Old Man Finzio. To be honest, the idea that I was somehow related to Old Man Finzio hadn't really sunk in, and I must admit it wasn't sitting especially well. Like I'd eaten an under-cooked pork chop or something, you know?

But that was the least of my worries, since Old Man Finzio was feeling sick pretty much full-time by then and probably wouldn't come anyway. No, what I had to worry about was that Julie and her mom and my mom and all the other moms out there in the Great Mom Network had also decided that this particular July 4th get-together should be held at our new downstairs apartment in the duplex. That would be the one that wasn't finished yet and, according to Julie anyway, might not be finished until two weeks after the day the earth plummeted into the sun. Especially seeing as how Julie and her mom kept coming up with new stuff that had to be fixed or changed or completed before we could move in. Worse yet, July 4th was on a Saturday that particular summer of 1953, and so I didn't even have a spare weekend on tap to try and scramble everything into shape before the onslaught of relatives on Independence Day.

Oh, joy.

Thanks to racing, I had a bit of experience throwing things desperately togeth- er at the last possible moment, going without sleep for days at a time, and gener- ally accomplishing the utterly impossible without the necessary time or materials. But this was different on account of there was no carrot of a green flag dangling out there in front of me and, even worse, no checkered flag, congratulatory beer and satisfied feeling of accomplishment in sight at the end of it. Not to mention that a Saturday afternoon with Ferraris and Allards and Jaguars and MGs was guaranteed to be full of noise and drama and excitement and good comradeship and generally a lot more appeal than listening to my old man telling me how to light the damn charcoal and when to turn the damn hamburgers or roll the blessed hot dogs and even how to mix my oldest sister Tina's loudmouth husband Roy another whiskey and soda. Not that he needed it.

"This is quite a place you got here," he said like he was looking at something on the bottom of his shoe. "You planning on adding some furniture any time soon?"

What with the painting and plumbing and electrical and everything, I kind of never had a chance to step back and realize that the bed and end table from my old room at home and the table and chairs from my Aunt Rosamarina's garage didn't exactly fill the place up. There was a sofa over there, too, but Julie wouldn't let me bring it over on account it was all moldy and covered with cobwebs and mouse poop and spider eggs. Plus it was kind of a pea-soup green and really wouldn't have matched up too great with the lilac trim. Not that it would have exactly filled the place up anyway. So I borrowed a set of folding chairs from Carson Flegley's family's funeral home (turns out not too many people want to get waked or buried on the Fourth of July) and he was even nice enough to bring them over while I was putting the finishing touches on the big barbeque grille Butch had welded up for me out of a 55-gallon oil drum. He made a really nice job of it, too. Even if it did take up nearly half of the patch of grass by the alley that Julie's mom optimistically referred to as a back yard and made the burgers taste ever-so-slightly like creosote.

Anyhow, I asked Carson to stick around for the party and, not really knowing any of my family, he agreed. My bossy oldest sister Ann Marie showed up first with her two squabbling kids and her nebbish, raw-materials-inventory-clerk husband Jerry in tow, and of course she was carrying a foil-covered dish of that awful cabbage, bean and peanut butter casserole she made for every family holiday on the calendar and that gave you the farts so bad you had to sleep with all the windows open and made everybody else in the neighborhood shut theirs. Even if it was 95 degrees out. And of course the first thing I had to do was take the whole bunch of them on a guided tour of our foyer (which is what Julie's mom insisted on calling the little three-by-three area between the front door and the coat closet, and which was barely big enough for a throw rug and a ceiling fixture at the same time) and our living room (which, what with the newly refinished floors and not much else, looked a lot like a bowling alley) and our dining room (ditto) and the bathroom with the freshly grouted tile I'd worked on all Wednesday night and the closed door to our bedroom where Julie was still getting ready and the kitchen that contained little more than a stove, a sink, an ice box, a folding card table with drink stuff on it and two of Carson's folding chairs, and the screened back porch where I had piled all the paint cans and grout cans and old plumbing pipes and what-have-you and covered them with a painting tarp. *"OhmyGOD!"* Julie wailed like it was the end of the world. *"That looks TERRIBLE!"* I couldn't believe she was so upset. I mean, I'd turned the cleaner side of the painting tarp out and everything. So I did my best to hide it behind a couple rows of Carson Flegley's folding chairs with the funeral parlor name, address and phone number stenciled on the bottom. Just in case some of them didn't find their way back home, you know?

I must admit I was feeling pretty tired by then. Like when you're kind of sleep walking your way through all the stuff you really ought to be paying attention to and everything people are saying to you sounds like it's coming through a phonograph speaker with a bad tear in it? And, speaking of phonograph speakers, Julie's mom was still upstairs getting ready, and she'd put her hi-fi right out on the back porch with the business end pointed out towards the alley, and she was playing that new Perry Como record she'd just bought over and over and over again with the volume knob turned right up to the redline:

"Don't let the stars get in your eyes,
don't let the moon break your hearrrrt...."

Don't get me wrong. I *like* Perry Como. I liked his new record, too. But not over and over and over again and so damn loud it was blowing the paint off the bricks in the alley and so blessed fuzzy on the bass end that it sounded like he was singing under water. About then my folks showed up with Sarah Jean and Mary Frances, and it really tore at me to see the sullen, defeated look on Mary Frances' face. She was wearing one of Sarah Jean's Catholic-girls'-school-approved high-necked jumpers again instead of her usual jeans and leotard tops, and you could see it didn't fit her right. At least her insides, anyway. I figured I was still the only one who really knew anything about what she'd been through—except for what I'd told Julie, of course—and it was obvious to me that living back at home and trying to be a regular person again wasn't really working out too well. I mean, once you've got a taste for that on-the-edge, up-all-night, flailing-away-at-the-truths-mysteries-and-contradictions-of-the-universe life in Greenwich Village, sharing a room with a meek, fearful little goody-two-shoes like my sister Sarah Jean and listening to our birdwatcher mom twittering all through breakfast about the monumental territorial struggle raging in our back yard between the robins and the blue jays is going to seem just a little bit dull and confining. And you could see in her eyes she was starting to chafe a little.

I wanted to talk with her, but this just wasn't the time or place. For one thing, I needed to wait until we had a little privacy. For another, I was already in full zombie operational mode following four straight days of finishing and straightening up the apartment (which still didn't look anywheres near finished, but then this impromptu Independence Day Party wasn't *my* idea) and it was already clear that I was going to spend most of the day showing off our foyer and bowling alleys and grout and the tarp and folding chairs on the back porch to one delegation after another of arriving family. Oh, and speaking of family, getting congratulated and pecked on the cheek and patted on the back and generally made to feel like a world-class pervert (and that I should be damn proud of it, too!) as word got passed around from one pair of lips to another that I'd gotten Julie in a family way.

"I think that's just wonderful," my quiet, stay-at-home sister Sarah Jean gushed, tears of joy and remorse welling up in her eyes.

"I'm really happy for you. Really I am," Mary Frances said unenthusiastically. It was like I'd somehow betrayed her by getting Julie pregnant after helping her get the abortion she'd decided she wanted and that nobody else was supposed to know about.

"It's the greatest joy on earth," my sister Ann Marie commanded like she was repeating a line from the Pledge of Allegiance. "And don't you forget it." Out back, I could see one of her kids chasing the other one around the barbeque grille with a hot dog fork. Like he was going to stick it in her eye, you know?

That's about when her henpecked, milquetoast little husband Jerry stepped in with one of those henpecked, milquetoast *"Well, here now!"* exclamations that parents who are used to being roundly ignored make all the time. The little girl hid behind his legs while he struggled to get the hot dog fork away from her brother. *"Well, here now!"* he said again as he wrestled for leverage. I swear, the little kid was damn near as strong as he was. And a lot more determined. But size ultimately prevailed as the hot dog fork jerked free. "There," he said proudly, showing it to the little girl behind his leg like it was a dead rattlesnake or something. She sunk her teeth into his calf clear up to the gum line to show her gratitude.

"It's *so* exciting!" my sister Tina said encouragingly. The baby in her arms seemed to agree, regarding me with a Buddha-like sense of joyful serenity as he crapped his pants for maybe the fourth time in an hour and filled the air with a stink that made the wallpaper curl.

"That was pretty fast work," her husband Roy observed appreciatively over the rim of his cocktail glass. Then he leaned in a little closer and nudged his elbow into my ribs. "You sure you weren't dipping into the cookie jar once or twice before the wedding?" Julie was really worried about that. You know, that the baby would come but the math wouldn't work out? I mean, there isn't a woman on this earth who can't count to nine. Or twenty-eight, for that matter. And all the while Perry Como was crooning the blessed paint off the brickwork in the alley:

> *"Don't let the stars get in your eyes,*
> *don't let the moon break your hearrrrt...."*

And then it would be time to get people drinks and have one myself and set out the appetizers and start the charcoal and get people more drinks and have one myself and get a couple for my funeral-home-folding-chair buddy Carson Flegley and my almost-a-nun sister Sarah Jean, who I noticed were off in a corner of the so-called yard together and actually talking to each other. Or maybe not. But at least they were standing in roughly the same place and looking off in opposite directions together. Right about then Julie's mom made her grand entrance, descending the stairs from her apartment with a fresh coat of lacquer on her hair, a freshly penciled-in arch to her eyebrows and a fuchsia-colored Vogue cigarette jammed into that two-bit imitation onyx cigarette holder of hers with the fake diamond trim. "Howz ever'body?" she asked with her head kind of cocked back like a loaded pistol. And I couldn't help notice that she was pointing it more or less right-between-the-eyes at my old man. He was looking at her kind of funny, too, and I got this queasy, wave-of-nausea feeling again that there was some ugly, dark, long-buried past between them that, sooner or later and no matter how cleverly or expertly I tried to avoid it, was going to rise up and kick me squarely in the balls. So I got myself another drink.

You would have, too.

The whole family was an awful lot of people for our little downstairs duplex with the four-by-six patch of grass out back for a yard, and so the festivities, such as they were, spilled over into the alley and up the stairway towards Julie's Mom's place and out onto the front porch, and what mostly I was doing was running back and forth and getting people drinks and serving the kids hot dogs and the adults hamburgers that tasted a little like creosote and making sure that there were plenty of buns and potato salad and potato chips and paper plates and paper napkins and mustard and piccalilli and of course that everybody had a drink (although I could pretty much count on Roy and Aunt Rosamarina to take care of themselves on that score) and maybe having another one myself. And of course by then we had fireworks and bottle rockets going off all over the neighborhood—naturally my asshole brother-in-law Roy brought a whole bunch of them—and we had the usual, family-issue, Fourth-of-July excitement when the now-you-see-it/now-you-don't fuse on the silver blockbuster bomb that Roy's jerkoff little boy was going to surprise everybody with by tossing it into the barbecue grille evaporated in an instant and damn near blew his fingernails off. The really nasty kids always cry the loudest and act the most betrayed, you know?

But even with all the gunpowder loads popping and sputtering up and down the alley and all the skyrockets sizzling across the sky, it was beginning to occur to me that I was so tired and used up and beat-to-shit groggy that I could barely drag myself from one end of the apartment to the other—I mean, I'd been up four days straight and working my damn ass off every minute of it!—and what I desperately needed more than anything was a small, quiet place to lie down.

Just for a minute, you know?

No question the bedroom was out. She'd find me and I'd catch hell. And lots of it, too. But there was so much going on with the fireworks and ice cream and all that I wondered if maybe I could find someplace to hide and catch a few winks? So I sneaked out on the back porch when nobody was looking and crawled under that painter's tarp with the paint cans and plumbing pipes and such underneath it. I really couldn't believe she'd gotten so blessed upset about it being out there for the party in the first place. I mean, gee whiz, I'd turned the cleaner side out and everything....

I was packing for Le Mans and Tommy Edwards and Cal Carrington and even Briggs Cunningham himself were waiting outside in Big Ed's white Eldorado convertible (only they'd painted a pair of wide blue stripes down the hood and deck so it looked like one of the team race cars) and you could tell they were real antsy and impatient on account of we had to catch the chartered plane over at Idlewild. The special one that was also painted to match the team cars and so big and well-equipped that it had its own race shop and machine shop and lunch counter and snack bar and an after-hours lounge with a pool table and a dart board and a live dance band—I think Guy Lombardo was playing this trip—plus a small, gauzily lit little room in the tail with a high, long, leather-covered table and satin pillows on it where Monique (you remember, the leggy French masseuse/interpreter with only one eye showing?) worked.

And, like I said, they were all waiting on me. Every blessed one of them.

And all I had to do was finish packing....

Only I couldn't *finish packing on account of I had every single person in my entire family—including four or five kids I'd never seen before but I knew for sure were Julie's and mine!—clogged up in the bedroom doorway asking me to do this or telling me to do that or complaining about something else. All at the same time, so you couldn't really make out exactly what any of them were saying. It was just this low, moaning hubbub of voices like one of those weird Gregorian chants you might hear passing a strange, ancient church with flying buttresses like bat wings and spires like scorpion tails and carved marble gargoyles on the eaves who follow you with their dead, stone eyes like patient vultures....*

I hear the horn honk impatiently outside.

But the Gregorian chant just gets louder and more impatient, and now I can make out little bits of it here and there, like woodwind solos.

Roy wants another drink.

Julie's mom wants me to repaint the wood trim with the right color lilac paint.

One of my kids needs his nose wiped and the baby needs something else wiped.

Old Man Finzio needs to take off for another doctor's appointment so I have to watch things at the Sinclair.

My dad wants me to mow the lawn and wash his damn Mercury.

Julie has to go to work at the Doggie Shake and needs me to watch the kids.

Then one of the kids gets his arm broken falling off the bike I wasn't supposed to let him ride yet and another one gets bit by the German Shepherd she was always teasing next door.

My sister Mary Frances wants me to take her back down to the alley behind that fancy doctor's office on Park Avenue so she can have her baby put back in.

Roy wants another drink.

And so does my Aunt Rosamarina. Only she just kind of holds her glass out in a trembling, bony hand and looks at me like a rabbit cornered by a pack of timber wolves on account of she's too shy and stiff already to actually ask.

Julie is screaming at me for something at the top of her lungs.

Oh, yeah. She wants me to wake up.

"WHAT THE HELL DO YOU THINK YOU'RE DOING, PALUMBO??!!" she screams at me in real life.

I mean, like it wasn't obvious....

7: A Storm Brews in Brooklyn

While I was enduring one of the most difficult and exhausting Fourth of Julys since the holiday was invented, the rest of the SCMA sportycar types were out at Strategic Air Command General Curtis Le May's Offutt Air Force Base just outside of Omaha, Nebraska, putting on one hell of a race meeting. To tell the truth, I didn't much care for airport races (although no question it would've been more fun than playing gracious host to that family menagerie of mine back in Passaic). I guess Tommy Edwards had sort of poisoned the well for me about how flat and dull and lacking in either scenery or drama those airport circuits were. You couldn't get really close to the action and there was no sense of speed or perspective or (and you have to excuse me for using this word) *danger,* you know? Not that I necessarily wanted racing to be dangerous. I mean, a lot of those drivers were my friends. But they were also my heroes, and the stature of your heroes is sort of directly proportional to the nature of the challenges they meet. It's just the way things are. And I surely didn't need to leave an angry wife and mother-in-law and Cast of Related Thousands behind just to drive two-and-a-half days cross-country each way so I could watch some nose-in-the-air creep like Creighton Pendleton the Third tool around the runways in that brutish 4.1-litre Ferrari of his. Especially when guys like him had their cars hauled out for them and looked after by "professional" race crews in fresh white coveralls like the Muscatelli brothers who worked for Carlo Sebastian. All guys like Creighton had to do was fly out—in his own damn private airplane with Sally Enderle sitting on his lap and maybe one or two of his well-heeled, silver-spoon buddies sipping scotch-and-sodas in the back—run the blessed race and then fly himself back home again. It made you want to puke.

I heard later from Barry Spline that it was quite a weekend out at the Offutt SAC base. According to published reports that came out in the sportycar press, it was the biggest damn SCMA race ever and drew over 50,000 spectators. At least according to the published reports, anyway. But crowd estimating had always been more of an art than a science with the SCMA (not to mention with General Le May's Air Force types, who were eager to make those races look like a huge success) and very few of the attending local press or traffic-directing State Troopers had ever been at anything much bigger than a high school football game.

Or, as Barry Spline put it with a wry smile: "H'it reminds me h'ov the story h'ov the two swell gents in a railway car going through the sheep country of Scotland."

"I don't know it," I confessed.

"Well, they passes by a fine stretch of pasture land with a bunch of bleedin' sheep on h'it, and, no sooner are they past but the one gent says to the h'other one: *'There's precisely sixty-two sheep in that field over there.'"*

"So?"

"So they goes on h'a bit further, and darn h'if they don't pass h'another bit a'pasture all covered with bleedin' sheep. And, no sooner are they past but the first gent says to the h'other one again, *'There's exactly fifty-seven sheep in that field over there.'"*

"And?"

"And so a little ways up they passes by a third bleedin' pasture—a great bloody huge one!—and this one's just covered with bleedin' sheep from one edge clear to the h'other. But no sooner are they past it but the first gent says to the second gent: *'There are precisely two hundred and ninety-eight sheep in that field over there.'"*

Barry paused for a moment to let the drama build.

"So what happened?"

"Well, the second gent is bloody well amazed. And so he finally breaks down and asks the first gent, *'Excuse me, guv'nor, but how in blazes can yer do that?'"*

"Do what?"

"Count all those sheep so bleedin' quickly?"

"Oh, it's just a silly trick," the first gent admits, *kind of embarrassed like.*

"A trick?"

"Sure. I just counts the bleedin' legs and divides by four...."

But no matter if it was 5,000, 15,000, or 50,000 spectators, the SAC base race at Offutt field was quite a deal. Omaha being more or less in the middle of the country, it drew SCMA racers from all over the place, and there was already a pretty heated rivalry going on between the East Coast and the West Coast (not to mention the South, Southwest, Midwest, Mountain states and every other identifiable or semi-identifiable local region you could imagine) about exactly who had the best drivers. Or the best cars, which often appears to be the same exact thing unless you really know what you're looking at.

Two guys I never heard of from Texas (of all places) named Carroll Shelby and Jim Hall came 1-2 in the 75-mile sprint for modified sports cars in a couple Allards. Turns out it was a real good circuit for Allards, what with a lot of hard accelerating out of slow corners and pavement that was flat as an ironing board, so all the wheels stayed pointed in roughly the same general direction. I guess Tommy was kicking himself that he didn't go, airport race or no, on account of SAC commander General Curtis Le May himself had taken delivery of the very latest new Le Mans-spec Allard with a brand new envelope body and was looking around for somebody experienced to drive it once it became clear that the bomber jockey he'd hand-picked for the job based on what he could do with a B-47 Stratojet was getting his clock cleaned by a bunch of spoiled, runnynose rich kids who'd actually had a little seat time in racing cars. Like Creighton Pendleton, for example. Or the scrawny, pasty-faced kid from Kansas City with thick glasses and an even thicker lisp who showed up with a C-type Jaguar and more raw nerve than was probably good for him. His name was Masten Gregory, and I remembered him from Sebring, where he handed out one large fistful of money to co-drive with Skippy Welcher in his C-Type and then coughed up a bunch more to buy another one just like it from Colin St. John the very next day—on the spot, can you believe it?—after The Skipper neglected to tell him that he'd used up the brakes and the pedal went clear to the floor heading into the hairpin on Masten's very first lap in the car. The amazing thing was how he stood up in the seat and bailed out over the side before the car went crashing through the haybales, bounded through a ditch, crossed the highway pretty much airborne, tore through a couple citrus-pickers' front yards in the trailer park across the way, collected several lines of drying laundry and then came to a very sudden halt against a derelict Ford pick-up some guy had up on blocks in his driveway.

I found out later that this Masten Gregory character came from a very substantial pile of mail-order life insurance money out in Kansas City that his mother and father had been fighting over tooth-and-nail ever since their divorce. But then the father died, and the mother very kindly set aside a little ostrich-sized nest egg for each of their children. Masten wasn't supposed to come into any of it until he was twenty-one, but he got married at nineteen and that somehow squirted him through a handy legal loophole so's he could get his hands on the cash and that's why he could go out and buy any damn car he wanted. I guess he was always kind of car crazy, and used to drag race a '32 Ford hotrod all over the streets of Kansas City (on both the Kansas and Missouri sides) and had also done a little crewing for his brother-in-law's racing team. So as soon as he had the money, he went out and bought himself a Mercury-powered Allard with a set of Ardun overhead-valve cylinder heads and decided to go racing. He blew a head gasket at his first race and, just like Tommy Edwards, figured he'd do a little engine swap and put one of those monstrous Chrysler Hemis in his car. Just to get a little more grunt. In fact, that's the car he originally took down to Sebring—for his second race ever, can you believe it?—but the car crapped out in practice and so that's when he forked over the money to rent the ride in The Skipper's car. And, in spite of the crash that damn near could have killed him, he liked that C-Type so much that he bought himself a little souvenir of the weekend in the shape of a very slightly used, ivory-white C-Type Jaguar that Colin St. John had just delivered to another customer a day or two earlier. Now as Big Ed could tell you, C-Type Jaguars were rare as hen's teeth and very hard to come by at the time. But Masten Gregory's pockets were so blessed deep that he had a special knack for getting around that sort of problem. If you know what I mean. Anyhow, he showed up at this little SCMA race in Stillwater, Oklahoma—driving the Chrysler/Allard again, on account of he'd lent the new C-Type to his brother-in-law—and damn if he didn't win it outright. Just like that! And everybody who ever saw him drive agreed that he was absolutely, positively fearless.

Only they kind of rolled their eyes when they said it.

He took the Jag out to California and won this big race at Golden Gate Park, and afterwards he graciously handed the keys over to the editors of *Road and Track* magazine so they could play around with (I mean, "road test") the fastest damn car they'd ever driven. Like car magazine writers everywhere, they tried very hard to make it sound all scientific and detached and professional in print, but the fact is they spent most of the afternoon getting their gongs off on balls-to-the-wall acceleration runs. And who could blame them? Not to mention that this particular C-Type was quicker off the line than most on account of it had a steeper, 3.92 rear axle ratio instead of the standard 3.31, so it was wound a little tighter than your average C-Type Jaguar. Not that you could call *any* C-Type exactly average....

So then this Masten Gregory kid and his tightly-wound C-Type show up for the Offutt Air Force Base SAC event in Omaha a couple months later and do it all over again in the big 200-mile feature race, coming in first overall against some of the top SCMA hotshoes in the country. Oh, Creighton Pendleton and some of the other fast guys chased him for a while, but they were all losing ground to this kid with thick glasses who looked like he'd just finished his first high school science project but drove like he was late for his own funeral. And a lot of the folks who watched him figured maybe he was. In fact, Creighton Pendleton got so flustered trying to keep up that he missed a shift and bent all the blessed valves in that incredibly-expensive-to-fix Ferrari engine of his. "Couldn't have happened to a nicer guy," I told Barry Spline.

"Made it worth the 'ole bleedin' trip," he grinned back at me. "Why, the valvegear in that car sounded like a mixmaster full of cheap cutlery."

Made me kind of sorry I hadn't been there to see it. And hear it, too....

Far as I could tell, the next event up for our Team Passaic guys out of the Sinclair wouldn't be until the Giant's Despair hillclimb rolled around again July 24-25. If we had any cars ready, anyway. Big Ed's 120 was out of the Greek's body shop, but you could tell he wasn't real keen on the notion of running it in the same event as Skippy Welcher now that The Skipper was supposedly getting his C-Type back. Plus that 120 of ours had been banged and bashed and bumped and blown up and had its synchros shredded and clutch and brake linings fried enough times that it had become kind of Used Goods in Big Ed's eyes, and you could tell he was more or less looking around for something new to replace it with. Even though I had it running just fine. I got the feeling that Big Ed was the exact same way when it came to wives. Or wives and girlfriends, anyway. But the upshot of the whole deal was that Big Ed was spending a lot of time on the phone with Carlo Sebastian about the seriously-pancaked Ferrari that Javier Premal and me went over a cliff with down in Mexico that was still undergoing (or supposedly undergoing, anyway) the world's longest and most extensive rebuild over at the Ferrari race shops in Italy. He was also making occasional trips across the George Washington in his Eldorado (or, if it was really hot out, in the black Sixty Special sedan with air conditioning) to talk to Colin St. John about any other interesting sets of wheels that might be coming down through the pipeline from the Jaguar factory over in Coventry, England. I got the feeling he had some sort of deal going, but he wouldn't tell me anything about it. He'd just kind of smile mysteriously, take a deep drag of one of those buck Cuban stogies of his, and blow out a smoke ring the size of a sugar doughnut. To tell the truth, I think he liked to keep me dangling.

And, speaking of keeping people dangling, Colin St. John was milking the Carson Flegley black Healey Hundred from Canada deal for all it was worth. He'd already taken two deposits plus a fifty-buck side bribe for the phony dealer up in Canada and it was amazing how much money he was making, over and above the advertised Healey Hundred retail price of $2985 (including heater and federal taxes) by *not* selling Carson the black one he already had in stock over at the windowless meat truck garage on the other side of town. Carson even offered to take off work and go up to Canada himself to make the trade, but Colin explained that the negotiations were at a very delicate stage relative to the phony

Canadian retail customer who was waffling between taking the black one or trading—with $ufficient incentive, of course—for the silver-blue model Colin had promised as a pace car the last weekend of August.

"But if things go our way," he assured Carson, "we'll have you on your way to Watkins Glen come September in that brand new, shiny black Austin-Healey 100."

It made Carson's eyes glaze over just thinking about it.

So I found myself stuck at the Sinclair with no race cars to run (and, worse yet, no racecar prep-and-repair money coming in) while the rest of the SCMA crowd headed off for Giant's Despair at the end of July and then to another of the SAC races at Lockbourne Air Force Base near Columbus, Ohio, on August 9th. It was widely publicized that all the proceeds at Lockbourne (if there were any, of course) were destined for the "Airman's Living Improvement Fund," which was a clever-as-hell angle-shoot whereby General Le May's pet jet jockeys could have a kind of hobby shop on the base where they could, oh, say, build a birdseye maple dining room set or make lamps out of old bomb casings or (but only if the mood struck them, right?) prepare the odd Allard or two so's they could keep their dogfighting skills sharp and maybe show those runnynose rich kids from the SCMA a thing or two. Which I guess was a pretty neat deal for all concerned. Except for maybe John Q. Public, Fred Average and Tom Taxpayer, who were kind of footing the bill for having government property turned into weekend playgrounds for a bunch of spoiled rich kids while air corps servicemen on Uncle Sam's payroll filled in as ushers and corner marshals and ticket takers and hot dog vendors and urinal swabber-outers and what-have-you. And don't think it had gone unnoticed in Washington. Especially by the pinko liberal "fellow traveler" democrat fringe, who kind of figured that providing freebies for rich people at the public expense was not exactly what the founding fathers had in mind when they wrote the Constitution. Not that you could prove it much one way or the other.

But, fortunately for the SCMA, "Tailgunner Joe" McCarthy had those left-wing types kind of pinned down under a covering fire of accusations and innuendo right about then, and, what with the war against the communists in Korea and the newspaper headlines all full of Julius and Ethel Rosenberg going to the gas chamber for spying and Uncle Joe Stalin dropping dead of a stroke in Moscow and his right-hand-guy/head-of-the-secret-police Lavrenti Beria getting the rug yanked out from under him (they charged him with "being an agent of capitalism," which was most definitely a capital sort of crime over there in Russia) plus a ragtag bunch of commie rebels led by this loudmouth Castro guy who really needed a shave making trouble for all the legitimate American businessmen down in Cuba, sticking your nose into and/or making rude noises about anything to do with the Strategic Air Command was not the most enlightened sort of thing you could be pursuing up on Capitol Hill. And the smart money knew it, too.

So the races went on.

Cal wanted to go to Lockbourne real badly, on account of he was hoping he might be able to land a ride in that V8-60-powered MG monstrosity that he'd driven at Elkhart Lake (Lord only knows why, since the damn thing almost killed him when it ran out of brakes the first time around) and he was really putting the pressure on for either me or Carson or Big Ed to go just so's he could tag along.

But I had all sorts of stuff to do at home and at the Sinclair (and, more importantly, no paying customers going to Lockbourne), so I had to beg off. Carson was of course still between sports cars (even though his new Healey Hundred was already waiting for him in Colin St. John's windowless meat truck garage on the other side of the bridge in Manhattan, needing only to have the cosmoline cleaned off and the windshield and bumpers put on to be ready to go) and it looked like Big Ed had more or less lost interest in running his oft-straightened-and-repaired XK 120. Especially when The Skipper would be showing up with his freshly rebuilt C-Type and most assuredly blow him in the weeds.

But Cal was not the sort of guy to easily be denied. And so he went through all the loose pocketbooks (not to mention pants pockets) back home at Castle Carrington and came up with enough nickels, dimes, quarters and half-dollars for one-way bus fare out to Columbus and maybe even a couple cheap meals along the way. He figured once he was out there, finding food to eat, a place to stay and getting himself back home would more or less take care of themselves. I mean, they *had* to, right? Typical Cal.

Well, that Frankenstein monster MG TC/Flathead Ford V8 thing never even showed up and Cal struck out landing any other sort of ride (word of his little "incident" with Carson's TD at Callicoon had kind of gotten around), and he was really kicking himself over not having Carson's black TD to drive when he watched a couple guys named Bob Fergus and Don Marsh finish one-two in the MG race. Hell, he could beat those guys blindfolded (although Barry Spline said he shouldn't be so sure about beating Fergus, on account of he was so slick and smooth that it was real easy to miss how genuinely *fast* he was). Things got even worse for the big car race. The Lockbourne layout was mostly a bunch of long straightaways (the start/finish stretch alone went for over one-and-a-quarter miles!), and so it was more than anything a wide-open horsepower festival. And who should show up with the biggest, heaviest hammer and anvil but our old buddy Creighton Pendleton, who had not only bought himself a bunch of brand new engine parts for his Ferrari (including the very latest Factory Team camshafts, carburetors and assorted hardware) but also paid to have them air-shipped over and then shoveled another wad of simoleons at Briggs Cunningham's own personal ace wrench, Alfred Momo, to have them put together properly.

Now this Alfred Momo guy had himself quite a reputation. As a kid back in Italy, he'd worked for some of the famous Italian car factories before the first war and even served as a riding mechanic at races like the Targa Florio—pumping gas pressure with one hand and hanging on for dear life with the other—when he was only sixteen. Doing stuff like that requires an unusual dose of faith in both the machinery under your butt and your fellow man (as represented by the guy with the crazy eyes in the seat next to you) and is definitely not for the queasy or faint of heart. Plus he was already a hell of a mechanic and machinist. His dad was a steam fitter who died when little Alfredo was only two, and so he'd been working on machinery since he was twelve and turned out to have a real knack for it. He served in the Italian Navy and did a lot of work on airplane motors. He left with a glowing letter of recommendation from his commanding officer, and they called him back in 1920 to serve as flight engineer on this record-setting Rome-to-Tokyo flight in their latest, tri-motor seaplane. And he saved the entire crew from a sure crash landing when one of the engines went sour over Albania by climbing *outside* the fuselage and fixing a busted fuel line. Can you believe it? Later on he came to America as a sales agent for FIAT, and wound up settling right here in New Jersey and running the Rolls-Royce factory's U.S. service shop. But his real passion was always racing cars, and so, after Rolls-Royce closed up that part of their stateside operation, he went to work for Carlo Sebastian and people started bringing him cars to prepare and modify for racing for them. Including Briggs Cunningham, who wound up kind of setting Alfred Momo up in his very own car business just so's he could have first dibs on his time. Everybody agreed he was a real genius when it came to figuring out mechanical things and his preparation was always meticulous, and that's because Alf Momo understood better than anybody that a successful racing car is made up of a kazillion properly-executed little details rather than some bright-idea demon tweak or radical notion that's going to turn the whole world upside-down and set it on fire in the bargain. Or maybe set it on fire first and then turn it upside-down.

But the point is that Creighton Pendleton had Alf Momo put all those new, trick pieces together for him and then he had Carlo Sebastian's Muscatelli brothers haul his freshly-rebuilt Ferrari out to Lockbourne for him while he flew out at his leisure to meet it (he even landed on one of the runways, honest he did!) and then he proceeded to effortlessly blow everybody and his brother into the weeds thanks to an engine that sounded like the howl of a jungle cat the size of Pittsburgh. That scary-brave Masten Gregory kid from Kansas in the ivory-white C-Type gave chase, but he was giving up six cylinders, one carburetor and more than 40 cubic inches to Creighton's hotted-up Ferrari, and, at least there on the long, high-speed straightaways at Lockbourne, it was simply no contest.

As per usual, our boy Cal wound up landing on his feet. Or, more precisely, taking off from Lockbourne in a private plane and landing at an equally private airstrip not more than six miles from Castle Carrington. And that's while the Muscatelli brothers and the car hauler carrying Creighton Pendleton's Ferrari (not to mention everybody else from our neck of the woods who drove to Ohio for that race) were still somewhere in the middle of Pennsylvania. He got the ride home from none other than Creighton Pendleton the Third (can you believe it?) and without a dime in his pocket, too. Typical Cal. Seems he made up some bullshit story about his own racecar breaking down en route, and Creighton, even though he didn't believe a word of it and didn't much like Cal in the first place and more-over thoroughly disapproved of the company he kept (and that would include absolutely all of the Team Passaic regulars), recognized Cal as a fellow member of the silver-spoon set whose family might well know and associate socially with families that might well know and associate socially with his own. And so Creighton was overcome with a fit of *noblesse oblige* and properly gracious about offering Cal a lift. "He didn't do it because he wanted to," Cal explained later, like it should be obvious to anybody. "He did it just to show me that he could." It was a difficult sort of thing for a grunt-level working stiff like myself to understand.

"But you don't even like each other."

"We hate each other, actually."

"But he was nice to you?"

"Oh, of course."

"And you were nice to him?"

"Absolutely."

"So wha'dja talk about?"

"Oh, this and that. You know."

If I'd known, I wouldn't have asked. "And how'dja get home from the airport?"

"Well, I couldn't very well ask him for cab fare, now could I?" Cal snorted, starting to sound just the least little bit exasperated with me. "So I told him I'd call the chauffeur to pick me up and then waited for him to take off again so I could hitchhike home. Got a ride right to my folks' door in less'n five minutes."

And that was the amazing thing about Cal Carrington. He always had this absolute faith that everything was going to work out for him. No matter what situations he put himself into or how brazenly he tempted the fates to squash him like a cocky little bug on a windowsill.

Like some famous guy or other once said, the rich are very different from you and I. And how.

But the race all the sportycar types in New York and New Jersey and all up and down the whole blessed Eastern Seaboard were jawing about—and the one Colin St. John's silver-blue Austin-Healey Hundred would be attending front-and-center as a pace car—was the "outlaw" AAA/FIA-sanctioned "professional" event that Sebring 12-Hour promoter Alec Ulmann was putting on at Floyd Bennett Field Naval Air Base on Saturday, August 29th. Right across the Manhattan skyline from us in, of all places, Brooklyn, New York! Needless to say, this had caused quite a stir among the devoutly-amateur clubby regulars of the SCMA (led, as you can well imagine, by ad-hoc committee chairman-for-life Charlie Priddle) seeing as how they figured sports car racing—and particularly sports car racing in and around the greater metropolitan New York area—was kind of their own private bailiwick. And they certainly didn't want to see it get all messed up with sponsors and advertising and commercial interests or hired-gun professional drivers with more skill than breeding. That would never do. And they didn't much care for Alec Ulmann and his Sebring race, either, since it paid actual prize money—can you believe it?—and counted points for the World Manufacturer's Championship. Which meant all those serious factory teams and even more serious factory drivers from Europe would come over and make some of the longstanding SCMA club regulars look like a bunch of three-ring circus bozos who couldn't find their ass with both hands.

But the *real* issue was whether the SCMA wanted just anybody to be able to drop in on their party. Or, worse yet, hold a sports car party of their own without such stringent (if not exactly specific or written down anyplace) admittance requirements. And the answer, unless they came from the right stock or knew someone who knew someone, was a resounding *"no."* Plus they didn't much want some other sportycar group—and especially a (horrors!) *professional* sportycar group—sending out entry forms to non-SCMA race events and possibly turning the heads or diverting the attentions of the rank-and-file racers.

Now you may wonder why they would care. But the fact is, for guys like Charlie Priddle and his steering and ruddering committee regulars, being bigwigs in the club was easily the single most important thing in their lives. It gave them power. It gave them prestige. It gave them stature. It gave them meetings to go to and committees to form and evaluation delegations to send out and strict and solemn driver tribunals to preside over. Why, it gave them the ability to make a brave, skillful and gentlemanly motoring warrior like Tommy Edwards—a man who embodied all the many things that they would never, ever, be—bow and curry favor and kowtow to them. Why, they could make guys like him squirm in their shoes if they really wanted to.

And believe me, they really wanted to.

But the best part of it was that they were invulnerable. Because nobody else—and certainly not the racers themselves—wanted any part of the time and effort and endless, thankless tasks it took to organize and put on their events. Hey, the racers just wanted to *race,* you know? So all those Charlie Priddle types just filled the vacuum. And they did it because that vacuum, in defiance of every known law of physical science, inflated them beyond all recognition. But there was a catch. Like all things massively inflated (and especially those massively inflated with nothing but hot air), the steering and ruddering regulars like Charlie Priddle knew they were only a tiny rip, tear, cut, leak or pinprick from shooting around the room like some little kid's birthday balloon—making a kind of squeaky, extended-play mouse-fart noise all the way—and winding up all shriveled up on the floor like a discarded condom.

And they were not about to let that happen.

So they got pretty damn vocal about just exactly what they were going to do to any SCMA member with the gall, cheek, insolence or temerity (or any combination thereof) to run this "outlaw" event at Floyd Bennett Field. By Jiminy, they'd lose their racing licenses! And their good standing in the club, as well. Why, they might not even get the regulation "Peace on Earth, Good Will Towards Man" Christmas cards that Charlie Priddle sent out every December on the club's behalf (which featured a jolly Santa in a green C-Type Jaguar with a sack of gaily-wrapped gifts next to him, a decorated Christmas tree strapped to an S. H. Arnolt luggage rack on the rear deck, and a couple elves in white coveralls wielding a floor jack and a brass-head knockoff hammer to change a flat right-front tire).

Well, you'd have to say that there were a bunch of sportycar types around with more than a passing interest in how this was going to work out. Particularly Tommy Edwards, who'd had it up to *here* with Charlie and his damn board members and steering committees and delegations of evaluators and driver review boards and was just looking for some way to explain, in the most delicate and yet most direct manner possible, that they could all take a flying leap at a rolling doughnut and let the rest of the world (meaning those with something worthwhile to do) get on with it. And so, even though he was anything but a political type or backroom power broker, Tommy Edwards had already arranged a ride for himself at Floyd Bennett field and was doing everything he could to talk up Alec Ulmann's "outlaw" event in Brooklyn to everybody he knew. And a surprising number of them were listening to him instead of the threats from Charlie Priddle.

Especially those who had seen both of them drive.

So there was quite a bit of anticipation going on, and I sure as heck didn't want to miss out on the action right there in our own backyard. Especially since Tommy would be driving again and Cal mentioned that he'd been down to see the guy who owned all those unsold Jowett Jupiters and that he just might be driving one again at Floyd Bennett Field. Not to mention that Big Ed was being real cagey about his own plans for the weekend. "Why don'cha meet me over there with the tow truck," he said, his cigar doing one of those wild, crazy-eight numbers between his teeth. "Just in case we need it, y'know?"

And that's why I was real careful about coming home in time for dinner and taking out the garbage and even complimenting Julie's mom on the broccoli she cooked until it was the color of a green olive and the chicken it went with that she'd kept in the oven until it was same approximate color, taste and texture as those Egyptian mummies you see on high school field trips to the natural history museum. Not that I'd ever actually chewed on one. But the point is that I wanted to go to that race over in Brooklyn in the very worst way and I moreover wanted Julie to come with me. Far as I could see, we'd had some of our best times together at those races (at least if you didn't count seeing Eddie Dearborn getting killed at Bridgehampton) and, looking ahead, it seemed like going away to the races with Julie was about the only place we'd ever be alone together and away from that nasty, mean-spirited, scheming, meddlesome, penciled-in-eyebrow, screeching banshee of a mother of hers.

Although I'm sure she had a lot of very nice qualities, too.

"Look, Julie," I whispered gently while we were nestled away all cozy and close together in the darkness of our bedroom, "this is going to be our future, see."

She didn't say a word.

"And I think it can be a real good one, too."

I knew she was listening, though.

"These sportycar people have loads of money. And they'll pay plenty for somebody who can take care of their cars and do a decent sort of job for them."

Still nothing.

"But I gotta *be* there, you know? Fixing the damn cars and sending them on their way just isn't enough. I gotta be the guy who's waiting to hand them a cold drink and ask them how it's runnin' when they pull in off the circuit. I gotta be the guy with all the parts and tools on hand to take care of emergencies. I gotta be the guy who sees to it that the cars get there and back home again—even when they're broken or wrecked or blown sky-high—so my guys don't have to worry about it."

Was that a snore?

"And I want *you* to be part of it. It'll be *fun,* too. You'll see. We'll get to travel together and see beautiful places and hang around with all these fancy rich people...."

"Who'll ignore us like we're furniture," she whispered back sleepily, "and treat us like the stable hands who sweep up behind their horses."

Yep, she was listening all right.

"But it's not like that at all," I protested, letting my voice come up to maybe half a decibel.

"*Sssh!* Keep your voice down. You want the whole damn neighborhood to know our business?"

Why, I was being so blessed quiet you could have heard an ant fart.

"Look," I whispered even lower, "this is something we can do *together.* Just the two of us, see..." I kind of scrunched in a little closer so I could feel her body all up and down against mine. "It'll be a chance for us to be *alone* for a change."

"Yeah," she snorted softly, "just you and me and that big loudmouth Baumstein and the nervous undertaker who gives me the creeps and your handsome, rich-kid friend who never has a nickel in his pocket and is just using you to get what he wants and...."

"But those are my friends!"

"SSHHH!"

"Sorry."

Julie kind of sighed and rolled over a little. I could just barely make out the top of her silhouette against the window shade. She had a hell of a shape on her, no lie.

"You know," I said so softly I could barely hear it myself, "I look around at all these old married couples. The ones that have been together a long time, I mean..." I was watching the gentle heave of her chest as she breathed in and out, "...and I just know that's not the way it's going to be for us."

"What do you mean?"

"Oh, you know. The husband goes off to work and the wife stays home and takes care of the brats and by the time he comes home they're both so worn out and aggravated and sick and tired of everything that all they do is snap at each other or yell at each other or not speak to each other because, deep down, they blame each other for how dumb and dull and useless and stupid and senseless their lives have become."

"You make it sound awful."

"It *is* awful!"

"SSHH!"

"It *is* awful," I repeated so softly you could barely hear. "But that's not how it's gonna be for us. Not us. We're gonna do things *together!*"

"Like going to the sports car races?" Julie snickered.

"Yeah, like going to the sports car races," I told her, trying to make it sound maybe a little more noble and worthwhile than it really was. I mean, there was no way you could confuse it with helping Albert Schweitzer take care of all those poor sick folks in Africa.

"You're such a boob, Buddy," Julie laughed. "I think that's why I like you so much."

"Because I'm a boob?" On the one hand, I guess I should have been insulted. On the other, I really liked the tone of her voice. It was kind of exciting, if you know what I mean.

"Oh, it's just that you're so...I don't know...such a boy scout."

"Now I'm a boy scout?"

Julie rolled back over and pulled me towards her, nuzzling her head against my neck and chest. "You can be awfully dumb and an awfully big jerk sometimes," Julie said softly, "but under it all you're basically a good guy and I know I can count on you." She kissed my shoulder. "That's worth a lot, I think."

"And so you like me?"

"Yeah. A little."

"But you just said you liked me a lot."

"When?"

"Just a second ago."

"That was then," she whispered playfully. "Times change." She was fooling around with my hair and driving me absolutely nuts. So I reached down for the elastic band on her pajama bottoms, but, as soon as I did, I felt her stiffen. *"SShh."* She hissed. *"She'll hear us...."*

Like I said, I had to find a way to get Julie away someplace.

8: Dog Days

The big official brouhaha over Alec Ulmann's non-SCMA event at Floyd Bennett Field had become pretty much *the* hot topic for all the sportycar types in the greater New York metropolitan area, and it was hard to find anybody who didn't have an opinion. He'd managed to get both the Triple-A (who sanctioned almost all the professional, open-wheel oval track racing here in the U.S. of A, including the Indianapolis 500) and the FIA (the *Federation Internationale d' l'Automobile* over in Paris, who sanctioned the World Grand Prix Championship and all the important professional sports car races in Europe, including the Twenty-Four Hours of Le Mans) to put their collective rubber stamps on his race at Floyd Bennett Field, and so it was looking very legitimate indeed. Plus he'd lined up sponsors with fat checkbooks like Shell gasoline and Castrol oil and Knickerbocker beer and K.L.G. spark plugs by promising them more than just a few cheesy cloth banners hung on the snow fencing. Because Alec Ulmann knew how to wheel and deal. Fr'instance he traded a bunch of signs and promised P.A. mentions and a nice article in the race program about Shell's new TCP fuel additive *("TCP: The Answer to Spark Plug Fouling")* in exchange for free gas for all the competitors and the understanding that, no matter what happened, they could tell the whole blessed world that the winner (no matter who the heck it was!) used Shell gasoline. Plus all the important brass from Shell and their families would get paddock passes and box lunches on race day and maybe—just maybe—a ride around the racetrack in a real, live racing car!

Alec Ulmann's sponsors ate it up.

All of which put the icy finger of fear up all the very tight assholes on Charlie Priddle's assorted steering and ruddering committees, and he made it abundantly clear that the SCMA would excommunicate *anybody* who entered, ran, or had anything to do with organizing the Floyd Bennett race in any way. But then somebody reminded him that only the Pope in Rome had the power to excommunicate people (and you had to be Catholic to boot, and not that many of the SCMA inner circle were). So Charlie changed it to "fired." Only then somebody explained to him that you couldn't really "fire" somebody from a club, on account of they really didn't work for you. So Charlie switched to the far more genteel "dismissed," which had always worked just fine for all the lazy servants, tippling chauffeurs and uncooperative chambermaids in the Priddle household back home. Only it turned out that "dismissed" was actually the same thing as "fired," no matter how much more genteel it sounded, and so that wouldn't work, either. "OK, then," Charlie snarled, "we'll *blackball* 'em!" And of course that was something well within the scope and sensibilities of club policy. In fact, they were rather good at it.

But a lot of the sportycar people around New York and New Jersey and New England were intrigued with the Floyd Bennett Field event—I mean, it was right in our own back yard, for chrissakes!—and, as rumors spread about who was committed to coming and who else was likely to show, the general wave of public opinion relative to Charlie Priddle's position boiled down to a sort of collective "screw him." And when none other than Briggs Swift Cunningham let it be known that he was bringing his famous team of homegrown, all-American challengers—winners at Sebring and freshly back from finishing all three cars an astounding third, seventh and tenth overall at the Twenty-Four Hours of Le

Mans—well, the floodgates were open. Charlie Priddle knew he could neither excommunicate, fire, dismiss or blackball the most important and influential single person in American sports car racing without raising a few eyebrows, so he did what any seasoned and experienced political expert would do and reversed his position 180 degrees without so much as the flicker of an eyelash. After all, you can only survive as a leader of public opinion if you make damn sure you're heading in the same direction it is....

"We're really pleased that Mr. Ulmann has chosen our fair city as the site of his race," Charlie told all the regulars who had nothing better to do than attend the general club meeting on the third Tuesday evening in August. "It's a chance to bring our sport to the people," he said earnestly, referring to all the grunt-level plumbers, printers, painters, post-hole diggers, Phys. Ed. teachers, peanut vendors and pipe fitters of assorted ethnic, cultural, political and religious persuasions who would never—ever!—be considered for SCMA membership, "a chance to show it off for all of our friends, families, relatives and all the wonderful local citizens of New York who may never have the chance to see us race at places like Bridgehampton or Watkins Glen." He smiled benignly from the podium at virtually everyone in the room. "And so we encourage all of you to do whatever you can to help make this event the huge success it so richly deserves to be."

Although, as far as Charlie Priddle could see, it wouldn't be such a bad thing if it maybe rained like hell or a gas main exploded or a terrible earthquake stuck that particular section of Brooklyn that day....

What with the heat of summer upon us and a lot of official, 9-to-5 Naval military takeoffs and landings going on at Floyd Bennett Field every day, Alec Ulmann and his crew wisely decided that practice would take place on Thursday and Friday evenings from about 5 PM until dusk so that all the racers could get used to the track (and vice versa) and all the inevitable glitches could get ironed out so's everything would run smoothly in front of the paying customers on Saturday. You had to admire the way these guys were handling things. But of course it's lots easier when you've got just one guy up at the top making all the necessary decisions and delegating all the necessary responsibilities the way he sees fit. Works a lot better than all those cumbersome steering committees and ruddering committees and boards of directors and solemn tribunals and such where there are always all sorts of personalities, hidden motives and pecking orders involved and the real issue often turns out to be who has the *power* to make decisions rather than the quality and timeliness of decisions themselves. But, as Big Ed pointed out, none of that should come as a surprise to anyone who understands the difference between a sole proprietorship and a publicly held company. Especially if you happen to own stock.

In any case, that's how I found myself tooling through Hoboken in the Old Man's tow truck a little after lunchtime on Thursday afternoon, August 27th, on my way to the Holland Tunnel and right across town to the Manhattan Bridge to Brooklyn and then down Flatbush Avenue all the way to Floyd Bennett Field for practice. I could hardly wait. The idea that we were going to have an actual sports car race right here in the heart of New York City was just too delicious. Why, for that one day, we'd be right up there front-and-center on the sports pages with the

New York Yankees and Brooklyn Dodgers instead of hidden back in the agate type next to the golf and tennis match stories and professional bowling scores. And I was sure you'd be able to hear the echoes of those howling Ferraris and thundering Cunninghams and blaring, brass-section Jaguars and lumbering, grumbling Allards all the way from Coney Island to Ebbett's Field.

And I was a part of it, too!

So I'd arranged to have Butch and Raymond and Tater and Old Man Finzio covering for me back at the station, and I'd even gotten Raymond to promise not to do anything he wasn't absolutely sure about on the customers' cars without having Butch check it first and I'd gotten Tater to promise to take his old hound dog Barney on all the parts runs with him and keep him tied up at the shop—even if he howled like hell—so's he wouldn't saunter out onto the sidewalk and hump the mailman's leg until it damn near came loose at the hip joint or put his head under passing ladies' skirts for a friendly little sniff (I swear, he'd even try to do that with nuns sometimes!) and I'd gotten Butch to promise not to piss Old Man Finzio off (not that there was any way he could much help it) and I even got Old Man Finzio to grudgingly agree not to fire Butch (or Raymond or Tater, for that matter) or threaten customers with that sawed-off baseball bat of his until I got back. And I had to do all that just to take off for a couple stinking hours Thursday and Friday afternoons and all of Saturday morning. Ever since I first started hanging around that Sinclair station on my way home from high school, I guess I'd dreamed about running a place just like it one day. What's that old saw your parents and teachers are always throwing in your face? You know, about being careful what you wish for, because one day you just might get it?

But I didn't care. I could deal with, worry about and fret over all that stuff come Monday morning. Until then, I was going to enjoy my few days of racing in Brooklyn, dammit. Even if it was hotter than blazes out already and, according to the radio, due to get even hotter for the weekend. But I could hardly feel it. Like I was immune, right? After all, I'd gotten Julie to agree to come with me on Saturday (and maybe even Friday evening, too!) and I'd heard that the guy with all those unsold Jowett Jupiters backed up in his warehouse was going to let Cal drive one again to try and pump up a little interest with the local citizenry. Not to mention that Big Ed left the Sinclair earlier in the day in the black Caddy sedan (the one with dark windows and air conditioning, natch, on account of it was so steamy out) with one of his scrapyard flunkies riding shotgun. "I'll meet you at the field around four or so," he told me. "I got some stuff t'do in the city first."

"But what about the 120?" I said. I mean, I had it parked over by the street lamp on the front corner of the lot, all polished up and looking sharp (at least over the fresh paint and body filler, anyway) and ready to go. I always kept it there whenever I had it in for service but wasn't actually working on it. As kind of an advertisement, you know? And people always stopped to look it over and marvel at it. A sleek, shiny XK 120 could still stop traffic on Main Street during that summer of 1953. "Well," I asked him, "you want me to bring it over for you so's you don't have to come back to get it?"

I had this picture in my mind's eye of me and Julie tooling across the George Washington Bridge in Big Ed's Jag (even though the Holland Tunnel was really the more direct route, but who wants to be stuck down in that dark, steamy, smoky tunnel in a Jaguar convertible when it's well over ninety degrees out?) and so I told him I'd be happy to take care of it.

"Nah," Big Ed said with a mysterious twinkle in his eye. "Just bring the usual stuff we need in the tow truck. I'll meet you there." And without another word, he was gone. Just like that. So I knew something was up and I couldn't wait to see what it was. Had Carlo Sebastian finally come across with a Ferrari for Big Ed? Boy, that would really be something if he did....

But it wasn't a Ferrari. Nope, it was maybe even better. And you should have seen the looks on all the faces—my own and Skippy Welcher's, in particular—when Big Ed tooled into the parking lot across from Floyd Bennett Field at the wheel of a brand new, shiny red C-Type Jaguar. Jeez, it was the color of wet lipstick and so new that the tire treads still had the same gloss as the sidewalls and the seat upholstery squeaked a little when ran your fingers over it.

What a car!

And did it ever look sexy in red, too. Boy, I couldn't wait for Julie to see it. Or for Big Ed to give me a chance to drive it! Oh, sure. I'd had plenty of seat time in C-Types when me and Tommy Edwards drove the first two in the country all the way from Colin St. John's meat truck garage in Manhattan to the races at Elkhart Lake. But that had been damn near a year ago, and, like eating my mom's Dutch Apple pie or fooling around with Julie, it was not the sort of thing you lost your appetite for. Not hardly.

"Boy oh boy oh boy," I gushed as I walked around Big Ed's new C-Type. "That's really *something!*" I ran my hand over the warm, smooth aluminum curve of the fenderline and thought about what a thrill it was going to be to work on a car like that. A *real* racecar, you know? I mean, garden variety XK 120s were wonderful *sports* cars—fabulous sports cars, in fact—but they were a little on the large and hefty side and maybe lacking a bit in the brake department for racetrack duty. And that's why the guys over in Coventry built the C-Types. They called them XK 120Cs so's all the regular citizens would identify them with the rank-and-file XK 120s on their dealer's showroom floor. But they were really pretty much all new and different from the pavement up. The engines were hopped up and the frame was all new and with lighter tubes and channels and a sort of third dimension to it to make it stiffer, the rear suspension was all new with transverse torsion bar springing and a little triangular torque reaction rod/lateral locator thing on the right side of the rear axle, and the whole blessed car sat a lot lower to the ground than a standard-issue XK 120. Plus that fabulous bodywork was all aluminum alloy, too. And that was the real trick about a C-Type. It weighed maybe seven or eight hundred pounds less than an ordinary, street-driven XK 120. Like I've said before, more power helps you out on acceleration and top speed, but light weight helps you *everywhere.*

"So when'dja pick it up?" I asked excitedly.

Big Ed made an elaborate ritual of unwrapping a fresh cigar and firing it up while a crowd began gathering around us. "Just this afternoon," he said casually, sucking on his brand new stogie and puffing out a perfectly formed smoke ring. The crowd around us was about four or five deep by then, and Big Ed made a real show of acting like owning a brand new C-Type Jaguar was no big deal at all.

You would have, too.

"That's a nice car you have there," this deep, strained, unfamiliar voice said. It wasn't the voice of a New Yorker. You could tell that right away. I wheeled around and here was this scrawny kid in a white tee shirt with a half-smoked Pall Mall dangling from his lower lip and a kind of banty-rooster jut to his lower jaw. I swear, he looked like a blessed high school student. And an underclassman, at that. But he carried himself like he was not about to be talked down to or dismissed like adults usually do to kids. No, sir. "I've got one just like it," he continued in his strange, Midwestern twang, the words all slow and deliberate like he had to work hard to make them come out right. "It's parked right over there." I looked over and, sure enough, here was this ivory-colored C-Type with big, kind of wavy black rectangles on the nose and sides with the racing number 58 inside them. Yep, it was Masten Gregory, all right. He wasn't listed on the entry sheet in the program—maybe he was afraid they'd turn him down if he sent in a mail entry on account of he was so young—so he just sort of showed up. I mean, it didn't even look like he was shaving yet. Plus he was already getting himself quite a reputation.

Like about how he'd been black-flagged for "wild driving" at the race at Chanute Air Force Base a few months earlier. And how he decided he'd show everybody exactly what he thought of that by painting black flags behind his racing numbers. Like he was proud of it, you know? Or that he picked 58 for his racing number on account of he was just 5 feet, 8 inches tall (and that was with thick-soled shoes on, believe me) and maybe 140 pounds dripping wet. But you couldn't mistake the look in his eyes. This guy was a *racer.*

About then the big Cunningham transporter swung into the lot, and of course everybody and his brother had to scurry over to watch the cars unload and take a gander at the all-American challengers we were all so proud of on account of they'd been running strong against the very best of the factory teams over in Europe. I knew a little of the story already, but I got the rest of it firsthand from Phil Walters himself—he remembered me from when Cal and I came over to congratulate him after he won that great race at Brynfan Tyddyn in Briggs Cunningham's Porsche—and you can bet I was hanging on every word. As were about three or four dozen other racers, crewmembers and diehard American racing fans who'd gathered around us.

"We had the new car over for Le Mans, and Briggs wanted John—that's John Fitch, of course—and me to drive it. Briggs had an awful lot of faith in that car."

"Oh? What was it like?"

"Well, to be honest, it turned out to be a bit of a sled. We had this idea that we'd try what the Indianapolis roadsters use and run solid axles front and rear. And it works just fine at Indy, where the road is smooth as a baby's bottom and you want the car to trim out real smooth and stable on those four long, fast sweepers. But a road course is something else again—it's got slow corners as well as fast, requires a lot of hard braking and sharp changes of direction, and there are places you have to transition from turning one way to turning another. So the car's got to be good at a lot more things. Plus the pavement's not smooth or regular like you have at Indianapolis, and we discovered that the more pitch and crown you have to the road and the more it dips and undulates, the more cumbersome a car like that can start to feel. Oh, don't get me wrong. It was fast as stink and a hell of a good racecar. Hell, *everything* that comes out of the Cunningham shops is a hell of a good racecar. But it was kind of big and heavy and a little bit numb, too."

"But I heard you guys did really well with it."

"Yeah, we did. It had a whole lot of grunt and I think it was maybe a little sleeker and slipperier through the air than the older cars, and it ran pretty much like a locomotive for the whole 24 hours at Le Mans. In fact, all three of the cars ran like that. But of course Briggs won't let you flog 'em. He and Alf Momo are real sticklers about that. They want you to run a pace that'll bring the cars home, and if you can't do that, you can't drive for Briggs Cunningham. No matter how the hell fast you are."

"I heard you got all three cars in the top ten."

"Yep. We took third, seventh and tenth overall. Won our class, too." He gave a helpless little shrug. "But that's not exactly what we were after, is it?"

We all knew what he was talking about.

"Briggs really wants to win Le Mans, you know. Win it outright. With an American car and an American engine." He looked straight at me. "That's a pretty damn serious undertaking for a sailboat captain. Even a really stinking rich one."

"But you almost did it this time."

"Yeah. Almost." He shook his head and laughed. "If we'd had the C-5R last year—or even a little better luck with the C-4Rs—we might have done it. But this year the factory Jags showed up with disc brakes and that was all she wrote."

"They're better, huh?"

"Oh, they'll be the next big thing. I'm sure of it."

"They make the cars stop quicker?"

"Not so much quicker as *longer.* If you think about it, a brake doesn't do much more than turn speed into heat..."

I'd never thought about it like that, but I could see as how he was right.

"...and the quicker you get rid of that heat—the quicker those brakes cool down—the more you have left under your foot the next time you stab at the pedal."

"I think I get it," I told him.

"Plus they don't seem so prone to snatching and grabbing and yanking the car all over the road so much when they get hot like ours do."

"So Jaguar really came up with something, huh?"

"Well," Phil allowed, "I can't say as they actually *invented* disc brakes. I mean, they've been usin' 'em on airplanes for quite some time and I think those little tin-shack Crosley things have tried disc brakes, too. But Jaguar's the one who made 'em *work* on a racing car. You gotta give 'em credit. They did a first-class job. They deserved to win."

I noticed that they'd only pulled the two older C-4R roadsters out of the transporter. "Where's the new car?" I asked.

"Haven't you heard?"

I shook my head.

"Aw, we got invited to do this 12 Hour race over at Reims, France, a couple weeks after Le Mans—right in the middle of the champagne country where they grow all those fancy grapes, right?—and the organizers were really nice and really wanted us to race there and all of our equipment was still in pretty decent shape after Le Mans and they were offering some pretty decent starting money because they figured all the French fans would really like to see these big, loud, lumbering white cars from America...."

"Starting money? What's starting money?"

Phil Walters looked at me like I was the least little bit of a rube. "See, over in Europe," he explained, "the race organizers pay you to enter their races."

"They *pay* you to enter?"

"Well, not just to enter. You've got to actually start the race. That's why they call it 'starting money.'"

That was sure a lot different from the SCMA, where you had to pay a pretty stiff entry fee just for the privilege of putting on the show that all the paying customers (assuming there were any) were forking over their money to see. "So how much did you get?"

"Well, that's the thing that nobody knows, see. They pay you according to how big a draw they think you or your team or your car or your star driver is going to be with the fans. And all the deals are done behind closed doors so nobody knows what anybody else is getting."

"But how much did *you* get?"

"Me?" Phil said incredulously. "I'm just a dumb old driver, Buddy. They pay me to sit behind the wheel and have the time of my life, and I don't ask questions except for which bed is mine, where's the bathroom, and what time do you want me down for breakfast."

He got a pretty good laugh from the crowd off that one.

"So what happened at this champagne race you were telling us about?"

"Oh, it was the damnedest thing you ever saw, Buddy. They set it up so the race didn't even start until straight-up twelve midnight. That's when it *started!* And before that—starting at eight o'clock—they had carnival rides and circus acrobats and dancing girls and cabaret acts from the most famous clubs in Paris—including the *Moulin Rouge*—and nine different dance bands playing and this huge fireworks display and..." his eyes kind of glazed over and his voice trailed off just thinking of it.

"And then what happened?"

"Well, after all that, right at the stroke of midnight, they waved the French flag and the drivers all scrambled over to their cars—it was a Le Mans start, see?—and the race was on."

We all leaned in a little closer.

"Behra and the Gordini came around in the lead at the end of the first lap. Hey, what do you expect from a Frenchman in a French car in front of his home crowd? And he was driving like an absolute madman. As usual." I remembered how spectacular Behra and the Gordini had been during the early stages of *La Carrera,* leading everybody—including the Mercedes-Benz and Ferrari factory teams—through the twisting mountain passes before he finally overestimated his brakes and shot off a cliff. "Not that I'm saying anything against him," Phil added quickly. "He's braver than Dick Tracy and one hell of a race driver. I don't believe there's anybody better when it comes to just guts, skill and speed." He paused for a moment, and you could see he was choosing his words carefully. "But our guys know all about those nickel-rocket acts, and we think it's maybe smarter to pick a pace and stick to it rather than fighting it out with all the crazies at the start. I mean, this Reims place figured to be a really good circuit for us—very fast and just perfect for a big, powerful car—and sure enough Maglioli in the 4.5 Ferrari passes Behra's Gordini by the next time around and my friend John has our C-5R all the way up in third already, so we were actually looking a little better than we'd planned at that stage of the game."

"Wow."

"And the crowd was loving it. You know, the French fans and press and everybody took a real liking to the C-5R at Le Mans. They called it "The Shark." And they loved how it recorded the highest top speed of anything out there. One-hundred-fifty-four-point-eight miles-per-hour heading down that long straightaway towards Mulsanne. And that's on the official clocks, too. Hell, we could out-*run* the factory Jaguars that wound up winning it, but we just couldn't out-*stop* them...."

"So what happened at Reims?"

"Well, like always, after a little gasoline and adrenaline burned off it settled down and the *real* runners started showing their pace. Behra had to come in to change a wheel—knowing him and the way he was driving, he probably clouted something—and, as the laps rolled off and the race started to get its real legs, it pretty much boiled down to us and the 4.5 Ferrari, duking it out for the lead."

You could have heard a pin drop.

"Oh, we weren't nose-to-tail or anything. The Ferrari was a little faster and we knew it. But we thought they were maybe pushing a little harder than we were and hopefully using up a little more brakes and gas and tires so they'd have to stop more often. And we didn't think they were getting as good pit stops as we were anyway. I mean, you should *see* those Ferrari pit stops!" Phil shook his head and laughed. "It's like a cross between a Keystone Cops movie and the grand opera in Rome." He shot me a playful wink. "I promise you, Buddy, it's better than anything you've ever seen at the circus."

"So what happened?" I asked breathlessly.

"Well, they had a long pit stop around 3 in the morning that put us in the lead, and we get the idea that maybe they're having some kind of charging problems with the generator or something. But we just keep holding our pace and the Ferrari retakes the lead when we come in for gas ourselves around 4. But then they come in again around five—just as it's beginning to get light out—and it turns out some of the corner marshals and race officials have noticed that they've been running around without their lights on. Which, according to the rules, you're not allowed to do until at least 5 AM. So a few of the French race officials come over to have a word with the Ferrari team manager. And when they get there, they find about a dozen or so Ferrari mechanics swarming all over the car and of course that's a lot more than the rules allow. So pretty soon there's an awful lot of arguing and arm-waving and shouting going on in French and Italian, and the Ferrari team manager—I think his name is Ugolini—is explaining to the French officials as how the lights were on when they really weren't and that the ten or twelve Ferrari mechanics climbing all over the car right in front of them really aren't ten or twelve mechanics at all. And then, right in the middle of all of it, the ten or twelve mechanics push the Ferrari to get it started and send it on its merry way." Phil paused a few heartbeats for dramatic effect. "And of course, according to the rules, anyway, you're not supposed to do *that,* either."

"So what happened then?" I couldn't wait to hear the rest of it.

"Well," Phil grinned, "first off there's *lots* more yelling back and forth in French and Italian, and the French officials are screaming, *'you push-started the car'* at the Ferrari team manager and the Ferrari team manager is screaming right back that they were only moving the car off some spilled fuel so they wouldn't set everybody—including the French race officials—on fire when they started it up, and of course we're loving every minute of it since the French and the Italians don't like each other very much anyway, and the more yelling and screaming and shouting we hear and the more arm-waving and nasty finger gestures we see, the more likely we figure it is that they'll get disqualified."

"And did they?"

Phil nodded. "Yep. The officials showed poor old Maglioli the black flag the very next time around."

"And that was it?"

"Oh, not on your life," Phil chuckled. "Ugolini's not having any part of it. So he goes out to the pit wall and waves to poor old Maglioli to keep going around."

"And?"

"And so they showed him the black flag again. And again. But he just keeps driving around and around anyway."

"What an idiot."

"Nah, it wasn't his fault. To tell the truth, Maglioli drove himself one hell of a race. A *hell* of a race! I'd drive with that guy any day of the week. So would John. But Ugolini is the head guy from Ferrari—his boss, remember—and he just keeps waving him on."

"So what happened?"

"Oh, the officials finally sent somebody over from timing and scoring to tell the Ferrari guys that their car wasn't being scored any more and that the laps weren't being counted, and, after a few more laps, they finally gave up and brought him in. I actually felt a little sad for them right there at the end. They'd really tried hard and ran a damn solid race."

I could see it all like I'd actually been there. "That left you in the lead then, didn't it?"

Phil nodded. "Yep. Things were looking pretty rosy for us right about then. But then John started to have some sort of problem with the steering. We noticed his lap times were getting fatter so we knew something was up, but we didn't have long until our next scheduled pit stop and so I guess John just decided he'd try to gut it out and live with it until our regular stop to see what could be done." Phil Walters took in a long, deep breath and slowly let it out. "And I guess that's about when the steering broke."

"The steering broke?"

"Yeah. And the brakes went, too."

I immediately remembered what Tommy Edwards had told me the very first time I met him. About how you can lose almost anything on a racecar—*anything!*—and still have a halfway decent chance at getting it safely off to the side of the road. Anything except the steering and brakes, that is. And poor John Fitch had apparently lost both of them right in the middle of some very fast, high-speed sweepers at well over 140!

"My God," I gasped, *"what happened?"*

"Oh, he had one hell of a wreck. One of the worst I've ever seen. Went off airborne on a set of fast swerves near a place they call Garenne. Flipped it over a couple times and landed upside-down in a field. Pretty much wrote the car off."

"Jesus! What happened to him?"

"Well, it was frankly amazing," Phil allowed, shaking his head, "I have no idea how, but damn if he didn't get away with it. As soon as the car took off, he had the good sense to head for the basement and stay there."

"Head for the basement?"

"You know. Dive for the floorboards and brace yourself in as best you can." Phil shook his head again. "It must've been like going over Niagara Falls in a beer barrel. But he made it! Oh, sure, he had a cut ear and a few bumps and bruises. But nothing major." Phil looked me square in the eye. "The way most of us figure, he's lucky to still be up here sucking oxygen on the sunny side of the grass."

"Wow."

Still, it seemed odd to me that any car would lose both steering and brakes at the same exact time. At least not unless the whole blessed front axle came off. And so I asked Phil about it. "We thought it sounded pretty odd, too. But John's not the kind of guy to make things up. And he knows enough about mechanics to pretty much figure out what he's feeling through the controls. But when we looked at the remains the next morning, the front axle was all bent to hell but still very much attached. And all the brake lines seemed intact, too."

"So what happened?"

"Well, not too many people know this, but I did a lot of the testing on the C-5R down in Florida. We'd wheel it out of the shop and look both ways to make sure there weren't any cops around and then kind of scoot off back into the coconut and citrus country where the roads are straight and empty and there's plenty of brush and undergrowth to hide what you're doing and most all you've got for company is egrets and alligators. And this one time I'm booming down one of these back roads at maybe 160 or so, and all of a sudden I'm looking back where I came from." He snapped his fingers. "Just like *that!*"

"Geez. What was it?"

"We never could figure it out. I mean, it happened so damn fast there wasn't a thing I could do about it. About scared the living piss out of me, too."

I let out a low whistle. It took a lot to scare the living piss out of a guy like Phil Walters. "And you never figured it out?"

He shook his head. "But we have an idea now."

"You do?"

Phil nodded. "We're starting to think maybe too much air got under the nose or something and it just, you know, *took off!*"

"Took off?"

"Yeah, took off. Like an airplane."

It was impossible to imagine something as big and heavy and married to the pavement as a Cunningham C-5R just taking off. But then, I was always of the school of thought that airplanes really shouldn't be able to fly, either. Especially big ones like that Boeing Stratocruiser Big Ed and me flew down to Texas on our way to *La Carrera.* "That would sure explain the loss of steering and brakes," I reasoned. I mean, neither of those things work especially well when the tires aren't touching the ground.

"Yeah, it would. But I don't think either John or I are particularly eager to do any more testing in that area to see if it happens again."

I supposed not. "He was lucky to get away with it then, wasn't he?"

"Yeah, it was a close one, all right. John could've got hurt real bad. And Briggs sure would've loved that first place cup, too. John and me would've liked it pretty much ourselves...."

I could feel it all swelling up inside me: the engineering, the emotion, the speed, the challenge, the expectation, the hard, gritty grind of it, the danger, and the stupid, sly, scheming twist of luck behind it all, and I knew more than ever what made racing so much grander and greater and infinitely more interesting than everyday life. "So that was the end of it?" I asked.

"Not quite. Briggs was still out there in the C-4R he was co-driving with your buddy Creighton Pendleton."

I looked around to see who all was listening and then drew in a little closer. "He's not really what you could call my buddy," I whispered in his ear.

"That's why Briggs was driving with him," Phil laughed.

I didn't get it. "Why's that?" I asked.

"So he wouldn't have to listen to him in the pits! Oh, he's a good enough 'shoe, as far as that goes, but, gee whiz, all he talked about was how damn much *better* his Ferrari was to drive than our cars. He's *such* a damn snob."

Creighton Pendleton was every bit of that, all right.

"Anyhow, the two of them ultimately came home third overall in the C-4R, and that was pretty damn decent, no matter what you think of either of them. And especially after the team did so well at Le Mans two weeks earlier."

"Yeah. And winning at Sebring in March, too," I reminded him.

Phil nodded. "Still, Briggs really wants one of those fancy tin cups from Le Mans. Wants it *bad.* He says we really need to bring it home here to America."

You had to admire a guy with that kind of ambition.

No matter how damn much family money he had....

Thursday evening practice at Floyd Bennett Field started right on the dot at 5:00 PM, even though the sun was beating down like blazes, the temperature was well into the 90s, and it was generally the kind of weather that makes you want to lie down in the shade and have a nice, tall, cool glass of lemonade. Not that you could find much in the way of shade at an airport circuit like Floyd Bennett Field. Hell, you'd be lucky to find a few tall blades of grass! But racers seem to have this knack for putting all that stuff out of their minds once the engines fire. It isn't until afterwards, when everything gets quiet again, that you realize just how blessed hot, dirty, tired, sweaty, greasy, grimy and thirsty you are and you drink the beer tapper dry. Not that beer is maybe the best thing for you when it comes to quenching a big thirst. But it certainly goes a lot further than water or lemonade when it comes to making you not care any more that you're so blessed hot, dirty, tired, sweaty, greasy, grimy and thirsty....

The runways at Floyd Bennett field were really wide, and that made it kind of difficult to follow where the course went at some points of the circuit. But, mostly thanks to SAC commander General Curtis Le May, all of our SCMA racers were getting pretty used to airport circuits and how flat and featureless they were. Plus it was great to have sports cars running flat-out and wide open and nipping around the course markers right there in the middle of Brooklyn. I'll bet it sounded like the blessed Bronx Zoo had burst open to all the people in the surrounding neighborhoods! Why, there hadn't been a road race anywhere around New York City since before the war. And that was the Vanderbilt Cup at Roosevelt Raceway way out on Long Island. I'd heard about it plenty from some of the SCMA regulars, about how it was held on this goofy, four-mile "road circuit" laid out by an architect who did mostly horse racing tracks. So it was made of hard-packed dirt and ridiculously wide and lined with wooden railings all the way around and doubled back on itself like a blessed small intestine so's it'd all fit right there in front of the grandstands. There was only one straightaway that really meant anything, and that was barely three-quarters of a mile long. I saw some press clippings once where the reporters complained you could go faster out on the Long Island Parkway than the best racers in the world could around Roosevelt Raceway. They only held races out there twice, in 1936 and 1937, and even though they put up a really huge wad of prize money to attract some of the top European teams, not too many people showed up to watch. Plus those who did got madder than hell on account of World War II was already brewing and *Il Duce* Benito Mussolini's pet Alfa Romeo team won it the first year and Herr Hitler's pet Auto Union and Mercedes-Benz teams—wearing swastikas on their headrests, no less—blew everybody into the weeds the second. Including the very best of the Americans. So they finally gave it up as a bad try and turned it into a harness racing track. With plenty of betting windows. And *that's* when they started making real money.

But, like I said, that was way the heck out on Long Island.

According to an article in the race program (written by none other than ace race promoter Alec Ulmann himself), they hadn't had any real motor racing in New York City proper since the grand old 2-mile board track over at Sheepshead Bay closed up in 1919. And I was astonished to read that the very first Astor Cup race there in 1915 (again according to the program, since it was way before my time) was won by some guy named Gil Anderson in a Stutz at the thoroughly amazing average speed of 102.6 miles-per-hour. No lie. And way before that, they held the very first 24-hour race ever in America just a few miles up the road from Floyd Bennett Field at some ancient and long forgotten dirt track at Brighton Beach on Coney Island. Can you imagine? In honor of those two great historical New York landmarks that nobody but maybe some of the grizzled old-timers who hang around the lion house at the Bronx Zoo in the wintertime would possibly remember, they'd christened the first race at Floyd Bennett Field (for stock, under-1500cc production cars like MGs and such selling for under $3000) "The Sheepshead Bay Trophy Race," and the second one (for over-1500cc production cars and under-1500cc cars that were either too modified or too expensive to qualify for the first group) "The Brighton Beach Trophy Race." And the top three finishers from each of those races got to enter the 100-lap feature "Floyd Bennett Grand Prize Cup Race" against all the big, hairy-chested modified racecars that was slated to cap off the action at 2:30 Saturday afternoon.

I noticed leafing through the race program that my English racer/fighter pilot friend Tommy Edwards was entered in the first race group driving something I'd never heard of before called an Allard Palm Beach, and entered by none other than Westbridge Motor Car Company, Limited, and our old buddy Colin St. John. Only I didn't see him or the new car out there when they turned the Sheepshead Bay Trophy tiddlers loose for first practice right on schedule at precisely five PM. But when they sent the second practice group out around 6, I was thrilled to see his familiar green helmet behind the wheel of this new, "smaller and more modern" Allard Palm Beach model. I guess it was the very first one in the country, and Sydney Allard himself had recommended they give it to Tommy to show off in front of the paying customers. It was kind of a handsome-looking thing—you could see they were aiming it right square at the Austin-Healey Hundred—but it was a little on the chunky side and not near so pretty as the new Healey model. And it didn't look terribly fast, either, if you want the honest truth of it.

Even with an ace like Tommy Edwards behind the wheel.

"So how's it runnin'?" I went over and asked him after the session was over.

"Hey, good to see you, Sport!" he grinned, extending a sweaty hand.

"Good to see you, too. How'd things go for you at Le Mans?"

"Oh, bloody spectacular," he laughed, rolling his eyes. "We had the new J2R, of course, and old Sydney decided that he'd run the first stint himself. Just to make sure I wouldn't break it or blow it up trying to stay ahead of the Jaguars and Ferraris." He shot me a wink. "And of course they had us gridded way up at the head end of the queue because they line them up according to engine displacement, and, when the tricolor fell, you should've seen old Sydney run! I don't think any of his cars go that fast."

"So he got a good start?"

"*Good?* Why, it was bloody well spectacular! He was still closing the door halfway down to the Dunlop Bridge!"

"Really?"

"Absolutely. And he was leading overall by the end of the first lap!"

"First place?"

"First place," Tommy nodded, holding up his index finger like it was the damn Empire State Building.

"Wow. And then what happened?"

"Oh, he ran it out of brakes in four bloody laps and we were out of it." He gave me a big, helpless smile. "They apparently got a bit hotter than they used to inside that new, envelope bodywork." He added a streetcorner New York shrug. "I didn't even get behind the wheel."

"Geez, that's too bad."

"Hey, that's racing. It was a nice free trip to France, though. And it's always worthwhile being at Le Mans, no matter what bloody well happens. Just to be a part of it."

"Boy, I'd sure love to do it one day!"

"Oh, you'll get your chance, Buddy. At least if I have anything to say about it."

I sure hoped he was right.

"So how's this new 'little' Allard running?"

"Outside of the fact that it can't get out of its own way, it's a genuine pleasure."

"Not good, huh?"

"Well, let me put it this way. Some sports cars are underpowered, and some sports cars are overweight. But with this exciting new Allard Palm Beach model, you get both!"

"So it's not very quick?"

"In a word, it's a bloody slug. Worse yet, Colin originally had it entered in the first race where we at least had some sort of a chance against the MGs. But then someone pointed out that the engine was seven cubic centimeters too big and we got booted up to the next group. It's really sort of a joke. Here, look for yourself." He opened the hood for me, and sitting there inside an engine compartment vast enough for a Jaguar straight six (or, with a big shoehorn and a couple five-pound jars of Vaseline, maybe even one of Sydney Allard's beloved American V8s?) was this tiny, wheezy little English Ford four-banger sporting a puny, single-pot Zenith carburetor of approximately the same size and fuel metering capacity as a sewing thimble.

"Hmm. Impressive."

"Yes, indeed. According to the sales brochures, it's got a whopping forty-seven brake horsepower at the flywheel."

"Forty-seven, huh?"

"Right-O. And only a single ton of automobile to haul around."

"Sounds like a potent combination."

"Oh, it certainly would be. If only they were normally-sized horses."

"Normally-sized horses?"

"Yes. These particular forty-seven horses seem to be more of the Shetland pony variety."

"I see."

"Not to mention that, as I believe I already mentioned, it comes in at a rousing seven cubic centimeters over the 1500cc limit, so it doesn't qualify to run against the MGs and such. Oh, no. I get to race this steaming turd against the bloody Jag 120s."

"Ouch."

"But what the hell, eh? It's a free drive and we'll just have to make the best of it."

"You Brits have always been good at that."

"I should say. Why, we bloody well invented the stiff upper lip...."

It was always great to see Tommy again. Even if his "free drive" was languishing uncharacteristically close to back of the time sheets, only just ahead of this upper-crust guy from Philadelphia named C.K. Dexter-Haven in a Jag 120 that Big Ed and Skippy Welcher used to chase after pretty regularly in their own XK 120s. The track layout wasn't helping much either, what with this one real long straightaway where all he could do was shift, keep his foot planted and watch helplessly while the Allard's tach needle crept pitifully towards the redline and Jaguar 120s roared by on both sides. But, like he said, at least it was free.

And speaking of free drives, my quick buddy Cal Carrington was indeed entered in the Sheepshead Bay race group driving one of those difficult-to-retail Jowett Jupiters for the guy who still had entirely too many of them salted away in a garage down by the shipping docks. As per usual, Cal was finding his way around pretty quickly and right up near the top of the "unofficial" time sheets that came out after the session was over. Typical Cal. I asked him how it was going, and he allowed as how the only problem with the Jowett was that you had to beat it around the head and shoulders with a two-by-four in order to get it to turn into a corner, and then it would hike up its skirts and spin the inside rear wheel something awful on the way out. Outside of that, it was fine....

The three of us shared a couple lukewarm colas together (it being a "professional" event and moreover run on government property, you weren't allowed to touch the beer until after the last session was over), and then I wandered over to make sure there was enough gas and water and oil in Big Ed's shiny red C-Type and just the right amount of air in the tires and that he moreover had his helmet on straight and his head pointed in more or less the right direction. That could be the hardest part with Big Ed, on account of he sometimes tended to get a little wound up before he drove. In fact, there were times I swear I could almost hear him hissing like an overloaded steam boiler. But then, finally, they'd give the order to *"fire 'em up!"* and everything would be all right again. Or at least I couldn't do anything about it any more.

It was well on towards dusk by then and not so breathlessly hot, and you could see the glow from the setting sun almost like a halo around the Manhattan skyline behind us. I must admit I was kind of eager to see what Big Ed Baumstein could do with that brand new red C-Type of his. And even more eager to catch a glimpse of that scrawny, dangerous-looking Masten Gregory kid from Kansas City in his infamous ivory C-Type with the black flag numbers on the nose and sides. Not to mention Phil Walters and Briggs Cunningham in those brutal, Chrysler-powered Cunningham C-4Rs just freshly back from Europe. So I joined Cal and Tommy over on this little patch of scrub grass not too far from trackside to watch.

It was quite a show, all right. There were more than forty cars in five different classes entered for the big feature race on Saturday, and an incredible fistful of fast, heavy iron squaring off for the overall win. Creighton Pendleton III was there with that fabulous, razor-tuned new engine in his Ferrari (and rumors were flying that it was really up from 4.1 to 4.5 liters—or maybe even more!) plus the two Chrysler-powered Cunningham C-4Rs for Briggs himself and Phil Walters, and then you had Skippy Welcher, Big Ed and Masten Gregory in a trio of C-Type Jaguars (not that either The Skipper or Big Ed figured to be much of a threat—except maybe to each other) and that Charles Schott guy was there with the cigar-shaped Jaguar special we saw him race and win with at Callicoon, plus another, really sharp and handsome-looking Jaguar special done up in perfect refrigerator white in the hands of that Walt Hansgen we'd seen race before in a regular-issue XK 120. Cal and I had marked him before as a guy to watch, and the car he'd put together was absolutely gorgeous. Built it with his own two hands, too (although I heard his dad had a bump and body shop someplace in Jersey, and I'm sure that helped). But it was brand, spanking new, and so he was going through the usual choruses of the New Racecar Blues. Which, by the way, get ever so much worse when you build the car yourself instead of buying one "off the shelf." But then, not everybody can afford the freight on a new C-Type. Or find one even if they can, for that matter....

There were also a couple J2X Allards—one with a Caddy motor, one with a Chrysler Hemi—and Perry Fina's squat, kind of Indy roadster-looking "Perry's Special" (also with a Cadillac V8 under the hood). Since it was already looking to be about the hottest weekend of the summer and the feature was slated to run for over 200 miles, some of the drivers were already scouting around for co-drivers (and some, like Walt Hansgen, already had co-drivers as a way to spread expenses out a little), and I was pleased to hear that Tommy Edwards might be drafted into a little late-inning cleanup work in one of the Allards come Sunday. And of course Cal had already been all over the paddock spreading horror stories about sunstroke, dehydration and heat prostration and casually mentioning that he did indeed have his helmet handy just in case.

Even against the bleak, wide-open emptiness of the Floyd Bennett Field runways, this looked to be about the biggest, deepest and most impressive field of racing cars I'd seen anywhere outside of Sebring and *La Carrera.* And those didn't really count on account of they were genuine, international-class events. Having this all happen right there in the middle of Brooklyn was enough to make you clench your teeth and fists and whoop at the sky. It was like we were planting our flag, you know?

Right from the start, you could see that the Cunningham guys were being pretty careful and methodical about learning the circuit and seeing which way it went and that Creighton Pendleton was fast as stink right out of the box (although it turned out he'd volunteered to help set up the course and had already been around it a few hundred times in his Rolls and more or less knew every inch of it already) and the Allards looked pretty cumbersome trying to get whoa'd down for the sharper corners and both The Skipper and Big Ed were finding ways to make a C-Type Jaguar look skittish, lurching and uncoordinated. Hey, you can buy any blessed kind of racecar you want, but you can't buy the skill, finesse and savvy it takes to drive it.

But the guy who caught everybody's eye was that Masten Gregory kid from Kansas City. I swear, watching him drive was like watching one of those circus guys in the gold silk bloomers juggling razor-edged pirate cutlasses and twelve-pound medieval battleaxes and flaming, double-ended torch batons in the center ring at P.T. Barnum. And, just like the guy in the circus ring, you got the sense that he wasn't worried about it at all. Oh, you could see he was still pretty green and maybe not as slick and smooth as my friend Cal Carrington (although he could afford the best cars—as many of them as he wanted, in fact—and that made up for a lot of rough edges), but no question he wasn't afraid of going fast. Not hardly!

And then, all of a sudden in the gathering gloom of evening with the big cars still roaring and howling and thundering and lumbering around the circuit, there was this *BANG!* and a huge sheet of bright orange flame erupted underneath Masten Gregory's C-Type—blown engine, no doubt about it!—and of course it immediately dumped all the oil out through the various jagged holes that the various jagged pieces of piston, connecting rod and crankshaft bits had poked through the block and oil pan and spread it right under his back wheels! He was going at a pretty good clip, too. So the car spun around and around on its own spewing-and-flaming puddle of oil and shot off the pavement onto the rough stuff and kind of launched itself over a jagged berm (that would've been what ripped the bottom of the gas tank open) and, silhouetted against the starburst of flames and with the car still very much airborne, we watched Masten Gregory scramble up to his feet on the driver's seat and bail out over the side.

It was the most incredible dismount any of us had ever seen.

Even more amazing, he got away with it! With no more than a bang on the knee where it hit the steering wheel or the dash cowl or something on his way over the side. The way I heard it—and with his crashed Jag C-type still a huge, billowing ball of flame right behind him—he stood up, kind of dusted himself off, sauntered over to the nearest flag marshalling station, and asked if anybody could borrow him a smoke. "I left mine in the car," he explained, nonchalantly pointing his thumb over his shoulder at the towering, gas-and-oil-fueled Jaguar bonfire behind him. Somebody said he didn't even look like his blood pressure was up.

Of course they black-flagged the session immediately and scrambled all the fire trucks to try and put it out, but it was burning pretty spectacularly and besides, everybody knew it was going to be a writeoff, so why waste a whole bunch of the Navy Department's fire extinguisher foam trying to get it out in a hurry. Not to mention that it was getting pretty dark by then and that burning C-Type was as good as any fireworks show you ever saw. Especially since nobody died in it....

Naturally I told Julie all about it and even talked her into switching nights at the Doggie Shake—even though Fridays were always good for tips—so she could come with me for practice the following night. But it was pretty dull and bland by comparison since the fizz and luster of something New and Different had already worn off. But it was nice to have her there anyway, and I was pleased at how Tommy Edwards made a nice fuss over her and teased her a little about the moron she'd married. It made her feel a little more like she belonged.

We got everything packed up a little after eight, and I couldn't help noticing that Big Ed was engaged in an obviously deep and serious conversation with that Masten Gregory character who'd almost turned himself into Castrol-basted barbequed ribs (and not very meaty ones, at that) the previous evening. And then he came over by me and asked where his XK 120 was parked back at the Sinclair. "It's locked up inside like always at night," I told him, hoping that Old Man Finzio or Raymond or—God forbid—Tater had fired it up and brought it inside at the end of the day like I told them to.

"Hmmm," Big Ed mused, rolling his cigar around in the side of his mouth. "Tell y'what, Buddy. I need'ja t'do me a little favor, see."

"Sure thing. Just name it."

"I wan'cha t'hitch up the 120 and drag it over here tomorrow morning, OK?"

"Sure," I shrugged. "But what for?"

"Nothin' special. I just want it here, that's all."

"Whatever you say, boss. You're payin' the bills."

"That's a good kid," he grinned, and stuffed a wadded-up tenspot into my shirt pocket.

"Look," I said to Julie as we climbed into Old Man Finzio's tow truck, "Big Ed just gave me a ten-buck tip. Why don't we shoot over by Coney Island on the way home?"

"Oh, I don't know," she sighed. "I'm so hot and tired and sweaty."

"Aw, c'mon. It'll be fun. Remember our first date at Palisades Park?"

I hadn't brought that up for awhile, you know? Not even to tease her about how she got sick over the side of the Ferris wheel and barfed all over the poor folks in the next gondola car below us. "C'mon, it's right on our way," I told her. "It'll be fun, honest."

So we went over by Coney Island and walked down the boardwalk together and played a few of those dumb carnival games that you never win (even though you see these damn little kids all the time carrying the huge stuffed lions and tigers and teddy bears you can only get with a perfect score) and we had a couple hot dogs and fries and I even talked her into going up on the Ferris wheel with me again. And it was really kind of nice. It was still pretty warm out but there was a nice breeze up there above the midway and you could see the lights of the Jersey coastline all shimmering and reflecting off the water way out there in the distance and hear the chug of a barge or tugboat or something out there in the darkness and carnival music filtering up from the boardwalk and the *crack!* of the rifles with the crooked sights in the shooting galleries and the faint wail of a police siren out there somewheres in the Brooklyn neighborhoods and, faintly but clearly, the sweet, strong voice of some 230-pound lady on a second story fire escape some-place singing opera arias in Italian. She was pretty good, too.

It was kind of a magic place to be.

"Y'know, Buddy, " Julie said dreamily, "it doesn't seem like we get any real time together any more. I mean, we're *with* each other a lot—when we're not working, anyway—but it always seems like we're hustling to do this or scram-bling to do that and never get a moment for ourselves." She looked out over the water towards Rockaway Point. "And it always seems like we're doing it to please other people and not ourselves...."

I knew exactly what she was talking about.

"It'll get better," I told her. Even though I wasn't particularly certain it would.

"I don't know, Buddy," she said, kind of burrowing her head into my shoul-der. "What if that's just the way it is when you grow up? You just keep doing the next thing you have to do and the next thing you have to do after that until the day you get too old and sad and sick to do much of anything any more?"

I kissed her gently on the top of her head. "That's a cheery way of looking at things," I teased her. But it wasn't really the right time for teasing. I knew she was feeling a lot of pressure and fear and uncertainty about the baby coming and everything else that was going on—or not going on—in our lives. And every now and then, like right at that very moment, I could feel it all welling up inside her and threatening to boil right over. So I pulled her in a little closer and kissed her again. Only it was a different kind of kissing than I'd ever known how to do before. Kind of sweet and understanding and, most of all, appreciative. And I could feel all that stuff inside her kind of level off and subside and then it was like she melted right into me and we were just this one warm, peaceful thing together for a few moments while the Ferris wheel went over the top and started to descend back down into the noise and lights of the midway. To tell the truth, I was pretty damn amazed I knew how to kiss like that.

Saturday, August 29th, was about the hottest day I have ever experienced in the greater metropolitan New York area in my life. And I have experienced a whole, heaping passel of blisteringly hot days in and around New York. I could tell it was going to be a scorcher as soon as I woke up, even though it was still well before dawn. Julie was lying there next to me, all deep asleep and peaceful, and I decided to let her sleep awhile longer while I went over by the Sinclair to hitch up Big Ed's XK 120 and load up the tow truck. So I was real careful to creep around on tiptoes in my stocking feet and not make a noise and of course that's when I tripped over the ironing board that usually wasn't there and sent it, me and the steam iron crashing across the floor. Not to mention all of our freshly folded clean clothes.

"JESUS, BUDDY, WHAT IS IT??!!" Julie gasped, snapping bolt upright in bed.

"I was trying not to wake you," I whispered by way of explanation.

"Oh."

"I was headed over to load up the tow truck. I thought I'd let you sleep a little longer."

"What time is it?"

"A little before five."

"Oh." Her eyes were open, but the way the words came out and the way her jaw was hanging made it sound like she was still asleep.

"Look," I whispered some more, *"why don't you just stay home and rest today? You don't have to come with. Really you don't."*

"But you want me to. You said so."

"Nah. It's not important. I'll just be doing a bunch of dumb car stuff anyway."

"But I want to come. I want us to spend more time together."

I have to admit, that made me go all warm and gooey inside. Especially since we'd shared a pretty special time together after we got home from that ride on the Ferris wheel at Coney Island the night before. Not that it's any of your business.

"Okay," I told her, *" if you're sure you want to…"*

"Sure I'm sure." She was full awake now. *"You think I want to hang around here all day and listen to my mother bitch about the paint in the bathroom and the fixture in the hallway and the curtains in the damn kitchen?"*

There was a sudden, loud squeaking noise from the ceiling directly above us, like somebody had dragged a chair with no rubber tips on it across a wooden floor. Julie and I looked at each other and fought hard to stifle a laugh.

"Jesus," Julie gasped, *"you think she heard us last night?"* She sounded kind of half-terrified/half-thrilled with the prospect.

No, I thought but didn't say, *there's always the possibility she went deaf.*

The air outside had a thick, steamy taste to it and my tee shirt was already sticking to me by the time I got done hitching up Big Ed's Jaguar and loading up the tow truck and heading back over to the duplex to pick Julie up. But traffic was light at that hour on a Saturday morning and we had the vent windows swiveled around backwards so there was kind of a warm, clammy draft through the cab as we made our way through early Saturday morning Manhattan and across the bridge into Brooklyn. The late night joints were already long closed and it was that empty time of day when the city first wakes up and you can catch the smell of freshly brewed coffee on every streetcorner and watch the guys with the drug stores and newsstands and smoke shops opening up and bringing in fresh bundles of *New York Times* and *New York Post* and *New York Daily News* and *The Wall Street Journal* to set out for the paying customers.

We got to Floyd Bennett Field by a few minutes after seven and unloaded the Jag, and by then the sun was already glaring down from the eastern sky like the business end of a blowtorch and I knew this was going to be one long, hot, sweaty and unbearable day. Big Ed showed up a little after eight in the black Sixty Special, and, before I could even ask him what was up, who should tool by without so much as a wink or a wave but that Masten Gregory kid at the wheel of Big Ed's brand new, shiny red C-Type. If you'd put a whole blessed grapefruit in my mouth, it would've fallen right out again. After all, that was *my* damn C-Type he was driving!

"W-what the hell..." I stammered.

Big Ed shrugged and put a match to the butt end of his cigar. "I made a l'il deal last night, that's all."

"A little deal. You mean you *sold* your brand new car? The one you worked and sweated and waited and schemed so long to get?"

"Hey," Big Ed smiled while putting a huge, meaty hand on my shoulder, "some deals are just too sweet t'pass up."

"No matter what?"

"No matter what," Big Ed nodded.

And that was the end of it.

It wasn't until later on that I managed to gather up all the details. Seems the original deal Big Ed made with Colin St. John for the new, red C-Type had one loose detail in the form of Big Ed's oft-crashed and even more oft-repaired XK 120. Which was, you remember, still barely more than a year old and very light on mileage thanks to all the down time it had enjoyed being pounded out and rebuilt. Not to mention that the speedometer had been on the fritz once or twice. But the point is that the real meat of any car deal involving a trade-in rests on the difference between how cheaply the seller can value that trade-in and how quick-ly and for how much more he can sell it to some other sucker somewhere down the road. And preferably not too far down the road, either. So all the loose talk about "suggested retail price" and "discounts for cash" and add-ons like taxes and document and transportation fees are just so much window dressing. The thing every car dealer *really* wants is to steal the trade-in.

But Big Ed was hardly a babe in the woods when it came to buying and selling (after all, that's what he did for a living) and so he reversed his field right at the end and offered to pull his ivory XK 120 out of the deal and put back in the meager cash value Colin St. John had offered him for it. Which of course would have taken a fat slice of the money pie of Colin's plate and so he had no choice but to up the offer on the 120 a little. Even if it was, as Colin put it, "in amazingly poor shape for a Jagyewahr of such recent vintage."

"Nah," Big Ed told him like he was just mulling it over for the very first time, "Y'know, I think maybe I'll just keep it. Give it to the little missus t'drive." This in spite of the fact that Big Ed Baumstein was about to be between "little missuses" for the third or fourth time as soon as the divorce papers cleared.

"Very well then," Colin agreed through clenched teeth. "Then all we need is to take care of the transportation and document fee details here, here, and here."

And of course there was a couple hundred right back in Colin's pocket. But Big Ed didn't mind. "You don't wanna waste your time and piss everybody off always trying to make the *best* deal, see," he often told me. "Just make sure you make a *good* deal. You do that enough times and you'll always come out on top." It was good advice, too.

And the point is that he did, indeed, get a damn good deal on that C-Type. Especially since they were in great demand and impossible to find and so any kind of a deal at all was a great deal on a C-Type. He was really looking forward to running the car, too.

And hopefully pinning Skippy Welcher's ears back.

Only then this Masten Gregory kid dropped out of the sky and almost killed himself blowing up and burning his own C-Type and then he came wandering over and asked Big Ed if maybe he'd like to sell his seeing as how the kid had his heart set on racing at Floyd Bennett Field. And preferably in a C-Type. Well, it was hard to take a kid like that seriously—like I said, it didn't even look like he was shaving yet—but he just kept upping the offer and upping the offer until even Big Ed Baumstein, who loved his cars more than just about anything, started thinking about just what he could do with all that extra cash. I don't know the exact numbers, but they were talking damn near Ferrari money when Big Ed finally caved in and said, "Okay, you bought yourself a car, kid."

And then the kid had to tell him, with an absolutely straight face, that he'd had his wallet underneath the seat cushion in the C-Type that burned and so Big Ed would have to wait for a transfer from Masten's trust fund in Kansas City on Monday morning in order to get the money. Now you and I probably would have balked at that, but Big Ed had asked around about this kid and knew that, whatever else he might be, he was good as his word. So they shook on it. At least after Masten threw in a few hundred more to sweeten the deal.

Hey, he had plenty, you know?

Not to mention that Big Ed got the burnt-out remains of Masten's C-Type for free as part of the deal (remember that Big Ed was a scrap dealer for a living) which he then proceeded to dangle in front of Colin St. John's nose like a dough ball in front of a carp seeing as how they both knew there were many hundreds of dollars—maybe even thousands?—worth of usable and re-saleable bits and pieces in there amongst the twisted tubes and melted alloy and thick layers of dried fire extinguisher foam. Big Ed wound up making Colin a pretty decent deal on the C-Type's remains—three hundred dollars, as is/where is—but it was all pure profit for Big Ed on account of he got it free for nothing. Fact is, that was probably the most successful single day Big Ed Baumstein ever had at a racetrack in his life. And the cars hadn't even fired up for the first race yet....

The main thing everybody remembered about that race day at Floyd Bennett Field was the heat. The newspapers and radio all said it was well up over 100 degrees in the city that day, and racing around out there on the baking white concrete runways and glistening blacktop service roads with the heat waves shimmering up off of them was like driving around on a damn skillet. And it was maybe even worse standing there on the sidelines without even the hot breeze over the windshield for comfort. But, like I said before, race drivers seem to have this knack for ignoring all that stuff while they're out there driving. Or at least the real ones do, anyway.

And there was plenty of raceday hoopla planned to keep everybody entertained and to keep all Alec Ulmann's sponsors happy. They had a really nice 32-page race program with plenty of paid advertising plus a bunch of feature articles that said wonderful things about anybody who had anything to do with the event and praised the sponsors' products to the heavens under the guise of informative journalism, and several local sportycar kingpins were using the event as a way to show off their latest wares. Colin St. John had brought the Allard Palm Beach for Tommy to drive (although he was having second thoughts now that the organizers had gotten wind that it was a 1507cc and not the 1495cc he'd told them it was on the entry form and had therefore been kicked it up into the Brighton Beach group with all the 3.8-liter XK 120 Jaguars) plus that silver-blue Healey Hundred pace car that he'd promised to send up to Canada at great personal effort and expense to swap for the black one he already had waiting over in the windowless meat truck garage for Carson Flegley. In fact, the only true part of the whole deal was that the silver-blue one was indeed already spoken for and headed towards Canada as soon as the Floyd Bennett race weekend was over. At least as far as Albany, anyway....

And you had to give credit to Donald Healey over in England and the way he did business. With the new 100, he was up against much the same problem that Tommy and Colin were having with the Allard Palm Beach. See, the Healey Hundred had this big old four-banger out of a mail truck or something with a stroke as long as your forearm, and, although it produced a heap of torque and pretty decent performance in the handy and lightweight new Hundred, it didn't have all that much top-end horsepower (or top end, period, when you get right down to it!) and measured in at a thoroughly odd and unusual 2660cc. Or, in other words, well over the two-liter class limit but a healthy measure shy of three. Not to mention that the three-liter class was chock full of multi-cam, multi-cylinder, multi-thousands-of-dollars-more-expensive Ferraris and Aston Martins and such that were pretty much out of the Healey Hundred's league. At least as far as heads-up sprint racing was concerned. So Donald Healey and his guys were real careful about exactly where and how they showed off their new baby. Like at

Sebring where they first introduced it here in the states and again that Saturday in front of the fans at Floyd Bennett Field. Both times, the new Healey Hundred was touted on the P.A. and featured in the race program, but was strictly on display and only used as a pace car as far as on-track action was concerned. Not that the Healey guys were afraid of competition. Not hardly. But they wanted to pick their shots, you know? Like by building a team of warmed over and hotted-up "special test" cars and signing up some really topnotch drivers and a crack team of mechanics and support personnel led by Donald Healey's son, Geoff, and this ace wrench named Roger Menadue to take on the big, high profile endurance races where preparation, ruggedness, consistency and rock-solid reliability were equally important as outright speed. Which is precisely how two of them came home a solid second and third in the 3-liter class and 12th and 14th overall at Le Mans that year.

Also on display at Floyd Bennett Field (and advertised in the program, natch) was the answer to the question that nobody'd asked in the form of a lengthened, four-seater MG TD. It was the bright idea of somebody over at J.S. Inskip in Manhattan, and it made you wonder what on earth anybody would want with a four-passenger automobile where it was damn near impossible to get into the back seat (and completely impossible if the top was up) and that had no legroom to speak of once you got back there. Not to mention no luggage space and the straight-line performance of a Volkswagen with a plug wire disconnected once you got four healthy adults crammed on board. But, like Colin St. John always said, *"There's an ass for every seat,"* and damn if they didn't take a couple deposits!

A pretty decent crowd showed up, especially considering the heat and the fact that both the Dodgers and the Giants were playing at home that particular Saturday, and the *New York Times* said it was as much as 50,000 people. But I think they maybe got that by counting the legs and dividing by two. But those that came got a heck of a show, and the first race for the Sheepshead Bay Trophy started right on time at 10:30 ayem and brought all the stock MGs out along with Cal Carrington in the Jowett Jupiter and a couple of those Singer things that had run so well at Callicoon. Including the one that won there, in fact, with that same exact, hired-gun speedway driver from California behind the wheel. His name was Lanny Lamereux, and he was a wiry, leathery little guy who was obviously cut from a smidgen tougher material than your average SCMA wheel-twister. And sure enough he'd grabbed the lead by the end of the very first lap and looked like he was off to the races. But my old buddy Cal worked his way through the MGs and got the Jowett up to second in a couple more laps, and then, ever so slowly, he started to reel in the Singer. To be honest, the two of them were both running about the same exact speed—and leaving all the MGs far behind—but, at least according to my watch, Cal was shaving the odd tenth or two off this Lanny Lamereaux guy every lap and gradually closing the gap. It was agonizing to watch and, since it looked like the Singer had maybe a little more grunt and its driver was far from a raw hand at this racing stuff, I wondered if Cal could get around him even if he caught up. As any real racing driver will gladly tell you, catching somebody and passing somebody are two entirely different things....

By the time the starter signaled three laps to go, Cal had the Jowett right up on the Singer's tailpipe and everybody watching from the paddock side—and especially me and Julie and Tommy Edwards and Big Ed—were going absolutely bananas, shouting and whooping and waving our arms in the air every time they went by. Only the next lap Cal came around all alone. Lanny Lamereux had sensed the motor tightening up in the Singer, and as soon as he saw the needle on the oil pressure gauge start to drop—like the pro he was—he switched off and pulled it over to the side before it poofed its engine. But he came over afterward to shake hands with Cal and congratulate him for a good drive, and you couldn't miss that they were both real disappointed they didn't get to race it out to the end.

"Think you could've got around him?" I asked Cal after he left.

"Around him or through him," Cal snickered like it was an absolute sure thing. But I wasn't all that certain. I was pretty sure from the look in Lanny Lamereaux's eyes that he'd kept a few speedway tricks hidden up his sleeve for those last few laps. Plus I didn't much like it when Cal got real cocky like that. And Julie didn't like it at all. Still, I was damn proud to count him as a friend and damn proud of how he'd won that race. Even if he could be a bit of a jerkoff about it.

Talent and humility don't always park in the same garage.

The second race for the Brighton Beach Trophy featured a bunch of Jag 120s—including Big Ed's—plus a couple of those little 1488cc Porsches that were too expensive to run in the first race and poor Tommy Edwards in the new "baby" Allard that was really way too slow and heavy to have any sort of chance. There was also this nifty little Kieft car from England in the hands of a very quick and experienced SCMA driver named Erwin Goldschmidt. Well, he was sort of an SCMA racer, anyway. Seems he ran into some of the same troubles getting into the SCMA that Big Ed did (and for about the same reasons, although Charlie Priddle supposedly told him right to his face: *"It isn't that we don't want you in the club because you're Jewish, it's that we don't want you in the club because you're a shit."*). But no matter what you thought of him, he was one hell of a good driver, and it was nice to see that Alec Ulmann had put a little piece in the race program about him as a way to grind Charlie Priddle and the rest of the "closed club" SCMA types about the way they conducted business.

Not that it did much good.

But, like I said, he was a hell of a 'shoe, and that's why they'd put him in this new Kieft to show it off. To tell the truth, it was like nothing anybody had ever seen before. It was built in England by this guy named Cyril Kieft, and it was real small and low and obviously intended exclusively for racing. Like an OSCA, you know? Only not nearly so pretty or well built. There was a hopped-up, 1467cc MG four-banger with more than 10-to-1 compression ratio under the hood, but the neatest thing was how the whole entire nose section hinged forward for service. It was made out of fiberglass, too, so it was really light. And the chassis had independent suspension on all four corners and there was even talk that you could get it with disc brakes like those winning Jaguar factory C-Types ran at Le Mans. Erwin Goldschmidt showed what it could do, too. Even though it was just a little one-and-a-half liter running against all the 3.4-liter Jaguar 120s, damn if he didn't jump into the lead on the very first lap and make it stick. Eventually the fastest of the Jag 120s caught up to him and stormed by, but he held onto second place all the way to the checker. It was a hell of a job, no lie.

And you had to be pretty impressed with those tubby little Porsches, too. Unlike the Kieft, they were real road cars—not pure racecars—and had to run in this group because they cost more than $3000 and were way too quick for the MGs and such in the first group. But they only had these dinky little 1488cc engines in back and so there was no way they could run with the Jaguars. Or at least not on a track like this, anyway. But all three of them were running together just outside the top ten, and they looked to be about the quickest cars of all through the esses. I swear, they took those corners like they were on rails compared to the Jags!

Meanwhile poor Tommy was mired about two-thirds of the way back in the pack in that overweight and underpowered Allard Palm Beach thing and having one hell of a dice with that C.K. Dexter-Haven guy and two or three other poorly driven XK 120s. Tommy would wail past the whole lot of them—sometimes picking them off two at a time under braking for the tight corners and then opening up a little daylight through the twisty stuff—but then they'd hit those long, runway straightaways and the Jags would roar right past him and he'd have to do it all over again. Plus he'd get boxed in or blocked all the time because the Jags were also fighting with each other and then they'd *really* open up a gap and he'd have to chase them down again a tenth or two at a time with superior driving. To be honest, it can be real entertaining watching a good driver in a lousy car up against a lousy driver in a good car. At least if you're not the poor sap behind the wheel, anyway.

And while all of this was going on, Big Ed was stumbling around at the back end of the field with a hole in his radiator that he was just too damn hot and busy and uncomfortable to notice dumping a steady drizzle of coolant under his own wheels. You think he'd have noticed the wisps of steam or the smell of hot coolant or the strange, snaky handling or when the temp gauge went up to the redline and then, even worse, went back down again (that's what happens when it finally runs dry and there's no water around the temperature sensor any more). But he did notice that the car seemed to all of a sudden handle a lot better when the cooling system stopped spritzing water under his tires when it went bone dry. Although he didn't get to enjoy it for long, of course, seeing as how it wasn't more than a lap or two later that the engine cried "enough" and locked up solid.

"Ahh, I was ready t'stop for a damn beer anyway," he said afterwards, mopping at his bald spot with a soaking wet handkerchief. But no matter how lah-de-dah nonchalant Big Ed tried to act, you could tell he was plenty pissed off about seizing up the engine in his XK 120. "I was gonna come in an' turn it over t'you," he added, casting a mean glare over Cal's direction. But I could tell he was just jerking Cal around. On account of he was so cocky and everything after he won that first race and also maybe because Big Ed was a little bit jealous of what he could do with a racecar. Maybe more than a little bit, even.

There was a "touring" parade for old classic racing cars after lunch, and naturally Charlie Priddle was right at the front of the line in his antique Bentley that was once a factory team car at Le Mans and looked massive and heavy as a damn steam locomotive. I couldn't believe they actually used to race cars like that, you know? And especially for twenty-four hours. Hell, scrawny little Charlie Priddle wore himself to a frazzle just trying to steer it around for a few brief exhibition laps. He was heaving and panting and pouring sweat like a blessed fire hydrant by the time he pulled in, and they had to about lift him out afterwards on account of he was too weak to work the door handle.

"He looks pretty well knackered," Tommy observed.

"Couldn't have happened to a nicer guy," Big Ed sneered, and we all nodded in agreement.

"He won't be the last to crumble in this heat," Tommy added. "This is the sort of stuff that separates the *real* racers from the pansies and ribbon clerks."

By the time they started lining up the cars up for the big, 100-lap Floyd Bennett Grand Prize Cup feature race that was scheduled for 2:30 PM, the temperature was up to over 100 degrees in the shade (not that there was any) and a whole lot more than that out on the racetrack. It was sweltering, all right, and Big Ed didn't even stick around to watch Masten Gregory drive that red C-type he'd owned—albeit briefly—just two days before. Nope, it was just too damn hot for that, and Big Ed climbed into his air-conditioned, black Sixty Special and headed for home. Which was really too bad, since Julie had been holed up in the Caddy enjoying the cool breeze out of the dash vents since the end of the last race, and she was none too happy about getting back into the frying pan with the rest of us. The only good thing about the weather was the effect it was having on the outfits on some of the young ladies in attendance. In particular, the luscious Sally Enderle was parading around the paddock in a pair of sunglasses, a flower print bikini top not much larger than the sunglasses, and some white shorts the approximate size of a small pocket handkerchief. Sure, I knew all about Sally and the petty, cheap, conniving, two-bit soul that lived inside her million-dollar exterior. But I couldn't help staring at her anyway.

"Who's that?" Julie asked with kind of a mean edge to her voice.

"It's nobody," I lied.

"If it's nobody, howcum you're slipping around in a pool of your own drool?"

"Look," I said, peeling my eyes away from Sally, "I can't help it if she's pretty."

"Pretty??!!" Julie snorted. "She's frickin' half-naked!"

I looked back over at Sally. "More than half, I'd say."

"Hmpf. You'd never catch me in an outfit like that."

You'd never fit into an outfit like that I thought but didn't say. My Julie had certainly padded on a few extra pounds since she found out she was pregnant.

Right on cue, Sally Enderle looked over our way and gave me this big, toothpaste-ad smile and a gushy little wave. She only did it because I was standing there with Julie. Just to bust my hump, you know?

"I thought you didn't know who she was," Julie said, glaring at me.

"Oh, I know w-who she is kind of," I stammered. "W-what I meant is I really don't *know* her, see."

"That's not what it looks like to me."

I didn't like where this was going. "Look," I said, staring Julie right square in the eyes, "her name is Sally Enderle, and she comes from some stinking rich, old-money family over in Maryland someplace and she's the girlfriend of that stuck-up Creighton Pendleton the Third jerk who races the Ferrari." I kind of left out the part about the nude swim and hopping in the sack with her that night at Elkhart Lake.

"So why did she wave at *you?*" Julie wanted to know.

"How should I know? I mean, I've seen her around before and stuff"—*God, was I ever a lousy liar*— "maybe she's just being friendly."

Julie was looking at me kind of sideways. But she wasn't saying anything, and so I figured it was an excellent time to change the subject. "You want an ice cream?" I asked in the sweetest, nicest, most thoughtful, caring and polite voice you ever heard. "I think I'm going to have one myself before the next race. Can I get one for you?"

The suspicious look in Julie's eyes never wavered. "Sure, I'll have one, too," she said in a voice that had nothing whatever to do with what she was thinking. "Make mine vanilla...."

Luckily for me, right about then they were getting the cars lined up for the big Floyd Bennett Grand Prize Cup Race. "Oh, let's go watch!" I said like it was the most exciting thing in the world to see sweaty racers and crewmembers pushing silent racecars onto this barren slab of concrete under a sun that was already set on Full Broil and getting hotter all the time. They were doing a Le Mans-style start and setting the cars out along the runway according to displacement, and that put those two Chrysler-powered Cunninghams and the Caddy-powered Perry's Special up ahead of Creighton Pendleton's Ferrari and all of the C-Type Jaguars and Jaguar specials, and the rest of the field was mostly smaller-engined modified and racing cars like OSCAs and Maseratis and Frazer-Nashes and such running for trophies and glory that nobody much noticed or cared about. At the very far end were four 748cc Crosley-powered racecars led by some guy named C.H. "Candy" Poole in something called a PBX that he'd built himself and one of those 745cc French D.B. "DoucheBag" things like we'd seen at Sebring. Cal could've entered in the Jowett again seeing as how he was one of the top three finishers in that first race, but the guy who owned the car figured he'd gotten exactly what he wanted already and there was no point tempting fate just to find out how many times his Jowett could get lapped by the Ferraris, Cunninghams and C-Types. But Cal was hopeful he'd catch on with somebody as a relief driver thanks to the heat. And he just might, too. It was that blazing hot out.

When the flag dropped right on the dot at 2:30, that small, skinny Masten Gregory kid sprinted across the track quicker than anybody and got away first in the gleaming red C-Type he'd bought from Big Ed. Phil Walters and Briggs himself were running second and third in the Cunninghams, followed by a few slower cars that made really good starts and then Creighton Pendleton's hotrod Ferrari, which had taken a moment to catch on the line but which was now sounding fabulous and going like stink. He cut through the slower cars in one lap and pulled up behind the two Cunninghams, and they in turn were chasing that Masten Gregory kid in Big Ed's ex-C-Type. It wasn't four laps before they were running into lapped traffic! That made for a lot of tight squeezes and close calls, and you could see as how this Masten Gregory didn't think twice before poking his nose in to get around somebody. In fact, some of the time it didn't look like he even thought once. But he was getting away with it, and I guess that's the real difference between genius and madness, right?

With their wealth of endurance racing experience to lean on, Walters and Cunningham were being a little more circumspect through traffic and not taking near so many chances. After all, 100 laps around the Floyd Bennett Field layout was well over 200 miles, and the secret to running a crack long-distance team is seeing all the way to the checkered flag rather than just to the next corner. And maybe that's why neither of them put up much of a fuss when Creighton Pendleton passed them in his screaming red Ferrari. Although afterwards, I noticed Phil Walters giving it a little more stick and hanging with him while Briggs, who would be the first to tell you that his hired-gun drivers Phil Walters and John Fitch were quicker than he, began to fall back and lose touch with the front three.

The Ferrari and the Cunningham both seemed to have more in the way of sheer grunt than Gregory's Jaguar, and they blew right by him on the straight-away after he got balked by a slower car that had no idea he was even there and damn near took the nose off his brand new racecar. But that didn't slow him down a bit, and he charged right back to challenge for the lead again before the rear end started making funny noises and he had to park it. Turned out one of Colin St. John's brilliant mechanics had drained the diff fluid in order to change it and then somehow forgot to refill it. Which of course meant that Colin could sell him back the higher-ratio diff out of his own burnt-out Ivory C-Type for something like quadruple what Colin had paid Big Ed for the entire hulk. At least once he got all that fire extinguisher residue cleaned off and gave it a quick-and-dirty respray of shiny black paint....

All of which left Creighton Pendleton in the lead with Phil Walters running smoothly and patiently a few lengths back, more than happy to let the Ferrari set the pace and clear the way through the lapped traffic. And you got the idea Creighton was maybe feeling the pressure just a little. I mean, here he was, leading the highly touted Cunningham team—the hands-down best damn sports car team in America according to everybody and their brother—and, if he drove a little harder, maybe he could just make it stick. So he was really pushing.

"Phil's playing cat-and-mouse with him," Tommy whispered in my ear. "And he's falling for it, too."

I'd kind of expected more from that Walt Hansgen guy who'd been so quick in an ordinary 120, but he'd let his co-driver start (and you can be sure there was likely some changes of checking account balances behind it) and so that pretty white Jaguar special was well down the field when the guy pulled in a little before half-distance and handed over to Walt. After that, it went like stink, but nobody except me and a few other people who were actually paying attention much noticed.

Not two laps later Skippy Welcher meandered into the pits in his C-Type, and you could tell he was pretty well fried by the way the car swerved and jerked and damn near picked off a couple flagmen on the way in. Skippy was drenched with sweat and his face was the color of a freshly boiled lobster. Milton Fitting came over to ask him what was wrong, but he just looked around like he was blind and couldn't see anything and then stuck his arm out and pointed his short, bony index finger directly at Tommy Edwards. *"You!"* He rasped, barely able to get the words out. *"Get in!"*

So Tommy strapped his helmet on and climbed in and took off in The Skipper's C-Type, and he put in a really nice drive over the second half of the race. Unfortunately, just like Walt Hansgen, he was so far back by the time he got in that nobody except Cal and Julie and me much noticed. And we had to point it out to Julie.

But meanwhile there was one hell of a race going on at the front, with Creighton Pendleton leading but looking like he was maybe running a little scared and Phil Walters right behind, applying all sorts of pressure and looking cool, calm and collected. Or at least calm and collected, anyway. And then we started to notice that Creighton was getting a little erratic, locking up his brakes or missing a downshift or getting all jerky trying to feed the car into the turns. "He's losing it," Cal said knowingly, tapping his finger against his forehead. Sure enough he looped the Ferrari a couple corners later and almost did it again two corners after that. By which time Phil Walters in the C-4R Cunningham was long gone. Creighton tried to tough it out for a few more slow, clumsy laps but finally pulled in on lap 64, looking even more used-up than The Skipper had. The Muscatelli brothers had to lift him out of the car and he looked genuinely dazed. But even so Cal was over there in an instant, helmet in hand, trying to talk his way into Creighton's Ferrari. And damn if he didn't do it, too!

By the time Cal wailed out of the pits in Creighton's Ferrari, they were down to fourth place and several laps behind with no chance at all of catching Phil Walters. But the C-Jag ahead of them and Briggs in the other Cunningham were another matter entirely. It took Cal about three laps to get the hang of the Ferrari—it was, by far, the best and fastest racing car he'd ever driven in his life!—and he made quick work of reeling in the third-place C-Type and taking off after the Cunningham in second. And what a job he did, chopping whole handfuls of seconds off the best Briggs could do every single lap! Plus there was drama up at the front, since the brakes on Phil Walters' Cunningham were starting to grab and lock up heading into the corners. I started to get this crazy idea that maybe Cal could actually *win* this damn race!

But Phil Walters was a pretty shrewd and experienced hand, and he was able to ease off just a little and drive his way around the problem and brought the car home in first place like a team-leading driver is supposed to. And you had to give him credit. But Cal did catch Briggs in the other Cunningham with just two laps to go and made an absolutely textbook-clean outbraking move to take second place. And that's the way they finished. Wow!

So it was pretty neat seeing Cal up there on the podium with Phil Walters and Briggs Cunningham and Creighton Pendleton and the luscious Sally Enderle. He'd done one hell of a job and everybody said so. In fact, he only did one thing wrong. He went a full second quicker than Creighton ever did in the car. Even though it was hotter than blazes and the track was greasy as a bacon griddle by the time he got in. And that meant for absolute sure that he would never, ever, get a chance to co-drive with Creighton Pendleton again.

I mean, there are some things you just don't do....

9:The Undertaker's Healey

Julie helped me load all the stuff and hitch up Big Ed's frozen-solid XK 120 after the races were over at Floyd Bennett Field, and I swear we were both so blessed hot and tired and grimy and soggy by then that it was all we could do to lift our arms to make rude gestures to each other. We were even too hot and tired to talk, you know? And of course nothing goes smooth or easy when you're beat to shit like that and your hands are so damn weak and sweaty and greasy that you can't hold a damn wrench or hammer without dropping it on your toe. And then it's like going off a damn high dive just to bend over and pick it up. But we finally got everything together and climbed into the cab of the tow truck—I swear, it was like a roaster oven in there!—for the ride back to Passaic. "Y'know, Palumbo," Julie said in a voice that sounded like it was coming from the next room, "you really know how to show a girl a good time."

"I thought it was kind of fun," I lied.

"It'll be fun when it's a distant memory. That's when it'll be fun."

"Coney Island was nice."

"That's already a distant memory." She wasn't really being mean or angry or anything. Just cranky and pissy and uncomfortable, which is something else entirely. Even if it looks a lot the same from the outside.

"Boy," I said, trying to drum up a little enthusiasm, "did'ja see the way Cal drove? He's really got it, y'know?

"Yeah. And he sure lets everybody know about it, too."

"Aw, he's just trying to get a few breaks for himself."

"Hmpf," Julie snorted, not sounding real convinced.

"I just wish I could see what he'd do with a *real* opportunity."

"What's it to you?"

"Look," I told her, "like it or not, this is gonna be our future. And these are my friends, too...."

"Don't be a chump, Buddy. These people are your friends because of what you can do for them. Because they *need* you. They'll dump you in a frickin' heartbeat if they get a better deal someplace else."

"Big Ed would *never* do anything like that!"

"Big Ed, maybe not," she allowed. "But I wasn't really thinking of him...."

And right about then is when I heard the safety chain drop and start skittering along the pavement behind us.

"What the hell was *that??*" I said, snapping bolt upright in the seat. I'd been just kind of doodling along and not paying too much attention—hell, I'd made this trip back to Jersey a kazillion times or more—and now here I was, smack-dab in the middle of the old George Washington Bridge, doing maybe 45 with Big Ed's Jag 120 hitched on the back and normal early Saturday evening traffic all around me and absolutely no place to pull over and see what was up. I glanced in the mirror and—*OH SHIT!*—Big Ed's Jag was kind of dangling all catty-wumpus off the hook and swinging back and forth like a damn pendulum. *"JESUSCHRISTALMIGHTY!"* I yelped through clenched teeth and slammed on the brakes. Which, in fact, turned out to be the exact opposite of what I should've done seeing as how the Jag swung forward and smacked against the back of the truck and then—just like *that!*—dropped clear out of sight. *"OHMYGOD!!"* I gulped, searching frantically for Big Ed's Jag in the rearview mirror. But it appeared in the side mirror instead, broken free of the hook and veering across four lanes of traffic all by its lonesome, ricocheting off the concrete wall on the far side, and kind of sashaying back the other way! At which point I swung my eyes over to the other mirror and watched it collect both the inside concrete wall and some poor doofus pharmacist from Hackensack in a '51 Buick Roadmaster the bank still owned half of. He'd done the typical thing and slammed on the brakes when he saw the Jag break loose, but of course then the damn Buick wouldn't steer any-more and so he couldn't help sliding right square into it when Big Ed's 120 came back across his bows. After which he promptly got rear-ended by the guy behind him in a Studebaker and the guy in the Studebaker got rear-ended by a guy in a DeSoto and the guy in the DeSoto got rear-ended by a florist delivery panel truck and the guy in the florist delivery truck got…well, you get the idea.

It was a real mess, all right, what with plenty of screaming and shouting and steam rising from busted radiators and somebody's horn stuck on and somebody else bleeding like a stuck pig from a split lip and, to tell the truth, there were an awful lot of people angry at me right there on the George Washington Bridge that evening. The only lucky break was that the pharmacist guy was built more or less like Masten Gregory—only maybe even smaller—and more of a whiner and whimperer than an *'I'll-part-your-hair-with-a-damn-tire-iron'* type. *"My God!"* he wailed. *"This is a brand new car!"*

I didn't think it was exactly the right moment to point out that his Buick was already two years old.

"Look at the grille! Look at the bumper!"

The front fenders weren't looking especially good, either. And neither was the back end, where he'd taken it up the tush from this printing press salesman and his family in one of those bullet-nose Studebakers. It looked like a damn V-2 rocket had crashed into the middle of the Buick's trunk. And the little florist guy near the back of the line was absolutely beside himself, getting all screechy and fluttery about how he was going to be late for a funeral. Or a wake, actually. And I didn't figure it would do any good to remind him that the guest of honor was hardly going to care.

Well, the cops came and we all swapped license numbers and insurance num-bers and I was already thinking about all the hot water I was going to be in with Big Ed and how this could radically change all the hopes and plans I had for a thriving sports car shop at the Sinclair. I mean, besides being sort of a partner, he was by far my biggest and best customer.

"Y'say the car came right offa th' damn hook?" Big Ed howled into the receiver after Julie and me got everything back to the Sinclair and I called him.

"Uh, yeah. That's kind of what happened," I said, sounding exceedingly lame.

"And how bad is it?"

"It's pretty bad," I admitted. In fact, it was probably worse than that. The chassis maybe only needed a little front-end work, but every single body panel on that Jag was junk.

"How'd it happen?" he wanted to know.

"I dunno. Maybe something broke. Maybe I was so damn hot and tired I didn't hitch something up right. I honestly just don't know." And I didn't, either.

"You think it's a total?"

I swallowed hard. "Yeah," I told him miserably. "I'm pretty sure it is."

"Why, this is *great!*" he whooped into the other end.

"It *is?*"

"*Sure* it is!"

"I don't get it."

"Well, I wanted t'trade that sonofabitch in on the C-Type, but that prick ratbastard St. John wouldn't give me a decent deal on it, see? An' now the insurance company's gotta come up with the full-boat replacement cost." He started chuckling on the other end. "An' they don't need t'know anything about that frozen-up motor, either!"

Turns out that our insurance agent buddy Mr. Bender had made a lowball pitch for a whole bunch of Big Ed's business, and all the new coverage was due to kick in on September 1st. So this represented a perfect way to say *"adios, muchachos"* to his previous agency. "They've sucked up an awful lot of my money over the years, and I sure as hell don't mind getting a little of it back. See, the insurance game is like casino gambling," Big Ed explained, "and it's always rigged in favor of the house."

"It is?"

"*Sure* it is. They're betting that everything's gonna be just fine and they've got you so damn worried and screwed up that you're betting against yourself that it isn't."

"Betting against yourself?"

"Sure. Betting that you're gonna crash your car or set your damn house on fire or get hit by a bus or a flood or a tornado or just suddenly keel over dead one day."

"So they always win?"

"No, not always," Big Ed said grimly. "But the catch is that _you_ gotta lose in order to beat them."

"That's a hell of a catch," I admitted.

"Yep," Big Ed agreed. "It's the best one there is."

It stayed beastly hot around New York and New Jersey for the whole blessed week after the race at Floyd Bennett Field—the *New York Times* said it was the worst heat wave in recent memory—and Julie was after me to buy an air conditioner and put it in. But it was a lot of money and I couldn't see my way clear to afford it and I sure as heck didn't want to buy it on time—I mean, it'd be fall and then winter soon enough and we'd still be paying on it, right?—but I did promise to put a good-sized extractor fan in the back kitchen window and another, smaller fan in our bedroom window so's we could get a little flow-through ventilation. I knew right where I'd get that extractor fan, too, since I'd seen one in Butch's front yard that he'd picked up from a factory building they were tearing down someplace. All it needed was a coat of fresh paint over the rust and a rewire job on the armature and maybe a new bearing or two on the shaft and it'd be good as new. "And just how long is *that* gonna take?" Julie demanded while fanning herself with a copy of *Better Homes and Gardens*.

"By the end of the week. I promise." And I meant it, too.

So I took the Old Man's tow truck over and picked up the extractor fan out of Butch's front yard and pulled the motor out and sent it over to be rewound and straightened up the frame a little (I even had Butch put a couple fresh new welds on it where the old spot welds were starting to pop loose) and I was just in the middle of painting it a bright, cheery, kitchen-appropriate shade of yellow when who should show up at the Sinclair but Carson Flegley in his brand new Healey Hundred. Seems Colin St. John had miraculously (and at great effort and expense, of course) managed to complete the phony "Canadian trade" for the shiny black Austin-Healey 100 that Carson wanted so badly and that Colin already had salted away in the windowless meat truck garage on the other side of town for six or seven weeks while he milked Carson for every available nickel. But that didn't matter to Carson one bit. In fact, you should have seen the smile plastered across his face when he came tooling into the Sinclair with the windshield folded down to the "racing position" like it showed on the third page of the owners' manual. Made the car look really slick, too. Even if folding the windshield down to that sleek and rakish "racing position" put the upper edge of it about even with your shirt pocket (or your tie tack or boutonniere, if you were going someplace fancy) which made it somewhat less than effective when it came to actually shielding anything much north of your armpits from the wind. Unless you were a midget or an eight-year-old kid, that is. And a short eight-year-old kid, at that.

"Whaddaya think?" Carson beamed, patting the Healey's cowling.

"You've got a yellow jacket in your teeth," I advised him. "But don't worry, he looks dead. Or at least pretty stunned."

Carson spit the remains of the yellow jacket out and delicately crushed it into oblivion with the toe of his shoe.

"So? Howzit run?" I asked.

"Oh my goodness," he gushed. "It's ten times the car that MG ever was. Maybe even twenty. It's absolutely *stunning!*"

You could see Carson was deep into the throes of New Car Rapture, and there may well be no stronger intoxicant on the face of this earth.

"How's it handle?" I asked.

"It glides like a soaring bird," he told me while picking a few more yellow jacket remnants from his bicuspid. "Wanna go for a ride?"

Well, he didn't have to ask twice. Only first I went inside to grab those aviator sunglasses that Cal gleeped for me on our way up to Grand Island. I mean, no way could I ask somebody in the throes of New Car Rapture to put the blessed windshield back up.

So we tooled off down Pine Street with Carson at the wheel, and after he got us a few miles out of town and kind of showed me where the steering wheel and pedals and shifter were, he pulled over and let me take the helm. And I must admit that his new Healey Hundred was one heck of a swell sports car. And one heck of a bargain, too. It was maybe even prettier than a Jag 120—I can't believe I said that!—and certainly a lot lower and lighter and handier. And Jeez, did it ever steer and brake and handle nice. At least so long as you slowed way down for potholes and railroad crossings and such, seeing as how the Healey was pretty low slung and didn't have an awful lot of ground clearance. In fact, as far as railroad crossings were concerned, it would sort of launch itself, sail gracefully through the air, and come down with the approximate impact of a B-29 making a crash landing if you didn't.

As far as sheer speed and power goes, the engine had lots more punch than Carson's old MG but was certainly no match for a Jag. Not hardly. Like I said, I'd heard a rumor someplace that the new Healey's engine came out of a damn milk truck or something. And I could believe it, too, since the stroke was as long as your arm and the redline was down below 5000rpm. But it had a lot of grunt and it was nice how you could damn near count the RPM by ear at tickover. I guess the three-speed transmission came out of that same milk truck, too. Only for milk truck operation it was a four-speed, but first gear was so ridiculously low that they'd blocked it off on account of it wasn't good for anything except pulling stumps out of the ground or wrapping the rear leaf springs clear around the axle housing like windowshades if you popped the clutch for a fast getaway.

You stirred the gears in Carson's new Healey with this long, trucklike shift lever that sprouted up out of the side of the transmission tunnel way down by the floorboards, and it came with a Laycock de Normanville—that name always makes me think of knights of the roundtable and castles and family crests and stuff, you know?—overdrive that you could use on second and top gears and pre-tend like you had a five-speed transmission. Not that you really needed it, since that lumbering four-banger under the hood had so damn much torque. But it was fun to play with anyway—"splitting shifts" was what all the Healey guys started calling it—and you could cruise real nice in overdrive top, doing an effortless mile a minute with the engine just loafing along at 2,500rpm. Plus using all those cheap, available, already-tooled-up-and-in-the-Austin-parts-bins driveline pieces is precisely what made the new Healey Hundred such a damn bargain. Besides which, being truck stuff by nature, it was all bloody hell for strong.

But the really amazing thing about the new Healey Hundred was the way it felt to drive. No matter what kind of plain Jane, blue-collar, shot-and-a-beer work-ing-stiff hardware was underneath the sheet metal, I have to admit I just flat fell in love with that car. It was just so blessed stout and sharp and handsome and handy and such a damn ball to drive.

Plus you had to just love that grin on its face....

"Yep, that's sure one heck of a nifty sports car," I agreed as Carson and me pulled back into the station.

"Yep," Carson beamed right back. "It sure is." I saw a kind of shiver go through him. "I just *love* it, you know?"

"Hey, you should. Enjoy it while you can."

"I had to pay through the damn nose for it," he admitted ruefully.

Of that I had no doubt.

But the sparkle came right back into his eyes no more than a heartbeat later. "I love it anyway, though. I think it's the best-damn-looking sports car I've ever seen!"

Yep. New Car Rapture, all right. No doubt about it. And it was an easy sort of thing to contract from a Healey Hundred during that summer of 1953. Why, it was almost an epidemic.

Speaking of new cars, who should roll into the Sinclair the very next day but Big Ed Baumstein at the wheel of one of the strangest damn four-wheeled creations I'd ever seen in my life. I knew what it was on account of I'd seen pictures in some magazines, but I'd never come face-to-face with an in-the-flesh Muntz Jet before. It was white, of course, and the bodywork looked like it was designed by the same guy who did those tubby little rocket ships in the old, black-and-white *Flash Gordon* serials with Buster Crabbe. You know, the ones that took off in a circle and fizzed little smoke-and-electrical-fire special effects out the back end?

"Whaddaya think?" Big Ed grinned.

It was hard to find the right words. Oh, I knew the story all right. About how famous Indianapolis racecar builder Frank Kurtis out in California decided to try his hand at a sports car. I mean, why not? The first ones he built weren't much more than one of his Indy 500 roadsters kind of widened up so's you could fit two seats inside and with some lights and cycle fenders and such slapped on to make it street legal. In fact, he called them 500Ks, and *Road and Track* did a road test of one with a hot-rodded GMC six under the hood and came away thinking it was a pretty keen deal. Almost like an all-American version of an Allard, right? And, just like Allards, you could get a Kurtis 500K sports car with just about any kind of engine you wanted. In fact, there was some guy named Bill Stroppe running one with a Mercury V8 out on the west coast and giving even the Ferrari guys fits. Honest. But the point is that Frank Kurtis had a real hefty supply of ambition, and he had this idea he wanted to build something more than just a thinly disguised Indianapolis racer. He wanted to build a *real* car with his name on the hood and decklid. And he wanted it to be something really special, too. Not so much a "sports" car as sort of a stylish, flamboyant, high-performance, super-exclusive and most especially head-turning "personal luxury car" aimed right square at rich, showy guys like, well, Big Ed Baumstein. What with the movies and all, it figured there were probably an awful lot of them running around in Hollywood. So he kind of knocked the walls back on his chassis design and added this bodywork that didn't look like anything else on earth (except maybe a half-submerged bullfrog with a severe underbite or maybe a hippopotamus in a chrome-plated catcher's mask) and made sure it had a few not-really-practical-even-in-sunny-California features to set it apart from the crowd. Like fr'instance a fully removable hardtop that you left back home in your garage anytime you wanted to try a little open-air motoring. The bad news was that it took at least two people to lift it off or re-install it, and there wasn't so much as an optional umbrella on board in case the clouds opened up while you were umpty-dozen miles from home. To be honest about it, that just sort of points out the difference between a racecar and a "real" car, and how the racecar is actually a lot simpler on account of all it has to do is get there first. A "real" car is expected to take care of the people inside it—regardless of where they're going or what the traffic is like or how bad the pavement is or what the weatherman is serving up—and believe me, that's a lot more complicated and involved than simply going fast.

At any rate, Frank Kurtis built a few of these things and even sold some, but they were all hand-built and so he was losing money on every one and also discovering that, for the exact reasons mentioned above, selling and satisfying his "real" car customers was turning out to be a lot tougher than keeping his Indy 500 racecar customers happy. After all, his cars won the Indy 500 in '50 and '51 and then again in '53, so he didn't really need any excuses where that was concerned. So Frank Kurtis finally decided to say "screw it" to the "real" car business and go back to what he was really good at.

And that would've been the end of it, if it hadn't been for Earl "Madman" Muntz.

Now you have to understand that Earl Muntz started out as a used car salesman in Elgin, Illinois, at the tender age of eighteen, and it wasn't six months before he owned his own lot. I kid you not. He was as red-white-and-blue American a character as Thomas Edison or P.T. Barnum, and there was a whole heap of both of them in Earl Muntz. Which is one way of saying you were never quite sure if he was some kind of genius electronic whiz kid or a snake oil salesman. But the point is that he had more ideas, ambition and *chutzpah* than any six or seven people you know. And like a lot of people with that kind of insatiable drive, Earl Muntz traveled out to California where such things tend to flourish and fester better in a land with no past and an oversupply of sunshine. He started out selling cars again, and pretty soon he became famous for the way he'd talk crazy on the radio and show this cartoon picture of himself in all of his ads, all dressed up in red flannel long underwear and wearing a three-cornered Napoleon hat on his head like he was nuts. He'd jabber out stuff like, *"I sell cars at wholesale and buy them at retail because it's more _fun_ that way!"* or *"I'd like to give 'em away, but my wife won't let me...She's _cra-a-a-zy!"_* all the time on the radio and, it being California, that sold him an awful lot of cars. But, like I said, he was also a pretty sharp and shrewd customer under that three-cornered Napoleon hat and knew a thing or two about electronics, and what really made his fortune was the Muntz TV. What he did was look at all the TVs everybody else was making and figure out what they could maybe do without. So he snipped out a bunch of electronic bits and gizmos that he didn't think were absolutely necessary and came up with a TV he could sell a lot cheaper than anybody else. In fact, the TV my old man gave himself for Christmas was a Muntz for that very reason. It was cheap. Oh, some people complained that the quality wasn't real good or that it wouldn't pull in signals worth a damn if you lived out in the sticks. But it worked pretty much okay if you lived somewheres near the broadcast towers—like probably half to two-thirds of the U.S. population did—and so "Madman" Muntz sold the living shit out of them.

I don't know exactly how Earl Muntz collided with Frank Kurtis' dead-in-the-water "personal luxury car" project, but the important thing to realize is that wanting a car with your own name on it is kind of an occupational hazard for rich, self-made, entrepreneurial types with a high tide of ego and ambition welled up behind their eyes. So "Madman" Muntz picked up the Kurtis deal and had him make a few more, and then he moved the whole shootin' match to a new factory in Evanston, Illinois—just outside Chicago—and also made some changes along the way. Like stretching the wheelbase so's a real person could actually sit in the back seat and switching from Cadillac to Lincoln engines and so forth.

To tell the truth, it was kind of hard to figure what a Muntz Jet was exactly good for. They were rare and expensive and genuinely hand crafted—hell, the bodywork was all hand-leaded, one car at a time—but they were also kind of heavy and impractical and Buck Rogers odd-looking and certainly not true sports cars like the original Kurtis 500K. Not hardly. But the one thing you knew for sure about a Muntz Jet was that it didn't look like anything else on the road and you sure weren't very likely to see one coming the other way. And I guess stuff like that counts for a lot with people like Big Ed Baumstein.

"Well," he asked again, "whaddaya think?"

"It sure is something," I finally answered.

"Yep, it sure is!" he grinned. "I think it may be the only one in Jersey."

"Do tell."

He patted it on the nose. "Yep, this baby gets a lot of attention all right."

Of that I had no doubt. And I must admit I was kind of worried about my future as I ran my eyes down the slab sides of Big Ed's new Muntz. I mean, no way was this thing ever going to be a racecar, and my budding sports car repair business at the Sinclair depended greatly on all the stuff I could count on Big Ed to want or break on his racecar. In fact, he was my meal ticket. "So," I finally asked, "is this gonna replace the Jaguar?"

He looked at me like I was nuts. "Oh, hell no," he told me, and started unwrapping a fresh cigar. "This is just a little something I picked up for the little woman."

"The little woman? I thought you were getting divorced again."

"I *am* getting divorced," he said like I was stupid. "I'm getting divorced *because of* the little woman, see. You met her."

"I did?"

"Sure y'did. It's that Rhonda I had with me up at Bridgehampton."

I remembered her all right. But it was going to take a lot of imagination to think of her as a "little" woman. Hell, I'd seen football linebackers smaller than her. And I'm talking real *professional* football linebackers, too—like with the Chicago Bears and New York Football Giants, not some of those Ivy League sissies out at Yale or Princeton. "So you're serious about this Rhonda?" I asked. I mean, speaking of "professionals," this Rhonda kind of looked and talked and acted like she might sort of be one.

"Buddy," Big Ed explained, clamping his arm around my shoulder, "you should get it by now that I'm not the kinda guy t'be particularly serious about anyone." He fired up his new stogie and took a few puffs. "I'm just out t'have a good time and enjoy myself, see?" he added thoughtfully. "A guy like me works hard for a living—I gotta bite and scratch and claw and fight the damn battle every day—and when I get the chance t'get away a little, that's exactly what I wanna do. Oh, it may sound kinda ugly and shallow and selfish, but I don't really care." He blew out another one of those perfect, Big Ed Baumstein smoke rings and watched it slowly drift away and dissolve. "I mean, look at me. Why would somebody wanna go out with me, huh?" He patted his back pants pocket knowingly. "But that's okay, I don't mind. I use them. They use me. That's what using's for, see?"

It just didn't sound right to me. But then I guess I'm not like some people when it comes to that sort of stuff. Still, I knew enough to keep my mouth shut. The first big lesson you ever learn about friendship is that, eventually, your friends are gonna think things and say things and do things that will absolutely make your skin crawl. And sooner if not later. And you've just gotta learn to keep your eyes focused high enough to look right over it. Otherwise they're not gonna be your friends much anymore. Or your customers either, for that matter. I think high standards are for people who can either afford them or keep quiet about them.

I decided to change the subject. "So, where'd you come by the Muntz?" I mean, I hadn't ever seen one around before.

"Aw, I saw this little number when I was looking at some distressed forging and finishing equipment out south of Chicago," Big Ed explained grandly. "Belonged t'the son of the guy whose business was going down the shitter. They worked together and were mad as hell at each other and blaming each other about the business going tits-up. That's always the way it goes. I think he sold it just to piss the kid off. Did it while the kid was off having a three-martini lunch with his lawyer or something. It was in the old man's name so there was nothing the kid could do about it."

"I bet he was mad."

"Oh, it was one hell of a scene when the kid got back. Hell of a scene." Big Ed shook his head and added a helpless laugh. "Only had a couple hundred miles on it, too."

"And you're gonna give it to Rhonda?"

"I didn't say I was gonna *give* it to her, Buddy. I said I was gonna let her *use* it, see? Weren't you listening?"

"I guess not."

"Yeah, I'll let her use it for awhile. And if she plays her cards right…"

"Yes?"

"…if she plays her cards right and keeps me coming back for more, who knows? She might just become my next future ex-wife."

I made a kind of sour face. I mean, I couldn't help it, you know?

"Hey, don't sneer at it, Buddy. Believe me, a lotta women are lookin' for exactly that sort of deal." He blew out yet another perfect smoke ring. "Hell, I got three or four of them on th' damn payroll already…."

Most all the people in the sportycar crowd were going up to Thompson Speedway in Connecticut the following weekend for a big SCMA national race—including Cal Carrington, who had sweet-talked himself into a ride up and a room-share deal with Carson Flegley and was running up the phone bill something awful over at Castle Carrington trying to nail down another drive in that V8-powered MG monstrosity—but it looked like I was going to have to take a pass. Carson was still breaking in his new Healey Hundred and had absolutely no intentions of racing it (a point he was careful to make exceedingly clear to Cal, as you can imagine), and Big Ed was between racecars and so I really didn't have any paying customers going up. I mean, you could never exactly classify Cal as a paying customer, even if he did come up with a drive.

Besides, it was still hotter than hell and I was plumb worn out from the Floyd Bennett Field race and I had a bunch of work stacked up at the Sinclair—real hot weather and real cold weather are always good for a garage business (at least if you can stand it)—and I'd promised Julie that I'd get that extractor fan mounted in the back kitchen window. And neatly, too. Not to mention that my mom had decided we should all get together for a nice family dinner on Monday evening on account of it was Labor Day and she figured nobody had to work. But of course that's because she didn't quite grasp the difference between having a factory job with a union contract and running a small corner gas station that people expect to be open on a day when half the damn population is traveling from one place to another to cook over charcoal grills and be with family. To be honest, Sunday would have really been better for me, but my old man and some of his union buddies had tickets to go watch the Giants play the Dodgers. It was a perfect kind of game for him because he was a diehard Yankee fan, and so he could scream and curse and hiss and boo and shake his fist threateningly at *both* teams and then come away happy no matter who lost. And afterwards he and his buddies always stopped by a local tavern to commiserate and analyze and argue with each other over all the dumb plays and stupid managers' decisions and ridiculous umpire calls. Sometimes they'd even get into screaming and shoving matches over it. But never fistfights. It was kind of a tradition.

But the point is that my mom wanted us to all get together as a family on account of there'd been a little friction (which is a nice, family-style word for yelling, screaming, door slamming and assorted rude Italian hand gestures) building up between my dad and my sister Mary Frances since she'd been living back at home. And especially since she'd started not exactly living back at home all the time and sometimes came home so late it was really early the next morning or even turned up missing for two or three days at a time. Bless her soul, my mom figured it might spread a little calming oil over the waters if we all got together for a nice family meal like we used to when we were little kids. Not that the meals we had together back then were all that nice, seeing as how my old man would usually arrive home glum or angry (or glum *and* angry, on a real four-star night) and then he'd maybe get a few snorts in him and start telling each one of us in turn (or all of us at once when he was in a really expansive mood) what was wrong with every single thing we did and why we'd never amount to anything. I know my mom always told us he only did it because, deep down inside, he really cared about us and worried about us and wanted the very best for us. But that didn't stop him from acting like an asshole.

So I was feeling pretty glum myself when Cal and Carson dropped by the station early Friday morning to fill up Carson's new Healey and say goodbye on their way up to Thompson Speedway. We had to pop the trunk to fill it on account of that's where the gas cap is on a Healey Hundred, and they had the back end of that car absolutely packed solid with clothes and beer and assorted race weekend gear. Geez, I wished I was going with them.

"You really oughta come with us," Cal said through his usual cobra grin. But I knew he was just needling me. He'd never really forgiven me for getting that free trip down to *La Carrera* while he got to stay at home and read car magazines, and so he figured it was sort of his divine right to tease me and taunt me and make me eat my liver as many times as possible any time he got to go to some cool sportycar event when I had to stay home. I mean, it was only fair, right?

"Nah, I can't," I grumbled, sounding fabulously envious. "I got a bunch of stuff I gotta do at home."

"The little woman needs you to put up some nice lace curtains?" He really knew how to put the knife in and twist it.

"Go to hell, Cal."

"Or perhaps you need to go shopping for some dear little baby things for the nursery?"

"The baby's not due until February."

"Oh, my. Married in June and the baby's due already in February? Let's see." He pretended to be counting his fingers. "My goodness, what fast workers you two are!"

"You can shut up any time," I told him. But it's not like I was angry. In fact, it was all I could do to keep from laughing. Cal just had this way of saying the most terrible, awful things so they came out funny. It kept him from getting that pretty nose of his flattened all over his face more times than I could remember.

"Carson," I said, "get this bum out of here before I do something he's going to regret."

Carson fired up that big, mail truck four-banger and snicked it into gear.

"Have fun," I told them.

"We'll do our best," Carson promised.

"And have a beer for me, too, OK?"

"Absolutely!" Carson nodded as he let out the clutch.

"WE'LL HAVE TWO!! AT LEAST!!!!" Cal shouted back over his shoulder as the loaded-up Healey squirted away, bottomed hard at the low point just past the edge of the lot, and growled off down the street.

I swear, it just took all the air out of me just watching them go....

10: A Weekend at Home

The weather finally broke in a big way on Saturday, what with heavy storms and lots of wind and it all came so suddenly and with such blinding vengeance that it caused a massive, chain-reaction, sixteen-car-and-one-bus accident on the New Jersey Turnpike. Fortunately without any fatalities or serious injuries. But at least it cooled things off some. Which made things a little easier for me Saturday evening after work when I finally finished mounting that big, cheery-kitchen-yellow exhaust fan in the back window for Julie and then discovered that it blew fuses every blessed time you turned it on! So, while my buddies were enjoying the heck out of themselves at the races up at Thompson, I spent most of my day Sunday screwing around with the fuse box and the wiring until I finally got it to where it would all work pretty decent (at least if you didn't try using the toaster or the iron on the same circuit, anyway) and you had to be impressed with the refreshing breeze through our apartment when you opened all the front windows and put it on "high." Not to mention the noise. Why, it sounded like a Grumman Bearcat was taxiing through the kitchen. But there was a nice little bonus in that it easily drowned out anything that might or might not be going on in the next room. If you catch my drift.

Anyhow, it was a job well done, and afterwards Julie and me decided we'd maybe go into the city and take in a movie that night—I mean, we really hadn't been out on anything like a date together since before we were married—and that little stop at Coney Island the previous Friday evening kind of reminded both of us why we got mixed up with each other in the first place. But of course then we had to decide what movie to see, and right away we were back arguing and being angry with each other on account of the male of the species and the female of the species are always attracted to entirely different kinds of movies. And don't think that Hollywood's not wise to it, either. She'd read in the papers how it was *"...one of the most captivating, delightful love stories to reach the screen in many years..."* and *"Completely enchanting..."* and so she wanted to go see *Roman Holiday* with Gregory Peck and Audrey Hepburn over at the Radio City Music Hall. Can you believe it? And on a night when we could just as easily go see *White Witch Doctor, Invaders from Mars, War of the Worlds,* or *It Came from Outer Space* (and that one was in 3-D, too!). We went back and forth for awhile and finally decided to just drive the Old Man's tow truck into town, park it, and then take a walk around the movie house district and see where we wound up. That was better than fighting and arguing all the way into Manhattan. And it turned out we were walking by the Trans Lux at 52nd and Lexington where this movie called *Lili* with Leslie Caron and Zsa Zsa Gabor had been playing for 25 weeks—it said right on the marquee: *"The Longest Run Hit in Town!"*—and we could see there was kind of a line and the previous show was just getting out and some of the women were sniffling a little and everybody was saying how wonderful it was and...

"BUDDY!"

I wheeled around and damn if it wasn't my sister Mary Frances. She was standing there in line with one of her old roommates from the apartment in Greenwich Village and—oh, my *God!*—that novels-in-Esperanto jerkoff Oliver Cromwell from N.Y.U. Boy, I wanted to punch him right in the damn nose.

"Buddy," Mary Frances said, sounding just a little uneasy, "you remember Suzanne and Ollie." It was only then I noticed that Ollie had his arm around her ex-roommate Suzanne's waist. "And *this,*" she continued, tugging at the sleeve of a kind of slender, bony, disinterested-looking guy in blue jeans next to her, "is Frederick." You couldn't miss how she was careful to enunciate all three syllables. He didn't look like much to me, what with a longish, tangled mess of dirty blond hair, no expression at all on his face and his spine in a kind of permanent, uncaring slouch. Mary Frances turned to Frederick. "Frederick," she said, "this is my brother Buddy and his wife, Julie."

It was like she was talking to a street lamp, you know? Or maybe a phone pole.

"Hi," I said, sticking out my hand and trying to look him in the eye. But it wasn't easy, on account of they were pretty much half-closed. I finally put my hand back down. Mary Frances leaned over towards me and whispered:

"Frederick's a little out of it tonight, but he's *really* a great guy..."

I could see.

"...Loads of fun..."

Oh, no doubt.

"...and," she leaned in even closer and whispered even softer, "he's an absolutely *brilliant* artist!"

Like that explained everything.

Well, nothing would do but that we go to the movie with them and I've got to admit it was pretty decent. Sappy as hell, but decent. And so naturally Julie and Mary Frances and Suzanne sprung a few leaks here and there and got all weepy and blubbery at the end. I may have even had a little sniffle there myself, but I'm sure it was just the air conditioning. By the time we were filing out of the theatre, Frederick had actually perked up enough to utter a stray syllable or two and say "OK" when Mary Frances asked us if we'd like to go over and visit his studio, seeing as how they had a bottle of wine and some peanuts and stuff over there and it was only a few blocks away. Julie and I looked at each other. I mean, I liked Mary Frances a lot and didn't want to just blow her off, but I wasn't exactly sure I wanted to know this Frederick character any better. Not to mention it looked like dear old Ollie would be tagging along (with his arm permanently attached to Suzanne, of course) and, besides making my skin crawl on general principles, Ollie could surely be counted on to critique, analyze, dissect, compare, contrast, put in proper artistic, social and historical perspective and generally ruin for everybody the sappy but still pretty decent movie we'd just seen. But thankfully Ollie begged off—in French, can you believe it?—on account of he and Suzanne had a lot of important work to do on a doctorial dissertation or something back over at his place.

Right.

So Julie and me and Mary Frances and Frederick went back to his studio together, and it was just this kind of big, disheveled, attic-like loft space that took up half the top floor of a building where they made belts and ladies' handbags during the daytime and so the whole place reeked of cowhide and tanning chemicals and such. Oh, and cats. Frederick had about a dozen cats running around.

And mostly of the alley rather than the windowsill or back porch variety. "They came with the place," Mary Frances explained. "They take care of the mice downstairs."

I noticed her overnight bag and shoes were over in the corner.

"Well, this is, uhhh...*nice,*" I told her.

"Yes, isn't it just *super,*" she gushed. *"Look!"*

She pointed upwards, and there above us were two large, ancient skylights with heavily frosted windows and chainfalls running down the walls to open them. Or maybe they weren't heavily frosted after all. Maybe it was just an inch-thick layer of pigeon crap.

"I'll go get the wine," Frederick said in a thin, scratchy voice, and disappeared behind a heavy steel door. It was by far the longest sentence we'd heard out of him.

"The light here is just *fantastic* for Frederick's work," Mary Frances cooed. And then she leaned in close and whispered again so as not to embarrass him in the next room. "He's got a one-man show opening at one of those fancy uptown galleries at the end of October. At least if it all goes through, anyway."

"What sort of things does he do?" Julie asked. I'd almost forgot that Julie was one heck of a sketch artist herself and had always wanted to do that for a living. Not to have gallery shows or anything, but just get paid to draw those fancy fashion models with the piled-up hair and elegant gowns and swanlike necks that you see arched over backwards in topple-over poses in the fashion magazines and Sunday newspaper supplements.

Mary Frances took Julie's hand and led us over to where Frederick had a big, gray tarp all spattered with paint kind of draped up against the wall and there in front of it were four small, stand-up easels. On each one was a little foot-square canvas—about the size of a damn floor tile, for gosh sakes—and the first one was just solid, semi-gloss black (with a brush and a gallon can of semi-gloss black paint sitting on the floor next to it) and the second one was kind of a dull gray (with a brush and a gallon can of dull gray paint sitting on the floor next to it) and the third one was kind of a deep, glossy orange-red (with a gallon can of deep, glossy orange-red paint sitting on the floor next to it) and the last one was smeared, speckled, splattered, dripped and spattered with every blessed sort of color you could imagine (with about fifteen or twenty smaller paint cans of various shades and colors gathered around on the floor next to it).

Julie and I stared at the four small, foot-square canvasses on their four separate easels for a long time without saying a word. I mean, what was there to say? About then Frederick came back in with the bottle of wine. And you couldn't miss the funny smell that more or less followed him into the room. I'd smelled it once before, wafting in off the fire escape at that New Year's Eve party in Greenwich Village.

"This is his masterpiece!" Mary Frances bubbled, sweeping her hand grandly through the air in front of the four small canvasses. "Isn't it just *magnificent?*"

I looked even harder. Like maybe I'd missed something?

"Well, what do you think?" Mary Frances demanded.

"Uhh, well...what's it called?" I finally broke down and asked.

"If I let you look at it long enough, you'll guess," she almost giggled. Like it was just *too* damn delicious, right? And then she stepped up, took a deep, dramatic breath, and pointed to Frederick's canvases in order from left to right: black, gray, orange-red and splattered. "This is Frederick's *Depression, Boredom, Anger* and *Anxiety!*" She proclaimed proudly.

Oh.

"But the real *genius* part is that he only works on this one when he's depressed, this one when he's bored, this one when he's angry, and this one when he's feeling worried or frightened or anxious. Isn't it just *marvelous?*"

"Looks to me like he's worried and frightened and anxious a lot." I observed.

"Oh, not at all. It just shows more on that one. *Depression* over there has more than…" she turned and called over to Frederick, "…*how many layers is it up to now, dear?*"

But it was like he didn't hear her, on account of he was making a real Life's Work out of getting the blessed cork out of that wine bottle. He'd somehow managed to break it off completely about halfway down the neck and was now digging out bits of cork one-by-one with a pocketknife that looked like it hadn't been cleaned or sharpened since the Roosevelt administration. And I'm talking Teddy here, not Franklin D.

She asked him again, only louder: *"How many layers is it up to now, dear?"*

He looked up from the wine bottle like a squirrel caught at a bird feeder. "Huh?"

"How many layers of *Depression* have you done?"

"Forty-six," he answered sullenly and went back to his wine bottle. Like it should have been common knowledge, you know?

Mary Frances' face absolutely lit up with admiration. "Frederick's *Depression* has forty-six separate layers of paint!" she exclaimed triumphantly. "And I think *Boredom* has even more!"

It was the sort of news that threatened to tilt the whole world off its axis. "Boy, it's really something," I admitted. "How long has he been working on it?"

Mary Frances pulled in close again and whispered, *"I'm not really sure. He was already working on it when we met and that was only a couple months before I moved back home…"*

"A couple *months?"*

Mary Frances nodded like it was a wonderful thing indeed. "Buddy wants to know how long you've been working on it, dear?" she called over to him.

"About nine months now," he grunted as the last, ratty plug of cork plopped down into the wine. "I'm about done with it, actually," he added as he brought the wine with all the cork fragments floating in it over and passed the bottle around. "All except *Anger.* That one needs a little more work."

"He rarely gets angry," Mary Frances beamed. "That's why that one is taking a little longer than the others…."

After we passed the bottle around a few times—I guess separate glasses were considered a needless, bourgeois frivolity in such artistic circles—Julie and I looked at each other and I knew it was time to tell them we had to be moseying on seeing as how it was getting late and we had a lot of important stuff to do the following morning. On the way home, we talked about Mary Frances and her new boyfriend. "He's kind of creepy, isn't he?" Julie observed.

"I don't think it's fair to call him creepy," I told her. After all, this was my very favorite sister we were discussing, and I wanted to give this new guy she'd fallen for every possible break. Besides, whatever else this Frederick was, he was a lot better pick than that pompous, know-it-all jerk Ollie Cromwell. "No," I said again, "calling Frederick creepy's just not fair. I think *weird* is more like it."

"I don't know," Julie sighed sadly. "Why can't she just find someone, you know, *normal?*"

And that was the real question. As far as I could see, the problem with Mary Frances was she was just too damn smart. Some folks envy smart people, but I don't. Not after what I've seen. Being smart doesn't necessarily mean you figure things out any better or find a lot of answers. In fact, more often than not, I think it just gets you into asking more and more difficult questions. Have you ever noticed how really smart people can shoot themselves up blind alleys, chase their tails around philosophical rats' mazes and paint themselves into little, tiny psychological corners that don't even exist for average folks? And they can drive themselves and everybody around them absolutely batty looking for Truth in things that aren't necessarily true and the meaning of things that just flat don't mean anything.

Or at least they don't to me, anyway.

Monday was Labor Day, and so I treated myself to not coming in until nine in the morning. Not that I slept any later. You get used to getting up at quarter-to-six and by God that's when you wake up. Alarm clock or no. Julie was still asleep, and you could feel the deep hum off that exhaust fan kind of vibrating through the apartment. On "low," it was like the engine of an ocean-going steamship, and I half-expected to look out the window and see the alley kind of gliding by like we were heading out to sea. It was nice being there alone in bed with Julie, watching her sleep, and for the first time I thought I could maybe just make out the new little curve rising on her stomach. It sent a kind of quick shiver through me. But it was a warm kind of shiver, not a cold one....

So I got out of bed real quiet so as not to wake her and sneaked outside and borrowed her mom's newspaper off the front walk—hey, I'd bring it up to her later—made myself a cup of coffee and went back to bed. It was nice, like I said, just sitting there reading the paper and sipping my morning coffee with Julie lying there all warm and cozy and half-asleep/half-awake next to me. The big news of course was that we were up against it with the communist Reds all over the whole blessed world. Marshal Tito from Yugoslavia was arguing tooth-and-nail with the Italians over who was gonna get Trieste and Chancellor Konrad Adenauer got himself re-elected in Germany (that was one for our side!) and they had this big prisoner-of-war exchange going on over in Korea and President Eisenhower was promising *45 million dollars* to the Shah of Iran (who was already filthy stinking rich with oil money) to help fight the communists over in his neck of the woods. Over in Washington, Senator Joe McCarthy was holding more hearings and promising to "name names" of the Reds and communist sympathizers working right there in the State Department and even the Pentagon. Can you imagine? Oh, and

Senator Louis B. Heller from Brooklyn wanted to bar the Post Office Department from sending Dr. Alfred C. Kinsey's new book, <u>*Sexual Behavior in the Human Female*</u>, through the mails until some of the senators had a chance to look it over.

I bet.

Here on the local scene, the manager of the Plaza Hotel either jumped, fell or got himself pushed out of the 16th-floor window of an unoccupied bedroom and came crashing down through the glass ceiling of the Crystal Room ballroom in the second-floor courtyard, doing neither himself or the glass ceiling any good at all. According to the article, he'd been under treatment for "some time" for "a nervous condition." Made me think about Mary Frances' new boyfriend Frederick and his *Depression, Boredom, Anger* and *Anxiety* paintings, you know? I also thought about him when I read about how "Federal and city narcotics squad authorities" had arrested this Greek guy who had only been in the country for about four months as he was trying to leave the Port Authority Bus Terminal with ten pounds of hashish in a suitcase. Agents said it was "impossible to place a valuation on the sixteen ten-ounce bricks confiscated because it was 'so rare in the market.'" By the way, the guy they arrested described himself as "an internationalist who travels all over the world."

Right.

And that's why I always save the sports pages and funnies for last. It's the only blessed good news you ever find in the whole damn newspaper. Even if you do have to hunt down around the polo results and minor-league baseball scores to find anything about automobile racing. Unless somebody gets killed, of course. Page One headlines were naturally about baseball (the world's most boring sport?) and it turned out the "pennant-bound Dodgers handed the forlorn Giants a 16-7 lambasting in front of 23,636 jeering onlookers at the Polo Grounds." And that certainly would have included my old man and his union buddies, who were nothing less than World Class when it came to jeering. There was also some heart-stopping news from the National Tennis Championships at Forest Hills and an edge-of-your-seat report from the big U.S.A. vs. Great Britain Walker Cup golf tournament at Kittansett Country Club in Marion, Massachusetts, where "refreshing breezes from Buzzards Bay" provided "excellent conditions." There was also a story (starting about halfway down the page, natch) about the limited and unlimited hydroplane regatta taking place on the Detroit River that weekend, and I must admit the thought of huge, streamlined speedboats powered by thoroughly unmuffled Rolls-Royce and Allison V12 aircraft engines chasing each other through choppy water and showering off enormous roostertails of spray sounded pretty darn interesting. The paper must have thought so, too, since that story actually continued on over to the next page. And right next to it at the top of Page Two was another waterlogged story about some damn yacht race off Long Island (I'm sure just all *sorts* of people follow yacht racing!) and next to that a breathless, action-and-drama-packed report on the 11th annual dog show at the Mid-Hudson Kennel Club, where liver-and-white English springer spaniel Champion Melilotus Royal Oak narrowly edged out the challenge from a feisty little wire-haired fox terrier named Champion Travella Superman of Harham to claim Best-in-Show honors.

I'm sure it was a real cliff-hanger all the way.

And then, about two-thirds of the way down the page (right next to those agate type Dog Show results, in fact) I finally located a tiny, three-column-inch piece with no photo about how Phil Walters in the Cunningham C-4R had chalked up yet another feature race win over Creighton Pendleton's Ferrari at Thompson Speedway (no surprise there!) in front of an estimated crowd of some 7000 people. To be honest, it was thoroughly amazing to me how sports writers could stretch a single, boring, nine-inning baseball game out to three or four entire columns (or a damn dog show to at least one) but insisted on summing up a whole SCMA race weekend with eight separate races and sometimes more than one class running in each into two brief paragraphs. Phooey. And right underneath was another inch-and-a-half motor sports story about how Juan Manuel Fangio of Argentina won the 270-kilometer *Gran Premio de Cortemaggiore* (whatever the heck that was) over at Merano, Italy, in an Alfa Romeo. I wondered how that managed to get any coverage at all. And then I read the next paragraph and found that Swiss driver Hans Ruesch's car had swerved off the road and plowed into the crowd on the very first lap and killed a 24-year-old *Carabinieri* named Ezio Saltori and hurt a bunch of other people besides. Including Ruesch, who got his chest crushed. Why, if it hadn't been for the dead and injured, that story never would've made the damn paper at all!

But there was also some good news from the racing world. Way down at the bottom of the page. None other than my favorite oval-track buddy Sammy Speed had won the Triple-A 100-mile national championship midget race at the Illinois State Fair at DuQuoin. Illinois, on the same exact Saturday all the sportycar guys were racing up at Thompson in Connecticut. According to the story, Rodger Ward led the first 37 laps and then Jack McGrath took over until he had to pit for a flat tire on the 42nd lap and then Johnny Parsons led until he ran out of fuel on the 79th lap and old Sammy took over and cruised her all the way home. Boy, that sure put a grin on my face!

After breakfast I went into work—it was only 8:15, but there was no sense hanging around just because I could—and I fixed a couple flats for people and pumped a lot of gas that day, so I was glad I went in. But I closed up early like my mom requested so we could be over at my folks' house promptly at 4:30 in order to help her and my dad get ready for a nice little "just us" family dinner. Neither of my married sisters and their families were coming on account of it was a long way to travel just for dinner and both their husbands had to work and the kids had to be back in school the following morning. And my Aunt Rosamarina had some civic librarians' group Labor Day picnic to go to at noon and therefore wasn't figuring to be in any shape to have dinner (or even string two syllables together, if you want the truth of it) by the time suppertime rolled around. And Julie's mom was invited out of common family courtesy, but she begged off, too. "Why I a-wanna go over dere to eat?" she said, glaring at me down the stairway like I'd murdered the blessed Lindbergh baby. "I'm a-got a-plenty to eat right-a here, boy."

"But Mom," Julie tried to explain, "Buddy's mom invited you."

"Shu' she invited me. She's-a always invite-a me. But that a-no gotta mean I always a-gotta go, eh? I be fine a-right a-here."

Well, there was no way I was going to try and argue her into doing something I really, deep down in my deepest heart of hearts, didn't want her to do anyway. "Okay," I told her. "We'll tell them you're not feeling well."

"I'm a-feel fine. I'm a-just a-no wanna go, that's all." She only looked slightly more resolute than the faces on Mount Rushmore. Except for Teddy Roosevelt, that is. He always kind of looked like he was smirking.

"We'll bring you something back," Julie promised.

"I don-a need a-nothing. I gotta some-a nice a-eggaplant right a-here."

"We'll bring you something anyway," Julie told her as I guided us out onto the front porch and let the screen door bang shut behind us.

"What the heck's with her?" I asked Julie as we headed up the street towards my folks' house.

Julie shook her head. "I don't get it, either. Honest I don't."

"You know," I told her, "the more I see other people in this family, the more I like you."

"That's my mother you're talking about," she reminded me.

"Listen, you can say the same thing about my old man if you want. Believe me, it won't bother me one bit."

So the "family dinner" over at my folks' house was down to my mom and my old man and my two unmarried sisters Sarah Jean and Mary Frances and Julie and me. That was the entire cast of characters. Only when we got there, Mary Frances and Sarah Jean were missing, too. Seems Mary Frances hadn't been around since Thursday afternoon. Not that it was any surprise to Julie and me. And my old man was plenty sore about it, too. "She wants t'stay out all night like a damn alleycat, that's just fine with me," he growled. "I don't really care one way or the other."

I could tell he'd had a couple belts already, so I didn't figure it would be the best time in the world to tell him that we'd seen Mary Frances and knew exactly where she was or anything at all about her artistic new boyfriend, Frederick. In fact, it was a great time to just shut up and listen and nod every now and then so he knew I understood what he was talking about. Not that either of us much cared.

"You do your best with kids, but what the hell good does it do?" he wailed to nobody in particular. "They just turn around and break your heart." He got himself another beer out of the refrigerator and asked: "You want one?"

Well, this was certainly a red-letter sort of Labor Day over at the Palumbo household. I don't believe my old man had ever offered me a beer before. Not once. Not that I didn't sneak one from time to time or pop the cap and drink one right in front of him when we were arguing and I was trying to piss him off. Not that pissing him off was ever any great challenge. And now here he was, asking me if I wanted to have a beer with him, and the lumbering, big-gutted heft of fatherhood washed over me like hot, soapy water. "Sure," I told him, trying to get my voice to drop a couple octaves. "I'll have a beer with you." I guess parental palship is one of the unexpected surprises about growing up and getting married and having a family of your own on the way. And, like a lot of those things, it somehow manages to make you feel good inside without ever actually being pleasant or pleasurable. To tell the truth, it's kind of confusing.

Meanwhile my mom was over at the sink chopping onions and celery and cooked potatoes and a little parsley for her famous mustard-and-mayonnaise potato salad, and so I eased over and gave her a nice little peck on the cheek and asked her where my sister Sarah Jean might be. "Oh," she kind of fluttered, "that nice friend of yours from the funeral home business came over to take her for a ride in his new sports car."

"He *did?*" I couldn't believe anybody had actually asked my sister Sarah Jean out. Or that Carson Flegley actually got up the stones to ask anyone out either, for that matter. It just seemed so unlikely.

"Oh, yes," my mom insisted. "He's called her up a couple of times, I think." She gave me this wide, vacant smile. "He seems to be such a nice, quiet, serious, grown-up sort of fellow."

Hanging around stiffs and funerals all the time will do that to you, I wanted to say, but I kept my mouth shut.

"Look," my mom urged, "why don't you boys go get the fire started and watch some television while we work on the salad and fixin's."

"I don't mind helping," I told her. What I really meant was that I didn't particularly feel like listening to my old man grumble and lecture and complain about his kids. After all, sooner or later, he'd get around to me. In fact, it was a sure thing.

"No, you run along," my mom insisted. "Men just get in the way in a kitchen." She looked over at Julie. "And we've got all sorts of things to chatter about, don't we? Now shoo."

I was coming to understand that the kitchen is the female clubhouse, and that men have no place in there except getting fresh ice or taking out the garbage. And that it gets very quiet and all the eyes follow you from the time you come in to do either of those things until the time you're safely out of earshot again. Not that it's a conspiracy or anything. After all, a conspiracy's got to have a point....

So I went outside and watched my old man demonstrate how easy it is to get a charcoal fire started with nothing more than a few stick matches and a half-gallon splash of gasoline (not to mention how you can damn near take your eyebrows off and move your hairline all the way back behind your earlobes in the process) and then we went back inside and plopped ourselves down in front of his new Muntz console model to watch a little TV. It being a Monday and smack-dab in the middle of the after-school time slot, there was a lot of kids' stuff on like *Junior Frolics* and *Gabby Hayes* and *Howdy Doody* and *Filbert the Flea* and *Rootie Kazooti,* so I decided it was maybe a good time to ask him about what the heck was up between him and Julie's mom. I mean, I knew I wasn't imagining it, because Julie'd noticed it, too. "Why the heck does she always look at you like that?" I asked him.

He started to get angry—I could see it in his face—but then it was like it all just boiled into thin air and evaporated and he kind of sunk back a little deeper into his favorite TV chair and sighed. "Aw," he said kind of apologetically, "I maybe went out with her once."

"You went out with her?" I gasped.

"Well, not so much like I actually went out with her...."

"My God! What do you *mean?*" I was on the edge of my seat.

"Look," he said angrily, "it's not like we went out together or anything...."

"Then what *is* it like?"

"Well, it's more like we—oh, whaddayacallit?—made out once at a party."

"You made out with Julie's mom??!!" I mean, I was getting sick to my stomach just thinking about it. *"MY GOD!!! When??? Where???"*

"Aw, it was at this beach party down by the shore, see?" He looked at me with these sad, surly, bloodshot eyes. "It was summer an' I was already graduated from high school a couple years an' she was fresh over from Italy and her family was brand new in the neighborhood an' she was a pretty cute l'il thing and couldn't hardly speak English or anything—y'gotta realize this was the twenties, and there were lots of parties an' all—an' I gotta admit I was lookin' pretty sharp back then an' already had a decent job lined up an' all an'..." his voice kind of trailed off.

"And?"

He looked down at the carpeting. "Well, see, there was a whole bunch of us an' we'd gone down by the shore an' we'd been drinkin' an' all an' there was all these stars up in the sky an' this big, huge bonfire..."

My stomach was churning. "And?"

"An' I guess me an' her went under the pier together."

"Went under the pier together?"

"Yeah. That's what you did t'find someplace dark an' private an' away from everybody else. You went under the damn pier together...."

I could see it in my mind. In fact, it was the kind of image you can't get rid of unless you have it surgically removed. "So what happened?" I had to ask.

"I dunno," he shrugged. "I swear I honest t'fucking God don't know for sure. Honest I don't. I was just s'damn drunk an' all."

"Was she drunk, too?"

"Aw, hell, son. She was damn near passed out."

"So you have no idea what happened?"

He sighed again, and for maybe the third or fourth time in his entire life, he looked kind of sad and guilty and uncomfortable. "It didn't matter what happened, see? All the kids saw us go under there together an' not come out again until later. That's all it takes."

"So what happened afterwards?"

"Well," he said miserably, "turns out that was just a week or so after I met your mom."

"You met mom?"

"Yeah. Just a couple days before, in fact. An' we started goin' out and goofing around together, an' I guess I never quite got around t'calling Julie's mom back or anything...."

"You mean you just *dumped* her?"

"Well, it's not like we ever went out on a date or anything. I mean, it was just this one night at a beach party, you know?"

"But you went under the pier with her! Right there in front of everybody!"

"She went, too, remember," he snapped defensively. "I mean, it's not like I *dragged* her or anything..."

"Well, thank goodness for that!" I said sarcastically.

"...although maybe I did have t'carry her a little."

And that was the end of it.

Well, that explained a lot of things. But Knowing The Truth is really kind of overrated, seeing as how lots of times it just makes things more confused and complicated and difficult instead of ironing them out for you.

A little later Carson Flegley's new Healey growled up to the curb with Carson and Sarah Jean on board, and of course nothing would do but that my mom asked him to stay for dinner. And I was glad of that, on account of I liked Carson and moreover having an outsider present inevitably tones down the usual barrage of accusations, arguments, taunts, threats of retaliation and parade of closet skeletons you normally get around the old family dinner table when only immediate blood relations are in attendance. It even worked pretty well on bossy, mean-spirited old farts like my old man. Usually, anyway. Plus it was nice to see how polite and thoughtful Carson was around my sister—even though it was hard imagining them together, even with the two of them right there in front of me—and I kept thinking back to what Colin had always told me about cars. You know, about how there's an ass for every seat?

After dinner the girls did the dishes and my old man went into his den to watch some more TV and Carson and me went out on the front porch with a couple cold Knickerbockers so he could tell me about the races at Thompson Speedway. "Well, that Phil Walters who drives for Briggs Cunningham won the big car race again."

"Yeah, I read it in the paper."

"But it wasn't much of a show. The new track up at Thompson is short and tight and *real* narrow, so the officials decided it would be smarter to run more races and have fewer cars in each race. There were only eleven cars entered in the big car race, and the Cunningham with Phil Walters on board was simply the class of the field."

"Anything good happen in the other races?"

"Well, let's see. In the first race there was a swell battle for the lead between a stock Porsche and a modified MG TC..."

That did my heart good.

"...and the TC won!" Carson added, looking pleasantly astonished.

But of course that's the difference between "stock" and "modified." It ain't so much what you start with, but what you *do to it afterwards* that counts. That and who they put you in against, anyway. "Like somebody famous once said," I told Carson, *"you may not be able to turn a pig into a racehorse, but you can turn it into a mighty fast pig."*

Carson nodded like he got it, but I could tell he really didn't. You had to be a real, certified racing wrench to understand that the badge on the nose is just the starting point. What happens between there and the starting line often determines who comes out ahead at the checker. Oh, don't get me wrong—driving still counts for plenty. But the higher up you go in racing, the faster all the cars are and the better all the drivers are and so the guy who starts out with the Better Mousetrap has one hell of an advantage. Especially if it's the only one around.

"So what else happened?" I wanted to know.

"George Weaver won the second race in that Oldsmobile-powered thing of his."

"The Healey Silverstone? That car's been around for quite a while."

"Everyone said it's getting a little long in the tooth. They let him run it in the Unrestricted Class and he got chased all over hell and gone by one of the DuPont kids in one of those little Cooper things with a motorcycle engine in the back and no passenger seat or fenders."

"A Formula III car?"

Cal nodded. "And then they had a race for stock Jaguars and then a race for those little bitty cars with the little bitty engines that sound like sewing machines."

"Crosleys?"

"Yeah, some of them. But also some little dwarf-size Italian cars I never heard of before."

"Bandinis?"

"I dunno. Bandinis? Stanguellinis? Etceterinis? What's the difference?"

"Damned if I know."

"Me, either," Carson agreed. "But Cal and I both thought the race for stock MGs was pretty exciting. In fact, he got a little testy about the way we hopped-up my TD so it couldn't run in the stock class any more." He gave me a helpless shrug. "Drivers like me need every edge they can get, but a talent like Cal just loves it when the cars are all equal. Then all he's got to do is out-drive the other people."

"Yeah. I know." But I also knew that you don't get much noticed by big-time car owners running around in a blessed stock MG. Or that's what I thought, anyway.

"Some fellow from Pennsylvania named Bob Holbert won that one. He was pretty darn good, too. There were drivers in other MGs all over him the whole race but he never left them so much as a sliver of an opening. Or at least that's what Cal said, anyway."

"What about the big cars?"

"They had a separate race for modified Jaguars, and that Masten Gregory was there with the C-Type he bought from Big Ed last weekend. But he had to start at the back."

"How come?"

"Well, the officials decided to grid all the races by pulling numbers out of a hat, and he just got a bad draw."

"That's so dumb."

"I think the point is that they want everybody to understand that it's all just for sport and fun and that no one should take it too seriously."

"Right."

"So he started at the back and got seriously boxed in at the start—as I said, the track is *very* narrow—and meanwhile that Walter Hansgen fellow in the specially-bodied Jaguar…"

"The pretty white one?"

Carson nodded. "…he took off and built up quite a lead. He was driving *very* well. But Cal said you could see how he was fighting the car compared to the way Masten Gregory was slicing around in that C-Type."

"So what happened?"

"Oh, once Gregory worked his way through the traffic, he was able to chase that Walt Hansgen fellow down in a few more laps. They went around nose-to-tail for awhile, but he finally slipped past and pulled away."

"That's too bad." Not that I had anything against Masten Gregory. Well, except for maybe his obscene wealth and the fact that he was probably even younger than me. But I'd seen that Walt Hansgen character drive a few times and was particularly impressed by the notion that he was driving a car he built with his own two hands out of a regular old, garden-variety XK 120, and was more-over running it heads-up against a genuine competition model like the ones the Jaguar factory team ran and won with at Le Mans.

"Anything else interesting happen?"

"Yeah. Briggs Cunningham let his son—that's Briggs the Third—drive that 1500cc OSCA of his in the last race and damn if he didn't win it…"

Oh, great. Another kid who probably wasn't even shaving yet.

"…but no question it looked to be the best car. By far." Carson looked at me. "Those OSCAs are real little jewels, aren't they?"

I nodded. "They sure are. Expensive, too. They're built over in Italy by the Maserati brothers. Did you know that?"

Carson shook his head, so I told him the *Readers' Digest* condensed version of the story about how the four Maserati brothers built machine tools and spark-plugs and some really swell racing cars over in Bologna, Italy. But then one of them died, and while the other three were still fantastic designers and engineers and fabricators and machinists, they weren't real savvy about the actual *business* end of the machine tool, sparkplug and racecar manufacturing business. And so they started going broke or threatening to go broke every blessed time they turned around. But, like I said, they made some really incredible cars and stuff. So this rich Italian industrialist guy named Omer Orsi, who *was* real savvy about the business end of business, stepped in and bought them out in 1937—lock, stock, and barrel—and signed the three remaining Maserati brothers to 10-year con-tracts. And they built some even better racecars after that seeing as how they didn't have to worry about going broke all the time. In fact, Wilbur Shaw won back-to-back Indy 500s in one of their cars back in 1939 and 1940. But during the war years, Orsi decided to move their operation up the road a ways to Modena and also hired some guy named Massimino as "chief engineer" over them. Only the Maserati brothers didn't like it much working for somebody else—in spite of the regular paychecks—and, like all Italians, they were maybe getting a little home-sick for the way they made the pasta and meat sauce back home in Bologna. So, the very day their ten-year contract with this Omer Orsi guy ran out, they packed up all their machine tools and hightailed it back to Bologna to build great racing cars and maybe go broke a few more times. Only they couldn't use the Maserati name, on account of Omer Orsi still had the rights to it. So they decided to chris-ten their new business OSCA, for *Officine Specializate Construzione Automobili* or something, and I figured their little MT4 was about the prettiest, quickest, best-designed and best built 1500cc racing car in the whole damn world.

"Boy, I'd sure like to get my hands on one some day," Carson said wistfully.

"I'd sure like to see *Cal* get his hands on one." I mean, it wasn't like I was being insulting or anything. Carson would be the first one to admit that Cal could drive blessed rings around him. Hell, he could drive blessed rings around just about anybody! "So," I asked Carson, "did Cal get to drive anything up at Thompson?"

"Yeah," he answered half-heartedly. "That fellow with the MG hybrid with the Ford V8 in it was there and gave him the keys. But it had to run in the same race as Phil Walters in the Cunningham C-4R and so he really didn't have much of a chance. Besides, it was overheating and running out of brakes every session and then it got stuck in top gear during the race and so he finished way at the back." Carson shook his head. "It was a pretty miserable weekend for him."

"You know," I said, kind of looking out over the trees and rooftops, "I always wondered what would happen if Cal ever got himself a shot in a real, topnotch racecar?"

"Why, he'd be so far out front they'd never even see him!"

Right about then Julie and Sarah Jean came out and joined us on the front porch. "Let me guess," Julie said, putting her fingers up to her temples and closing her eyes like it was taking great powers of concentration: "You're talking about cars and racing."

"That's amazing," I gasped. "How do you do it?"

"I cannot reveal my secrets. It must remain a mystery."

"We were just talking about the races up at Thompson," Carson added meekly.

"What a surprise."

"And there's another one up at Watkins Glen in two weeks."

"Oh, I can hardly wait."

"It's really pretty nice up there," I tossed in. "Real pretty country for sketching and hiking and boating and stuff. You'd like it."

"Right. And I'm sure I'd get a lot of sketching and hiking and boating done on one of your race weekends. *Hah!"*

"Well, you might..." I offered weakly.

"Hmpf," Julie snorted. "You'll be off with your racing friends drinking beer and talking about carburetor jets."

"I don't know," Sarah Jean said timidly. "It sounds kind of...*interesting."*

And now I was beginning to get the gist of things. Carson wanted Sarah Jean to come up to Watkins Glen with him, and I got the feeling that maybe she wanted to go real bad, too. But the only way either of them could even dream of making that happen was if a whole group of us went up together and there was somebody of the female persuasion—like my Julie, fr'instance—for her to share a room with. I mean, there was just no way she (or my father or mother, for that matter) would ever consider it any other way. Not to mention that I doubted he'd ever have the stones to just walk up to her—eyeball-to-eyeball, you know?—and simply *ask* her.

But I had to admit it was sounding like a pretty good idea to me, too. After all, since Julie and me had gotten ourselves married, I'd missed the race at the Offutt Air Force Base outside of Omaha and the Giant's Despair Hillclimb in Wilkes-Barre, PeeAy, and the race at Lockbourne Air Force Base near Columbus and even the SCMA Labor Day weekend bash practically right in our own back yard at Thompson, Connecticut. Not to mention that the Watkins Glen races coming up in two weeks were going to be the final event on the East Coast SCMA racing calendar before everything got buttoned up for winter. So it was kind of a Last Chance sort of deal. Although to be honest, if you hang around with racers long enough, you'll come to find that—each in its own special way—damn near *every* race weekend finds some way to qualify for Last Chance status. It's just the way the bug works.

Besides, what with the baby coming and all, it'd be nice for Julie and me to maybe slip away by ourselves one more time. And especially if I could talk Sarah Jean into staying by herself once we were up there so's Julie and me could share our own little cabin together at the Seneca Lodge. That would really be nice, you know? Or at least I thought it would, anyway.

So I started working on her a little on the way home. "Y'know," I told her in the world's most reasonable voice, "it might actually be nice for us to go to that race up at Watkins Glen together. You'd like it up there. Honest you would."

She didn't say a word.

"It's real pretty and scenic, and there's waterfalls and Lake Seneca and this big log cabin lodge building at The Seneca."

It seemed like my voice was passing right through her.

"And besides, this is the last race of the season. And I didn't get to go to the races at Omaha or Columbus…"

"Okay, we'll go."

"…or Giant's Despair or Thompson or…"

"I said we'll go, Buddy."

It took a moment for it to register. "We *will?*"

She looked up at me and gave me that same great, movie-magazine smile she used to flash at me over the counter at Old Man Finzio's gas station before we ever even went out together. "Why not?" And then she gave me a nice little kiss on the cheek. "You're a pretty good guy sometimes, Palumbo."

Well, I can't say as I'll ever figure out women and their moods (and pregnant women most especially) but, right at that moment, I knew exactly and for certain why I'd married Julie Finzio. And I was damn glad I'd done it, too.

11: The Outback Glen

Most folks figured there would never be any races at Watkins Glen again after the disaster in '52 when Tommy Edwards' Allard had to swerve to avoid that idiot Skippy Welcher's car and sideswiped the crowd at the south end of Franklin Street and that poor little nine-year-old boy got killed. Especially after all the newspapers and state legislators and general-purpose do-gooders got done rolling around in it like a hound in a sweet-smelling pile of shit and *Life* magazine ran a grisly two-page photo spread that made your guts churn just to look at it. In fact, there wasn't even a race date listed for Watkins Glen when the SCMA calendar came out in the spring. But that was also on account of this long-running political war that was raging in the SCMA about just exactly what sort of organization they were going to be. On the one side you had all the snooty Charlie Priddle and Creighton Pendleton types who wanted to keep sportycar racing their own private little club and not let any of the riffraff in. Especially the professional factory teams and paid drivers from Europe—or, worse yet, those cigar chomping, gum smacking, shot-and-a-beer grease monkey yokels and ruffians from our own, home-grown Triple-A oval track and Southern stock car circuits—who would most certainly spoil the fine, upper-crust ambience and atmosphere at our races. And most likely blow a lot of those rich, privileged, well-bred and equally well-mannered SCMA "amateurs" into the damn weeds while they were at it.

The other faction wanted to open the sport up all the way to the throttle stops, including a few real professional races with prize money and everything, and moreover trying whatever they could to entice the top European teams and drivers to come over stateside and compete. That bunch was led by Alec Ulmann, the guy who promoted the race at Floyd Bennett Field and also pretty much founded the big 12-hour race at Sebring—which was the only real, internationally-recognized sports car race in America—along with his good buddy Cam Argetsinger, who got those very first open road sports car races going up at Watkins Glen in 1948 and had been at it ever since. So those were two pretty sharp guys with a lot of ideas and drive and clout and moxie and moreover plenty of friends all over the sportycar world. Anyhow, the squabble between those two camps had been going on for quite awhile and had boiled over and gotten nasty a bunch of times. Like when the club stripped Ulmann of his duties and position as Activities Chairman and then called him up before one of Charlie Priddle's beloved tribunals and told him in no uncertain terms to either keep his damn opinions to himself or resign his membership.

Alec Ulmann told them precisely where they could stick it.

So they sent back his membership renewal form—his *lifetime* membership, right?—along with his $100 dues check and he was out of the club. Just like that. Blackballed. And oh-so-conveniently just before nominations closed for the upcoming club elections, for which Ulmann and Argetsinger had put together their own slate of candidates.

But meanwhile the racing went on. Political brushfires are kind of an ongoing thing in racing—all types of racing, in fact—because you've got so much power and greed and big money and even bigger egos and all these private angles, simmering hatreds, seething envies and deep green jealousies involved. It's just the way things are. And, after Tommy's tragic accident in '52 and all the awful publicity it generated, Charlie Priddle and his buddies got together and decided that there was absolutely no way that they could possibly allow their club to be involved with anything as dangerous, ill-conceived and socially irresponsible as the race they themselves had been sanctioning, supporting and promoting for the previous five years.

Even worse, Cam Argetsinger and the Watkins Glen organizers had lost the cooperation of both the Department of Public Works and the State Police after the wreck in '52. And the New York state legislature had come down like a ton of bricks and decreed that there would be no automobile racing of any kind on any New York state highways. Ever. Period. Full Stop.

But there were a lot of people who'd had a really swell time at those races up at Watkins Glen from 1948 to 1952—racers and spectators alike—and no question the local businessmen and chamber-of-commerce types wanted those races to keep going on account of they pumped an awful lot of greenbacks into the local economy. Having the racers and their fans swoop into town rented out an awful lot of tourist rooms and filled up an awful lot of campgrounds and sold an awful lot of ham-and-eggs breakfasts, ham-and-cheese, salami and egg-or-tuna-salad sandwich box lunches, full-course sit-down dinners and countless, groaning truckloads of soda pop, suntan oil, Kodak film, paper plates, penny candy, cigars, cigarettes, chewing gum, chocolate fudge, salt-water taffy, band-aids, popcorn, Cracker Jacks, pretzels, dill pickles, lemonade, licorice sticks, ice cream and beer. And I mean *lots* of beer....

But keeping the races going would take a lot of doing. No question running the race down the hillside into town (where a big, plate-glass shop window awaited you if you misjudged the turn or ran shy of brakes) and through the heart of Watkins Glen on Franklin Street was finished. There was just too much stuff to hit and no way to control the crowds and no place to put them even if you could control them except right along the curbs and sidewalks just a scant few feet away from where the cars hurtled past—some of them doing better than a hundred miles-per-hour! And even if you could somehow get all that figured out, you still had that law to deal with about no racing on state highways, seeing as how Franklin Street was also Route 14 and the charge up Old Corning Hill was Route 329 and that daunting, endless, sweeping right-hander way up over the treetops and overlooking Lake Seneca was Route 409. So that obviously wasn't going to work.

But Cam Argetsinger and Alec Ulmann and all the diehard Watkins Glen organizers and supporters on the Grand Prix Committee were not the type to give up easily. No sir. They found a patch of rolling farmland up on a hilltop near the town of Dix—just a few miles away from the original circuit—and got to work setting up a new racetrack. Nevermind that the roads were narrow and mostly all dirt. At least they were *town* roads (as opposed to State-of-New-York roads) and they could always be paved and widened. All it took was a little time and money. Neither of which, by the way, were in especially abundant supply. But the good folks from the Town Board of Dix didn't need much convincing that the races were plenty good for the local supply of greenbacks, and they offered their full cooperation.

Which is more than you could say for the SCMA The club sent a delegation of high muckity-mucks up from Manhattan to take a look at the proposed new track (led by one Charles Winthrop Martingale Priddle, natch), and they decided unanimously and with great conviction that they didn't want anything to do with it. In fact, if there somehow was indeed a race (and, at that point, it didn't really look too likely) they were going to do everything in their power to discourage holders of SCMA racing licenses from participating. At least if they wanted to continue holding onto those SCMA racing licenses, anyway.

Plus there were a few other niggling little problems. Like there were less than forty days to go before the planned race dates on September 18th and 19th and the roads still had to be widened and paved and grandstands had to be built and a control tower had to sprout up out of the ground and P.A. wiring had to be strung and speakers had to be mounted and snow fencing had to be run around the whole blessed 4.6 miles—outside *and* inside!—to keep the spectators back and parking areas had to be established and admission gates had to be figured out and, well, there was a *lot* of stuff to do. And damn little time or money to do it with.

But somehow the folks up in Schuyler County got it all done and, despite all the puffing and sputtering and saber-rattling from Charlie Priddle's bunch, the Glen group had received over a hundred entries. This in spite of a widespread rumor (and you can figure out for yourself who was spreading it!) that the track wasn't finished and the races were going to be cancelled. Followed by yet another, eleventh-hour bullshit story that they'd been postponed until the following weekend.

So we really didn't know what to expect at all. But at least we were going, and I was glad of that. Turns out Big Ed had booked up a block of cabins at the Seneca Lodge as soon as the dates were announced (although that was when he still had the C-Type Jag on the way that he sold to Masten Gregory at Floyd Bennett Field and before I managed to drop his XK 120 into the lap of that poor doofus pharmacist in the Buick Roadmaster on the George Washington Bridge), but he decided that we all ought to go anyway. I mean, it *was* a Last Chance sort of deal. And our Brit friend Tommy Edwards was going to be driving a brand new, Chrysler Hemi-powered Allard J2X that Colin St. John had just sold to a guy named Juan Perona (not to be confused with Juan Peron, the Argentine dictator who was also a sportycar nut) who owned the swanky and infamous El Morocco nightclub over in Manhattan. And of course we all wanted to see Tommy drive. Not to mention that it was a great opportunity to support Cam Argetsinger and the blackballed Alec Ulmann and all those hardworking people up in Schuyler County, New York, and simultaneously thumb our collective noses at Charlie Priddle and his bunch, and that was certainly a worthwhile sort of thing to do. Besides, Big Ed wanted to take his new girl Rhonda on a nice little spin through all the pretty fall foliage in his brand new sports car.

"You mean the Muntz?" I asked him while I wiped down the windshield and checked the tire pressures on his creamy white Eldorado.

"Nah, that's not a sports car. Besides, I bought it used. And it's her car, anyway."

"Well, what car are you talking about?"

"You'll see," he grinned. "You'll see."

And sure enough, what comes gliding into the station the very next day but a brand new Chevrolet Corvette with Big Ed Baumstein at the wheel. He looked damn good in it, too. It was his kind of car. To be honest, it was the first Corvette anybody around Passaic had ever seen. I mean, they'd just come out and Chevrolet was only building a handful of them in '53—to kind of test the waters and get the bugs out, you know?—and all most anybody had seen was pictures and stories in the car magazines about them.

To be honest, I had kind of mixed feelings about the new Corvette. On the one hand, it was great to finally have a real, all-American sports car. On the other hand, it *was* just a Chevy, and it had all the usual, standard-issue Chevy bits and pieces underneath. Like the engine was just a warmed-over version of the old "Stovebolt Six" car and truck motor that Chevy had been building pretty steadily since 1929. Oh, I know it was a big deal when it was first introduced—*"a six for the price of a four"* and *"valve in head/ahead in value"* was the way Chevy touted it back before I was born—and I've got to admit I liked working on them because they were simple, stout and solid as a damn sledgehammer. And they were hell for strong. Why, even the blessed *pistons* were made out of cast iron on the older ones. Plus everything was easy to get at when you had to put a wrench to one. In fact, they called it the "stovebolt" on account of all the tin on the engine was held on with slotted-head bolts. And, sure, they'd hogged it out and updated it a couple times over the years. In fact, just a few years back in 1950, Chevy punched it out to 235 cubic inches and renamed it the "Blue Flame Six." Like it was a brand new motor, right? But everybody who owned a tool box and a work bench knew it was just the same old lump of iron with a few more cubes and ponies under the rocker cover.

For the Corvette, Chevy had pretty much done the same exact thing the Brits did to turn truck motors into sportycar engines. They'd given it a little higher-compression pistons and a little hotter camshaft and hung some side-draft carburetors off the head, just like the Brits did (only Chevy used Carters instead of S.U.s). And they even went the English one better by sticking no less that *three* of those carburetors on the Corvette, and then topped it all off with a freed-up dual-exhaust system grumbling out of two chrome cannon barrels sticking out right through the rear bodywork. It looked pretty sharp, no lie. And that bodywork was pretty special, too. It was all made out of fiberglass, and you had to be impressed with the bird-strainer gratings over the headlamps and the four tiny little Buck Rogers tailfins over the rear lights. The new Corvette only came in one color—Polo White—and I've got to admit it was a pretty sexy piece.

The only thing I couldn't decide was if it really deserved to be called a sports car. I mean, sure it had two seats and three carbs and dual exhausts and even side curtains instead of regular roll-up windows. But it had that big, heavy lump of a six under the hood and lots more standard-issue Chevy stuff under the fenderwells and, most telling of all, you could only get it with an automatic transmission. And a damn two-speed Powerglide, at that. We used to joke that the Powerglide automatic could sap the strength of even the strongest motor, on account of when you floored it, it made that engine torque and strain and wheeze until you were near dizzy from it. And then, finally, it would shift. And drop the engine revs damn near down to idle. Like a turd falling into a bucket of mud, you know?

I wasn't sure you could really *have* a sports car with an automatic transmission. And particularly a Powerglide.

I mean, stirring gears and learning how to heel-and-toe and double-clutch downshift properly was a big part of the sportycar game. And *Road and Track* had about said as much in a less-than-breathless report on Chevy's new Corvette in their August issue. Then again, you had guys like Big Ed Baumstein who were never particularly arty with a stickshift but who desperately wanted to see themselves (and, more importantly, have others see them) as genuine sportycar types with a genuine sportycar aura about them and genuine sportycar *savoir faire* oozing out of every sweat gland and hair follicle. And that's precisely what made the new Chevrolet Corvette just *perfect* for a guy like Big Ed Baumstein.

Like I said, it was his kind of car.

"Whaddaya think?" Big Ed grinned.

"It's sharp-looking," I said honestly. "What's it like to drive?"

"Smooth as glass," he crooned, kind of floating his hand out in front of him like he was caressing the air.

Yep, it was his kind of car, all right.

No question about it.

Well, not five minutes after Big Ed and his new Corvette went gliding back out onto Pine Street, the phone rang and I immediately recognized Spud Webster's voice on the other end. *"Hey!"* I damn near shouted into the receiver, "long time no see!"

"Not since Sebring last year."

"Yeah."

"How things been goin' for you?" Spud asked.

"I can't complain."

"I heard you got married."

"Can't complain about that, either."

"That's good. That's good. And take it from a old married man, Buddy. It don't do enny good if y'do."

"So I've heard."

We got a nice laugh off that.

"I saw in the paper where Sammy won that midget race over in Illinois."

"They had it in a paper way up in New York?" He sounded pretty impressed.

"Well, y'had to kind of squint to see it."

"Figures."

"But it was still great to see he won."

"Yeah, Sammy had a real good run in that midget. Drove himself a smart race. It was hotter'n blazes that day. An' dusty, too. But we got hosed again in the big car race on Sunday. When it really counted, y'know?"

"What happened?"

"Aw, some guy offered Sammy a real nice Lugie Lesovsky car with a brand fresh engine in it t'drive on Sunday after he did so good on Saturday in the midget. It was better'n what I had on the trailer, so I didn't mind. But Sammy got bumped hard from the rear not two laps in and went right through the fence..."

"Jeeez!"

"…an' one a'them fence posts split the tank wide open and she burned to the ground."

"My God! Was he hurt?"

"Nah. Just a couple singes here an' there. You know Sammy." I heard him sigh into the receiver. "But that was th'end of maybe the best damn shot we've had so far."

"Easy come, easy go."

"Yeah, I s'pose…"

It was tough to imagine the kind of life they led, towing from one racetrack to another all over the country and trying to live on the prize money until they could attract the attention of some rich car owner. "So," I finally asked him, "you probably didn't call me up here in Passaic long distance just t'pass the time of day?"

"Nah, we need something off you. Otherwise we sure wouldn't've spent the dimes and nickels."

"Just name it."

"Well, we're stuck up here around Syracuse—we ran the big race up here on the 12th…"

"I read about it in the paper. Tony Bettenhausen won, didn't he?"

"Sure did. Driving the Belanger car. They got that thing working like a dream on dirt."

"But you're still there?"

"Yeah. Like I said, we're kind of stuck, actually. We got a race on the 26th at the Indiana Fairgrounds an' I gotta find somebody who can weld up and machine a cracked engine block somewheres in between."

"That shouldn't be so awful tough."

"It's been patched up a few times before…"

That made it a little tougher.

And then it came to me. *"I've got the guy!"* I almost screamed.

"You do?"

"Yeah! His name's Roman Szymanski, and he can do damn near anything with a chunk of metal."

"Any kind of metal?"

"Absolutely."

"And he'll work fast?"

"Lickety-split."

"And he'll work cheap?"

Well, that was something else again. "Well," I allowed, "he's kind of a friend of mine and I send him a lot of work. Maybe I can call in a favor or two…."

And so I called Roman and called Spud back at this pay phone outside a pawn-shop in Syracuse and made arrangements to meet them at Watkins Glen on the weekend—hell, they weren't that far away—and then, come Sunday, they'd follow me back down to Jersey and over the two bridges to Roman's shop in Brooklyn. He'd agreed to open the place up for us around five in the afternoon on Sunday and stay for as long as it took to get the job done. To tell the truth, underneath that quiet, pale, pudgy and unemotional exterior, I think Roman Szymanski had a little touch of the racing bug himself. It's an easy thing to pick up. Anyhow, I told Spud they should yank the motor out and strip it down and get the block all squeaky clean and ready for surgery and I'd meet up with them at the Glen.

I couldn't wait to see Sammy and Spud again.

The way the whole deal worked out, Big Ed and Rhonda would be driving up in his new Corvette on Thursday to kind of reconnoiter the area and set up shop for us, and Carson Flegley would be coming up with my sister Sarah Jean in the Healey on Friday after he got done with a couple funerals. I'd had some second thoughts about leaving poor Sarah Jean all by herself up at the Seneca, so after I closed up the Sinclair Tuesday evening I went into the city and dropped by Frederick's studio to see if maybe Mary Frances wanted to tag along and share a free room with her. Mary Frances hushed me as soon as she opened the door. *"He's working,"* she whispered.

I looked over her shoulder and, sure enough, Frederick was agitatedly splattering yet more different colors of paint on *Anxiety.*

"Let's go down for a coffee," Mary Frances said in a voice that was barely audible.

So we went down to this Greenwich Village coffee house just down the street where all sorts of artists and poets and philosophers and Jazz musicians and "fellow traveler" communist sympathizers and agitated political types and other assorted champions of the downtrodden, purveyors of truth and beauty, over-educated bullshit slingers and out-and-out phonies hung out and ordered ourselves up a couple demitasse espressos that were thick and black as molasses but tasted more like sour tree bark.

"So, what's up with you and Frederick?" I was careful to use all three syllables.

"Oh, he's absolutely brilliant," she answered. Only without too awful much enthusiasm, you know?

"No question about it," I agreed with even less enthusiasm.

"His work will hang in all the great galleries one day."

"Don't artists generally have to keel over dead before that happens?" I mean, I don't know art, but....

"Oh, of course. And it's even better if they starve to death or go mad and disfigure themselves or commit suicide." I was getting the idea that, just maybe, Mary Frances was getting a little clearer picture of what a future with this Brilliant Artist character Frederick was actually going to amount to.

"Tell me," I asked her, "what exactly do you do while he's busy doing all this brilliant artistic creating?"

"Oh, my," she said airily, "I read and I write and I draw…"

"You never knew how to draw."

"I didn't say I draw *well.* I just said I draw…."

"Sounds like just mounds of fun."

"And sometimes I even help him with things."

"How rewarding that must be!"

She looked down into her espresso and added, almost apologetically, "And sometimes I sneak off to a movie."

"All by yourself?"

She nodded. "Sometimes I don't even think he even knows I'm gone." She shook her head in faint disbelief.

"Look," I told her, "a whole bunch of us are going up to Watkins Glen for the races next weekend. Sarah Jean's even going. Why don't you tag along? It'll do you good to get away."

"You just want me to play chaperone for Sarah Jean with that undertaker guy." I could never fool her. Not ever.

"So what if I do? It'll still do you good to get away and have a few laughs. We can spend some time together, you and me and Julie and even Sarah Jean."

"I don't know..." she said uncertainly. I could see she was wavering.

"C'mon!" I told her. "You deserve some time away. It'll give you a little perspective."

She looked up from her coffee and, very slowly, her face opened up into a lukewarm shadow of her old smile. "What the hell, why not?"

"That's *great!*" I damn near shouted. "I mean, it's not like you're gonna be *missing* anything...."

Her smile faded. "I know," she said miserably. "I know...."

Back at the studio, we found Frederick standing in the middle of the floor staring at *Depression, Boredom, Anger* and *Anxiety.* "It's finished," he said solemnly without looking up.

"That's wonderful, dear," Mary Frances told him. But it was like he didn't hear her.

And then, suddenly, he wheeled around and eyeballed me right in the face. And his eyeballs were pretty wild and bloodshot, too. "You know people who cut metal, don't you?" he asked in kind of breathless, desperate tones.

"Huh?"

"In the car repair business. You know places where they cut metal. What do you call them?"

"Machine shops?"

"That's it! A machine shop!" He said it like he'd just discovered a cure for polio.

"What about machine shops?"

All of a sudden this sly, almost slippery look came into his eyes. "I need you to get a piece of metal cut for me. Can you do it?"

"Sure," I shrugged. "Why not?"

"And you can have them cut *any kind* of metal?"

"Sure I can. There's always a way."

"And into any shape I want?"

"I got a guy who can whittle a damn saxophone out of a diesel engine block if you really want him to." I was thinking of Roman Szymanski, of course.

"Very well. Very well." Frederick continued, rubbing his chin. "Here. Follow me. I need you to help me with something for my next project."

And that's when he led us downstairs and the three of us stole a New York City Bureau of Streets and Sanitation manhole cover right out of its hole in the street and put it in the back of Old Man Finzio's tow truck. But not before old

Frederick stared at it under the streetlamp in the alley for about twenty minutes, rolling it this way and that and turning around and around so he could see it from all angles. And then, finally, he took a piece of chalk out of his pocket and marked off the exact and precise foot-square chunk he wanted carved out of that manhole cover. To be honest, I was scared we were gonna get shagged by the cops the whole time. But this Frederick guy never even batted an eyelash. I mean, it just didn't bother him. Like it was *his* blessed manhole cover to begin with. And I could tell Mary Frances got a charge out of it. That was just like her. In the name of all the artists and poets and politically oppressed of this world, she'd stood up to the evil, corrupt, decadent and bourgeois government of New York and come away victorious! And we had the damn manhole cover to prove it, too....

"Listen," I kind of whispered from back in the shadows, "don'cha think we ought to, you know, put something in there so nobody falls in the hole?"

"Of course," Frederick agreed. "After all, we're not barbarians."

So he went upstairs and came back down with some pieces of a busted easel (I think it was the one he started *Anger* on and he maybe got a little carried away), and set them over the hole. Only it was pretty dark there and you couldn't see real good and I didn't think it was enough. So he went back upstairs and rummaged around and finally came down with a fistful of wire clothes hangers and a set of red flannel, union-suit underwear. You know, the kind with the button flap in back like that cartoon character of Madman Muntz with the Napoleon hat wore in all of his used car lot ads out in California. And I've got to admit that Frederick was, indeed, a very artistic type of guy. In just a few moments and with just a couple quick twists and bends of his coat hangers, he had it looking like this invisible man in a union suit was climbing up out of the New York sewer system. And with the back flap down, of course.

Fact is, I kind of wished I'd been there (only where I could see them but they couldn't see me, of course!) when the next patrol car made its rounds....

As you can imagine, Cal Carrington had been trying every line, pitch, schmooze and angle in his entire repertoire in order to get Carson Flegley to let him race his new Healey up at Watkins Glen, but Carson wasn't buying any of it. To begin with, he really *loved* that new Healey—hell, he'd only had it a couple weeks—and besides, it said right there in the official Austin-Healey 100 service manual that you should keep maximum revs down to 3000rpm for the first 500 miles and 4000 for the next 500 miles. Not that me and Carson hadn't maybe stretched it a time or two already. But that was a lot different from letting a razor-edge 'shoe like Cal go chasing after Ferraris and Jaguars with it. Not to mention that I got the feeling Carson wanted to spend a little quiet, eyeball-to-eyeball time with my sister Sarah Jean, and the middle of a noisy, teeming racing paddock (and especially when you're letting some far handsomer, cleverer and more talented guy drive your brand new sports car!) is hardly the best spot for that sort of thing.

Fact is, I found myself getting more and more comfortable about the notion of Carson and Sarah Jean hanging around together. I mean, I liked both of them, and Carson sure looked like a better proposition than our sister Ann Marie's nebbish of an inventory clerk husband, Jerry, and easily twice or three times as good as our other sister Tina's loudmouth drunk of a wholesale paint salesman husband, Roy. So I was glad to see they were going to be spending a lot of time and miles together on the Watkins Glen weekend. At least so long as she stayed in the room with Mary Frances at night. I mean, I had to worry about more than one kind of stiff when I thought about Carson Flegley and my sister. Sure, he didn't look at all like the romantic type. But take it from me, given the right place and the right circumstances, there is not a single male creature on this planet—regardless of species—that is incapable of being the romantic type.

In fact, sometimes they don't even need the right circumstances....

But the point is that Cal had struck out with Carson and the guy with the MG/Ford Flathead V8 thing wasn't coming and neither was the guy with all those unsold Jowett Jupiters and so he was shit out of luck as far as finding a ride was concerned. Or even a ride up there, when you get right down to it, seeing as how he was *persona non grata* and just about Grounded for Life back at Castle Carrington. Not that he much cared about or even listened to whatever his folks had to say. So the obvious answer was that Cal would ride up with me and Julie and Mary Frances after I finished up at the shop around 3:00 or 3:30 or so on Friday. Big Ed had offered to borrow us a car, and he even gave me my choice of which one. I was tempted to ask for the Muntz, on account of it was really pretty quick and powerful—I mean, it *was* based on star Indianapolis 500 racecar builder Frank Kurtis' original design—but I didn't like the idea that you either had to put on that Godawful metal top or leave it at home. Not to mention that, with the top on, there was damn little headroom in the back seat. Or legroom either, when you got right down to it. But no question the Muntz attracted lots of attention. Only it was a little different than the kind of attention you'd get in a Jaguar XK 120 or Big Ed's new Corvette. In the Jag or the Corvette, people would look at you with longing and envy swooning in their eyes.

In the Muntz, they'd just look at you.

So I settled on the Eldorado—hey, I'm just a ragtops and roadsters kind of guy when I have the option—and I had the four of us off and on the way to Watkins Glen by quarter after three on Friday afternoon. It was a little chilly, but not so cold that you couldn't keep the top down (at least not if you were in the front seat and had the heater going full blast, anyway), seeing as how Big Ed always carried a big, red plaid stadium blanket in the back for the rear seat passengers. But they had to share it. And that's why I kept one eye peeled on the rearview mirror to see if anything might develop between Cal and Mary Frances. To be honest, I really thought I could see those two as a match there. I mean, outside of Julie, they were probably my two most favorite people in the whole world. And no question they were both as smart and quick and sarcastic and funny and ballsy as God ever made anyone. So it made perfect sense to me that they would maybe get together. Oh, sure, I knew he was an irresponsible, ne'er-do-well, Rich Kid racing bum. And she'd been hanging around and maybe even gotten herself a little bit infected by those philosophically, psychologically, politically, intellectually and most assuredly artistically infatuated phonies and posers over at the epicenter of the known universe in Greenwich Village. But, hey, one day Cal was gonna come into a load of cash (although both of his folks would probably have to keel over dead first) and how much better a deal was that than hanging around with that genius, novels-in-Esperanto creep Ollie Cromwell or a strange, struggling young artist like Frederick Frumpt who most likely had to either die or go nuts or cut off an ear or a gonad or something if he ever wanted to really make it big in the retail fine art racket?

But you can't always tell about people or think you know what's best for them. In fact, they can get pretty damn indignant about it if you try. For whatever reasons, Cal and Mary Frances mixed about as well as Girling Crimson brake fluid and a double chocolate malted milk. Or, in other words, not very well at all. There was always this kind of sneering edge and challenge in the air when those two got anywheres close to each other. And maybe for the same exact reasons I thought they'd click so well together. You know, because they were the two sharpest, brightest, ballsiest, funniest and most sarcastic people I ever knew. I guess what it comes down to is that you need a little contrast and difference and balance between two people for that sort of thing to work out. Not to mention that most male/female relationships are only equipped with a single spotlight, and, while it's always important to remember to share it, there's hardly any way you can share it at the same time.

So it was pretty quiet back there in the back seat of Big Ed's Eldorado. Even after we stopped and put up the top to kind of cut down the noise from their teeth chattering. We stopped again for gas and a couple soda pops and sandwiches just outside of Binghamton around eight, and Cal offered to take over the wheel for the final, two-hour-and-change run up through Elmira and Horseheads and on up Route 14 to Watkins Glen. I was a little worried about handing over the keys to Big Ed's Eldorado—I mean, Cal only had one speed, and that was pretty much flat out—but I was tired and starting to see giant Saint Bernards and brontosauruses and stuff lurking behind the roadside billboards, so I figured I ought to maybe let him drive. Besides, it was real nice to cuddle there in the dark in the back seat of Big Ed's Cadillac with Julie. At least so long as I didn't lift my head up and see the needle on the speedometer pointing in the general direction of the rearview mirror. Like I said, Cal only had one speed. But if I kept my head down, it was almost like Julie and me were all alone back there in the dark, all snuggled up in that red plaid stadium blanket with the wind rushing past the window glass like the roar of a subway tunnel and the heavily padded canvas top above us flapping and fluttering and the steady, rolling drum of the Caddy's tires across the pavement coming up through the leather upholstery beneath us until it was like we were burrowed deep inside our own, private, cozy little world. And I'm not about to tell you what went on in that cozy little world, either. I mean, it's really none of your business.

All I will tell you is that neither Cal or Mary Frances had the slightest idea.

Anyhow, we rolled into the parking lot at the Seneca Lodge just a few ticks after ten, and I'm sure Cal set a brand new record for the run from that gas station just outside Binghamton to the bar at the Seneca Lodge. Or at least in the four-passenger American luxury convertible class, anyway. As per usual on a race weekend, the place was packed and noisy and chock-full to the rafters with smoke, racing stories, lies, liquor and laughter.

"Jesus, it's crowded in here!" Julie shouted in my ear.

"Who are all these people?" Mary Frances shouted in my other ear.

But I was already picking up little snippets of racing conversation all up and down the bar. In fact, I was about being devoured by them:

"I've put that new set of needles in the carburetors but I've still got a damn flat spot around 4,000rpm."

"Did you try raising the float levels?"

"Did you try lowering the float levels?"

"Did you try raising the jets?"

"Did you try lowering the needles?"

"Did you try lowering the jets?"

"Did you try raising the needles?"

"Did you try putting 90-weight in the dashpots?"

"Did you try putting brake fluid in the dashpots?"

"Did you try running the dashpots dry?"

"Did you try taking the springs out?"

"Did you try heavier springs?"

"Did you talk to that Joe Curto guy?"

"DID YOU TRY PUTTING YOUR DAMN FOOT DOWN?"

That last one triggered a barrage of laughter followed by the hearty clinking of glassware. And there was more, too, just a few stools down:

"It was great to have an actual practice day today. A chance to learn the track and all."

"They need to do that at all the races. A couple lousy warmup laps before they flag you off just isn't enough. Especially on a track you've never seen before..."

"Like they did here last year!"

"Like they've done here every year!"

"...it's just not enough, y'know?"

"It's asking for trouble!"

And from the next stool:

"Jeez, I can't believe what they got done up here in 40 days!"

"Built the whole damn circuit."

"It's amazing, isn't it?"

And next to that one, a genuinely wobbly and inebriated celebrant was swaying gently from side-to-side on his barstool: *"Ahh, it'sch nott'sho damn amazsh-ing,"* he observed. *"Why, it shays right in the Shaint Jamesh Bible that God made the whole damn univershe in jusht sheven..."*

"He did it in six, you besotted heathen. Didn't they teach you anything in Sunday school? God rested on the seventh!"

That just made the drunk indignant: *"If He'sh God, whysh He gotta resht at all, huh? Anwsher me that!"*

"Oh, go to bed. You're stiff."

He was, too.

And further down:

"It's too bad they didn't get a better turnout."

"I heard they got a hunnert cars."

"Yeah, maybe. But none of the really BIG guys are here."

"HEY, I'M HERE!" It was Big Ed's voice. There was no way you could miss it.

"Yeah, but you're not even racing. And Cunningham's not here. And neither are any of the Ferraris or the C-Jags or..."

"It's that rat-bastard Charlie Priddle and his bunch."

"They think they own this bloody sport." That was Tommy's Edwards' voice. I'd know it anywhere. So naturally I headed over towards it.

"I heard a rumor the race was cancelled."

"Me, too."

"I heard it was postponed till next week."

"Like I told you, it's that rat-bastard Charlie Priddle and his bunch...."

I broke through between two shoulders and there was Big Ed with Rhonda kind of draped all over him and looking like she'd been ready for bed about two or three hours ago—I guess she'd been pretty much alternating between Pink Squirrels and Sloe Gin Fizzes—and Tommy right next to her with three gin-and-tonics lined up in front of him on the bar. I had to do a kind of double-take when I saw him because his face was about the same color and texture as a seriously overcooked Thanksgiving turkey. "Jesus, where the hell have you been?"

"Hey, Sport! Good to see you!"

"Good to be seen."

"Barkeep!" Tommy shouted. *"Another drink for my friend!* Here," he said, pushing one of his gin-and-tonics over in my direction, "have this in the mean-time. You could bloody well die of thirst waiting for a drink around here."

That didn't seem too likely. Not at the Seneca Lodge.

"So where'd you get the tan?" I asked him. "Florida? California? Cuba?"

"Bonneville."

"Bonneville?"

"Bonneville bloody Utah, Buddy. The salt flats." He let out a grim little laugh. "Garden spot of the west. Bloody vacation paradise. All beach. No water." He shook his head ruefully. "Talk about dying of thirst...."

"What the hell were you doing at Bonneville?" I mean, I'd heard about the famous speed record runs out on the salt flats of Bonneville. Why, everybody who knew how to gap a damn sparkplug knew about Bonneville. But I always thought it was all California hotrod types running long, skinny streamliners and tiny little cars called "lakesters" made out of aircraft wing tanks and old Ford roadsters with no fenders and big, honking, supercharged V8s under their louvered hoods. That didn't exactly sound like Tommy Edwards' cup of tea, you know?

But what I didn't know was that there are literally thousands of different speed records on the books at Bonneville. And they're all certified and official and confirmed in writing by the Triple-A and the FIA and therefore just about cast in stone. Although a lot of them have been around for an awfully long time and are just sort of there for the taking. At least if you're willing to spend the time and money and effort it takes to go after them. Which is precisely why that crafty old Donald Healey sent one of his hopped-up, "special test" cars over (along with a razor-tuned "stock" Healey Hundred) to see if they could maybe rack up a few

World and American Records and pick up a little easy publicity. Like I said before, those Healey guys were pretty damn smart about just where, when and how they wanted to show off their new baby.

And it turned out they invited my very own British buddy Tommy Edwards to be one of the team drivers for those record runs out at Bonneville. Which kind of explained why Tommy's face looked like a rasher of crisp bacon, seeing as how there wasn't any shade at all out on the Bonneville salt flats. Unless you brought it with you, that is. So naturally Cal wanted to know how he'd come up with the Healey ride.

"Oh, it was mostly dumb luck," he shrugged. "I knew a bloke over at Healey's, and it was cheaper to put me on than to pay for another plane ticket over from England."

"Wow," I said over my third gin-and-tonic. "That sounds really *neat!*"

"Oh, I suppose," Tommy allowed, swirling the ice around in his glass.

"What was it like?" Cal wondered, craning his neck forward across the bar.

"Oh, I reckon everyone should do Bonneville at least once in their lifetime. Just to see what it's like." He sucked up the last of his latest gin-and-tonic. "But I should think once is probably a lifetime supply, thank you very much."

"Not much fun, huh?"

"Oh, *God!* It's bloody hot and barren and the sun blazes down like a bloody blowtorch and there's no shade at all and that blasted salt gets into absolutely everything."

"Sounds awful."

"It is."

"But you get to go so *fast!*" Cal insisted.

"Well, it's hardly any great, keen test of driving skill."

"It isn't?"

Tommy laughed. "After awhile, you don't even feel it. You just keep your bloody foot on the firewall and mind the gauges and try not to drop off to sleep." And I could see in his face how it could get pretty darn hot and uncomfortable—not to mention boring—droning around some huge, flat, empty, 10-mile circle in the middle of the Bonneville Salt Flats under a broiling August sun. Which is precisely why the Healey record runs at Bonneville required so many drivers, seeing as how they were running two cars and going after all sorts of different records. Including some of the real long-distance marks like 12 and 24 hours. Not to mention that there was a little "marquee value" to having an established stateside 'shoe like Tommy Edwards on board. And even more to famous Hollywood actor and onetime child star Jackie Cooper, who was bitten by the sports car bug as bad as anybody, had done a fair bit of racing, and also got invited to take a few turns behind the wheel of the new Healey Hundred at Bonneville. So long as he posed for all the pictures that went out with the press releases, that is.

Turns out they set over 100 outright World Speed Records with those two Healey Hundreds (in their classes, anyway) including a thoroughly astonishing flying mile run at 142.636 miles-per-hour in the "special test" car! Which was, truthfully speaking, a good thirty-five or forty mph faster than you could ever hope to go in an ordinary, showroom-issue Healey Hundred unless you drove it off a cliff. But, like sharp car business guys everywhere, Donald Healey understood that most people don't know the first damn thing about automobiles, and so if you parked a new Healey Hundred in your driveway (like our friend Carson Flegley, for example) and your doofus neighbor with the buck teeth and fat wife and noisy kids who picked their scabs and noses all the time came over and asked you, *"Hey, Bub, wot'll she do?"* you could look him right square in the eye and say, *"Well, one just like it went one-hundred-and-forty-six-point-six-three-six miles-per-hour at Bonneville last week!"* and watch his jaw drop right off his blessed face.

It was better than elevator shoes, you know?

"That reminds me. Where the heck are Carson and my sister?" I looked around the bar and couldn't see them anywhere. Not that you couldn't easily hide two people in that mob. Or three or four or five or six or eight, for that matter.

"Oh, they went into town," Big Ed explained. "Guess they wanted a quiet little dinner all by themselves."

Cal went through a suggestive, explicit and thoroughly disgusting series of gestures with his fingers.

"Jesus, Cal, knock it off. Julie's here."

"No, she's not."

Which is about when I looked around and realized that both Julie and Mary Frances had left the bar.

"They've been gone for an hour."

Uh-oh. Trouble.

It seems Julie and Mary Frances had gotten tired of all the noise and smoke and endless racing chatter and gone for a little walk outside. It was pretty chilly, but at least they got to see the cabins and the trees and all the sports cars parked out front and the cool little sliver of a moon hanging up in the sky and, in fact, all the things that made the Seneca Lodge at Watkins Glen so special to all of us. Then they came back and I guess maybe we were still talking about the Healey Record Runs or something and so they went to the desk and got the keys and went back to the cabins. Julie was sitting up in bed when I got there, kind of doodling on her sketchpad under the dim light of the lamp on the bedstand next to her. She looked really pretty in that light. Almost like she glowed, you know?

"Nice of you to drop by," she said without putting any real anger or energy into it.

"Sorry," I told her. "I didn't hear you leave."

"You wouldn't have heard a bomb going off! Boy, when you're around those racing friends of yours, it's like nothing else gets through."

"I dunno," I said, listening to my own voice kind of backing itself into a corner, "it's just that I haven't seen them for awhile and I wanted to catch up on what's going on and I was, you know…" I really needed to find something here, "…still so charged up from our ride up here together in the back seat of the Cadillac and…"

"Hmpf. And how many drinks have you had?"

"I dunno. A couple, maybe…."

"How many?"

Well, at least that explained the glow.

But Julie wasn't really mad. Not really. She was just busting my hump because that's what wives do. For recreation, you know? Just to let their husbands know they're not getting away with anything. And she snuggled up right next to me after I hit the can and tossed my pants in the general direction of the floor and came to bed.

"It's nice up here, isn't it?" I whispered.

"You drink too much when you're with those racing people," she whispered back.

"But it is nice, isn't it?"

She shrugged up against me. "Maybe a little. At least if you ignore the bugs and the animals I heard prowling around out there and all the damn drunks in the bar talking about racing until I swear I could scream..."

"But outside of that, it's nice, right?"

"Maybe a little."

"See, I told you."

"I saw Carson and your sister Sarah Jean come home."

"What time?"

"Oh, about an hour ago. While you were still off drinking the bar dry with your friends."

"I wonder why they didn't come in?"

"Maybe it's because they're normal and don't like all that stupid car talk."

"Carson loves talking about cars."

"Maybe he loves something else, too."

"You think so?"

I felt a giddy little shiver go through Julie's body. "They just sat out in the car in the parking lot for the longest time."

"Were they necking?" I had a hard time visualizing that one.

"NO!" Julie insisted, sounding hurt and disappointed I'd even think such a thing. "They just sat there and talked...It was kind of sweet. Really it was."

"Did he kiss her good night?"

There was another giddy little shiver. "I think he wanted to. He brought her up to the door of the cabin and they just sort of *stood* there...."

I could see it. The hemming and the hawing and Carson and Sarah Jean both with their eyes down and toes kind of digging in the turf.

Julie snuggled in even closer. "Are you excited about the baby?"

To be honest, I hadn't really thought that much about it. Not that I was about to admit something as damning as that to Julie. "I'm not *worried* about it, if that's what you mean." And that was the truth. I mean, I just had this sort of blind, dumb, instinct-driven Male Optimism that everything was gonna to be okay. Nature was just supposed to take care of all that stuff for you. And if it didn't, what the heck could you do about it anyway?

"Which do you want, Buddy? A boy or a girl?"

That was another thing I hadn't thought much about. I mean, it wasn't like you had a choice, right? Not like you do with ice cream flavors or anything.

"Oh, I guess either's all right," I told her.

"You sure you wouldn't rather have a boy?"

"Yeah, sure," I admitted without thinking. "I guess."

"You mean you wouldn't want a girl?"

Boy, was that ever a trick question!

And to think I didn't see it coming!

"Look," I told her, "I don't care one way or the other, just so long as it's happy and healthy and smart and clever and beautiful and handsome and lucky and fortunate and loves us terribly and then grows up to be terrifically successful at something so we can get out of the damn garage business and retire to that island villa I promised you in the Caribbean."

"That's all you want, huh?"

"That and a little sleep is all."

And I was halfway there, already. Three-quarters, even....

"If it's a boy, what do you want to name it?" I heard Julie ask from a distant shore. This could go on all night.

So I pretended to already be asleep until I actually was.

But it was still nice being there in bed with her in that dark, cozy little cabin at the Seneca Lodge, what with the smell of the evergreens all around us and the faint, hollow cry of a hooty owl somewhere up in the oak or maple trees and soft little night critters rustling around on the carpet of fallen leaves and pine needles. Every once in a while, you'd hear the warm, predatory growl of a sports car returning home to the lodge from some late party or other. I could always tell what it was just from the sound. And then it would switch off with maybe a quick *chuff-chuff* of run-on from a hot spot in one of the combustion chambers and you'd hear the doors slam with a tinny *thunk!* Followed by footsteps across the gravel and two voices you couldn't quite make out as they headed over to the bar for a nightcap and then the muffled wave of noise and laughter as they opened the door and went inside....

Like I said, it was nice. Real nice, in fact.

12: One Hell of a Race Day

Race day dawned cold and windy at Watkins Glen, and somehow we all managed to wake up early and got together for a little breakfast at the lodge around 6:30—God, it seemed quiet and peaceful and innocent there in the daytime!—and after breakfast Big Ed and Rhonda and Carson and Sarah Jean headed up to the track while Cal and Julie and Mary Frances and me took Big Ed's Eldorado down into town to pick up some race-day supplies. You know, ice and soda pop and sandwiches and cigarettes and beer and maybe a coffee or hot chocolate or two against the chill. Then we turned around and headed back South down Franklin Street—following the old course that used to run right through town—and swept right on 329 just like it did to climb Old Corning Hill. That was where Tommy had his terrible accident the year before, but I wasn't about to say anything. As we climbed the hill, Cal and me started pointing out features of the old circuit to Julie and Mary Frances. First came the sweeping climb up 329 under a canopy of trees and then how it leveled off a bit and then dipped blind under the railroad overpass and then kind of opened up into a long, flat-out straightaway heading towards that fast, daunting, deceptively simple high-speed, right-left ess where Sam Collier skated on some gravel and went off the road into a meadow full of wildflowers while leading the second lap of the Grand Prix in 1950. He was guest-driving Briggs Cunningham's new Ferrari at the time, and Cal and me both knew that he flipped end-over-end a couple times and died later in the hospital from his injuries—the first driver ever to get hurt seriously at Watkins Glen—and we also knew enough to keep quiet about it around the girls. It just wasn't part of the story that needed retelling, you know?

We turned left on Glen School House Road—right where the old track made a hard right into the State Park and descended the steep, woodsy downgrade into White's Hollow and across the old stone bridge at the bottom where Denny Cornett spun off and rolled his MG two-and-a-half times down into the creek during that first-ever race at Watkins Glen in 1948. But we could tell the girls about that one, seeing as how he walked away from it with barely a scratch. Still, they didn't seem particularly impressed. At least not like most guys would.

The organizers had the start-finish line and the race paddock set up on a gently sloping straightaway between Wixon Road and Wedgewood Road and, unlike some of the SCMA races we'd been to, we flashed our race credentials and got right in. They even had a place nearby for us to park. The bad thing was that the whole circuit sat on this high, rolling sort of landscape on the very top of some hills, so the wind kind of raked right across it and, what with all the construction that had been going on, that wind was pushing an awful lot of grit and dust and dirt and even gravel along with it. Plus it was damn cold. Even for late September.

"It'll warm up," I said encouragingly.

"I'm staying in the car until it does," Mary Frances said flatly.

"Me, too," Julie agreed.

So Cal and me got out and wandered around the paddock to see what was up. And I wondered as I walked into that wind with my face buried down into the shoulder of my windbreaker if maybe the girls weren't the smart ones. But once you get around the racecars, the chill kind of evaporates. Or at least you don't notice it so much anymore. To be honest, the turnout of cars wasn't nearly as good as the Glen race the year before. Or even Floyd Bennett Field, come to think of it. But maybe that was to be expected, what with all the in-fighting and last-minute rumors and confusion. Anyhow, I finally got a closeup look at the nifty white Jaguar Special that super-fast Walt Hansgen guy was driving. Like I said before, he built it himself out of a standard XK 120 that he'd been racing—and doing pretty well with—although there was a behind-the-hand rumor going around that he didn't come from a whole heck of a lot of money. Someone said his dad ran a bump shop someplace over in Jersey, and that he'd actually put a second mortgage on his house to buy that Jaguar. Without telling his wife and family about it, either. It was the kind of thing you'd expect Cal Carrington to do.

And, also just like Cal, the better he did in that stock Jag, the more he felt himself being drawn towards deeper and deeper water. That's just the way it is when you've got the hunger for it and it turns out you're any good. Well, no way could this Walt Hansgen guy even think of affording something like a C-Type—hell, he still owed an arm and a leg on his XK 120—so he kind of yanked the body off and built a sort of tubular third dimension to the frame and did a little of this and that with the driveline and suspension. Including fabricating this odd little triangular locator/torque-reaction arm on the top right-side of the rear axle that he'd copied directly off the factory C-Types and that the factory subsequently gave up as a bad try and tossed in the trash heap after they found out it made the cars awful squirrelly. But the real point is that he'd made it with his own two hands, and the aluminum body they'd built for it—remember, his dad had a bump shop—was both very handsome and terrifically original. It really impressed me that a person could build a car like that—right there in your own shop, you know?—and have it come out good enough to run heads-up against the best the overseas factories had to offer.

I could feel the itch to maybe do something like that myself one day.

Not far down from Walt Hansgen's Jag Special we found Tommy Edwards next to John Perona's brand new Allard J2X that he'd be driving. The one with the big, hot-rod Chrysler Hemi under the hood. It was painted silver with red trim, and Tommy looked real pleased with it. "How's it runnin'?" I asked him.

"It's got bloody monstrous power," he said with a rare combination of awe and enthusiasm.

"And what's the track like?"

He mulled it over for a moment. "I suppose it's safer than the old one. And they've done a decent job of keeping everybody back. But I've got to say I rather liked the old one better. Even after what happened."

"Any dicey spots?" Cal wanted to know.

"Oh, there's a couple blind hills and places you could really use a bloody escape road. Just in case. And the last corner is a bit of a bitch. The entry is downhill, so the braking is iffy. And if you miss it and go off, you sail right into outer space."

"Wow."

"So how do you size up your chances?" Cal asked. We'd all been around long enough to understand that *what* you were driving was never near as important as *where* you were driving it or *who* you had to race against.

"It's a hard one to call," Tommy said evenly. "There are a lot of long straight-aways with slow corners leading onto them, and that should work in our favor. I think we've got the legs on bloody everybody when it comes to sheer power…"

"But?"

Tommy laughed. "But that which speeds up must eventually slow down again, mustn't it? And all those wonderful, long straightaways seem to end in those same, sharp corners. So you've somehow got to get rid of all that terrific speed you've gained if you want to keep the car out of the bloody landscape."

"And how are the brakes?" I asked.

"Oh, they're the usual Allard brakes, Buddy," Tommy laughed. "They'd be absolutely brilliant on a car with half the weight and capacity."

Still, you couldn't miss the gunfighter glint in Tommy's eye. Unlike his sadly humorous run mired deep in the pack in that pig of an Allard Palm Beach at Floyd Bennett Field, you could tell that Tommy knew he was in with a chance here at Watkins Glen. Sure, the Cunninghams weren't here and Creighton Pendleton wasn't here and that Masten Gregory kid in the C-Type wasn't here. But what did that matter? When it's race day and you've got a good, clean shot at coming first under the checker, that's all that matters. No matter if it's the twenty-two minutes of Podunk or the Twenty-Four Hours of Le Mans.

About then I could feel my morning coffee getting to me and I started look-ing around for someplace to, you know, let a little of it back out. And that's always a big problem at racetracks out in the country. And especially up here in the new Watkins Glen paddock, which was really pretty much in the middle of open farm-land without so much as a stunted tree or a moderately-sized shrub you could stand behind. "Is there a can around here anyplace?" I asked.

"I believe you'll find a hastily-erected *pissoir* over next to the control tower."

Sure enough, just about twenty paces past the newly-built tower (which was really not much more than a Paul Bunyan-sized stepladder made out of two-by-fours and clad in plywood sheeting) I found a little eight-foot by twelve-foot box made out of the same exact 2x4s and plywood. And, even this early in the morn-ing, it already had a line in front of it. Fact is, there was already a pretty decent crowd (and more sure to come!) and you couldn't help wondering how they were possibly going to take care of everybody with a few little makeshift outhouses like this one. And I said as much to the guy standing in line in front of me.

"Don't worry," he told me, "the line moves pretty fast."

"But how?"

"They've got a trough inside."

Sure enough, when I got inside, I had to marvel at the simplicity and ingenu-ity of the sanitary engineering. There was just this big, galvanized tin gutter thing going all the way around the walls (and of course on a slight downward angle) so that every blessed inch could be put to good use. And I suddenly realized that the sight, smell and sound of eight or fourteen guys packed together shoulder-to-shoulder while peeing into a galvanized tin gutter was as much a part of the great Race Weekend experience as cold, overpriced hotdogs and vicious morning hang-overs. Just out of curiosity, after I was done, I took a quick peek out back to see where, exactly, that gutter wound up. And it looked like it just went out about ten or twelve feet and dumped into this hole in the ground where I doubted anything would ever grow again. Or at least nothing green, anyway.

"What happens if you have to do the other thing?" I asked my outhouse expert acquaintance as we headed back towards the paddock.

"The other thing?"

"You know. Or if you're a girl?"

"Oh, they've got a couple two-holers scattered around here and there and there's a couple farmhouses where you could maybe find something to use if you asked nice." He looked at me and grinned brightly. "Most people just decide to hold it."

Ah, another Great Lesson in Racing! No question about it.

We got the girls out of the car and lined up along the fences (thankfully with our backs to the wind!) for the Seneca Cup Race at 10:30, and Julie'd brought that plaid blanket out of the back of Big Ed's Caddy to put around us. But it was still pretty damn cold. The race was a good one, though. It was for "unrestricted category" cars (meaning anything that didn't fit anywheres else) and so you had everything from one of the DuPont kids and a couple other masochists in those tiny, 500cc, motorcycle-engined, chain-drive Cooper Formula III open-wheelers that looked like some little kid's pedal car on up to George Weaver's Maserati Grand Prix car (the same car-and-driver combination that won the Seneca Cup Race in 1951) and Phil Cade in another old Grand Prix Maserati, but with a big, honking, 5.6-liter Chrysler Hemi stuffed under the hood! And believe me, they must've had one hell of a shoehorn to get it in there, too. Plus there were a bunch of stock and modified XK 120s led by none other than race organizer Cam Argetsinger himself and some quick young transplanted South African doctor out of Pennsylvania named M.R.J. Wyllie. Personally, I thought the guys in those little Cooper FIII cars were nuts, mixing it up in a race group where some of the drivers in the big cars probably couldn't even see them. Like little tin kittens in a cattle chute, you know?

But everybody played nice and so things worked out all right. The field trundled off for a pace lap—a couple guys had to push-start the little Coopers on account of they didn't have starters on board—and of course Colin St. John had one of his brand new Healey Hundreds out there in front as the pace car. He even got famous comedian Fred Allen to drive it in return for agreeing to sell him (at full list and then some, of course) his "only example of the new model." Fact is, it was the same exact silver-blue Healey Hundred that Donald Healey showed off at Sebring in March and that had served as the pace car at Floyd Bennett Field and that Colin claimed to have swapped to Canada for the black one Carson was driving. And then supposedly sold on the sly to some guy in Albany. Only the deal fell through because the guy in Albany didn't have the money (or his folks wouldn't give him the money or he couldn't get his hands on his trust fund or something) and so Colin had it back again. But he had no problem at all telling Carson (and Fred Allen!) that it was a brand new one he'd "just got in." And I knew it wasn't for sure, on account of I'd noticed this little tiny dink in the chrome down at Sebring and noticed it again at Floyd Bennett Field. But Colin wasn't above unscrewing the speedo cable so's it wouldn't rack up any miles. I swear, that Colin St. John could shit on a plate and have you thinking it was chocolate layer cake. What a salesman!

Well, the green flag fell and the cars thundered and blared and howled (or popped and blatted, in the case of the little one-lung Coopers) away in a cloud of swirling dust and tiresmoke and the smell of burning castor-bean oil and whatever wild sort of fuel concoction the Coopers were using. Mary Frances made a face when she got a good whiff of it, but I thought it smelled better than any perfume. The race order was a complete shambles at the start seeing as how they were still pulling the grids out of a hat but, like always, it only took until the first long straightaway for things to sort themselves out. It was that George Weaver guy in the Grand Prix Maserati in front the first time they came around, and he pulled out a huge lead by the sixth lap or so and it was looking like a laugher. But then he blew a piston or threw a rod or something (whatever it was, it left a pretty impressive hole in the side of the block afterwards!) and all of a sudden it got interesting again, what with that Phil Cade's Chrysler-engined Maserati duking it out tooth-and-nail with M.R.J. "Doc" Wyllie's "factory lightweight" Jag 120. No question that big, hulking V8 in the Maserati had the legs on the Jag six down the straightaways, but you could see that the Jag was a bit handier and that, at least the way I saw it, this "Doc" Wyllie guy was driving the blessed wheels off of it. And Cal and me tried to explain all of that to Julie and Mary Frances as we stood there along the snow fencing with the wind whipping at our backs. "It's just a bunch of noisy cars running around in circles going nowhere," Mary Frances observed with about the same degree of bubbling excitement your average male reserves for flower-arranging contests, fashion shows and two-hanky, tearjerker movies.

"I'm cold," Julie said through lips that did indeed look slightly blue.

"You girls want to go back to the car?"

"Oh, no," Julie said sarcastically. "And maybe after this race, we can go build a snowman or something."

"But only if we get to wear shorts or swimsuits," Mary Frances chimed in.

Well, the point of it is that you can't expect somebody else to like and get enthused about something just because it sets your own pants on fire. And that goes double for your wife or sister or girlfriend. If you've got a real, deep-gut *passion* for something—and I don't care if it's ski jumping off mountain cliffs or collecting the top fly buttons off the second pair of pants that come with two-pair-of-pants blue serge suits—you tend to forget that other people may not exactly share your feelings. Although you catch yourself wondering how they could possibly *not* get excited over, well, a bunch of noisy cars running around in circles going nowhere....

So the girls went back to Big Ed's Caddy and took the red plaid blanket with them while Cal and me hung on the fences and watched the race come to a really thrilling conclusion. Like I said before, the last corner was a real booger, what with a difficult, downhill braking area and nothing but a big bunch of Wild Blue Yonder waiting for you if you missed the turn. So naturally that's where "Doc" Wyllie decided to make his pass. It was one hell of a piece of driving—even Cal said so—on account of he was patient and waited and waited until the very last moment to pop out of that Chrysler/Maserati's slipstream and dive down the inside. He damn near didn't make it, as the Jag kind of skittered out in a big pendulum slide and kicked up a big cloud of dust at the very outside edge. But he got it done, and that's what separates the real *racers* from the guys who merely drive fast. "That was a hell of a job!" Cal whooped. "If he'd showed that move any earlier, the guy in the Maserati would've just streamed back by on the straightaway and then pulled inside to block on every corner after that." Cal shook his head admiringly. "One *hell* of a job!"

But I was thinking about something else. What if you had a car with the power of one of those big American V8s but the brakes and handling of a really lightweight Jag 120? Or maybe even a C-Type, you know? And what if you built it yourself with your own two hands—like that Walt Hansgen guy did with his car—and put a certified Ace Racer hotshoe like my great-but-perpetually-broke-rich-friend-who-was-always-looking-for-a-damn-ride Cal Carrington behind the wheel? What would happen then?

What, indeed....

Anyhow, the second race of the day was the 22-lap, 101.2-mile Queen Catherine Cup for under-1500cc tiddlers, and the field was full of stock MGs and modified MGs and MG specials and a couple Porsches and a Singer and a few Crosley-powered Siatas and such and two of those jewel-like OSCA MT4s the Maserati brothers built over in Italy and that Carson and me (and everybody else, for that matter) liked so much. Right on cue, Carson joined us on the fences to watch. "Where's Sarah Jean?" I asked him.

"She's back in the car with the other girls. She said she was cold."

"Can you believe it?"

"With a race about to start?"

It seemed incredible, you know?

"Geez," Carson asked, kind of swiveling his head around, "anyplace I can take a quick whiz before it starts?"

"Right over there," I told him, nodding in the general direction of the little eight-by-twelve, plywood-and-two-by-four structure with the long line in front of it.

"But I'll never make it back in time!" he sort of groaned.

"Sure you will. It goes real quick. They've got a trough in there."

So he went and sure enough he got back just as the little tiddlers came to the end of their pace lap and lined up for a dramatic standing start that was probably the bright idea of somebody (like Colin St. John, for instance?) who sold replacement clutch linings, pressure plates, throwout bearings and second-gear synchro rings for MGs. The field got away with a birdlike chirping of tires, and it was obvious right from the start that the two OSCAs in the hands of George Moffett and Henry Wessels the Third had the legs on everybody. But they put on a good race between themselves—even trading the lead a couple times—while they pulled further and further away from everybody else. But there was other stuff to watch. Like when the guy in the Singer finally made the mistake that everybody'd been dreading and went off the outside of that last corner and went for a wee bit of a flying lesson before coming back down to earth and rolling over. Twice.

Fortunately the cops got over there in a hurry and helped him out and the crowd stayed back where they belonged behind the snow fencing and the amazing part was that, although the driver was a little shaken and goose-egg-eyed, he wasn't hurt at all. And, even more amazing, he was able to drive the car home the following day. Albeit without the windshield glass. Or the headlamp glass. Or the taillight glass. Or the rear-view mirror. Then again, he probably didn't want to be looking at himself much on the way home....

Meanwhile the two OSCAs just kept stretching it out even while they battled each other for the lead—boy, those were some swell little cars!—but all the drama got sucked out of it with only a lap or two to go when Wessels' car went sick (I think it was the rear axle or something) and he had to limp home a distant second.

We got ourselves some sandwiches out of Big Ed's trunk and absolutely insisted that the girls join us on the fence to watch our friend Tommy Edwards drive John Perona's Allard in the big feature Watkins Glen Grand Prix that capped off the day. And fortunately the wind had died down a little and it had warmed all the way up to maybe the mid-40s or something, so they really couldn't complain. Even though they did.

"Where's Big Ed and Rhonda?" I asked them.

"Oh, they went back to the lodge hours ago."

"Yeah," Mary Frances added. "Looks to me like they're the smart ones."

It also looked like Big Ed was getting his money's worth out of that Muntz. But of course I didn't say anything.

I must admit that the race was pretty damn swell. Even the girls enjoyed it. But of course it helps to have somebody to cheer for. In fact, that makes all the difference in the world. And here was our good friend and buddy Tommy Edwards running a close second to that nifty homebuilt Jaguar special of Walt Hansgen and staying just ahead of another Allard (only this one with a Caddy engine) in the hands of a guy named Delavan Lee. And I was absolutely thrilled to see our buddies from the next pit at Sebring, Hal Ullrich at the wheel of Brooks Stevens' Excalibur, running about mid-pack and going very nicely. It looked like that car handled really well (in spite of all that Henry J hardware under the sheet-metal) and you had to be impressed with how it was sneaking up through the pack as the faster cars started running into trouble. And all that with just a warmed-over version of that anemic, boat-anchor Willys six under the hood!

Meanwhile at the front, Walt Hansgen and his Jag special were slowly but surely inching away from Tommy Edwards and Delavan Lee in the two Allards. It looked to me like Tommy had the other guy pretty much covered and was only driving fast enough to stay ahead. I guess he'd either given up on chasing down Hansgen or he was playing a little game of "wait-and-see" and making sure he had plenty of car left for the end of the race. Especially brakes. After all, it's not the first five or ten or twenty miles that matter in a 100-mile race. It's that last five or ten or twenty *feet*....

But I guess the other guy thought he was in the race of his life up against the great Allard 'shoe and sometimes factory Le Mans driver Tommy Edwards, and so he was really hanging it out to dry. And right about then some guy well back in the pack in an older Healey Silverstone with an Olds engine in it skated off the black part, got into a bit of a tank-slapper and ricocheted back onto the racing sur-face right in front of another car. And that poor guy about put both feet through the firewall trying to wake the brakes up and so he looped it, too. And that's about when Tommy and the other Allard came around, fighting for second. Well, Tommy saw all the yellow flags and the cars pointed every which way in front of him and did exactly what you're supposed to do. He raised his hand to let the guy behind him know something was up, glanced in the mirror to make sure he wouldn't get punted squarely up the backside when he did it, and lifted off to slow down. Which, as sometimes happens, the other guy took as a gift-from-God opportunity to pass the great Tommy Edwards. He made it, too. Even though he had to kind of slalom his way through stationary racecars and scattering corner workers in the process.

Well, the organizers took a more or less dim view of that (as well they should!), showed him the black flag and brought him in for a little wrist-slap and talking-to from pit marshal John Burns. Now John Burns is a kind of lanky, bony, slow-talking and deliberate sort of an individual who would be well over six feet tall if he ever stood up straight. He also has the longest, most amazing and multi-jointed index finger you have ever seen (I swear, there must be at least six or seven separate bones in it!) which he can shake, wag, point or even corkscrew at an offending driver like the business end of an auger bit. And, as every driver who has ever been called in to see him will surely attest, the best thing to do with John Burns and the end of his finger is just say "yes, sir," "no, sir," and "no excuse, sir," and let it go at that. Hanging your head in shame a little bit doesn't hurt, either. Because the more you try to argue or make excuses or, worse yet, start getting indignant and maybe even making certain types of rude or impatient hand gestures at John and his finger, the slower he talks and the longer you sit there.

The guy in the Allard sat there a long, long time.

While all this was going on, that "Doc" Wyllie guy who won the first race pulled in with a slipping clutch (no wonder he wasn't running better!) and Hal Ullrich in the Excalibur had sneaked his way up to a distant fourth place. And then that long-running penalty to the Allard driver escalated him to third. It was a pretty amazing performance, even if he hadn't exactly done it with brash moves and bravado. That's okay, the agate-type results on the back page of the *Times* sports section reads the same no matter how you managed to get there.

And then we had all sorts of drama at the front when, with just a couple laps to go, Hansgen's Jag special slowed and you could see Tommy was catching him up in a hurry. *"He could WIN this!"* I shouted to damn near everybody in Schuyler County.

Well, we all wondered what happened, and it turned out that Hansgen had run out of fuel in his main tank and switched onto reserve, but there didn't seem to be any there, either. And so while he was fiddling desperately with the switch and flipping it back and forth from "Main" to "Reserve," Tommy caught him up and passed him. But it just must've taken a little time for the fuel to refill the line, and a second later Hansgen's Jag special barked to life on "reserve" and he took off after Tommy and the Allard. And there were only two laps to go!

What a show they put on! Like I said, Tommy'd wisely saved the brakes on the Allard, and he still had a lot more grunt from that big Chrysler Hemi. But no question Hansgen's Jag special could go into corners much deeper. And for two solid laps they passed and re-passed, Tommy churning out of the corners and passing on acceleration down the straights, and Hansgen nipping down the inside to re-pass him going into the corners. And never once did Tommy pull to the inside and try to block. "That's just not the way it's done," was the way he put it afterwards.

So Hansgen out-braked him at the end of the backstraight on the very last lap and held Tommy off by a scant two carlengths at the checker, and everybody agreed it was one hell of a race. And run the right way, too. In fact, you should have seen Tommy and Walt Hansgen shaking hands and toasting each other and slapping each other on the back when they handed the trophies out afterwards. It made you proud to be a part of it, you know?

It was nice that the races were on Saturday so we could all go back to the Seneca Lodge and have a little wind-down party and then get up the next morning to limp back home at our leisure. And I do mean limp. Why, you should've seen all the sports cars parked around the Seneca when we pulled in! And right there in front was Spud and Sammy's old Ford rig with their AAA "Win-Some Special" championship dirt car lashed on the back. You could look right through behind the front wheels and see the engine was already out, and I really couldn't wait to see those guys again.

"You want to go in for a little dinner?" I asked Julie.

"I gotta tell you, Buddy, I'm really bushed." I looked into her face and for maybe the very first time I saw the strain and drag of carrying another person around inside you. "And I sure as heck want to take a shower while there's still some hot water left."

"Are you hungry?"

"Famished."

"Would you like me to maybe get you something and bring it back to the cabin?"

"Oh, that would be *great.*" Her eyes looked really, really tired.

"What would you like?"

"Oh, just maybe a turkey sandwich. Or, no, make that some roast turkey if they've got it. With gravy and mashed potatoes and cranberry sauce. And maybe some peas or carrots or corn or something. In fact, make it peas *and* carrots *and* corn. And maybe a nice little salad. And some soup if they've got it. But not too much. Oh, and a couple pickles and green olives, too. And maybe some black olives and celery...."

You get the idea.

So I went into the lodge and ordered Julie what amounted to a Thanksgiving dinner to go and went back into the bar for a drink while I was waiting. As you can imagine, the place was lit up with noise and packed to the rafters, and who should I run into as soon as I walked in but Brooks Stevens and Hal Ullrich and the rest of the Excalibur team. Of course Brooks had polio and couldn't get around real good, and so they had him sitting at a table kind of holding court. He recognized me and acted real happy to see me, and that was nice.

"Sit down, sit down," he smiled graciously, and asked Hal to order me a drink. Hal Ullrich was a big, strapping guy with blonde hair, a granite jaw and a tank commander's look in his eyes. "So, how has the boy wonder been?" Even though he couldn't walk very well, Brooks had this easy grace and charm about him that you just couldn't miss. Listening to him talk was like watching Fred Astaire glide across a polished marble dance floor.

"Oh, things have been going OK, Mr. Stevens."

"Call me 'Kip,' Buddy."

I was kind of flattered that he remembered my name. "Boy, you guys had yourselves one heck of a run today."

"Oh, you know how it is," Brooks shrugged. "The cream always rises to the top."

"Only today we got lucky," Hal Ullrich laughed, pushing a cold Knickerbocker in front of me. "The cream sank."

"Didn't it though!" Brooks agreed, and they clinked their glasses together.

"It's good to see you guys again," I told them. "You just up for the races?"

"Actually, I had to be in New York last Wednesday for the grand opening of this car show display at the Museum of Modern Art. It runs through October 6th."

"Cars at an art museum?"

"Why not? They're probably about the most useful kind of sculpture around."

"I never really thought of it like that."

"Well, somebody did. And you should have seen it. All the lah-de-dah, hand-kerchief-up-the-sleeve 'experts' and 'critics' were there." He looked at me with ridiculously sad, serious eyes. "Why, the very air was perfumed."

"I dunno. Those artsy types make me kind of uncomfortable. Like itchy underwear, you know?"

"I do, indeed. And you show excellent taste and judgment."

"So what kind of cars do they have?"

"Oh, like everything in the art and design world, it's very political. They had mostly the work of Italian coachbuilders because we've got this big National Phobia that the Italians know more about style than we do."

"Do they?"

"Probably. But you don't have to go around admitting it to everybody, do you?"

"I guess not."

"The only American cars that got in were the Cunningham road car and Ray Loewy's Studebaker Starliner coupe."

"That's a really sharp-looking car," I agreed. "Especially for a Studebaker."

"Well, it's certainly an improvement over those dreadful, 'which-way-is-it-going' things with the chrome torpedo heads in the nose."

You got the feeling that Brooks was just the tiniest bit jealous about Loewy's Studebaker getting picked for the show.

"And how about the Cunningham?"

"Oh, it's really just another Italian job. At least as far as the bodywork goes. And I doubt Briggs really believes he's going to sell very many. I think he's just trying to convince Uncle Sam that what he's doing is a business, not a hobby."

"What's the difference?"

"Well, depending on whom you have for a lawyer and a tax accountant, maybe around 50 percent."

"Still, it's nice they put those cars in an art museum, isn't it?"

"Yes, I think it is. Justifies the medium. But, of course, now we'll have to have critics."

"Critics?"

"Oh, you can't have art without critics. It's just not done."

"Y'know, I always wondered," I asked Brooks, "how does a person get to be a critic?"

"No one seems to know. It's apparently something that just sort of happens to certain people. Like being struck by lightning. One day they put their hand on a rock, look up into the heavens and decide that they either know more than anybody about everything or more than everybody about anything."

"Are you talking about *writers?*" a familiar voice said from behind my shoulder. I twisted my neck around and found myself eyeball-to-belly-button with my old *La Carrera* scribe buddy, Hank Lyons.

"Hey!" I damn near shouted. "What the hell are you doing here?"

"Trying to make a living."

"You doing any good at it?"

"Not so's you'd notice. I'm doing a story for *Wire Wheel* out in California."

"I never heard of it."

"You probably never will. Some land development guy and his printer brother-in-law decided they could make themselves a quick million or two by cashing in on this hot new sports car craze that's sweeping the country."

"Howzit going for them?"

"Oh, I figure them to be going broke just about the time my check clears. At least if I'm lucky, anyway."

"But at least you're getting paid to do what you want."

"Not very much," Hank assured me with a grin. "But the real beauty part is that we don't get expenses or benefits, either."

"You guys need a union," I told him. "I'll fix you up with my old man. He'll have you getting union scale for doing nothing in no time at all. And time-and-a-half on weekends, too."

"Sounds like a plan."

"Want a drink?"

"Does a chicken have lips?"

So I ordered him a beer and introduced him around the table.

"You know Brooks Stevens?"

"I know all about him, but I've never had the pleasure." He turned to Brooks. "We think you're a pretty special guy out in California."

"So kind of you to say so," Brooks kind of blushed, and extended a weak but graceful hand. "You're that writer fellow, aren't you?"

"Guilty. And that reminds me. What were you just saying about writers?"

"I believe I was talking about critics, not writers."

"What's the difference?"

"Same phylum," Brooks explained, "but entirely different species."

"How so?"

"Well, to be a proper critic," Brooks continued, waving an imaginary silk handkerchief through the air. "I think it's imperative that you first fail miserably at whatever it is you plan on criticizing. And it helps if you have no talent. Or, better yet, have some talent but never have the gumption or fortitude to believe in it."

"And that's important?"

"Oh, absolutely. That's where the cruelty comes from."

"But how is that different from writers?" Hank asked, egging him on. You could tell he was getting a real kick out of Brooks Stevens. We all were.

Brooks pondered it for a moment. "Well, with a writer, at least you get a good story along with all the slings and arrows and puffed-up personal opinions. With a critic, all you get is the arrogance, bile and venom."

Hank nodded his head approvingly. "You know," he laughed, pointing his thumb in Brooks' general direction, "this guy really knows what he's talking about!"

Brooks looked down in his lap and you could see another little blush of color rising up his neck. What a nice guy. And a real gentleman, too.

"So," I asked Hank, "what kind of story are you working on?"

"Oh, it's just a race report. I'm trying to get my byline around a little so I can maybe pick up a few assignments for *Road and Track* and *Popular Science.*"

"You think you can?" I mean, you saw those magazines on every newsstand.

"Well, I've got all the qualities they're looking for. I'll work cheap, I always meet my deadlines, I've got no self-respect, I'm sick in love with racing, and I actually know how to put a subject in front of a verb to make a simple, declarative sentence." He took a quick swig of his Knickerbocker. "Although that last one's not really all that important."

"Because you have editors, right?"

"No." He looked at me with pained exasperation. "See, in the magazine business," he explained, "editorial content is only there to keep the ads from crashing into each other."

I'd never thought of it that way, but I could see it made sense.

"So you came all the way out here from California just to cover a damn race for a magazine you think is going broke?"

"Hey, I always told you I was a writer—I never said I was a *smart* writer. Besides, a lot of sports car folks out in California wondered if there was actually going to be a race here at Watkins Glen this year. There were a lot of ugly rumors going around…."

"It was a lot of stupid politics," I told him.

"Oh, yes," Brooks smiled. "This is the *Salon de Refuses* of sports car racing."

"The *what?*" I asked.

"Oh, it's very famous. At least as far as art history goes."

"Tell me about it." I mean, you don't generally pick up a lot of high culture in the gas pumping and foreign sports car repairing business. Besides, Brooks always told a great story, no matter what it was about.

"Well," he started in, kind of lowering his voice and drawing us all in like it was some scandalous secret, "it seems the French Academy of Art had a certain way of doing things. Very classical and overdone, you know, with lots of deep shadows and heavy velvet draperies and little cherubim and seraphim running around all over the canvas like midget clowns at the circus."

"I think I know the kind you mean. I saw them when Julie made me take her to the art museum in Manhattan."

"Now this was back around the time of Napoleon the Third, and these classical, Academy of Art painters had a pretty good thing going. They'd get commissions to paint flattering portraits of rich people in the classical style or to do paintings of great moments from history or the bible or mythology—there were some pretty strict rules about exactly what sort of subjects you could paint—and the good ones were so busy they had squads of assistants and apprentices running around filling in backgrounds and putting flowers in vases and dotting the eyeballs of all the warriors and cherubim and seraphim in these huge, famous battle scenes."

"So?"

"Well, there was this other bunch of painters who just wanted to paint from real life. Just the way it was. Even more important, what with photography just coming on, they wanted to show through painting what you could never capture by just snapping a picture."

"Like what?"

Brooks knitted up his brow. "Let's just call it the feelings and emotions of a scene. Like the swirling smoke inside a glass-ceilinged railroad station."

I thought maybe I'd actually seen that one once. "So what happened?"

"Well, the Academy people didn't like it much at all," Brooks said gleefully. "And, being very French and very stuffy, they simply said *'zut, alors!'* and refused to hang their paintings."

"That's kind of a raw deal."

"Ah, but there's more to the story. Those new painters—we call them 'Impressionists' today—got together and decided to do exactly what we did here at Watkins Glen."

"I don't get it."

"They put on their own show! And it was called the *Salon de Refuses* because the French Academy had refused to hang their paintings…"

Boy, it's amazing what you can pick up around racing bars!

"…and there was this one painting, *'Luncheon on the Grass'* by Edouard Manet, that caused quite a stir with the academy. In fact, all over Paris!"

"What for?"

"It showed a couple artists and their models having a picnic lunch."

"So what's wrong with that?"

"It seems the young ladies didn't have any clothes on."

"But haven't I seen, you know, *lots* of naked people in paintings?"

"Indeed you have. But the Academy people had some very strict rules about it. The subjects had to be goddesses or Madonnas or out of the bible or Greek mythology. Or about to be killed or raped and pillaged in some famous historical battle. That would work, too."

"And this was different?"

"Oh, sure. This was just a couple frisky young women with no clothes on having lunch on the lawn with a couple healthy-looking young men and a bottle of wine. It was a different sort of message, don't you see?"

"But did the men have their clothes on?"

"Oh, of course. Otherwise it would be dirty. After all, this was supposed to represent some young French artists and their models having lunch."

"Running around nude on a lawn?"

"Lounging would be more like it."

"Well, I don't know art," Hank tossed in, "but I sure like frisky young women without their clothes on."

"Me, too," I agreed.

"And that was the point exactly."

About then the lady from the front desk came in with Julie's dinner—Jesus, it filled a whole damn corrugated carton—and so I paid for it and excused myself and took it back to our cabin. Julie was in her bathrobe, just drying her hair.

"Well, here you go," I said, trying to lay it all out on the little end table by the bed.

"Thank you."

"They didn't have any carrots, but I got you peas and corn."

"That's fine."

She sat down and started unwrapping the tinfoil and I was just kind of hovering there with my underwear on fire, dying to get back to all my racing friends at the bar.

"Are you having anything?"

"I think I'll just get a sandwich or something."

Julie looked up at me kind of sideways. "You're going to go back in there and get drunk with all your friends, aren't you?" It wasn't really a question the way she said it.

"Absolutely not!" I assured her, my eyebrows fairly jumping off my face.

She rolled her eyes.

"Well, y'wanna come *with?"* I asked her lamely.

She shook her head. Boy, she looked tired. "No, you go ahead. I'll get our things packed."

I started for the door.

"Just don't stay out real late and don't come home drunk. I hate it when you do that."

"I'm just gonna meet up with Spud and Sammy, that's all," I mumbled as I went through the door. "I'll only have a couple and then I'll be right back…."

Boy, did I ever feel married.

Back in the lodge I found Spud and Sammy at the far end of the bar with Cal and Carson and Tommy Edwards and Barry Spline. Tommy bought me a drink. In fact, he bought a round.

"You're celebrating pretty good for a guy who came second," Spud grinned.

"And why not? The right bloke won."

"It's nice to be able to afford that kind of attitude," Sammy said with just a little taste of a sneer in his voice. He couldn't believe the sportycar racers didn't run for prize money.

"So, how've you guys been?" I asked Spud.

"Well, we're doing better than we should with the equipment we've got…"

"And what does that mean?"

"It means we're eatin' beans and sleepin' in the damn truck most nights," Spud laughed.

We had another beer and made arrangements to meet in the morning for the caravan ride into Jersey and over to Roman Szymanski's shop in Brooklyn to get their block welded up. "Who's gonna be driving the lead car?"

"I guess I am," Cal said. "Big Ed and Rhonda already took off."

"They did?"

"Yeah. She said she'd had about enough roughing it for one weekend."

"Yeah," Cal snickered. "And Big Ed looked about worn out, too...you guys can probably use their room tonight if you want to." He shot Sammy a wink. "But I'd maybe turn the mattress over if I were you."

"And b-burn the sheets," Carson added.

"My God! Carson made a joke!"

Well, that certainly called for another round of drinks.

"Now I want you to take it easy on us tomorrow," Sammy told Cal. "That rig of ours is kinda old and it runs outta breath at sixty-five or so."

"Yeah," Spud added. "And I run out of nerve at about fifty."

"It doesn't tow real great?"

"Not with the engine out of the racecar and sitting in the back of the truck. I think we've got us a sort of negative tongue weight situation."

"Can't you roll it further forward?"

"Not without bashing in the grille."

"Those things cost money," Sammy said into his beer bottle.

We talked a little about this and that and I bought a round because I hadn't yet, and eventually we got around to the subject of Tommy Edwards and the Healey record runs at Bonneville and, naturally enough, to Carson's shiny new black Healey Hundred parked right outside. "Seems like a pretty odd sort of engine displacement, doesn't it?" Spud asked about the long stroke, 2660cc four in the new Healey model.

"I'll tell you the whole bleedin' story on that engine," Barry Spline announced grandly. "Got it right from the bleedin' guv'nor 'imself, Donald 'ealey. And may the Lord strike me dead if it ain't all exactly as I say it is."

We all leaned in a little closer.

"It's like this, gents. Back in the thirties, Austin penned themselves up this big, stout old six-cylinder motor for some great monster saloon or truck or whatever they had planned. Four bloody liters worth. And the really odd an' mysterious thing h'about it was that it bore an h'uncanny bloody resemblance to the six-cylinder Chevrolet engine you yanks were building over 'ere in the States."

"You mean the Stovebolt Six?"

Barry nodded. "Nut for bloody nut and bolt for bleedin' bolt." He drained the rest of his beer. "It was a bloody heist job, all right."

"Wow."

"So what happened?"

Barry Spline looked at the empty beer bottle in front of him. And pretty soon we got the message. Tommy ordered us another round.

"Well," Barry continued, kind of drawing us all in, "th' bloody depression was on and petrol was dear and old Hitler and Mussolini were already struttin' around and stirrin' the pot over h'across the channel in Europe, and there was also that bloody awful 'taxable 'orsepower' mess from the government to deal with. So h'it never got built."

"But you're talking about a six-cylinder engine. The Healey's a four."

"I'm gettin' t'that, mate. You'll see." Barry took a deep breath and dug into the rest of the story. "Well, then the bleedin' war came and none of the 'ome manufacturers were building much in the way of cars at all. It was all bloody tanks and trucks and military transports and such. And meanwhile of course the damn yanks came over—sorry, mate—and we 'ad American Jeeps running all h'over the bleedin' island. Like bloody ants they were."

"Military Jeeps?"

Barry nodded. "We 'ad Willys Jeeps and Ford Jeeps and Army Jeeps and Air Corps Jeeps in great bloody supply. Well," he continued after another gulp of beer, "comes war's end and the English pound is flat as a bleedin' kipper there's no cars t'be 'ad even if yer 'ad the bleedin' money, and pretty soon every mother's son on the island wants t'get 'is 'ands on one a'those leftover yank Jeeps." He looked around the group. "Yer gotta understand that there was 'ardly any steel or aluminum about ter make new cars out of and the h'econonmy's in such dire bloody straits that yer can only get 'old of that stuff if yer plannin' to h'export all the bleedin' cars yer build t'the colonies and get some of those nice, fat, sturdy American dollars in return."

"So what does all that have to do with the Healey Hundred?"

"I'm gettin' to it. I'm gettin' to it." He took another pull off his beer and it was time for another round. I got that one. "Well," he continued, "'round about then some of the engines in those lovely American Jeeps we 'ad running around all over the place—and mind yer, cars of h'any kind were still bloody 'ard to come by—started wearing out and needin' the odd repair. And you yanks raped us royal for the parts we needed t'keep 'em runnin'."

"We did?"

"Oh, I don't blame yer. H'it's business, that's all. If I need something an' yer've bloody got it—an' h'especially if I've got no other bloody place ter go for h'it—well, h'it's just my bad luck an' yer good fortune then, h'isn't it?" I could see how that notion had developed into a real cornerstone philosophy for Barry Spline and Colin St. John over at Westbridge.

"And what made matters worse was there was so little 'ome money on tap to go h'out and buy new Jeep parts and Jeep engines from you yanks. England needed to *sell* more things to you Americans, not *buy* bloody more."

"So what happened?"

"Well, the lads at Austin decided what England *really* needed was a new, 'ome-based, all-British replacement h'engine to stick in those sick American Jeeps. And they looked in the closet and 'ere was the prints and prototypes for this big bloody six that never got h'itself built, all ready t'go and nice as you please. So they up and hacked two cylinders h'out of the middle and 'ad the blokes over at Rolls-Royce tool up a bloody new crank for it—four-cylinder cranks are always the bleedin' easiest because they're all flat in one plane, see?—and that's where the motor in that new 'ealey 'undred came from. It's two bloody thirds of that four-liter six that Austin nicked off Chevrolet back in the thirties, but never got around t'building."

"So you're telling me it's really two-thirds of a Chevy Stovebolt Six and it started out as a replacement engine for Jeeps?"

"Trust me. It'll bolt right in."

"Boy," I said, "that's one heck of a story."

"Right it is," Barry agreed. "And h'it doesn't end there, either. Austin stuck that same bloody lump of iron in all bloody manner of trucks and taxicabs and milk floats and postal wagons and Lord only knows what else." He straightened up a bit. "A'course, for the bleedin' new 'ealey 'undred, they hung a pair of S.U.s and a rorty exhaust on it t'try and kid it into thinkin' it was a sports car engine. But it gets to thrashing pretty 'ard and running out of breath if you get h'it up any-wheres close to the redline."

"LAST CALL!"

"Jesus, what time is it?"

"If it's last call, it's got to be about one."

"Oh, jeez," I said, kind of sinking into my barstool. "I absolutely *promised* Julie I wasn't gonna do this."

"Might as well have one more before you go face her," Cal offered. He even bought, can you believe it? And brandy, too. Even if it was the cheap stuff.

Judging by the gash through my eyebrow, the gravel up my nostrils and the clods of grass in my teeth, I'd say I was maybe a wee bit unsteady as I made my way back to our cabin that night. In fact, I think I also had kind of a hard time finding it. But finally I did and I tried to be real careful and quiet and creep in on stocking-foot tiptoes so's I wouldn't wake Julie up. Although I maybe would've been better off if I hadn't knocked the chair and the bed table over. With the remains of her turkey dinner on it, too. But I guess Julie had decided that she was just going to lie there in a clenched-up little ball and pretend to be asleep rather than to waste her time getting mad at a moon-eyed drunk who was struggling mightily just to undress himself. And that's when it occurred to me—as the room swirled around and around and the events of the day wheeled past on the insides of my eyelids like newsreel footage of Macy's Easter Parade—that what I really needed was to take a leak and let some of the beer and gin-and-tonics and brandy and whatever else out of my system. And I knew just the place, too.

"MY GOD, PALUMBO!" Julie screamed from somewhere far off in the dis-tance behind me, *"WHAT ARE YOU DOING??!!!"*

"Don' worry, Honey," I told her from atop a pair of tall, rubbery legs, *"there'sh a trough over here, shee..."*

If you must know, I was peeing into our suitcase....

13: My Bright Ideas

Needless to say, the drive back to Jersey the following day was among the most silent in recorded human history. Or at least it was in the back seat of Big Ed's Cadillac, where Julie was pretty much making a life's work of looking out the side window. And one part of me—that would be the throbbing head and the tongue that had apparently been licking a dead goat all night—felt absolutely terrible and was happy to just leave it at that and wallow in its misery. But another part of me (which I expect is likely just some leftover altar boy/cub scout residue that stuck to the inside of my skull somewhere along the way) felt terribly guilty. And believe me, it's lousy when you're feeling terrible and terribly guilty all at the same time. Plus I had the other little guy—you know, the one with the horns and pitchfork and the protruding lower jaw—whispering in my cranium that she had no *right* to be mad at me. I mean, what did I do? Go out and pass a little time at the Seneca Bar with my racing buddies? Have a few laughs? Blow off a little steam? Get so stinking drunk that I peed in our suitcase?

That would be the one Julie'd just packed, too.

I mean, she had to understand the way things were on those racing nights in the bar. Why, I'd never been involved in anything so neat and special and interesting in my life. And I was *part* of it now, too. People like Tommy Edwards and Cal Carrington and Brooks Stevens and even Barry Spline and Colin St. John talked to me like they cared what I thought about things. And I sure cared what *they* thought about things. Besides, it was educational. Where else besides the Seneca Bar would a guy like me ever find out about that Cars as Art show at the Museum of Modern Art or where the engine in the Austin-Healey Hundred came from or that 'Lunch on the Grass' painting with the frisky naked ladies on it that caused such a stir at the *Salon de Refuses* in Paris back when Napoleon the Third was alive? And also how that had something or other to do with the non-SCMA race we'd just attended at Watkins Glen, although I couldn't exactly remember what. Anyhow, the trip home seemed to be taking an awfully long time—even with speed demon Cal at the wheel—on account of we had to go slow enough for Spud and Sammy's rig to keep up and it was pissing rain the whole time out of an ugly gray sky. Not to mention that silent rides always seem to take longer.

I found a copy of the previous Thursday's *New York Times* folded up under the front seat and, for lack of anything better to do, I started thumbing through it. I already knew there was a heavy fog on Wednesday that caused a bunch of chain-reaction accidents and fouled up traffic on the New Jersey Turnpike for hours. But I didn't know that a Dr. Ben E. Senturia had dropped an absolute bombshell at the annual meeting of the International College of Surgeons in St. Louis by claiming that ear wax was really an antiseptic. I mean, who would've guessed? And the crown prince of Japan (who the *Times* described as "a slim, grave-faced young man") was in town "to view a variety of America's wonders." Including a color TV set and the second game of a Yankees doubleheader. And next to that was a small piece about an eerie greenish glow that the U.S. Coast Guard had observed in the surf off the Rockaway Beach in Queens for the past few weeks. "Look at this," I chortled feebly. "Looks like maybe the Martians have finally landed."

Julie didn't even blink. And I know, because I was looking.

"Says here two Siamese twins are going to be separated."

I hoped they'd be the only ones.

"And that Army clerk Senator McCarthy said was '100% Red' got suspended. Even though her lawyer said she never even considered party membership. Says she had access to classified documents, too. About food shipments to Korea and Indo-China. Who knows what those communist reds might do with top-secret information like that!"

Not even a lip curl.

"6,500 people showed up to see that new Cinemascope movie, *The Robe*. Victor Mature's in it. Maybe we oughta go see it?"

I might as well have been talking to the Washington Monument.

We dropped Julie and our seriously aromatic suitcase off at the apartment under her mom's place so she could get cleaned up and take care of a few things while I navigated Spud and Sammy and their rig across Manhattan to Roman Szymanski's machine shop. I mean, there was no way Julie wanted to go over by Roman's shop with us and listen to another three or four (or five or six) hours of car-and-motor talk. And especially not with me. "I'll be back in a couple hours, Honey," I called up to her as she climbed the front steps.

"Suit yourself," she said without turning around.

Well, at least we were talking again.

Cal had taken off already to drop Mary Frances back at Frederick's studio in Greenwich Village in Big Ed's Eldorado, and he'd promised to come by Roman's shop to pick me up a little later and take me home on account of they might be there all night—and then some!—and I had to be at the Sinclair at seven sharp the next morning. To be honest, I kind of hated depending on Cal for my ride back to the duplex. I mean, it wasn't a question of whether he'd show up or not. No, it was more a question of *when*. And I was already in enough trouble at home, thank you very much. Before they left, Mary Frances made a point of coming over to Spud's and Sammy's truck and thanking me personally for inviting her on, to use her own words, "one of the dumbest, dullest, most boring and uncomfortable weekends I've ever enjoyed."

Remember what I said about how some people just don't get it when it comes to racing?

"It's just a bunch of spoiled rich kids showing off their toys..."

I couldn't very well argue with that.

"...and rich old men trying to pretend they're spoiled rich kids again..."

Or that either.

"...and they're all playing *dare/double dare* and risking their stupid lives as if...as if..."

"As if it meant something?"

Mary Frances glared at me. "Well it *doesn't!*" she snapped angrily. "I mean, how much dirt, dust, grease, grime, noise, lies and beer can a person *stand* in one lifetime?" To be honest, I couldn't understand what set her off. And then it dawned on me. She really didn't much fancy going back to Frederick's studio! No matter how dumb, dull, boring and uncomfortable her weekend at Watkins Glen had been, at least she was with a bunch of decent people and it was lively and fun and there was excitement and the scent of The Unexpected hanging in the air. I got the feeling that hanging around with an Out There artistic genius like Frederick could get a little lonely at times. Even when he was right there in the same blessed room with her.

"You take care of yourself, okay?" I told her. And that's when her eyes went all gooey on her and the anger crumbled right off her face.

"You stay in touch," she warned me softly, tears starting to well up in her eyes.

"Sure thing."

"And don't you dare miss Frederick's gallery opening," she swiped a knuckle across her cheek, "I'll have to kill you both if you don't show up."

"We'll be there," I promised her.

She looked down at me with a final little sniffle and smiled. And then I saw the tears starting up all over again. "I really enjoyed talking with Julie," she whispered, her voice all choked up with emotion.

"I'm glad."

"She's really a special kind of girl."

"I know."

"You better treat her right," she warned sweetly.

"I know that, too."

"You'd better!" She sniffed. Then she rubbed her eyes one more time, straightened up her spine, took a deep breath, and headed back over to where Cal was waiting across the street in Big Ed's Cadillac. He had the radio on, and—wouldn't you know it—I could hear they had that sad, sappy Les Paul and Mary Ford hit *Vaya Con Dios* playing.

"You got somthin' in your eye, kid?" Spud asked as they pulled away.

"Nah," I told him. "It's nothing."

And, after maybe five or ten minutes, it was.

We stopped by the Sinclair to pick up that damn stolen manhole cover of Frederick's that I'd promised to take over to Roman's shop to have whittled down the way he wanted—it wasn't the easiest thing in the world to try to explain to Spud and Sammy—and then I passed the time on our way over to Brooklyn showing them the sights and kind of thinking out loud about building my own racecar. "I mean, it wouldn't be so hard to do…" was I believe the way I started in. "Big Ed's got enough scrap hardware lying around from all the cars he's run through to just about do the trick. He's got the frame and suspension off that crumpled-up Jag 120 that fell off the back of our tow truck in the middle of the George Washington Bridge—the motor's blown and it looks like hell, but I think the chassis' fine—and he's got a nice, low-mileage Caddy V8 engine inside that crushed-and-pulverized '52 convert that some pissed-off employee dumped a load of farm-route garbage all over and then he had one of his other guys push it all around his scrapyard with a bulldozer just to make absolutely sure the insurance company would total it…."

"He's quite an operator, isn't he?" Spud observed.

"He's a Jersey guy," I shrugged. "He only wants what's fair."

Spud shot a sideways glance over at Sammy. "That's exactly the kind of guy we need for a team owner, Sam. By the time he got done, we might actually *make* money doing this."

I'd actually thought of that myself. I mean, no question the best racetrack duty for a guy with Big Ed's talents was team owner. In fact, that applied to more than a few of the drivers I'd seen in the SCMA. Starting with that crazy asshole idiot Skippy Welcher. But that wasn't something you could just blurt out and *tell* any of them. And especially a guy like Big Ed Baumstein. At least not if you wanted to stay friends with him, anyway.

"You think it'd be hard t'build my own car?" I asked Spud.

"Well," he said, kind of clearing his throat, "I suppose I've got as much experience as anybody when it comes t'fooling around with racecars. Let's see if I can muster up a little sage advice for you."

I was all ears.

"First off, doing it yourself from the ground up is always ten times harder than working on something somebody else built."

"But why should that be?"

"Because you come to find out that you're not so damn smart after all."

"But I've already got the frame and the engine and..."

"You also," he cut me off, "find out that it takes ten times as long and costs ten times as much as you ever imagined."

"Always?"

"Always." And he said it like there weren't any loopholes, either.

But of course the thing about enthusiasm is that it's like a pot boiling over on the stove, and so long as there's stuff in the pot and flame coming off the burner, it's just gonna keep on boiling over. "Let's just say I wanted to try it anyway. How do I do it? Where do I start?"

Spud looked over at me and smiled. "Well, there's basically two ways to build a racecar." He held up one finger. "The first is the design-and-engineering method."

"How does that work?"

"You lay everything out on paper and try to noodle it out in your head first, checking and measuring every component you've got—twice!—and pretty soon you have this big, impressive stack of drawings and plans and notes and charts all over the workbench next to the same useless pile of junk you started out with."

"Why's that?"

"Because the paperwork never seems to come out quite the same in the metal. Or at least not the first time, anyway. Like you leave plenty of space for a nice, big radiator, but it turns out you've got a damn frame channel right in front of the water outlet, so you can't get the hose on it. Or the carbs fit perfectly, but there's no room for the damn linkage. Or you can't get the exhaust headers to find their way around the steering box. Or the springs you figured would work just perfect either have the bellypan dragging on the ground or the whole car is jacked up three feet in the air. Like it's on stilts."

"But you can fix all that stuff."

"Oh, sure you can. Easy as pie. Why, all it ever takes is just a little more time and money. And then a little more time and money after that. And then a little more..." he looked over at me and winked. "You get the idea."

That didn't sound like a very good way to go. Especially since I was never much good at drawing out plans. Even for simple stuff like Christmas sleigh table centerpieces or horse head bookends in cub scouts. "What's the second method?"

"Why, it's the old 'whoosh-bonk' approach."

"How does that work?"

"Well, you just wheel out your chassis—*whoooosh!*—and simply drop that old engine and driveline right down the middle—*bonk!*—and then just hit the old starter button and drive her away. Just like that!"

"That sounds a lot simpler. How well does it work?"

"About the same. You still run up against all this stuff that doesn't fit or doesn't work or won't line up because the hole's a sixteenth off where you thought it would be or you've got two male fittings or two female fittings trying to go together instead of a matched male-and-female set or you've got ¼-twenty coarse when what you really want is a machine screw thread or you've got S.A.E. when what you really need is pipe thread…believe me, it never ends."

"But you didn't answer my question. Which way is best?"

Spud reached over and put a fatherly hand on my shoulder. "Neither."

He sounded like he knew what he was talking about, too.

We got to Roman's shop about quarter-after-five and he was right there at the back door, waiting for us, looking kind of like a pale Humpty Dumpty doll with a thinning patch of reddish-brown hair on top and his usual wire-rimmed bifocals with the flip-down magnifying lenses for close inspection work. I introduced him to Spud and Sammy, and he'd apparently heard of them both. Not that Roman was the sort to make a big fuss over it. "You have engine block?" he asked.

"Yep," Spud said proudly. "All stripped down, scrubbed clean and rarin' to go." He took the tarp off the pickup bed, flopped down the rear panel and there was the naked block of that big, hefty, 220-cubic-inch Meyer-Drake four-banger all wrapped up in swaddling clothes. It was really pretty light—especially considering it was cast iron and all—but bulky as hell on account of the head and block were all cast up in one piece the way Meyer-Drake did things. "Makes it tough doing a valve job," Spud allowed as we hefted it inside. "Like building a damn ship in a bottle…" he grunted as we lifted it onto Roman's steel-topped work table "…but at least you never hafta worry about head gaskets."

"Is very good design," Roman smiled approvingly as he unwrapped the engine. "Same like Offenhauser and Miller American engines and even French Peugeot long time before. Very good for…" he stopped, searched for words, and then made a little oval in the air with his finger.

"It's not just the *best* damn mousetrap," Spud nodded. "It's the *only* damn mousetrap."

But a dark scowl spread across Roman's face as he continued to unwrap the engine. He looked at Spud, then back at Sammy, and back at Spud again. "This you call *clean?*" he asked incredulously. Neither of them answered. Roman ran his finger around the inside of one of the cylinder bores and held it up so we could all see the tiny gray smudge on the tip. "Would your mother call this clean?" he asked Spud and Sammy. "Your grandmother, maybe?" He shook his head, sighed heavily, and had me grab the other end so's we could move it over to the middle parts-cleaning tank. Roman had no less than three parts-cleaning tanks. The first one he called "Mine Sewer," because that's where all the really ugly degreasing and de-gumming took place. The middle one he called "Good Enough," because the parts that came out of it were good enough to at least look at. And the third he called "Bridgeport Clean" after his favorite American machine tool, the Bridgeport Mill. He'd finally picked one up surplus (and in excellent condition) from a Navy shipfitting outfit that was going into mothballs up in Maine, and it was by far the newest piece of equipment in the shop. All the rest of it was tough old German stuff from before the war. "Old German machine is maybe better," he'd whisper so the machines couldn't hear him, "but I rather work American machine." I guess he barely made it out of Poland with the shirt on his back in 1938, and his folks didn't make it out at all.

"Here," he said to Spud and Sammy like they were little kids who had to clean their mess up, and handed them each a wire-handled bristle brush. "When is done *here,*" he pointed to the middle tank, "you call me. If is *right...*" he nodded towards the third parts-cleaning tank, "maybe I let you go here." He turned and shot me a wink where Spud and Sammy couldn't see it. "And you come with me outside."

I started to say 'no,' on account of I figured I really ought to stay and help Spud and Sammy, but Roman shook his head. "Is *good* for them," he whispered in my ear, and then chuckled all the way as he led me out into the alley in back. It was right around six on Sunday evening with the last painted colors of the sunset visible over the Manhattan skyline behind us and a brisk September chill in the air, and you could smell corned beef and cabbage with carrots and potatoes cooking someplace nearby and hear some kids chasing each other up and down the wooden back stairway of a three-flat where a radio was playing the new Dean Martin hit record *That's Amore:*

> *"Whennnnnn thaaa...*
> *moon hits your eye*
> *like a bigga pizza pie*
> *that's a-morayyy...."*

Dean crooned. And the chorus answered him right back: *"That's a-morayyy"*
It was a heck of a song, you know?
"So, you are okay?" Roman asked.
"Yeah," I told him. "Sure."
"Married life is good?"
"Yeah. Mostly."
"Mostly is still good," he nodded, and I watched the corners of his mouth curl up an eighth of an inch or so. That amounted to a knee-slapping belly laugh for a serious-faced guy like Roman Szymanski.

> *"Whennnnn thaaa...*
> *stars seem to shine*
> *like you've had too much wine*
> *that's a-morayyy"*

Dean crooned some more. And the chorus answered back: *"That's a-morayyy"*
I was thinking about Julie, you know? I mean, I'd been kind of a jerk to her. In fact, come to think of it, there was no "kind of" about it. Not hardly. After all, she was my wife now and she was walking around with my kid—*MY KID!!! JESUSCHRISTALMIGHTY!!!*—in her belly and here I was running around doing car stuff on a Sunday night—and not even *customer* car stuff, just "favor for a friend" car stuff!—after we'd already spent the whole damn weekend doing car

stuff up at Watkins Glen and I'd be off to do more car stuff at the shop first thing the following morning. A towering, fourteen-foot tidal wave of guilt poured and pounded over me and I was almost sucked away by the undertow. It made me want more than anything to be back at the duplex with Julie, bringing her a glass of wine or a nice, hot cup of coffee and maybe even giving her a back rub or a foot massage while that same exact Dean Martin song played on the radio:

"S'cusa me
but you see
back in old Napoli
that's amore!"

But of course I had to wait for Cal and Big Ed's Caddy first. Which might take some time, seeing as how he was only fifteen minutes late. So I told Roman my idea about building a racing special out of the chassis from Big Ed's wrecked Jaguar and the engine out of his smashed-to-shit Cadillac. "You think I could do it?" I asked Roman.

He shrugged. "If you *want* to, you can do. No problem." But then he looked me in the eye and asked: "But why want to?"

"I dunno. It's like this itch I have."

"Is huge big job," he warned.

"I know."

"Much work. Much detail. Much make parts. Much money."

"I don't think we'd have too much in the 'much money' department."

Roman curled his lip and thought for a moment. "Maybe I help you a little anyway," he said slowly, like he had to drag each syllable out of himself. "But only when time is free," he added quickly. "Not to interfere with pay work."

"Deal," I said. And we shook on it.

And that's the amazing thing about youth and enthusiasm: it just doesn't know any better. And that can be worth an awful lot when it comes to picking out impossible projects for yourself. Especially when you're trying to run a gas station/auto repair business for somebody who's rarely around anymore and still fairly freshly married and you're moreover expecting your first kid. But the Boy Racer side of your brain can know all that stuff and even nod its head like it's paying attention to every single one, and yet just go on dreaming and scheming and making crazy, wild-assed racing plans....

It's a sickness, if you want the truth of it.

"Oh," I suddenly remembered. "I've got something else out in the truck for you."

I led him over and showed him the cast iron manhole cover and the chalk marks and scrawled notes on it showing exactly where and how Frederick wanted it cut and finished. To my surprise, Roman didn't even once ask why or what it was for. It was just another job as far as he was concerned. All a machinist like Roman needed to know was how you wanted it.

It was already well past seven when we rolled Frederick's manhole cover into the shop, and so I decided to just go back outside and wait for Cal to come and take me home. And then I waited some more. And the longer I waited, the madder I got—I mean, all he had to do was drop my sister off in Greenwich Village and shoot across the damn bridge into Brooklyn!—and the more I started wondering just why the hell I wanted to bust my hump sweating and begging and bleeding together a damn racecar just to give my spoiled, thoughtless, don't-care-a-damn-about-anybody-else jerk of a Rich Kid friend Cal Carrington a chance to make a name for himself? Only pretty soon it'd been so long and gotten so late that I started to get genuinely worried. Like maybe something terrible had happened? And I started to have visions of Big Ed's Cadillac crushed under a semi-trailer on the Riverside Parkway or—worse yet—cruising through Harlem with one of the dangerous street sharks from Sylvester Jones' favorite crap game at the wheel. And neither Cal or my sister Mary Frances anywhere to be seen! Only then I'd catch hold of myself, remember it was Cal Carrington I was thinking about, and get mad all over again.

Meanwhile Spud and Sammy and Roman were hard at work in the shop, vee-ing out the crack in the block with a grinding wheel and making a heavy steel fixture to bolt the block to so's it wouldn't twist or warp when Roman welded it. I was thinking maybe I ought to call Julie. Only what was I gonna say, you know? *"Hello, dear, I'm over in Brooklyn screwing around with car stuff again and the only reason I'm not right there by your side is that my very best car buddy—you remember, he was Best Man at our wedding!—has kind of left me stranded and, no, I don't know exactly when, or if, he's ever coming back. But I'll see you soon, okay?"* And right about then is when Cal and Big Ed's Eldorado squealed around the corner and swung over to the curb in front of me. Right around ten PM, can you believe it?

Turns out my friend Cal had decided to drop by that Scalabrini's Italian Restaurant in Brooklyn for a little dinner. All by his lonesome, right? And just because it belonged to the father of the beautiful Angelina Scalabrini that he'd met at the New Years' Eve party at the apartment my sister Mary Frances shared with a couple other girls (not to mention that great asshole intellect Ollie Cromwell) in Greenwich Village. I knew Cal and Angelina had gone out a few times, but then she and her mother pretty much dropped off the face of the earth. At least as far as New York was concerned, anyway. I guess he'd tried to get in touch with her once or twice, but the trail went dead cold at the foot of the Brooklyn Bridge and her father was no help at all. Even when Cal went into the restaurant like he did that night and spread some of his parents' money around to try and get some information. "She's a-no here..." her father told Cal in the most agreeable voice imaginable, "...an' I'm a-no have any idea where she might-a be. You wanna soup with that?"

"Geez, you could've at least called!" I snarled at Cal as I climbed into Big Ed's Caddy.

"I didn't have any nickels or dimes left."

"You had enough to buy yourself a damn spaghetti dinner."

"That's why I didn't have any nickels or dimes left...I left a nice tip."

"Jesus!" I fumed. "You're a damn deadbeat!" No question Julie was gonna be furious at me all over again! And she had every right to be, too! *Dammit!*

We drove across the Brooklyn Bridge in a dead, stony silence. And then, about halfway through Manhattan, Cal looked over at me again with these sad, apologetic, Bassett-hound eyes. "Buddy?" he asked in contrite, humble tones.

"Yes?"

"Have you got any gas money on you?"

14: Things Change

Fortunately for Cal's perfectly-shaped nose, I had a dollar and some loose change left in my pocket and so we stopped for gas at the station right at the entrance ramp for the George Washington Bridge. I always hated stopping there because they had the most expensive damn gasoline on the entire Eastern Seaboard. Hell, they knew you'd never stop there and pay New York prices unless there was no way you'd ever make it over to the Jersey side without putting a little something in the tank. Plus they were open twenty-four hours, so you had to pay through the nose for that, too. But I held back a few coins so I could call Julie from the pay phone and tell her I was on the way. "I'm just on the way home," I said into the receiver.

"Okay," she said without any emotion at all in her voice. I couldn't believe how far away she sounded.

"I didn't want you to worry."

"Why would I worry?" She sounded like maybe she'd been crying.

"Well, I just thought…"

—click!—

Jesus, I felt miserable. "I wish I had some flowers or something to take home," I said to no one in particular.

"I can do that for you!" Cal beamed as he gunned the Caddy out of the station.

"But it's late, Cal. Nothing's open. And I spent my last money on gas."

"No problem!" he grinned. And I knew right away we were off on another crazy and dangerous Cal Carrington adventure. Sure enough, he took us on a little detour over by Carson Flegley's family's funeral parlor in East Orange on the way home. "You wait here," Cal whispered, raising his finger across his lips. "And, whatever you do, don't turn the lights on or play the damn radio. And if the cops come by, get your head down!" And with that he closed the door gently and disappeared off into the darkness.

Well, I honestly don't know which is worse, going along with the perpetrator when he actually does the crime or waiting out by your helpless lonesome in the getaway car, wondering what you'll do if you're suddenly surrounded by patrol cars and frozen in a crossfire of police spotlights. Believe me, I was nervous as hell and even thinking about maybe taking off and just leaving him there. Hell, it'd serve him right! Only he'd apparently already thought of that and so he took the keys with him. *Damn!* I couldn't read the clock on the dash and I was afraid to turn the interior light on to see, but the one in the window of the rug and tile company across the street looked to be around straight-up midnight. Only it didn't seem to be moving, you know? But I sure moved when I heard the crash and tinkle of breaking glass. In fact, I damn near punched a hole the size of my head in Big Ed's convertible top. But just as quickly it went quiet again and all I could do was sit there helplessly and wait. And maybe sweat a little bit, too….

And then there he was, sneaking out of the bushes all crouched over like an Indian brave with this enormous heap of dark red roses gathered against his chest. "I think I tore my damn pants climbing through the basement window," he whispered as he tossed the flowers in the back and slipped into the driver's seat.

"Did you steal those?"

"No. I paid for them at the cash register on the way out."

"Oh, God," I moaned. "I don't even want to know where you got them."

"No, you don't. But believe me, the people I got 'em from won't miss them at all."

"Jesus, Cal..."

"Hey! You needed flowers? I *got* you flowers! And I didn't take them out of any of the arrangements, either. Nobody'll ever be the wiser."

"But if they didn't come out of the flower arrangements, where'd they come from?"

"Out of the caskets, of course. Sometimes they stuff a whole bunch of 'em down in the caskets with the bodies. All around 'em. I just took a couple out of each one. Just one or two. Nobody'll ever know. Besides, Carson's our friend. He'd *want* you to have the flowers!"

"Oh Jesus, Mary and Joseph!"

"We were just lucky they had so many stiffs on deck to be planted tomorrow."

That was the thing about my friend Cal Carrington. No matter the situation, he could always find something to be thankful for....

We got back to the duplex around twelve-thirty, and all the lights were out in our apartment except for this faint, flickering glow from the back bedroom window. I'd never seen anything like it at our place before, and it made me go all strange and hollow inside.

"Think I can come in and flop on a couch or something?" Cal asked.

I knew that this was neither the time or place for an extra set of eyes and ears in our apartment. And especially not Cal Carrington's.

"Not if you had two broken legs and a sucking chest wound," I told him.

"But I can't go home. Jesus, my folks're home, and they'll be waiting for me with torches and pitchforks."

I guess maybe Cal had made a quick run through the family pockets and purses before heading off for Watkins Glen.

"I don't care if they draw and quarter you. You can't stay here. Not tonight." I started gathering up the flowers out of the back seat, and I could feel Cal's eyes on me. "Look, why don't you go over to the apartment over my Aunt Rosamarina's garage? You can stay there."

"I can?"

"Sure. Just remember to park on the next street and sneak in from the neighbor's yard in back. And keep it quiet. If she hears you, she'll call the cops for sure."

"How do I get in?"

"There should be a key over the door."

"But what if there isn't?"

"You can shinny up the tree and go in through the window."

He could see that it was a perfect Cal Carrington sort of caper.

"Hey, thanks."

"Just remember to keep it quiet, okay?"

"Sure thing."

"And have Big Ed's Caddy over to the station before eight. I need you to wash it and clean it up for him before he gets there."

"I've gotta wash the car?" he asked incredulously.

There was only one Cal Carrington. That was a fact.

Our apartment was all dark inside and, as I tiptoed down the hall with Cal's stolen bunch of memorial roses cradled in my arms, I could see that the weak, flickering glow I'd noticed in the window was a sad little votive candle that Julie had set on the floor by the bed. It made for strange, unworldly shapes and shadows. She was laying in a heap on the edge of the bed, staring down at the flame, and in that light her body looked like the carcass of some poor, dead animal like you see by the side of the road. I could tell by the little wads of Kleenex all around the candle that she'd been crying. Jesus, it just tore my heart out. I felt Cal's roses slip out of my arms and heard them softly scatter across the floor—it was like everything was happening in slow motion, you know?—as I eased my way over to the bed and sat down next to her.

"I'm so sorry..." I started in.

"You don't have to be sorry," she said in a voice as dead as yesterday. I'd never really seen her like this before. She was just all empty inside. Cried out. Hollow. Nothing left. Jeez, I couldn't have felt worse if I'd slugged her in the mouth.

"Oh, God," I groaned miserably. "I feel like such a...such a..."

"Jerk?" There was just the faintest little flutter of a laugh in it.

"Jerk doesn't even cover it, Julie. I've just been so...so..."

"Thoughtless?"

"Boy, that's the word for it. And I've acted like such a damn...such a damn..."

"Inconsiderate asshole?" I could feel her perking up a little. Thank God for that!

"It's just I get so damn, ah..."

"Obsessed?"

"Yeah, I guess. I just get around racing stuff and I, uhh, just..."

"Forget everything else?"

I started to say something, but there just wasn't anything left to say. She knew me. She had me dead to rights. She understood it all. "Yeah," I agreed, letting out a heavy sigh, "that's it."

I'd been expecting, well, an argument or something. Maybe even a screaming match. Maybe even flying china and cutlery. But not this. She kind of scrunched around on the bed so her head was resting on my thigh and I put my hand on her head and stroked her hair. Even all drawn and tired and cried out like that, she looked beautiful in the candlelight. Sad, but beautiful. "You really look beautiful in the candlelight," I told her.

"Oh, right," she scoffed quietly.

"No. You really do."

She gave a little sniffle. I let my eyes follow down to her middle. You could see it for sure now. The little bulge that was more than a tummy.

"I really need you to be with me now," she said in a faraway voice as her eyes followed the dance of the flame.

"I know."

"I just feel so all alone."

"I know." I leaned over and kissed the top of her head and the smell of her hair filled my nostrils. "The season's over. I'm done with it. It's just you and me now."

She rolled her head up and looked at me with two very skeptical eyes. "Don't bullshit yourself, Buddy," she smiled. "Face it. You're an addict."

And that's the thing about being married. If it's any good at all, they know you better than you ever know yourself. And that's a comforting kind of thing to realize, even if it is a little scary. In any case, we slept really well that night, just kind of wrapped up into each other with that little votive candle flickering on the floor beside us and casting the shadows of children's dreams and nightmares all over the walls and ceiling....

In the morning when I got up to go to work, I noticed a folded card and envelope made out of fancy, embossed linen paper sitting on the bedstand next to us. "What's that?" I asked.

"Oh," Julie said dreamily, "that's an invitation to the opening of Frederick's one-man show at that gallery over in Manhattan."

I couldn't think of anyplace I'd rather not be.

"It looks really interesting," Julie continued. "It's supposed to be one of the most *avant garde* galleries in Manhattan. I've read about it in the paper a few times."

I picked up the card and stared at it. It was kind of like a wedding invitation, only it used this really artsy typeface where all the letters were upper case and like they belonged carved over the doorway of a mausoleum or something. It read:

THE PENDLETON-CARRINGTON GALLERIES
TAKE EXTREME PRIDE
IN PRESENTING A PREMIERE ONE-MAN SHOW

FROM NOVEMBER 1ST THROUGH NOVEMBER 30TH, 1953

THE PAINTINGS, SCULPTURES, AND MIXED-MEDIA CONSTRUCTS

OF

FREDERICK FRUMPT

YOU ARE CORDIALLY INVITED TO ATTEND THE GALA OPENING

ON SATURDAY, OCTOBER 31ST, FROM 7 TO 10PM

DRESS ACCORDINGLY - RSVP PLEASE

Well, it took less than a heartbeat to recognize the two gallery owners' names at the top of the invitation, and not two seconds more to realize that was the same night as Carson Flegley's now-to-be-annual racer's Halloween bash over at the funeral home in East Orange. The same one where I'd asked Julie to marry me in the darkness inside that oversized, lardbucket-edition casket on the coffin show-room floor. "But honey..." I started in. But I caught myself.

"What?"

"Nothing. I was just wondering what you wear to one of these things?"

"You've got that nice blue suit I bought you for Christmas."

"Oh. Yeah. And what will you wear? It says 'dress accordingly.'"

"I'll have to get something I guess. I mean," she looked down at her stomach, "even if I had something, it wouldn't fit me now."

Boy, I was dying to say something about Carson's party. But I bit my tongue. For once.

"You ever heard of the Pendleton-Carrington Art Gallery over in Manhattan?" I asked Cal when he showed up to wash Big Ed's Cadillac around 10:30 the next morning.

"How'd you ever hear of it?"

"We got an invitation to an opening there."

"You *did?*" He looked genuinely shocked.

"Yeah. It's Mary Frances' new boyfriend. Or whatever you want to call him. He's some kind of Out There artist and they sent us an invitation to the opening."

Cal rolled his eyes. "Oh, brother."

"So is this Carrington guy any relation of yours?"

Cal let out a sigh. "Yeah. He's my oldest brother."

"I never heard you talk about him."

"Well, we make a big point of not talking about him. He's really just my half-brother. From my dad's first marriage."

"Gee, I didn't know your dad was married before."

"We don't talk about that much, either."

"What happened? Divorce?"

"No."

"Then what?"

"She fell out of a window." Cal made a little high-dive arc with his finger and let it fall —*splat!*—against the fender of Big Ed's Caddy. "Forty-second story. Right on Park Avenue." He looked me in the eye. "Most everybody thinks she jumped."

"That's awful. Geez, I'm sorry."

"Hey," Cal shrugged, *"I* never knew her. It all happened long before I was born." He leaned in closer and whispered. "From what I hear, she was supposed to be nutty as a fruitcake anyway." He made a screwy-in-the-head motion with his finger.

"Then what about your brother?"

"L.C.?"

"Elsie? Like in 'Elsie the cow?'"

"No, but that might work." Cal looked down at the floor. "See, he's kind of a fruitcake himself..."

"I don't get it."

Cal made a little mincing move and struck a dramatic, toppling-over-backwards pose like a fashion model.

"Oh, I get it." That explained why they didn't talk about him much. "So what does L.C. stand for, anyway?"

"You're not gonna believe it."

"Try me."

"It's for Lochinvar Charlemagne..."

"Lochinvar Charlemagne?"

"Yeah. I guess she was quite the reader."

"Boy, you gotta hate kids t'do something like that."

"Well, I mean, it's not *all* bad. Lochinvar was this great, brave knight from a Sir Walter Scott poem and Charlemagne—you've heard of him, haven't you?"

The name did ring a bell. But not a very large or loud one. "Wasn't he the guy from that *Knights of the Round Table?*" I'd taken Julie to see that movie with Robert Taylor, Ava Gardner and Mel Ferrer, and I kind of thought one of them might have been Charlemagne. Only not Ava Gardner, of course.

"You're only off by a couple hundred years, a country and a language."

I was pretty proud of myself anyway. "Okay, smartypants. So who was he?"

"Now I only know this because I looked it up once," Cal kind of half-apologized, "but Charlemagne was the King of the Franks..."

"You mean hot dogs?"

"No. It was this big tribe or country or something over in Europe."

"Still, it seems strange to name a country after a sandwich."

Cal rolled his eyes. "Anyhow, he kind of got in cahoots with the Pope down in Rome and became emperor of the Holy Roman Empire."

"The Pope, huh?" You had to be impressed with anybody doing business directly with the Pope. Everybody in our neighborhood says that's not an easy thing to do. "So how'd his mother come to name your brother Charlemagne?"

"I guess she'd been reading something called the *Song of Roland.* It's an epic poem."

"What's an epic poem?"

"I dunno. I guess it's a poem that's too damn long to read."

"Did you ever read it?"

"I said I looked it up once. I never said I made a life's study out of it."

"Lochinvar Charlemagne Carrington...wow," I said, letting out a low whistle. I mean, it didn't exactly roll right off the tongue. "So how'd he get hooked up with Creighton Pendleton?"

"It's not Creighton. It's his cousin, Eric." Cal made another little mincing move with his feet. "I mean, they're not bad guys or anything, just..."

"I get it."

Cal went back to washing Big Ed's whitewalls. To be honest, he did such a lousy job of it that it made you want to snatch the bucket and brush right out of his hands. But of course that was the whole idea.

"So how'd they wind up, uhh, together?"

"How should I know? L.C. had some of his own money from his mom's family and he couldn't wait to get out of the house once my dad decided to remarry. I think he lived with an aunt or something for a while and then took his own apartment over in Manhattan. I've been there once or twice. It's pretty nice, but..."

"But what?"

"I dunno. I just don't feel real comfortable there."

"So you never see him?"

"Not much. Oh, he's over around Christmas and like that every once in awhile—you know, somebody like my mom or sister makes a phone call and invites him—but he always wants to bring Eric, and that makes my dad drink even more than usual. That goes for my mom, too, come to think of it." Cal shot me a big, cheery smile. "In fact, I kind of envy how embarrassed and upset he makes them."

"You're one hell of a kid, you know that?"

"Look. That's just the way it is in the land of long driveways. You push 'em out of the nest as fast as you can. Or, if they insist on hanging around, then *you* take off and go to Paris or London or Bermuda or Palm Beach or wherever and leave 'em alone with some hired maid and the keys to the liquor cabinet."

"That's really kind of sad."

"Hey, it's no big deal. Someday my folks'll kick off and I'll have the life of Riley. At least if I don't manage to get myself disinherited first."

Money or not, it still didn't sound like the rosiest of futures. Not hardly.

A couple evenings later, on Thursday the 24th, heavyweight champ Rocky Marciano made headlines again by knocking some poor stiff—I mean "the challenger"—clear through the ropes and then proceeding to beat him senseless when he had the questionable judgment to climb back into the ring again. And I remember it so well on account of that was the headline on the sports page sitting face up on the counter by the cash register the next morning when Old Man Finzio called me into the office to have a word with him. That was kind of unusual, since he didn't hardly speak to anybody any more unless it was to argue or complain or cuss them out about something. And even then, he didn't have much energy for it. Even though I'd seen him around the station a lot over the past several months, this was the first time in ages that I'd really taken a good, solid look at him. And it was pretty scary. He was sitting behind the counter with the newspaper spread out in front of him and Tater's old hound dog Barney sitting next to him, head stretched out over his thigh so the Old Man could scratch him behind the ears. Barney'd sit there for hours like that if the Old Man would let him. Anyhow, it was kind of a shock to see how Old Man Finzio's cheeks and eyes had sunken way in and it was almost like you could see contours of his skull coming right through the skin. And his complexion had gone all sallow on him. Like spilled candle wax or something. Except for these two reddish smudges like cheap rouge underneath his cheekbones. But the worst part of it was his eyes. They were staring out the window towards Pine Street, but it was like they didn't have any sight left any more. Like nothing was registering....

"What's up?" I asked.

"The Doc says I gotta go inta th'hospital," he said without looking at me.

I felt a gust of cold wind go through my guts. "What for?"

His bony shoulders gave a faint, quarter-inch shrug. "He says they gotta cut." *Oh, Jesus!* "When?"

"He says I gotta go in next week." His voice was just a dull, hollow monotone. Like he was dead already, you know?

"Well, don't worry about the station," I started in. "I'll be sure..."

Old Man Finzio shut me up with a feeble wave of his hand. "You think you might do me a favor?" he asked hoarsely. In all the time I'd known him, he'd never asked me or anybody else for anything. Not once. Not ever.

"Sure," I told him. "Anything you want."

"Talk to that Jew Baumstein fr'me. See if he'd maybe like t'buy out my stake." He was still staring out the window without seeing anything, and I swear I thought I saw tears starting to well up in his eyes. In Old Man Finzio's eyes, can you believe it?

"Sure I will," I kind of gulped. "And, if there's anything else…I mean, if there's anything I…if you…"

His head snapped around and suddenly his eyes were focused on me like gunsights, all full of their old fire and venom. *"I don't need nothin' else!"* he snarled. "Now git back t'work, dammit. I can just see what's gonna happen t'this place when I'm in th'damn hospital getting' my damn guts ripped open…."

To be honest, I never knew exactly what kind of deal Old Man Finzio had with Big Ed. I knew they'd had lunch that one time and afterwards Big Ed sent that irritating little Jewish lawyer around with some papers—including an employment contract for me—and then those tough Italian friends of Big Ed's from Graziano Construction showed up and knocked back the wall and built us two more service bays and put in a second hydraulic lift. After that, I was never exactly sure who owned what—or what part of what—at the station. But I did have a talk with Big Ed the next time he dropped in and he said, sure, he'd go see Old Man Finzio and get things ironed out. "You're gonna be runnin' this place for real now," Big Ed said cautiously. "And believe me, runnin' a business is one big, never-ending pain in the ass." He was looking at me in a very serious way. "You're gonna hafta learn how t'*manage*, see? An' that's the biggest ass-pain of all. It ain't enough t'know how to do yer own job. Nah, that's the *easy* part. Y'gotta learn how t'coax an' threaten an' nursemaid all these other people. And not *one* of 'em will ever do things th'way you would or th'way you want 'em to. People just don't *care*, see? They'll show up late or drunk or sometimes they won't show up at all! They'll cut corners and sneak stuff out the back door and tell you they've done stuff when they really haven't. And if you ever find a good one that you really, *really* trust…nine times out of ten they'll either quit an' go inta business against you or steal you blind…"

He wasn't exactly making it sound attractive.

"…and there's nobody else t'turn to, see? It's *you* who's gotta point th'way and crack the whip and fire all the lazy jerks who can't cut it and deal with all the friggin' mooches and deadbeats." He looked me square in the eye. "Think you're up to it?"

"S-sure I am," I told him, my voice cracking just a little. And I was pretty sure I could, too. Just as long as I had Julie there to back me up. Or stand behind, as the case might be.

"Well, for whatever it's worth, I think y'can, too, Buddy." He put his hand on my shoulder. "In fact, I'd bet money on it."

"You are betting money on it," I reminded him.

"Don't remind me."

And then he gave me this really nice smile. In fact, it was the nicest, warmest, most sincere sort of smile I'd ever seen out of Big Ed Baumstein. Kind of like he was proud of me, you know? "Good luck, kid," he said, and he stuck out his hand

and we shook on it. "You just do what you think is right and always keep one eye on th'money and you'll do just fine." Then he turned and started to lower himself back into his Corvette.

"Uh, t-there's, uhh, one other thing..." I kind of half-mumbled.

"What's that?"

"Well, I kind of had this idea, see?" I licked my lips. "About how I could maybe build a race car...."

"*Build* a race car?"

"Yeah. Like some of those 'specials' we've seen at the races. Like the one that just won up at Watkins Glen?"

Big Ed looked kind of interested. Or at least curious.

"See, I was thinking..." I crouched down a little so we were eyeball to eyeball, "...you've got this wrecked Jaguar 120 back here with a blown engine that the insurance company's already settled on—I mean, the engine's blown and the body's all beat to shit, but I think the chassis's just about perfect..."

"So?"

"...and you've still got that crushed-up '52 Caddy convert over at one of your scrapyards..."

"Don't remind me."

"...and I don't think the engine had more than six or seven thousand miles on it..."

"Six thousand, two hundred and fifty eight."

"...and I think that original Caddy engine out of Tommy Edwards' Allard is still up against the shop wall at Westbridge someplace with that four-carburetor manifold and the hot cam and everything still on it..."

Big Ed's cigar was starting to roll around in his mouth and make tiny figure-8s in the air. "So what's your idea?"

"It's easy!" I said like it was nothing more than nailing a set of skate wheels to the bottom of an orange crate. "We'll strip the chassis down to nothing—make it as light as we can!—and then shovel that Caddy engine inside and throw a few pieces of sheetmetal on it and go clean everybody's clock."

"With something made out of junkyard scrap?"

"Absolutely."

The figure-8s got bigger and grander. "Y'think you could whip something up that could beat Skippy Welcher's C-Type?"

"With The Skipper driving?"

Big Ed nodded.

"Not a doubt in the world."

"Out of junkyard scrap?"

I nodded.

A big grin spread out over his face. "And about how long d'ya figure all this would take?"

"I dunno. It's the off-season now so I won't have a lot of race work lined up. And Roman Szymanski said he'd help out some." I shrugged, rolling it over in my head. "Maybe a couple of months. We could maybe have it ready in time for spring."

"And how much d'ya think it would cost?"

"I dunno," I shrugged again. "Not much..."

Big Ed took a deep draw on his stogie and puffed out another perfect smoke ring. "Sure," he said dreamily, watching the smoke ring rise and dissolve in the air, "why the hell not?"

"You mean it?"

"Sure. It'd be friggin' *great* t'grind Skippy's nose in it with something you made up yourself," he chuckled. "And especially made outta junkyard scrap!" He swiveled his head and looked at me. "Any idea what you'd call it?"

Of course I'd thought about that part a lot. "I was thinking maybe we'd call it The Jagillac." I said proudly. And then I looked down at my shoes. "Or maybe even the Palumbo Panther?" I added kind of sheepishly.

Big Ed mulled it over. "I think I like Jagillac better. But we'll see."

"Yeah. I mean, I gotta build it first."

"Just remember," Big Ed growled, pointing a forefinger the size of a Kosher frankfurter at me, "this is just a side deal, see? The garage business hasta come first."

"Of course it does."

"It's easy t'get yourself blind and sidetracked over stuff you really like..."

"I know."

"...you forget about what's important..."

"Sure."

"...you neglect th'things you really need t'pay attention to..."

"That'll never happen here," I assured him.

"It better not."

"It won't. I promise."

Big Ed nodded sternly. And then I watched his eyes kind of melt and go all dreamy on him. "So," he added absently, his cigar doing a kind of slow Dutch roll from one side of his face to the other, "y'really think you can build something faster than Skippy's C-Type?"

"I sure think I can give it one whale of a try."

I hate to say it, but the blessed New York Yankees wrapped up yet another World Series on October 4th—their fifth straight, can you believe it?—by beating the Brooklyn Dodgers 4-3 in the sixth and final game. And of course there was no hearing the end of it around my folks' house on account of my old man was such an enormous and loud-mouthed Yankees fan. In fact, I'd wear my Dodgers cap just to needle him a little while the series was going on. But after the Yankees won, he'd take to turning it around sideways on my head or flicking it clear off with his thumb and forefinger just to rub it in. And I guess I had it coming, too. But the amazing thing was that we actually watched one of the games together on his TV and downed a couple Knickerbockers while we were at it. I mean, it wasn't like I was actually getting to like him or anything. Not hardly. I just wasn't so preoccupied with hating his guts anymore. Some people think you become more tolerant as you get older and wiser and more mature, but I really think you just start running out of gas. It takes a lot of energy to fuel a really decent hatred....

Meanwhile my mom and Julie and my sister Sarah Jean were getting thick as thieves as the time for the baby got closer. I'd never really witnessed or understood before about what a Communal Female Activity having a baby is, but I can tell you for certain it's a Members Only, closed-shop kind of deal, and even when you're right there in the same room with it, they make it painfully clear that you are on the outside with all the other males in the universe who Don't Understand At All and furthermore it's all your fault anyway so why don't you just go pop open another beer and watch dumb sports on television with your top pants button undone and your fly unzipped about halfway down.

We'll be in the kitchen doing the dishes and feeling terribly in-the-know and superior....

Over in Manhattan my sister Mary Frances was hard at work with the gallery people on the opening of Frederick's one-man show, and she was really enjoying getting active and putting something together for a change. I talked to her once or twice and she seemed genuinely smitten—gobsmacked, even—by some of the snazzy, upper-atmosphere people she was meeting and talking to and making arrangements with in the high-flying circles of the New York art gallery scene. Oh, she knew it was mostly all phony bullshit, but it was hard not to get blinded by the glint off the glitter and gold and diamond earrings, you know?

And while I was stuck in Passaic running the shop and taking care of things at home and getting ready for Frederick Frumpt's big Grand Opening party that I really couldn't have cared less about at the Pendleton-Carrington Gallery, the really affluent and mobile local New York-area sportycar folks who never actually had to work for a living were traipsing all across the country to run a pair of SAC-base races a week apart at Stead Air Force Base near Reno, Nevada, and the second annual big SOWEGA meet at Turner Air Force Base near Albany, Georgia. And it pained me even more than the Yankees winning another World Series to hear that Creighton Pendleton and his blessed Momo hot-rodded Ferrari won the feature races at both events. Damn. I guess the Reno event wasn't too huge and it rained like hell on top of it, and after that Masten Gregory kid—who my scribe buddy Hank Lyons had already nicknamed "The Kansas City Flash" after his white C-Type with the black-flag number panels on it went up in flames at Floyd Bennett Field—broke an axle in the red C-Type he bought off Big Ed, it was just no contest. Phil Hill gave chase in one of Ernesto Julio's Ferraris, but it was just a puny little 2.9-liter, and up against the rumored 4.5 (or maybe even more?) in Creighton's car, it was all Phil could do to come home a distant second. And that was the thing about airport circuits. The corners were almost always tight, fiddly little hard-90 rights or hard-90 lefts, and then you had these long straightaways in between. So, as long as your brakes could keep up with it, it was just a bunch of damn dragstrips strung together, one right after the other. And no question Creighton's car was all big muscle and lean meat when it came to wailing down a straightaway. Hell, you could even *hear* how strong it was!

Worse yet, he went down to the SOWEGA race in Georgia the next week and beat the whole blessed Cunningham team. Can you believe it? Oh, it wasn't all pure merit. Briggs had Phil Walters in that new, freshly rebuilt, solid-axle C-5R that'd finished a strong third overall at Le Mans but then crashed so badly just before dawn at Reims, and even though Phil allowed as how it wasn't the handiest thing in the world, it was good enough to scrap back-and-forth with Creighton Pendleton's Ferrari for the first few laps and then slowly draw away for a pretty solid lead. But Phil'd had a blowout earlier in the day on the abrasive concrete runways and, what with the engine starting to sputter and spit back through the carburetors, he made a pit stop for fresh tires and to have the mixture adjusted. And that was all Creighton needed. John Fitch chased after him in the older Cunningham, but it just wasn't enough, and damn if that nose-in-the-air, Bermuda-tan jerk Creighton Pendleton the Third didn't cop his second big feature win in as many weekends. It was enough to make you puke, and I was almost glad I hadn't been there to see it in person. Almost....

I can honestly say I never attended any social function remotely similar to my sister Mary Frances' far-out-in-the-cosmos boyfriend Frederick's gala opening party for his one-man show at the Pendleton-Carrington Art Gallery on 57th near Park Avenue in Manhattan. Over at the duplex, the build-up had started several weeks before, seeing as how Julie had always wanted to have herself some kind of a career as a fashion artist and she figured this might be a great way to meet some people and make some contacts in the art world. Although I wasn't exactly sure that those were at all the same kinds of art. And then I had to leave work for most of a morning and all afternoon to take Julie out shopping for something to wear. And I knew going in that it was going to be a Certified Matrimonial Ordeal on account of Julie'd been feeling all fat and sad and disgusted and uncomfortable and mopey and depressed as hell and crying over nothing at all for quite some time. Not that it was any surprise, seeing as how women just seem to do that when they get good and pregnant, and there's nothing you can (or should!) try to do about it. Just act nice and pleasant and considerate and thoughtful and, as much as possible, stay the hell out of the line of fire. Being in another room is a good idea. Being in another building is even better.

On top of which I wasn't particularly thrilled with the prospect of laying out good money (and, most likely, lots of it) for a dress or whatever that she would only ever wear once—I mean, exactly how many 57th-and-Park Avenue functions would we ever attend in our lives that just happened to roll around when she was five months pregnant?—and the very worst of it was that she wanted me to go with her to pick it out. Personally, I would much rather have just handed over a fat wad of cash and let her go out with her mother or something. Or my mother. Or maybe even my sister Sarah Jean or Mary Frances. I'm sure they would've been happy to go. Any one of them. And then they could have cooed and twittered and clucked their tongues and examined and tried on every damn dress on every damn rack in every damn ladies' store on both the East and West banks of the Hudson River and it would've been just fine with me. So long as I didn't have to go along. Only that's not what Julie wanted....

Let me take a moment to explain to you the difference between the way men shop for clothes and the way women shop for clothes. A man will have a general idea of exactly what he wants before he goes into the store. As in: *I need a pair of pants because the seat has ripped out of this one* or *I need a dress shirt because I have to go to a funeral on Friday and there's a marinara stain on the one I have that's so big the tie won't cover it* or *I need a nice sweater because they look at me funny when I wear my sweatshirt to church on Sunday*. And so the male of the species will enter the store (and it usually doesn't matter much which one) and make a beeline for the rack, shelf or table where the particular article of clothing he's looking for is displayed. At that point he will narrow it down by finding the stack or section with his size in it. And then he will further narrow it down by looking at the price tags and eliminating a good half the remaining field right there. Only then will he get down to actually looking at the garments themselves. In the case of pants or jackets, he will be looking for a nice, comfortable fit and enough pockets for all the stuff he needs to carry around. In the case of a dress shirt, he wants to make sure the collar is a good half-inch or even inch bigger than his neck on account of they always lie about the sizes. And if it's a sweater, he wants to be absolutely sure that it's not that awful itchy, scratchy stuff that your relatives always buy you for Christmas. And that's it. He's back out the door in five minutes—tops!—and the only time color or style ever enter into it is if one of those painfully polite salespeople stick their noses in and try to be helpful.

I mean, who cares?

Women, on the other hand, think that shopping for clothes is a great and miraculous adventure. A glutton's orgy of style, fabric, color, cut, haunting second thoughts and mind-numbing indecisions. A chance to enhance themselves beyond their wildest dreams if they can just find that *perfect* thing. That one shining, magical, shimmering confection of cloth or silk or lace that will instantly render them younger and slimmer and wittier and more attractive and appealing and arousing and purer than the very angels in heaven than they ever were. And they're not above traipsing through every damn clothes rack in town to find it, either.

"Do you like this one?"

"It looks fine. How much is it?"

"Don't you think it makes me look fat?"

"It looks fine. How much is it?"

"You do think it makes me look fat, don't you?"

"I said it looks fine."

"Although I did like the one with the lavender-and-orchid trim."

"I liked that one, too."

"It did look nice on me."

"It looked fine."

"It's too bad they don't have the lavender-and-orchid trim on this one."

"Maybe they do."

"I'll ask the saleslady. But I doubt it…"

And of course they don't, because those two dresses were made by two different dress companies just across the street from each other in the garment district. And even though the guy who owns the first one is the second cousin of the guy who owns the second one and even through the designer who works for the second one is second cousin to the designer who works for the first one, none of them have been speaking to each other for years. And of course that means that neither of those dresses will do. Which naturally means that now you're off to yet another blessed dress shop or department store.

"I'm sorry it's taking so long."

"It's fine."

"But I just want to find the right thing."

"That's okay."

"I don't want to buy just *any*thing."

"God forbid."

"And it has to be the right sort of color."

"Oh, absolutely."

"What do you think of this one?"

"It's fine. How much is it?"

"Don't you think it makes me look fat?"

And you're off to the races all over again....

The important thing to remember is to keep your hands in your pockets the whole time so she can't see them strangling imaginary baby bluebirds and bunny rabbits.

Julie finally wound up compromising for a very pretty, kind of church-choir-robe-cut outfit in pewter satin with a pale rose-colored vest over the top that she planned to wear with matching shoes and a matching handbag and a matching band in her hair and maybe her mom's string of cultured pearls. Personally I didn't get it about the shoes. I mean, the dress came damn near all the way to the floor and I swear she could've worn beach sandals or steel-toed work boots or even big, webbed yellow Donald Duck swim fins and nobody would've been the wiser. Unless they saw her getting out of a car or something, you know? But, outside of the fact that the whole outfit cost more than what I normally charged for a Jaguar valve job and took just as long as that valve job to find and settle on (and I'm including runs to the machine shop here), I have to admit I kind of liked it, too....

The Pendleton-Carrington Art Gallery was located on a swank stretch of 57th Street just off Park Avenue and not too far from where Mary Frances got her abortion, and they even had a doorman in brass buttons out front to park your car and show you the way inside. Big Ed had been kind enough to borrow us the big Caddy sedan so's we wouldn't have to pull up in Old Man Finzio's tow truck, and I must say that a car like his Sixty Special didn't even merit a raised eyebrow in that particular neighborhood. Not hardly. The gallery itself had a marble-framed front window with polished brass trim around it and you could hear the clinking of real crystal and the titter of refined laughter—*oh, my, that must have been a good one!*—coming through the open doorway. And that's about when I realized that everybody was in costume. Everybody but us, that is. Unless we came dressed as a couple of geeks from New Jersey. And you should have *seen* some of those getups! There was a cowboy in a big ten-gallon hat and tooled leather boots and a matching, tooled leather gun belt with nickel-plated, pearl-handled revolvers on either side. But the really amazing part was how he was kind of "wearing" this papier mache horse around his waist that looked like it was lifted right off a carnival carousel! I wondered how the heck he ever went to the can, you know? And there was this slender young lady (at least I was pretty sure it was a lady) in the most incredible flamingo outfit with big, pink satin wings at her hips and this skullcap of a hat with eyes sewn on the sides and this huge, pink-sequin flamingo beak for a bill. And right across from her (or him, or whatever) was this angel all in flowing, gauzy linen with a battery-operated, rotating, neon-illuminated halo and wings that looked like they were made out of genuine, pure white bird feathers. And next to him was a devil that turned out to be some *really* muscular guy wearing nothing more than a rubber mask, a coat of red grease-paint, and a sort of loincloth thing with a damn tail hanging off the back. Jeez, didn't he get *cold?* And here was some *very* attractive young blonde done up as a mermaid and not wearing anything but her own hair (and maybe some double-sided carpet tape where you couldn't see it?) from the scales up. "I'm feeling a little uncomfortable here," Julie whispered in my ear.

"Me, too."

"Meow!" someone whispered in my other ear as a set of long, catlike fingernails raked softly down the back of my neck. I spun around and there was Mary Frances. All dressed up in a tabby-stripe cat suit with painted-on whiskers and padded cloth ears.

"Jesus! You didn't tell us this was a costume party!"

"It said 'dress appropriately' on the invitation," she frowned. "What could be more appropriate for Halloween?"

"But you could've said *something.*"

"Oh, stop whining. Not everybody dressed." Sure enough, she nodded over to a corner where her boyfriend Frederick was standing there all by his lonesome, looking just as lost, befuddled and preoccupied as ever and wearing the same, paint-spattered tee shirt, denim jeans and denim jacket outfit that he always wore. Of course, they expect that sort of thing from an artist. In fact, it's kind of the basic uniform. "Besides," Mary Frances continued, "this isn't really supposed to be a costume party."

"It isn't?"

"Not really. This is kind of a pre-party. After all, it's only 7:30. People at a place like this are usually just dropping by before they go off to their *real* parties."

"Their real parties?"

Mary Frances nodded and took a sip of her champagne. "This is kind of like an appetizer, see? Go out and mingle a little. See what's new on the art scene."

"And who is *this,* pray tell?" A catty new voice purred into my earlobe.

I turned and here was yet another cat costume. Only this one was on a man. Sort of. He was a tiny, skinny, dainty little guy wearing a skin-tight black leotard with a long, black velvet tail attached, matching, long velvet gloves and boots, and a black velvet skullcap with black velvet ears. And he had what looked like real cat whiskers sticking out of his face—right out of his damn cheeks!—not simple, painted-on ones like Mary Frances. "Meow," he said in a lilting voice, and pawed the air in her general direction.

"This is L.C. Carrington," Mary Frances explained.

"And you must be the mechanically inclined brother," he purred some more.

"Uh, yeah," I said, and hesitatingly stuck out my hand. At least he had gloves on. "And this is my wife, Julie." He ran his eyes down her coyly, and stopped short at her middle.

"You're the one with the little bun in the oven, aren't you?" he cooed, arching his eyebrows.

Julie blushed.

"Well, you just have a look around," he continued daintily. "There's plenty of hors d'oeuvres and champagne. And be sure to let me know if you see anything you like." And with that he kind of pranced off towards where this tall, strong, Hollywood Leading Man type in an artists' smock and a cocked blue beret was standing, holding up an artists' palette with two glasses of champagne on it.

"That's his, uuh, *'partner,'*" Mary Frances whispered.

"You mean Eric Pendleton?" I could see the resemblance.

To be perfectly honest, this didn't exactly look like the kind of crowd where Julie might run into anybody who could help jump-start her career as a fashion artist for the newspaper. Especially the guy in the King Neptune outfit wearing a clear vinyl jacket filled with blue-tinted water with real, live goldfish swimming around in it.

"Well," I told her, "we might as well go look at the pictures."

So we moseyed around through this unbelievable crowd in their unbelievable costumes and listened to the unbelievable things they had to say and the unshakable opinions they had about the artistic works of Frederick Frumpt. The four small canvasses of *Depression, Boredom, Anger* and *Anxiety* were arranged in a circle, and there was a decent crowd gathered inside of it giving them all a looksee. And who should be there right in the middle of it all but our old tweed-jacket genius, novels-in-Esperanto, Expert-On-Absolutely-Everything buddy Ollie Cromwell.

"This one seems to reach out to a meaning well beyond its deceptively simple base concept," Ollie was explaining to a handful of wealthy idiots who actually seemed to be hanging on his every word. "It forces us to look inside ourselves." He caught me out of the corner of his eye and favored me with a faint smile of recognition along with benign astonishment that I should ever be discovered in such a place. "And this one..." he said, continuing on to *Anger,* "...is filled with the hapless human fury that ultimately ferments in its own futility and dissolves into..." he nodded in the direction of *Anxiety,* "...and we become captives of our own angst, alienation, appetites and indecision—running around like rats trapped in the maze with all ends closed and no way out—and that of course leads us back to..." he nodded in the direction of *Depression* again. "...and the endless, eternal cycle comes full circle again."

Boy, was he ever full of shit.

"It would be a shame if they were ever purchased separately and the set were broken up," he declared. "The meaning would be lost."

"This gray," some other overeducated doofus chimed in knowingly, "why, it's almost *too* gray of a gray."

"Yes!" another agreed excitedly.

"It's almost as if..." Ollie Cromwell shrewdly and cannily observed, "...it's too much of a muchness."

"Ah, yes," they all agreed, and moved on to the next group of paintings.

I kind of liked the next one in a creepy sort of way. It was called *The Three Faces of Death,* and it was just three more little foot-square gold picture frames, each one mounted on one side of this sort of triangular display column set up on a slowly-rotating turntable. Like a blessed postcard rack. Anyhow, the first one was nothing more than a gold frame around that foot-square chunk of cast-iron manhole cover Frederick asked me to have Roman Syzmanski whittle out for him. You could see that heavy waffle-finish and the cast in letters "SANIT" arranged on kind of a curve. It was from "SANITARY DISTRICT," you know? But of course all the "art experts" on hand nodded and conversed knowingly about how it was maybe the word "SAINT" purposely misspelled? Or short for "SANITY," but not all there....

Obviously you can find lots of meaning in things if you look hard enough.

Anyhow, the second gold frame on the next panel had a foot-square block of wood inside it painted a dull, dark red (maybe paint left over from *Anger?)* with a couple weathered old hinges on one side and this creepy old antique brass doorknob mounted on the other. The knob turned and everything, but the hinges didn't work and so you couldn't really open it. And I know, because I tried it and damn near pulled the whole blessed thing off. It was just hanging on a damn picture hook.

But the most astounding piece in Frederick Frumpt's *The Three Faces of Death* was on the third panel. Why, it was just an empty gold frame with nothing in it at all! Just an empty frame, can you believe it? Oliver went on for a good half-hour about that one.

To be honest, I didn't get a lot of what was going on with Frederick's artwork. I mean, I'm not stupid. I understood a little of what he was getting at. What I didn't understand was all the fuss. Why he had one called *Love* that was just a damn junkshop mirror in one of his gold frames. And a sculpture he called *Aphrodite* that was nothing more than a mannequin's arm with a boxing glove on the end sticking up out of a big, yellow-and-green-painted glob of plaster-of-Paris.

And who should walk in through the front door about then but Skippy Welcher and his nineteen-year-old Oriental masseuse, who was looking even more bored and disgusted than usual in spite of her glittering silver lamé Tin Woodsman outfit or The Skipper's highly professional Cowardly Lion. I think it even had genuine fur. Or at least it smelled like it, anyway. And of course L.C. and Eric fluttered right over the instant that Skippy came in.

"How *are* you?"

"So good to *see* you!"

"What a *stunning* pair of outfits…."

So. The Skipper collected modern art. Somehow that figured.

"Look," I said to Julie. "I don't know anything about this stuff, but isn't art supposed to be, you know, *pretty?"*

"Pretty?" I heard someone scoff from behind. Oh, Jesus. It was Ollie. "Great art," he explained grandly, "is hardly a matter of *'pretty.'"* He said "pretty" like it was some disease you might catch off a dead rat or something.

"Then what is it?" some idiot asked.

"Truly *great* art…" and he made it clear that he was one of the chosen few who would actually know the difference, "…is a guidepost to where we've been and where we're going. A mirror reflecting our most deeply treasured beliefs, our joyous joys, our sorrowful sorrows, our hidden fears and futile foibles. A pathway that leads us to the very precipice of human experience and dangles us danger-ously and deliciously over the void. Great art makes us ask those difficult and eternal questions that can never be answered…"

Personally, I always figured *answering* difficult questions was a lot better deal than asking more questions you couldn't answer at all. After all, it's not too hard to stump human beings. I mean, we're just people, you know?

"Great art," Ollie proclaimed to the heavens in a pounding crescendo, "should be layered like an onion with mystery, meaning and the mortality and morality of man." He held up an imaginary onion and sliced it right there in mid-air for all to see.

"D'ya think I can get mine grilled?" I muttered over my shoulder as I aimed Julie and me in the general direction of the door.

It was still pretty early when we left the Pendleton-Carrington Galleries on 57th Street and, to be honest, I really wanted to stop by that party at Carson Flegley's family's funeral home in East Orange on our way home to see how all my racing biddies were doing. But I could tell Julie was tired. I'd fed her a couple glasses of that champagne—hey, it was free, right?—and I could see it was all she could do to keep her eyes open. Plus it must not be easy lugging an additional person around all the time. Especially when you never get a chance to set them down. Still, it being Halloween and all and after the end of the racing season, this represented yet one more of those Last Chance deals that racing is so full of. *Last Chance to See Everybody until Next Spring* was the way I heard it inside my own head. And so I finally broke down and asked Julie about it. "Think we could maybe stop by Carson's party on the way home?"

She let out a long sigh. "I'm really kind of bushed."

"It's where we got engaged last year…" I reminded her.

"How could I ever forget?"

"We'd only stop for a couple minutes…." I lied.

"If you really want to," she said without enthusiasm. To be honest, I think she was just too damn exhausted to argue about it.

But she'd dozed off to sleep by the time we got to the Flegley family funeral home. I could see the lights glowing in the little ground-level slit windows to the basement and I could hear some muffled laughter and music—the rumor was Carson had hired a live band this year—and I wanted so badly to go inside and see all my racing friends and wrap myself up in all those good jokes and lies and conversations about what happened last year and what we were all planning and scheming and counting on for next. I especially wanted to tell everybody about the new special project I had in the works. Get their comments. Get their opinions. Get their enthusiasm behind me. What a great antidote that would be for all the leftover distaste I'd accumulated at that nauseatingly intelligent and over-wrought art gallery party in Manhattan.

Only Julie was asleep beside me in the front seat of Big Ed's Caddy. Deep asleep, you know, with her breath rolling in and out like a soft, tiny snore and even a little trail of drool running down her chin. I must've got ready to reach over and tap her shoulder to wake her up a half dozen times. But I didn't. I just took one long, last look around the funeral home parking lot—there was Carson's black Healey Hundred and there was Big Ed's new Polo White Corvette and there was what's-his-name's MG TD and Cal's mom's brand new, gleaming baby blue 1954 Packard Caribbean convertible that I'm sure she had no idea was out of the garage, not to mention a fistful of other TCs and TDs and a handful of XK 120s and a sinister new Aston Martin coupe and….

And it was time to let my eyes take one more longing, lingering sweep of the parking lot, put Big Ed's Caddy softly in gear, and ever-so-gently, so as not to wake her, head for home…

15: The Quicksand Effect

Every major racecar project starts out like a house afire. You're all full of notions and enthusiasm and you're working ideas around in big, fat chunks and, particularly if it's an engine-swap hybrid like what I had in mind, most of what you're doing in those early stages amounts to demolition work. And, as any kid who ever carried a slingshot in his back pocket will tell you, that sort of work is really *fun*. I'd kind of filled Cal in on the basics of the project (and even hinted that there might be a steady ride in it for him somewheres down the line once I convinced Big Ed that a guy of his talents was much better off as a team owner than a driver), and so Cal was dropping by the station pretty regularly that late fall of 1953 to see what he could do to help. Which wasn't much, when you get right down to it, since Cal really didn't have a lot of mechanical skills or stick-to-itiveness and was moreover lazy as hell to boot. That tends to happen when you grow up with servants and chauffeurs and cooks and housemaids and such scattering rose petals in your path everywhere you go and then sweeping them up behind you when you're gone. But he talked a great fight and kept the pressure on me to keep wailing away at it, and he really enjoyed torching the old, bent-up body panels off Big Ed's crashed-out XK 120 once I showed him how to use a cutting torch. In fact, it was a little scary how much he enjoyed it. Especially seeing as how he wasn't real particular about making distinctions between stuff that should be stripped off and discarded and things that we might actually need to use again.

I'd decided what I really needed to do was drop by Westbridge and try to make a deal with Sylvester to go over to the scrapyard where Big Ed's crushed-up Caddy was and pull the motor out of it like a dentist pulls a bad tooth. To be honest, what I was really trying to do was get Sylvester interested in maybe doing a few side jobs for me again over at the Sinclair. I mean, he'd tried it before and given it up as a bad deal on account of the travel and the way the Old Man snarled at him all the time and the fact that nobody in our neighborhood much cared for colored people. But it was different now. The Old Man was in and out of the hospital and when he wasn't there he was back in his apartment all by his lonesome feeling angry at the world and sorry as hell for himself—and who could blame him?—and so I was pretty much running the show. And I was amazed how much work we were getting. Sports cars and ordinary stuff, too. I mean, all I ever did was try to be honest about what was wrong and do my best to fix the cars properly and treat people decent so long as they did the same to me and stand behind my word and come through as best I possibly could when I'd promised something. I had no idea that was such a rare thing in the car repair business.

Not that you can always please people. In fact, that's one of the hardest lessons in life. Sometimes, no matter how hard you try, things just go to shit on you. Like the time Tater dropped his second cousin's old '46 Kaiser off the lift when he was just trying to do a little after-hours, emergency dangling-exhaust-system repair as a kind of favor. Broke every piece of glass on the car. "Tater," I told him, "whatever else may or may not be true here, *this did NOT happen in my shop!*" Or the time Raymond was trying to braze a little seam crack in the radiator filler neck of Mrs. Muccianti's faithful old Pontiac and set the torch down on the fender—just for a second, you know?—to check his work. We wound up having to pay the Greek to refinish the whole damn fender. And it still didn't match.

Especially in sunlight. Even the second time. And some people are just not about to be satisfied. It's just the way they are. And the more you bust your balls and try to make things right for them, the more angry and ornery and suspicious they get and the surer than ever they are that you're taking advantage of them.

There's just nothing you can do.

But fortunately you've got the law of averages working in your favor, which says basically that most average people will be satisfied with average repair work done in an average amount of time. And particularly if it comes in at slightly below-average prices. But it was the sports car work that was more and more ringing the old cash register and paying the bills. Those customers didn't seem to mind paying a little extra (in fact, thanks to Colin St. John and Barry Spline, they more or less expected it!) and they were always amazed (ditto!) when a job was actually completed on time. Plus we were starting to do pretty good with a little accessory business I'd started, putting sorely needed luggage racks on the back of MGs and badge bars and driving lights on the front and either Maserati air horns, *ah-ooo-gah* horns, or *ding-dong* Bermuda bells under the hood. Sportycar people loved being able to fuss over their cars, and so every little doodad and doohicky I could find wound up in the resurrected old glass cigar case I'd put across from the cash register. We even started carrying Wakefield's Castrol oils and brake fluid and such along with our regular line. To be honest, our local Sinclair guy wasn't real happy about it. But I explained to him as how the British car manufacturers specified it right there in the factory service manuals. Besides which, I could charge a little extra for using the imported stuff. And my customers loved it, too, because it made them feel like they were doing something above-and-beyond-the-call-of-duty special for their cars.

Anyhow, we were busy as hell, and, like I said, what I really needed was somebody like Sylvester (or Butch, before he got hurt) who I could just hand a tough job off to and walk away knowing they'd do it just as good as I would. Maybe even better. But that kind of talent is hard to find in the car repair business, and it usually comes with either bad habits and surly attitudes or a little too much ambition and imagination. Those would be the guys who try to make side deals with your customers and then sneak stuff out of the parts room to do back-alley jobs on the cars they used to fix in your shop. Or, worse yet, open up across the street from you and then spread rumors all around town about what a dirty, lying cheat you are. It's all part of the game.

"Wuf'fo you wants me t'come t'work in Jersey agin'?" Sylvester asked through a mouth full of hot sausage sandwich in the alley out behind Westbridge.

"I need somebody I can count on."

"Y'caint count on me," he reminded me. "Din'tcha learnt nothin' th'last time?"

"Maybe I can't count on you, but at least I can trust you."

"Y'caint trust me, neither. Hell, son, *ah* cain't trust me sometimes…."

"How about weekends? You could just come over and work on weekends."

Sylvester eyed me suspiciously. "Y'don't git it, do you? Th' only reason ah works is t'git myself t'the weekends, see. Them is mine."

"But all you do on the weekends is drink and shoot dice and get in trouble."

"Yeah. But it's *mah own* trouble. That's the damn point, see?"

I didn't see, exactly. But I knew that look in Sylvester's eyes. It said "don't push me, don't bug me, and, for God's sake, don't con me." There was no place to go with him once he got that look. No place at all.

"So I hear y'all's gonna be turnin' inta' a daddy soon," Sylvester giggled without looking up from his sandwich.

"That's the rumor. Sometime around the first of March or so, I guess." Julie and me were telling everybody "sometime around the first of March" on account of even people in our neighborhood who never graduated kindergarten could count to nine.

Sylvester grinned and shook his head. "Sheeeee-*it!* Little snot-nosed piece a'shit like you is gonna be a daddy." He shook his head again. "Don't that beat all."

"We could really use you over at the Sinclair…"

"We'll see. We'll see. But don't y'all be countin' on it, son."

But he did take the deal to cut the engine out of Big Ed's Caddy for me, and sure enough he showed up over at the scrapyard early one weekday morning when he'd called in sick at Westbridge and by lunchtime he'd burrowed right through all that twisted metal and had that Caddy V8 sitting on a wooden shipping pallet and ready to haul over to the Sinclair. Whatever else you could say about Sylvester Jones, he knew how to get things done. And he knew how to do it out in the field, too, not just cozyed up to a workbench someplace with all his favorite shop tools close at hand.

Meanwhile, with a lot of yelling and screaming and other assorted high-decibel advice from Butch, Cal had gotten the body pretty much stripped off the XK 120, and I'll never forget that Saturday afternoon when the Caddy engine showed up in one of Big Ed's dumptrucks and we wrestled it over onto the pavement next to that stripped Jaguar chassis and started trying to figure exactly what to do next. That "what to do next?" part is a real key, since probably 50% of all great car projects stall out on exactly that sort of problem. And another 30% or so peter out from a simple oversupply of beer. But I had Roman Szymanski drop by late in the day and he was right away running his eyes all over everything and whipping out his pocket measuring tape and scratching his head and making notes in this little spiral notebook he always carried in his shirt pocket. The obvious thing was that the blown-up Jag six we'd yanked out of that hulk was one hell of a lot longer and taller and skinnier than the American Caddy V8 we were planning to put in. And it was also obvious, just looking at the stuff in front of us, that there was a lot of excess, unnecessary length in general from the pedal assembly forward on the Jag chassis. In fact, the way Roman saw it, there was a lot of unnecessary length, period. "You cut here and here," he said, making chalk marks on the frame channels indicating just shy of a foot-long chunk of the Jag's frame, just ahead of the crossmember. "Shorter is better. Turn quicker."

So we did what he said and cut the frame in two, and right about then is when I had the very first pang that says: *Just what the hell do you think you're doing here? It looks like you're cutting it up for scrap! What ever made you think you could build your own racecar?* And of course it didn't help any to see the two ends kind of sitting out there behind the station in the rain like two large abandoned rickshaws when I came to work the next morning. And then the rain turned to snow.

It stayed shitty and cold for about a week after that and Julie insisted we go visit Old Man Finzio in the hospital again to try and cheer him up. I argued that such a thing was not possible even when he wasn't so sick, but she just glared at me and that was pretty much the end of it. To be honest about it, I've never been much good at going to see sick people in the hospital. Even Butch, right after his accident. I just feel so blessed useless and dumb and like I'm not doing any good for anybody and making myself miserable in the process, you know? Plus I hate hospitals in general. I hate the antiseptic smell and the fluorescent lights that don't cast any shadows and the way the doctors whisper out in the halls and the squeak of the nurses' rubber-soled shoes on the linoleum floors. It gives me the creeps, honest it does.

I think women, generally speaking, are much better than men when it comes to that "visiting the sick and dying" stuff. I know my mom was always genuine World Class when it came to that. Why, she could go over and chitchat for hours on end to a neighbor or relative who looked like they ought to be getting the last rites instead of a new recipe for braised pig knuckles or some hot backyard news about the nice new family of Baltimore orioles who were nesting in our apple tree. You know my mom and her birds. But the point is it never seemed to bother her that the person she was talking to just laid there looking up at the ceiling like they were staring out over the edge of the Grand Canyon and never said anything back. And Julie turned out to be much the same way. Although she didn't twitter on and on about birds or braised pig knuckle recipes like my mom. Thank goodness. But she had this way of finding something or other to say and sounding a little encouraging even when there was no reason to be. And there was sure no reason to be when it came to Old Man Finzio. In fact, it was frankly amazing to me how he could continue to look sicker and feebler every time I saw him when I was sure he was already about as sick and feeble as anybody could ever get without cashing their chips in. The scariest part was always when Julie got done and it came time for me to go over and say something. I'd kind of mumble a few words in the general direction of the windowshade or the pitcher of water on his bedstand or the nurse call button next to the Old Man's pillow. You know, about how many gallons of gas and quarts of oil we'd sold or the cars we had in for service or how good the sports car business was going. And then, without really meaning to, I'd catch myself looking at him. And it curled me up inside like a rotten piece of bacon on a grill. But the worst of it was when, out of nowhere, he found my eyes with his and strained upwards like he wanted to lift his head up off the pillow and his thin, purplish lips trembled as they rasped out, *"I ain't afraid t'die, sonny,"* underneath the most terrified eyes I had ever seen. Afterwards, on the way home, I remember it was kind of raining and snowing at the same time, and not the sort of moment when you dared to switch on the radio. And so we drove along without saying anything, just listening to the slow flap of the windshield wipers and the harsh, grating whirr of the defroster fan and wondering inside just what on earth was keeping the Old Man going. I think it was maybe fear.

A few days later it got decent again, and Roman came over that Sunday and we spent the entire day just getting set up to weld the frame back together. He'd brought over a bunch of heavy steel plate and angle iron and used our heavy H-lift as a kind of platform to make a jig and bolt everything down so's the frame wouldn't warp or distort from the welding when we put it back together. And then he spent maybe four hours just measuring and checking and dropping plumb bobs like a damn bricklayer and making chalk marks and notes right there on the damn floor. When it came time for the actual welding, I went over and got Butch—even with his bad hand and the fact that you had to kind of prop him up and brace him in position for every bead, he was still the best damn welder I'd ever seen. And especially on that tough vertical and overhead stuff. Roman even came up with some channel section and triangular gusset pieces to make sure our new, short-ened frame was even stiffer than before, and it was damn near five ayem by the time we had the thing disengaged from the H-lift and rolled back out behind the shop and covered up with a tarp again. And that's the bad thing about trying to build a racecar in a regular commercial repair shop. You absolutely have to get all that racecar shit packed up and back outside before you open up then next morn-ing or you are simply not going to be able to earn a living. Which means that, no matter what, you've got to work on each little stage of the project until you're actually done with it. No matter how late it gets.

Or how early.

"Where the hell have you been?" Julie moaned sleepily as I dragged myself into bed for a quick half-hour's shuteye before I had to get up and open the shop again.

"I had some racecar work to do."

"In fricking November?"

"It's a big project. For Big Ed."

"Well, I sure as hell hope you're getting paid for it...."

That was as good a time as any to drop off to sleep.

There was this supposedly "International-Grade/European-Style" sports car rallye scheduled for the Thanksgiving weekend—Wednesday November 25th through Sunday, November the 29th—starting right out of downtown Manhattan, and it'd been written up in all the magazines and club newsletters and had become the subject of animated bar and cocktail lounge conversations among all the SCMA regulars for a variety of reasons. It was titled "The Great American Mountain Rallye," and it was causing quite a stir because European-style rallying and American-style rallying as practiced by the SCMA were two completely dif-ferent sorts of animals. In a typical SCMA rallye, you wanted a nice, sunny, top-down kind of day so's you could enjoy a little open-air motoring while you fol-lowed these simple, logical, easy-to-understand route instructions made up by some guy who probably beats his wife, kicks his dog and pulls the wings off flies just for the fun of it. Along the way, you maybe have to answer a few silly ques-tions about signs or buildings or things you may see—kind of like a treasure hunt, you know? And, if it's a really *serious* rallye, you also need to maintain a very specific sort of average speed (down to two or three decimal places will do) and always be right on time so that you won't get penalized for being early or late when you're suddenly and unexpectedly confronted by a checkpoint. I'd been on one or two American-style rallyes with Big Ed, and I'd have to say it's a fun thing to do so long as you don't carry any sharp objects in the car with you and avoid going with your spouse, fiancée or anyone you ever might consider as a prospective spouse or fiancée. Because there will be arguments. And maybe even a few stab wounds, if you bring anything sharper than a ballpoint pen along with you. But it can also be a fun way to waste an afternoon if you don't get too damn serious about it.

Like the Europeans do, for example. See, over in Europe, their rallyes run for several days straight—not to mention several nights!—and the general idea is to try to maintain an exceedingly brisk average speed through the highest, iciest, twistiest and most snowbound mountain passes, across the sloggiest, muddiest, slipperiest and slimiest water crossings, and generally around and about the narrowest, most inaccessible, rutted and poorly surfaced country back roads that Europe has to offer. And believe me, they've got some real beauts over there! And it's considered even better if they luck into a really awful onslaught of rain, sleet, snow, fog, blizzards, earthquakes, tornados, floods, quicksand, tidal waves, plague epidemics, border wars, volcanic eruptions or any combination thereof in order to spice things up just a little. In addition, there's generally no penalty for being early at any of the checkpoints and not too much in the way of enforced speed limits over on that side of the Atlantic, and so European-style rallying can get to looking an awful lot like a flat-out, balls-to-the-wall *La Carrera Panamericana* run through a heavy winter storm across the frosty top edges of the Alps. And, just as in *La Carrera,* it's a regular sort of thing to see cars getting stuck nose-first in ditches or fetched off into the trees or falling off cliffs or running out of brakes on the steep downhill runs, and the fact that you have to keep at it for several days and nights makes it quite a difficult challenge indeed for the drivers and crews. Plus a lot of the European carmakers consider it a real important way to show the public—who turn out in large numbers to watch the cars pass through their local neighborhoods and follow the results closely in their morning newspapers—just what their cars can do. So they sign up a lot of top racing drivers—like Stirling Moss and John Fitch, for example—who were both hired to drive those handsome, kind of upright-looking new Sunbeam Alpine things that were never much good as actual racing cars but did just fine on rallyes.

In the right hands, anyway....

Well, the notion that this kind of rallying was coming to the old U.S. of A. was pretty big news. And even moreso on account of it was going to be sponsored and sanctioned by the definitely *non*-SCMA Motor Sports Club of America and the Triple-A and that a lot of the top European teams were coming over to show all of us heads-up-our-butts colonials just exactly how it was done. Better yet, the organizers had made a deal with the famous Alpine Rallye over in Europe (which runs across five different countries and through thirty-one of the highest mountain passes in France, Italy, Switzerland, Austria and Germany, and where they award you one of these fancy *Coupe des Alps* cups just for finishing without penalty) so that the winning car and crew from The Great American Mountain Rallye would get a free entry into the Alpine Rallye over in Europe in 1954. Which was a heck of a deal. At least if you didn't count the cost of getting yourself and your car over to the starting point in Marseilles in the first place.

But the point is it sounded like a new and exciting kind of sportycar adventure—not to mention yet another way to stick a small and hopefully uncomfortable thorn in the side of the SCMA—and so Big Ed had signed up to run his new Corvette and Carson was going to run his new Healey and of course Cal was going along with Carson on account of he figured he'd maybe get to drive if it got a little too icy and slippery for Carson through the high mountain passes and he could maybe even impress some of those European factory teams to hire him on. And meanwhile Big Ed was all over me to go with him because he was going through a little bit of a rough patch with Rhonda—she wanted a ring and the future divorce settlement that went along with it and Big Ed was having second thoughts on account of somebody he knew thought he'd seen her out someplace with some other sugar daddy—and besides, she wasn't really much of a stopwatches, maps and notepads kind of girl.

"I dunno," I told him. "I mean, the Old Man's not fit t'come in anymore an' I gotta kind of look after things at the shop an' Julie's home pregnant an' I just don't know if I oughta be takin' off from Wednesday through Sunday to run some international sports car road rallye." I mean, when I stepped back a few paces and took a good, solid look at what I was saying, it was almost scary. What the heck had happened to me, anyway?

"What th'hell's happened to you?" Big Ed echoed. "You're th'boss now, see? You can do any damn thing you want."

"But I gotta keep an eye on things, you know?" *Who the heck is this new Buddy Palumbo,* I wondered to myself, *and what's he done with the old me?*

"You mean you're never gonna be able to take off again *ever?"*

"It's not like that," I told Big Ed, and the words sounded like bullshit to my own ears even as they passed over my lips. "It's just things are kind of, I dunno, *busy* right now, and...."

"They're *always* busy, Buddy. It never stops. Not ever. Y'gotta make time t'do th'things you really wanna do, or you'll never get t'do 'em at all." He held up a warning forefinger. "Always remember this, Buddy: *whatever you wanna do in this life, y'better DO it, because you're a long time dead."*

It was not the kind of advice you could easily ignore.

The amazing thing was that Julie was all for it. I'd noticed as the weeks went by that she was spending more and more time with her mom and my mom and my sister Sarah Jean and her old girlfriends from the Doggie Shake and that I was feeling a lot like a fifth wheel around the apartment and maybe even like I was walking on eggs a little every time I was around her. But a lot of that was on account of you never knew whether you were gonna find yourself with the sweet Julie, the sad Julie, the happy Julie, the forlorn and depressed Julie, the giddy Julie, or the Julie who wanted to march through downtown Passaic with your head on a stick. "You go ahead," she told me. "It's Thanksgiving weekend anyway, and so we'll all be doing family stuff over at your folks' house."

That sounded like another excellent reason not to be around.

"Then maybe Saturday I'll get together with the girls and we'll have coffee and go see a movie together or something."

It was almost like she was looking forward to it, you know?

"You go ahead," Butch agreed over at the Sinclair. "I can keep an eye on things."

"Y'all go ahead," Raymond Tuttle nodded. While behind him, on the lift, the fresh oil he was just putting into Big Ed's Sixty Special was running out all over the blessed floor because he'd forgotten to put the damn drain plug back in.

"Yeah, c'mon," Big Ed grinned. "It'll be like old times."

And so I took a deep breath, packed up a few things in a small duffel bag (there wasn't a hell of a lot of luggage space in Big Ed's new Corvette), left a shit list a yard long for Butch and Raymond and Tater to look after, and hopped into the passenger seat next to Big Ed for the ride into Manhattan. "Well," I said, "here goes...." as I watched Old Man Finzio's Sinclair slowly slip away and then disappear completely as we rounded the corner and headed east towards the New York City skyline.

The Great American Mountain Rallye started in the parking lot of the 79th Street Yacht Basin on the Upper West Side, and I must admit I was kind of astounded by the turnout. That Erwin Goldschmidt guy who didn't have much use for the SCMA (or vice-versa) had brought a nifty-looking Cadillac-engined Studebaker coupe put together by Bill Frick's shop over at Frick-Tappett Motors in White Plains, and there were more American cars mixed in with the MGs and Jaguars and Healeys and such than I expected. Then again, this *was* supposed to be a winter event, and although there's a lot to be said for nimble European chassis and fine European roadholding, the bare fact is that Detroit builds the best damn heaters, defrosters, wind-up windows and weather-stripping in the business, and that can be worth a lot more than a well-carved apex or two when the thermometer takes a nosedive. And, speaking of heaters, another team showed up with one of those strange-looking little Volkswagen things that count on the heat off the air-cooled engine blowing up these channels inside the doorsills to keep the inhabitants warm and the windows defrosted. Sort of. But you had to be impressed with how simple and clever and straightforward and unusual it all was. Even if it did sound like a damn fart in a bathtub.

But the most impressive thing of all was just how *serious* and *professional* some of the visiting Europeans seemed to be. And particularly the Brits. They considered rallying a great way to show off just how tough and rugged and reliable and dependable their cars were. Which is precisely why Sunbeam-Talbot sent over a full team of their Sunbeam Alpine more-or-less "sports" models and even hired our old nose-in-the-air buddy Creighton Pendleton to pilot one of them (and you could see how that was making my friend Cal Carrington eat his liver!). There was also a thing called the *Coupe des Dames* in international rallying, which was a special and very prestigious prize for the top all-female team *("see, our cars are so easy to drive in difficult conditions that even a WOMAN can do it"),* and so they'd also sent along a very nice and obviously very competent lady rallye driver named Sheila Van Damm, who had done really well for Sunbeam on the European rallying scene. And that presented a bit of a problem for the organizers, seeing as how the old Triple-A simply did not offer competition licenses to women. I mean, it had just never come up before, you know? At least not on the dirt-track fairgrounds circuit or even, I don't think, at the Indy 500.

As you can well imagine, there was a fine old British flap about it, and it got even worse when one of the Triple-A guys, in an honest effort to fix things up and keep everybody happy, suggested that maybe this Sheila Van Damm person could do the navigating and that her assigned navigator—a kind of college-professor type named Ron Kessell with ordinary, male-type personal plumbing—could sit on the business side of the front seat and do the actual driving.

Well, the notion that they couldn't front up the driver they wanted (and, worse yet, that it didn't really matter who drove…at least so long as it wasn't a woman, anyway!) upset the British Sunbeam team quite a bit. In fact, they were already in the middle of writing up the first of what would ultimately be a whole fistful of self-righteous and indignant protests when the organizers finally caved in and said—*heh-heh*—why don't we just make everybody in the cars "co-drivers" and let it go at that, okay?

Fair enough.

And you had to be impressed with how much this Sheila Van Damm lady knew about cars and racing and rallying. Why, it was like she was wired right into the whole worldwide motorsports scene! And then I found out that she wrote articles about rallying for this English magazine called *Autosport,* which came out every Friday—every blessed *week,* can you believe it?—and covered every kind of motorized competition you could imagine all over the world. Including The Great American Mountain Rallye!

And while it was fresh news, too!

Plus it was a real treat to lean your ear over and listen in when she was talking to a couple of her Sunbeam teammates: "I say, did you see the results from Mexico?"

"It was Fangio in the new Lancia D-Two-Four, wasn't it?"

"Clean sweep for Lancia, old boy. First, second and third."

"I bet that raised a few hackles over at Ferrari."

"No doubt."

"Hackle-raising is one of their specialties."

"That Fangio is incredible, isn't he?"

"Smart, too. He didn't win a single stage, but he was there at the end when it counted."

"Well, it's his type of event, isn't it? I mean, he cut his eyeteeth running old jalopies up and down the mountain ranges in Argentina."

"And that D-Two-Four looks to be a nice piece of kit, doesn't it?"

"They hired Jano away from Alfa Romeo to design it for them."

"Sad business, though. Fangio's teammate Bonetto got himself killed on the fourth stage and two other Eyeties did themselves in with a Ferrari."

"Dangerous, that…I say, do you happen to know who was first Brit home?"

"I'm afraid it was 'England out naught' again."

"Bloody shame. The lads at Jaguar really ought to see about making some sort of effort down there with the C-Types."

"Show the flag a bit, eh?"

Boy, the 1953 edition of *La Carrera Panamericana* had wrapped up just two days before, but this Sheila Van Damm and her buddies already knew all about it! I noticed one of them had a copy of that *Autosport* magazine she wrote for, and I asked if maybe I could see it. "Not this one. I just got it, old boy," the guy with the magazine said apologetically, "But I brought along a few old issues to catch up on during the plane ride over. You're welcome to them."

He rummaged around in his luggage and handed me about a half-dozen copies of *Autosport*. Well, at least I'd have something to read in the hotel room at night while Big Ed practiced up on his snoring....

But the point is that Sheila Van Damm and the rest of the people on the Sunbeam team took this Great American Mountain Rallye thing pretty seriously. And that turned out to be kind of a problem, seeing as how the people from the AAA and the Motor Sports Club of America who were running the damn rallye weren't nearly so professional or persnickety or well-prepared or tight of sphincter as some of the highly professional, persnickety, well-prepared and exceedingly tight of sphincter European teams who had traveled one hell of a long way across the ocean and had spent one hell of a lot of time and money and effort just to be there. And this was destined to cause a bit of friction. Starting off with the Great Mileage Correction Fiasco. Seems the organizers asked everybody to give them a mileage correction factor to even-up the mileage as shown on their own personal odometers with the Official Route Mileage as laid out by whoever the hell set the rallye route up in the first place. Only problem was that the official mileages as listed on the route instructions weren't at all accurate or consistent. Or at least not by tight-of-sphincter professional European rallying standards, anyway. And then there was the little matter of our local American speed limit laws, and so you got penalized—and I mean *heavily!*—if you somehow happened to show up early at a checkpoint. And the top average speed listed for the rallye—the very *top,* mind you!—was a measly 40 miles-per-hour. You should have heard how the Europeans scoffed and snorted at that! And it was made even easier on account of the weather didn't cooperate at all. Sure, it got cold up in northern Vermont and New Hampshire on the second and third days, but we were shit out of luck as far as ice and blizzards and closed mountain passes and border wars with Canada were concerned. In fact, as far as Big Ed and me and a lot of the other American entrants saw it, The Great American Mountain Rallye was nothing more than a nice, long, boring, scenic, early winter drive through the countryside. Or, in other words, a typical American rallye....

But the worst of it was the fuss over the timing and scoring. Seems some of the checkpoints actually showed up a few miles sooner than they indicated on the route instructions, which meant that you tended to arrive early unless, like Big Ed and me, you were already running late. Worse yet, the "official clocks" (which looked to me like they got filched off the scoring stand at a local high school basketball game) didn't much like the cold weather. In fact, my most lasting memory of the entire five days was the look on the face of this one British navigator when, right in front of him at a checkpoint up near Lake Champlain close to the Canadian border, the "official clock" froze solid. Just like that. And so the checkpoint official gave it a whap with his fist. At which point the hand jumped about four minutes and froze solid again. "Look here," the checkpoint official offered, " why don't you just use the time off my wristwatch. It's usually pretty close...."

The British navigator actually started to turn colors and sputter just a little. Like a teapot coming to a boil.

Still, it was nice to get away, even if it did amount to spending several clear, cold days stuck in a two-seater car with Big Ed Baumstein on a bunch of scenic country back roads and low mountain passes that didn't impress the European teams one bit. But I liked it. We got to travel all over Connecticut, Massachusetts, Vermont, New Hampshire and Upper New York State, and Big Ed even let me drive some of the time, and that was fun. I'd have to say that the Corvette was really pretty comfortable compared to an MG or something. And especially in cold weather. But the fiberglass body kind of rattled and clunked and creaked like an old wooden buckboard over rough roads, and it wasn't maybe the most powerful or handiest sort of sports car I'd ever driven.

Plus I got to thumb through those old copies of *Autosport* every night in our hotel room while Big Ed snored so loud he made the wallpaper flutter and again in the morning over breakfast or after breakfast while I was waiting back in the room for Big Ed to finish his regular Artillery Barrage morning constitutional. I lined them up by date and read them in order—cover to cover!—and it was like a whole new world opening up to me. Here was a two-page race report on the September 19th Watkins Glen event—complete with pictures!—that appeared in the October 2nd issue. Hell, you wouldn't see anything in *Road and Track* until the December issue at least! And on the very next page was a John Bolster test report on a "preposterously fast" new sports car called a Lotus. I'd never seen anything like it. Why, there was nothing to the damn thing! It didn't even have doors! But it was so light they had a picture of this John Bolster character holding up the whole damn frame in the crook of his blessed elbow. It was built by a guy named Colin Chapman, and I guess he'd already had some success building and racing his own cars over in England and he was getting quite a reputation as a clever and inventive sort of gent. Why, he didn't even paint the car—just left it in bare polished aluminum—on account of how much a can of paint weighs.

Still, I have to admit that new Lotus looked a mite on the frail and fragile side to me. But, at least according to the article, it was also fast as stink. And that always counts for a lot in a sports car. The astounding thing was that this Chapman character seemed to want people to take it seriously as a road-going automobile. Can you believe it? Hell, there was no way to even get in or out of the thing with the top up. And the only way a guy like Big Ed could ever sit in it was by straddling the damn transmission tunnel with one leg down each footwell. But you could tell this John Bolster guy really liked it, and you had to love the way he wrote it up. And I quote: *"As Mr. Chapman has no intention at present of invading the Rolls-Royce and Bristol market, he has given a little less attention than those two manufacturers to sound deadening and exhaust silencing. In consequence, particularly at peak revs, with the hood up, one can definitely hear the machinery at work..."*

I bet.

And I got absolutely absorbed by all these *Autosport* race reports and rallye reports and trials reports (trials are these strange English events where the basic idea is to drive these tall, tippy-looking roadsters up muddy hills and across soggy cow pastures and through cold, swampy peat bogs in terrible weather with the top down) from all over Great Britain, the continent and, in fact, the whole blessed rest of the world. Plus you got to read all the latest motorsports news flashes, rumors and gossip. Like there was always some Great New British Challenger in the works that was finally and once-and-for-all going to show the blasted Italians (and the blasted Germans, and the blasted French, and the blasted Americans...) just how it was done. Or some promising young British driver on the horizon who was finally and once-and-for-all going to show the bloody Italians (and the bloody Germans, and the bloody French, and the bloody Americans, and the bloody Argentineans...) just how it was done. In fact, flipping through the pages of *Autosport,* it was hard to avoid the notion that there might be just a wee bit of pro-British, Home Team sentiment left over in England after the war. Just a smidgen, you understand....

But it was neat reading John Bolster's test of the fabulously fast, expensive, exotic and complicated supercharged Pegaso from Spain and looking at a teaser shot of the new, fuel-injected Mercedes-Benz 300SL coupe that had the same, swoopy gullwing doors we'd seen on the factory racecars down in Mexico but that you could actually buy and drive on the road if you had enough money. Not to mention the cover shot of the strange new Bristol 450 coupe race and record car with its flattened-down front end and plastic headlamp covers like a pair of eyes and these two aerodynamic fins down the back that made it look like some weird brand of flounder you might catch off a Jersey pier. Inside was a fascinating cutaway drawing of the tall, handsome, all-British Bristol six under the hood. It had become a tremendously popular 2-liter racing engine in Great Britain, even if it *did* look suspiciously similar to a certain prewar BMW six that mysteriously disappeared from Germany—along with its chief engineer—after the war....

And I loved the reports on all the new British and European cars on display at the Paris Salon and the Earls Court Show in London. Including the handsome new Jowett Jupiter roadster with its startling all-plastic bodywork (which, by the way, looked one hell of a lot better than the old metal one) and a sharp new A.C. "Ace" sports car prototype and overleaf from that the new Alfa Romeo sedan and the new Aston Martin 2/4 coupe. Naturally Donald Healey had pictures and stories about the Healey Hundred plastered all over the place (you knew he would!) and MG was countering with a new sports model of their own, the TF, which had faired-in headlamps and a chopped and tilted-back grille that I thought looked very rakish indeed. Especially compared to their old TC and TD models (although I could hear the whining and whimpering from the diehard old upright-grille TC and TD types already). MG also had themselves a new four-seater sports sedan called the Magnette. It was named after some famous prewar MG racing car (more whining and whimpering), but I thought it looked really keen. And English car company Standard Triumph was unveiling their jaunty new TR2 roadster, which *Autosport* said would do an honest 100 miles-per-hour and touted as *"one of the lowest-priced high-performance machines in the world."* I kind of liked the way it looked, what with its cut-down doors and bulging frog eyes and the grille sucked way inside its own opening like it was swallowing something.

But the car that absolutely blew me out of my chair was the stunning new Arnolt-Bristol. I'd never even heard of it! Oh, I knew all about the S.H. Arnolt Company in Chicago that supplied parts and accessories for British cars, but I never knew they built cars, too. And you should've seen the picture! It had this smooth, flowing shape with these swoopy, razor-edge creases along the tops of the fenderlines and the two headlights stuck down low and mean inside the grille opening. It said in the caption that it was a Bristol chassis with Italian bodywork by some outfit called Bertone, and that it was being built specifically for export to the U.S. "Look at *this!*" I said to Big Ed as he came out of the can.

"What is it?"

"It's some special car with an English engine and chassis and an Italian body that they're making for the U.S. market only."

Big Ed peered in over my shoulder. "Sounds t'me like they're going through an awful lot of trouble."

"Yeah. But isn't it *neat?*"

Big Ed peered in a little closer and gave a mild grunt of approval.

He was getting tired of his Corvette. You could tell.

As always on long trips with somebody you know pretty well but don't actually live with, Big Ed and me had our long, edgy silences and moments of agitation with each other and times when we wondered just why the hell we wanted to be out there together in the middle of nowhere. But it was kind of refreshing to be far away from Passaic and Old Man Finzio's Sinclair and the duplex with Julie and her mom and the baby on the way and my folks' house and everything else that seemed to be closing in around me back home like one of those fly-eating plants you see in those flickering 16mm educational films with the hair-spider jumping around in the corner of the frame in high school biology class. And I told him about it. About how, all of a sudden, it seemed like I had a lot more than I ever bargained for going on in my life, what with the shop to run and all the customers to keep happy and the damn gas to pump out front when I was already in the middle of something and the phone ringing all the time and the payroll to get done with Julie every week and poor Julie getting bigger and more uncomfortable every day and winter setting in and the onslaught of yet another Family Holiday Without Letup season with my mom and dad and Julie's mom and my married sisters and their husbands and Sarah Jean (and maybe Carson Flegley?) and Mary Frances and her Lunar Orbit boyfriend Frederick and more damn work at the shop than I could believe and all this stuff to buy and set up at home for the baby and Old Man Finzio to go see whenever he was back in the hospital—I hated doing that, on account of all he did was stare at the wall and curse and grumble, but Julie said we had to since he didn't have anyone else to visit him in the hospital and sit there in the room with him and watch him stare at the wall and listen to him curse and grumble—and I was coming to realize that all the commitments and responsibilities and places I had to be and things I had to do were kind of dragging me around by the nose instead of the other way 'round. "It's the quicksand effect," Big Ed explained as we thumped across a covered bridge over a half-frozen trout stream someplace up near Lincoln Pass.

"The what?"

"The quicksand effect. One day you're a kid without a care in the world and, next thing you know, you've stepped in a damn pool of quicksand and it's all you can do to keep it from sucking you under."

"Boy, that's it exactly."

"Get used to it, Buddy," Big Ed chuckled. "You'll find it's pretty much like that from here on out."

"You're joking."

Big Ed shook his head. "I wish I was. But I'm not."

"That's a cheery thought."

"And it's not the responsibilities," he assured me.

"It isn't?"

"Uh-uh," he held up his index finger. "It's the *being* responsible that does you in."

"But I don't *like* being responsible."

"Nobody does. It's no fun. It screws up everything," Big Ed unwrapped himself a fresh cigar. "In fact, it plain and simple stinks."

"And there's no way out?"

"Eventually you die," he said like it should make me feel better.

"And that's it?"

"Well," he allowed, "you can try to be a rich bum like me, but I can't say as I really recommend it. Besides, I don't think you got what it takes."

"I don't?"

"Nah. You're too nice. You care about people. You try to do the right thing." He shook his head. "Yer just not cut out t'be a prick. It's just not in the cards fr'you."

"So what do I do?"

"Same as you're already doing."

"But it's grinding me down, y'know? Every day it's grinding me down."

"Aw, you're not even through the top layer a'skin yet," Big Ed laughed. "Trust me, Buddy. It's barely even started...."

And of course he was right.

"...But here's the important thing, see. Y'gotta plan. Y'gotta plot. Y'gotta decide what it is you wanta go after in life an' then y'gotta go get it for yourself...."

We'd turned onto a side road heading up a steep hill, and it was all packed with flattened-down snow and patches of ice and the back end of the Corvette was sliding all over the place while the rear wheels spun helplessly and our forward progress slowed to a crawl. Even with Big Ed mashing the gas until 80-to-100 miles-per-hour was waving back at us on the speedometer! Like I said before, Big Ed Baumstein was not one of your more skill- or finesse-oriented sportycar drivers. Not hardly. He was more of the Babe Ruth/Rocky Marciano, ham-fisted-but-with-very-large-hams school of high-speed motoring.

"...y'gotta think about the *future,* see?" Big Ed continued as he spun the steering wheel one way and then the other like a damn ship's captain, right foot still mashed to the floorboards so that all three throttle plates in those Carter sidedrafts were thoroughly horizontal. "Things don't generally just fall in your lap in this life..." Big Ed hollered over the fringes of valve float, "...at least not unless you've worked yer damn butt off puttin' that lap of yers in the right place first…" and with that, the back end of the Corvette kind of slewed out sideways one final time, teetered on the verge, and then eased itself gently yet inexorably down into the ditch. It felt exactly like that quicksand Big Ed had been talking about.

And right about then is when that funny-looking little 1200cc Volkswagen powered right past us, carving up through the snow like it was nothing thanks to the weight of that air-cooled engine hung out over the rear wheels where it could actually do some good. It disappeared away up the hill, motoring along just as nice as you please, blowing those unmistakable, fart-in-a-bathtub noises back at us out of its little pea-shooter exhaust pipe the whole way. Damn!

16: Car Shows, Cribs and Coffins

By the time Christmas and New Years rolled around, Old Man Finzio amazed everybody by rallying enough to be wheeled out to the sitting room at the end of the hallway in his hospital wing every now and again, where he'd sit for a half hour or so staring silently out the window like he hated everything he could see and then they'd wheel him back again. Once a week or so we'd go over and do the wheeling for them. Julie insisted on it. And I wasn't about to argue with her, on account of she'd gotten to that stage where she was real big and uncomfortable and couldn't wait to squeeze the kid out just to get rid of the damn burden of carrying it around. Watching her go through all that stuff was difficult (although I'm sure not so difficult as being the person with the additional person stuck inside), and I was learning that the only thing you could do under those circumstances was maybe bring her a cup of tea or a jar of olives or a gallon tub of ice cream when she wanted it and try to keep my head down in the process. You really don't want to be getting into a difference of opinion with a female creature of *any* species when they're seriously pregnant. It's just asking for trouble.

So for Christmas I bit the bullet and surprised her with a brand new, not-quite-top-of-the-line, last-year's model Zenith TV set with an illuminated "Spotlight Dial" feature so's you could tell what channel you were watching even in a darkened room (which I bought on time, of course, even though I hated to do it and it was against my better principles). At first Julie got mad at me for spending the money, and even madder that I'd bought it on time, but then she started watching it a little and then a little bit more until finally she was pretty much ignoring me. Which, if you want the honest truth of it, was kind of a relief. Of course the bad thing about television is that it brings the whole damn world into your own, private apartment, and while Dave Garroway and Gary Moore and Arthur Godfrey and even J. Fred Muggs might be a bit more entertaining than the person you happen to be married to (and when you think about it, they *should* be—after all, they're professionals), I prefer my news and comment when *I* decide to pick up a newspaper, not when some network yahoo decides it's time to blast me with it out of the TV screen. And there was a lot of stuff going on in the world right then. "Tailgunner Joe" McCarthy was continuing to roll down Capitol Hill like a damn avalanche, showing off lists of "communists in our government" that he never actually read out loud and pointing fingers in all directions and warning everybody and their brother about the dirty Reds who—at least according to him—were absolutely everywhere in the State Department. And some people, like Senator Pat McCarran and TV newsman Edward R. Murrow, had had about enough of it and even said so in public. Meanwhile the *real* communist Reds over in Russia had themselves a little political rethink and stood Stalin's old second-in-command and the ex-chief of the Soviet Secret Police Lavrenti Pavlovich Beria and six of his best buddies up against a wall in front of a firing squad. But they didn't stand for very long, as I'm sure you can imagine. The Navy launched the world's very first atomic submarine, the *Nautilus* (which hopefully gave the Russians a little something more to worry about), famous New Zealander Sir Edmund Hillary and his faithful Sherpa guide who never got any credit were traipsing all over the Himalayas looking for the Abominable Snowman, Marilyn Monroe married Joe DiMaggio, and everybody you passed on the street or got stuck behind in the checkout line at the grocery store was humming *"Stranger in Paradise"* from the hit show *Kismet* or whistling *"How Much is that Doggie in the Window?"* over and over and over until you wanted to smash their teeth in. I mean, there's a limit to just how much *cute* you can take, you know?

Towards the end of January, the whole bunch of us—Cal, Carson, Big Ed and me—snuck our way over to Manhattan on a Sunday to run our eyeballs over the World Motor Sports Show at Madison Square Garden and the General Motors "GM Motorama" display at the swanky Waldorf-Astoria Hotel just twenty blocks away. The Garden show was neat on account of they had television star and show promoter Herb Shriner's fantastic Phantom Corsair parked right out front, and I swear it looked like something out of a Batman comic book. Honest it did. And they also had this sort-of homemade armored car that, to quote the *New York Times,* "crashed through the Iron Curtain last summer to carry eight Czech refugees to freedom." Unfortunately, it didn't do quite so well up against normal, everyday New York traffic, since it broke down on its "heroic tour of the city" and had to be towed the rest of the way to Madison Square Garden. Honest it did. They ran a picture of it in the paper and everything. But it was great to be there in person and run my eyeballs and fingertips down the fenderlines of all those fantastic cars I'd seen on the pages of *Autosport* magazine. Including the same exact Lancia D24 racecar that Juan Manuel Fangio used to win *La Carrera Panamericana* in November (and it was extra neat being one of the only people there who really knew what that meant). They had the new, production-issue Mercedes-Benz 300SL "gullwing" coupe making its World Premiere up on a big, rotating turntable right by the front entrance. It was the final, civilized, over-the-counter version of the cars that had won both Le Mans and *La Carrera* in 1952, and it sure looked mean and slick and fast and immaculately finished and solid as a damn bank vault. It should, for a whopping $6,820 Ca$h American! And there was a waiting list, can you believe it? On the floor next to it was the 190SL "wife's car" you could get to go along with it if you really needed a matched set. You could also talk to this nice guy with a bad limp named Rudi Caracciola, who I guess was some big famous racer for Mercedes-Benz before the war. To be honest, he looked kind of bored and tired to me. Then again, that's what real racers always seem to look like when they're out of the car and away from the track. Even if they've given it up. Or if it's given them up, too....

"You oughta get yourself one of those," Cal told Big Ed, pointing an envious finger at the slippery-looking silver 300SL up on the rotating turntable.

"Nah, I don't think that'd be such a swell idea."

"Too rich for your blood?"

Big Ed's lip curled. "It ain't that at all. I can afford any damn car I want, see?"

"Then what's the problem?"

"It's German."

"You won't own a German car?"

"Hey, I don't give a shit. The war's over as far as I'm concerned. The Germans got a big head and stepped out of line and they got what was comin' to 'em. I made a lotta money on it, too. I'm not gonna be a damn hypocrite."

"Then why not buy yourself one? You deserve it."

"I'd love to," Big Ed said wistfully. "Only I got family and friends t'think about, see...."

"They don't approve of German cars?"

Big Ed looked at Cal like he'd just fallen off a turnip truck. "Look, it's like I said. The war's over as far as I'm concerned. Finished. Kaput. Ancient history. Next case. There's nothing you can do t'change or undo any of it, see?"

"I see."

"But some people don't think that way. In fact, a *lotta* people don't think that way."

"And they're *your* people, aren't they?"

"Yeah," Big Ed said disgustedly. "They're my people, all right." But then he turned around and faced all three of us. He looked angry. "Now don't go gettin' me wrong here. I know who I am and I know where the hell I came from. And I feel as bad as the next guy for anybody who had to go through all that shit inna war. I give plenty to charity..."

None of us said a word.

"...but I know people who've made a damn life's work outta reminding the world over and over again about stuff we'd be better off sweeping under a rug and forgetting." He rolled his palms up helplessly. "I mean, fr'chrissakes, it just doesn't do any *good...*"

Cal and Carson and me looked back and forth at each other.

Big Ed's eyes gradually lowered to the floor. "I guess what really pisses me off is that the loudest and shrillest and angriest ones are people it never touched at all, see? The people who spent the whole friggin' war here in the states having paper drives and scrap drives and charity auctions and never suffered so much as a loose hangnail!" He looked up at us again. *"They're* the ones who feel guilty, dammit! Because they missed out on all that misery." He sighed and shook his head, and you could feel the cloud of anger kind of pass over and melt away.

"So you can't have a German car, right?"

"Yeah, that's about it," Big Ed snorted disgustedly. "I'd just have to take too much crap from too many people if I did."

"You think, umm, *people like yourself* will ever buy German cars?"

"Nah," Big Ed sighed. "I can't ever imagine it happening. No way...."

Across from Mercedes was the Rootes display, which featured a special, cream-colored Hillman "Californian" sedan up on a dramatically sloped platform and a bright red Sunbeam Alpine like Sheila Van Damm and her teammates drove on their disappointing Great American Mountain Rallye. But they had a big sign on it anyway trumpeting all the other major rallye successes they'd enjoyed over in Europe. I don't think they realized that most Americans think a rally is something you have before a high school football game.

A red Healey Hundred was on display right in the middle of the Austin of England stand, and Donald Healey himself was there in person to press the flesh and answer your questions. He was sure one hell of a promoter, no question about it! Jaguar didn't have anything much in the way of new models, but the XK 120 roadster, coupe and drophead on the stand all had dazzling chrome wire wheels and right in the center of it all was the much-publicized "Golden Jaguar" XK 120, which was all done up in gleaming Olde English white with matching white leather upholstery and genuine, 18-karat gold-plated accessories, fittings and trim. You could almost feel Big Ed's eyes bug out when he saw it. I was happy to see Triumph had their gutty new TR2 sports car up on a turntable that actually rivaled Mercedes'—you just knew they were going to sell a ton of them here in the states!—and our old buddy Colin St. John was showing off a new MG TF in light gray with red leather upholstery and a flamboyant red Bentley Continental that could be yours for a paltry $17,320. Or, in other words, not quite twice what an average house went for.

Hudson of all people had this monstrous "Italia" dream car on display, Kaiser had their pursed-up Darrin two-seater with the grille that looked like it was sucking a lemon and the doors that slid forward into the fenders (now why on earth would you want to do that?) and Packard showed off their huge "Panther Daytona" roadster prototype with an all-fiberglass body that didn't look real likely to make it into production. I mean, who the heck needed a two-seater automobile with a 122-inch wheelbase and enough luggage space for a trip across India? Alfred Momo had a stand where you could buy yourself a swell hop-up kit for a Healey Hundred engine that had Carson drooling all over his shoes (and Cal right along with him!) and our friend Carlo Sebastian was displaying the special single-seater the Ferrari factory was planning to enter at the Indianapolis 500 that year (he seemed pretty confident they were going to win, even though they weren't exactly sure who was going to be driving it yet), plus a new 250-series three-liter "Europa" coupe, a monstrous 4.5-litre "America" roadster and a nifty little 2.7-liter "225 Export" coupe with bodywork by Vignale. I noticed Big Ed went over and had a few words with Carlo Sebastian, and then Carlo led him over to that sharp little 225 Export coupe and Big Ed tried to get himself inside. And then he tried again. Finally Carlo shrugged—*what can you do?*—and that was the end of that particular Ferrari fantasy as far as Big Ed Baumstein was concerned.

All the others, of course, were already spoken for....

But the exhibit that knocked me flat was the Arnolt display. Turns out this S.H. Arnolt guy was quite a character. They called him "Wacky" on account of he always wore this big, Texas-sized 10-gallon cowboy hat and a matching set of tooled leather cowboy boots so he looked every inch the county fair sideshow hustler. But I found out later he was also incidentally the largest single employer in the entire state of Indiana and also part owner of Bertone bodyworks over in Italy and quite the entrepreneur in general. And if that reminds you in any way of the story of certified Genuine American Character Earl "Madman" Muntz with the red flannel underwear and Napoleon hat, you're not the only one. Anyhow, what this S.H. "Wacky" Arnolt did with his life was pretty darn amazing. He started off as a salesman, see, and wound up selling this little "Sea Mite" outboard engine for some company in Wisconsin. But then they went broke and owed him a lot of back commission money, and so he settled on the rights to the Sea Mite engine. And then the war came and he somehow managed to talk the U.S. government into buying up a few kazillion Sea Mite engines for Our Boys in Uniform and he was on his way. He branched out into a lot of different businesses during and after the war—including imported sports cars—and no question underneath that massive 10-gallon hat was the head and heart of a genuine car-nut enthusiast with a serious case of the old sports car disease.

Meanwhile, over in Italy, this Nuccio Bertone guy had a coachbuilding shop in Turin that had been around for many years but had fallen on hard times after the war and was just about ready to go tits-up. As a kind of last-ditch, desperate effort, they built themselves a couple handsome and well-proportioned envelope bodies on a pair of MG TD chassis, one coupe and one convertible, and stuck them on the stand at the Turin Auto Show in hopes that somebody—hell, *anybody!*—might want to buy them. Well, up walks "Wacky" Arnolt in his 10-gallon hat and says: *"That's a damn fine-lookin' pair of MGs you got there!"* and he orders himself up a couple hundred. Just like that.

Well, as you can imagine, old Nuccio Bertone and his people are about falling all over themselves! And so they start building the cars and shipping them over and even getting some interest from other manufacturers after they do a couple show cars and this far-out-in-the-ozone "aerodynamic study" on an Alfa Romeo chassis called the B.A.T. (for *Berlinetta Aerodinamica Tecnica)* 5 all done up in sinister, gunmetal gray with these wild, science-fiction tailfins curving up around the rear window like the petals of some all-alloy space flower. Well, old Wacky sees it and likes it and decides to buy it and, pretty soon, he's part owner of the whole blessed company. And what do you do if you're a big-time, all-American entrepreneur who owns part of an Italian coachbuilding house that needs more work but go into the damn car manufacturing business yourself? And that's precisely how S.H. "Wacky" Arnolt wound up ordering himself a bunch of very nice Bristol running chassis over in England and having them shipped down to Italy so's his buddies at Bertone can put the most beautiful production-car bodies I'd ever seen in my entire life on them. I mean, they looked like they swooped right down out of the future! Or they did to me, anyway.

"Wacky" called the new cars Arnolt-Bristols, and he had one on the stand along with that incredible B.A.T. 5 aerodynamic study and a couple of the Arnolt MGs, and I'd have to say that I spent darn near an hour just wandering around those cars and gawking at them. Big Ed seemed pretty interested, too. Even after he tried to sit down in the Arnolt-Bristol roadster and discovered that he could only get one cheek at a time into that stylish little bucket seat that was obviously designed for skinny little ginzos who look good in tight Italian pants. "We can make whatever kind of seat you need," the salesman assured him. "Right at the factory."

Big Ed liked that kind of service. Then again, he was never exactly what you would call an "off-the-rack" kind of guy....

After the International Motor Sports Show we dropped over by the GM Motorama at the Waldorf Astoria, and of course the crowd was enormous on account of admission was free and you always get a boatload of rubberneckers whenever you advertise something free at a swank address like the Waldorf Astoria (although the ads did tell you to use the 49th Street entrance so's the Great Unwashed wouldn't interfere with the hotel's regular guests). Anyhow, it was quite a change to see General Motors' view of the future compared to what we'd seen at the other show. The star attraction was GM's incredible new turbine-powered "Firebird" dream car, which looked exactly—and I mean *exactly!*—like the rocket-powered Douglas D-558-2 Skyrocket that had just set a new world record by flying twice the speed of sound back in November. Only the GM version had a little bit smaller wings. Oh, and four wheels, too. Chevy division showed off a "concept vehicle" station wagon version of the Corvette called the Nomad, and I could see Big Ed's opinion of his own Corvette going sourer and sourer even as he stood there looking at it. I mean, it was a damn *station wagon,* for gosh sakes! And each of the other GM divisions had their own "sporstcar study" two-seater dream cars like the Corvette. Buick's was called the "Wildcat" (which, to be honest, looked pretty sharp, if just a wee bit on the gaudy side) and Olds had its "F-88" and Pontiac showed off a "Bonneville Special" in a kind of deep metallic chestnut color with a plexiglass bubble roof, a pair of big chrome racing stripes down the middle and what appeared to be the business end of a solid-fuel rocket for a rear end treatment. And there were bigger dream cars, too. *Really* big. But, like I said, all of that was pretty tame stuff compared to the "Firebird" turbine car. I mean, did the brass at GM really figure we were all gonna be cruising around Levittown one day in four-wheeled, bubble-canopied jet fighters? Or would it go the other way to huge, flamboyant, longer, lower and wider All-American Land Yachts with extravagant scoops and enormous tailfins and two-tone paint and matching Living Room Sofa interiors? The problem as far as I could see was that there just weren't any *real* cars in between....

Meanwhile Old Man Finzio had gotten worse again and his doctors decided to cut him open and dig the worms out of his guts one more time—God only knows why—the first week of February. And so now he was back staring at the ceiling without really seeing it in the Intensive Care ward and I don't think he even knew when somebody else was in the room. But Julie said I had to go anyway, on account of they know you're there and it makes them feel better not to be alone even if they can't show you or tell you how they feel. And maybe she's right. It was hard for her to go because she was so huge and uncomfortable and about ready to pop herself, and the strange part is I didn't really mind it so much as I thought I would. I'd sit there and read the paper or a copy of *Road and Track* or something for a half hour or so and Old Man Finzio would just lay there and wheeze and gurgle and stare up into space. But I noticed he really did wheeze and gurgle more comfortably when I was in the room. Sometimes he'd even close his eyes and drift off to sleep, and it frankly amazed me how good that made me feel.

The baby finally arrived in the early, pre-dawn hours of Sunday, February 14th—Valentine's Day, wouldn't you know it?—and naturally we'd been up all night in the hospital just waiting for it to arrive. In fact, I thought everything was gonna happen in a big hurry when Julie called me up all frantic and panicky at the shop on Saturday afternoon to tell me it was time. Boy, I was out of there like a shot in the Old Man's tow truck and then falling all over myself back at the duplex trying to gather up all the things I thought we might need. "Why on earth are you bringing *that?*" Julie half-gasped/half-demanded as we headed out the door.

It was hard to know what she was talking about, since both my arms were full of stuff.

"That!" she repeated, and pointed to the thing in my hand.

"It's the baby's rattle," I explained. "My mom gave it to you at the baby shower, remember? I thought maybe we might need it...."

Julie rolled her eyes. And then she got another pain that blew them wide open. *"Oh JESUS!"* she damn near screamed.

I almost tipped the Old Man's tow truck over just trying to make the blessed corner at the end of our street. Hell, I thought she was about ready to have the kid right there on the front seat! But that was just the beginning....

We got her to the hospital and checked her in and the whole time she was wincing and grimacing and biting her lip and digging her fingernails into my arm—I still have the marks, honest I do!—and then they put her in this little room to wince and grimace and bite her lip and dig her fingernails into anything that was handy some more. Jeez, it was tough watching her go through all that. I'd walk into the room to see if maybe I could do anything for her, but one look at her face and I couldn't wait to get back out of there. I mean, I can take it when *I* get hurt. Hey, you put up with it, you know? But watching somebody you care about when they're hurting and in pain is something else entirely. It just tears your guts out. Plus I could tell she didn't much want me around watching, and it was actually a relief when her mom showed up an hour or so later and threw me out of the room—staring flamethrowers at me the whole time like all of it was something I'd done to Julie on purpose—and then I just kind of meandered around the hospital corridors feeling tired and scared and more than anything utterly useless. And it didn't help matters one bit that the damn baby'd decided to show up more than a week early so that everybody in the neighborhood who could count to nine would enjoy themselves a nasty little behind-the-hand snicker over it. But at least it was healthy and normal when it finally decided to poke its way out around 3:30 ayem, a seven-and-a-quarter pound boy with a black thatch of pureblood Italian hair on his head already and an exceedingly well-developed set of lungs. I swear, you could probably hear the echo all the way over in Times Square.

We thought about calling him Valentino for being born on Valentine's Day and all, but decided it was maybe too hokey (besides, a kid named Valentino in our neighborhood was either going to get into an awful lot of fistfights or turn into a florist or a hairdresser or something), and we finally settled on Vincent Anthony after Julie's dad that she hardly knew. I'll never in my life forget the moment when she handed him over to me for the very first time. My legs were shaking so bad you could almost hear the knees knocking together, and I was so afraid I'd drop him or crush him or hold him too loose or squeeze him too tight or put my thumb clear through that soft spot in his head they always warn you about. Jeez, he was such a tiny, helpless little thing and it made me go all hollow inside at the thought that he was mine to look out for and provide for and take care of forever and ever. I don't think you ever really know pure, cold fear in your heart until you hold that first little baby in your arms.

Which is precisely why I insisted we make Big Ed the baby's godfather. I figured he was the one person we knew who could actually do the kid some good here and there or maybe help him out of a jam or two while he was growing up. And you would not believe how surprised and embarrassed and grateful and emotional Big Ed got when I asked him. "Boy, that's really something," he said over and over again. "That's really, really something." And he went right out and bought little Vincenzo a couple hundred bucks worth of toys. Including a Lionel electric train that I didn't think he'd get around to playing with for a few years yet (and that we had no room in the apartment to set up anyway) and a brand new, top-of-the-line, 100th Year Commemorative Edition Schwinn Black Phantom bicycle complete with cantilever frame, chrome fenders, chrome horn, chrome tank with a cast aluminum horn button in the side, girder front fork with a chrome coil spring, whitewall tires, head and tail lights, rear luggage rack, deluxe sprung seat and red, white and blue plastic streamers coming out of the rubber handlebar grips. "Don't you think it's maybe a little big for him?" I asked Big Ed.

"Well, it's got training wheels, see...."

People will tell you that a lot of wonderful, magical, heartwarming things happen when you bring a new baby home. And especially when it's your first. To begin with, everybody starts treating you with a new kind of warmth and respect and understanding. Even hardcore jerks and assholes like my old man and Julie's mom, can you believe it? Of course, the other thing that happens is that you don't get to sleep any more. Babies, I was soon to discover, operate on this special internal clock that is always set to go off precisely whenever you find yourself finally falling into a deep, velvety sleep. And, like I said, little Vincenzo Anthony had himself quite a set of lungs. Plus he could swing a really mean kick if he didn't figure his lungs were quite getting the job done. In fact, I was thinking maybe he'd grow up to be a football placekicker for the Giants or something.

But the point is that your schedule changes completely when you bring that first baby home. All of a sudden you're on *his* schedule, you know? And so the only time *you* can sleep is when *he* sleeps. Only he sleeps when you're off fixing engines and towing in sick cars and changing oil and pumping gas and arguing with cheap mooch customers over their bill. So when you get home after working late on some dumb school principal's Plymouth so you can get up early and be there so he can pick it up before he has to be at school in the morning, little Vincenzo is wide awake and raring to go and sure to wake you up at least a couple dozen times to be fed or changed or just for the damn mischievous fun of it.

"You look tired," Cal observed one day when he dropped by to try to borrow enough gas money to get his mom's new Packard back home to Castle Carrington before she noticed it was missing.

"Yeah, I'm pretty bushed," I admitted as I shuffled around the shop on dead zombie feet. "I haven't been sleeping real good."

"You need to get your rest," Cal offered, like it was my choice or something.

"Thanks for the advice. Everybody says it'll get better."

"When?"

"Oh, maybe when he starts dating...."

All of which put the Jagillac project on the back burner for several months while I tried my best to keep up with the valve adjustments and 2am feedings and gear whines and baby whines and tires changes and diaper changes and pumping gas and burping gas and all the other stuff that tends to turn your life into some kind of Hollywood Special Effects blur that you find yourself stumbling through on plodding, exhausted feet when you've got a business to run and a wife and customers and family to keep happy and a new baby in the house.

But then he'd look at me with one of those gurgly, goo-goo smiles or, better yet, reach out and take hold of my fingertip like it was some kind of lifeline off the back of the Titanic and I'd melt into just another dumb, googly-eyed new daddy telling everybody who'd listen about the way he smiled or the sweet little noises he made or just exactly how he took hold of the end of my finger or batted at his rattle or what a lovely little dump he took right square on the back of my hand when I was in the middle of changing him.....

To be perfectly honest, I wasn't too much use when it came to changing little Vincenzo. Oh, I could *do* it. If I really, really had to. But it made me gag and hack and act like it was going to make me puke so bad that Julie'd get all mad and disgusted and say, "Here, let *me* do that!" and push me right out of the way. Apparently I'd learned a thing or two from Cal Carrington, if you know what I mean.

But the thing you don't see—the thing you never realize or appreciate at the time—is how the minutes and hours and days are so full of all the stuff you have to do that, even though you're busy as hell and doing more than you've ever done in your life (and on less sleep, too!), the weeks and months start all melting together and you can't believe it's late spring already and the damn Jagillac project is sitting out there behind the shop under a tarp just the same way you left it a few weeks before the baby was born. I mean, we'd missed any chance of making the early-season races and I was also starting to realize how difficult and time consuming all the damn little details of building your own car can become. Why, once I got started on it again, Roman and me must've farted around for three solid weeks just trying to get the damn motor mounts right. And then of course the exhaust manifolds wouldn't clear the frame or the steering shaft. I thought about swapping them around—you know, pointing them upwards and forwards on the opposite sides?—but it wouldn't bolt up that way, either. Plus it would've looked a little screwy, you know? So that meant we had to make header dump pipes out of tubing. And don't even get me started about what kind of damn job *that* was. Plus adapting the front end of the tranny out of Big Ed's Jaguar to the flywheel end of Big Ed's Caddy engine turned out to be a real major undertaking. Roman finally solved it by literally bolting the two flywheels together and doing a little machining here and there so's they'd weigh less than seventy pounds and made us a nice adapter plate so's the Caddy starter would still work on the front side and the Jag clutch arm and bellhousing would work on the back end. It was a pretty genius piece of field engineering, if you want the truth of it. Even though we were both thinking the Jag gears and synchros might be a tad marginal against the torque of a hotted-up Caddy V8. Why, Big Ed could shred 'em up even with the stock Jaguar six installed....

Old Man Finzio finally passed away early in the morning of Tuesday, March 2nd, and I can remember it so well on account of it was the day after the U.S. exploded the biggest Hydrogen Bomb ever someplace in the middle of the Pacific Ocean and a handful of Puerto Rican fanatics opened fire from the gallery of the House of Representatives in Washington and wounded a bunch of U.S. Congressmen. And I know all that for certain because it was on the front page of the early-edition newspaper I read and re-read over and over while I was waiting at the hospital to help out with the paperwork and make "the arrangements" for Old Man Finzio's body. I mean, there was nobody else to do it, right? Anyhow, according to the newspaper story, this new bomb was "so powerful that scientific measuring instruments could not record its full effects, and radioactive debris was hurled far beyond the safety zone set for the test." They said it was a full 600 times more powerful than the A-Bomb the Enola Gay dropped on Hiroshima back in 1945 and damn near wiped the whole blessed city off the face of the earth. It also said the U.S. Armed Forces were already stockpiling these things and were planning to set off even bigger ones in the next series of tests. And that was a scary thought indeed when you had a new baby at home and also knew for certain that if *we* had something, the Russians were sure to want one of their own sooner or later. Plus I couldn't believe that people had actually pulled guns and sprayed bullets around in the House of Representatives. Nobody could. It was like the whole world was made of sand and it was leaking out through an hourglass right under your blessed feet.

And besides that, Old Man Finzio was gone, and that gave me the same exact kind of feeling. I'd never exactly gone through all the stuff you have to go through when somebody dies—I mean, I'd never been old enough or directly in the line of fire before—and the amazing thing is how numb you feel and how you can't really get your head and heart around it. It's almost like sleepwalking. Thankfully Carson came over when I called and he was an enormous help. He even got us a swell wholesale price on the casket and the room and the flowers and the mass cards and all the other fixins' you need for a proper wake and funeral. The sad part was nobody much came to the wake outside of me and Julie and Julie's mom and my mom and dad and my sister Sarah Jean and short, ten-minute visits by Butch and Tater and Raymond and of course Big Ed. I actually had to call Cal Carrington and some of our better sportycar customers over at the station to get enough pallbearers to make it look right at church the next day. And the worst part was that Julie's mom asked me to say a few words at the funeral. Jeez, that was the last thing in the world I wanted to do. Not to mention that I had no idea whatsoever what I could possibly say. I mean, the whole idea at funerals is that one or two people who knew and loved the deceased are supposed to stand up there in front of God and everybody and rattle off a few teary-eyed nice things about them. But, to be brutally honest about it, there weren't too many nice things you could say about Old Man Finzio. I asked Julie about it (or, more precisely, I asked her if there was any way in hell I could possibly get out of it!) but she got that look she has like the foot-thick door of a solid steel bank vault and told me I was gonna have to do it and to just to say something nice and simple and be done with it. But the idea of standing up in church and lying through my teeth didn't really sit too well—especially in front of God and Butch and everybody else who really knew Old Man Finzio—and I didn't sleep a wink all night agonizing over it.

Fortunately the church was damn near empty for Old Man Finzio's funeral—just the immediate family and a few charitable customers from the Sinclair—and I squirmed and fidgeted all the way through the part where you alternately sit down and stand up and sit down and kneel while the priest mumbles along in Latin that you don't understand and then drones on into a bunch of

English that you don't understand either, the whole time just dreading the moment when I'd have to go up there and climb those rose-colored marble steps to that dark, serious-looking oak podium and "say a few words." And then the time finally came and Julie's mom got up first and she strutted her way up there and cocked her head back with those beady, bird-of-prey eyes of hers flicking around from one near-empty row of pews to another. "He was a good man, my brudder-in-law," she said proudly, almost angrily. "He always kept a nice t'ought for us after my husban' got machine-gunned dead by a Jap pillbox inna Philippines." She looked directly over at Julie and me. "He took carra my Joolie an' me anytime we needed anything, an' he put that husban' of hers to work an' gave him a wunnerful opportunity." She said it like pumping gas and fixing cars at the Sinclair was a royal commission or something. And then, just like that, she stepped down and strutted back to her seat and turned her cold, fierce eyes at me like a pair of Ming The Merciless ray-gun beams.

Julie nudged my leg. *"Go on!"* she hissed under her breath.

So my legs kind of stood me up and I walked like a condemned man on the last twenty paces to the gas chamber up to that somber-looking oak podium, took a deep breath, turned around, and faced the few scattered people out there in that tall, vast, empty and intimidating sanctuary. And then I caught Butch's eyes, looking right at me. He was hard to miss, what with his wheelchair out in the middle of the aisle. "W-well," I began, my voice kind of cracking, "my mother-in-law is right about Ol...I mean, Mr....I mean...*him* giving me an opportunity." I looked around the room desperately for help. And there was Big Ed, looking back up at me, kind of urging me along with his eyes. I swallowed hard and, without even thinking about it, started talking more about Butch and Big Ed than Old Man Finzio. "I learned an awful lot from him. Not just about fixing cars, but about people and growing up..." And then it was like I caught myself and this little voice inside said, *"you'd better watch it, Buster, you're in church,"* and I desperately tried to think of something real and honest and yet not too terribly ugly or damaging or mean-spirited I could say about Old Man Finzio now that he was gone. I cleared my throat and started in again: *"The thing everybody who knew him remembers about this man..."* I began grandly. And then I kind of ran out of words and found myself stranded. I looked desperately at Julie and then Butch and then Big Ed for assistance. And then it came to me, and I straightened my shoulders and addressed that meager crowd with renewed confidence: *"...is that he treated everybody the same."*

And that seemed as good a time as any to stumble back to my seat and sit down. *"Good job,"* Julie whispered in my ear. *"Thanks."* That by itself made it kind of worthwhile.

No doubt it would've pissed the Old Man off something awful if he'd known Cal Carrington was one of the pallbearers carrying his earthly remains, but I'm sure he was far too dead to care. And so me and Carson and my dad and Big Ed and Cal and Raymond and Tater and Butch kind of rolling alongside the casket as best he could took the Old Man's coffin out of the silver-and-black Cadillac hearse, brought it over to the fresh hole in the ground at the cemetery, listened while the priest said a few more words that didn't mean anything to anybody who actually knew Old Man Finzio, and then we all laid our gloves on top of the casket and watched as they lowered it down into the ground and that was pretty much the end of it.

And I remember I kept thinking: *"so now I'm really on my own now."* But the funny part is, it didn't feel all that much different. But I guess that's the way it is with change and growing up. It all happens so fast and yet so gradually that you never really catch it while it's happening. It's only later, when you look back on it. Or when you look in the mirror one day and wonder where the heck the kid went....

Elkhart Lake's

ROAD AMERICA

···*INAUGURAL*···

Road Races

SEPTEMBER 10-11, 1955

**OFFICIAL
PROGRAM
50¢**

*Sanctioned
by the*
**SPORTS CAR
CLUB OF AMERICA**

"Old Speckled Hen" is a strong, fine ale created by Morland of Abingdon, Oxfordshire, England. the home of the MG sports car. Morland developed their special traditional ale to 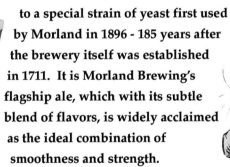 commemorate MG's 50th anniversary, employing all the skill and enthusiasm you would expect from a centuries-old country brewery.

The ale was named after a unique 1927 MG saloon car. Canvas covered, painted gold and flecked with black, the car was known fondly as "the old speckled 'un." The name evolved over time into "Old Speckled Hen"— and the rest is history.

The ale owes its distinctive character and smooth, dry taste to a special strain of yeast first used by Morland in 1896 - 185 years after the brewery itself was established in 1711. It is Morland Brewing's flagship ale, which with its subtle blend of flavors, is widely acclaimed as the ideal combination of smoothness and strength.

In addition to brewing exceptionally fine English ales, the brewery owns and operates over 1700 picturesque town, country and riverside pubs - the heart of hospitality in Britain!

Elkhart Lake

America's Road Racing Capital

SCCA Road Races
September 10-11

SEE the revolutionary *new* four-mile course!

SEE cars & drivers from all over the world compete!

Road America, Inc., Elkhart Lake, Wisconsin
N7390 Hwy 67 - Dial 2-4576
www.roadamerica.com

3

Author / racer / ride mooch
B.S. Levy in the process of
mooching yet another exciting
ride from well-known Canadian
racer, team owner, organizer,
friend and enthusiast without
peer Dick Baker. "Dick's the
kind of guy who gets things
done. He's got ideas, energy,
determination, enthusiasm,
follow through, and the
motivational ability to get
better than what they believe
is the beat out of others.
It's special people like Dick
who make our sport work
and move it forward into
the future!" *Burt Levy*

World-famous host, promoter,
showman, restaurateur, racing
driver and motorsports enthusiast
nonpareil Joe Marchetti with one
of his beloved Ferraris. Joe's
insiration, hard work and creativity
have given his events a unique
ambience and unmatched sense
of style. It was Joe who first
offered author / racer B.S. Levy
a true,world-class racing car to
drive and write a story about,
and he is pictured above with
the Ferrari 250LM he co-drove
with Burt at his Chicago Historic
Races International Challenge
event at Road America in July
of 1987.

WISCONSIN RACING

Photography by
KENNETH B. MELDRUM

MG TC at the Kettle Moraine Hillclimb

Road America - MGs & VWs

Elkhart Lake Street Race

Jaguar & MGs

Arleen Meldrum - Jaguar XK120

Road America - Spectator Parking

Road America - Trio of AC Aces chasing Jaguar

Road America • Ferrari followed by D-type Jaguar

Kenneth B. Meldrum

Road America • Front straight at start / finish

Road America Archives

"Racers Tom DePagter and Earl Goddard swap lies and excuses after the dust settles on another fine day's racing at Elkhart Lake."

COMPETITION PROVEN

holman moody ®

Johnny Allen
Donny Allison
Chris Amon
Sir Gawaine Ballie
Johnny Beauchamp
Bob Bondurant
Jo Bonnier
Jack Brannan
Bob Burdick
Jim Clark
Roy Crawford
Darel Dieringer
Walt Faulkner
George Follmer
Larry Frank
Frank Gardner
Paul Goldsmith
Henri Greder
Dan Gurney
Walt Hansgen
Graham Hill
Jim Hurtubise
James Hylton
Innes Ireland
Bob Jane
Bobby Johns
Parnelli Jones
Connie Kalitta
Bo Ljungfeldt
Tiny Lund
John Mantz
Denise McCluggage

Bobby Allison
Bill Amick
Mario Andretti
Lorenzo Bandini
Lucien Bianchi
Phil Bonner
Jack Bowsher
Ronnie Bucknum
Neil Castles
Ceasar Cone
Chuck Daigh
Mark Donohue
Tim Flock
A.J. Foyt
Buck Fulp
Richie Ginther
Jerry Grant
Tommy Grove
Ann Hall
Paul Hawkins
John Holman
Dick Hutcherson
Jacky Ickx
Bobby Isaac
Ned Jarrett
Junior Johnson
Alan Jones
Elmo Langley
Freddy Lorenzen
Alan Mann
Banjo Mathews
Bruce McLaren

John Holman (center) and Bruce Thomas carry Chuck Stevenson

For 50 years, John Holman and his company helped men and women race all over the world. Lee Holman continues that great racing tradition.

Ralph Moody • Jochen Neerpasch • Norm Nelson • Bob Olthoff • Augie Pabst • Eddie Pagan
Marvin Panch • Jimmy Pardue • Jim Paschal • David Pearson • Richard Petty • Roy Pierpoint
Tom Pistone • Dick Rathmann • Jim Rathmann • Brian Redman • Jim Reed • Lance Reventlow
Peter Revson • Les Ritchey • Fireball Roberts • Pedro Rodriguez • Gas Ronda • Lloyd Ruby
Johnny Rutherford • Troy Ruttman • Eddie Sachs • Swede Savage • Jo Schlesser • Skip Scott
Vern Schuppan • Wendell Scott • Jack Sears • G.C. Spencer • Nelson Stacy • Chuck Stevenson
Jackie Stewart • Bill Stroppe • Dick Thompson • Mickey Thompson • Curtis Turner • Al Unser
Bobby Unser • Bill Vukovich • Larry Wallace • Rodger Ward • Joe Weatherly • Bob Welborn
Don White • Sir John Whitmore • Glen Wood • Cale Yarborough • Lee Roy Yarbrough • Brock Yates

To add *your* name to this list please call

Holman Automotive, Inc.

P.O. Box 669351 • Charlotte, NC 28266
Ph: 704 394-2151 • www.holmanmoody.com

9

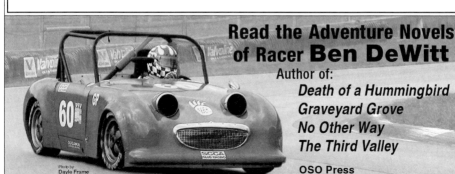

Great friend Archie Leach takes Bob Lucurell's favorite Allard out for a spin

Art Eastman

Elkhart Lake's new Road America • 1955

Road America Archives

Road America • Race day

Road America Archives

Elkhart Lake • Phil Hill • C-type Jaguar

Elkhart Lake • Allard

Road America • Stirling Moss • Aston Martin DBR2

Every racer
needs a keeper...

...and this one's
a keeper

Anne & Glenn Sipe

14

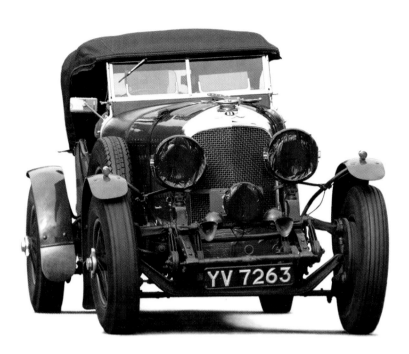

Road America • Augie Pabst • Bentley

Elkhart Lake • Kettle Moraine Forest Hillclimb • MG TC

Kenneth B. Meldrum

Robert H. Fergus

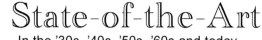

Elkhart Lake • Robert Fergus / MG TC

Robert H. Fergus Estate

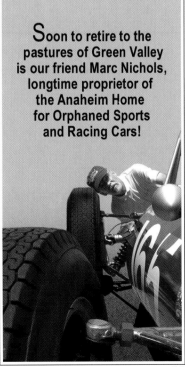

ENTRY LIST
ROAD AMERICA INAUGURAL RACES, SEPT. 10-11, 1955

TIDDLERFEST TROPHY RACE

DRIVER	ENTRANT	CAR
Henry Adamson	Mensa Racing	Amilcar 1100
Mike Argetsinger	C. Argetsinger	MG TC
Kent Bain	Vint. Racing Svcs.	Lotus 6
Gary Barnhardt	Same	MG TF
Dave Bean	Dave Bean Eng.	Lotus 7 (1172)
Craig Bielat	Team Thicko	Lotus 3-wheeler
Kurt Byfield	Same	Jowett Jupiter
Joe Curto	J. Curto Racing	MG TD (sprchgd)
Tom DePagter	DRE	TR Shitfire
Ben DeWitt	OSO Press	Bugeye Sprite
P.J. Fitzgerald	Katy Racing	Saab 850 M.C.
John Gorsline	The Gorsline Co.	Mini Cooper S
Neil Harmon	Quick-Time Inc.	EZ-GO Golf Cart
Sy Kaback	Grand Prix Imports	Lotus Six
Ken Koules*	Pluto Division of	MG 1100
Paul Ranieri*	Elmer Fudd	"
John Summers*	Industries	"
Bob Kullas	Krause & England	Alfa Romeo
BS Levy	Allpak	Alpine A110
Linda Lloyd	Pandora Racing	OSCA MT-4
Henry N. Manney	Same	Alfa Guilietta
Don Marsh	MidVo	Lester MG
Kelly Marsh	K. Marsh Racing	BMW 328
Pete McHugh	Motorhead Ltd.	Triumph 1800
Rob Orander	R.L. Orander DDS	MG TD
Bill Parish	Zapata Racing	A-H Sprite
Dan Poindexter	Team Passaic	MG TF
Ross Robbins	Willie Tingles Racng	Cooper T-11
Bill Siegfriedt	Cmmdtre. Promisco	Ferrari 125S
Mike Space	Ludicrous Racing	Lancia Fulvia
W. S. Thompson	Team Thicko	Red Rat Spl.
A. Tristano	Jean & Pearl Rcng.	Moulton GP
Gus Vang	Driving Impressions	Karman-Ghia
Duck Waddle	Ruptured Duck Rcg	Bobsy SR1
C. Williamsen	P. Williamsen Rcng	Austin-Healey
A. Williamsen	Kiki Williamsen	Hillman Minx
Bob Zecca	OMP USA	Fiat Abarth

ERNESTO JULIO FINE WHINE CHALLENGE

DRIVER	ENTRANT	CAR
Bobby Brown	Scuderia Ferrari	Ferrari 312 T4
Phil Harris	Truechoice	Ex-Amon Ferrari
BS Levy	Think Fast Ink	Lotus 79
Tom Sedivy	TomSed Corp	Lola Indycar
Steve Simpson	HSR/SVRA	Lola F5000
Paul Walter	Metropolitan Mspts	Reynard Indy
Ted Wenz	MWE	McRae GM1

MONOPOSTO MEDALLION RACE

DRIVER	ENTRANT	CAR
Pete Aaron	Yamura Racing	Yamura V-12 F1
Gary Anderson	British Car Mag.	Lotus 25 F1
Ian Baas	Scuderia Sharon	Training Wheels
"Stretch" Bol	Lotus Lane Rcng.	Lotus 24 F1
Steve Brooks	The Atlanta Hawkes	Hawke DL2B
G. Bruggenthies	Tempo Racing	Lotus 20
Phil Cull	Judy Cull	Zink FVee
Dan Davis	Victory Lane Mag.	Offy Midget
Peter Egan	Woodwind Rcng.	Lotus 31
John Gardner	Blue Pencil Rcng.	Gemini FJr.
Earl Goddard	Fred Goddard	Repco-Brabham
Jeff Hailand	Lotus Lane Rcng.	Lotus 69
Dan Hayes	Irish Racing	Lotus 51
"Sparky" Kluck	Lotus Lane Rcng.	Royale RP3A
Phil Lamont	Vintage Tyre Ltd.	Lotus 18 FJr.
BS Levy	Mellow Motors	BRM H-16
Alan Lewis	Flush Racing	Formcar Fvee
Ali Lugo	MC Taylor Rcng.	Scarab F1
Stirling Moss	Rob Walker	Lotus 18 F1
Marc Nichols	Marilynn Nichols	Keift FJr.
David Payne	Endless Road	Gurney Eagle
Mike Rand	Tracy Rand Rcng.	Lola
Bert Sadock	Bob Blain	Ausper FJr.
J.P. Sartre	SEFAC Manetta	Manetta F1
Kevin Smith	Lotus Lane Rcng.	Titan Mk. 6B
Scott Stoddard	Jordan BRM	BRM F1
Jack Velden	The Atlanta Hawkes	Hawke DL2B
Johnl Weinberger	Continental Motors	Ferrari F2 Tasmn
Bob Woodward	Mouldy Racing	Lola Mk. 2 FJr.
Eoin Young	Down Under Rcng.	McLaren Tasman

MULSANNE MARATHON FIA LOOPHOLE LAPS

DRIVER	ENTRANT	CAR
Lowell Blossom	Scuderia Sharon	Elva 3-Wheeler
Michael Delaney	Gulf-Porsche	Porsche 917
Andy Greene	Andy Greene Rcng	Royale RP4
Peter Gulick	Lee Chapman Rcng	Isetta HSR
Bob Harrington	Harrington Photo	Dailu/Chev
John Higgins	Rick Grant Racing	Fabcar/Porsche
Richard Howland	Smashed Frog Rcng	Elva Mk. VI
Lucky Jordan	Shorty Farnsworth	Elva Mk. 6
Mike Kaske	Kaske Racing	Causey P3
BS Levy	Mellow Motors	Ford GT40 Mk. II
Joe Marchetti	Como Inn	Ferrari 250LM
Gordn Medenica	Lee Chapman Rcng	Chevron B6
Jason Miller	Wynnfurst Ltd.	Wynnfurst Typ 1
Jeff Miller	Wynnfurst Ltd.	Wynnfurst Typ 2
Ron Pace	Wynnfurst Ltd.	Porsche 917/20
Brian Redman	Square A Motrcars	Chevron B-19
Johann Ritter	Gulf-Porsche	Porsche 917
Vito Scalise	SEFAC Ferrari	Ferrari 512
Glenn Sipe	Gear & Machine	PBS
Erich Stahler	SEFAC Ferrari	Ferrari 512
Glen Stuffers	Autodelta	Alfa T-33
Jonathn Williams	SEFAC Ferrari	Ferrari 512S

20

ENTRY LIST

GOLDEN AGE FOREVER YOUNG CUP

DRIVER	ENTRANT	CAR
Cam Argetsinger	Mike Argetsinger	Jaguar C-Type
Steve Ave	Flush Racing	Devin SS
Dick Baker	Baker Racing	Auto Sport Spl.
Big Ed Baumstein	Team Passaic	Jagillac Special
Gino Borghesa	Lion's Mouth Rcng	Boano Sport
Bud Bourassa	Ecurie Stephanie	Jaguar C-Type
Jack Boxstrom	Prancing Teddy Rcg	Sadler Mk. V
Danny Burnstein	Upside-Down Rcng	Jaguar XK-120C
Tom Calhoun	Same	Jag D-Type
George Camp	Scuderia Faux Pas	"lost" C/D-Type
Larry Cope	Biddle-Ridley Rcng	Lincoln Pan-Am
Jimmy Dobbs	Dobbs Motorsport	Allard J2
Jon Donohoe	Grand Prix Imports	Lotus Mk. IX
Dennis Eade	Comprep	Wombat Mk. I
Lt. Tom Edwards	Team Passaic	Cad/Allard
John Fergus	Robert Fergus	Lotus 15
John Fitch	Briggs Cunningham	Cunnighm C4R
Geoff Fleming	Bridgehampton HS	Nash-Healey
Mike Gagliardo	Midwest Mtrsports	BMW 328
Michael Galati	SCCA Pro Racing	Maserati 450S
Don Gilkison	Mel-Don Racing	Ferrari 410S
Bob Gillespie	Glenspeed.com	Jaguar C-Type
Les Gonda	Battle of Britain rcg	D-Type Jaguar
R.H. Grant III	Siebken's Resort	Ferrari Monza
Masten Gregory	Same	Jaguar C
Dan Gurney	Max Balchowsky	Ol' Yaller
Walt Hansgen	Same	Hansgen Jag
Charlotte Harris	Wire Wheel Sptscrs	Tojeiro/Climax
Phil Hill	Ernesto Julio	Ferrari 750
John Hurabiell	Jay Chamberlain	Lotus Eleven
Bill Keith	Bill Keith Motors	Porsche 550RS
Brian Kullas	BK Racing	Ferrari TR
Adam Levy	Mellow Motors	Lister/Chev
BS Levy	Think Fast Ink	Scarab
Bob Lucurell	Chris Lucurell	Allard K1
D. McCluggage	Full Court Press	Ferrari 250swb
Ken Meldrum	Equipe Arleen	XK120MC
Brad Merlie	Smashed Frog Rcg	Jaguar D
Myles Miller	Karen Miller Rcng	Porsche 1500RS
Paul O'Shea	O'Shayzul Racing	M-B 300SL
Augie Pabst	Meister-Brauser rcg	Scarab
C. Pendleton III	Carlo Sebastian	Ferrari 375+
A Quattlebaum Jr	Pamela's Eskadale	Muntz Jet M110
Bud Schaefer	Norcar	Jag 120 Coupe
Syd Silverman	Vintage Connection	Allard J2X
Jeff Snook	Snook's Dreamcars	Lotus Eleven
Scott Starr	Aargus Plastics	Aston Martin
Thor Thorson	Ghetto Engineering	Ferrari 500TRC
Hal Ullrich	Brooks Stevens	Excalibur
H. von Seelen	BVS Racing	Jag 120C
Fred Wacker	8-Ball Racing	Allard J2X
J&J Webster	Classic Impressions	M-B 300SLR
John Weinberger	Continental Auto	Ferrari 375+
Skippy Welcher	Milton Fitting Rcng	C-Type Jaguar
David Whiteside	Loti Racing	Lotus 17
Janos Wimpffen	Time & 2 Seats rcg	Aston DB3S
Wdy Woodhouse	Briggs Cunningham	Cunnghm C-4RK
Bob Ziner	BeeZee Racing	Porsche Spyder

OIL-DRI BRITISH EURO CHALLENGE CUP

DRIVER	ENTRANT	CAR
J.A. Austhof	JAVA Racing	MG EX-182
Mikr Belfer	Beverly Belfer	Triumph TR3A
Steve Bicknell	Team Healey	Austin-Healey
Spr Dve Bondon	Splinter Grp. Rcng.	Morgan SLR
Dave Burton	Blue Flag Racing	Porsche 356
Bob Calhoun	Same	Healey 100S
Cal Carrington	Team Passaic	Healey 100
John Chatham	Team Healey	A-H 3000
Beth Conlon	Castrol USA	Alfa Veloce
Mike Cook	Group 44	Triumph TR4
Phil Coombs	Fourintune	Healey 3000
Dick Davenport	Same	Alfa Tubolare
Keith Denahan	Walter Denahan	Porsche 356
Bill Dentinger	Beady-Eye Racing	Triumph TR3
Mike Engard	Ragtops & Rdstrs	Triumph Italia
Bob Fergus	Driving Machines	A-H 100S
Paul Hardiman	Brit Twit Racing	Humber S. Snipe
David Hardy	Team Healey	Austin-Healey
Ed Henning	McDonald's Racing	MGA
Peter Kuprianoff	Team Healey	A-H 3000 Tank
BS Levy	Mellow Motors	Triumph TR3
David Long	Team Healey	Austin-Healey
Wild Bill Lyman	Bond Corp	A-H 3000 Mk. III
Richard Mayor	Same	Austin-Healey
Dick Meldrum	Rose Racing	MGB
"Wacky" Mittler	S.H. Arnolt	Arnolt-Bristol
Kevin Murphy	Murphy & Guaetta	A-H 100 LeMans
John Mutchner	JT Mutchner Ent.	MGA 1622
Jay Nadelson	Investor's Capital	MG EX-182
Roly Nix	Team Healey	A-H 3000
Colin Pearcy	Team Healey	Austin-Healey
Dan Pendergraft	Fourintune	Healey 100/6
John Reed	Crystal Tack Cloth	Triumph GT6+
Harvey Siegel	VIR	Elva Courier
Chris Silvestri	Scuderia Silvestri	Elva Courier III
Hal Sternberg	Star Hill Stables	Healey 3000
Tim Suddard	Grassroots Mtrspts.	TR3
John Targett	Dana's Killer Bees	MGB
Ed Tillotson	C.O.R.T.	Lotus Cortina
Sam Tomaino	W. Suburban Impts.	Alfa Duetto
Rob Vang	Driving Impressions	AC Bristol
Mike Windsor	Team Healey	A-H 3000
Teddy Worswick	Team Healey	Sebring Healey

GROUND-POUNDER FLYING FIBERGLASS FRACAS

DRIVER	ENTRANT	CAR
Big Effin' Al Cole	Zapata Racing	Shelby Mustang
Chuck Gutke	Cobra Restorers	Cobra 289
Craig Harmon	Kim&Neil Harmon	BMW 3.0 CSL
Terry Larsen	Bad News Rcng Tm	Pont Firebrd 400
Burt Levy	Arrow Labels	Corvette GS
Larry Ligas	Predator Racing	Jaguar XK-E
Tim Michnay	Michnay Automtive	Corvette SC
RpdRay Mulacek	Quicksilver Racing	BIG-block Vette
Carroll Shelby	Shelby American	FIA Cobra
Paul Zimmerman	Motorsport Collectr	Cobra Daytona

21

ENTRY LIST

COUNTRY BACON CHEATIN' SWINE CHALLENGE

CAR	ENTRANT	CAR
Duncan Baker	Baker Racing	Lotus Cortina
Mike Besic	Besic Motorsports	Alfa GTV
Richrd Brunning	Brit Twit Racing	Caterham 7
Dick Carlson	ATR Ltd.	Lotus Super 7
Ellie Chan	Saabnet.com	Saab 900 Turbo
Kevin Clarke	BritishBeers.com	BMW 2002tii
David Hinton	Leaping Cats Rcng	Jag120widebody
John Holman	Holman & Moody	Studebaker Lark
BS Levy	Mellow Motors	Lotus Elan 26R
J.A. Mahoney	Ken Keefe	Porsche 911S
Matt Morris	Mojo Racing Prod.	Datsun 240Z
Barb Nevoral	Bull Frog Racing	Alfa Romeo
Eric Prill	Fight MS Racing	Lotus Super 7
B. Refenning	901 Shop	Porsche 901
J. Refenning	901 Shop	Porsche 901
D&L Respecki	D&L Mtrsprts Ltd.	Datsun 510
Nika Rolczewski	Racerchicks.com	Ferrari Dino
Tony Scalzo	W. Suburban Imprts	Alfa Romeo GTA
Peter Stark	Hollywood or Bust	Alfa Canguro

BUCK ROGERS CAN-AM COMMEMORATIVE CUP

DRIVER	ENTRANT	CAR
Bob Akin	Bob Akin Racing	Porsche 962
Bob Blain	Squint Racing	Shadow Can-Am
Don Braaten	Team VDS	VDS Can-Am
Mark Burgard	Mathews Racing	McLaren M8F
Pam M. Burgard	Mathews Racing	McLaren M8D
Lee Chapman	Lee Chapman Rcng	Lotus 40
Simon Hadfield	Lee Chapman Rcng	Lotus 30
Cap Henry	HMC Ltd. Internet	Porsche 917/20
BS Levy	McKee Engineering	McKee Can-Am
Pete Lyons	Big Bear Racing	Chaparral 2C
Greg Mathews	Mathews Racing	McLaren M20
Harry Mathews	Mathews Racing	McLaren M6A
Mark Simpson	Penske Motorsports	Porsche 917/30
Dan Tinley	Maureen Markoff	McLaren Can-Am
Bob Woodman	Woodman Tire	Lola T-70

QUEEN VICTORIA KAISER WILHELM CUP

DRIVER	ENTRANT	CAR
Art Eastman	Scuderia Ferrari	Alfa Monza
Les Halls	Glockenspeil Rcng	M-B 125 GP
Burt S. Levy	Mellow Motors	Bugatti 35B
S. Quattlebaum	Brass Monkey Rcng	AutoUnion Dualy
AQuattlebaum III	Driving Machines	Marmon Wasp
Bob Brzezinski	Spare Change Rcng	NashMetro V-12
PD Cunningham	Real Time Racing	Acura NSX
Mike Gourley	McClenagan Racing	Ferrari512BBLM
Tom Hnatiw	Dream Car Garage	Hemi Cuda 6-pk
Mike Keyser	Toad Hall Racing	Porsche RSR
BS Levy	Team Passaic	Dekon Monza
Doug Liebhardt	Liebhardt Mills	WOO Sprinter
Jim Marinangel	Chi. Region SCCA	Ferrari F-40
Alton McBride	Last Lap Restrtions	NASCAR stocker
Rob McClenagan	Mike Gourley Rcng	Hertz Town Car
Tom Meunier	Exotic Car Transport	Peterbilt Semi
David Moody	Telephone Msg Cntr	Porsche 928
Bernie Nevoral	Bull Frog Racing	Sherman Tank
Dale Phelon	Dale Phelon Mtrsprt	NASCAR Ford
James Redman	Targa 66	Funbus
Howard Turner	Bob Wagner Racing	G44 XJS
Bill Warner	Amelia Island Cncrs	G44 TR8

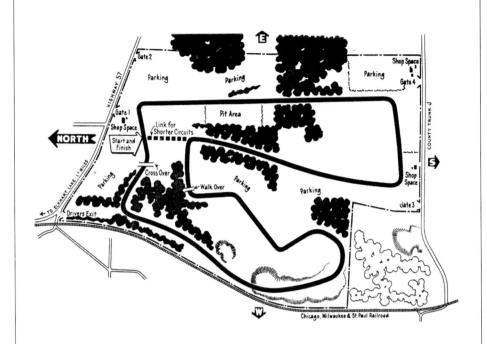

Road America

Elkhart Lake • Briggs Cunningham's team of three Cunningham C-4Rs arrive

Peter Laun

Road America • Crosley Hot Shot

Art Eastman

Rare Racer Returns

— by —
Dewey Dellinger

Famous Italian refrigerator magnate (not to be confused with magnet) Renzo Rivolta's tiny but revolutionary Isetta was first shown at the Turin Auto Show in 1953, and immediately stirred up a true tempest in a teapot among the motoring press. Being an Italian car, it had to be raced (the Italian's would race ironing boards if they only had wheels and engines) and a factory-supported team of five was entered the 1954 Mille Miglia. Although not yet a threat to the dominating red cars from Ferrari, Maserati and Lancia, they did manage to finish 176th, 177th, 178th, 179th and 181st overall out of 182 listed finishers, and the first Isetta took only twice as long as Ascari's winning Lancia D24 to complete the fabled thousand miles.

Obviously a bit more power was needed. The answer came in the form of the ubiquitous Chevrolet "smallblock" V8, first introduced in America in the 265-cubic-inch form in 1955. By 1957, working in utmost secrecy, Rivolta's engineers were busily creating an Isetta "Homologation Special" powered by the famous America V8. As can be imagined, there were many problems to overcome, but the car was finally finished in mid-1959 and taken to Monza for a top-secret test in the hands of regular factory test driver Nino Barlini, who joined the priesthood immediately thereafter.

Test drivers who calmed down sufficiently to talk about the 5.0GT/HSR after driving it remarked that it had the approximate power-to-weight ratio of a 44-magnum bullet but that the brakes and handling "left something to be desired." Still, it was an undoubtedly promising combination, and who knows what might have happened had not the car (and, in fact, the entire Scuderia Isetta team transporter) been stolen while double-parked in front of a pizza joint in Palermo. Rumors abounded that it had been surreptitiously spirited off to Maranello, Coventry, Stuttgart or Dearborn, but, once the insurance company settled, the project was pretty much forgotten. Although no question the 5.0GT/HSR concept pointed the way towards Renzo Rivolta's famous Chevrolet-powered Iso Rivoltas and Iso Grifos of the 1960s.

The fate of the single Isetta 5.0GT/HSR prototype remained a mystery for over 40 years, until it was rediscovered by the famous Anglo-American restoration and race preparation team of Simon Hadfield and Lee Chapman, who have made quite a name for themselves digging up great but obscure race cars that nobody much remembers. "Simon found it in the courtyard of a lovely old mold and liverwort farm in the south of France, being used as a garden planter," Chapman explains, "and we knew such an important piece of Isetta history needed to be resurrected and preserved."

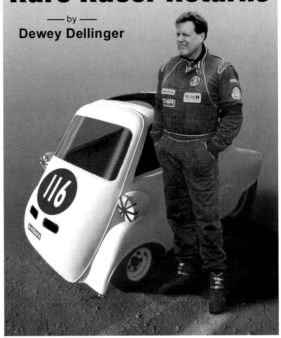

Popular vintage racer Pete Gulick ponders his future with the recently re-discovered and restored, Chevrolet smallblock-powered Isetta 5.0GT/HSR (Homologation Special Racer).

The project found its "angel" in Pete Gulick, a longtime Chapman customer well known for his speed, sportsmanship and enthusiasm, and the car was beautifully restored for American vintage racing. "Oh, we've made a few updates like Wilwood disc brakes and such in the interest of safety," Chapman allows, "and the Chevy smallblock is pretty much an off-the-shelf item set up according to current standard American vintage practice. You know, billet crank, Carillo rods, forged pistons, aluminum flywheel, multi-disc carbon clutch, aftermarket heads, double-pumper 850CFM Holley carburetor, roller rocker cam and a little shy of 14-to-1 compression and 400-cubic-inches total displacement. Just the usual vintage stuff." How will the resurrected racer fare on the vintage circuit? "Well," Pete allowed after his first test run, "it's not real fast yet, but it sure is scary."

Know Your Flags!

Green
The course is clear!
Start racing! (unless you already have)

Yellow
Someone else has screwed up for a change! Possible primo over-taking opportunity!

Double Yellow
(Full course) Slam on your brakes immediately with-out checking your mirrors. Whoever's behind you will think twice about ever passing you again!

Blue / Orange Stripe
There's somebody right behind you trying to get past. Turn your mirrors down and block like hell!

Yellow / Orange Stripes Check your oil pressure gauge. You may not have any.

White
Slow moving or emergency vehicle ahead. Proceed at full speed and see how close you can come without hitting it.

Black
Either the fellow just ahead of you or the one behind has done something bad. Also known as the "Who, Me??? flag.

Black / Orange roundel (meatball) Some-thing has fallen off your car. Slow down and look for it.

Red
The guy you hit has spun and caught fire and is blocking the track, so the race has to be stopped.

Checker
Time to start thinking up excuses!

26

Road America • Jaguar SS100

Art Eastman

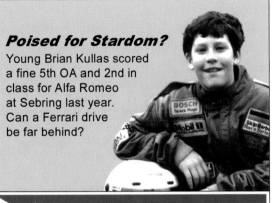

Poised for Stardom?

Young Brian Kullas scored a fine 5th OA and 2nd in class for Alfa Romeo at Sebring last year. Can a Ferrari drive be far behind?

Road America • Wet Bugatti *Art Eastman*

L.L.R. LAST LAP RESTORATIONS

SPECIALIZING IN:

- **COMPLETE GROUND UP RESTORATION OF AUTHENTIC WINSTON CUP & GRAND NATIONAL CARS FROM 1950 TO PRESENT ERA**
- **CHOOSE FROM OUR INVENTORY OF MANY CAR PACKAGES AVAILABLE OR BRING US YOUR EXISTING CAR FOR RESTORATION**
- **LEASE / RACE PROGRAMS AVAILABLE NOW**
- **ANNUAL LEASE PROGRAMS AVAILABLE FOR WESTERN AND SOUTHERN HISTORIC RACES**
- **YOU CAN HOUSE YOUR HISTORIC CUP CAR AT THE LAST LAP FACILITY IN THE WORLD CENTER OF STOCK CAR RACING - CHARLOTTE, NC**
- **RACE TRANSPORTATION AVAILABLE AS WELL AS TRACKSIDE SUPPORT**
- **COMPLETE FABRICATION FACILITY / MAJOR WRECK REPAIR & BODY HANGING SERVICES**
- **FORTY YEARS EXPERIENCE IN STOCK CAR BUILDING AND RACE COMPETITION**

Last Lap Restorations, Inc.
744 Crosspointe Drive, Denver, NC 28037 • (704) 489-4343 • www.LastLap.cc

WINNERS OF THE BRUMOS DAYTONA CONTINENTAL HISTORIC RACE - NOVEMBER 4, 2001
4 Entries in Daytona Race, out of 28 car field - 1st place, 5th place, 7th place, & 11th place

Elkhart Lake • Bugatti Race 1987   Art Eastman

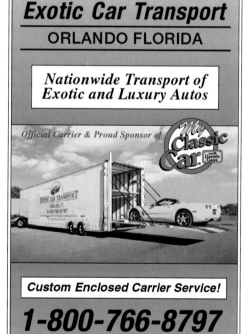

Exotic Car Transport
ORLANDO FLORIDA

Nationwide Transport of Exotic and Luxury Autos

Official Carrier & Proud Sponsor of My Classic Car

Custom Enclosed Carrier Service!

1-800-766-8797
www.exoticcartransport.com

30

Elkhart Lake • Kettle Moraine Forest Hillclimb • Alfa Romeo

Kenneth B. Meldrum

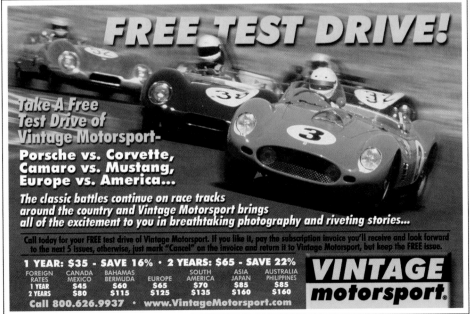

Road America • Briggs Cunningham's D-type Jaguar and the Cunningham C-6R

Peter Laun

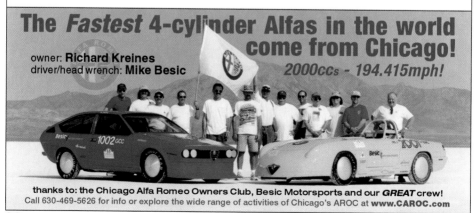

Elkhart Lake • MG meets the spectators!

Kenneth B. Meldrum

Little seven-year-old Donny Braaten of Van Der Stratten Elementary School in Sheboygan thinks *this* is what race cars will look like in another 25 years.

Elkhart Lake   Road America Archives

39

Meanwhile racing season was upon us full blast. Sebring came and went in the middle of March, and Cal and Tommy and Carson and of course Creighton Pendleton went down, but I had to stay home and do what you have to do when you're a new young father with a family to take care of and a damn gas station and garage business to run. And, according to them anyway, I missed one hell of a show. Lancia had sent over a whole team of the V6 D24s that'd swept *La Carrera Panamericana* in November—including one for World Grand Prix Champion Juan Manuel Fangio—and the Cunningham team was back with the C-4R that had won The Twelve Hours the previous year and a 375 Ferrari that'd been gone over with a fine-tooth comb in Alfred Momo's shop and repainted the usual Cunningham refrigerator white with two wide blue stripes down the middle. Also wearing the Cunningham colors was Briggs' nifty little 1500cc OSCA MT4, to be piloted by the famous English driver Stirling Moss and Bill Lloyd. Now Stirling Moss had already built himself one hell of a reputation over in Europe, but he was under contract to Jaguar and they weren't doing the Sebring race (I guess the way Jaguar figured, there was only one blessed race in the world worth winning, and that was the Twenty-Four Hours of Le Mans—period!), and the fine print in Stirling's contract said that he could drive other cars for other teams so long as they weren't direct competitors to Jaguar. Which is how one of the two best drivers in the whole damn world—I mean, people like Hank Lyons who followed it regularly figured it was pretty much down to him or Fangio—wound up driving Briggs Cunningham's little peanut-sized 1500cc OSCA at the biggest damn sportycar race in America.

Creighton had somehow worked himself a deal to drive for Ernesto Julio in his new 375 Ferrari (hey, he knew better than to take twelve tough, hard hours out of his own car if he could drive somebody else's!), but I guess he was a little upset when he found out his co-driver was going to be Phil Hill again. After all, he'd spent most of the off-season grousing and whining to all of his high-toned friends about how this Phil Hill character from California had wrecked his old Ferrari at Sebring (without bothering to mention that it was actually he, Creighton Pendleton the Third, who'd somehow managed to run it clear out of brakes first!), not to mention that he already knew for a fact that Phil was quicker than he was and that is the last thing *any* racing driver wants to look forward to heading into a big race. All of which made you very happy indeed if you knew and disliked Creighton Pendleton.

Tommy was going to be driving with the Healey guys again in one of those very special "Special Test" Healey Hundreds—which were now fitted with disc brakes just like the factory Jaguar C-Types that'd won at Le Mans—and Cal had somehow talked Carson into entering *his* Healey Hundred for the two of them to run in its very first race. They really wanted me to go, too. To kind of run the team for them, like I'd done the year before. But there was just no way. And then Tommy stepped in and got them a sort of friendly, informal type of deal to be the orphan stepchild entry of the factory Healey team. Which meant they could get a helping hand now and then (at least when one was available, anyway), plus a few parts here and there and plenty of sage advice from Geoff Healey himself and that

Roger Menadue guy who pretty much did everything from figuring stuff out to fabricating parts to fine-tuning the engines to folding up the dirty laundry for the Healey factory race team.

Well, the race looked to be another clean sweep for Lancia, what with current World Champ Fangio and previous World Champ Alberto Ascari and the old "Silver Fox" Piero Taruffi as lead drivers in the first three team cars plus a fourth entry for a pretty decent Italian 'shoe named Gino Valenzano, who they teamed up with infamous millionaire playboy Porfirio "Rubi" Rubirosa as kind of a publicity stunt. Not to mention that a large wad of cash may have changed hands under the table someplace, seeing as how this Rubirosa character had made a sort of life's work out of marrying rich women. He came from the Dominican Republic, where he more or less started off his career in the high-end womanizing business by marrying the not-so-beautiful daughter of local military/political strongman and soon-to-be dictator-for-life (at least until they threw him out, anyway) Generalissimo Rafael Trujillo. You remember, the same guy who bought that $29,500 Pegaso right off the stand at the International Motor Sports Show at the Grand Central Palace in Manhattan. But marrying the *El Presidente's* daughter was just a start for this Porfirio Rubirosa guy. Later on he hitched up with this famous French movie star named Danielle Darrieux, and then he kind of changed direction a little and married himself off to American tobacco heiress Doris Duke, who was figured by most of the gossip columnists to be the second richest unattached female in America. Not that she ever stayed unattached for very long with that kind of money. And you'd think it might be hard to trade up from the second richest eligible female in America, but that's precisely what "Rubi" did, getting himself divorced and re-hitched to the *first* richest unattached female in America, Woolworth five-and-dime heiress Barbara Hutton, in 1953. And the whole time he was pursuing, courting and marrying up with these morsels of American commerce, he was running around all over the place with all these other beautiful women. Like during the whole, whopping 53 days he was married to Barbara Hutton, he was apparently using the plane she'd bought him to run back and forth to New York or Hollywood or wherever to carry on a little side-action slap-and-tickle with Zsa Zsa Gabor. And that's not even mentioning the affairs he was supposed to have had with Marlene Dietrich and Veronica Lake and Ava Gardner and Marilyn Monroe and Jayne Mansfield and Dolores Del Rio and even Evita Peron. I kid you not. And so you may find yourself wondering, as I did, just exactly how this joker managed to turn himself into "The Romeo of the Caribbean" (or that's what the papers called him, anyway) and what, precisely and exactly, women found so damn irresistible about him?

"Well, umm..." Carson started in, but then all he could do was kind of turn beet-red and look down at his shoes.

"They say he's hung like a horse," Cal explained, more or less filling in the blanks. "Why, some friends of my parents said they'd heard Zsa Zsa Gabor say at a party that a night with 'Rubi' was 'the nicest present a woman can give herself.'"

Wow.

And I was surprised to discover that Julie had heard all about this Rubirosa character, too. "They say he's hung like a horse," she told me.

"My God," I half-gasped, "how the heck does stuff like that get around?"

"It just does," she explained. "All the girls I worked with down at the Doggie Shake know about it. I bet your mom and sisters do, too."

"Even Sarah Jean?"

"Sure."

I shook my head. And then something else occurred to me. Something I was just dying to know but really didn't know how to ask. "Does it really make that much difference?"

"What?"

"You know." I made a hand gesture that ended somewhere down around my knee.

"How would I know?" she said flatly. Which, when I stopped to think about it, actually asked as many questions as it answered....

But we were talking about the race I didn't get to go to at Sebring, weren't we?

"So this Rubirosa guy is quite a hand with the ladies, huh?"

"Yeah, he's a World Class cocksman, all right," Cal allowed. "But the sono-fabitch can't drive a lick."

"He can't?"

Cal shook his head. "Oh, he looks the part okay, but he sure as hell can't play it." Cal shook his head disgustedly. "He had first and second gears stripped out of the car before his first stint was over. And all the drivers in the faster cars were saying that the only time he ever looks in a mirror is to check the damn knot on his tie."

"Boy, that's a shame."

Cal nodded.

"So what happened?"

"Well, it started out looking like a full-tilt Lancia benefit, what with the team cars of Taruffi and Fangio and Ascari tooling around in the top three spots with only Phil Hill in that Ernesto Julio's new Ferrari to keep them honest."

"He can really drive, can't he?"

"Yeah," Cal allowed, "and it was really nice the way it ate at Creighton that he couldn't quite keep up."

That put a smile on my face.

"But the guy who impressed the shit out of me was that Stirling Moss from England."

"The one driving the little OSCA?"

Cal nodded and Carson added another nod for good measure. "Jeez, you should've *seen* the way he went around corners. It was like watching a damn ballet."

I'd never seen that look of awe and admiration for another driver in Cal Carrington's eyes before. Not ever. And it's a testament to Stirling Moss that it actually lingered there for two or three heartbeats before Cal's normal, cocky atti-tude flooded back.

"So then what happened?"

Cal shrugged. "They started dropping like flies. Beginning with us." He and Carson looked back and forth at each other. "We weren't twenty minutes into the race when the aluminum bracket or adapter or whatever you call it that holds the damn oil filter on broke. Just like that!"

"The same thing happened to the other privateer Healey. It just cracked and pumped all the oil out."

"Did'ja hurt the motor?"

"Nah," Cal grumbled. "I smelled it and saw it on the gauges and switched it off. But it was sure one heck of a long walk back to the pits."

"Yeah," Carson added glumly. "And we couldn't get it from where Cal left it until after the race."

"Sounds pretty disappointing."

Cal rolled his hands up in the well-known New Jersey *what can you do?* pose.

"At least the car was okay," Carson tossed in.

"So did the same thing happen to Tommy in the factory Healey?"

"Not hardly," Cal snorted. "It seems they've done a bit more fiddling and fine-tuning and finding things out on that one."

"It's almost like it's not the same car," Carson grumbled. "It just looks the same."

Well, that would be the idea, wouldn't it?

"Anyhow," Cal continued, "it was a pretty interesting race. The Lancias played around with each other for a couple hours and then they started falling out, and then around two in the afternoon Phil Hill brought Ernesto Julio's Ferrari in with a chewed-up pinion gear and they were out—and was Creighton ever a class-A jerk about not being the one behind the wheel when it happened!—and then the Cunningham Ferrari that was running second broke a valve spring and retired and the Cunningham C-4R went sick in the engine and it fell out, too, and that pretty much left Taruffi in the third team Lancia way the hell out front and the Valenzano/Rubirosa Lancia with only the top two gears left way down the charts and nothing but a swarm of little tiddler cars in between."

"Tommy and Lance Macklin had the factory Healey all the way up to third overall by the time the sun went down!" Carson said with an amazed look in his eyes.

"And Moss and Lloyd in the little Cunningham OSCA were running second overall!" Carson shook his head. "On 1500ccs, can you believe it?"

"And then it got even better right at the end. The leading Lancia broke out on the circuit with less than an hour to go, and poor old Taruffi had to push it all the way back to the pits. And he's not a real big guy."

"Yeah, it damn near killed him. And it didn't do him any good, either. The car was finished and so all they could do was sit and watch while that little white Cunningham OSCA with Moss and Lloyd in it cruised around to the checker."

"What happened to the Lancias?"

"Oh, that Valenzano that was teamed up with Rubirosa drove his ass off for the last couple hours trying to catch up—with no first or second gear, remember—but he was still five laps back at the end. And Taruffi's co-driver pushed their car down pit lane and across the finish line at the end to try and salvage second, but I guess they'd gotten a push-start or something earlier after a pit stop, and so all they got for their trouble was a damn disqualification."

"Cal and I made out better by a couple places just by dropping out early and starting in on the beer!" Carson giggled.

"Yes sir. Old Carson and myself were in pretty rare form by the time the fireworks rolled around after the race."

"It was something to see, all right."

Boy, I sure wished I'd been there!

And that of course got me all fired up and jump-started on the Jagillac proj-ect again. And so I'd work on it whenever I could—and sometimes even when I couldn't—and Big Ed and me would make plans to have it ready for each upcom-ing race date, and then of course the weekend would come and go and I'd still have things scattered all over the shop in a million pieces and a million kazillion ten- and twenty-minute jobs yet to finish. Plus I had other race customers to take care of, like Carson who'd gone out and bought himself one of those Momo hop-up kits for his Healey Hundred and this new guy Buster Jones who'd bought him-self a slightly used Jag 120 and got recommended to me and a couple of the MG regulars I'd originally met at Giant's Despair who were coming by for service and race prep pretty steady and some spoiled little rich-kid friend of Cal's named Danny Poindexter who'd gotten himself one of those rakish new 1500cc MG TFs and wanted absolutely *everything* done to it. Including a hot cam and richer carb needles and having me order, air-ship all the way from England and then imme-diately bolt on a super-duper Laystall–Lucas all-alloy aluminum cylinder head that he'd seen advertised in a copy of *Autosport* when he was over in England for some famous horse race or other. Danny Poindexter always seemed to have a lot of ready cash in his pockets (which is probably why my forever-broke rich-kid friend Cal Carrington liked hanging around with him) but he tended to be one of those whiny, forever disappointed Privileged Brat types who never quite get things exactly the way they want. And they let everybody know about it, too. Then again, when you don't really have to work or go to school or anything—I think Danny had been through more than one or two exclusive prep schools with-out a lot of success on either side—there's really not much to do except sit around and complain and be disappointed about things. Which, to be honest, he was extremely good at. Danny Poindexter was a short, wispy little guy with thick black hair that was always perfectly trimmed and matching glasses with thick black Clark Kent frames that somebody somewhere must've told him made him look forceful. He dressed correctly and immaculately for every occasion and I bet several of the pairs of shoes he owned cost more than our television set.

Anyhow, according to that ad in *Autosport,* the bolt-on Lucas-Laystall all-alloy cylinder head conversion for MGs promised an instantaneous "20% increase in B.H.P." thanks to a "9.3 to 1 compression ratio," "improved flow," and "stage II valves and springs" (whatever the heck that meant). And I have to admit I was skeptical. But I was happy to do it because it was race work and paid good, and you have no idea how nice it is working inside a new, squeaky-clean engine com-partment instead of rooting around in the goo and glop and blackened sludge that most mechanics have to put up with on a daily basis. Plus having all these new sportycar types around meant plenty of sportycar bull sessions almost every night when they came to pick their cars up or just to stop by and see how things were progressing. I even started to carry a little rack of a half-dozen or so copies of *Autosport* on the counter by the cash register. I had a friend of Tommy's airmail them to me direct from London just as soon as they came out, and we were never much more than a week behind the very latest news from Europe. I almost always sold them out. Not that I made that much on them, what with the air freight and all. But it sure gave me something to read in the john every week, and it was a way for all my guys to keep abreast of the latest developments over there in the real heart of the sportycar world (not to mention maybe spot some new gizmo or go-faster goodie that they just *had* to have and that I could possibly get paid to find and install for them).

Plus it made us all feel like real *insiders,* you know? And so we'd have long discussions some evenings while I worked on the Jagillac (and, if somebody brought over a sixpack of cold Knickerbocker—or even Blatz or Rheingold or Ballantine's Ale—they could turn into some really *long* discussions) about what was going on and who was doing what to whom and, more importantly, with what. Like we were all amazed at how this team of those new Triumph TR2 roadsters had absolutely steamrollered everybody—including the Jaguars and Porsches, can you believe it?—at the RAC Rallye over in England. Not that you should ever confuse a genteel form of competition like a road rallye with a genuine, wheel-to-wheel race. Still, TR2s finished first, second and fifth and took the Ladies' Class award as well, and you would have thought they won the blessed Twenty-Four Hours of Le Mans or something based on the amount of ink they gave it in *Autosport.* Then again, even though I absolutely loved that magazine and the way it whisked me off to a whole new world every week, the editors could tend to run on a bit if a particular car or driver happened to be from England....

Speaking of Le Mans and magazine articles and such, we were all absolutely thrilled when the April 26th issue of *Time* came out with none other than Briggs Swift Cunningham on the cover and a big story inside about his efforts to win Le Mans with an all-American car driven by all American drivers. I swear, I wanted to staple that cover right to my forehead just so's I could walk around and tell people I knew that guy. I even took a copy home to show my old man. But he just squinted at it and leafed through a couple pages and snorted out his opinion that, *"rich people can get away with any fool thing."*

It was true, of course.

But it wasn't exactly the point.

I got a call out of the blue from Sammy Speed the last week in April (or, more correctly, from Spud Webster with Sammy Speed standing right there next to him but, as per usual, not saying much of anything), and it turned out that Sammy had a ride lined up for the Indianapolis 500 and Spud was putting a sort of impromptu, race-day pit crew together and decided to give me a call. It was damn nice of him, too. "Is the car any good?" I asked him.

"It sure oughta be. It's got the most powerful damn engine in the field."

And that could only mean one thing: Sammy was going to be sitting behind one of those famous, monstrous, centrifugally-supercharged Novi V8s. The engine with the legendary banshee wail that had promised to thoroughly dominate the Indy 500 ever since it was first introduced in 1941, but had never yet delivered on that promise. Even though it was reckoned as the most powerful damn racing engine that the Brickyard had ever seen. Spud told me the whole story, of course, about how Ed and Bud Winfield (who were longtime oval-track guys and already pretty well known for the Winfield carburetors used on most of the oval-track engines) were looking for a new engine for team owner Lew Welch's old, front-drive, flathead Ford V8-powered Indianapolis car back before the war. Now Welch was a pretty well-to-do guy thanks to a highly successful Ford V8 engine rebuilding business up in Novi, Michigan, and so they commissioned Leo Goossen—the same guy who designed the Offy four-banger—to draft them up a new engine. Only it had to be a V8 on account of that's what would fit in their chassis and also because rebuilding V8s was what gave Welch the deep pockets to fund the deal in the first place. To nobody's surprise, the engine wound up looking an awful lot like two little Offy midget engines stuck together on a common crankcase, and there was this big centrifugal supercharger hung high up on the back end to press as much fuel and air into the cylinders as they could stand. Welch called the engine a "Novi" after his hometown, and the wild, turbine whine of the supercharger impeller and its flat, single-plane crankshaft and the oddball firing sequence that went along with it are what produced the sound that made the Novi famous. "Y'ever heard one?" Spud asked at the other end of the line.

"Not really."

"It'll make the fillings in your teeth ache."

"Wow."

But of course there was more to the story. The new engine showed up in the Winfield brothers' old front-drive car at the last Indy 500 before the war, and it was obvious right away that it had a lot of potential. But also that it was maybe way too much motor for the chassis, and the best they could do with it was tenth on the grid and a fourth-place finish. But nobody who heard it run would ever forget it.

After the war the Novi showed up again with even more horsepower and a brand new, front-drive Kurtis chassis, and it was hands down the fastest thing on the speedway. No question about it. But it was thirsty and drank a lot of fuel, and so it had to have great big fuel tanks and therefore weighed a lot and ate up front tires something awful. Oh, the Novis were fastest qualifiers and on the front row more times than you could count—two of them side-by-side on the front row in 1949, in fact—and the crowd in the stands and the newspaper reporters looking for heart-tugging, hard-luck Cinderella stories absolutely loved 'em. But they never had the goods or the guts or the just plain luck to still be in front at the end of 500 miles. "You think this year'll be any different?" I asked Spud.

"Well, we heard they've done some work on the cars. And they've found even more power out of the engine...." Although, to be honest, power out of the engine was never exactly a problem with the Novi V8.

"So what's the deal?"

"Well, if we make the show, I'd sort of like to recommend you for the pit crew. You know how to change a tire, don't you?"

"I've been known to."

"And you can carry a can of gas or oil without tripping over your own feet?"

"If it's not too heavy."

"Then I'd say you're qualified."

I couldn't believe it! Why, I might actually be going to the biggest damn race in America: *the Indianapolis 500!* But of course I wanted to be just a tiny bit cool about it. "So," I asked real carefully and casually, "whazzit pay?"

"Gas money and hot dogs."

"With mustard?"

"Nah. The mustard's extra."

It sounded too good to pass up, you know?

Meanwhile back at the Sinclair, more wannabe racers hanging around and dropping by pretty regularly for race prep and hop-up work meant I had to go off on more and more race weekends when what I really wanted was to stay home and work on finishing the Jagillac. But I knew I had no choice. Hey, if I didn't go with them and look after their cars and hold their hands, they'd for damn well sure find somebody else who would. So I had to traipse down to Andrews Air Force Base near Washington, DC, the first weekend in May and then off to Cumberland, Maryland, for another SCMA race two weeks later. And Cumberland was kind of interesting since it was held on this airport (only a regular country airport this time, not a SAC base) that was built up on this sort of plateau overlooking the Potomac River and just across the water from West Virginia. It was pretty country and a tight, flat, slow and twisty little 1.6-mile course with no less than two 90-degree corners and two hairpins, but a lot of the drivers—and my guys in particular—were a bit spooked by the fact that one of the curves was a kind of diminishing-radius deal at the end of a half-mile straightaway, and, if you misjudged it, you went off a sort of cliff at the edge of the plateau and plunged about 200 feet straight down into the Potomac River. So, if you somehow survived the fall, you might very well drown. Or at least that's what all the fast guys were winking and nudging each other about around the beer tapper, anyways.

At least the SCMA had re-shuffled their race groups a little so that the Healey Hundred was in the same race with the Porsches and MGs and those new Triumphs I knew we'd be seeing a lot of, so that was good news for Carson and all the rest of the Healey owners. But, to tell the truth, I'd gotten to the point where I really didn't enjoy going to the races all that much unless I had somebody in the group with the balls, talent, skill and moxie to actually have some chance of winning. I mean, to do all that excellent engine work on Carson's Healey or little Danny Poindexter's fire-breathing TF and then see them muddling around in the middle of the damn pack with what should have been first-place machinery was just a little bit disheartening. Even if it was putting beans on the table and taking care of the payments on that new Zenith TV. Oh, Cal tried like hell to get Carson to let him drive the Healey, but I guess the memory of the MG disaster at Callicoon was still a little too fresh in Carson's mind, you know? So some other guy in a Healey won the race and that Dick Thompson dentist guy finished second in a 1500cc Porsche coupe and one of those gutty-looking new TR2s finished third and here was my buddy Carson running back around twelfth or so, just behind the fastest of the MG TCs. I mean, it was just plain *embarrassing*. But at least he was ahead of our new recruit Danny Poindexter in the hopped-up TF, who it turned out couldn't find his ass with both hands when it came to driving a damn racecar. Why, he made even Big Ed Baumstein look smooth. Oh, he was a nice enough guy and was usually polite and mild-mannered outside the car (or at least when he wasn't getting all pissy about something), but I guess he had a sort of excitable streak and he'd get real flustered and jittery and try to do too many things at once whenever he strapped on a helmet and went out on a racetrack. I mean, the racing game is all about *letting* the car do things, not *making* the car do things. But of course if you told him that, he'd just try even harder. And I know, because I did and he did.

Our other new guy in the Jaguar, Buster Jones, was kind of a College Quarterback Letterman type with a big handsome smile and even bigger biceps and the mechanical sympathy of a peeled turnip. I could see right off that he was destined to join that great, teeming mass of drivers who muddle around somewhere between the idiots, no-talents, doofuses and ribbon clerks like Big Ed and Skippy Welcher and Carson Flegley and the Certified Fast Guys like Cal Carrington and Phil Hill and Phil Walters and, I hate to say it, even Creighton Pendleton. If he worked at it, I could see Buster Jones developing into a sort of Perpetual Top-Ten kind of racecar driver, but never quite a Perpetual Top-Five. And, seeing as how he didn't really like or understand the mechanical stuff, he was a pretty good bet to lose interest and wash out after a season or two. Or maybe even less. I mean, sportycar racing isn't for everybody. It's expensive and time consuming and, yes, even a little bit dangerous. Maybe even more than a little bit. And that's why you get a crop of newcomers every single year who stick their toe in the water, swish it around a little, and then draw it right back out again. Or, as we insiders say, *"O.S.B.—Other Sports Beckon."*

But probably the worst part of those two weekends at Andrews Air Force Base and Cumberland was watching Creighton Pendleton notch up two more feature wins in that damn hot-rod Ferrari of his. I mean, the Cunninghams didn't show and Masten Gregory was off to Europe someplace and there just wasn't much of anybody to challenge him. So I got to watch the handsome Creighton Pendleton with his Bermuda tan and Brylcreem hair and toothpaste-ad smile carry the checkered flag and the luscious Sally Enderle with the gorgeous everything and the heart of solid brass around on yet two more Ferrari victory laps.

And I'd had a lifetime supply already, believe me!

Less than two weeks after I got back from Cumberland it was time to pull up stakes again and head off for Indianapolis, and you can bet Julie was getting pretty damn sick of how much time I was spending away. Naturally I lied just a little and told her I was getting paid to do it (although I didn't exactly mention how much!), and also explained as how this was another one of those Once-In-A-Lifetime, Desperate-Last-Chance Opportunities that seem to crop up just about every other weekend during racing season. But I bought her some flowers and avoided her eyes and felt guilty as hell for at least an hour or two (at least if you added it all up, anyway) before Cal and I headed off west again in the wee hours of Saturday morning, May 29th, so's we could do the eighteen- or nineteen-hour drive straight-through to Indianapolis (or sixteen or seventeen hours with Cal at the wheel!), catch a few hours' shuteye, go through registration to get our credentials and be ready for pit stop practice in Gasoline Alley with the rest of the crew just after lunch on Sunday so's we'd be all set for the race on Memorial Day Monday. Cal had absolutely begged me to get him a pit pass, and Spud finally obliged after I explained as how Cal was pretty handy with a stopwatch and could write legibly on a pit board and also as how he would likely run me over with the tow truck if I didn't bring him along.

But I was glad to have the company for the long trip west and besides that, Cal's folks were out of town again and he'd managed to hot-wire his old man's new air-conditioned Chrysler Imperial so we were riding in style. Albeit a little blind on account of I'd also disconnected the speedo cable so's we wouldn't rack up a lot of unnecessary miles that his father might notice when he and Cal's mom returned from Paris or Venice or wherever. And that of course meant Cal had absolutely no idea how fast he was going. Not that he had much of anything besides a passing gear under any circumstances. All I know is that it was a nice-riding car and real quiet and sumptuous inside and the cars and trucks we were passing—especially on the Pennsylvania Turnpike—all looked like they were parked.

We talked a lot about cars and racing along the way, and of course about how Cal really wanted to make it as a racing driver—you could hear the ache and hunger in his voice when he talked about it—and how we'd both like to make it to that big show at Le Mans one day. We also discussed the Jagillac project, and how great and fast and handsome it would be when I finally got it done and how even greater it would be if I persuaded Big Ed to let Cal drive it and if he actually beat that rich, Bermuda-tan asshole Creighton Pendleton the Third with it. Beat his stinking Ferrari with a car I built with my own two hands! Boy, that would really be something! And of course we talked the most about Indianapolis. The 500 wasn't exactly our kind of racing, but it sure was American racing, all right. In fact, the Indy 500 was like the sacred shrine of American oval-track racing, and there was nothing else like it anywhere in the world.

To begin with, it goes on for almost a whole blessed month, what with practice and qualifying taking up three full weeks and "carburetion day" on the Thursday before the race and then this strange, agitated, almost vibrating rustle of activity as the biggest damn stadium you ever saw—bigger than ten Rose Bowls!—fills up with a crowd of farmers and shopkeepers and factory workers and insurance agents and gas station owners and machine shop operators and car dealers and families and neighbors and, in fact, a cross-section sampling of the whole rank-and-file population of the great, dull and trustworthy American Midwest. It's a yearly pilgrimage for a lot of them—for many the only race they go to or care about at all—and they've got high school marching bands with pretty, dimple-cheeked drum majorettes and flags and pennants rippling in the breeze and picnic baskets loaded to the brim with sandwiches and side salads and home made fried chicken. And there we were, Cal and me, just two more tiny ants in the middle of this huge, teeming, party-decorated all-American anthill, looking up from pit lane at the immense crowd filling up the stands across from us and feeling all their eyes looking down at the hundreds of people like us down in the focused bottom-center of this huge concrete cauldron, all of us waiting nervously and feeling the sizzle in the air and trying to look like we actually have something important and worthwhile to keep us occupied. But the truth is we were just waiting, too....

I couldn't believe we were actually there, if you want the truth of it, all dressed up in crisp yellow coveralls with red-and-blue trim to match the car Sammy was driving. Only it wasn't the Novi he'd been signed up for going into qualifying. And that was another story. It turned out the old front-drive Novi had gotten a little long in the tooth, and, even though it still had more flat-out power than anything else at the Speedway, the rear-drive, Offy-powered cars—and especially the nifty new Kurtis 500 "roadsters" like the creamy-gray number 14 "Fuel Injection Special" Billy Vukovich used to win the '53 500 with ease (and damn near won the '52 race with as well)—had simply gotten so good that they were too quick for the Novis now. Oh, there was talk of a new, rear-drive Kurtis chassis for the Novis, but it was still in the hot-air stage, and Sammy knew from the first day of practice that he was riding the wrong horse. "Aw, I could still pass guys going down the straights if I was light on fuel," he shrugged, "but they'd eat me right up through the corners if the driver was enny good." He shook his head. "An' that thing was like pushing a barge around with a damn tugboat with a full load of fuel on board."

"So wha'dja do?"

"He played possum," Spud said with a wink.

"I could'a qualified it pretty easy—maybe not even too far back—but race day would'a been pretty grim fer us."

"*If* we lasted," Spud added.

"Yeah. *If* we lasted," Sammy agreed. "The last time a Novi ever finished this race was back in 1948."

"And some other guys with empty cars—*good* cars!—had been nosing around and hinting about Sammy maybe driving fr'them."

Sammy looked down at the concrete. "So I kind of laid her down in qualifying." You have to understand that qualifying at Indianapolis takes two whole weekends—one car at a time for four flying laps each—and the average of those four laps is what puts you in the show. Or doesn't. Each car gets a maximum of three qualifying attempts at Indianapolis. "I'd run one or two laps as fast as I could—just to remind everybody I could still drive here—but then I'd, umm...."

"...have a problem," Spud whispered, like somebody might be listening.

"I gave it a clutch job on the second try," Sammy admitted. "It wasn't a real nice thing to do." A "clutch job" is where a driver purposely dabs the clutch at full speed. Just enough to let the engine over-rev and blow up. Or at least bend a few valves. You could tell he felt pretty bad about it. "But you only get so many shots at this place, and there were still a lotta good seats going begging."

So the old front-drive Novi didn't qualify and Sammy spent the days between the first and second weekends of qualifying making the rounds of the garages in Gasoline Alley trying to line up a more promising ride. And found one with bird-seed-and-hamster-feed magnate Les Gonda's Sun Seed team out of Ohio. Les was a sharp, earnest, friendly, straightforward little guy who always looked like he'd been working on heavy equipment but had built himself a very successful seed and feed business somewhere near Bowling Green, and had been a big Indy 500 fan ever since he could remember. "My dad brought me here every year right up until the war when they stopped having races. He died before they started up again. But I've never missed one since." Les was one of many well-to-do Midwestern car owners who only made this one race every year. They weren't in anywhere near the same league as guys like California oil baron Howard Keck or Atlanta multimillionaire Lindsey Hopkins, but they'd buy themselves a decent car from a year or two before and have some grizzled old racing wrench on the company payroll to look after it and get it ready. And then, as the month of May approached, they'd put a pit team together out of friends and employees and pick some young local hero, seasoned old hand or promising rookie right out of the sports pages and try to make the show.

Like Les said, "It sure beats sittin' in the stands."

For that year's race they'd picked up a couple-year-old Kurtis-Kraft 3000 chassis and hired on an Ohio farm kid named Ricky Laidlaw who'd been making a sort of reputation for himself in stock cars and midgets and such on the local bullring dirt ovals of Ohio and Pennsylvania—just another punk kid racer with wide eyes, big dreams and a cocksure, banty-rooster attitude—but it was obvious early on that he wasn't ready yet for the big show at Indianapolis. "He's a good little racer," was the way Spud put it, "but you kinda gotta sneak up on this place. You try to grab it by the scruff of the neck an' it'll rip your arm off."

And that's the way it was at Indy. It was so big and so fast and you couldn't drive it by the seat of your pants, throwing the car into the turns sideways like you might on a quarter-mile dirt oval. "You gotta thread the needle at this place. Four times every lap. And you gotta do it smooth and you gotta do it clean and you gotta do it calm." Spud looked me right in the eye. "And you can't even see the walls."

"Jeez, isn't that kinda hard?"

"So are they. An' that's what makes it so tough. Oh, you gotta *feel* 'em out there. And you gotta get so close you can almost reach out an' touch 'em! But if you *see* 'em, you'll get spooked. And you'll stop looking way ahead like y'gotta at this place. An' that's when you start getting all tight in the car and the track starts jumping at you in bits and pieces instead of all flowing together like it has to if you don't wanna wind up hurting yourself." And of course that was the other thing about Indianapolis. People got hurt and died there. That's just the way it was.

In any case, Ricky Laidlaw came in like a lot of young kids, what with a confident, cocky grin on his face and a chip the size of the Rock of Gibraltar on his shoulder. But by the end of his first practice session around that vast, fast, intimidating speedway surrounded by unforgiving concrete walls marked here and there with ominous black smudges and grandstands that towered up over the racetrack like steel-and-concrete tidal waves, his smile looked pretty much pasted on and that chip on his shoulder had crumbled to dust. Oh, he tried to gut it out—pride'll do that for you—but the more he tried to force himself the spookier it got, and Les had to cut him loose after he spun three times in one session trying to force himself up to speed. It was just dumb luck he didn't hit anything. "He'll make it back if he sticks with it," Spud assured me. "I've seen him on the dirt and he's got enough raw talent. But the key word there is 'raw.' And that's not what you want or need here at Indianapolis. This is a real special sort of racetrack and you need a real special sort of driver to take it on. At least if you plan to be around come the finish, anyway...."

Of course the Indy 500 driver everybody and his brother was talking about that year was Californian Billy Vukovich. They called him "Vuky" and "The Mad Russian" and "The Silent Serb" and "The Fresno Flash," but, whatever it was and whatever it took, Billy Vukovich was dead-solid-exactly the kind of driver you needed at the Indianapolis 500. Sure, he had great equipment and a great team behind him—most of the folks in Gasoline Alley reckoned that his mechanics, Jim Travers and Frank Coon, were simply the best and savviest in the business—but, the way Spud Webster put it, he had something else, too. "Just about any race driver can come out here, grit his teeth, hold his breath and make it through Turn One a time or two. And the better ones get used to it enough so they can get through the four laps of qualifying without shitting their pants or collecting the wall. But lemme tell you, this place puts the fear of God inta you like no other. It's just *so* damn fast, and y'gotta be so calm and cool in the car. Here at Indianapolis, it's a question of how fine you can slice it and still feel relaxed and have your hands nice and soft on the wheel. And, for whatever reason, Billy Vukovich can do that better—and for longer—than anybody I've ever seen. It just doesn't seem to faze him…."

And then Spud told me about how Billy showed up at the Speedway the previous year in Howard Keck's new Kurtis K500 "roadster" chassis and just flat drove away from everybody. What made the new car so different was that Frank Kurtis had moved the engine damn near a foot left of center so's the weight of the driveline would be closer to the inside on left-hand turns—and of course all the turns at Indianapolis were left-handers—plus it made for a lower profile and center of gravity on account of they'd canted the engine over 37 degrees from vertical and those things allowed them to get the driver down out of the breeze a little better since the driveshaft on a Kurtis 500 ran alongside his hip rather than directly underneath the Family Jewels. Which is another reason why you had to be a pretty brave guy to even think about racing at Indianapolis. Billy only qualified down in eighth on account of he didn't get a proper run in on pole day, but he was faster than the polesitter by the flick of an eyelash. In fact, the only car faster than him in qualifying was Chet Miller in the Novi, and he was way down towards the tail end of the field because they didn't get it qualified until the final day. And, typical of the Novi, they ran qualifying with a lot of extra boost out of the supercharger and maybe even a healthy dose of "pop" (which is what they call nitromethane around Gasoline Alley) mixed in with the methanol. No way could it run that quick in the race, and everybody knew it.

But Billy and the Kurtis 500 could. Oh, it took him a bunch of laps to work his way to the front, but then he just breezed away from everybody. It wasn't even close. And remember, just about everybody was running the same Offy engine and the same Firestone tires, so it had to be something about the car and the driver and the guys who set it up. But that's the way it is in racing. Sometimes—rarely—all the planets line up for you and it's like you can do no wrong. Everything's so effortless and easy that you catch yourself wondering just what the hell happened to everybody else. And then, leading by a country mile and with just nine laps to go, a bolt in the steering gear popped and Billy banged the wall and Troy Ruttman lucked into the win. But the handwriting was right there on the wall along with the black marks from Billy Vukovich's new Kurtis.

The team came back in '53 with the same exact combination. Only now there were a lot of other top drivers and crack teams with new Kurtis 500 "roadsters" in the field. But it didn't make any difference. Billy Vukovich put the "Fuel Injection Special" on the pole and simply ran away with the race. It was hotter than blazes that year, the race went just shy of four hours and Vuky was one of only five drivers who managed the full distance without needing relief. So he was tough as nails as well as smooth, calm, fast and consistent at the Speedway.

And this year he'd had a few problems in qualifying the first weekend and everybody had a bad time with wind on the second—and that can get pretty serious at upwards of 150!—so Vuky and the "Fuel Injection Special" were way down in 19th position on the inside of the seventh row of the grid. Or just four rows ahead of Sammy Speed in our yellow-blue-and-red Sun Seed Special, which Sammy had pushed solidly if unspectacularly into the field on the final day of qualifying. If you can call 137.987 miles-per-hour unspectacular, that is.

According to the newspapers, the favorite was polesitter Jack McGrath, who'd cracked off the first 140-plus qualifying run ever at Indianapolis in one of the brand new Kurtis 500Cs. In fact, he was almost two miles-per-hour clear of the next fastest car. And the papers made a big deal out of how that could add up to several whole laps by the end. But you know how the papers are. The fact was that anybody with one of the new Kurtis 500s (or maybe an Eddie Kuzma chassis like the one Jimmy Bryan had put on the outside of the front row) and a strong-running Offy under the hood was in with a chance, and it would all come down to driver, pit crew, and—of course—racing luck....

And here I was—down in the sunshine/spotlight glare of it all in what felt like the center of the whole blessed universe—waiting while the stands filled up and the bands played and the dignitaries paraded by and my palms all sweaty with anticipation. My gut was in a knot, and I could only imagine what the drivers were feeling. And then, finally, it was time to roll Sammy's car out to our 29th spot in the middle of the tenth row, and it was a thrill how all the cars in the field were gleaming and glistening from wax and polish. Why, every nut, bolt, washer, exhaust pipe and suspension link was either painted and shined to a perfect gloss or plated over with chrome or zinc or nickel or cadmium. Oh, the paintjobs were maybe a little garish by European sportycar standards—maybe a little more like circus wagons than racing cars—but you had to be impressed with how beautifully finished and detailed they were. Especially the way they glinted like they were made of colored glass under that brilliant Indiana sun while the crews milled around them and exchanged nervous, useless little snippets of small talk and the drivers did their best to look off someplace else and not catch your eye and walk like it was just a blessed stroll in the park when the time came for them to head for their cars. Like Bill Vukovich did as he ambled past us, looking somehow taut and loose-jointed at the same time. He was a wiry, tough-looking little guy with halfback shoulders and those sad, faraway, gunfighter eyes that all the great drivers seem to have. And the thing you noticed most was that he looked as calm and relaxed as if he was walking down his driveway to get the Sunday paper—as if he didn't see or hear or even feel all the noise and tumult and jabbering faces and hooting fans and band music swirling all around us. I remember he shot Sammy a wink as he went by.

A few minutes later they played the National Anthem while we all stood at kind of a fidgety parade rest around the cars—you could feel all those eyes looking down at us and almost hear the heartbeat of the guy standing next to you—and as the *"home of the brave"* part came over the P.A. system, there was thunderous cheering and applause that seemed to be coming right up through the ground! And then some famous guy sang *"Back Home Again in Indiana,"* and after that there was even more cheering and applause and whooping and hooting and then, as it died just a little, this solemn voice crackled over the P.A.:

"GENTLEMEN, START YOUR ENGINES...."

Spud stuck the nose of the electric starter into the little socket tube sticking out of the nose while crews around us all did the exact same thing and there was this chorus of grinding, clattering whirrs from all the starters around us while the noise from the stands pounded in against your eardrums and made the hairs on the back of your neck stand on end....

One engine sputtered and cracked to life.

And then another.

And another,

And then ours popped and banged and splattered its noise up there, too, sending a wisp of bluish oilsmoke up into the atmosphere. Spud figured you wanted just a little oil creeping in through the valve guides when the engine was sitting. Just to keep everything slick, you know? He looked in at Sammy.

"See you in 500 miles."

Sammy gave him the thumbs-up and we scrambled back over the pit wall. Even with all those unmuffled engines barking and roaring right in front of us, you could still hear the noise from the stands. In fact, it was damn near overpowering. And it got even louder as the bright yellow Dodge Royal convertible pace car led the field around on a couple parade laps. It was a pretty special sort of Dodge, what with wire wheels and a Continental kit on the back and of course "Indianapolis 500 Pace Car" lettering all up and down the sides. The morning newspaper said it was Dodge's first-ever appearance as the Speedway pace car, and that they did it to celebrate Dodge's 40th anniversary and also to show off their high-performance Red Ram V8 (which was really not much more than a three-quarter-size edition of the big Chrysler Hemi, if you want the truth of it). You got the feeling that a lot of favors and cash might have to change hands if you wanted your particular brand and model to be selected as the Indy 500 pace car. But you sure got your money's worth, no question about it!

The field rolled around on their parade laps and I couldn't believe how the noise and tension and excitement kept building and building, and just when I thought it had reached a final peak from which it couldn't possibly go any higher, the pace car swooped into pit lane and the green flag waved and the field roared past like a sideways avalanche and the fans in the stands roared right back even louder and screamed and stamped and stomped until the concrete underneath them shook and shuddered like it was a blessed earthquake!

You've never seen anything like it in your life.

And it stays like that—at a damn frenzied, fever pitch!—for a whole bunch of laps while everybody yells themselves hoarse and the field jostles and jockeys for position and the hard chargers carve their way towards the front. But it's not the kind of thing you can sustain, and, eventually, people start sitting back down and ungritting their teeth and unclenching their fists and it slowly begins to dawn on everybody that this is one long, *long* race.

Meanwhile the field streams by every sixty-some seconds—slowly but surely stringing itself out with the Fast Guys still in a knot up at the front as the slower cars and drivers gently slip further and further behind. Vukovich's gray number 14 with the red wheels and number circles was already up to eighth after just seven laps, and Spud nudged me in the ribs as he went by. "You keep an eye on him," he hollered into my ear over the roar of the open exhausts. "He's headed for the front." To be honest, you couldn't really see all that much from where we were in the pits, but you'd hear the crowd noise turn up like there was a rheostat someplace and then, moments later, McGrath would charge past with Jimmy Bryan and Vuky not too far behind, the three of them pretty well clear of fourth place, and you'd maybe even catch Vuky poking and probing around on the inside of Bryan as they headed out of our sight towards Turn One and the noise rheostat would turn up again at that end of the Speedway.

Meanwhile Sammy was soldiering on in Les Gonda's older Kurtis, putting in good, solid laps and maintaining his pace and looking, more than anything, like he was planning to be around when the money got passed out. Sure, it's disappointing when a good driver doesn't find himself matched up with a winning car. Or at least not unless a bolt of lightning shoots down out of the heavens and zaps about twelve or fifteen other cars. But it turns into a different kind of challenge. Can you find a nice, smooth, comfortable groove at a difficult place like Indy, pick guys off when you can and get the good pitstops and the good breaks in traffic and maybe even get a top-five finish out of a tenth-place car or a top-ten finish out of a twentieth-place car? And that's exactly what Sammy was doing, getting by the guys he could and taking care of the car while all the hotdogs and heroes banged the wall or busted and burnt up their equipment....

I have to tell you I was nervous as hell before our first pitstop. "Don't worry about it," Spud whispered in my ear. "You've changed tires a million times before."

"Yeah," I agreed. "But never with 100,000 people staring at me."

"I think it's more like 175,000," he grinned, and gave me a pat on the shoulder.

And then it was time and the car swept into the pits—Spud and Les had decided to pit a little early to avoid all the congestion when everybody's tanks started running dry, and also to get Sammy out on an empty stretch of track where he could put more solid laps in away from heavy traffic—and I swear it was like everything was in slow motion and my hands were all thumbs when the car jerked to a stop and our Nose Man shoved his jack under the front and yanked it up off the ground. I got the right-front off quick enough, but then I bobbled the big, three-eared wheel nut and it clanked down on the concrete and then bounced right back into my lap, and I had to scramble like I was on fire to get it and then almost whiffed it when I finally got it back on the spindle and took a swing at it with the hammer—Jesus, this was taking *forever!*—and then all of a sudden I was done and I looked up and Spud was just finishing his wheel and the fuel hose came out a heartbeat later and Les tapped Sammy on the helmet just as he dropped the clutch and peeled away. Jesus, my mouth was dry as old toast, my heart was pounding and I was shaking so bad I could hardly walk as we clambered back over the wall.

"Nice job," Spud hollered over the noise.

"I dropped the wheel nut," I hollered back at him.

"Yeah? But y'didn't *lose* it. That's th' main thing. Mistakes are gonna happen. The important thing is t'keep 'em *little* mistakes...."

Our second pitstop went a little better—at least I didn't drop anything!—and meanwhile the race at the front droned on. It was pretty clear that Vukovich, McGrath and Bryan had the legs on the rest of the field. And that meant it came down to the speed and consistency of the driver and the speed and consistency of the crew on pitstops. Not to mention strategy. Vuky started with lots of fuel on board and his guys had the engine trimmed out about as lean as it would go, and that's how they managed to do the whole race on just two pitstops. Everybody else needed at least three. And that's why, by three-quarter distance, Vukovich had taken the lead and was starting to stretch it out. There's a psychology to it, really. It's not enough to simply get ahead of the other guy. No, you've got to break his heart. Get ahead and then, when he's trying everything he can to catch up, keep pulling away. And that's exactly what Billy Vukovich was doing. To everybody.

Meanwhile Sammy had inched us up into the top ten—which was pretty good, considering how many cars were still running—and, as is kind of traditional at Indy, there was drama right there near the end. Sam Hanks had pulled the No. 1 Bardahl Kurtis into the pits and handed it over to his teammate Jim Rathmann—I guess it had a split exhaust header that was gassing him pretty bad—and Rathmann went out in this car he'd never even sat in before to finish up the race. Now you may think that these cars are all the same just because they look the same, but there's a lot of fiddling and adjustments you not only *can* make on an Indianapolis racer, but that you *have* to make. You gotta make some choices, that's all there is to it. And that means that no two cars ever feel or handle exactly the same. In fact, according to Spud, they never feel or handle the same even when you try to set them up nut-for-nut and bolt-for-bolt identical. Don't ask me why. But the point is that, with just nine laps to go, Jim Rathmann came off the last corner in this car he'd never so much as sat in before and lost it in a *big* way. Maybe he hit a patch of oil or something—who knows?—but he came spinning right down the middle of the front straightaway with smoke pouring off the tires and wound up more or less parked sideways across the track right in front of the main grandstand!

To tell the truth, it must've been pretty embarrassing.

But the crowd gave him a huge hand for not hitting anything (not that the driver can do all that much about it once the world starts rotating!) and it sure perked them up for the finish. In the end it was Vukovich by almost exactly a lap over Jimmy Bryan (who'd been getting the living hell pounded out of him ever since a spring and shock broke) as "The Mad Russian" chalked up his second-straight Indy 500 win. Wow. And if it hadn't been for that busted steering bolt while he was leading in '52, it could very easily have been his third in a row! Like I said, he was a pretty special kind of driver running for a pretty special kind of team when it came to the Indianapolis 500. He'd set a new speed record, averaging 130.840 miles-per-hour, and he got kissed on both cheeks in the winner's circle—his wife Esther on one side and actress/race queen Marie Wilson on the other—and told the horde of reporters and photographers crowded all around that he'd like to win "two or three more" before retiring to a 40-acre grape farm he'd bought himself out near Fresno.

As for our team, Sammy never put a wheel wrong all day and brought the old Sun Seed Kurtis home ninth overall, and we all went nutty as hell over going the whole distance and notching up a top-ten finish. Why, it paid almost Seven Thousand Dollars! $6,985, to be exact! To finish *ninth,* can you believe it? And Spud also reminded us that this had been a really clean, safe year at the Brickyard, and so we had a lot to be thankful for. "When everybody who walked in through those front gates gets t'walk out again under their own power, it's been a good race."

That night Les Gonda took us all out to dinner and spread a little bit of that cash around. But not too much, on account of he was already trying to figure out how he could work himself a deal on one of those newer Kurtis chassis for next year....

18: Sportycars and Stock Cars

One really nice thing happened the Tuesday morning after I got back from Indianapolis. Some high school kid wandered by the shop while I was working on one of the Jaguars, and you couldn't miss how he kind of froze in his tracks and his eyes bulged out when he saw it. I knew that look, on account of I'd been wearing the same exact one when I saw my first Jaguar tool up to the pumps not all that many years ago. I watched out of the corner of my eye while he slowly inched closer and closer to the open garage door, his head kind of craning forward like it was on a stalk. "Hi," I said, and he damn near shot out of his shoes. "What's your name?"

"J-Jasper," he stammered, his voice cracking like shaved ice. "J-Jasper Mitchell. But everybody calls me J.R."

"What's the 'R' for?"

He looked down at the concrete. "Rudolph."

"Like Rudolph Valentino?"

"I guess." Jesus, this kid had never heard of Rudolph Valentino! I took a quick glance in the fender mirror to see if I'd sprouted any gray hair.

"You like sports cars?"

"Boy, do I *ever!*" He sounded like he was about ready to wet his pants.

"Think you could wash this one for me for a quarter when I'm done working on it?"

"Could I??!!"

And that, in a nutshell, is how I came on probably the best damn worker to ever spend his after-school and summer vacation hours at the Sinclair since another starry-eyed kid named Buddy Palumbo what seemed like a hundred summers ago. J.R. Mitchell would do anything you asked him to, and could pick up just about anything you showed him how to do. And once was usually enough. Plus he seemed almost guilty about taking the quarters and half-bucks and dollars I'd dole out to him for the work he did.

But he was still just a kid, and what I really needed was somebody to more or less serve as my backup around the shop. Somebody who'd do things the way I wanted them done—the way I'd do them myself, you know?—and watch over things when I had to go off to the races and such. I took another run at Sylvester Jones over at Westbridge, but he just wasn't interested in being on foreign soil over here in Jersey and, more importantly, further away than a short drive uptown from his home turf in Harlem. I had Cal coming around pretty regularly to do this and that on the Jagillac and he'd help out here and there, but the fact is he really didn't care about anything but going racing, and on top of that he had the work ethic of a three-toed tree sloth. So, while it was nice having him around just to lighten things up a little and do some of the grunt work, his asset value was kind of marginal. But then, I wasn't paying him very much, either.

Raymond Tuttle had turned out to be exactly what he'd appeared to be from the very beginning: an honest, earnest, hardworking and well-meaning kind of guy who didn't have the least little cause-and-effect idea in his head about how car stuff actually worked. Oh, he could do something pretty well once you'd showed him how (and so long as it was absolutely *exactly* like the one he'd done before), but there was no getting around that he was a natural born Parts Replacer by genetics, talent and temperament, and would never, ever, be anything more. And that left Butch. Good old, crippled-up Butch. Still the meanest, orneriest guy at the station (at least now that Old Man Finzio was gone) but also the one guy, besides myself, who knew what he was doing, knew what was going on and, moreover, really seemed to give a shit about how the work got done. Then again, he didn't have a lot of other stuff going on in his life, either. He'd kind of given up on going to the therapy sessions at the V.A. hospital and didn't even try to use his crutches much anymore—just rolled around the shop in his wheelchair and even out to pump gas now and then once we'd made a little wooden ramp for him so he didn't fall flat on his face trying to roll on and off the pump islands. But the main thing was I could count on him to show up and be there and take care of the mechanical stuff the same way I would—or maybe even a little better—and the only thing I had to remember was not to let him get too involved with handling the customers. As bad as Old Man Finzio ever was, he was never as bad about suffering fools and putting up with ignorance as Butch. But then, Old Man Finzio always enjoyed taunting and demeaning and sneering at people. It was kind of a hobby with him. Butch just wanted to be left alone.

But, like I said, I could count on him. Every morning Mean Marlene would drive by in whatever beat-up old Ford Butch had worried and fussed together for her and damn near push him and his wheelchair out the door and take off with a wheezy rattle from the exhaust and a pitiful little chirp from the tires and not so much as a wave, smile or "how-are-you" to anybody. And most nights she'd pick him up, too, always acting like it was the biggest damn chore in the world to load him and his wheelchair back into that rattletrap Ford. Some nights I'd take him home or Tater Tuttle'd kind of hang Butch's folded-up wheelchair on the back of his oil-devouring Crosley wagon and drop him off on the way to whatever bar, pool table or large-breasted female with hair almost as big as his own was awaiting him. And I got the feeling that sometimes they maybe stopped off and had a few together along the way.

And then things changed.

You know, you never realize how much you grow to lean on and count on and believe in the simple, familiar, ongoing, day-to-day routine of things. Even stuff that drives you nuts or bores you silly or gets you so damn irritated you want to put somebody's nose through a meat grinder. Like Tater Tuttle disappearing for three hours just to run five or six miles up the highway to pick up the re-cored radiator you need for the corner grocer's never-washed International Travelall that he needs to pick up fruit at the produce market at 5 ayem the next morning and that you promised to have done by six tonight. Or Butch getting mad as hell on the phone at the auto parts guy you buy all your ordinary belts and hoses and sparkplugs and such for American cars from on account of he sent over the wrong gasket set for the carburetor on some foot doctor's DeSoto. Or one of our mooch regulars dropping by to try and negotiate a better price on a grease-and-oil change if he brings his own grease and oil. Or Barry Spline trying to tell you that retail is really wholesale on a bunch of parts you need for a Jag or MG you've got torn apart in the service bay and actually expecting you to believe it. But the point is that you're fighting the everyday battles on your home turf and according to your own schedule and priorities, and there's a certain comforting regularity and rhythm to it—even to the aggravation and anguish—and you start to feel just the tiniest bit safe and secure wrapped up in that routine.

And then, like I said, things change.

And it always comes from the blind side, too....

This particular deal started when Butch didn't show up for work one morning. I didn't think too much about it at first. I mean, people get sick or hungover or whatever and it wasn't actually something you'd read in Butch's character that he'd call in or anything to tell you about it. Still, it was the first day he'd missed since I'd talked the Old Man into re-hiring him back after his accident. Saturdays included. And then it got even more mysterious the next day, when he showed up about an hour late in a blessed taxicab. A taxicab, can you believe it? Now, I knew what I was paying Butch, and even with those nice, fat disability checks he was getting from Uncle Sam, a taxicab was just not the kind of thing you'd expect out of Butch Bohunk's budget. Not hardly.

"Aw, Marlene's got a new job," he grunted by way of explanation. "She's workin' evenings as a cocktail waitress over by The Pines."

Now everybody in town knew The Pines was a place over near Hackensack where businessmen in suits went for a quick one with the boys on the way home from work and generally stayed until closing time once or twice a month. Luckily for The Pines, there was a vast supply of these businessmen, so they could survive and prosper even though the regulars only dropped by once every few weeks. Plus it helped that The Pines was rumored to have an "upstairs room" where you could play cards or dice for money and likewise meet girls in fishnet stockings who'd do things for money that your wife maybe wasn't real keen on doing any more. If she ever was. "How'd she ever get a job over there?" I asked.

"Aw, she met a guy who knew a guy. A cook or something." He looked at me kind of sideways. "She's workin' *downstairs* over there, y'unnerstand..."

Nothing else ever crossed my mind.

"...but the tips're real good an' she seems t'like it pretty much..." I could tell Butch wasn't one-hundred percent pleased with this new situation. Two or three percent would be more like it.

"So she works nights now?"

"Yeah. She gets in around two or three most nights..." he looked down in his lap "...makes it a lil' tough fer her t'drop me off in the mornings..."

"I can fix that up for you," I told him. "No problem."

But of course it was a problem on account of I had Julie and the baby at home now and I was generally up most of the night—or most nights, anyway—and the last thing I really needed was to have to get up at five ayem just so's I could leave the duplex at quarter-to-six, drive way the hell over by where my old man worked at his chemical plant job in Newark, pick Butch up at his ramshackle house with the front lawn that looked like one of Big Ed's scrapyards, and get us both back to the station in time to open up right on schedule at seven o'clock. And it was an iffy kind of deal asking Tater to do it, on account of his idea of a full day's work started somewhere around ten or ten-thirty (and that was on a good day!), and Raymond usually took the bus to work. And Cal was absolutely out of the question seeing as how *his* idea of a full day's work started around where Tater's left off and went due south from there.

It occurred to me that what I really needed was another vehicle around the station. I mean, using the Old Man's tow truck for Julie and my personal transport was wearing a little thin anyway and, although I didn't feel too hamstrung about taking a customer car or two home for a little test drive (for purely professional diagnostic purposes, you understand), I got real nervous about giving one out to Raymond or Cal or, God help me, Tater. But if I had another vehicle, I could maybe lend it or the tow truck out to Raymond and have him pick Butch up and thereby get my allotted half-hour of sleep between when the baby finally stopped crying around five-fifteen or five-twenty and when the alarm went off at ten-to-six.

"I got just the thing for ya!" Big Ed grinned from behind the wheel of his white Eldorado. It was a beautiful spring day and this was the first time all year he'd had the Eldo out with the top down. "We got it as part of a scrap deal on some forging-and-heat-treating company over in Pittsburgh. C'mon over by the shore yard on Thursday or Friday. I should have it by then."

So Tater drove me over to Big Ed's scrapyard overlooking the Hudson on Friday afternoon and he took us around back and there was this adorable little '47 Willys CJ2A "Civillian Jeep" painted several different shades of bright lipstick red with a wind-up power winch over the front bumper and a white canvas top and side curtains. Oh, it was maybe a little rough here and there, what with some serious fender and rocker cancer bubbling up through what was obviously a very quick & thick respray job. And the top and side curtains weren't so much white as the color of an old pair of kid's sneakers with a couple rough summers on them—and maybe frayed a little around the edges, too. But it was still cute as hell, and I knew that Julie would just love it. Especially compared to the Old Man's tow truck. And Big Ed had even had the guy who did his trucks put some fancy gold lettering on both sides of the bodywork, just below the canvas side-curtain/doors and well above the worst of the rust. It read:

Finzio's Sinclair
Expert Towing & Repairs
plus the address and phone number on one side and:

Alfredo's Foreign Car Service
Sports Car Specialists!
plus the same address and phone number on the other.

"Who the hell is Alfredo?" was the first thing I wanted to know.

"It's my sister's Saint Bernard," Big Ed said like it made perfect sense. "I figured we had'ta make it sound like maybe more than it was to attract new customers, see?"

"But *'Alfredo's?'*" I mean, I was thinking why not *'Buddy's Foreign Car Service,'* or *'Palumbo's Performance Palace'* or something, you know?

"I dunno. I had the sign painter here and I was just tryin' t'come up with something, you know..." Big Ed waved his hand through the air like he was scattering stardust. I rolled it over in my mind a little. Come to think of it, *"Alfredo's"* did sound a little classier and more exotic and, more importantly, more expensive than *"Buddy's."*

"But what do I say when somebody wants to talk to Alfredo?"

"Y'don't unnerstand anything about business, do ya?"

"I don't get it."

"Don'cha see? *Alfredo* is the genius foreign car expert that nobody ever gets to talk to. He's the brains of the outfit, see?"

I still didn't get it.

"Sure," Big Ed continued grandly. "He worked for Ferrari over in Italy. Or maybe Jaguar over in England. Or maybe Ferrari and *then* Jaguar. With maybe a little stint at MG or something beforehand, when he was a teenager."

"But why go to all that trouble?"

"Because y'can *charge* more with a guy like Alfredo around. And especially if he's never around for the customers t'actually talk to..."

It was beginning to come to me.

"...He just left a half-hour ago," Big Ed demonstrated in a Fawning Toady example of a falsetto voice. *"You just missed him. But Alfredo said your engine needs a complete overhaul..."*

It was like something like you'd expect out of Colin St. John over at Westbridge.

"...Oh, if you want to discuss the bill, you'll have to take it up with Alfredo. But he's just left for Europe. Won't be back for six weeks...."

Yep, Colin St. John for sure!

To be honest about it (and maybe right there was the problem!), I wasn't too wild about the idea. And yet I had to admit I kind of liked the way *'Alfredo's Foreign Car Service'* rolled off your tongue.

"I got somethin' else here that'll tickle ya," Big Ed grinned, and led me around to the front of the Jeep. "Just feast yer eyeballs on *this!"* He popped the two spring-loaded T-latches and raised the hood. Underneath it was a V8-60 Ford Flathead engine sporting an Offenhauser intake manifold with two Stromberg 97s and these cute little chrome hot-rod air filters on top. You could see it was kind of a homebuilt, back-alley sort of engine swap, what with loose wires and cables dangling all over the place and a throttle linkage worthy of old Rube Goldberg himself. But you could tell from the dirt and oil film that it'd managed a bunch of miles already, and so you had to figure it'd be good for a few more.

"Looks like an awful lotta motor for a damn Jeep," I allowed, rubbing my hands together in anticipation. "How's it drive?"

"Like a stick a'dynamite with a short fuse!" Big Ed grinned right back at me. "Here," he chuckled, tossing me the keys, "see fr'yerself."

Well, while Jeeps may have been exactly what Uncle Sam's Army had in mind when it came to climbing muddy hills, fording rocky streams and standing up to all kinds of weather and terrain (not to mention multiple hits from enemy gunfire!) all over the Pacific, African and European theatres in World War Two, they are not exactly the most comfortable or livable sort of vehicles for New Jersey parts runs or commuting. And especially when fitted with an engine sporting roughly two-and-a-half times more horsepower than the designers ever intended. The best way to describe this cute but vicious little beast is to simply explain that it had roughly the power-to-weight ratio of a Jag 120 in a narrow, short-wheelbase chassis that stood about as high over its wheel centers and handled around corners about as well as a Radio Flyer coaster wagon.

It sure was fun, though! And it got damn near as many head swivels and tongue clucks as a blessed Jag 120. Can you believe it? I let Cal take it for a spin when he dropped by Saturday to help cut the Swiss-cheese holes Roman had recommended in the Jagillac's frame *("you cut everything from here to here,"* he said, pointing at the X-ed in section from the firewall back to the rear springs, *"make lighter!")* and it kind of shook me the way he squealed out of the lot with the Jeep tilted way up on its two outside wheels. He came back about fifteen minutes later with a shell-shocked smile on his face. "Whaddaya think?" I asked him.

"Well," he allowed cautiously, "it's sure as hell no sports car."

I guessed not.

"But it's a lot of fun seeing how far you can get the inside wheels up in the air without tipping it clear over...."

And it was, too. Only I never got it near as high as Cal Carrington did. And that was just fine with me.

In any case, I started using Big Ed's overstimulated Jeep mongrel as my everyday driver (at least when I wasn't, ahem, *"road testing"* some customer or other's far more interesting, comfortable, desirable, benign and generally less-lethal-to-the-operator type of automobile). But the main thing was that it was entertaining as hell, and I could hand the Old Man's tow truck over to Raymond most nights so's he could take old Butch home and pick him up again in the morning. And that worked out pretty good, so I was home safe and clear with all my ducks realigned in a row and a new routine in place. Just like things have to be. Plus Julie absolutely loved that new Jeep. Just like I knew she would. Or at least she did until she got her first ride in it anyway. *"Jesus, Buddy!"* she hollered over the racket as we leaped, hopped, banged, skittered and jittered our way down the street, *"This is like being kicked down a flight of stairs!"*

"Yeah!" I shouted back enthusiastically. *"Or maybe more like a fire escape!"*

June 12th and 13th there was an SCMA race at the Westover Air Force Base near Springfield, Massachusetts, but none of my guys were going on account of we figured it was gonna be a pretty lame weekend, what with all the heavy runners over in France doing the Twenty-Four Hours of Le Mans. All of 'em except us, anyway. And that Le Mans race was shaping up to be one heck of a contest, seeing as how Jaguar had this brand new model called the D-Type coming out and, at least according to Barry Spline and Colin St. John, it made the C-Type look like an old lady's shoe. I found that pretty hard to imagine. And Ferrari was countering with this monstrous 375 Plus model, which was likewise a lot sleeker and slipperier than any previous Ferrari and also just happened to have its engine hogged out to 4.9 liters. It was actually a little odd, since the way Ferrari numbered his cars was always by the displacement of one cylinder. Like that pretty little "225" coupe Big Ed couldn't fit in at the World Motor Sports Show had 12 cylinders at 225ccs each for a total of 2700ccs or 2.7 liters (or roughly 165 Cubes American, to put it in lingo any streetcorner pump jockey can understand).

Likewise the "250" Ferrari was a three-liter and the big-block "340 Mexicos" we'd seen down at *La Carrera* and the "340 America" Carlo had on the stand at the show were 4.1 liters. It all made sense, you know? And so did punching the "340" out to "375" (for 4.5 litres total, like Creighton had in his car) for a little more oomph. But of course the only thing you can really count on out of Ferrari (aside from maybe the consistently best damn all-around racing cars in the world) was that you couldn't count on anything. And that's why he called his new, 4.9-liter Le Mans challenger the "375 Plus." Just to screw everybody up. But, whatever it was, it was sure to be fast as stink. Especially down that long, undulating, three-and-a-half mile straightaway heading towards Mulsanne. Sure, Cunningham would be there with the C-4Rs and that much modified, blue-and-white Ferrari of his, but the Chrysler-engined cars were getting kind of long in the tooth and didn't figure to have the speed or brakes or handling to win it outright any more against the latest stuff from Ferrari and Jaguar. But they were solid and reliable and figured to be around at the finish, and that counted for a lot in a grind like the Twenty-Four Hours of Le Mans. And he had Creighton Pendleton over there driving for him again, which was enough to make you puke. I mean, here was a guy who could easily afford to race any damn thing he wanted out of his own pocket—not to mention a guy who'd rubbed the entire Cunningham team's nose in it a few times—and he gets offered a free ride, all expenses paid, to the biggest damn sports car race in the world. And meanwhile guys like my friends Cal Carrington and Sammy Speed, who could drive damn rings around him, are begging rides and counting raindrops back here in the States. It just didn't seem fair....

Speaking of Cal and Sammy, while all that high-octane activity was going on in Massachusetts and over at Le Mans, Big Ed and me sneaked down the road to Linden, New Jersey—just a little ways south of us and pretty much directly across from Staten Island—to watch our buddies Sammy Speed and Cal Carrington drive in a most definitely *non*-SCMA Money Race put on at the Linden Airport by this southern-fried group of stock car racers called NASCAR They were the same bunch who'd been running around making circles in the sand down at Daytona Beach since 1948 or thereabouts, and the head honcho was a guy named Bill France who actually seemed to think he could make a living putting on stock car races. Can you believe it? Anyhow, this was their first-ever attempt at an airport road race, but they'd laid out a pretty decent two-mile racetrack on the concrete runways of the Linden Airport with no less than five real sharp turns on it. Which meant it was for sure gonna be hard on brakes. It was also the first time NASCAR had ever allowed European sports cars to run against their usual all-American Detroit iron. For real ca$h prize money, too! In fact, that's how Cal finally got Carson to let him drive the Healey. Charlie Priddle and his gang from the SCMA had made it perfectly clear that anybody who accepted something as crass and ungentlemanly as (horrors!) *Prize Money* for competing in a contest of speed would no longer be considered an amateur (or a gentleman, for that matter) and might very easily find themselves no longer welcome at the SCMA's sportsmanlike and Simon Pure amateur events. Harrumph. How exactly that squared with people like Briggs Cunningham going over and running the biggest and most professional sports car races in the world with the same exact team he brought to

SCMA events was a little beyond some of us, but then the last thing you expected out of all Charlie Priddle's steering committees and ruddering groups and star-chamber tribunals was consistency.

But the point was that my buddy Cal finally had a ride in Carson's Healey (and I had it running like a bear with its fur on fire, if I do say so myself), and it was great to see our old friends Sammy and Spud again. Seeing as how he'd had a little road racing experience on the runways of Sebring in Big Ed's Jaguar back in the spring of '53, Sammy'd gotten himself hooked up on a one-race deal driving a brand new Hudson stock car for some wrench-spinner from Daytona Beach named Smokey Yunick. Now this Smokey Yunick guy was quite a character. He was crusty, shrewd and leathery as they come, and always wore a porkpie hat with the sides kind of rolled up and his sunglasses stuck up over the brim whenever he wasn't actually wearing them. They called him Smokey because he generally smoked a straight-stem pipe and always sucked on it and thought a moment before he said anything. And then he said just exactly what was on his mind. And the way he explained his opinions and observations about things could get very colorful indeed. To give you an idea, he called his car shop down in Daytona Beach simply "The Best Damn Garage in Town." And you can bet it was, too.

Anyhow, Smokey's regular driver was a tough, lanky, ex-truck driver from Sanford, North Carolina, named Herb Thomas, and between this Herb Thomas' undeniable driving ability and the way this Smokey Yunick bolted those Hudsons together, they'd won themselves the NASCAR championship outright in 1951 and again in '53 after finishing second in 1952. Smokey allowed as how that was sort of an off year for them. The car Herb drove for Smokey wore No. 92 and had "Fabulous Hudson Hornet" slathered down both sides like a blessed four-wheeled billboard. Now I already knew about Hudson's big but ancient 308-cubic-inch straight six and the optional "Twin H-Power" dual-carb setup you could get for it, and it was easy to see how Hudson's low-slung, "step-down" build gave it maybe a lower center of gravity than most of the other Detroit sedans. I'd even heard of the special "Severe Usage Equipment" package you could get right from the factory if you wanted to go race a Hudson stock car. But I had to admit I had a little professional curiosity going about exactly what made this particular Hudson Hornet such a successful racecar. So I asked that Smokey Yunick character about it. You know, one garage operator/racing mechanic to another. "Aw, hell," he told me after a long, slow draw on his pipe. "We just pull the back seat out, pry the hubcaps off an' paint the numbers on it, same as anybody."

Right.

Anyhow, a lot of people who followed stock car racing had noticed just how fast and rugged and reliable Smokey's Hudsons were, and one of them (who had a little money in his pocket thanks to a couple dozen chicken ranches around Gainesville, Georgia) asked Smokey if he could maybe build him a Hudson like the one Herb Thomas was driving. And that's where the second car came from. Smokey had just finished it, and wanted to give it a little shakedown run before he turned it over to its new owner. Besides, this Linden race paid a thousand dollars to win, and it certainly didn't hurt to double your chances with a second fast Hudson in the hands of a fast, seasoned race driver with a little airport road course experience.

"So," I said to Spud, "Sammy's car is the same as the one Herb Thomas is driving?"

Spud rolled me a fisheye. "I said Smokey promised to build a car *'like'* the one Herb Thomas is driving. That's not necessarily the same as *'identical to.'*"

"It isn't?"

"Oh, don't get me wrong. I'm sure it's real close. Why, it wouldn't surprise me at all if it was damn near the same as the Hudson Smokey was runnin' back when that chicken farmer ordered up a car. But that was last year, and if there's one thing you need t'know about Smokey Yunick, it's that he never stays in one place for very long. He's always up to something," Spud chuckled. "It's one a'the things you can pretty much count on."

It was obvious there was a bit more to this stock car racing business than pulling the back seat, prying off the hubcaps and painting your car like a highway billboard.

Still, they were all big, lumbering American sedans that mostly ran on these bullring ovals down south—and mostly dirt ovals, at that—and so I really didn't see how any of them had much of a chance running against Jaguars and such on a road course. In fact, I was ready to start looking around the paddock for some-body with a pleasant southern drawl in order to place a small, gentlemanly sort of side wager on the outcome. I mean, I knew from *La Carrera* that no stock car was ever going to keep up with a genuine sports car. Not on a road circuit, anyway. Only I hadn't taken into consideration that guys like Smokey Yunick built them-selves some pretty damn special Hudsons and Dodges and Oldsmobiles, and that the guys they had wheelin' 'em around were hardly what you would call raw hands at this line of work.

At the start, I was thoroughly amazed to see some guy named Buck Baker in an Oldsmobile Rocket 88 take the lead and hold it for the first ten laps. But he was being pressed hard by Herb Thomas in Smokey's "Fabulous Hudson Hornet." They were going at it hammer and tongs and the best Jaguar in the race was a strangely painted, two-tone XK 120 coupe down in about fourth or fifth place. The driver was a local Jersey boy—a mechanic out of Bloomfield named Al Keller who'd done a bit of oval track and stock car racing in his time—and I guess he worked on it now and then for its owner. Who turned out to be none other than big, famous jazz bandleader Paul Whiteman. And I do mean *BIG* famous bandleader. He was quite the sports car nut, though, and you could hear Paul Whiteman cheer-ing up a storm every time Keller slipped past this guy or stormed past that guy, moving his way up through the field from seventh starting slot. That was one real sweet-running Jaguar, too. You could hear from the exhaust note that somebody who knew what he was doing had been running a set of wrenches over it.

Meanwhile Sammy was playing it pretty cool in the other, more-or-less-but-probably-not-precisely-the-same Smokey Yunick Hudson, running about fifth or sixth and taking it easy on the brakes. In fact, he was taking it easy on the whole car, seeing as how Smokey had been pretty damn explicit about how the car was already sold and they were just there to cruise around and wring it out for the new owner and hopefully pick up a little extra prize money. Blowing it up, abusing it or wrecking it was most definitely *not* part of the plan. And our boy Sammy was doing exactly as he'd been told.

There was simply too much straightaway at Linden for Cal to ever challenge the leaders in Carson's Healey Hundred, but it was nice watching him pick off a hotrod Dodge or Hudson or Olds (although, just like Tommy Edwards in that gutless Allard Palm Beach at Floyd Bennett Field, sometimes it took him three or four tries to make it stick). Up at the front of the pack, Thomas in the Smokey Yunick "Fabulous Hudson" led for two laps and then Baker in the Olds 88 muscled back in front and then Thomas barged past him again—I mean, this was more action than you usually got in a whole blessed race weekend at an SCMA event!—but you could see that Keller in the Paul Whiteman Jaguar was slowly but surely running them down. He finally sneaked past into the lead right around half-distance on the 23rd lap. You could see as how the two heavy stock cars were starting to run a little shy on brakes by then. But these guys compensated by just hurling the damn things sideways to slow them down for the corners! Can you believe it? And they didn't much care if they used a couple yards of the dirt if they needed a little extra room. Like I said, these stock car guys weren't exactly raw hands when it came to the race driving business. Not hardly.

But the Jaguar was simply a better car—at least on this kind of track, anyway—and at the end of the fifty laps and 100 miles it was Al Keller in the Paul Whiteman Jaguar coming home first and pocketing the thousand bucks, and the only car on the same lap with him at the end was our boy Sammy Speed in the second-string Smokey Yunick Hudson. I think he was the only stock car driver to have anything much in the way of a brake pedal by the end. Buck Baker in the Olds had slipped and struggled his way back to third, a lap down, and then came three more Jaguars (led by a pretty decent driver and Jaguar dealer from Nyack named Bob Grossman) and a thoroughly disappointed and brakeless Herb Thomas in the other Smokey Yunick Hundson in seventh. Which is not too bad, considering about 40 cars started the damn race. As for my buddy Cal in Carson's Healey Hundred, he drove a hell of a smart, smooth race and wound up 11th overall and right on the back bumper of this '54 Dodge with a big number 42 on both sides that he'd been chasing and catching and even passing now and then but never staying ahead of for very long throughout the whole last half of the race. Cal won himself a hundred bucks ca$h American for his efforts—real prize money, wow!—but he didn't care at all about the money. In fact, he just handed it over to Carson. Just like that. And Carson gave twenty bucks of it to me as a sort of a tip, which was real nice of him. But the only thing Cal wanted was to find out who the heck was driving that number 42 Dodge he'd been racing against. "I gotta tell you," he grinned admiringly, "that guy was one hell of a shrewd customer. He figured out right away where the Healey was better than him and then he just made it so I couldn't hardly use it. Anybody know what his name is?"

"Says here in the program he's some guy from Randleman, North Carolina named Lee Petty."

None of us had ever heard of him, you know?

Well, I have to admit they had a pretty nice little four or five column-inch writeup about the race at Linden in the sports section of the Monday *New York Times*. Keller and the Jaguar had averaged 77.58 miles-per-hour over the 100 miles and, according to the *Times,* anyway, the show played to some 23,000 spectators. Although I think they may have arrived at that number by counting the legs and multiplying by two instead of dividing. But it was nice to see a little coverage, even if it did only list the top ten finishers in the agate type down at the bottom so Cal's name didn't quite make the list. What can you do? And right next to it was an eight or nine column-inch report from the Twenty-Four Hours of Le Mans, where two seemingly mismatched drivers I'd read about in *Road and Track* and *Autosport*—a burly, heavyset guy from Argentina named Froilan Gonzalez (who they called "the wild bull of the pampas") and a slight little Frenchman named Maurice Trintignant—took the win in one of Ferrari's monstrous new 4.9-liter 375 Plus racers in a real nail-biter finish in the pouring rain over 1953 winners Tony Rolt and Duncan Hamilton in the last surviving D-Type Jaguar. I guess Stirling Moss managed to keep pace with the Ferrari early on in one of the new Jaguars, but his car fell out and so did the third new D and so, in fact, did most of the field. Only eighteen cars were listed as finishers out of the nearly sixty cars that started, but I guess there was plenty of drama anyway, what with a monsoon of a rainstorm right near the end and the Gonzalez/Trintignant Ferrari way out front, but then it wouldn't start at the end of its last pitstop thanks to wet electrics or something and I could just imagine the Ferrari mechanics going totally berserk and running around like their pants were on fire, scrambling all over the back of each other trying to get it fired while the second-place Jaguar prowled closer and closer to the lead. But finally it caught and fired and the Ferrari headed out into the rain again and hung on to win by just a single lap after more than 2500 miles of racing. Wow! I was happy to see the Chrysler-powered Cunninghams came home third and fifth, even if prize asshole Creighton Pendleton was sharing the driving chores in one of them. Those strange-looking, flounder-faced Bristol 450 coupes with the twin tailfins down their backs finished first, second and third in the two-liter class and an amazing seventh, eighth and ninth overall. And that was with an engine and chassis pretty darn close to the one in that Arnolt-Bristol *Bolide* I'd liked so much at the Motor Sports show. A little tiddler 750cc French DB "DoucheBag" took 10th overall and won the Index of Performance for the Greater Glory of France, and it was nice to see one of those new Triumph TR2s finishing 15th in its first major race. Even if it was only good enough for fifth in class behind the three team Bristols and a Bristol-powered Frazer-Nash.

Oh, and the other thing that happened while I was off with Big Ed and Cal and Carson and Spud and Sammy Speed at Linden was that little Vincenzo said his first real words. Or Julie said they sounded like words, anyway, even if she couldn't exactly make them out. But whether it was just a bunch of gobbledygook or *"would you please put a little more cornstarch on my bottom, this rash is killing me,"* it was kind of a shame that I missed it.

I think it was two days or so after the race we were back in the shop working on the Jagillac again, and I remember it was around lunchtime and I was trying to show Cal how to use this big hole saw to cut lightening holes in the Jagillac's frame without having the circle of metal fall to the inside so's you couldn't get it out. If that happened, you didn't lighten the frame very much at all (although you did, indeed, make it weaker!) plus you didn't particularly want to wind up with a racecar that sounded like it was carrying a load of tiny manhole covers every time it went over a bump in the road. And then, all of a sudden and thoroughly out of nowhere, I heard the compressor pump start to make an unusual and thoroughly unearthly sort of clatter. Now let me take a moment to explain that shop compressors (and almost anything else with an oscillating, pulsating, up-and-down, round-and-round or cyclical monkey-motion sort of operational movement) always make a lot of noise. That's just what they do. But when you live with a particular one for an extended period of time (as you would around virtually any car shop) you get used to it and it just becomes part of the normal, background hum of everyday business. In fact, you don't even hear it.

Until the noise changes, that is. Say, develops an ugly new *knock!-knock!-knock!* kind of clatter that was for sure never there before. When that happens and it's your car shop, it pricks the hairs on the back of your neck up to attention and you know right then and there that *SOMETHING'S BAD WRONG!* And you also know that, no matter what, you'd sure as hell better drop whatever you're doing and switch the damn thing off and then get about fixing it *right away* on account of an air compressor is pretty much the life blood of any self-respecting car shop and you damn well can't live without it. Or at least you'd rather not, anyway.

So I pulled the pump off and took the cylinders apart and sure enough we had a serious rod knock from a bearing that was all hammered out of its connecting rod like some poor little tin soldier that'd gotten itself run over by a diesel locomotive. And I kind of wondered where we'd get a replacement, seeing as how that compressor dated back to around the landing of the Pilgrims at Plymouth Rock. In fact, I wouldn't be surprised if they brought it over with them. As ballast. Far as I knew, it'd come with the place when the Old Man bought it and it was for sure secondhand even then, and I don't think me or anyone else I ever knew in the car shop business had ever heard of the Pimplenicht & Goldfhardt Compressor Company out of East Bumjump, Massachusetts, before. And of course I started having minor seizures about the down time and how much a new compressor was going to cost, and immediately after that started wondering if maybe Roman Szysmanski could make me something that would put it right again.

And just what the hell was I going to do in the meantime?

"Don't worry about it, Buddy," Butch grumbled. "I got most of a compressor like this'n took apart over t'my house that might work. We'll just hafta rig up a l'il ole adaptor plate is all."

So I piled Butch in the vicious little Jeep Big Ed had bought for us and we headed over to his place in Newark just after lunchtime. We had to leave his wheelchair behind on account of there was no room for it in the back of the Jeep if we were planning on bringing the compressor parts back with us. And as soon as we got there, I could sense something wasn't right. There was this sad-looking old beige Plymouth kind of sagged way over to one side on its worn-out springs parked behind Mean Marlene's equally beatup old Ford, and I could feel fire and ice starting to simmer up together in the passenger seat before I even got us over to the curb. "You go up on the porch fr'me," Butch rasped in a desperate whisper.

"What for?" I asked him even quieter. I felt this cold, withering hollow opening up in my gut and I knew that, no matter what, I sure as hell didn't want or need to know what was going on in that house. And I even more sure as hell didn't want to come back and face him if by some stray chance I found out.

"Y'gotta go up there," he told me, his eyes fixed like searchlight beams on the front screen door that was hanging off one good hinge and one with maybe only two wallowed-out screws left holding it. "The compressor parts is in those two wood boxes under the table."

I could see the boxes sure enough. And there was no way to tell him I didn't want to go on account of what I was damn sure we were both thinking. At least not without letting on that I was thinking it, too. So I got out and closed the door real quietly and kind of tiptoed through the front gate and the front yard that looked like a Boeing Stratocruiser full of old industrial machinery had crash-landed into a hardware store. Before I was even up on the porch I could hear the unmistakable grunting, groaning, squealing and gasping for air kinds of sounds that can only come from a wild Amazon pig being crushed to death by a giant anaconda or two very overweight, out-of-shape and thoroughly inebriated middle-aged human beings rooting around in the sheets and pillowcases together. I swear, it stopped me dead in my tracks. I started to turn and head back to the Jeep, but I could feel Butch's eyes searing a hole through my back and so I forced myself to creep the rest of the way up the front stairs and tried my damnedest to avoid peering into the window as I eased the boxes of compressor parts out from underneath the table. Then again, it's kind of hard to ignore the sight of a very large, very fat and exceedingly hairy ass—and we're talking a few curly gray hairs as well as curly black ones—desperately bobbing up and down just on the other side of the windowsill. Or Marlene's shrill, unmistakable voice choking out the sweet, tender words: *"Yew stop an' I'll make you wish you hadn't, Honey!"*

It was enough to turn your stomach inside out, honest it was.

Butch pretty much disappeared for three or four days after that. I hadn't said a word when I got back to the Jeep with the compressor parts, but one look at my face and Butch knew what I'd seen and heard up on his front porch. And I got the feeling that it wasn't the all-fired rude shock I thought it might be. Like maybe he'd been suspecting something, you know? But I could see it tore him up something awful. Which is why as soon as we got back to the Sinclair and I got him back into his wheelchair, he asked me for ten bucks out of the till and then just rolled off down the street and vanished. I have no idea where he went or how he got there but, judging by the shell-shocked look in his sullen, bloodshot eyes and the wavering shake of his hands and the sick, grimy smell of a heavy Lost Weekend bender coming off of him when he finally returned, he sure as heck got his money's worth of oblivion out of that tenspot.

"You look awful," I told him.

"I feel awful," he groaned back.

"You need to go home and sleep it off."

"I already slep' it off."

"Then you need to go home and get cleaned up."

"I ain't goin' back there. Not never." He said it like he meant it, too.

Like I said once or twice before, Butch was one of those guys who lived according to a sort of redneck, blue-collar, ex-Marine, shot-and-a-beer/hillbilly-music Code of Ethics, and one of the prime stipulations of that code was that you didn't get caught fooling around once you were married. Emphasis on the "get caught" rather than the "fooling around," of course. In fact, it was The Original Great Unforgivable Sin if you did (and where in creation would country-and-western music ever have been without it?). But the point is that one of the most basic things "a man didn't do" according to Butch's sacred code was go whimpering back to somebody who you knew was cheating on you. It simply wasn't done.

But that leaves a few little practical and logistical problems to sort out if you happen to be stuck in a wheelchair with two busted-up legs and a bad right wing and no place special left to turn. I knew for sure I couldn't invite Butch home to the duplex to stay with Julie and the baby and me. That was another thing that simply wasn't done. At least by the Sacred Code as I understood it over at our house. And Raymond had his own house full of redneck relatives already, and pawning Butch off on Tater looked like a lousy prospect seeing as how they were a lock to start going out boozing together and that meant I'd have two useless, hungover rummies showing up sometime between 10:30 and straight-up noon every day instead of just one.

And that's the thing about running a damn business instead of just being another grunt working-stiff auto mechanic with a wrench in your hand. All of a sudden you've got all these damn People Problems to deal with instead of just car problems to fix. I guess that's what Sylvester meant way back when he told me I had to start acting more like a boss. But it's tough when the people who work for you are also your friends. I mean, it's not like you plan it that way or anything. It just happens. And now I felt like it was somehow *my* blessed responsibility to find someplace for Butch to stay and somehow help him through this mess until....

And then I had a great idea!

"You can stay in my old apartment over by my Aunt Rosamarina's house!" I blurted out without thinking. And then I remembered that steep stairway up the side of the garage to that little pup tent of an attic apartment with the sink and shower stall and toilet all lined up in the center because it was the only place you could stand up straight. There was just no way Butch could ever get up and down those stairs.

"Bullshit," Butch snorted. "Let's go take a damn look at it."

So we did. And it wasn't ten minutes before old Butch had a tape measure out and had me running up and down that stairway taking measurements and then up to the front door that my Aunt Rosamarina would only open a tiny crack with the chain lock still on to make a deal with her about renting the place out. And letting us do a little free-form carpentry and mechanical work on the stairway out back, too.

"Is he a n-nice man?" my Aunt Rosamarina asked in a weak, trembling voice. She obviously hadn't started in on her daily dosage of sherry yet.

"Well, he's kind of laid up in a wheelchair from a car accident," I told her like I was actually answering her question.

"The poor man. Can he get around by himself?"

"Well," I allowed, "he's pretty stubborn about being self-sufficient."

Boy, was that ever an understatement!

"Good for him," she said, and you could see this frail little shudder of exultation go through her. Thank God she hadn't met him yet!

By the time I got done with my aunt, Butch had it all planned out, and by the middle of the following afternoon we had wood planking nailed down over the stairs to make this terribly narrow, steep sort of ramp up the side of the garage with two lines of 2x4s running down it for wheel guides and a bunch more 2x4s strung up in a sort of cross-braced framework to reinforce the stair railings. Then all we had to do was pirate the winch off the front of that scary red Jeep Big Ed had more or less donated to the cause (I mean, I wasn't planning to yank any stumps or pull any stuck hogs out of a bog hole any time soon) and bolt it up real solid underneath the floorboards on the top landing where it wouldn't be in the way. I mean, there just wasn't room for both it and Butch's wheelchair up there in front of the doorway. At least not if he wanted to be able to rotate himself the necessary ninety degrees to get in through the door. So the winch had to go under the floorboards. But we had to somehow get the cable pulling the other way and from a high enough point to clear the ramp, so we hung a small guide pulley off the bracing for the floorboards and bolted this big, industrial-strength, cast-iron guide pulley off the top railing. We'd found them both in Butch's front yard when we went over while Mean Marlene was at work to get some of his things, along with a battered-up, heavy-duty truck battery and the rusty old battery charger with the missing faceplate we wired it to. The rest was simple. We ran the winch cable over the bottom pulley and around the top pulley and attached the business end to this sawed-off piece of plumber's pipe with a cap on each end so's the cable couldn't slip off—like a water skier's tow rope, you know?—and all Butch had to do was get the wheels on his wheelchair lined up just so, take hold of that plumber's pipe handle, hit the START button we'd installed at the bottom of the stairs, and hope like hell he could hit the STOP button up at the top before the winch pulled both Butch and his wheelchair right through the railing.

"You think this is safe?" I asked him.

"It's like any piece of machinery," he allowed like I was stupid not to know. "It's as safe as the guy who operates it."

That didn't exactly put my mind at ease.

But Butch was real happy with what he'd done, and even happier that Aunt Rosamarina lived close enough to the Sinclair that he could actually wheel his way to work and back home to the apartment over my aunt's garage all by himself on nice days. Not to mention that there was a cozy little corner tavern with a decent hillbilly jukebox in it right along the way. Sure, Butch was still real gloomy about Marlene—I mean, that's just not the kind of thing you easily get over—but you could see it was really doing his spirit a lot of good discovering he could actually get around and take care of himself pretty much all by his lonesome. For a guy who more than anything just liked to be left alone, that was a pretty terrific thing to find out....

Meanwhile, over at the duplex, little Vincenzo had figured out how to hold his head up and roll over all by himself, and then how to sit up and even look around like he was taking it all in. You have to have kids yourself to understand what huge, miraculous, life-changing sorts of events those are. Not that anybody else much cares or has any idea why you get so damn googly-eyed when you talk about it. I have to say that I was really starting to enjoy having the baby around. Especially watching it change from this terrifyingly fragile little foreign object that only knew how to scream, squeal, shriek, spit up, shit, shred and soil into what was obviously turning into its own little person with its own little personality, and who moreover knew exactly who I was and also seemed, on the basis of no solid evidence whatsoever, to genuinely like me.

That's a special kind of feeling, no lie.

And things were going pretty well between Julie and me, too. Except for the regularly interrupted sleeping when little Vincenzo decided he needed to put something in one end or let something else out the other. But you get accustomed to it. Even if it drives you absolutely nuts and helps you begin to understand those horrible people you read about in the newspaper who smother infants with pillows or strangle them with electrical cord or beat them senseless with their own nursery-rhyme books or crib mobiles. In fact, I think the New Parent business is probably more about clenching your fists and gritting your teeth and somehow *not* doing those things rather than all the kissing and cuddling and cooing and caring-for you see displayed so lovingly in the Ivory soap and diaper-service ads in the Sunday magazine supplement.

But, like I said, you grow accustomed to it. And you also, very slowly, get used to the idea that babies only know one thing—*I WANT!*—and likewise understand only one particular aspect of time. Which is always *RIGHT NOW!* The raw, unvarnished truth of it is that babies are the most selfish and demanding creatures on the face of the earth. Bar none. Why, they make Ming the Merciless look like a blessed church usher. But you can't get mad at them—or at least not for very long—on account of they're so little and helpless, and moreover have this way of looking at you in this very special way that makes you feel guiltier than Judas Iscariot and his thirty pieces of silver. And that's even after you've been up all night doing every blessed thing you can think of to satisfy those *I WANTS!* and *RIGHT NOWS!*

The other thing that keeps you from doing bodily harm to the helpless little things is that they sleep now and then and even have their peaceful and placid moments when they're awake and can also become totally absorbed and amused for five to ten minutes at a stretch playing with their crib toys or seeing how many toes they can fit in their mouth at one time or finding out what the paint on the baseboards tastes like or going outside for a little sunshine and fresh air. Although that last one is inevitably bracketed by a solid half-hour of parental struggling trying to dress and undress the little darling in appropriate sunshine-and-fresh-air outdoor clothing—I mean, you simply *can't* have the kid rolling around on the lawn in his blessed birthday suit! Even though, as a young parent, you will most certainly come face-to-face with that exact situation one day. Probably more than once, in fact.

But the point is we were starting to get used to it, and I could see as how Julie really enjoyed taking care of little Vincenzo. Even if it occasionally left her slightly frazzled and upset and headachy and ready to jam a meat fork three inches deep into my forehead and then twist it back and forth a few times by the time I got home from the shop every day. Still, she was finding time to do a little sketching now and then when the baby was asleep, and she'd dress him up and bring him over to the shop once or twice a week in the fancy French stroller buggy with real leaf-spring suspension that Big Ed bought for us. Julie'd park him out by my bench in the shop and he'd watch me work on the cars while she went over the books and neatened up the office and the john a little. And I'd talk to him and try to show him what I was doing and maybe even give him something big enough that he couldn't swallow it and smooth enough that he couldn't cut himself on it to play with—like the hollow brass float out of an S.U. carburetor, fr'instance—while he sat there in the stroller buggy with those huge baby eyes of his glistening at me.

"This is the top off an S.U. carburetor," I'd tell him, holding out the lid of the S.U. float bowl I was working on so he could see it. "And right here inside is the needle-and-seat valve. It shuts the fuel on and off like a cork in a bottle." I worked the hinged brass fork arm up and down for him and then demonstrated by making a small "O" with my lips and then plugging it with a forefinger that reeked of gasoline—I might as well have sucked on a damn fuel line!—and then pulling it out again. "But the important thing…" I continued hoarsely after spitting a few dozen times, "…is that these S.U. needle-and-seat assemblies are not especially well made and you can count on them to wear out eventually." I removed the little brass pin and the forked arm and let the tiny needle fall out in my palm and showed little Vincenzo the telltale ring of wear around the tapered tip of the needle. "And the great thing about that is it makes the car run absolutely awful," I told him gleefully, "but it's very cheap and easy to fix if you know what you're doing." I demonstrated by unscrewing the seat part of the valve with a quarter-drive ratchet, putting in a new one with a new fiber gasket, sticking the new needle part in the hole, replacing the brass fork arm with the brass hinge pin, eyeballing the float level and then screwing the lid back on the carburetor. "What did that take me?" I asked little Vincent. "Two minutes? And I'll spend another two minutes on the back carburetor." I leaned in close so nobody could overhear us. *"And then I'll charge twenty dollars for it!"* I whispered in his tiny ear. *"And the guy who owns the car will be absolutely thrilled that his MG runs great again for only twenty dollars!"*

Jesus, I was starting to sound like Colin St. John and Barry Spline!

So I straightened up for a little heart-to-heart with my son.

"But you don't want to be in the garage business," I sighed while the baby rolled that cool brass float happily across his cheeks. "It's hard and it's dirty and the work never ends, and you try and you try, but you just can't keep some people happy. They think you're trying to cheat them whether you're trying to cheat them or not. Just because you run a damn garage, see? And so then you start thinking *'Why not?'* and *'What's the point?'* and maybe it'd be nice to have a little steak on the table now and then instead of just hamburger…" I took the float away and pulled in close and looked little Vincent right in his wide, glistening eyes. "Nah, you want to be something else. Go to college maybe. Be a bigshot lawyer or judge or congressman or something. You can steal people blind in that line of work..." Come to think of it, that was just the same thing all over again. Only with diamond pinky rings instead of raw knuckles and split fingernails. "You should be a doctor!" it suddenly occurred to me. "That's a great line of work. You fix people up and make them better, see? And you get Wednesdays off and the weekends, too. And it pays good if you work in the right neighborhood..." And that made me think of sitting in the tow truck waiting for my sister Mary Frances in the alley behind that fancy doctor's office on Park Avenue. Plus who wanted their kid to be around sickness and sadness and despair and disease and death all the time? "I don't know," I finally admitted. "Maybe you could write a book."

Then he reached out for the carburetor float I'd taken from him, and he started bawling something awful when I wouldn't give it back to him. *I WANT! RIGHT NOW!* But I couldn't give it to him on account of I needed it to put the second carburetor back together. And of course then he torqued it up to a full-fledged scream. You know, the kind where they turn beet-red and you worry that they're going to strangle themselves with their own vocal cords.

"Jesus, Buddy, what did you do to him?" Julie hollered at me as she rushed into the shop to save her beloved baby from the vise I was obviously crushing him in.

"I didn't do anything," I told her lamely. "We were just having a little talk."

"Well, you must've done SOMETHING!" she snarled at me as she picked little Vincent up out of the stroller and cradled him in her arms.

"I just took this away from him because I needed it is all." Like an idiot, I showed her the brass carburetor float.

"You let him play with THAT??!!"

And that, of course, was just the beginning.

But even so it was nice having Julie and the baby coming around every now and then, you know? It made me feel like, no matter what I was doing, it was somehow worthwhile.

Tommy Edwards stopped by the shop one afternoon after he got back stateside just to say hello, and you could tell he was pretty disappointed by the fact he'd gone over to co-drive with Sydney Allard at Le Mans again in the J2R, but there were problems getting everything ready and the car never made the race. "We would've been bloody well out of it anyway," he said with a twinge of regret. "The car's just past it compared to the new Jaguars and Ferraris and there's really not anything you can say." It had to rankle him even more that our old asshole buddy Creighton Pendleton the Third wound up sharing the Cunningham that came home fifth overall at the end. But he did have an interesting story to tell. "You know, Briggs had bought this 375 Mille Miglia Ferrari for his team to run, and then he had Alf Momo and his chaps go over it like it was nothing but a bloody starter kit."

"What did they do?"

"Well," Tommy laughed, "you know I'm not particularly mechanically inclined, but I do know one thing they did was put a set of water-cooled brakes on it."

"Water-cooled brakes?"

Tommy nodded. "I'd never heard of it either, but damn if they didn't have two great bloody holes cut in the nose to feed air to the brake radiators and a bloody thermometer right in the middle of the dash to keep track of the brake temperatures."

"How'd it work?"

"Oh, I guess it worked all right. But I'll wager that Jaguar's discs are just as good, and a hell of a lot less complicated. But the point is that Briggs thought enough of the car to put his top drivers—you know Johnny Fitch and Phil Walters..."

"Sure I do."

"...to put them in the Ferrari and leave the old Chrysler-powered Cunninghams to the second and third string."

"So what happened?"

"Oh, the Ferrari ran fairly well off the start, but then it broke a bloody rocker arm and limped around for a few hours before they finally retired it with something else gone wrong."

"Retiring at the Twenty-Four Hours of Le Mans is not exactly front page news," I reminded him.

"Too true. But the funny part came afterwards."

"Oh?"

"Seems Briggs and Alf Momo went down to Maranello after the race to have a bit of a word with old man Ferrari about the valve rocker that had broken. But old Enzo insisted that 'Ferrari valve rockers do not break.' Even after Briggs took it out of his pocket and laid the bloody thing right square in the middle of Signore Ferrari's desk!"

"Wow. Did he at least give them another one?"

"Not on your life. He made Briggs bloody well pay for it. Nine dollars and ninety-five cents American!"

"And that's on top of the trip down to Italy?"

Tommy nodded, laughing.

"So what does it all mean?"

"I think it means we won't be seeing Team Cunningham buying many more Ferraris!"

In a way, that was good news. You sell the best and fastest cars to the smartest, most experienced, best-funded team and it tends to take a lot of the drama and suspense out of the racing. Not to mention the color and character.

Meanwhile the Jagillac project was progressing a little. Although not so's you could really notice. That's one of the things you learn about a big, up-from-the-ground car project like that. It becomes an endless series of little start/stop/start-again/stop-again details that you either never figured on or never figured out properly the first time around. And while all of that is going on, it's real easy to lose track of the overall thing you wanted to build in the first place. Imagine burrowing into a piece of wood when you have no idea how thick it is. All you can do is keep burrowing and burrowing and hope you're heading pretty much in the right direction and hope even more that someday, some way, some when and somehow you're going to break through on the other side and be finished. Or, as Barry

Spline put it: *"H'it's the first bleedin' ninety percent of the job that takes the first bleedin' ninety percent of the time. But h'it's that last bloody ten percent of the job that always takes the other bleedin' ninety percent of the time."*

He knew what he was talking about, too. But there are little rewards along the way, like when you finish up one bit or another and allow yourself to step back for a coffee or a smoke or (if it's after closing, anyway) pop the cap off a cold bottle of Knickerbocker and enjoy a brief Appreciation Moment. It sure helps keep your spirits up. Like the day we finally got the engine and tranny installed (and then discovered we hadn't left enough clearance for the front U-joint where the driveshaft had to disappear into the center section of the frame). Or the day we got the basic plumbing and wiring done and decided to fire it up—just for the hell of it!—working the carburetor linkage on the four Stromberg 97s by hand with me doing the left two and Cal doing the right two. Just so's we could hear the roar out of those eight tubular downpipes and the great way it splattered back at us off the concrete floor. Or howabout the day we got the square-tube firewall frame erected off those Swiss-cheesed chassis channels so we could hang the steering column onto something solid and hook up a few gauges and start figuring out just how the hell and where the hell we were gonna run the throttle linkage.

And may I say right here and now that it's the little things you never think of—like U-joints that don't fit where they need to go or the monkey-motion throttle linkages you have to dream up out of thin air—that turn simple little "whoosh-bonk" shop projects into major-league, extended-play hair-pulling marathons. *You* try to figure how to turn the downward press of a human toe way down by the floorboards into a horizontal-to-vertical, 90-degree rotation of four separate throttle shafts in four separate Stromberg 97 carburetors staggered all over the place on the cast aluminum Detroit Racing Equipment intake manifold that we got off Tommy Edwards' old derelict Caddy V8 that we found leaned up against the back wall of the Westbridge shop (and that I had to pay Barry Spline a double sawbuck for even though I think it actually still belonged to Tommy!). Not to mention that the whole, spindly apparatus you finally come up with has to be bolted to an engine that is going to shake and rock and get hot as blazes and want to twist itself right off its blessed mounts every time you crack those throttles open....

It can drive you just a little bit nuts.

But, if you keep at it and never look too much farther ahead than the next bolt to be tightened and the next problem to be solved, eventually you get someplace. And for Cal and me, that someplace was the early evening of Sunday, July 4th, 1954. Or exactly two years to the day from the night we tried to simultaneously set off about six or seven fistfuls of skyrockets in the driveway in front of my Aunt Rosamarina's garage and damned near burned it (and Cal's worthless old '47 TC that we had inside) clear to the ground. But of course that was when we were young and foolish, you know?

The story was that we'd been working on the Jagillac pretty much all day that Sunday while the rest of the hardcore sportycar crowd was off enjoying themselves at the SAC-base race weekend at Offutt Air Force Base just outside of Omaha, Nebraska. And we were making some serious headway, what with the engine and driveline all installed and buttoned up and a big Ford pickup truck radiator all fastened down and supported here and there by Swiss-cheesed shelf bracing and plumbed up to the engine with only four or five cobbled-up Auto Parts Store hoses and angles and reducers. Not to mention that we had all four wheels on the ground and the tires full of air and brake and clutch pedals that actually seemed to *do* something when you stepped on them and a steering wheel that made the front wheels turn when you twisted it this way and that, and a genuine, working shift lever poking up out of the tranny and, after about three solid days of maddening, painstaking and thoroughly thankless work, a gas pedal that actually made the throttle plates in those four Stromberg 97s stand up to perfect vertical attention when you mashed it to the floorboards. Well, most of them, anyway. And I wasn't being exactly literal when I mentioned floorboards, either, seeing as how you could look clear down to the shop floor from the prospective driver compartment of our new Jagillac.

But that didn't bother Cal Carrington.

"What we really need to do," Cal whispered in my ear while the first, tentative afternoon volleys of Fourth-of-July M-80s and Ladyfinger bricks started going off here and there around the neighborhood, "is take it for a spin."

Now let me explain that, while the Jagillac was surely a lot more than just a chassis and an engine at that point, it wasn't a whole lot more. In fact, it probably looked a lot like those Bristol "running chassis" from England that "Wacky" Arnolt shipped down to Turin to have those sexy Bertone bodies put on. Only maybe not quite so well finished, and with perhaps a few things—like the ignition switch, for example—more or less dangling in mid-air. And I suppose what *should* have been circulating through my mind right about then was all the various and sundry ways in which the Jagillac, in its existing state of completion, failed to meet the equally various and sundry provisions of the New Jersey Motor Vehicle Regulations and Licensing codes regarding operation of appropriate vehicles on public streets and highways. But instead I found myself wondering what we could use for seats and how I could hook up that dangling ignition switch and do something with a battery so's it wouldn't fall right off the frame and bounce along the ground if we happened to get a little rambunctious around a corner.

I fixed the seat problem with a piece of plank we used as a ramp now and then fastened directly to the frame rails with a couple stove bolts and then tied the cushions off the moth-eaten old green couch in the office on top with twine to get the driver high enough so's he could actually see over the steering wheel and engine block. And all it took was a length of plumber's strap with a tensioning bolt to hold the battery down on the frame. And the Caddy ignition switch we'd gotten out of Big Ed's wrecked '52 convertible was a snap, too. I just hooked up the blessed wires and taped it to the steering column with a fat wad of electrical tape. And I remembered in the nick of time to put a clamp on the fuel line where it fastened up to the tank on account of we were in such a hurry we'd really just pushed it on when we fired up the engine that first time.

I remember evening was starting to settle in, and you could hear the crackle and snap and fizz of Fourth-of-July fireworks and the whistle-and-pop of Fourth-of-July bottle rockets going off all around us. Why, if ever there was an absolutely *perfect* time to take a harmless little spin in a brand new, all-American racing car that you'd put together with your own two hands....

Well, there was no question that I should drive first. I mean, after all, I was the official Dr. Frankenstein on the project, right? So I settled down on the couch cushion and peered up over the wheel rim at the naked throats of those four hungry Strombergs. "You ready?" I asked Cal.

"Roger."

"You got anything to hang onto over there?"

"Yeah. I can kind of hang onto the frame over here."

"OK, then...*CONTACT!*" I turned the key of the Caddy ignition switch I'd taped to the steering column—kind of holding it with my other hand so's it wouldn't twist right off—and we listened to the motor grind. And then it ground some more. "It's cold. I think it maybe needs a little choke."

So Cal scrambled out and put his palms over two of the Strombergs like I'd showed him. The Caddy engine sputtered and popped once or twice. He moved hands to the other two carburetors. The Caddy choked and stumbled. He pulled his hands off again and there was this tremendous backfire—I swear, the flash of flame was two feet long and damn near singed Cal's eyebrows off—but then it caught a little, stumbled for a second, and then it all came together as the engine roared to life. God, what a sound! Between the carbs and the cam and the shave job Roman had put on the heads for more compression and the unearthly racket and reverberation from the Caddy's eight dump pipes, it was enough to make you wet your pants. And I was just about to push the clutch down and shove it in gear when Cal screamed: *"WAIT!"*

"FOR WHAT???" I shouted back over the engine noise.

He didn't say a word, but ran into the office lickety-split and came back with those two pairs of mirrored aviator sunglasses he'd gleeped for us on our way to Grand Island. And he brought my Dodgers hat, too. I put it on backwards. For aerodynamics, you know?

"READY NOW?"

Cal nodded.

"WATCH YOUR ELBOW ON THAT U-JOINT THERE!"

He nodded again.

And we were off.

I took it pretty easy as we tooled out onto Pine Street, keeping one terrified eye peeled for the cops and the other one on the temp and oil pressure gauges—we didn't have a tach figured out yet, and I didn't see any reason for a speedometer on the Jagillac. I mean, it was just extra weight, right? To be honest, the Jagillac felt kind of nervous and jumpy under me. Like it was poised hair-trigger to do something sudden and crazy and totally unexpected. Of course, part of that could have been because I was sitting up on top of a fairly loose couch cushion tied to a plank that was obviously none-too-securely carriage-bolted to the frame rails and so I was pretty much hanging on by the steering wheel any time I gave the throttle a tiny nudge. I turned up Polk and cut over to Mulberry to stay off the main streets where I figured the cops might be, and all over the neighborhood we saw kids and their dads gathered in driveways, setting off firecrackers and launching rockets and aerial bombs into the gathering gray of the evening sky while the moms stood off to the side with their hands clamped down tight over their ears or maybe just grimacing on account of they were using their hands to hug the littlest child into their aprons, away from the noise. But they all stopped dead in their damn tracks—froze solid!—when Cal and me rumbled past in the Jagillac. And I could understand why, since it looked like some crazed mechanical beast out seeking vengeance on whoever had skinned it alive and then turned it loose like that—nothing but raw guts and skeleton with occasional spits of flame and that fearful, carnivorous noise rattling out the dump pipes and shattering back off the pavement....

"LET ME GIVE IT A TRY!" Cal hollered over the noise. And of course there was no way I could refuse him. I mean, in a lot of ways, this whole damn project was all about him in the first place. So I pulled into a handy, trash can-lined alley behind a dry cleaning shop and we real quick ran around and switched positions. And then Cal glanced over at me with this cheerful, confident and only slightly maniacal grin on his face and advised me to hang on.

Which I did.

Even so, he damn near spit me over the side as he tevved her up, popped the clutch and roared out of the alley in a perfect, roostertail-of-gravel-into-peal-of-squealing-rubber powerslide onto Mulberry Street and kept the throttle buried all the way to the next intersection. The noise was deafening as the torque of that hot-rodded Caddy V8 squashed the rear end down all squirrelly into the pavement and jerked the front end skyward and it was all I could do to keep my fingers curled around the edge of that plank in a damn death grip so's I wouldn't get back-flipped over the rear axle and crack my skull wide open on the concrete. Jesus, if *feeling* Godawful fast had anything whatsoever to do with *being* Godawful fast, then my Jagillac was sure going to be one *hell* of a fast racecar. And Cal was just about to reach for third gear and show me even more as he blasted across the intersection of Polk Street without so much as a flinch on the gas pedal. Coincidentally taking us right across the bows of a police cruiser out looking for underage kids shooting off fireworks without adult supervision. I must admit, the officer inside that car had some pretty decent reaction times. Why, he had the siren switched on and the red mars light on his roof fired up and rotating even before we were clear of the intersection.

Damn!

Well, I looked over at Cal and he looked back at me and I could see in his eyes that he was about to make a run for it. So I did the first intelligent thing I'd done all evening, reaching over and ripping that taped-on Caddy ignition switch clear off the steering column. Just as Cal was planting his right foot and sending the throttle plates in those four Strombergs straight-up vertical. Only I'd pulled the plug. The thunder cut in mid-peal, the nose crashed back down towards the pavement, and all you could hear was this massive, wet pumping noise as those eight large and hungry cylinders sucked in as much gas and wind as four wide-open Strombergs could feed them, compressed it by a factor of around ten, and then dumped it out—unfired—through those eight organ-pipe exhausts aimed down at the concrete. You could smell the raw fuel. I wondered if it was maybe running a little too rich, you know? And then something else occurred to me:

Jesus, were we ever in *trouble!*

To be honest, it turned out kind of funny. At least afterwards, anyway. The cop was this short, scrawny and extremely serious-looking little middle-aged guy who I remembered used to come around to our high school and give talks about crime prevention and Civil Defense and also prowl the grounds and chase after kids who cut class or snuck out to have a smoke behind the gymnasium. And he was pretty serious about all that stuff, too. In fact, we used to joke that he never cracked a smile in his entire life. And surely *never* on duty! Well, he took a quick once-around the Jagillac and then another, much slower tour and you could tell he was short-circuiting a little from the smorgasbord of infractions and illegalities we'd laid out in front of him. He really didn't know where to begin. Why, at the very least he was gonna have to run us back to the station house for more citation books. Finally he took a deep breath, straightened his shoulders, and stepped up on Cal's side as if there was actually some kind of door—or a car body in any conventional sense of the word—between them.

"May I see your license and the registration for this vehicle?" He said it dead serious, but also with a little sarcastic edge. Like he knew we didn't have it, right? And I figured I'd better start explaining as how this was a genuine Race Car and how we'd just finished putting the final touches on it and just needed to take it out for one quick little test spin to make sure everything was hooked up correctly and working properly and not leaking and....

And that's when Cal told the cop: "We left it in the glove compartment."

Well, it didn't take a master detective to deduce that there was no glove compartment on the dashboard of the Jagillac. Or a dashboard, come to think of it.

"Do you realize this is a public thoroughfare?" he said like maybe we didn't.

"Sure we do!" Cal told him enthusiastically. "This is Mulberry Street. And the one over there is Polk." Jesus, I wished he'd shut up. But I guess Cal figured we were dead meat anyway, and so he wasn't about to take the load of shit this tinstar cop wanted to dish out along with it.

"Do you know this, ah, *'vehicle'* is in violation of several New Jersey highway safety codes and automobile regulations?" It was pretty hard to argue with him from our position on top of a pair of couch cushions on top of a wooden plank sitting behind eight silent but still steaming and thoroughly unmuffled exhaust pipes with no headlights ahead of them or taillights behind them and no fenders of any kind over the four wheels around them.

"I'm sure it is, officer," Cal sassed right back.

And right about then is when some unsupervised kids fooling around with a box of fireworks in a nearby driveway launched a low-trajectory skyrocket that whooshed over our heads trailing a showering, yellow-orange comet trail behind as it spiraled into the lilac trees in someone else's front yard.

"Kids," the cop snorted, like we were the ruin of this nation.

Still, it was nice to be included in as a kid again....

Well, I called home from the cop station and of course Julie was furious on account of we were supposed to have gone over to my folks' house for our Fourth-of-July family barbeque—geez, I'd forgot all about it—and besides that the baby was sick and throwing up all over the place and couldn't keep anything down and her mother was driving her nuts that she should feed him sassafras root and fresh garlic mashed up in cod liver oil and what the hell was I doing down at the frickin' police station anyway?

"Uhh, well, see, Cal and me..."

And of course that was all it took to launch her off onto another wholesale barrage about my good-for-nothing rich racing buddy Cal Carrington who never had a dime in his pocket and was forever taking advantage of me and..."

"Uh, Honey? Honey? D'ya think you could maybe give Big Ed a call for us?"

Click!

Fortunately Cal still had a call coming, and we were lucky that he caught Big Ed at home on a holiday when you might expect he'd be out somewhere watching fireworks and raising hell (not to mention a couple dozen gin-and-tonic tumblers) and having a little fun. Only Cal allowed as how that might be what he was up to anyway. At least going by the background noises, which Cal said included the sounds of ice clinking in glasses, Nat King Cole on the hi-fi and the tittering and giggling of several young female voices. I thought we were sunk, but damn if Big Ed didn't drop whatever (or whomever) he was doing and drive over in the Eldorado to bail us out. I could tell he'd had a few when they came to let us out of the lockup, but I guess he always bought a lot of tickets to the policemen's ball or something and he somehow got us off without any charges being filed. Why, he even got the police tow truck to haul the Jagillac back over to the Sinclair station for us. Then again, there were always rumors around that Big Ed knew a few people who knew a few people (if you know what I mean) and that some of them, just like me, were basically in the repair business. Why, they could fix damn near anything.

"Geez, how'd you do it?" I asked Big Ed as he drove me back home in the Caddy.

"You're good at fixin' some things an' I'm good at fixin' other things," he said through an annoyed but self-satisfied smile, his cigar doing a sort of slow-rolling pirouette from one side of his face to the other. "Who's the idiot asshole who decided t'go for a lil' drive?"

I looked down at the deep-pile carperting.

"It was that wiseass Cal, wasn't it?"

I didn't say a word.

Of course the other thing that happened on the Fourth of July was that it started to rain later in the evening, and Big Ed had to disgustedly put the top up on his Eldorado when he stopped to drop me off at the duplex. And meanwhile old Butch was over at that cozy little tavern I told you about around the corner and a block-and-a-half down from my Aunt Rosamarina's place, celebrating the birthday of this great nation and the signing of the Declaration of Independence by sitting in a corner all by his lonesome and listening to sad hillbilly songs on the jukebox while he drank himself cockeyed. As the clock closed in on midnight, one by one the other rummy regulars unsteadily rose off their barstools and waddled, staggered or stumbled out the door. And eventually Butch decided it was time for him to go, too (which is another way of saying his cash supply ran out and the bartender wouldn't let him run a tab), and Butch was further dismayed to find rain pelting down as he wheeled himself over to the door. "Damn, ish rainin'" he observed.

"Yeah," the bartender agreed without looking up from the bar he was wiping. "Ain't a fit night out for man nr' beast, izzit?"

So Butch had no choice but to suck in a deep breath, tuck his head down between his shoulders, give it the old "Geronimo" heave and start wheeling his way up the street towards my Aunt Rosamarina's place. As you can imagine, he was soaked clear through by the time he got there, but at least wheeling through the rain had sobered him up a little so's he could try to line his wheelchair up real straight and careful against the two-by-four guide runners on that steep ramp we'd built up the side of my Aunt Rosamarina's garage. But, like I said, the roll over had only sobered him up a little, and he'd been a lot more than a little drunk. And so he didn't get it quite right and it all went terribly wrong about a third of the way up, when the outside wheel caught one of the railing supports and kind of pivoted Butch's wheelchair around sideways and jammed it into the railing. But the winch kept winding and threatened to topple him clear over, and so he dropped the plumber's-pipe tow handle to keep something terrible from happening.

But it happened anyway....

Instead of falling free and just getting dragged the rest of the way up the ramp and leaving Butch stranded there helpless a third of the way up and stuck against the railing—hell, he could wait that one out until morning, even in the rain!—the damn handle caught on part of the wheelchair and started trying to pull it sideways and also mash Butch *hard* into the railing and maybe even bring the whole blessed stairway down at the same time. Maybe even the whole damn garage, too, seeing as how the Fourth of July had never been an especially lucky day for it. To tell the truth, Butch could easily have been crushed to death like some unfortunate victim in a medieval torture-chamber story. Or maybe buried like some poor old miner in the collapsed wood splinters and timbers if the staircase came down. But, fortunately, that old, rusty battery charger out of Butch's ex-front yard wasn't much good and neither was the old battery we got there, and so the winch couldn't get quite enough juice to actually kill him or bring the building down.

It did make him holler a bit, though.

And of course that's when my Aunt Rosamarina came rushing out of the house with the genuine Cape Cod nor'easter rain slicker she always kept hanging by the back door for emergencies thrown on over her housecoat, the flashlight with batteries she changed religiously every month clutched in her hand and that big brass Industrial-Grade fire extinguisher she kept under the basement stairs banging and clanging along behind her. She obviously hadn't forgotten the Fourth of July Cal and me set her garage on fire just a few years before. But of course none of that fearful preparation readied her at all for seeing an ex-Marine hardhat diver with a very colorful command of the language stuck in a wheelchair about a third of the way up her back garage stairway and being damn near crushed into hamburger meat by a clicking, squealing, panting and wheezing ex-Jeep CJ electric winch that was just too damn feeble to get the job done properly.

"W-what should I do?" she shrieked up at him.

"Hit the button, dammit! Right there on the railing! Hit th' Goddam button!!!

My Aunt Rosamarina looked around frantically to find it, and when she did, she jabbed it so hard that she damn near dislocated her finger. And—just like that—the plaintive electrical moan from the winch stopped cold and suddenly the only sounds were the hard patter of the rain and the damp creaking from all the straining two-by-fours and planking and, above it all, Butch's alternately pained, pleading and colossally pissed-off cussword exercises in five or six different languages.

Well, my aunt was a thin, scrawny, bony little woman, but she had the finger strength and determination of a nun hanging onto a misbehaving twelve-year-old, and damn if she didn't climb right up that slippery, creaking, teetering ramp in the driving rain with her flashlight clutched desperately in her hand and, with Butch's screaming, agonized and thoroughly abusive instructions ringing in her ears, help him get free.

"Y'needta get a little slack in th'Goddam line, G'dammit!!"

"Climb up and flip the Goddam switch th'other way!!!"

"Jesus Fucking Christ, not THAT way!! Yer KILLIN' me up here!!!"

"NOT SO MUCH, DAMMIT! NOT SO FUCKING MUCH!! WHAT'SAMMATTER WIT' YOU, YOU STUPID FUCKING BITCH??!!!

To be honest, I don't believe anybody had ever talked to my Aunt Rosamarina that way in her whole entire life.

The strange part was, she seemed to kind of like it.

20: Onward and Upward

I never knew all the details of what happened that rainy Fourth of July night over at my Aunt Rosamarina's house—not that I really wanted to—but I do know between the two of them they somehow managed to get old Butch back down the ramp and up her back kitchen stairs into the house, and both of them (in separate rooms or at least looking the other way, I'm sure) into some dry clothes or blankets or something. And then I guess she asked him if he maybe wanted a little glass of sherry to warm him up and he maybe asked if she had anything that might warm him up just a wee bit warmer and she allowed as how she might also have a bottle of brandy handy and so they sat up at her kitchen table until around dawn polishing both of them off together.

And damn if Butch didn't pass out first!

In fact, he was kind of embarrassed about it when he showed up bruised, late and wobbly at the Sinclair on Monday morning. "I just can't understand it," he told me. "A'course, I had a pretty good head start on her earlier in th'evening...."

There was a genuine look of amazement—admiration, even—in Butch's bloodshot eyes.

And that's when he started staying in the house with my Aunt Rosamarina. In the spare room, of course. And they were real careful to make it look right for the neighbors by spreading the word that she was helping take care of this poor, decent Christian man in the wheelchair as a way to do good works and earn a little much-needed income to supplement her retirement pension from the library. They were real sticklers about splitting up the workload and expenses around the house, too. She took care of the gas and electric bills and he brought a little take-out food home every few nights from the sandwich shop across the street or the pizza and pasta joint on Polk Street. And a bottle or two, of course. On rainy evenings, she'd walk down to the Sinclair in her Cape Cod rain slicker with a big umbrella under her arm and insist on wheeling him home. And then he'd get all angry and embarrassed and cuss her out something fierce—*"I don't need no damn nursemaid!"*—and she'd fuss and scold him right back and he'd yell at her and she'd yell at him and sometimes he'd even say terribly cruel and private things right there in front of anybody and make her cry.

I can't remember ever seeing her so happy.

She even got after him about going back to those therapy sessions that never seemed to be doing any good over at the V.A. hospital. Well, Butch told her exactly where she could stuff it on account of how the hell was he gonna get over there since there was no way you could get a guy in a wheelchair on a bus and he was damned if he was gonna skip work and pay cab fare all the way over to East Orange two or three days a week just so's a bunch of doctors and nurses who didn't give a shit about him could fuss over him and poke at him and make him try to do stuff he knew he just couldn't do anymore. And she told him: "Fiddlesticks."

That was pretty strong language for my Aunt Rosamarina.

And that's how they decided in maybe the middle of their second bottle at her kitchen table one night that he'd be willing to go over to those therapy sessions at the V.A. hospital if she'd learn how to drive and take him there. Actually, it wasn't so much of a "decision" as a "dare/double-dare" type of deal, but those work just as well so long as you follow through on them. Of course, there was the little problem of just exactly what they were going to do for a car, and that's why I had to sneak over to Butch's old house real early one morning—I cadged a ride with my old man and one of his union-buddy pals on their way to work at the chemical plant at six ayem—to hotwire his old Ford and bring it back while Marlene was still asleep. To be honest, I didn't much like the idea—I mean, why kick a hornet's nest just because it's on the ground in front of you?—but I owed Butch a lot of favors and really depended on him around the shop and he couldn't very well go do it himself in his blessed wheelchair and there wasn't really anybody else he could turn to, you know?

It's a sad fact of life that your friends wind up getting you in a lot more trouble than your enemies ever do.

And so it really came as no surprise when none other than Mean Marlene herself came snarling and stomping off the bus that stops across the street from us about three that very afternoon. She made a beeline for the shop like she was going 300 miles an hour with her hair on fire, and Butch saw her coming and instinctively did what he'd learned when trouble started and he was badly outmanned and out-gunned in countless seedy waterfront bars all over the Pacific back when he was a hard-hat diver with the Marines. He ducked out the back and wheeled himself up the alley as fast as his arms could carry him.

"Where's Butch??!!" Marlene screeched at me from beneath a hairdo the approximate shape and color of a copper scouring pad.

"I dunno," I shrugged.

"Don't shit me, Buddy. The car's gone an' don't think I don't know where it went."

"Maybe you better talk to Butch about it."

"HE didn't steal that car! And don't think for a minute I don't know who did!" She jangled the Ford's keys in front of my nose while her eyes blasted through me like double-barreled Tennessee death rays. Jesus, I didn't need this....

"Well," I offered lamely, "it *is* his car, isn't it?"

Before I could move she struck like a timber rattlesnake, grabbed two fistfuls of my shirt and dragged me in so close I was staring directly into the caked-on orange textures of her makeup and all the dental work she'd never gotten done and could feel her breath on me like the exhaust vent of a crematorium. *"Lissen here, Buddy Palumbo. I need that car t'git to work. Ya unnerstand me?"*

Boy, I hated being in the middle of this!

"Now I ain't leavin' 'til I git it back, see?" She let go of my collar and pushed me away disgustedly. And then, just like a woman, she got all hurt and squishy and vulnerable right there in front of me. She even started to cry. "Ah always

loved ya lahk a son, Buddy," she sniffled. "Lahk a damn son!" She looked up at me like she was deserving of the deepest and most heartfelt sympathy. "Ah took good carra Butch, even after his wreck an' all."

Yeah? And you lived pretty good on his pensions and disability money, too! I thought but didn't say.

"Ah need him back, Buddy," she whimpered in a hillbilly twang.

Well, why didn't you think of that before you started screwing around with the guy with the fat, hairy ass? And right in your own damn house where he was bound to find out about it, too! But of course I just kept my mouth shut and didn't say that, either.

So we stood there kind of squared off at each other and I got the feeling that she wasn't going anywhere unless she was driving there in Butch's old Ford. And it occurred to me all over again what a lousy idea this had been and so I finally told her to take the damn thing—I mean, she had the keys and it was parked right out back and the only reason she hadn't already grabbed it and disappeared was that we had the foot doctor's DeSoto wagon parked behind it and blocking it in. Butch made me do that, too....

So I moved the DeSoto and Marlene got into the old Ford and fired it up—Jesus, it sounded like a damn threshing machine—and she looked over at me before she took off and I could see another fat set of crocodile tears welling up in her rattlesnake eyes. *"Yew be sure an' tell Butch ah want him t'come home agin,' okay?"*

I promised I would.

"Look," I told Butch when he wheeled himself back in from the alley, "this just isn't gonna work." I knew he'd been behind the back door so's he could listen in while me and Mean Marlene were talking.

"It isn't?"

"Nah. I'll steal the damn Ford from her and then she'll come over here and interrupt things and waste a lot of time and make everybody miserable until she gets it back. It just doesn't do any good, see?"

He could see I was right.

"And there's another thing. What kind of true-blue friend hightails it out into the alley as soon as he gets a whiff of her and leaves me to face her, huh?"

Butch looked up at me with a strangely soft and apologetic look in his eyes. "She won't cut you, Buddy." And that's when I saw all over again that terrifying scar that went from the hairline of his Marine crewcut clear down through the arch of his left eyebrow and even continued on a little further down his cheek. You tend to stop seeing stuff like that when you're around it every day. Like an old, ugly piece of furniture you just get used to and don't much notice anymore. But no question Mean Marlene had been on the other end of the blade that did it. She was capable of stuff like that when she got riled up. And that was back when Butch had two good fists and his feet under him so's he could fight back, too.

"Lissen," I told him. "I got an idea. If you're so damn dead-set on teaching my aunt to drive, why not use the blessed Jeep?"

"The Jeep?"

"Sure! We don't use it much in the afternoons after Tater shows up with the Crosley. And I've always got the Old Man's tow truck if I need a set of wheels in a pinch. And besides," I swept my hand around the shop, "I can always take somebody's car out on a test drive."

Butch looked at me uneasily. He wasn't the type who much relished favors or charity. "You sure it's okay?"

"Sure it is."

"I'll pay for my own gas," he kind of growled.

"You bet your ass you will," I growled right back. And that seemed to satisfy him.

Which is how it happened that ex-Marine hardhat diver and ace mechanic in a wheelchair Butch Bohunk wound up teaching my retired librarian Aunt Rosamarina how to drive in a rough, jumpy, short-wheelbase, high-center-of-gravity and exceedingly skittish and hair-trigger Jeep CJ2A with a Ford V8-60 under the hood. The only good thing—what with all that torque and those hard, knobbly, skinny Jeep tires without much bite to them—was that it was extremely difficult to stall. Even for a beginner. Still, Butch maintained that teaching my aunt to drive was about the scariest thing he'd ever done. Including anything that ever happened to him in the Marines and the knife fight with Mean Marlene. On the other hand, besides learning how to drive, my Aunt Rosamarina picked up and occasionally started using a few brand new words....

The other thing occupying my attention about then was the Jagillac project. After our little Fourth-of-July "test drive" that landed Cal and me in the hoosegow, I was more convinced than ever that I'd built a genuine, short-fused rocket of a racecar, and I only had to do a few little things—like fr'instance rotating the front torsion bars by relocating the splines where they go into the muff and then adjusting the brass-barrel adjustor nuts so the front end was no longer pointed skyward like a damn bullfrog in mid-leap—and neaten up the plumbing and wiring to finish it off. Oh, and come up with some kind of a body for it....

And that's the funny part. Because when you're a car-crazy kid in high school, all you do all day long is draw pictures of cars. Especially in history and geometry class. But it's always the outside—the shape—that you're sketching. Sure, you know what kind of stuff you plan on putting inside of it. Like, say, a supercharged Jaguar six with a four-speed transmission mated to a Willys four-wheel-drive system and Porsche suspension, for example. But that's all in your head. The stuff the teacher catches you scribbling is always the bodywork.

But then you finally find yourself inside a project like that, all wrapped up in the radiator plumbing and the flywheels and clutches that don't match and the bolt holes that don't quite line up (or even come close!) and the kazillion other little details that, piled one on top of the other in a perfectly straight line, will finally bring that running, moving and hopefully fire-breathing racecar you've always dreamed about to life. And then, after all that's done, you've still got to figure out what to put over it.

So, after I lowered down the front and dropped the rear an inch-and-a-half to match by putting a couple thick aluminum pads that Roman made for me between the springs and the back axle, I went for an extended walk around to try and decide just what sort of bodywork we needed for the Jagillac. In my mind's eye, I envisioned this low, sleek, smooth-looking sports/racer with a man-eating grille opening—even bigger and meaner than Creighton Pendleton's Ferrari!—and an aerodynamic fin off the headrest, and all of it made out of hand-hammered aluminum alloy like they do over at those *carrozzeria* body shops in Italy. And it had to be painted black, of course. A shimmering, glistening, liquid-pool black with a shine as deep and dark and evil as the gleam in the devil's eyes. And with a little gold leaf trim, too. Just for color. I mean, after all, this *was* the Palumbo Panther, wasn't it?

But the more I walked around that thing, the more I realized that, although I maybe knew a little bit about mechanics, I sure as hell didn't know much of anything about bodywork. And it was occurring to me more and more that it was obviously a very different sort of thing to just pick up out of the blue. Not to mention that Big Ed and me had decided we wanted to take the Jagillac on its shakedown run at the Giant's Despair Hillclimb out by Wilkes-Barre, PeeAy, at the end of the month and there was hardly any time left at all. And no way would the gnarly, chunky, broad-shouldered metal chunk of the Jagillac fit inside the low, smooth shape I saw in my head. Even if I knew how the heck to build it. Why, that big Ford pickup truck radiator alone was going to make the front end look more like a baseball diamond backstop than the low, sleek, man-eater of a racecar I'd envisioned. And what with the seats way back there butted up damn near against the rear axle, there really wasn't going to be any room for that long, sexy, faired-in headrest with an aerodynamic tailfin on it. At least not unless it looked like the tailfin off some kid's stamped metal toy airplane from Japan, anyway. You know, the kind that spit sparks and whine when you roll them across the carpet?

I went to see the Greek who did bodywork for us and he came over and looked at it and the best he could do was tell me it'd cost at least a thousand dollars for him to build me a body—and that was the insider, wholesale price, too!—and it'd take him at least three or four weeks to do it. Outside of that, he recommended the best thing might be just to nose around a few junkyards and see if I could find anything that might fit. I mean, I knew how to drill and bolt as well as the next guy, and I always had Butch available if I needed a little serious welding done. And, fortunately, I just happened to know somebody in the scrap business.

So I called Big Ed and went over to one of his scrapyards to nose around, and it was neat how he was starting to get a little more enthused about the project as it got closer to completion. Turns out he'd ordered himself one of those fabulous-looking Arnolt-Bristol things we'd seen on the stand at the World Motor Sports Show at Madison Square Garden (I'd been egging him on about it and showing him the clippings about those mechanically similar but incredibly ugly, bottom-feeder faced Bristol coupes that had done so well at Le Mans) but he wanted one of the Deluxe models that they hadn't actually started building yet and so it was going to take a little time. You have to understand that the standard Arnolt-Bristol model was called the *Bolide* (which means a large meteor or fireball—especially one that blows up!—and I know, because I went to the library and looked it up) and it was kind of a stripped-for-racing, bare-bones sort of sports car without some of the little niceties and accoutrements that you got on the Deluxe model. Like a heater and a top and side curtains, for example. So Big Ed had put in his order for a Deluxe with a special, Lard Bucket-edition drivers' seat mounted way down low so's he could actually fit in the thing with the top up (well, sort of, anyway), but they told him it was going to take a good six or eight months to arrive and so he was more or less between automotive love affairs at the time. And other types of love affairs as well, seeing how things had more or less broken off with Rhonda on account of he was pretty sure she'd been two- (or maybe even three-?) timing him with some other sugar daddies, and he'd even sold the Muntz through one of the salesmen he knew at the local Caddy dealership who had just the right guy for it. Hey, like Colin St. John always said, *"There's an ass for every seat."* And of course the good part was that both Big Ed and the Caddy salesman wound up making a little on the deal on account of Big Ed had bought it so right. But then, that's what he did for a living, you know?

But the main point was that Big Ed was about cocked and ready for another automotive adventure. And he'd also decided, being kind of "between positions" as far as his love life was concerned, that parading around as a real live racing driver again might pad his mystique and *savoir faire* a little. Besides, he was just plain bored and needed a little something to juice up his life again. And, at least until his new Arnolt-Bristol arrived, the Jagillac looked like a great way to do it. Especially after the cops told him how loud and fast it was when he came down to bail Cal and me out down at the police station.

So he told me to go ahead and look around his yards and take anything I might need and he even sent me over to this friend of his' place that was more an automotive rather than an industrial boneyard and, slowly but surely and much in the fashion of the creepy Dr. Frankenstein's gallows-and-graveyard spare-parts monster, the Jagillac's body began to take shape. Although, I must admit, not that pleasing a shape. Not hardly.

The front end turned out to be easy. We still had the bent-up and oft-repaired front hood off of Big Ed's totaled-out Jaguar, and the Greek said he could hammer it back fairly cheap and straight so long as he didn't have to match it up to anything else and I wasn't too picky about what it looked like underneath. I allowed as how that would be fine, and he could remove as much of the under-bracing as he wanted to lighten it just so long as it remained strong enough not to bend over double in a stiff breeze.

"A stiff breeze or a *really* stiff breeze?" the Greek wanted to know.

"Make it a *really* stiff breeze," I told him after a little consideration.

Of course the sexy, chrome-bar grille from Big Ed's car was pretzelized beyond salvation, so we went with some hardware-store expanded metal in a nice little diamond-shape pattern to put in the hole at the front of the hood, and then just kind of hung the whole shebang out over the engine and radiator like the kids out in California do with their hot rods. It actually fit pretty nice once we chopped a few inches off the back end and decided it was okay to have the front of the hood sticking out past the front wheels. And we had to kind of lean the radiator back a bunch to make it all fit (which meant the filler neck was now angled back in an uncoordinated position so's you had to jack the back end of the car way up off the ground any time you wanted to top off the water) but we figured we could live with that. So I had Butch weld me a couple nice tabs in the cowl we'd built and another, longer one off the front where we used a standard Jaguar hood catch with a short, flat little handle made out of a cheap box-end wrench from a standard MG factory tool kit that wasn't much good for anything else. I even drilled a couple lightening holes in it. And then, for the *piece de resistance,* I put on the hood emblems. Now what I should have done was waited until we had the thing all painted (or at least primered) but I'd picked up one of those chrome "V" emblems off the bull nose of an old Cadillac in Big Ed's friend's junkyard and I just had to see what it would look like. So I drilled two holes and mounted it just above the grille. Got it dead center, too. Just with my eyeballs. And then, right above it, I put that fabulous bronze Jaguar medallion that came on the nose of every XK 120. Unfortunately, the one off Big Ed's car had the mounting pins broken off the back, so I had to kind of drill a couple holes and screw it down with a couple sheet metal screws (or maybe it was one wood screw and one sheet metal screw, on account of I was in such a hurry to see the finished product) but I figured we could always go back later and put a new one on the right way when we had the time. And that's kind of a constant, bottomless pit of self-deception you fall into when you get anywheres near close to the end of a big car project. You're so damn impatient to see what it's gonna look like that you maybe get a little ahead of yourself. Maybe more than a little, even....

At the back of the hood I used a couple ordinary hardware-store gate hinges, but I made a mental note that we were going to have to maybe come up with something to make that hood fully removable on account of it made these ugly, creaking, metal-being-forced-to-go-some-way-it-didn't-really-want-to noises when you tried to raise or lower it and then it hung all limp and funny when you tried to prop it up on account of the Greek maybe didn't understand the difference between a stiff breeze and a *really* stiff breeze after all. But I must admit it looked mean and dangerous. Even if not especially sleek, what with that big, angled-back Ford pickup radiator sticking out a good eight or ten inches on either side. And so

I awarded myself an entire six-pack Appreciation Moment that evening before I went home to bed. And thank goodness Julie was already asleep when I got there.

The rear end of the car was a little tougher, on account of I couldn't find much of anything that looked like it would fit from the dash cowl and firewall back. I mean, it was just a big, empty space with sheet-aluminum floorboards and a pair of MG seat cushions on it out of an old wreck I'd found. But they were better than those moth-eaten old cushions off the sofa in the office. I had Butch weld up another kind of rear cowl out of more square tubing and we made it so's it'd fit a matching MG seatback and we pop-riveted another sheet of aluminum on it and ran a few Swiss-cheesed braces and that part was done. And by that time there was only about a week to go before Giant's Despair, and so naturally it all went into panicky fast-forward. We welded in a few angled lengths of Swiss-cheesed shelf bracketing between the front and rear cowl hoops and pop riveted some more aluminum sheeting onto them and then did the same from the rear cowl hoop back to the end of the frame. It made the back end look a lot like the business end of a very short, stout and ugly aluminum chisel, and I resolved that I would certainly have to do something to dress it up a little whenever I had the time. But there wasn't any time—none at all!—and so I went on to the next thing, making up these flimsy little five-inch-high doors (just to meet the regulations, you understand) out of aluminum sheet and some perforated strap and channel out of the enormous Master Builder Erector Set kit Big Ed bought for little Vincenzo when he was about three days old. But it was good stuff—plated against rust and corrosion and *real* light!—and I hung those doors on two more sets of hardware-store hinges so they pivoted up and down from the bottom in a kind of reverse Mercedes Gullwing effect. And then I stepped back, took a deep breath, and realized that—*voila!*—the Jagillac had a body! Even if it did look like a tin outhouse that'd been run over a few times by an angry steamroller. But it was a body nonetheless.

Oh, sure, there were a few details yet to finish. Like I needed some headlights and taillights. So I made a quick run over to Big Ed's friend's automotive bone-yard and picked up a couple bucket-style headlamps in good condition that almost matched off a '33 Ford and a '35 Dodge and made some simple brackets that only took three hours apiece to mount them down low on the frame staring out on either side of that expanded-metal Jaguar grille. I have to admit, it looked a little lopsided when I was done, but I told myself it was simply an authentic sort of Pirate Leer and let it go at that. I also found some very nice and easy-to-mount taillights off some other old wreck and had to more or less bolt them on and wire them up from the underside seeing as how I'd pop riveted everything shut on top and I wasn't about to start taking anything apart at that stage of the game. Even though maybe it would have been easier and quicker if I did. But you get into this sort of *Damn The Torpedoes, Full Speed Ahead* line of thinking when you're caught up in a project like that, and the one thing the *Damn The Torpedoes, Full*

Speed Ahead operational approach lacks is any kind of a reverse gear. I mean, it's simply not available....

"Y'know, you're gonna need a set of fenders," Cal reminded me. And indeed, according to the rules, you had to have some kind of fenders. And that was going to be a bit of a problem. Fenders off some wrecked road car would be way too big and heavy and wouldn't fit very well anyway, and the aluminum sheet we had was just too damn flimsy. What I *really* wanted was a set of those swell, nicely rolled and perfectly finished cycle fenders like I'd seen on the Kurtis 500S roadsters and also on some of the hotrods they were running on the dry lakes out in California. Only we had to be shoving off for Giant's Despair the very next evening, and so there wasn't time to do anything except head over by Big Ed's scrapyard one more time with the idea fixed dead-center in my skull that somehow, some way I had to return with a set of fenders for the Jagillac. And I looked and I looked and I looked. There was a big, round metal shroud from an enormous industrial fan that would take me hours to cut down and reshape to the right curvature, and they'd still be lumpy and jagged and heavy as hell when I was done (not to mention sharp as a damn switchblade if I tried to smooth the edges down with the grinder). And then I saw them. They were all over the place, in fact. Why, I couldn't believe I hadn't noticed them sooner.

"You're gonna make the fenders outta *trash cans?*" Cal said incredulously.

"These aren't just *any* trash cans!" I grunted as I hefted two of them off the back of the Jeep. "These are extra-big ones, see? They're short, but big enough around to clear. I measured 'em. They got rolled edges, too. And *look,*" I beamed proudly, dinging on the metal, "they're even *galvanized!*"

It was hard to argue with. Especially when we had less than 24 hours to go.

So we got the hacksaw and the rotary grinder out and I cut two kind of wide, two-thirds-round rear fenders complete with mounting straps out of two of the galvanized trash barrels and two narrower, kind of half-round front fenders without mounting straps out of the third. I'd already figured how I was going to take the front wheels and brake drums off and bolt a couple lengths of 3/16ths steel strap I had directly to the brake backing plates and then just put the drums and wheels back on and kind of bend that strap around until I could mount the fenders. And then maybe I'd drill a few lightening holes in the strap. Just for the hell of it. Although I have to admit I was starting to worry it might look just a wee bit cobbled-up by the time I was finished.

But I was wrong.

It looked much worse than that.

But at least it was done, and now all we had to do was put a little paint on it to try and cover up all the different kinds of metal we had going (not to mention all the weld bead, braze and body filler showing all over the place, and especially on Big Ed's much-straightened and modified Jaguar hood. So I had Cal run over to the parts store just before it closed to pick up some primer and a couple cans of gloss black paint. Only I really didn't know enough about paint and metal surfaces to understand that there's primer for steel and another kind of primer for galvanized steel and still a third kind of primer you need to use on aluminum. And Cal knew even less about primer, which is why he came back with one can of black primer and one can of red primer and a third can of gray primer. "I didn't know which one you wanted," he explained proudly, "so I got one of each...."

They were pretty small cans, too.

I figured it wouldn't matter, you know, on account of all that primer would be covered with this gleaming, shimmering, foot-deep coat of gloss black paint that we would spray on the next morning and that would hopefully be dry enough to travel by the time we took off for Pennsylvania later that night. Big Ed had a business deal going and some machinery to pick over at a foreclosed tea strainer and potato peeler plant in Cleveland, and the plan was he would meet up with Cal and Carson and me and the rest of our gang at the registration table for the hillclimb in Pennsylvania early in the morning on Saturday the 23rd. All we had to do was get there.

And it looked like we were going to make it in fine shape, too.

Or at least it did until I went to clean up the three-colored primer coat on the Jagillac early the next morning and get it ready for that final, foot-deep layer of shimmering, gloss black paint. And that's when I discovered that the primer hadn't exactly taken much of a bite into the aluminum and galvanized panels. In fact, it was sluffing off in sheets! All of which is why the Jagillac headed off for its very first event at Giant's Despair painted three different shades of primer plus a lot of dirty-looking bare aluminum and galvanized patches here and there where the primer'd just come right off.

I can say with both deep pride and absolute certainty that it was about the ugliest damn racecar you ever saw in your life.

And it didn't help any that we were hauling it dangling off the back of Old Man Finzio's tow truck. But we didn't have much choice, seeing as how it didn't have a license plate or mufflers or anything and we already knew what an all-fired Cop Magnet the Jagillac was. The important thing (I kept telling myself) was that we were *On Our Way,* and that it didn't much matter what the new car looked like. Hell, if it was *fast,* it'd be beautiful....

Naturally it rained most of the way to Wilkes-Barre that night, and I insisted on doing most of the driving on account of I wasn't quite sure I trusted Cal Carrington with the tow rig. I mean, there was no question he could drive it—and surely get there one hell of a lot quicker than I could—but I had my new baby hitched on the back and, ugly though she was, she was mine. So I figured it would be less nerve-wracking for me to just plod along at a nice, comfortable pace rather than hang on for dear life while my buddy Cal experimented around with six-wheel drifts and four-wheel steering.

We got into Wilkes-Barre a little before dawn and parked outside a little truck stop diner we knew for a half-hour of fake shuteye before we got coffee and headed over to registration. Only it turned out to be real shuteye—I guess I didn't realize how worn out I was and that you never have as much energy as you think you do—and next thing I knew Cal was shaking me awake and handing me a cup of coffee on as beautiful a summer morning as you could ever imagine. "You want any breakfast?"

"Jesus, what time is it?"

"Relax. It's just coming on eight o'clock."

"Eight o'clock??!! My God!! Registration starts at seven!!"

"Hey, why be in such a hurry just to wait in a damn line so you can register just so you can wait in another damn line to get the car tech'd just so you can wait in another damn line for gas and air, just so you can go over and wait in the longest and slowest line of all for another two hours just to get a lousy minute and a half run up the damn hill?"

Which was another way of saying that Cal was hungry and didn't have enough money in his pocket for anything but coffee. But I had to admit, he had a point. So we went inside for a couple house-special Triple Play breakfasts (three eggs, three sausage links, three strips of bacon, three buttermilk pancakes, three slices of buttered toast and three pounds of hash browns), and I even took the time to peruse a few old copies of the local morning newspaper I found tucked away up on the hat shelf over the coat rack in front. In a way, I was kind of enjoying the idea that we were going to show up a little late. I mean, Cal was right—we weren't really gonna miss anything. And this way, we could make a kind of Grande Entrance. Plus it was nice to catch up on all the news I'd been missing while I had my brain buried so deep inside the Jagillac project I was like an ostrich with its head in the sand.

Turns out the communist Reds had kicked the French out of Dien Bien Phu (wherever the heck that was) and meanwhile old Tailgunner Joe was protecting us from all the communist Reds right here on our own doorstep by holding lots of hearings and laying down an absolutely withering fire of accusations and innuendo. His latest target was the U.S. Army, and you got the feeling from the newspaper articles that some people on Capitol Hill were getting just a little bit sick of it. But you had to be careful, on account of the same thing that happened to that physicist J. Robert Oppenheimer could just as easily happen to you. He'd had his security clearance pulled, even though everybody agreed he was "a loyal American" and pretty much led the team of scientists who developed the atom bombs we dropped on Hiroshima and Nagasaki to knock the Japs out of the war. But then he'd gone and spoken his mind about what a terrible, dangerous sort of weapon it was and how it maybe wasn't such a great idea for us and the Russians to be building and stockpiling bigger and bigger bombs and more or less waving them around and pointing them at each other like blessed cap pistols. It made sense to me. But you had to be a little bit careful about what you said and who you said it to when it came to National Security. Meanwhile, just up the road, the U.S. Supreme Court poured gasoline on a hornets' nest and then tossed a lit match at it by setting aside the "separate but equal" ruling the same blessed court made in 1896 and ordering school integration. Personally, I'd never thought too much about it one way or the other, but I guess some people felt pretty damn strongly about it. And it sure figured to make a lot of white folks down south unhappy. I mean, for a lot of them, the Civil War wasn't all that over yet. And even those who did know it was over figured the wrong side had won and had never gotten real used to the notion of taking orders from Washington.

A skinny Brit named Roger Bannister broke the four-minute mile and Boeing rolled out the Dash-80 prototype of their new, four-engined jet airliner that could carry 219 passengers and cruise at 600 miles-per-hour and a company called International Business Machines introduced this incredible electronic brain that could do more than ten million calculating operations in a single hour. Can you believe it? In the picture, it looked like some kind of huge short-wave radio that filled an entire room and the article said IBM was going to lease them—not sell them—for an astounding $25,000 per month! Wow! And they already had orders for thirty of the blessed things! Oh, and the guy who invented the zipper died.

You see how you take things for granted?

Anyhow, after breakfast we gassed up and headed over to the SCMA registration area at the base of the hill, and of course by that hour the place was packed with sportycar people, and you should have seen the expressions when we rolled up in the Old Man's tow truck with the Jagillac hanging off the back. Why, you would have thought we were the Evil Witch dropping in uninvited on Sleeping Beauty and Prince Charming's coronation ball. I particularly enjoyed the look on Charlie Priddle's face. It was like he'd eaten some spoiled meat or something.

Well, we parked and unhitched, and about then Big Ed wandered over and found us and I must say he showed commendable restraint when he got his first real look at the Jagillac. "Is it finished?" he asked.

"Not exactly," I told him. And then I explained the part about the primer and the part about the two headlamps that didn't quite match and...

But he was just kind of walking around it, staring at it, not really listening and trying to make some sense out of it. He wasn't the only one, either. In fact, quite a sizable crowd had gathered. The same kind of crowd you get when somebody steps off a curb in Manhattan and gets mowed down by a bus and they're lying there in the gutter with blood all over and arms and legs pointed every which way, still faintly twitching.

"What is this thing?" somebody asked.

"We call it the Jagillac," I told him proudly.

"Hmpf. Looks more like a trash wagon to me."

Everybody laughed, and I felt my cheeks and ears starting to glow like they were in a blessed blast furnace. Big Ed came to my rescue.

"You just wait and see how th'sonofabitch goes up that hill!" he snarled at the crowd. "Then we'll see what kinda 'trashwagon' it is!"

But of all the people who didn't much care for or approve of the car, naturally Charlie Priddle didn't care for or approve of it the most. And he made it damn near impossible for us to get it through tech inspection. First off, we didn't have seatbelts—Jesus, I'd forgot all about it!—but my buddy Carson came through again and said we could borrow the set out of his Healey Hundred so long as we swapped them back and forth between runs. And then Charlie didn't like some of the gaps and holes in the firewall, and so we had to take some aluminum sheet that I'd thankfully brought along and make a bunch of little odd-shaped patches and fasten them in place with sheet metal screws and pop rivets. And after that Charlie didn't like the fact that we had bare, unpainted metal showing on the car. But I countered by reminding him about that clever Colin Chapman guy and his new Lotus cars over in England, and how he didn't paint them as a way to make them lighter and the British clubs let him run.

I don't think Charlie expected me to know anything about that, you know? And it was all thanks to those people from the Sunbeam team and their old copies of *Autosport*.

But Charlie wasn't finished with us. Not by a long shot. The next thing he didn't like was the dump pipe exhausts. He said it was "dangerous for the driver" because of the fumes, and we'd have to make something that brought the end of the exhaust pipes at least as far back as the drivers' head. By that time it was obvious he was just screwing around with us and that he'd just keep finding things wrong until he found something we couldn't possibly fix. So Big Ed decided to challenge him. I mean, what did we have to lose?

"Show me where it says that in the damn rule book," Big Ed demanded, his cigar pointing up out of his mouth like the barrel of a Howitzer.

So Charlie got out his rulebook and sure enough it said the exhaust had to be pointed "away from the driver."

"It *is* pointed away from the driver!" Big Ed argued. "Down is away!"

Well, there was an official huddle of armband people and by now we had a pretty decent crowd gathered around—hell, there's nothing much else to do and a lot of standing-around time involved at a hillclimb—and eventually Charlie had to give in. "But," he warned, shaking a bony finger at Big Ed and me, "you can bet your life that rule will be re-written by the next event!"

Of that I had no doubt.

I suppose it would be nice to say that we sent Big Ed up the hill a few times in the Jagillac, and that then he let Cal give it a try and of course Cal took Fastest Time of the Day on his very first attempt and then everybody shook my hand and applauded and by the time we left on Sunday evening I had a fistful of orders for Jagillac copies to build for other racers. Only it didn't quite work out that way. By the time we fought our way through tech inspection the morning runs were pretty much over, and because we were a late entry we had to go to the back of the line for the first runs of the afternoon. I explained over and over again to Big Ed that the Caddy engine had a lot more torque than the Jag ever did and so he had to go a little easy on the driveline, and I swear it made my skin curl when I watched him rev it up and drop the hammer for that first run up the hill. The car rocked back on its haunches and crabbed all catty-wumpus sideways while rubbersmoke boiled off the back tires and I think it actually scared the piss out of Big Ed—hell, he'd never even sat in the thing before!—because you could hear him pedal out of it almost immediately and then just kind of spurt and putter his way up the rest of the hill. To be honest, he looked a little shell-shocked when he came back down. "How was it?" I asked.

"It handles a little funny," he more or less mumbled.

"Whaddaya mean?"

"I mean it don't steer so good."

"It doesn't want to turn?"

"Nah. The other thing."

"The other thing?"

"Yeah. When you steer it, it's like it turns way too much…."

As you can see, Big Ed had a real analytical approach to the science of vehicle dynamics. But to be fair, his knees were sort of shaking and he looked a mite unsteady as he clambered out of the car and made his way over to the cooler for a cold drink. I followed after him. "But is it *fast?*" I asked over his shoulder.

Big Ed stopped in his tracks, turned around, and rolled his eyes like Donald O'Connor. "We ain't got no problem in that department," he assured me shakily. "No problem a'tall."

Well of course I wanted him to give Cal the last run of the afternoon, but Big Ed had his heart set on trying it again (even though it obviously scared him, and I guess more power to him for giving it another shot), and this time he was just a little more tender off the line—the black streaks were only five or six feet long and didn't hardly snake at all—but you could still hear he was taking the hill in a series of short, hellacious bursts and then just about shutting it down when he got scared and tiptoeing his way through the corners. Still, he set a time better than the guy in the fastest supposedly-bone-stock MG and for Big Ed Baumstein, that was one hell of an accomplishment. It was one hell of a run for the Jagillac, too.

Meanwhile my other guys were doing their usual lackluster job in some really top-flight equipment (if I do say so myself), what with Carson mired down past the middle of the time sheets and well off the pace of the quickest hopped-up MG, Buster Jones in his bone-stock Jag 120 a few places ahead of him, and Danny Poindexter's hotrod TF with its Lucas-Laystall cylinder head even further back. To be fair, the TF wasn't running all that great on account of it had gotten a little fussy about the kind of gasoline it swallowed ever since I installed that new cylinder head, and I'd had to dial back the timing a skosh to keep it from pinging like hell up towards the top of the hill. Typical of a lot of fledgling racers with an undersupply of raw talent, Danny was sure it was the car and that the answer—as it inevitably always is to guys like him—was *More Power!* In fact, he asked me about maybe fitting one of those Shorrock superchargers that he'd heard about from one of the other MG guys. I allowed as how I didn't know all that much about it, but I figured doubling up a blower on top of that 9.3-to-1 compression ratio that was already detonating like crazy even on the best Ethyl we could find was probably not such a grand idea. And then I suggested one of the truest things you can ever tell anybody in this sport: *"Why don't you just go out and buy yourself a faster car?"*

To be honest, this was not very smart advice coming from a mechanic who made the bulk of his beans and burgers modifying and race-preparing customer cars. Because if I wouldn't bolt on a Shorrock supercharger just so's he could blow the whole damn thing sky-high, well, for sure he'd find himself somebody else who would. But I guess I figured it wasn't such a good idea to let people do dumb, idiotic things with their money, even if it included handing a big, fat wad of it over to me. Why, I was damn near a disgrace to the profession.

Outside of Big Ed scaring himself silly in the Jagillac, the high point of the day was when Carson let Cal take a run up the hill in his Healey. True to form, Cal was right up there with the fastest of the Healey Hundreds, damn near neck-and-neck with that Bob Fergus guy out of Columbus who used to be so blessed quick in an MG. Like Carson, he'd put his MG out to pasture (only not by having Cal and me push it off a cliff!) and gotten himself a new Healey. As I said, the two of them were darn near dead-even, and right up there among the faster Jaguars! After the runs were over, Bob Fergus wandered over to say "Hi" and introduce himself. He was a long, lanky kind of guy with those faraway, pilot's eyes that all real race drivers seem to have and a big, careful smile underneath them. He looked pretty young—mid-twenties, maybe—but I guess he already had himself a foreign car dealership in Columbus in partnership with his Ohio racing buddy, Don Marsh. There was an easy, unhurried grace about the way this Bob Fergus moved and talked, and he reminded me a little of those honest, straightforward, right-thinking "a man's gotta do what a man's gotta do" hero types you see in old westerns. I liked him right away. Cal liked him, too. But there's always kind of an edge in the air whenever two genuine Fast Guys get together. Oh, they smile and joke and laugh and maybe even glow off a little admiration for each other. But there's always a certain wariness and evaluating going on behind their eyes. You know, like two gunslingers sizing each other up from the opposite ends of some dusty Hollywood main street in Tombstone or Dodge City.

That night Big Ed took the whole gang of us out for dinner at that Chinese restaurant we'd never been able to find the first time we came to Wilkes-Barre and, after a few too many Manhattans, I got him to agree to let Cal give it a try on the final run the next day. I also called Julie from the pay phone back by the john and it was nice to hear her voice again—even if she did seem a wee bit peeved that I was off having a swell time screwing around with all my racing buddies and pretending it was work—and I got a special little charge I'd never really felt before when she put little Vincenzo up next to the receiver to make some drooling and googling noises at me....

When we arrived at the bottom of the hill the next morning, we saw that somebody had arranged themselves a little prank at our expense. They'd gleeped some trash can lids out of an alley someplace and hung them over the wheels like hubcaps and even taped a fifth one down on the Jagillac's ugly, bumpy, chisel-shaped aluminum deck like some kind of spare tire Continental kit. And they'd painted "TRASH WAGON" above and below the handle with a spray can of shiny silver paint. Big Ed looked angry at first, but then, all of a sudden, his face blossomed out into this big, happy smile. "Say," he asked me, "were you plannin' t'paint this thing when we get home?"

"Sure I was. I mean, just *look* at it..."

"Don't."

"Don't?"

"Yeah. Don't paint it. Leave it look just like this."

"But…"

"Nah, it's perfect. Leave the Continental kit, too. Bolt it down or something."

"I don't get it."

"Hey, they *hate* it."

"So?"

"So I *love* it!"

"You do?"

"Yep. An' the more they hate it, the more I'm gonna love it," he grinned.

You couldn't deny that there was a certain perfect, elliptical logic to the whole idea.

So I bolted down the trash can lid like Big Ed wanted and then he took two more runs up the hill that morning, going a little quicker each time. But it was still always a wild burst of noise and then silence, a wild burst of noise and then silence, and Big Ed was even getting to the opinion that it was maybe something more than him just backing out of the throttle. Although he couldn't be sure, seeing as how he was still way behind the car and more or less hanging on for dear life. So we put Cal in for the first run after lunch and he made an absolutely perfect, silky-smooth launch and damn near exploded up towards the first curve and then, all of a sudden, it was like the engine cut. And then, a heartbeat later, it cut right back in again and blasted another fifty yards or so before it cut out again.

So it wasn't just Big Ed, after all.

Even with the engine cutting out, Cal turned in a pretty damn respectable time—seventh or eighth overall, I think—but he was also absolutely at a loss as to what was wrong. As you can imagine, I went over every damn wire and electrical connection on the car looking for the problem—ignition switch, distributor, coil, fuel pump, even the blessed battery cables!—but I couldn't find anything wrong. What I really wanted to do was take it for a little test drive, but they had a couple state troopers plus some local cops right there, and so that was pretty much out of the question.

"Well then *you* take it up the hill," Big Ed told me.

"*ME?*"

"Sure you. You're the guy who's gotta figger out what's wrong."

"You did it two years ago in my car," Cal reminded me.

"I blew the damn thing up!" I reminded him.

"Well, just don't do it again, okay?" he grinned at me.

So I climbed on board and fired up that big Caddy engine and chuffed my way up closer and closer to the front of the line and it got time to strap Cal's helmet on and I swear my mouth was dry and my palms were sweaty and I was getting this feeling like I really wanted to be anywhere else at all. And I mean *any*where. Sure, I loved racing and I was about as sick with it as anybody you'll ever know. But I wasn't a natural-born driver like Cal, and I could feel it all the way down to the pit of my guts. I just worried too much, you know? Worried about the car and worried about Julie and the baby and worried about the gas station that needed me and worried about the two flywheels coming apart where we'd bolted them together and the fuel tank maybe rupturing and catching fire and, more than anything, I worried about being just plain stupid-ass bog slow up that hill. And that's when Cal leaned down and tapped me on the helmet. "Hey, relax. It's just another test drive."

That made it a little better. In fact, that made it a lot better.

The luscious Sally Enderle was there at the starting line again (what else?), and she smiled at me with her eyes all suggestive and dreamy like she just might take me down to the beach at Elkhart Lake again for a little midnight skinny-dipping some time—she was the type who liked keeping everybody in heat, just for the fun of it—and then the flag waved and I took it real easy off the line like I knew I should to save the driveline, and then I floored it. It was absolutely shattering how that car leaped forward! Or at least it was until the massive intake of air through those four wide-open Strombergs sucked the Greek's flimsy *"stiff breeze"* edition of a Jaguar hood right down on top of them. Which is precisely what was causing the engine to choke itself off just when it was really starting to sing. By the time I got to the finish line, I'd already figured out exactly how and where we were gonna have to cut the holes (and maybe even add a scoop or something?) to keep it from happening.

You live and you learn.

21: Discovering Columbus

There was a SAC-base race coming up at Lockbourne Air Force Base just outside Columbus, Ohio, a couple weeks after Giant's Despair, and we'd decided it was going to be the Jagillac—er, pardon me, the Trashwagon's—big wheel-to-wheel debut. It figured to be one hell of an event, since there was already a pretty good regional rivalry going on between the East Coast racers and the West Coast racers (not to mention the Midwest racers and the Southern Fried racers and even some North of the Border racers from Canada) and, what with the road races at Elkhart Lake shut down thanks to the Wisconsin State Legislature, Lockbourne looked as good a place as any to have a no-holds-barred shootout and settle things once and for all.

Or at least until the next race, anyway.

I'd already heard that my old pirate-shirt *campadre* Ernesto Julio was coming from California with his new Ferrari and Briggs Cunningham was coming with his whole trailer-full of goodies, and there were a bunch of C-Types entered (although, with the coming of the new D-Type at Le Mans a few months earlier, the C-Types—as eventually and inevitably happens to every great racecar—were starting to look very much like last year's model). Plus there were rumblings that Creighton Pendleton might have something new up his sleeve. To be honest, the idea of Big Ed Baumstein taking all that scalding-hot iron on with our Trashwagon sounded pretty damn laughable. But, if I could just get him to put Cal in the car....

Anyhow, I had a lot of prep work backed up at the shop getting ready for the Columbus race (and, just like always when I had a lot of race work going, it seemed like every blessed hod carrier, hairdresser and heating contractor in the neighborhood needed a clutch change for their Chevy or a water pump for their Willys), and I was real happy we had that J.R. Mitchell high school kid dropping by every day to help out. He was a quick study and had a natural knack and feel for mechanical things—how they actually *work* as well as how you take them apart and put them back together—and if I put him on a job with Butch maybe wheeling by and looking over his shoulder every now and then, I knew I didn't have anything to worry about.

He reminded me a little of myself, you know?

Plus he had The Bug—just like I did back then—and even though he wasn't the kind of kid to do a lot of talking or wisecracking or asking of favors, you could see in his eyes that he really wanted to go off to the races with us. But there were a lot of reasons why I figured that might be a bad idea. To begin with, there were a few things going on during your typical race weekend that might not exactly be suitable for an innocent and impressionable young high school kid. Not that they ever did me any harm. But the point is that J.R. had himself a set of parents someplace who might not appreciate somebody pointing their kid down the pathway to motorized, alcohol-fueled, high-speed perdition and then giving him a gentle shove in the back. I mean, you just knew he'd love it all the more once he saw it and heard it and smelled it in person. Same as I did. And you also wonder if you really want to be responsible for introducing him to that sort of desperate and overpowering addiction. Plus there was the little matter of being responsible for a kid that age on a race weekend when you've got a million other things going on. Not that he figured to be the kind to get in trouble. But the most important thing was that I really needed him back at the Sinclair when I was gone. He got things done. And equally important, he was always polite and straightforward and honest and respectful when he talked to our customers. Even the jerks and assholes.

Speaking of our jerk customers and all the work we had backed up, it didn't help matters any that Danny Poindexter had burnt up a couple exhaust valves and melted a little aluminum off the top of a couple pistons in his hot-rodded TF on the way back from Giant's Despair—like I said, that engine didn't care much for most of the pump gas you could find—and I was even thinking about stacking up two or three head gaskets under that lovely Lucas-Laystall cylinder head when I put it back together to kind of ease back the compression a wee bit. "You think that'll work?" J.R. asked me.

"I dunno," I told him. "But have you ever seen a motor blow three head gaskets at once?"

Neither had I.

Meanwhile Danny had taken my advice and headed over to Manhattan to see about a faster car, but he had a little string on him seeing as how his folks wouldn't even think about letting him get a Jaguar. It just looked too damn powerful and cost too much money. Nope, he had to get something "cute," or it was no go as far as his parents were concerned. And that's how he wound up with a bright, shiny-red Triumph TR2. Only problem was that the trade-in Colin St. John offered him on his almost-brand-new (not to mention expensively hopped-up but currently not running) MG TF was something less than half of what he'd paid for it just a few months before. Not that his family couldn't afford it. His dad ran a respected and well-connected accounting firm and he'd made a ton of money making his wealthy clients even wealthier and even more if they went down the old lemonade barrel on account of a few secret partnerships he had going with some Chancery Court judges so they could snap up the odd prime real-estate parcel for nothing more than back taxes before anybody else even knew about it.

But nobody likes to get jobbed, and so Danny came by all moaning and whining and cranky about the lousy trade-in deal Colin had offered him on the TF. And it *was* a lousy deal indeed. Seems little Danny Poindexter was learning four of the Basic Insider Truths about the retail car business. To wit:

1. Depreciation-wise, there is no more expensive ten feet in motoring than that first ten feet you drive out of the dealer's lot. You might as well set fire to a fistful of fifties as soon as you clear the damn curb.

2. The difference between "retail" (what the dealer is charging you for the new car) and "wholesale" (what the dealer is offering you for your trade-in) is the basic reason why car dealers' wives wear sable coats and vacation in Florida and live in big brick houses in a nice part of town where gardeners mow the lawns and trim the shrubbery.

3. Anything you do to "improve" a car (and especially anything expensive) can be counted on to reduce that car's resale value by somewhere between two and twenty times the amount you spent "improving" the car in the first place.

4. If your car is not running and needs some service attention and you are torn between trading it in "as is" or paying somebody to fix it before you trade it in, let me put your mind at ease by assuring you that you lose either way.

Now, these lessons in automotive life were not sitting especially well with little Danny Poindexter. And, seeing as how the offer Colin made him should have legitimately been accessorized with a revolver and a stick-up mask, the old wheels started turning and I called Big Ed and, just like that, I was in the used sports car business with Big Ed as my not-so-silent partner. I knew what to do, too. I pulled the cam and carb needles and that lovely Laystall alloy head off the motor and put all the bone-stock stuff back on, and then I had Julie make me up a real nice little FOR SALE sign so's I could put it out front next to the free-standing "Sinclair" sign and maybe even take it to the races with us and set it up like that someplace conspicuous in the paddock. And then I had J.R. clean off all the parts I'd removed and put them back in their original boxes and I had Julie make me some little FOR SALE signs for them, too. But, per Big Ed's explicit instructions, I was careful not to put a written price on anything.

"Y'don't wanna leave any of the possible gross on th'damn table, see?" he explained, kind of huddling in next to me like we were plotting the overthrow of Yugoslavia. "An' the other thing y'gotta remember is that *the first guy who names a price loses."*

"Why is that?"

"'Cause it's like drawin' a line in th'sand, see. You know that the very next thing that's gonna happen is that some sonofabitch is gonna step over it." He took a long draw on his cigar and exhaled in a series of smaller smoke ring puffs. "Either that or run full-tilt th'other way."

"But what do I do when somebody asks me how much something is?" I mean, I'd been around the world of automotive buying and selling long enough to know that the very first question on everybody's lips is inevitably 'How Much?'

"That's where the selling part comes in, see? Y'turn the tables on 'em."

"Turn the tables?"

"Sure."

"But how?"

"Ah, it's easy. Y'start by flattering 'em a little. Y'say: *'You seem to be an intelligent, experienced, streetwise and aware sort of individual. Tell me, because I'm honestly new at this and I don't really know—what do YOU think it's worth?'"*

"But what if they give me too low a number?"

"Doesn't matter. What you really want is th'damn *commitment!"*

"The commitment?"

Big Ed nodded. "Once they name a price, that means they've decided to buy th'damn thing. In their head, I mean. All that's left is the negotiating."

"Yeah. But I don't know *how* to negotiate."

"Lotsa times you won't even have to. But when y'do, just give me a call."

"Give you a call?"

"Sure. Say, *'It sounds fine to me, but I gotta go check with the car's owner.'"*

"But what if I can't reach you?"

"Doesn't make any difference. In fact, you don't even haf'ta really call."

"I don't?"

"Nah. Just let 'em see you on the phone is all, see? Pretend t'dial if you have to."

"But what do I do then?"

"Oh, that's the easy part. You come back and say, '*Geez, I'm sorry. It sure sounded good to me. But the owner says your offer is a little too low.*'—and here's where you roll your eyes like th'car's owner is the biggest asshole in the whole damn world—'*If you could just maybe see your way clear to making your offer a little more realistic...*'" Big Ed looked me in the eye. "...Th'important thing is that *you're* the good guy and the jerk on the other end of th'phone he never sees is th'bad guy, see?"

I saw.

Boy, Big Ed Baumstein had only ever sat on the customer side of the desk in car dealerships, but he sure as hell picked up a lot about how the game works.

As far as the flimsy Jag hood getting sucked down and choking off the air to the carburetors on the Trashwagon was concerned, I cut four nice, neat, perfectly round holes in the metal—each one lined up absolutely perfect over the throats of those four Stromberg carburetors—and then I hogged them out just a wee bit bigger and maybe not so perfectly round anymore when I discovered that they weren't quite so perfectly lined up as I'd thought they were. But it looked kind of unfinished. And that's about when my old buddy Spud Webster happened to call to ask about the dates for the Watkins Glen race that year on account of he and Sammy were planning on running the 100-mile AAA dirt race at Syracuse on September 11th and he wondered if maybe I'd like to come along and crew there, or maybe we could meet up at the Seneca Lodge again. Sure enough, I checked the calendar and the Glen race was a week after Syracuse, same as the year before. "I kinda doubt I can make it up, though," I told him. "I got all sorts of stuff goin' on down here and the baby at home and all, and we got the race at Thompson, Connecticut, the week before, so I'll most likely be thrashing to get stuff pounded out and put back together in time for Watkins Glen."

"Some other time, then," Spud assured me. "So, what else you got goin' on besides way too much?"

So I told him all about my progress on the Jagillac project and how it had finally had its first Trial By Fire (and incidentally turned into the Trashwagon, which Spud thought was pretty darn hilarious), and also about the flimsy hood problem and the unfinished look of the four now more or less irregular holes I'd carved in the hood.

"What you need is a set of velocity stacks."

"Velocity stacks?"

"Sure. You know, those air horn things some of th'guys put on their carburetors and injection units at the Speedway."

"Where would I find some?"

"I actually think I might got a set that'll fit four Strombergs back home in Texas. They're pretty nice ones, too."

"What d'they look like?" I wanted to know.

"Oh, these are the real deal, no kidding. They're cast aluminum with these neat, curved-horn tops—they look *great!*"

"Do they do any good?"

"Who knows? But at least they don't hurt nothin.'"

"How d'ya mount 'em?"

"Oh, it's easy enough. I'll call home and have m'wife ship 'em to ya."

"How much d'ya want for 'em?" I mean, you always need to know how much.

"Just pay the shipping, okay? If you like 'em an' want to keep 'em, we'll fig-ger something out later."

Sure enough, a heavily-taped cardboard carton containing four gorgeous and carefully wrapped air horns showed up about a week or so later. And, just like Spud said, they were easy as pie to mount on the carburetors. They looked absolutely fabulous, too. But I had to locate Spud and call him out on the road to ask him a very important question:

"Which way d'ya point 'em? Facing forwards or facing backwards?"

"Well," Spud chuckled into the receiver, "there seems t'be two different schools of thought on that."

"How so?"

"Well, some guys think you need t'aim those horns forwards, so the forward motion of the car will really *push* that air down into the carburetors. Kind of like a supercharger, see?"

That made sense.

"But some other guys figure you need to rotate 'em around the other way so's you've still got an unrestricted suck of intake air but you're not gulping all kinds of sand and dust and rocks and insects and stuff down into your engine."

That made sense, too.

"What do *you* think?" I asked him.

"Me? It's like I told you before. I think they look *great!*"

Well, the great Which Way Do You Face The Air Horns debate raged hot and heavy at the regular, after-work Team Passaic wrenching and bench-racing semi-nars at Finzio's Sinclair for weeks. And, like a lot of such racing-related mechan-ical conundrums, the more we thought and argued about it, the more muddy and confused the issue became. Just listen:

"I like that supercharger effect! We could always put some window screen or something over the throats t'keep the rocks out."

"Yeah, but then you're breaking up the flow with the screening. Besides, it'll look like hell, and they're the only neat-looking thing on the whole damn car. I say turn 'em around the other way."

"I don't care which way you turn 'em, if you've got one carb in front of the other like we do, the air horn on the front one's gonna block the airflow to the back one."

"Then why not turn the two front ones forward and the two back ones backward?"

"Aw, that'll never work. With that Supercharger Effect you were talkin' about, you'll get way more air in the front carbs at high speed than the back ones, and either the front half of the engine'll go lean and maybe burn a piston or the back half'll get so rich and fat it won't hardly run."

"Maybe we could jet the front carbs richer than the back?"

That didn't sound right.

"Maybe we could face the air horns *towards* each other?"

"Nah, then they'd be suckin' air right out of each other. That's the exact oppo-site of what we wanna do here!"

In the end, after many hours of discussion and countless bottles of Knickerbocker and Rheingold for fuel, it was unanimously decided that we didn't have a clue. So we resolved to try it each different way we'd thought of at the racetrack and see which worked best. In the meantime, I set them up kind of staggered, with the front two on each side rotated precisely 40 degrees inward from dead straight ahead and the back two rotated outward exactly 60 degrees the other way. "If anybody asks you about it," I told my guys, "just wink and say it's a secret, okay?"

Hey, if you can't dazzle 'em with brilliance, baffle 'em with bullshit, right?

A whole bunch of my guys were planning to go to those SAC-base races out by Columbus, Ohio, and that created a lot of transportation problems for me, seeing as how the Trashwagon was hardly what you could call street-legal roadworthy and so it had to be carried somehow and Big Ed had just taken delivery of his shiny new Arnolt-Bristol Deluxe (which showed up in a dazzling and elegant shade of deep metallic red—kind of a wine color, really), and so of course he wanted to drive that. Not to mention that I wanted to bring our nearly-new, ex-Danny Poindexter MG TF so we could park it in a conspicuous spot in the paddock with a FOR SALE sign on it and, what with Danny bringing his new TR2 and Buster bringing his Jag 120 and Carson bringing his Healey and a bunch of my MG guys bringing their cars, I really needed to tote damn near half of my shop along just so's I could take care of them all. Which meant I was gonna have to borrow one of Big Ed's trucks again to carry stuff. And even that big pickup he kept at home kind of smelled. Plus it was obvious I was going to need more hands than just the two at the end of my own, personal arms to take care of all the wrenching and fixing and track tuning and back patting and hand holding that would have to be done. And every extra pair of hands I brought would need to be fed and given a place to sleep and....

I was beginning to understand that success in business is kind of like a roller coaster ride. It starts with this long, hard, uphill climb where you can't even see the top. And then, after you've clawed and scraped and suffered and expended more time and energy than you ever thought you had, you finally go over this blind little hump where your guts get all light and then, well brother, it all starts happening faster than you can keep up with and you're just hanging on for dear life. And it was also starting to occur to me that bigger isn't necessarily always better. It's just bigger, is all....

Why, I even thought about bringing Julie and the baby along—you know, so Julie could help out with some of the hand holding and keeping people off me so's I could get some blessed work done—and we could maybe even set little Vincenzo up with a lemonade stand or something to rake in a little extra cash. But Julie brought me down to earth in a big hurry. With a crash, in fact. "Sometimes I wonder if you gotta brain in your head, Palumbo," she snarled at me. She had the baby clutched under one arm, smiling and gurgling and joyfully pulling her earlobes and yanking her hair while she tried to stir the tomato gravy on the stove with the other so's it wouldn't stick. You couldn't miss how there was sauce all over the place. Baby food, too. Oh, and apple juice. "Look, it takes me half a frickin' hour just to get Vincie ready to go up one frickin' flight of stairs to see my mom. And then I can only stay fifteen minutes before he needs something else, understand? And now you want to take us halfway across the frickin' country? Are you frickin' *nuts??!!"*

Come to think of it, maybe it wasn't such a great idea. Especially the lemonade stand part. "I'm sorry. I was just thinking…"

"Well, there you go thinking again," she growled at me. To tell the truth, Julie was not in a particularly great mood. In fact, she'd generally been in a pretty damn abysmal state of mind ever since a few days after we came home with the baby. Oh, she was happy in those few nice, peaceful, right-off-a-Hallmark-greeting-card family moments when we'd sit together on the rug in front of the television set with little Vincenzo kind of rolling around between us and he'd gurgle and smile and coo and we'd talk right back to him in that goofy *goo-goo-gaa-gaa* language that seems to come naturally to parents and grandparents with young babies but makes everybody else want to throw up.

Unfortunately, you could wad up all those precious, priceless, placid family moments we'd enjoyed since we brought the baby home into about the length of your average Rocky Marciano heavyweight title defense. The rest of the time Julie and me were running around like crazy taking care of the next thing that had to be done—either her at home with the baby or me down at the shop with the blessed cars—and, if I was really honest about it, I could see as how she got even less breaks or Appreciation Moments out of the average day than I did. No matter how much new moms love and adore their babies, I don't think they can help feeling just a wee bit trapped by them, too. In fact, maybe more than a wee bit. Plus I think you get a little nuts stuck inside the same four walls with the same demanding—*I WANT! RIGHT NOW!*—cellmate twenty-four hours a day….

"I dunno, Julie. I was just thinkin' it'd do you some good to get out a little, y'know?"

"Sure, it'd do me some good!" she snapped. "But how can I? You see what I've got going on here."

"I dunno," I said again. "Maybe we could at least go out to dinner together sometime. Just us, you know?"

"Oh? And who's going to look after the baby?"

"Maybe your mom?"

She looked at me like I'd just clawed little Vincent's eyes out.

"I just feel so guilty, you know?" I told her. "Traipsing off all over the country while you're stuck back here at home…."

"So you feel guilty, do you?"

"Yeah."

"Real guilty?"

"Yeah. Real guilty."

"Good!"

And that was the end of it.

After much deliberation, I wound up actually hiring Cal to work for me on the Lockbourne weekend (although it wasn't much more than what I'd lend him anyways for food and such and never see again, and also with the understanding that he got time off on the spot if he was able to talk Cal or Big Ed—or, in fact, anyone else—into letting him drive). But I also knew I'd have to bring somebody else along to help out. A real mechanic, you know? And that's why I went over to Westbridge and begged and pleaded with Sylvester to come along with us. I knew he'd be free, seeing as how Barry Spline made it a point never to bring Sylvester to the races. Or, as Barry so delicately put it, *"We don't h'exactly want to h'advertise that we've got a bleedin' jungle bunny working on people's Jagyewhars."*

Plus there was the little matter of the weekend-long boozing, blues music, dice games and all-purpose hell-raising Sylvester liked to participate in up in Harlem. Occasionally followed by gospel church services with his wife and kids on Sunday morning and then a little more all-purpose hell-raising come evening. "Whuffo I wants t'go along with you?" Sylvester snorted at me. "They ain't gonna like me there."

"They don't like you here."

"That's why ah likes t'git back t'Harlem on mah weekends. T'git away fum you folks."

"Am I such a bad guy?"

Sylvester regarded me with angry, suspicious eyes that had seen way too much in their time. "No, you isn't," he said finally. "You has always been straight wit' me."

And that's when I offered him damn near what he earned in a week at Westbridge. And I knew, too, on account of I'd snuck a peek inside his pay envelope one time.

"All that jest fo'a weekend?"

"Well, we gotta leave early Friday morning in order to get there. It's six hundred miles."

"An' when we gits back?"

"We'll drive all night coming home. With any luck at all, we'll be back in time for work Monday morning."

"With no fuckin' sleep?"

"You don't sleep on the weekends anyway!"

"How d'*you* know that?"

"I've seen you come in on Monday mornings. Besides," I lied through my teeth, "we can drive in shifts and sleep in the cars on the way back."

He didn't look too sure.

"I really need you," I told him.

The words hung there in the air for a moment and then, finally, he shook his head and laughed. "Aw, whuttha' fuck. Ah kin miss one dice game in mah life. It ain't gonna kill me."

"Great!" And then I thought of something else. "Ahh, there's one more thing?"

"Whazzat?"

"No drinking."

Sylvester's eyes narrowed down to angry slits. "Lemme ast you somethin.'"

"What's that?"

"Is *you* gonna drink?"

I started to answer, but realized he had me dead to rights. "Uh, what I m-mean is," I kind of stammered, "I don't want you drinking during working hours, see?" It was hard talking that way to a guy like Sylvester who was older than me and had brought me along as a mechanic and taught me so much. But I'd seen the way he came in on Monday mornings and could only imagine how wild and wasted-away he got himself over the weekends.

Sylvester eyeballed me for awhile, and then his face blossomed out into a wide, fatherly smile. "You r'member whut I tole you about actin' like a damn boss?"

"Sure I do."

"Well, sonny, you just up an' done it." He shook his head, laughing to himself, and then reached out and messed my hair a little. "Who'd a'ever thunk it?" he grinned, "Who'd a'ever...."

At any rate, the Team Passaic Columbus Caravan left Team Passaic H.Q. precisely around three hours late on account of, well, on account of having to have entirely too many people and parts and bits and pieces to hassle together and too many ducks to get lined up in a row. And even then Cal hadn't showed yet. But I called him at home (and got him out of bed, I think) and left the keys to our FOR SALE MG with J.R. Mitchell and told him to be sure Cal had a few dollars gas money in his pocket and to warn him to for gosh sakes not speed in order to catch up to us. I mean, the last thing I needed was to have to double back and bail him out of jail. Fact is, I thought about leaving Big Ed's parts-and-tools truck behind for him—hey, he deserved it!—but we needed all that stuff at the crack of dawn the next morning at Lockbourne, and the most expendable set of wheels we had going was the MG. Oh, Cal would've been there before the blessed roosters crow if it'd been *his* damn racecar or if we were off to some race *he* was driving in. But that's just the way he was.

And so we set off. Big Ed was in his shiny, almost-maroon Arnolt-Bristol Deluxe along with this new girl named Nanette he'd come up with someplace. She was a bouncy, big-boned type with curly black hair along with the usual, Big Ed-size brassiere cups and a laugh that made your eardrums want to curl up in a dark corner. She didn't talk much and, judging from her laugh, that was probably a big plus. I was driving the Old Man's tow truck, carrying the still-three-shades-of-primer, tarnished galvanized and bare aluminum Trashwagon with the trash-can-lid Continental kit on the rear deck dangling from the hook (I was gonna *have* to come up with some better way than this to haul it around!), and I had Sylvester in Big Ed's pickup with all the tools and parts and stuff in back. Carson was there in his glistening-black Healey Hundred with the hotted-up motor under the hood, and I'd had the Greek cut in a couple sexy-looking louvers to help it run cooler by either bringing in fresh air or letting hot air out—I could never decide which—and Carson'd even made a deal to bring my sister Sarah Jean along seeing as how I was going to be there to sort of chaperone. Not that either Carson Flegley or my sister Sarah Jean much needed one. Those two struck you more or less as one of your Self-Chaperoning kind of couples. Buster Jones was smiling and ready to go in his Jaguar and Danny Poindexter was sharing the cockpit of his brand new, British Racing Green Triumph TR2 with some equally bored, spoiled, well-dressed, well-coifed and chronically dissatisfied Social Register pal of his named Foster Thornton-Throckberry. Danny said everybody called him "Fos," but I really think you had to have the right kind of clothes, bank account and social standing to really pull it off. They even had the damn top up on the Triumph so their hair wouldn't get too mussed—on an absolutely gorgeous day, can you believe it?—and no doubt they'd keep themselves entertained by complaining the miles away all the way to Ohio.

Well, the first thing I learned about traveling to the races caravan-style is simply this:

Don't!

Because you can never get any sort of consensus on how fast or slow you should be going and then somebody needs to stop for gas and somebody else needs to pee a half hour later and every stinking mile is taken at the speed of the absolute slowest runner in the group over that particular stretch of road. Before we even reached the Pennsylvania line Big Ed had sprinted out ahead on account of this Nanette was maybe playing a little finger hockey in his lap and so he got a little anxious to find a room—hell, a scenic overlook would do—and Buster Jones took off after them because he thought it was a chase game of some kind and that's what you were supposed to do and Carson and Sarah Jean wanted to get just far enough ahead so's I couldn't see down into the Healey's interior in case they were maybe holding hands or something and Danny and his buddy 'Fos' were stopping at every damn drugstore on the way trying to find some special suntan lotion with a French name and cocoa butter in it in case they decided to stop for another five or ten minutes to put the top down. Like good old Coppertone wasn't good enough, right?

What with all Danny's stopping and meandering, Cal and our ex-Danny Poindexter FOR SALE MG caught up with us about forty miles into the Pennsylvania Turnpike—he'd started a good hour and a half behind us, so that should give you some indication exactly how briskly he'd been progressing and how opposite-of-briskly we'd been motoring along—and then who should come roaring up in my mirrors but Big Ed and Nanette in the Arnolt-Bristol. I guess they maybe found a little "rest stop" along the way. Only not two minutes behind them came the ever-smiling Buster Jones, who apparently never figured out that he was kind of a fifth wheel and had stopped to enjoy the scenery with Big Ed and Nanette every time they did. You could see as how Big Ed looked like he was under a little pressure.

Anyhow, when we all stopped for gas, it was decided that we'd maybe swap vehicles around a little just to ease the boredom. Carson was happy to let Danny and his nose-in-the-air friend try the Healey and I ordered Cal into the tow truck—I mean, we were headed into the mountains pretty soon and it was getting dark, and so I figured it was time to put my first-string driver in the trickiest rig to drive—and Carson was eager to try our FOR SALE MG on account of he'd never driven one of the new TFs before and he was curious as to how different it was from that black TD Cal and me had pushed off that cliff for him. Not to mention that you sit pretty cozy in an MG. And, speaking of "cozy," Big Ed had soured a little on the seating arrangements in his new Arnolt-Bristol and wanted to take over his own scrapyard pickup truck with all the parts and tools in back (plus its enormous front seat where at least one of the occupants could more or less, umm, "stretch out," if you know what I mean...). And that meant Buster Jones got a chance to try out Big Ed's rare and sexy new Arnolt-Bristol that he'd been chasing after all day and sucking into impromptu, third- and fourth-gear drag races that the Jaguar always won easily. Still, he wanted to see what the Arnolt was like. All of which left me and Sylvester to chauffeur Buster's Jag 120 and Danny's new Triumph, and, seeing as how I had a lot of miles in Jags but had never driven one of the new Triumphs, I offered Sylvester the Jag. In fact, it made me feel kind of good to offer him the keys to the classier, faster and more expensive ride. He didn't say anything about it—you could tell he felt a little wary and out of place in this crowd—but I could see he seemed pretty happy about it when he slipped behind the wheel of that XK 120 and adjusted his rugged old engineer's cap in the rearview mirror.

I have to say I really liked the feel of that new TR2. I mean, it was just such a gutty, jaunty little thing. Sure, like the Healey Hundred, the four-banger motor in the Triumph started out as something less than exactly a genuine Sports Car type of motor. In fact, it was first cousins with a Massey-Ferguson tractor engine, if you want the honest truth of it. But they'd followed the usual, blue-collar British sports car recipe by pumping up the compression just a tad and putting slightly bigger lumps on the camshaft and then frosting with a pair of S.U. carburetors and a wonderfully noisy exhaust system where the mufflers didn't amount to much more than a little goiter-swell in the pipes. Thanks to light weight (achieved to some degree by using body panel material only slightly stouter than your average, grocery-store tunafish tin), low gearing and a nice rush of midrange torque, the TR was pretty darn snappy off the line. The ads said it would do an honest 100 miles-per-hour, and I, for one, believed them. Especially once I got the chance to try it out myself after it turned dark and nobody could see what I was doing. Oh, it took a pretty fair open stretch of roadway (and maybe even a slight downhill slope) to get it up there, but eventually I saw the magic "ton" on the speedo dial. Or something around the magic "ton," anyways, seeing as how the needle on the speedometer kind of wavered back and forth at me like the blessed wand on a metronome. You could feel Danny's TR straining and shuddering to make it, but damn if it didn't! And it braked and handled pretty decent, too, as I discovered when I spied what might have been the headlights of a Highway Patrol police cruiser trying to catch up to me in the little ladies'-purse-sized mirror the engineers at Standard Triumph conveniently stuck up on the dash. So I took Immediate Zigzag Evasive Action up a handy off-ramp that was damn near in my lap at the time. It was a pretty hairy maneuver, if you want the truth of it, what with one of those ever-worsening, high-speed pendulum deals that inevitably include repeated armfuls of desperate steering lock (first one way and then the other and then the first way again and then...you get the idea) and a rondo chorus of screeching rubber (first one side and then the other side and then...) plus a hefty and lucky ricochet *BUMP!* off a curb or something that kept me from sailing right down a blessed ravine. No question I left a nice, pointy new peak in

Danny Poindexter's driver's seat upholstery by the time it was all over. But we somehow got through it, and I was sure right then and there that I would hardly be the last guy on earth to go on the Ride of His Life in a Triumph TR!

But when I parked down under the turnpike crossover where I was pretty sure the cop would never find me and got out to check the car over, I was horrified to see a huge, caved-in dent in the right-rear fender, just behind the wheel. Oh, *SHIT!* Danny Poindexter was gonna have himself a blessed conniption fit! And the worst part was, he'd have every right to. Plus then I'd have to fix it. I reached my hands down to the bottom edge of the caved-in metal—they were still shaking a little from that wild, sashaying ride down the exit ramp—and, just for the heck of it, I gave a little tug. And that's when—*POP!*—that right-rear fender just popped right back to its original contours. Just like *that!* And all of a sudden I saw a brand new magic in making body panels out of grocery-store tuna-tin type material....

In any case, there was no doubt that the TR2 and Healey Hundred represented a new generation of English sports cars, and if I were to sum it all up (as I did many times up at the bar and around the beer tapper before the weekend was over), Carson's Healey had a little more grunt down low and a little wider stance so it was maybe slightly more stable in long, fast sweepers, but Danny's Triumph was a narrower and had more quick *snap!* to it—maybe even a little too much sometimes?—but that made it better at the nimble kind of cut-and-thrust-through-the-tight-stuff maneuvering you expect out of terriers and border collies and such. And the TR2's shifter was an absolute delight! Just this stubby little lever jutting up out of the transmission tunnel—right under your hand!—with nice, short throws and a wonderfully direct and solid feel to it. Quite an improvement over the long, snaky and shaky "school bus" wand in Carson's Healey Hundred. But the best thing about the Triumph—bar nothing!—was those nifty cut-down doors. Why, you could reach out easy as you please and touch your fingertips right down to the blessed pavement! You simply couldn't do that in any other kind of car. It was better than forty more horsepower, honest it was.

And that, all by itself, earned the new Triumph a special place in my heart.

The only real problem with that car—like a lot of other cars I would come to know and work on over the years—was the loose (or, in Danny's case, overly tight) nut behind the steering wheel. Danny Poindexter was just not a particularly likeable kind of guy. Especially with the way he talked down to everybody—and most especially to Sylvester Jones—and didn't even know he was doing it when he did! But I guess that's what happens when you grow up with everything handed to you and being told that your shit doesn't stink and your ass is made of angelfood cake. Besides, you learn early on in this business that neat cars have no control over the assholes, jerks and idiots who own them. I mean, just look at Charlie Priddle and Skippy Welcher and all the swell automobiles *they* had! The good part was that Danny Poindexter would surely get bored and disgruntled with his Triumph soon enough and move on to some other toy—maybe even a Ferrari or Maserati or somesuch one day after his parents keeled over dead—but that meant that maybe some ordinary, lunchbucket guy who never figured he could afford a real sports car could pick it up used and enjoy the living hell out of it. And that was the key to the whole deal on a Triumph: they offered an awful lot of real sportycar guts and feel and performance for not very much money at all. And that's why the factory over in England had geared up to produce a ton of 'em! Like I said before, I figured they'd sell every one they could make.

Our caravan got a little strung out going through the mountains at night, what with all of our differing speeds and comfort zones and priorities (not to mention top-speed test runs and evasive actions), and I decided I maybe ought to pull off at a decent vantage point and make sure the whole convoy was still making head-way in the proper direction. And they all went by within the next ten minutes or so. Except one. Where the heck was Sylvester in Buster's Jag 120? I started pic-turing the worst (including Sylvester stopping someplace or other for a few bot-tles of sweet wine and all the terrible things that might happen as a result), and so I went on another Triumph top-speed run to catch up with Buster in Big Ed's Arnolt-Bristol, flashed my lights and then waved for him to follow me up the next off ramp, down the other side, and backtrack east again, looking for the missing Jag. To tell the truth, I was pretty damn worried. I mean, you never think of all the bad things that might happen when you set one of these deals up—you're always surfing along on this tidal wave of energy and enthusiasm and, well, *con-fidence* that it's all gonna be fine—and then, once you start to worry a little or maybe even panic about what might go wrong, you begin to see the never-ending Domino Effect of Disaster you might well have set in motion. What if the car was blown up? Or wrecked? What would you do then? And what if Sylvester was hurt? Or even killed? My God, who'd take care of his wife and kids in Harlem???

Fortunately, it wasn't that bad. Sylvester had simply turned off for a little gas and to take a pee in Breezewood, and there happened to be a cop car at the station (maybe the same one I thought was chasing me?) and the officer inside got maybe a wee bit Cop Curious about exactly what an individual the likes of Sylvester Jones might be doing in an XK 120 Jaguar? In fact, he was in the process of put-ting handcuffs on Sylvester by the time we pulled in.

Well, it didn't take long to sort it all out, and the cop was actually a little apologetic. To Buster and me, anyway. In fact, he leaned in close and explained to us matter-of-factly as how he was just looking out for our interests and thought the car might easily have been stolen. And meanwhile Sylvester was standing over by the pumps with no expression at all on his face, just rubbing his wrists a little where the cuffs had been.

"I'm sorry," I told Sylvester after the cop had left.

"You ain't got nothin' t'feel sorry about," he said without looking me in the eyes. "You didn' do nothin'…" Sylvester's voice was real cold and faraway, and I was starting to wonder if it had been such a great all-fired idea to bring him along in the first place.

The SCMA race at Lockbourne Air Force Base turned out to be a real mon-ster of an event, what with five races scheduled and damn near two hundred cars entered. Including no less than three four-litre-and-above Ferraris, the whole blessed Cunningham team, several C-Type Jags, "Smilin' Jack" Ensley in his hot Kurtis 500, and more damn production-class MGs, Jag 120s, Healey Hundreds, TR2s and Porsches than I'd ever seen in one place in my life! Plus, out of

Chicago, a team of three white Arnolt-Bristols with blue racing stripes down the middle—just like the Cunninghams!—with Fred Wacker as one of the drivers and another car in the hands of old tooled-leather-boots, ten-gallon-hat "Wacky" Arnolt himself. He'd even entered himself as "Wacky" in the race program, can you believe it? But they made the Arnolt-Bristols run in the two-liter "E Modified" rather than the two-liter "E Production" class on account of they hadn't built very many yet and they were a solid 50% pricier than Triumph's new, two-liter TR2. Of which—just like I figured—a whole eager bunch showed up.

So it was a pretty spectacular entry, and the weather even cooperated with beautiful blue skies, mild breezes and plenty of sunshine. And yet I'll always remember Lockbourne as "the weekend when everything broke," on account of my guys proved to be certified Disaster Magnets from the moment we checked through registration until I made arrangements to have the last Dead Indian hauled back to Passaic. It started off with Carson's Healey, which had been running like an absolute champ since the day he got thoroughly overcharged for it by Colin St. John and took delivery. Only now the damn overdrive quit working. And while I was messing around with that, Buster Jones came in with steam pouring out and the radiator boiling over in this Jag. Turns out it was just a simple thing. Somebody (and I'm not saying who, but his initials just might be Cal Carrington) had somehow neglected to properly tighten down the mounting bolts on the generator when he adjusted the fan belt tension like I'd showed him, and so it'd kind of worked its way loose and threw the belt. Easy enough to fix. I even had a spare. But what you couldn't know was if anything got seriously cooked in the process, seeing as how Buster was not real great about checking his gauges (although he was better about it than Big Ed, but that's not saying very much), and he only came in when it started to smell like he was maybe passing a foundry or something. And then I had to go through one of those angel-whispering-in-one-ear/devil-whispering-in-the-other-one deals about whether to tell Buster it was my fault or not. I mean, if you run a shop, you're more or less responsible for the work your people do. And if worse came to worst, we could be talking a complete Jaguar engine overhaul here. And Buster Jones would be completely within his rights to expect it on the house, too.

And while I was agonizing over that, who should come in on a hook—ass-end first!—but Danny Poindexter's TR2 with one of the rear wheels missing. Or *most* of it missing, anyway. Seems the pie-plate-sized center section that bolts onto the brake drum was still solidly attached right where it was supposed to be. But the remainder of the wheel and the tire around it had apparently torn loose and headed off in the general direction of Cleveland. And there was no escaping that it was the same right-rear I'd bounced off Something Solid coming down that exit ramp on the Pennsylvania Turnpike in a series of life-or-death slides. The strange thing was, I felt absolutely no compunction whatever to tell that sniffy, tight-assed little Danny Poindexter about it and own up like a man to my angel-on-one-shoulder/devil-on-the-other responsibilities. But I did wind up telling Buster Jones about the loose generator-adjusting nut on his Jag. He just smiled that big, toothy College Letterman smile of his and said, "Hey, that's okay. We all make mistakes."

I suppose there's a lot of important thinking and philosophizing you could do on exactly what that all means (no doubt somebody like Ollie Cromwell could talk you a whole blessed encyclopedia about it!), but the point is that you can't avoid a little off-the-cuff/behind-home-plate umpiring in the sportycar race prep and repair business and, just like the guys in the major leagues, you gotta call 'em as you see 'em....

And then you've got to move on to the next thing. Which, in this case, was Big Ed coming in with a slipping clutch on the Trashwagon. I put Sylvester on that one, seeing as how it would get him under a car where people wouldn't be staring at him all the time. I mean, you couldn't miss that he was the only black face in the whole blessed crowd, and anytime he looked one way, everybody on the other side would stare at him. Then he'd turn his head and they'd all look away real quick like there was suddenly something *very* interesting someplace else, and meanwhile all the people and their brother on the other side would crane their necks and swivel their eyes around to stare at him. It was a little like watching a damn tennis match, honest it was.

I managed to get the overdrive back working again in Carson's car and had Cal put the spare on Danny Poindexter's Triumph so he could venture out again (and you can bet I checked those lug nuts and made sure they were on plenty tight, too), although you could see Danny was regarding his car with a new and wider set of eyes since it had snapped at him. Good. But now it was time to bite the bullet and check over Buster Jones' Jag to see if we'd done any lasting damage. With Cal hovering over my shoulder, I checked the oil—it looked and smelled OK, thank goodness—and then checked under the radiator cap for that foamy, chocolate malted milk-looking stuff that means oil in the water and, most usually, a blown head gasket. But it all looked right, so I pulled the spark plugs and looked them over—they all looked fine—and then I spun it over on the starter with the plugs out to listen for any ugly noises in the bottom end and watch for telltale bubbles coming up in the radiator. And I have to say it looked like we'd gotten away with it! Of course, something like that can easily come back to haunt you later—I mean, no question getting an engine that toasty hot and boiling doesn't do it any good—but there's kind of an unwritten law in mechanical circles that if the patient gets up and walks away under his own power and without a noticeable limp, you're off the hook.

Poor Sylvester was really struggling with the Trashwagon clutch on account of we'd kind of thrown the bodywork up in a hurry over a pretty much finished chassis and engine and never gave much thought about having to dig back into it some day. And may I say that made the Trashwagon's innards none too easy to get at. In fact, "thoroughly impossible" might be a more accurate description. But he kept after it, grunting and cursing as he took apart in the space of a scant few hours what it had taken me so many months of effort and agony to create. "Buddy," he called up to me from under the car, "does you know the differments b'tween an engineer an' a damn mechanic?"

"No," I answered honestly.

"Uh-huh," he nodded. "That's a-zackly whut ah thought."

So overall it was a pretty miserable weekend for Team Passaic out at Lockbourne. Poor Cal never got a single chance to drive. He wanted me to let him out in the FOR SALE MG—"You know I'll do good in it, and it'll help you sell the car," he pleaded. But I just didn't think it was a good idea. Not to mention that, unless you happen to be a genuine racecar driver looking for a genuine racecar, you want a car *just like* the one you saw win the big race, not the same exact one you just saw somebody flogging within an inch of its life (and, most likely, taking well beyond the prudent redline on all available dash gauges) earlier in the afternoon. Plus we seemed to be in one of those operational modes where everything we were sending out on the track was coming back on a hook. Besides, that tall, lanky Bob Fergus guy from Columbus who was so blessed fast in his MG and his Healey came over and seemed genuinely interested in the MG I had for sale.

"How much you want for it?" he asked.

"I dunno," I said, following Big Ed's instructions to a "T." "What do *you* think it's worth?"

Bob Fergus' lips spread out in a big, appreciative smile. "Don't try to bullshit a bullshitter, Buddy," he beamed at me. "I'm a car dealer here in town…"

"I know."

"…and I just might have the perfect guy for this car. So how much do you want?"

I thought for a second, did a few calculations in my head, and quoted him a price about three-hundred-and-fifty dollars over what we had in it.

"That's a pretty fair retail price," he allowed, rubbing his chin, "but there's really nothing left in it for me. I'm a dealer, Buddy, and so I've got to get the *wholesale* price so I can make a little something on it, too."

I could see right away that I was in way over my head, so I excused myself and went looking for Big Ed. "So where'd you leave it?" he asked as I steered us back over to the MG.

"I didn't leave it anyplace."

"Did you quote him a price?"

I looked down at the ground as we walked. "Yeah. I kinda did."

I could almost hear Big Ed's eyes roll. "How much?" he finally asked.

I told him.

"Hmm," he mused, the wheels obviously turning. "That's not too awfully bad."

"It isn't?"

"Nah."

"Really?" I was feeling pretty proud of myself.

"Hey, I didn't say it was *'great.'* Just not too bad."

I figured that was still pretty decent, you know?

And then I got to sit in the peanut gallery and watch firsthand as Big Ed and Bob Fergus slowly circled in around a deal. No question Bob wanted that particular MG and figured he could sell it, but the problem was going to be how you got two decent profits out of two sales on the same damn car? They talked about a split deal and they talked about doing a direct sale to Bob's customer with some kind of appropriate "finder's fee," and you could see neither one of them were particularly thrilled with half the baby. And then Bob threw something new into the mix. "You see that brand new Volkswagen parked under that tree over there?"

Sure enough, there was a shiny gray Volkswagen Beetle parked under a tree next to Bob's Healey and MG just across the paddock from us. It had Ohio dealer plates on it.

"Yeah, I see it," Big Ed nodded.

"Well, I'm the Midwestern Volkswagen distributor now—they want me to try and set up a few dealerships for them—and how about if I throw that car in at flat wholesale as part of the deal and you give me the MG for two hundred less."

"But what do I need with a damn Volkswagen?"

"It's a heck of a car," Bob said earnestly. "It'll cruise all day at top speed, it's light as a feather to drive, great in snow because the engine weight is hung out there over the back wheels, and it's air-cooled so there's no radiator to ever boil over." That was something a previous Jaguar 120 owner like Big Ed could genuinely appreciate. But he still didn't look real convinced. So Bob just eased on into a little more folksy, matter-of-fact, low-key salesmanship. And that always starts off with flattery. Only you have to kind of slip it in so the guy on the other side of the bargain doesn't notice. "For guys like you and me who really know cars," Bob Fergus continued, "the best thing about a Volkswagen is that it's simple and built solid and easy to fix. And they don't change models every year, so the same parts that fit last year's car will also fit next year's car. Pretty soon you'll be able to get parts and service everywhere in America."

You could see Big Ed was getting a little intrigued. Bob Fergus could see it, too.

"And remember this," Bob Fergus continued without either hurrying or skipping a beat—jeez, you had to love his timing!—"that MG of yours is a *used* car and the one I'm offering you in the deal is *brand-spanking new*. It's never even been titled." Bob drew in for a little quiet, just-between-you-and-me stuff. "Don't know if you know it or not, but that car over there is one of the new 1200s. Brand new this year. It's got *twenty percent* more horsepower than last year's Volkswagen."

I was impressed.

"Oh, yeah?" Big Ed asked. "So how many is that?"

"Thirty-six!" Bob beamed. Like it just as well might have been three hundred, right? "And it'll cruise all day long at the highest speed limit in the nation and get thirty-five miles per gallon of regular on the way. Go ahead," he urged Big Ed, "take it for a spin."

So Big Ed did, and I went along—just out the paddock and up the road a few miles and back—and I've got to admit it was kind of fun. Oh, the engine sounded like we had a forty-five-pound bumblebee trapped under the rear deck and the shifter was kind of rubbery, but it did feel both light and solid at the same time. And I liked how even though it was cheap and simple it was obviously put together real well—I mean, the paint on the metal dash was as thick-looking and well applied as I'd ever seen anywhere—and I got the feeling we were going to be seeing a lot more of these Volkswagen Beetle things on American roads before too long.

I have to admit, the deal was sounding pretty good to me. And I think it was sounding pretty good to Big Ed, too. But he knew better than to just let himself get led by the nose down the old garden path. That's just not the way a real pro negotiates. No, a seasoned player like Big Ed knows the way it's done is to let the other guy ramble on and shoot his wad and then pretend like you're gonna walk away. Not walk away *mad,* you understand. Just walk away....

"I dunno," Big Ed mused, his cigar doing a kind of slow log roll across his lower lip, "it sounds real tempting, but I still got this problem about what th'heck a guy like *me* is gonna do with a damn Volkswagen."

"You keep it at a steal of a wholesale price or you sell it back home and make a profit."

Big Ed thought it over for a moment. "You'll show me the paperwork from the factory?"

"Sure I will."

Big Ed took a long, slow draw on his cigar. "Okay, howabout this: invoice wholesale on the Volkswagen and a hundred less on the MG?"

"It's the old squeeze play," Bob Fergus grinned. "Let's say a hundred and seventy five."

"Let's say a hundred and twenty-five."

They were eyeball-to-eyeball now, serious and wary but smiling the whole time.

"Okay," they said almost in unison, "let's make it a hundred and fifty off on the MG."

Big Ed stuck out his hand. "Deal."

"Deal," Bob agreed.

And that's how we got our first Volkswagen.

After it was all over, they both seemed pretty happy and satisfied, and Bob even took the time to share a little of his automotive retailing philosophy with me. "You don't always need to be trying to make the *best* deal, Buddy," he explained. "Just make a *good* deal. Where everybody walks away with something. And then just make *lots* of them...."

By the way, besides buying the MG and selling us that brand new Volkswagen 1200, Bob Fergus also copped a class win each in the Healey and MG that he entered. In fact, I was sorry Carson didn't turn Cal loose in the black Healey to give Bob a little run for his money. That would've been a heck of a good race! As it was, Bob's Healey finished fifth overall behind four XK 120s and well clear of all the other Healeys, Jags and TR2s behind him. And it was a nice touch that, because of engine displacement, the Jag 120s ran in Class C and the Healey Hundreds ran in Class D and the Triumph TR2s ran in Class E in that race, so each camp got a class winner out of it and a trophy to admire and something to cheer and brag about. Which went right along with the long-standing SCMA policy that Everybody Oughta Win Something. Not that I got to see much of that race, since I spent most all day Sunday stuck underneath or burrowed deep inside the engine compartment of one busted car after another. So I missed seeing a pretty little 1100cc OSCA walk away with the tiddler race and three more 1500cc OSCAS finishing 1-2-3 in the third race and that super-quick dentist from Washington D.C., Dick Thompson, lead a four-deep Porsche sweep of the under-1500cc Production Car race, while Bob Fergus cruised home to another fifth overall and his second class win of the day in his trusty old MG TC.

Meanwhile Sylvester and me had worked our damn asses off putting a new Jaguar clutch in the Trashwagon and then screwing it back together any way we could with tape, baling wire and a whole shitload of sheet metal screws and pop rivets in order to have it ready for the 150-mile feature race for big-bore modified cars at the end of the day. And, wouldn't you know it, who should Big Ed wind up right next to on the third from the last row on the grid but our old pal Skippy Welcher in his oft-crashed-and-flattened and subsequently much-repaired C-Type. And it was about to need a little fender-straightening again, seeing as how Big Ed and The Skipper got together in a slight, umm, "competitive misunderstanding" at the very first corner. In fact, eyewitnesses said they hit three times. First kind of by accident when they bounced off each other trying to bull their way into the same exact hole in the atmosphere, and then a second time coming out of the corner when an obviously pissed-off Skippy Welcher simply used Big Ed as kind of a bank-shot cushion in order to make the rest of the turn, and a third time when Big Ed returned the favor by using the back end of Skippy's C-Type as a Brake Enhancer going into the very next corner. It was hardly the sort of gentlemanly, sportsmanlike and genteel racecar driving the SCMA had in mind when they wrote their bylaws! But it sure was fun to watch. Unfortunately, it didn't last very long, seeing as how Big Ed managed to strip all the damn teeth off second gear and so he was done and out of it before the first lap was even over. Damn.

Meanwhile it was quite a jumble at the front of the pack—Creighton's Ferrari and Phil Walters in the Cunningham Ferrari (now back to standard without those weird water-cooled brakes) had both taken evasive action to avoid a scuffle at the first turn and so they were back a ways further than expected—but after everything sorted itself out, it was those two running first and second and local Ohio driver E. B. "Ebby" Lunken in his 4.1 Ferrari holding down third. And that's the way they finished, with old Creighton the Third notching up yet another win.

I was getting just a little sick of it, you know?

Not that I really got to watch much of it, seeing as how Buster Jones' Jag finally started running hot and showing a few telltale bubbles in the radiator that probably spelled H-E-A-D-G-A-S-K-E-T during his race. So we parked the Jag and started stripping it down and then snooty little Danny Poindexter spun off and hit the only protruding chunk of concrete for miles around during his race and trashed the front end of his new TR2 bad enough that I'd have to find some way to get him and it and his buddy 'Fos' all back to New Jersey. Luckily Bob Fergus stopped over at the end of the day and, after a little friendly dickering with me and Big Ed, arranged for all of our dead-in-the-water automobiles to be hauled over to his dealership and then transported back to Passaic on one of the car haulers that brought his VWs out to him from New York. He negotiated us a pretty good deal on it, too.

In fact, by the end of the weekend, the only Team Passaic people driving home in the same cars they came in were Carson and Sarah Jean in the Healey (which Carson drove to a safe, sane and thoroughly uninspiring eighth in class and seventeenth overall in his race, but at least he didn't crash or break anything) and Big Ed and Nanette in the Arnolt-Bristol that hadn't turned a wheel all weekend except going back and forth to the motel. Which it did fairly often. And which is also why Big Ed wanted to swap out for his pickup on the ride home (for reasons we don't really need to go into here), leaving me and a thoroughly worn-out Sylvester Jones in the Arnolt-Bristol and Cal all by his lonesome in the tow truck. Which most certainly could've done with a couple extra hooks to haul off our dead and wounded!

Everybody else had to pile into the Volkswagen.

Turned out it was kind of a lucky break that we bought it!

And then, just to top things off, who should drop by while we were loading up but that asshole Charlie Priddle, carrying a written protest about Big Ed's driving along with yet another shit-list of reasons he'd dreamed up as to why our Trashwagon "wasn't suitable for competition" with the SCMA He still didn't like the exhaust, and he called the trash can lid on the rear deck: "a dangerous protrusion that might easily come off and endanger other drivers"—even after I showed him how solidly it was bolted down!—and then he showed us this new rule that said cars had to be presented in "a neat and clean condition with no primer showing" and wrote in our log book that it had to be fixed by the next race. And who should be following right in his footsteps but that clown prince of paddock assholes, Skippy Welcher and his equally squirrelly squire-cum-sidekick Milton Fitting. We hadn't really seen much of Skippy for awhile, and I'd almost forgotten what a colossal jerk and pain in the ass he could be. And naturally he was the guy who had lodged the protest about Big Ed's driving. Which meant, seeing as how it was late in the day and everybody—including most of Charlie Priddle's armband entourage—had gone home, that Big Ed was most likely going to have to appear and humble himself in front of one of Charlie's infamous Drivers' Committee tribunals. Which is apparently why The Skipper was feeling so damn cocky and proud of himself.

"So," he chuckled as he gave the Trashwagon a once-over, "anybody die in this wreck?"

Now Cal or me or even Big Ed himself could say something like that about the Trashwagon and it would've been funny. Hilarious, even. But the way The Skipper said it made you want to punch him square in the nose. And that would only be fair, seeing as how Skippy had personally installed the fresh dents and crumpled fenders all down the left side of the bodywork. Not, in all honesty, that you could much tell. So Big Ed told Charlie Priddle *he* was gonna enter a counter-protest against Skippy Welcher's wheelmanship and sportsmanship and such for essentially driving right into the side of him. On purpose.

Well, that naturally didn't go down very well with The Skipper, and so he turned to Milton Fitting and damn near hollered, "You ever see such a pile of junk?" right in his ear. Like he was pretending to whisper it, right?

"This is a fast car, Bub," Big Ed glowered at him.

"I see it's going extremely fast right now," Skippy snickered right back.

"It's just broken a little, that's all," Big Ed sneered.

"Looks to me—*heh heh*—like it's broken a lot."

Well, it didn't take more than ten or fifteen seconds for Big Ed and The Skipper to be squared off nose-to-nose and eyeball-to-eyeball (although Big Ed had to kind of look down in the general direction of Skippy's shoes to make it happen) and yelling at each other like they were about to explode. And of course all that excitement made The Skipper start sputtering up spit like an upturned water fountain. Right into Big Ed's face! I couldn't exactly hear all of it, but the general gist of the conversation boiled down to one of those little kid's playground *"IS NOT!"/"IS TOO!"* deals about which was really faster, The Skipper's C-Type or Big Ed's Trashwagon. But they just as easily could've been arguing about metric versus British Standard socket sets or the price of rice in China or Jane Russell's bra cup size. When you get to the level of personal distaste, dislike and disrespect like we had going between Big Ed and The Skipper, the subject of the disagreement hardly even matters any more. We finally had to pull them apart before either The Skipper got himself a well-deserved split lip or Big Ed drowned in Skippy's sputtering saliva shower.

"You haven't heard the end of this, Baumstein!" The Skipper screeched back at us as Milton and Charlie Priddle led him away.

"Neither have you, asshole!" Big Ed bellowed after him. *"Neither have you!"*

The ride back to Passaic with Sylvester in Big Ed's Arnolt-Bristol started out pretty nice, but then turned into one of those long, sullen, edgy, silent trips when you feel all sweaty and scratchy and clammy and unkempt and can barely keep your eyes open and no matter how fast you risk it with the gas pedal, you just don't seem to be making any headway. Poor Sylvester was about cashed out after working damn near all night on the Trashwagon, and he was a little shaky and raspy on top of it from going all weekend without his usual dosage of sweet wine. So we stopped a hundred miles or so out of Columbus for a couple sandwiches and I even bought Sylvester a nice little pint bottle of muscatel for dessert. Hell, he'd earned it. "Y'all want enny?" he asked once we got rolling again.

"Nah," I told him. "I don't 'spose I better. We got one hell of a long drive ahead of us."

"Suit'cher self," he shrugged, and unscrewed the cap and started to lift the bottle to his lips. But then he stopped. "Y'all gonna wan't me t'drive a l'il?"

"Nah. I'm fine for now. You go ahead."

So we cruised on eastward in the Arnolt-Bristol with the sun going down in a brilliant sunset behind us and Sylvester gently guzzling his wine as the green, rolling, deep-shadowed Ohio farmland wheeled past. In spite of all our problems on the weekend, it was a pretty damn nice place to be. But then it got dark and those clouds that made for such a beautiful sunset caught up with us and we had to stop and put the top up when it started raining just past the Pennsylvania line. No question the top on that Arnolt-Bristol was kind of an afterthought once Bertone got done with all those fabulous, swoopy curves, and I knew right away that Big Ed was gonna have a hell of a time trying to fit inside that thing with the top up. And then it started raining even harder and so we had to pull off under a viaduct to put the side curtains in. But it was still early August, so it was warm out even though it was pouring rain, and that made the cockpit of that Arnolt-Bristol into its own little pup tent of a steam bath. Don't get me wrong, I liked that car. I liked it a lot, in fact. But there are some trips that just aren't destined to be any fun no matter what you're driving. They only get fun later, when you're telling people about them over drinks. Then the worse they are, the better.

Sylvester dozed off most of the way across Pennsylvania on the Turnpike while I flogged us through the rain and the mountains and then, finally, struggled our way around Philadelphia at about 4:30 in the morning and picked up the Jersey Turnpike for that last, easy stretch back home. "Y'all want me t'drive?" Sylvester asked, bleary-eyed, as he swiveled his head around and tried to figure out exactly where we were.

"Nah, I'm all right," I told him. I mean, he looked pretty ragged. And it didn't take him thirty seconds to be deep asleep again with his engineer's cap pulled down over his eyes and snoring just a little.

To tell the truth, I was maybe a wee bit tired myself. So I stopped very gently so as not to wake Sylvester and quietly removed the driver's side curtain for a little fresh air to maybe sort of wake me up and took off again. I could just barely see that purplish-gray glow of early dawn starting to grow off to the east, and I got this feeling that if I could just make it through till sunrise, we'd be okay. And so I tried to keep myself entertained by pretending I was racing through the night at Le Mans. And when that got dull, I looked around inside the cockpit and down over that sexy, curving hood with the big power scoop in the middle to clear that tall Bristol engine and tried to explain to myself just exactly where Big Ed's Arnolt-Bristol fit in the greater sportycar scheme of things. Just like old Esperanto novelist Ollie Cromwell would about art or literature or wine or philosophy or, in fact, any damn thing. So why not cars? Besides, who was there to stop me?

So I inhaled deeply of its aroma, felt the slender grace of its riveted woodrim steering wheel with my fingertips, and gave it a shot. Just like those *Road and Track* and *Autosport* writers who get their gongs off all day long thrashing the living tar out of all these fabulous sports cars (that, incidentally, always belong to other people!) and then sit down and write about them in the dry, detached third person like they're discussing unique rock formations or unusual species of fish. Something like this: *'No question the Arnolt-Bristol has more style and stature than commonplace, mass-produced sports cars. It's beautiful and unique, and feels stronger, solider and more refined to the touch than either the Austin-Healey Hundred or the Triumph TR2.'* Hell, it *should* for that kind of money! But you sat kind of way up in the air compared to either of those two, and it had this long, willowy shift lever that just kind of sprouted up from underneath the dashboard and the whole thing seemed, well, just *different.* Plus, even with a six under the hood, it was still just a two-liter and didn't really have the punch and power of a Jag or anything and...

...and that's about when I dozed off and damn near killed old Sylvester and me. It happened on the blessed New Jersey Turnpike, can you believe it? On this smooth, flat, arrow-straight stretch of road after I'd already gotten us through the damn mountains and the rain and all the tough stuff was behind us. All I had left was this straight, easy shot up the Turnpike to home. But of course the mountains and the rain keep you nervous and scared, and that helps keep you awake. It's those long, boring, droning runs down that endless ribbon of highway that seems to dangle from the horizon one moment and then change into a flat, motionless stalk of concrete sticking out in front of you the next.

In any case, we must've been doing better than 90 on account of I'd been fighting off sleep by going faster and faster to try and keep myself interested ever since we got on the Turnpike, and so we were really traveling when I felt that first mighty, thumping jolt that blasted me wide-eyed awake and froze my guts solid in a heartbeat as Big Ed's Arnolt-Bristol went bounding down into the median ditch at breakneck speed....

"HOLY SHIT!" I screamed as the car bounced through the bottom showering off huge, squishy clods of dirt and careened up the other side.

"WHUT TH'FUCK???!!!" Sylvester screamed right back as he woke up to find us on a crazy boblsed ride through the ditch and barreling up the other side like it was a damn launching ramp. Naturally I slammed the brake pedal clear to the floor, but the brakes just don't do all that much good when you're on wet grass. In fact, I think it may have actually speeded us up a little. Or at least that's what it felt like, anyway.

And those brakes do even less when you're airborne....

Well, we came out of that median ditch like a sideshow act you'd pay cash money to see, launched clear over some guy in a Chevy going the opposite way (by that time it was all happening in terribly slow motion, and I remember looking down like I was in a low-flying Piper Cub and casually noticing that it was a blue 1950 Fleetline Deluxe and that the driver had his arm hanging out the window and he was wearing a shortsleeve white shirt and a gold wristwatch), and then we hit ground all catty-wumpus, bounced twice like a rookie carrier landing, rocked up on two wheels so we were tilted at maybe a 45-degree angle with Sylvester kind of falling over into my lap while a terrifying, elongated shriek of rubber-against-concrete seared our eardrums and then it banged down *HARD!* onto all fours again and I had the brakes locked up solid as it spun around one way, caught, and the spun around the other like the damn Tilt-A-Whirl ride at Palisades Park. And then—just like *that!*—it was over....

We'd come to a halt at the end of a hundred-yard series of smoking, near-incomprehensible skid marks facing more or less backwards (or, in other words, pointing in generally the right direction, seeing as we were now kind of half-on/half-off the inside traffic lane aiming back towards Philadelphia) with the engine ticking over at a nice, comforting idle and not a single blessed scratch on the car.

Not one!

Sylvester looked up at me from the general direction of my lap. *"Yo' wants me to mebbe drive fo' awhile?"*

When you think about it, I was pretty damn lucky to get away with not one but *two* near-cataclysmic road disasters on my way to and from the Lockbourne races. And you'd think that might have had some kind of sobering effect on me. But, to be honest, the only real effect it had was to give me two more great race-weekend road trip stories to tell at the bar or around the beer tapper when neither me or the people around me were feeling the least bit sober at all. Sure, crashes are a terrible and dangerous thing. But *getting away* with crashes is a way to know that God really loves you. Or that He's setting you up for something even worse down the line.

It can go either way....

In any case, we got back to Passaic with no more than flat spots serious enough to shake the fillings out of your teeth on all four of Big Ed's tires and a pretty visible ding in the right-front wheel rim from my initial, single-point landing on the Philadelphia-bound lanes of the New Jersey Turnpike. But I didn't say anything much about it. I just put the spare on the right-front and went out and bought three fresh tires out of my own pocket and stuck the bent rim with the best of the flat-spotted tires on it in the trunk and walked away. I figured Big Ed wouldn't be hanging onto that car too awfully much longer—he'd get bored with it and want something else—and I was going to wait until a little time had passed before I told him the story. I mean, it wasn't like I was *never* gonna tell him. It's just I wanted to wait for the right moment. Say, over drinks at Watkins Glen. In maybe a year or two.

Speaking of Big Ed, he was plenty nervous about his coming run-in with Charlie Priddle and his armband wolfpack at the big Drivers' Committee tribunal, and he was even toying with the idea of bringing his lawyer along. But Tommy Edwards, who'd been there, advised against it. "It's not about who's bloody right or wrong, Ed," Tommy explained. "It's about making you squirm and crawl."

"I've never been real good at that," Big Ed grumbled.

"Well, you'd better learn if you want to keep your bloody license."

So Big Ed went in to the SCMA general membership meeting on the third Tuesday of the month all prepared to kowtow and grovel and lick the soles of the shoes of whoever he had to—Charlie Priddle included—in order to keep his ticket. Of course I went with him, on account of I wanted to give him a little moral support and I also wanted to see for myself what was going to happen. In fact, we all did; Cal and Carson and Tommy Edwards and even Buster Jones and Danny Poindexter. Which meant it was also a perfect excuse to sneak out for a night with my racing buddies—er, *'best customers'*—seeing as how Julie's mom was spending most of her free time down at our apartment "helping out with the baby." And she had a *lot* of free time.

Don't get me wrong. Having Julie's mom right upstairs was a great help when it came to little Vincenzo. She could watch him so Julie could pop out to the store without lugging him around with her and she helped Julie with the dishes and the cooking, and they even washed clothes together in the machine Mrs. Finzio had upstairs and then hung them out to dry together over the little patch of grass by the alley I laughingly referred to as our back yard. But she was around all the time, and the longer and better I got to know Julie's mom, the surer I was that she hated my guts. Oh, she never *said* anything. But she had this way of following me with those beady, weasel eyes of hers and giving me motherly smiles that looked suspiciously like sneers. As if *I* was the reason why Julie and her weren't off on a tropical island somewhere, wearing silk underwear and satin gowns and gold shoes and diamond tiaras and being fawned over and catered and kowtowed to by some fairytale prince from Never-Never Land. And that can wear a little thin after awhile. Not to mention that, when she did hiss at me—I mean, talk to me—it was always to remind me about something I hadn't done or hadn't gotten around to yet or to point out that so-and-so's husband just got a promotion or so-and-so and her husband were taking a vacation in Europe and so-and-so's husband—who was a damn garbage collector!—got to wear gloves all day so at least his hands were *clean* when he came home from work.

Like I said, it could wear a little thin after awhile.

And it was like pulling a damn stump out of the ground to get her to go back upstairs at night. And I'm talking way past dinnertime here. Of course, the culprit was that Zenith TV I was making payments on. I mean, who wanted to go upstairs and listen to the radio when you could be watching *Amos n' Andy* or *You Bet Your Life* with Groucho Marx and rooting for the contestant to guess the Secret Word? And just a twist of the dial switched you to real-life crime dramas like *Treasury Men in Action* or *Dragnet* with Jack Webb as Sergeant Joe Friday:

"I just want the facts, ma'am. Just the facts...."

Why, I was even thinking of going deeper into hock just to get the old bat her own TV set!

But there were pluses, too. Once little Vincenzo got past those helpless first six months and started looking like the Central Permanent *"I WANT!"/"RIGHT NOW!"* fixture in our lives, Julie and me even talked now and then about how nice it would be to sneak out for a hamburger or a movie or something all by ourselves. Only when she said it, it came out like lovely, wishful thinking. When I said it, it sounded like child abandonment and criminal negligence. But of course that's just the difference between men and women, and you'd better get used to it if you ever want to have a family. Not that you ever can.

Still, I had a few weekends home in a row in August and so, after a lot of agonizing over it one way and the other, Julie and me decided we'd grit our teeth, leave a list of phone numbers for everybody from the fire department to the pediatrician to the projectionist booth at the movie house and went out together on a Friday night to see the Alfred Hitchcock movie *Rear Window* with Jimmy Stewart and Grace Kelly. And it was a heck of a show, all right. Even though Julie kept digging her fingernails into my arm all the time whenever it got real scary and suspenseful and whispering in my ear, *"You think I ought to go out to the lobby and call my mom to make sure everything's all right?"* whenever it wasn't. I don't want to give it away, of course, but in the end, Jimmy fights the murderer (it's the jewelry salesman, natch!) by popping a bunch of flashbulbs in his eyes and the police show up in the nick of time just as he gets pushed out the window and breaks his other leg. You should really go see it for yourself....

But it was nice being out with Julie again—just the two of us, you know?—and, once Julie'd called home a couple dozen times to make absolutely sure things were okay, we even went over to the Doggie Shake for Cokes and fries and of course all the girls wanted to know how we were doing and how the baby was and all, and I know it was nice for Julie to be the center of attention like that. Even if I did feel kind of like the frog at the end of the log the whole blessed time. But I gutted it out and did my very best to show a good profile and look like the sort of strong, silent, trustworthy, loyal, helpful, friendly, courteous, kind, obedient, cheerful, thrifty, brave, clean and reverent husband all the girls at the Doggie Shake would want when they went shopping in the matrimonial market. Then we stopped over by Weederman's and split a double butterscotch sundae—they always had much better ice cream than the Doggie Shake—and afterwards we went out and parked out back behind the Sinclair like we used to do when we were dating and listened to the radio and made out a little. Not that it's any of your business.

But that night didn't change things much over at the duplex, where I was feeling more and more like *I* was the outsider. There was Julie and her mom and all this heavy-duty hormonal female mothering stuff going on, and I was just the guy who came and went with the dirty socks and the pay envelope and fixed the plumbing when it backed up and got dragged by the ear to go to family things that were always like all the other family things I'd ever been to in my life and featured the same exact cast of characters every time and, worse yet, you'd hear the same blessed stories over and over again until you were ready to go batty from it. Only for some reason the women seem to really enjoy all that dullness and boredom. They must, or otherwise why do they keep planning more and more excuses to "get the family together" to celebrate every damn birthday, anniversary, baptism, confirmation, graduation, marriage, religious occasion, seasonal festivity, get-out-of-the-hospital party, wake, funeral or local, regional or national holiday recognized in even the remotest sort of way by anybody on the entire blessed family tree?

Not that I'm complaining, you understand.

At least it was nice that Carson Flegley had advanced to the status of Possible Prospective New Family Member by continuing to date and hang around with my sister Sarah Jean, so at least I had somebody to talk cars with when the family got together. Butch, on the other hand, was most definitely left off the whispered guest list for family gatherings on account of what a neighborhood scandal it was that he was actually living in the same house with my Aunt Rosamarina without benefit of clergy (and, to make it even more scandalous, he was rumored to still be married to that Other Woman who lived over by my old man's chemical plant in that ramshackle house with the front yard that looked like a couple planes had crashed in it).

"Tell 'em t'go fuck themselves," was the general reaction Butch expressed through my Aunt Rosamarina. Only not quite in those exact words.

I'd have to say my aunt was having what appeared to be quite a positive effect on Butch as well. She was taking him to the therapy sessions at the VA Hospital twice a week no matter whether they seemed to be doing any good or not (and whether he wanted to go or not, either!). She was also seeing to it that he took a little better care of himself and made himself a little more presentable—why, sometimes she even got him to shave two or three times in a single week! And, in return, he was sharing a bottle or two of sherry (or something slightly stronger) damn near every night and teaching her important life lessons like how to tell people to go fuck themselves. So they were both getting something out of it.

But I was always worried that Mean Marlene would come back into the picture somehow and that my dear old Aunt Rosamarina would wind up getting shafted. If, in fact, she wasn't getting shafted already. In which case she'd be getting shafted even worse. In fact, one day I even took Butch aside and asked him about it. He gave it a long, hard think, looked me right square in the eye, and told me to go fuck myself.

I guess I had it coming, too. I mean, of all the things you can't do anything about, how some people you know and like manage to make other people you know and like either happy or so forlorn and angry and miserable they're about ready to kill themselves (or each other) has to be right at the top of the list. And if you do bite the bullet and throw your two cents in, the most likely thing that's gonna happen is that *neither* of those people is going to want to know you or like you anymore. So the only thing to do is just shut your mouth, hopw for the best and look on the bright side. Praying a little can't hurt, either.

And, speaking of people you know and like making themselves happy or miserable, my other unmarried sister Mary Frances had finally gotten sick and tired of that out-in-the-vast-beyond Genius Artist boyfriend of hers, Frederick (and it was easy to see how that could happen if you'd ever met him!) and she'd moved back in with those girlfriends of hers who had the Greenwich Village apartment where Julie and Cal and me had attended that New Years' Eve bash with the great jazz band and the strange, smoky smell out on the fire escape. But my sister was never one to go for very long without somebody to thrill and excite and then, inevitably, disappoint her, and this time she'd taken up with this sawed-off Jewish political chump named Leonard Putzman, who was bald on top, shaggy on the sides, and wore a goatee "just like Lenin's." He had an I.Q. up there in the "pure genius" range but the common sense of a wooden soup spoon, and he made no bones about the fact that he was out to topple the U.S. government, replace it with a true, democratic "people's republic" (led by him, of course), socialize industry, redistribute wealth, uplift the oppressed, and right all the world's wrongs, injustices and inequalities in the process. And he'd be happy to start with you if you happened to be sitting next to him.

I think what attracted my sister to him was that he wasn't afraid to come right out and brag that he was "a Socialist" (as opposed to a "Communist," although I personally had a hard time getting the gist of the difference) and to call many of our democratically-elected government officials—including the president, vice president, and most especially Wisconsin Senator "Tailgunner Joe" McCarthy—"a bunch of lying, cheating, bourgeois, fascist, capitalist swine" at the top of his lungs to anyone who would listen while carrying protest placards through rush-hour traffic around Times Square. No question you have to be pretty damn committed to do something like that. Or maybe you just should be? But my sister really liked the idea that Leonard was planning to fix up the world for everybody (which, when you get right down to it, was mighty thoughtful of him), and you had to be impressed by the dedication and fervor with which he pursued his lofty goals, joining radical political groups and volunteering for committees and then getting into important political or philosophical differences of opinion about just exactly how the eight or ten of them should go about toppling the U.S. government and socializing industry and redistributing the wealth (plus occasional side disagreements concerning vital issues like personal hygiene and who was sleeping with whom), and so eventually and inevitably the committee would reach a massive loggerhead stalemate and break up and then the minority—sometimes even all three of them—would go off in a huff and join or form some other either more radical or less radical new group and volunteer for committees and....

Well, at least it kept them out of trouble.

But the thing I started noticing about Leonard and all the other radical socialist and communist *intelligentsia* types that my sister was now hanging around with in the cheap bistros and coffee shops of Greenwich Village was that, although they all pounded any available tabletop and spouted vehemently about how totally committed they were to their cause, not a one of them seemed to really believe they could pull it off. And of course the *reason* they couldn't pull it off—at least according to Leonard—was that Certain People in the group didn't see the Obvious Right Way to Do What Needed To Be Done. Which is another way of saying they disagreed with him. But I think that's because they were pretty darn sure in their own minds that *they* were the ones who really saw and understood the true revealed word on the Obvious Right Way to Do What Needed To Be Done. Plus there was always a lot of time devoted to squabbling over how, exactly, they were going to carve up the world and redistribute all that wealth once they got their hands on it.

All of which meant that every last one of them was pledging allegiance to something not a single one of them really believed they'd ever get done. And you could tell by how bitter and angry and cynical they all were. It made you wonder what the point was? Or it did me, anyway. But I guess that's what happens when you decide the only way to make yourself happy is to fix the entire rest of the world. It's not something you can really expect to happen, you know?

The funny part was that this Leonard Putzman was really kind of a nice guy when you were just sitting there shooting the breeze with him and he wasn't out trying to fix the world. He even brought my sister flowers on her birthday. Roses, even. But toppling the U.S. government and fixing up the world was kind of a big job and so he couldn't take a whole lot of time off. After all, there was oppression to ease and injustices to redress everywhere you looked. Not that Leonard, personally, ever had to deal with much of it. He'd managed to narrowly escape all that oppression and injustice—by the skin of his teeth, mind you!—on account of being raised in a well-to-do Jewish suburb and attending expensive private schools all his life.

And he resented it plenty, believe me!

Speaking of justice, Big Ed's (and Skippy's) Drivers' Committee Tribunal rolled around on the third Tuesday of August, and, like I said before, we all went down to offer a little moral support and have ringside seats for the fireworks. Only it turned out you couldn't *get* ringside seats seeing as how meetings of the Drivers' Committee were conducted strictly behind closed doors. But you could wait in the bar and shoot the shit until either the black or the white smoke went up. And it turned out both Big Ed and The Skipper got a huge break when Charlie Priddle didn't show up to head the lynch mob on account of he was stuck home with a high fever and a terrible case of food poisoning. It couldn't have happened to a nicer guy. And I will always believe that, somehow or some way, Big Ed was involved. It was the kind of thing certain friends of his could easily make happen. Especially if Charlie ever went out for Italian food with maybe a nice glass of wine on the side.

All of which left two of Charlie's favorite lap dogs pretty much in charge. And, typical of the kind of brains and talent Charlie Priddle regularly surrounded himself with on his favorite committees, neither one of these guys could think their way out of a brown paper bag. At least not on their own, anyway. The senior one (who worked for Lucas because he was somehow related to somebody important back in England, and had been sent over stateside after the war to get him out of everybody's hair) was an elegant, refined, well-mannered, well-dressed, proper old-school British gent named Cedric Thistlewhite, who had a marvelous sweep of gray hair, a matching mustache, could wear a silk ascot without looking foppish and had an Armstrong Siddeley Sapphire touring car as his daily driver. It was one of only a handful in the country. I remember I asked him one time at the Seneca Lodge just what the heck an Armstrong Siddeley was, and he told me: "It's for the gentleman who wouldn't presume to drive a Bentley."

"Oh? And what's a Bentley for?"

"Why, a Bentley is for the gentleman who wouldn't presume to drive a Rolls-Royce."

"Oh? And what's a Rolls-Royce for?"

"It's for the gentleman who wouldn't presume to drive, and would prefer to have his chauffeur do it for him."

In any case, put a half-bottle of scotch in him and old Cedric could go on for quite a spell about Armstrong Siddeleys. Starting with how the company first came about with the merger of two smaller car companies, Armstrong-Whitworth and Siddley-Deasy, and produced its first car in 1925. But "Armstrong-Whitworth-Siddeley-Deasy" was a bit of a mouthful (not to mention that all those chrome letters on the nose and decklid might require stiffer springs), so they pretty much flipped a coin or drew straws or something and Whitworth and Deasy were the odd men out. "Armstrong Siddeley have always built good, solid, *quality* motorcars," Cedric Thistlewhite would go on with a tear welling up in the corner of his eye. "My own dear father drove an Armstrong Siddeley Special Mk. II before the war—damn fine thing it was, too—and I myself had a Hurricane and then a Lanchester before I came over here and got the Sapphire."

By then the tear would be rolling down his cheek.

His inner circle of friends on the various SCMA steering, ruddering and Driver Tribunal committees called him "Mawky" because of the way he'd go on about his family's wonderful lineage of Armstrong Siddeleys or his dear old father who was killed in The Blitz or the lush green of the English countryside or the white cliffs of Dover or the red, red roses his dear sainted mother used to raise in the garden just outside the kitchen window at their family summer home. But, to tell the truth, besides going on and on about those things, uttering the odd *"harrumph!"* or *"tsk! tsk!"* or *"I say!"* and ordering himself another double scotch, old "Mawky" Thistlewhite couldn't pee a hole in the snow without Charlie Priddle there to unzip and hold it for him.

Word around was that he was great friends with Colin St. John. But then, Colin needed to stay on the very best of terms with the SCMA hierarchy. Not to mention wanting the very best deals and occasional extended terms on all the parts he needed from Lucas. Besides, they had a lot in common seeing as how they were both Brits and they both liked good scotch. Especially when someone else was buying. Cedric Thistlewhite's second-in-command this particular evening was the ne'er-do-well third-cousin heir to one of America's great bauxite mining fortunes, Hugh Freestone Tinpenny, who looked like the Christmas goose in a Charles Dickens story and was already half in the bag when he showed up. Or maybe even a little more than half. Hugh Freestone Tinpenny was a man of red, rosy cheeks, few words and very noisy breathing, and you could always tell when Hugh Freestone Tinpenny was in the room on account of it sounded like somebody had parked a steam engine behind the draperies. I must admit he did know quite a bit about the family business that had left him with the sort of wealth that made him terribly attractive to pretty young women even though he wasn't, and, if you asked, he'd kind of gasp and wheeze his way through stories about the great bauxite scare of ought-two, the great bauxite scandal of 1918, and of course the great bauxite hoax of '23. And that's not even mentioning the great bauxite glut of '29 that darn near ruined the company before the war came along and made his family a thousand times richer than they ever were. And they were plenty rich before. In any case, I could tell just by watching the way he gently wavered back and forth like a very fat palm tree with way too many coconuts up top that Hugh Freestone Tinpenny didn't want much more out of the evening than maybe a half dozen more nightcaps and for it to be over. So it was anybody's guess how the proceedings would turn out once the doors slowly closed on the Drivers' Committee meeting.

Only the club bylaws said you had to have three presiding club officials at a Drivers' Committee tribunal (just to make sure there were never any deadlocks, although when Charlie Priddle presided, it was inevitably always unanimous), and I was pleased to see that Cedric Thistlewhite picked none other than our old buddy Colin St. John to serve as third man. I mean, I figured Colin would think twice before dropping the axe on a good customer. Even though Big Ed hadn't been buying too many cars from him of late. In fact, I thought I even saw Colin shoot Big Ed a wink as they filed into the private meeting room where the Drivers' Committee did its business. But I couldn't be sure.

There was nothing for the rest of us to do but sit in the bar and chew the fat while we were waiting. And, you'll be happy to know, not just about cars and racing stuff, either. I mean, some of us took the time to actually read a newspaper every now and then. After all, you gotta read *something* on the john. So most of us were aware as how "Tailgunner Joe" McCarthy's assault on domestic communism was kind of running out of steam after accusing everybody and his brother in the government of being a damn red and then making the mistake of taking on the U.S. Army. And now all of a sudden his chief counsel, Roy Cohn, had up and resigned as a way to avoid getting caught in the crosshairs of public opinion himself and being maybe ruined for life (the same way he and Senator Joe had been doing to other people for months on end), and so "Tailgunner Joe" was running out of friends fast on Capitol Hill. Like rats off a sinking ship, you know? Bigger and more important news was that the last of the U.N. troops (who were mostly Americans, don't kid yourself) were finally coming home from Korea after three years of fighting, a half million dead and, as far as most of us at the bar could see, not much else accomplished.

There were car things to talk about, too, of course. Like fr'instance how the ride back from Ohio went for the four Team Passaic guys who got stuck in the Volkswagen. Amazingly, they all complained about the engine noise and the back seat legroom and the ventilation and the lack of power going through the mountains with four full-sized (or, in the case of "Fos" and Danny Poindexter, nearly-full-sized) people on board and the damn near zero luggage space up front—and then allowed as how they all *loved* it! Like I said, whatever else might be true, it was a fun car to drive.

And Danny Poindexter was kind of interested in maybe getting something like Big Ed's Arnolt-Bristol for himself, seeing as how it had the same size engine as the slightly rearranged Triumph his mother already allowed him to buy (although I'm sure she didn't know he was racing it!), but it was ever so much more stylish and expensive and exclusive. And right away the old wheels started turning, seeing as how I was pretty sure Big Ed would get bored with it on account of it didn't have enough grunt or muscle for him and here was maybe another chance to make a few bucks off a car deal. And having that brand new but slightly bent TR2 in the mix made it all the more interesting to an aspiring motor trade wheeler-dealer like myself.

About then the behind-closed-doors Drivers' Committee meeting broke up and you could tell by the scowls coming out through the doors that nobody was much happy. They'd given Big Ed a 30-day suspension—which really meant just skipping the race meet up at Thompson Speedway in Connecticut on Labor Day weekend—and slapped The Skipper's wrist with a meaningless 30-day "probation" that he still considered a disgraceful injustice. To be honest about it, they were both damn lucky that Charlie Priddle wasn't there, seeing as how Skippy would've probably gotten a life sentence and it would've been *"hanged by the neck until dead"* for Big Ed.

We all maybe should've known better than to hang around after the big Drivers' Committee tribunal was over, since everybody'd already had a few and Big Ed and The Skipper were glowering at each other like stray dogs in an alley. But, hey, we were talking cars and even current events every now and then and enjoying each other's company and for sure didn't have anything especially better (or at least more interesting) to go home to. And that would be about when we heard voices rising and squabbling going on behind us. Sure enough, it was Big Ed and Skippy again. They'd somehow circled around to that same, dumb, How Many Angels Can Dance On The Head Of A Pin argument that started it all. You know, about which was faster, The Skipper's C-Type or Big Ed's Trashwagon. And, judging by the look in their eyes and the spit stains all over Big Ed's collar, this time they might really come to blows over it. Which would have been bad for Skipper seeing as how he would most likely get his nose broken, his ears cauliflowered, a matching set of black eyes and all of his front teeth knocked out. But it would be even worse for Big Ed, since it would look more like a wholesale beating than a fair fight and he might very easily lose his racing ticket forever for doing such a thing at a club meeting. And that's not even considering the possible civil and criminal charges that might follow.

So I stepped in.

"Look," I said in the most reasonable voice since that Dutchman offered the Indians twenty-four bucks worth of beads for Manhattan, "you're making a scene here, standing at the bar yelling at each other."

"It's okay with me if we take it outside," Big Ed growled without taking his eyes off The Skipper. The look in them was very scary indeed.

"That suits me *fine!*" The Skipper whined right back. You had to give the little weasel credit for balls, no question about it. But I guess if you're genuinely nuts, bravery is no real problem. In fact, maybe it's not even bravery at all.

"Going outside won't settle anything," I argued. "That won't have anything to do with whose car is faster."

They both swiveled their eyes towards me.

"What you need," I told them as I fumbled for ideas, "is, umm, some kind of, umm..." I was about to say 'race,' but then I realized they were already racing each other on a fairly regular basis. Besides, what with driver talent and skill to consider (not that either one of them had much to speak of) that still wouldn't tell you for sure who had the faster car.

"What we need is a *bet!*" Big Ed snarled defiantly.

"You got it!" The Skipper spit right back.

And that's how, on around towards midnight in a swank hotel bar in Manhattan on the 17th of August, 1954, Reginald "Skippy" Welcher wagered Big Ed Baumstein a fat thousand dollars Ca$h American that his C-Type Jaguar was faster than Big Ed's Jagillac-cum-Trashwagon that I'd put together with my own two hands.

We all drank to it, too.

23: California Horsepower

Gossip about the bet between Big Ed and Skippy Welcher spread through the sportycar community in and around the greater metropolitan New York area like a bacterial infection and, like any great and stupid challenge that too many people have heard about, it started snowballing and developing a life of its own and, generally speaking, turning into something that would, one way or the other, come to pass. Not to mention that a thou$and bucks was a lot of money back in 1954. Even if you could afford it.

Only problem was, "faster" can mean a lot of different things to a lot of different people. Fr'instance, "faster" on a normal SCMA weekend usually meant who could make a lap around some makeshift pylon, trash barrel and haybale "race circuit" on a bunch of concrete SAC-base runways in the least number of minutes, seconds and tenths. At the Twenty-Four Hours of Le Mans, you had to stretch that same idea out over an 8.384-mile loop of undulating French country roads and two complete tours around your wristwatch. Over at the Indianapolis 500 on the first day of the first weekend of qualifying, it came down to who had the best car, the best engine and the best setup (plus the best break on the weather and track conditions and a driver who could hold his breath for ten miles) for threading the needle around four high-speed, hair-raising laps of the biggest, most glamorous and equally most dangerous oval of them all. To those drag racers who were starting to run standing-start, one-on-one, head-to-head quarter-mile shootouts against each other out in California, it meant who could get the nose of their car from sitting dead still at the flash of the green to the finish line first. So it was all about acceleration and reaction times, really. That and not jumping the start. To the wild and woolly guys who ran *La Carrera*, it was a much longer, more drawn-out question of who could get from one blessed end of Mexico to the other quicker than everybody else without going so fast or being so brutal on the equipment or simply running out of lucky pills that you ran out of near-misses and didn't make it to the end.

So, like I said, whose car is "faster" could mean a lot of different things. And, if you wanted to make a really fair test out of it, you had to figure something that would pretty much take driver skill out of the equation. Which was always a good idea anyway when you were talking about the likes of Skippy Welcher and Big Ed Baumstein. And so, in a meeting of "seconds" that included myself and Milton Fitting and Tommy Edwards and Hugh Freestone Tinpenny to arrange the duel between the C-Type and the Trashwagon, we went round and round quite a few times before finally settling on the agreed-upon format:

Top speed.

Plain and simple.

And, as everybody and their brother knows, there is only one place in America where you have all the room in the world to let those carburetor throats open wide and suck to their hearts' content and allow the engine to creep and struggle and strain its way up to those final few rpm and accurate, checked-and-certified timing equipment that will capture that blinding flash of speed and chisel it indelibly into the granite of history—to three decimal places and going both directions, if you want to make it stick—and that place, of course, is the Bonneville Salt Flats out in Utah. And, as fate would have it, the annual Bonneville Speed Week time trial runs were scheduled to start the very next week!

Although there were of course a few little details to work out....

"You're going *where??!!*" Julie screamed at me.

"Uhh, Bonneville. Out in Utah. See, Big E—"

"Utah??!!"

"Yeah. See Bi—"

"What the hell is out in UTAH??!!"

"Well, they've got Mormons and the Great Salt Lake and..."

"Don't get cute with *me,* Palumbo!"

So I explained to her as best I could about Big Ed and the bet with Skippy and how Bonneville, Utah, was really the best place to settle it. Maybe the *only* place to settle it. And then I told her the other part. That Big Ed had promised me a full half-interest in the thousand-buck prize—that would be five hundred dollars right direct in Julie's and my pockets!—if we managed to pull it off and beat The Skipper's C-Type. That would be the biggest one-lump pile of cold, solid cash we'd ever laid our hands on. And that softened her up just a little.

"How long will you be gone?"

That was another thing I didn't know yet. I mean, I'd looked in our Rand McNally road atlas and, best as I could figure, it was a solid three days of driving—maybe even three-and-a-half—each way to get out to Bonneville and back, since it's right smack-dab on the Utah/Nevada state line a couple hours west of Salt Lake City. On top of which, from what I'd learned from a few phone calls—including one to Chuck Day, that hotrod/sportycar wrench wizard from California who I'd met at Elkhart Lake and who I furthermore knew had been to Bonneville a time or two—you don't just show up, take the spare out of the trunk, fold the windshield down, make your run, load everything back up and head for home. No, there was apparently a lot more to it than that.

So, even though it was looming up barely a week or so away, the trip to Bonneville was taking on all the characteristics of a Major Campaign. We even toyed with the idea of trying to ship the Trashwagon out by train, but there was a lot of stuff I needed to do on it before we left and it maybe would've been a great idea if only I'd had more time. As it was, I wound up getting a meeting together with all my guys and told them I had to take off for maybe as much as ten days but that Julie would be by every day to check things out and keep her eye on the till and that, if anything needed settling or deciding, I'd make sure to call in and talk to Butch and J.R. at least three times every day.

What more could I do?

And then I had to hustle over to Big Ed's to get his pickup truck (he was planning to fly out and meet us there, natch) and over to this friend of his in the scrap business' place to borrow a decent trailer (for a change) and then over by the duplex to pick up the suitcase of clothes and the paper bag of sandwiches Julie'd packed for me—*"You'd sure as hell better come back with five hundred bucks in your pocket!"* she told me in no uncertain terms as she kissed me goodbye at the door—and then it was back over to the Sinclair to start loading things up and calling Cal to make sure he'd be there in time so's we could miss rush-hour traffic and then, in this frantic, goofy whirlwind of activity that seemed to have no top, bottom or center to it, I suddenly found myself in Big Ed's pickup cab with Cal

Carrington on the seat next to me and the Trashwagon strapped onto the trailer behind, heading southwest on the New Jersey Turnpike towards the longest damn road trip of our lives!

You have to understand that there's a certain pace you have to find for long-distance, over-the-road travel—truckers know all about it—where you sort of lengthen out your stride and your attention span enough to cover the whole, stretched-out expanse of hills and mountains and forests and farmland and big-time cities and little whistle-stop towns and steel mills and milking barns and cement plants and cemeteries and kids on bicycles with dogs chasing after them that make up this great and expansive country of ours. You've got to work hard at taking it easy if you want to take it all in and not have it turn into drudgery. But it's only the *new* and *different* that really startles you and fires you up, and, unless you find that pace I was talking about, eventually the miles start wearing you down like some kind of Chinese Water Torture.

Cal was a pretty good guy to travel with, on account of he loved driving and long distances and that special sense of freedom you get out on the road—hey, as long as you keep moving, nothing can touch you—and we also talked about a lot of stuff from time to time. About how desperately he wanted to become a *real* racing driver and how much that meant to him. "This is the only thing in my life I've ever been really serious about," he said dreamily as he cruised our rig smoothly, almost gently through the eastern Pennsylvania mountains in the middle of the first night. "Hell, it's the only thing I've ever been really *good* at…."

We talked about my life, too. About Julie and her mom and my sisters and family and little Vincenzo—who I was already missing—and how the kid in me had suddenly found itself all sealed up inside this apparently adult human being that actually seemed to know where it was going and what it was thinking of doing next. And yet, deep down inside, I knew I was still just that same little kid, you know?

I asked Cal about that, too. About what was going on with him and girls and dating and stuff and maybe even one day having a family. He allowed as how he always had these spoiled party girls from the social set he could go out with—hell, aunts and cousins and friends from his parents' country clubs were always trying to fix him up—and sometimes he even did and some of them even put out. But they were all silly and petty and didn't care about anything important, and it was just too much effort to try and act interested. He also kind of hinted that he thought a lot of my sister Mary Frances—even though it was clear they were like oil and water whenever they were around each other on account of they weren't interested in any of the same things and, more importantly, they were too much alike—because he liked her spark and spirit and the defiance that flared up in her eyes anytime she figured somebody who didn't deserve to was talking down to her. "She's always looking for something in these weird guys she meets," I tried to explain, "but the truth is she knows more than any of them." And then I kind of dropped my guard and told Cal about the baby that never was and our trip together in Old Man Finzio's tow truck to that grim, silent alley behind Park Avenue. Geez, it seemed like an awfully long time ago. When I was done, I felt kind of empty inside. And then I looked over and said, "Outside of me and Julie, you're the only one who knows. And if you ever tell *anybody*…."

"Don't worry about it. I know how to keep a secret." He said it too easily, though, and that worried me. I figured I needed a secret from him, just to keep the scales balanced. And I told him so.

"I don't have any secrets," he said matter-of-factly. "I'm completely transparent."

"Iron-clad is more like it. Nobody gets inside you."

He looked out at the oncoming headlights and licked his lips. "One person did."

"Who's that?"

"You know."

"I do?"

"Sure."

I only had to think about it for a second. "It's that Italian girl whose father owns the restaurant. The one you met on New Year's Eve."

"Angelina Scalabrini," he nodded, savoring each syllable.

"But you haven't seen her for more than a year."

"Nobody has."

"Whatever happened to her?"

"I guess her mom was some kind of minor-league singer or actress or something and she took Angelina out to California to try and make a star out of her."

"How'd you find that out?"

"I got a letter from her once. Not really a letter. Just a postcard."

"What kind of postcard?"

"Just a typical California tourist postcard. You know. *'Wish you were here'* and a picture of some palm trees or something."

"Didn't you ever write her back?"

"No return address."

"How about her father?"

"Don't really know. I used to go over to his restaurant now and then when I had money and spread a few tips around to find something out, but it closed a few months back and I haven't really gone looking for him."

"That's too bad."

"Yeah. It was a damn good restaurant. It'd been there since before the war. I think his folks used to run it."

"That's a shame." I thought about it for awhile. "You ever think about going out to California and trying to look her up?"

"Nah, what for? Even if I could find her, what would I do then? Show up on her doorstep like some raggedy lost puppy and beg her to let me inside? Nah, there's no future in making an ass out of yourself like that."

Like I said, iron-clad. But at least we were even on secrets.

It was quiet for a few hours after that—just kind of a nice, sweet, melancholy feeling as we rolled down out of the mountains and on into the rolling farmland of Ohio while dawn was coming up behind us and spreading its rich, golden light over the corn and alfalfa fields. We filled up and got a couple bacon-and-egg sandwiches to go at a truck stop in Zanesville—once you get that good, long-distance pace going, you don't want to stop for any longer than you have to on account of you don't want to lose it—and Cal bought himself a cheap tin harmonica out of a little wicker basket up by the cash register. Or he said he paid for it, anyway. I took over at the wheel and Cal just kind of leaned himself up against the doorjamb and ran that thing slowly back and forth in his mouth for the next couple hours. I think what he had in mind was the sort of plaintive, mournful tune the grizzled old cowpoke in those black-and-white westerns plays for the battle-weary cavalry troops gathered around the campfire...generally just before he gets shot right through the gizzard with the first Indian arrow of the next attack. Only Cal's version came out more like a duck and an alleycat being fed into a sausage grinder.

"That's awful," I told him honestly.

"It'll get better."

"I'm not sure I can last that long."

Which is why I made a slight detour through Columbus to stop by Bob Fergus' dealership to see about maybe picking up a cheap radio for the truck. Luckily Bob was there and he was happy to help us out. "I think I have just what you're looking for out back." He led us around the side of his building—geez, he had a lot of Volkswagens!—and there on the business end of a tow hook was a damn near brand-new Volkswagen Beetle that'd obviously had itself a pretty bad wreck. In fact, it was worse than pretty bad, seeing as how some guy and his daughter got killed in it. You could tell from all the dried blood and the shattered windshield and how the license plate was mashed damn near back to the dashboard, Which was mashed damn near into the back seat. I mean, there wasn't an awful lot in front of you in a Volkswagen—except for the gas tank over your knees, that is—and this one got folded up pretty comprehensively when it got into an argument with a delivery truck over who had the right-of-way. Then again, that doesn't mean the guy and his daughter would've come out any better in a damn Cadillac sedan. Sometimes it's just a question of whether you get crushed to death by the other fellow's car or your own.

"You can have the radio out of this one if you've got the stomach for it. We're cutting it up into parts anyway, and the glass in the radio is busted so I can't very well resell it." Bob Fergus had a very matter-of-fact attitude about it. But then he used to be a fighter pilot, and you learn pretty fast in that line of work the difference between what's possible and practical and all that other stuff that you can't do anything about.

So I got my tools out and kind of crawled in through the shattered side window to get the knobs and nuts off and then pried what was left of the front hood off and got it out. It didn't take long at all. I pirated the antenna, too. But I had to buy a speaker from Bob's parts department and borrow some wire and connectors from one of his mechanics, and then we were on our way with Cal driving while I fished under the pickup's dash for a hot wire and rigged up a ground wire and set about making the radio work. It looked a little crude once I was finished—especially the antenna jammed into the vent window on my side and held down with about four pounds of tape—but it worked and we could at least listen to a little music as we drove across country. Or at least sometimes we could, seeing as how the reception wasn't real good out in the boondocks and stations would get all crackly with static and fade in and out on us all the time. But even that was better than Cal and his old cowpoke harmonica. And sometimes at night, we'd all of a sudden be pulling in big-city stations like *"the 50,000-watt, clear channel voice"* of WGN in Chicago or KAAY down in Little Rock clear as a bell, and we'd marvel over how the heck that could happen. But then Chicago or St. Louis or wherever would start to get all fuzzy and crackly and then you'd twist the dial and try to pick up Davenport or Des Moines or even Denver. Which was no good if we were trying to listen to a variety show or, worse yet, follow one of those creepy radio mystery plays like *The Shadow....*

"...Who knows what evil lurks in the hearts of men?"

But then, right when it was getting good, you'd lose it. Or get interrupted by a damn Wildroot Cream Oil hair tonic commercial.

Which is maybe why most big-city stations were simply playing music with a break for news, weather and sports every hour. And the amazing part was that most of those stations—all over the whole blessed country!—were playing the same exact music. Like *"Hey There, You with the Stars in Your Eyes"* and *"This Ole House"* by Rosemary Clooney and *"Three Coins in a Fountain"* from that mush movie that Julie kept asking me to take her to and *"Hernando's Hideaway"* from *The Pajama Game* and that infectious, whistle-along, Val-de-ri-Val-de-ah *"The Happy Wanderer"* tune that Cal and I sang along with maybe the first two-hundred-and-forty-seven times we heard it but then started switching off after that. There was *"Moonlight and Roses"* and the instrumental version of the theme song from that John Wayne movie, *"The High and Mighty"* (which, by the way, you should never go see if you're planning an airline trip anywhere), and a pumping, thumping new chart climber titled *"Shake, Rattle and Roll"* from a band that'd played a few dates around the New York/New Jersey area called Bill Haley and the Comets. But the biggest song in the country—the one every D.J. and his brother was playing over and over and over again—was this damn near incomprehensible thing with hardly any words to it (or not many you could understand, anyway) titled *"Sh-Boom!"* by a group called the Crew Cuts. Still, I thought it was pretty catchy.

"That stuff hurts my ears," Cal groused.

"It's better than your damn harmonica."

"Maybe it is. But those guys are getting *paid.*"

"If I win that five hundred bucks, I'll pay you *not* to play."

The two of us traded off driving every once in awhile and slept—or tried to kid ourselves into thinking we were sleeping—along the way, and only stopped for gas and to pick up some sandwiches or something and take a commode or urinal break as necessary. To be honest, I'd never been further west than that time Tommy Edwards and me drove the first two C-Type Jaguars in the whole damn country up to Elkhart Lake and, even though I'd looked in the road atlas plenty of times before we left, I was amazed at just how much blessed *country* there is out there in the good old U.S. of A. And also how much of it looks so much the same from about the foothills of Eastern Pennsylvania until you see the Rockies looming up out of the mist on the horizon about an hour or so east of Denver. Makes you realize just how small and densely packed New York is. Kind of like a cage full of rats.

And nothing you ever knew back there in New York or New Jersey really prepares you for your first face-to-face look at the Rockies. There's something wrong with you if it doesn't make you go all hollow inside. We stopped for a gas fill-up on the west side of Denver—the snowcapped Rockies towering off to the west of us like the very judgment of God—and the old-timer in a cowboy hat who ran the place suggested we'd make better time by doubling back and then heading north towards Cheyenne and then west through Rawlins. But we figured he didn't know what he was talking about on account of any fool could see the straight-through-the-mountains run was much shorter on the map. Although, if you think about it, a road map only shows east-west, north-south and left-right sorts of distances. Up and down—and especially *way* up and *way* down—doesn't much register. Or at least not for the first couple hours, anyway.

But I was kind of glad we made the wrong choice, since it was really something to see. Especially snow at the side of the road at the end of August and scenic overlooks where you could pull over and stare halfway back to the old George Washington Bridge. Or that's what it seemed like, anyway. It was also something to see how the constant climbing and the high altitude just sucked all the suds out of the pickup's motor, and it got to where the engine was pinging and the radiator was steaming and the fuel was damn near percolating in the carburetor. Cal even suggested we take the Trashwagon off the back and one of us could drive it to kind of ease the load. But I knew who he meant by "one of us" and I was damned if I was gonna let him enjoy the Trashwagon on this fantastic road while I struggled along with the pickup and an empty trailer dancing around behind it. So instead I had him pull over and I retarded the timing just a tad. Which didn't do much for what little zip was left in the engine, but at least I hoped we wouldn't burn a piston.

The ugly part was that I knew the scariest and most difficult section was still ahead of us. I mean, whatever goes up must eventually come down, and I was pretty darn sure the brakes on the pickup wouldn't much fancy the steep downgrades that went on forever or the trailer in back trying to sneak its way around us like a cracked whip anytime we got on them hard. I took over from Cal at the highest point at Trail Ridge (12,183 feet according to our map), and then just took it real easy going down and even pulled over where I could to let the brakes cool a little. Even so, I was smelling baked lining material plenty and standing on the damn pedal with both feet by the time we hit the next place where the road finally flattened out again.

We went through Salt Lake City a little after midnight and it seemed pretty quiet. Then again, those Mormons aren't exactly known for their wild parties and nightlife, are they? And of course Cal knew the whole story about how Brigham Young and his followers and a few spare wives came out that way looking for a place to stay and freedom to live and worship the way they wanted to, and he picked Salt Lake City on account of he could turn his wagon around on Main Street. But then the locusts came and ate all their crops and they were thinking they were going to have to leave when—just in the nick of time!—a huge flock of seagulls arrived and ate all the locusts and then of course they shit all over the desert out a ways west of Salt Lake City and that's why the salt flats are all white. Or at least that was Cal's version, anyway.

But you couldn't really see all that much on account of it was still dark when we rolled into Wendover on the Utah/Nevada border an hour or so before dawn. There wasn't much in the way of lights—or anything else, for that matter—in the town of Wendover. Just the biggest damn expanse of nighttime sky I'd ever seen in my life. It was actually kind of eerie, having traveled all that distance across maybe three-quarters of the whole blessed country and then finally arriving at our destination and switching the pickup's engine off and realizing how really strange and numb and floaty it felt not to be moving any more. In my guts it was like we were still on the road, and every time I'd close my eyes and try to drop off to sleep, I'd see oncoming headlights on the insides of my eyelids and startle myself awake to keep from doing what I'd done with Big Ed's Arnolt-Bristol all over again. Besides, I wasn't really tired. Not really....

The roar of a GMC-supercharged Oldsmobile Rocket V8 with dump pipes blasted me awake like a land mine going off under the seat upholstery, and I was suddenly looking out the windshield at the biggest, widest, flattest, most desolate stretch of landscape I'd ever seen in my life. It was more flat and barren than any desert I'd ever seen (or seen pictures of, anyway), and the landscape had all the color and charm of the residue in the bottom of a Bromo Seltzer glass as far as you could see in every direction. Water mirages rippled the atmosphere off in the distance on imagined horizons and, beyond that, rising out of a mist as thick as a rainstorm, this towering, purplish mountain range shoved itself into the sky like huge, crude spikes hammered upwards through the earth's crust. None of it looked real at all, and I half expected to see a flying saucer passing overhead or one of those fizzy, crackly little *Flash Gordon* space rockets to come circling in for a landing....

"Hey! Welcome to Bonneville."

I wheeled around and there in front of me was none other than Chuck Day, the California sportycar wrench and hot-rodder I'd met at Elkhart Lake in '52. He was still chewing gum and sporting a blond crewcut and looking calm and unexcitable as ever.

"Good t'see you."

"Good t'see you, too." His eyes went back to the trailer. "You build that thing?"

I nodded sheepishly.

"I looked it over. It's really not too bad underneath." He shot me a sideways look and as much of a grin as you could ever get out of Chuck Day. "You're not much of a body-and-fender man, are you?"

I felt my face flush. "Aw, I was in kind of a hurry. I figured I'd go back later and maybe nicen it up a little, but Big E—I mean, Mr. Baumstein..."

"I remember him."

"Well, those asshole armband idiots from the SCMA absolutely *hated* it. So now Big Ed won't let me change it."

"Just to piss them off?"

"You got it."

His grin spread out into a genuine smile. "I like it!"

"Yeah," I told him. "But I'm gonna have to do something before the next race. Paint it at least. I guess they passed a new rule that you can't have any primer showing."

"Just for you guys?"

"I guess."

"Boy, you must've *really* pissed them off!" he said with obvious admiration.

We walked back and around the trailer and, like anybody who's built their own racecar and is showing it off to another top wrench, all I could see was what I should've done differently. But Chuck seemed pretty impressed. "I like this," he said, pointing to the trashcan lid Continental kit on the back deck. "It's a nice touch."

Turns out Chuck was there with some of his Sepulveda Boulevard hotrod buddies who were running a wing tank with a hopped-up flathead Ford in back and also, of all people, Ernesto Julio.

'Ernesto Julio's here at Bonneville?" I asked incredulously. I mean, it didn't really look like his kind of place.

Chuck nodded. "He just took delivery of a new Ferrari road car a month or so back—a 375 America coupe with a 4.5-liter engine—and he wanted to see what it could do. I mean *really* do. You can't go by the speedometer in a Ferrari."

"You can't?"

"Nah. It's like their horsepower numbers. Lotta horses, but they tend to run small."

"So I've heard."

"And *this*," he continued, sweeping his eyes around the endless Bonneville horizon, "is the world's greatest no-bullshit dynomometer."

"It is?"

"Yes sir," Chuck nodded affirmatively. "Better than any test rig, better than any road course, better than any drag strip."

"Why's that?"

"Well, first off you've got the room to really stretch a motor out. Right out to the edge of what it'll do."

I could see that.

"And the other thing is the difference between *acceleration* and *top speed.*"

"Could'ja maybe explain that a little?"

"Sure. Acceleration—once you've got traction, anyway—is all about multiplied torque against weight."

I could see that.

"But top speed is all about horsepower against frontal area. You look around at the lakesters and streamliners here. None of 'em are built light like you'd do a dragster or a road course car. But they're sure as heck skinny and slick."

Looking around under all the trailer awnings and suspended tarps in the paddock, I could see what he was talking about.

"And speaking of that," he added, walking around to the front of the Trashwagon, "you really oughta do something about the radiator hanging out in the breeze like that."

"I think we need it t'keep it cool," I told him.

"Not here you don't. You're not gonna be runnin' all that long at a stretch. Why, a lot of the drag-race guys don't even run radiators at all any more."

"They *don't?*" I asked incredulously.

"What for? At a strip y'start it and get it up to temperature and then you only run for maybe fifteen seconds or so. Who needs a radiator?"

Already the wheels were turning.

Who else should I meet out on the salt but Tommy Edwards. Of all people! He was out there with the Healey crew again, who'd come out with some more rather "special" Healey Hundreds to try and set a few more World Records and grab another fistful of publicity. "Hey, good to see you," I told him.

"Good to see you, too. What brings you out to this garden spot of the west?"

"Oh, Big Ed and Skippy Welcher have a bet going about whose car is faster."

"I heard about it. But I'm actually a bit surprised you came all this way."

"On short notice, too. But it's a thousand bucks."

"Really?"

"Yep," I nodded, "cash on the barrelhead."

"Who's holding the money?"

"I don't think Big Ed's got that worked out yet."

"Well, he'd better, or you'll never see a nickel of it. At least if you win, that is."

I looked him in the eye. "We didn't come here to lose," I told him.

"You know, this isn't a bit like circuit racing. It's a whole different thing, Buddy. And there are lots of little tricks to it. Maybe I should introduce you to some of the Healey boys. They've made a pretty decent show of these things."

"Geez, would you?"

"No problem at all. Glad to do it. Besides," he leaned in closer and whispered, "there's an awful lot of standing around with nothing to do here at Bonneville. Fresh company is always welcome." He led me over by the Healey trailer, which had a big, slanted tarp awning off the side and angled to protect the cars and crew from the morning sun while the trailer itself blocked the even hotter afternoon variety.

"This is a pretty nice setup," I told him.

"Well, we're not exactly raw hands when it comes to making the best of desert conditions, are we? Just ask old Erwin Rommel."

There were two Healeys under the awning, a fairly standard-looking Hundred with a couple extra slots under the grille to feed air to an oil cooler but a bunch of really special hardware under the hood including an all-alloy cylinder head with bigger ports and valves and a hotter camshaft and a cold-air box for the bigger S.U. carburetors. "That's the prototype for the new 100S competition model," Tommy half-whispered. Like somebody might be listening, you know? "It's a hell of a car, really. Lighter than the standard model, disc brakes all 'round and uprated suspension underneath, four-speed gearbox with overdrive plus a solid 130 horsepower and bags of bloody torque. Oh, it won't be giving the Ferraris or the D-Types any frights for overall wins, but it'll be in there at the end and surprise an awful lot of people." He looked at me and smiled. "It's a bloody great thing to drive, too."

But I was more interested in the thing parked next to it: a kind of Healey Hundred streamliner with a long, smooth nose tacked on the front and an even longer, sleeker tail section behind the rear wheels. It had a neat-looking driver headrest with a fin on the back and a plexiglass canopy that made it look like a jet fighter. "That one's got a supercharged engine under the hood." He leaned in even closer and whispered: "They say it's got more than 200 bloody horsepower."

Then Tommy introduced me around and I actually met Donald Healey him-self—who was even going to do some of the driving, can you believe it?—his son, Geoff, who pretty much ran the "Special Test" Healey factory racing program, their ace wrench Roger Menadue and a couple of the other drivers. Including this lanky Texan in bib overalls with lots of curly hair, a slow drawl, an easy laugh and a handsome, Dean Martin kind of smile that put you at ease in a heartbeat. You could tell Tommy really liked him. "And this supposed gentleman is Carroll Shelby." Carroll stuck out his hand. "He's a bloody chicken farmer by trade, but he occasionally attempts to moonlight as a racing driver."

"Howdy. Nice meetin' ya," Carroll grinned. "And don't take no crap off this limey sumbitch. You listen t'these guys long enough, they'll have y'thinkin' it was them saved *our* bacon in the damn war, 'steada the other way 'round."

"They can't help it," I tossed in. "They've just got that one little island and I think it's given them kind of an inferiority complex."

"I wouldn't be a'tall surprised."

"Well," Tommy answered with a sarcastic edge, "we surely have nothing as vast and empty and godforsaken as this bloody place."

"Hey," Carroll argued patriotically, "this is the best damn racetrack in the whole world."

"It is?" I asked.

"Sure it is. You can go as fast as you want for as long as you want and there's nothing to hit for fifty miles."

I could see his point.

"Plus it's got the one thing that every great racetrack needs."

"What's that?"

"Nobody around t'complain about the noise!"

There were actually quite a few Brits at Bonneville that year, seeing as how MG had sent a brand new, knee-high streamliner over called the EX-179, and they had that Captain George Eyston we'd seen at Sebring there to drive it, along with that expatriate-Brit Californian with the hawk nose and gunfighter eyes named Ken Miles. Miles had been making quite a name for himself with an MG special out on the west coast, and you could see right away he was the real thing. Like Austin-Healey, the MG folks wanted to sell as many cars as they could here in America and take as many of those solid Yankee greenbacks as they could back to England. And they'd learned that the most crucial single question asked in driveways and at curbsides and out by the pump islands at gas stations all across America amounted to three simple words:

"Wot'll she do?"

And both MG and Austin-Healey were keen as hell to give those slack-jawed colonial yokels something to talk about.

My friend Chuck Day was helping out a little with another British car, a pret-ty little motorcycle-engined Cooper streamliner in light blue and white that the owner—another guy from California who'd actually gone to England to pick it up from the Cooper factory—was planning to run in three different classes with three different engines. And that of course meant an awful lot of wrench work and engine-swapping. But, as I was soon to find out, that's pretty much the norm out at Bonneville anyway.

I'd have to say I picked up a few insider tips from the Healey guys and Chuck Day about things I could do to maybe make the Trashwagon a little faster for our big showdown with The Skipper. So as soon as I got everything unhitched, I sent Cal to take the racecar through tech inspection—and these guys made the tight-asses of the SCMA look like amateurs—while I took the pickup into Wendover to try and find a gas station or scrap yard that might have a little smaller radiator I could maybe make fit and some thin sheetmetal—preferably aluminum—that I could use to make a full-length bellypan under the car. I didn't have a lot of time, either, seeing as how The Skipper was sure to show up pretty soon and I didn't think he'd be real pleased with the idea that I was rebuilding the car a little espe-cially for Bonneville.

Fortunately Wendover wasn't much of a town and had accumulated quite a bit of automotive scrap over the years. I mean, if you've got a cheap, piece-of-shit car that's not worth repairing—or that you don't have money to fix—and it craps out in a Godforsaken place like Wendover, Utah, you don't have much choice but to sell it to the local garage for bus fare or just leave it where it lies. Plus the salt is pretty rough on body panels, so local cars tend to rot right down to the pave-ment around all their mechanical bits. I managed to find a perfect little radiator out of a derelict Crosley (albeit, like the rest of the car, with a few serious holes that looked surprisingly similar in diameter to .22 caliber rifle bullets), but I got the guy at the gas station to borrow me his torch and some brazing rod and I just plugged 'em up. I mean, it was just like Chuck said: We wouldn't be needing a lot of cooling because the engine wouldn't be running all that long. I was also planning—as Chuck advised—to fit a bigger water pump pulley if I could find one and run the belt real loose. And maybe even pull the guts out of the genera-tor if I had a chance. As for the belly pan, I couldn't find any sheet aluminum, but I did locate some thin galvanized tin from a couple big old metal signs like they put up on barns and fences and stuff out by the highway. These particular ones were for some very special Christmas and Easter week shows by the Mormon Tabernacle Choir over in Salt Lake City.

Back out at the salt flats I got the radiators swapped (with the help of the Healey guys and Chuck Day, who helped me make a few neck-down adaptors and some mounting brackets that were actually a lot neater and better engineered than the ones I'd originally cobbled together myself back at the Sinclair) and the new one spray-painted black so's you could hardly tell unless you knew what you were looking for. But it took damn near a foot of width out of the frontal area, and that had to be a good thing. Oh, and I pulled the fan blades off, too, while I was at it.

Then Chuck and Roger Menadue helped me cut up those big, sheet-tin Mormon Tabernacle Choir Christmas and Easter Show highway signs to make a fairly decent bellypan that went from the front of the frame rails all the way back to where the front of the rear leaf springs anchor with just a nice, rectangular cutout for the bot-tom of the oilpan and a kind of rounded, triangular one for the bellhousing.

"You better drill some holes in it around the firewall," Chuck Day suggested.

"Why's that? Won't it spoil the airflow under the car?"

"Well, if the engine blows or springs a leak or something, you're liable to have all kinds of gas and oil spewing out that just might catch fire. You want to be carting that stuff along with you at a hundred-and-fifty-plus or let it bleed out on the salt?"

"You got any larger drill bits?" I asked after thinking it over.

We put another, smaller belly panel under the fuel tank (this one with *lots* of holes along the rear edge!) and right about then is when The Skipper and Milton Fitting showed up in the C-Type, both of them wearing these goofy red-felt "Souvenir of Estes Park, Colorado" cowboy hats with white lettering and trim. Then again, the C-Type didn't have anything much in the way of weather protection and even less when it came to shielding your head from the sun, and these were the only hats they could find with both a wide brim all the way around and a little cord chin-strap deal with a slip-up Indian bead to keep them from blowing right off your head when you got up to anything over forty miles-per-hour. They still got quite a bit of sun between the East Coast and Estes Park, Colorado, and Milton and Skippy's faces were both about the same color as those hats. You had to kind of give them credit for making the trip straight through in the C-Type, but then The Skipper started in bragging about how fast they made it and it occurred to me all over again that it's probably easy to do stuff like that if you're just plain nutty.

"Made the whole trip in forty hours flat!" The Skipper lied through his teeth. "Cops chased us a couple times, but we just fed 'em our fumes. Left 'em in the dust. Blew 'em in the weeds. Sucked their—*heh heh*—headlamps out."

Now everybody knows there's no way in hell to drive from New York City to Wendover, Utah in forty hours without rocket assist, but there just wasn't any point in calling him on it.

"Yessir, I had her flat to the floor in top from one end of Kansas to the other. I'd say we were averaging at least a hundred and sixty. Came through the Pennsylvania mountains flat in top, too. Hit a hundred-and-eighty or so on the downgrades...."

He was just *so* full of shit.

And that made it even more important that we beat him here at Bonneville. Not to mention the money, which, after some heated haggling, had been turned over to Tommy Edwards for safekeeping until the thing got settled. Only things didn't look too rosy for us at all after the first series of runs. What with the altitude and all, The Skipper's C-Type wheezed through the traps at a less-than-startling 146.325 mph. But the Trashwagon was even worse, struggling hard to top 138. To be honest, it sure sounded to me like Big Ed was pedaling out of it about halfway through the run, and I found out why when he came back from halfway to the horizon with his face about the same color as the surrounding salt. "What's wrong?" I asked him.

"I dunno. It felt like the steering went out...."

I reached in and twisted the wheel and watched how both front tire treads swiveled from left to right just like they were supposed to. "Looks fine to me," I told him.

"Well, maybe it came back, see?" he grumbled, looking very agitated indeed.

I was kind of thinking that maybe the raw speed just spooked him, you know? "Here," he protested like he knew exactly what I was thinking. *"You* try the sonofabitch!"

"I'll drive it for you!" Cal offered eagerly before Big Ed's words even dissipated into the atmosphere. Hell, he'd drive anything—any place, any time—so long as he could keep his foot mashed down, shift and steer. He was what Tommy and all his pilot buddies call "a natural-born stick-and-rudder man," and there was simply nothing else in his life that he could do as well or that made him feel anywhere near as good. Or as at peace with himself, if you want the strange, ironic truth of it.

Which is one of the reasons Cal was so eager to take that hellishly long road trip and come out to Bonneville with me. Not that he had anything better to do. Because you've got a lot of heavy-duty racing people of all possible breeds and species out at Bonneville. Plus a lot of waiting time and sitting around time between runs. I mean, for an honest-to-goodness, World Record top-speed run, you want the time of day to be right and the wind to be right and the temperature to be right and even the blessed salt to be right—and believe me, it changes!—plus you've gotta present your car to the officials for a pretty serious once-over before and after every run to make sure you haven't slyly slipped a bigger motor in when nobody was looking. And don't think people haven't tried.

But the point is that you do a lot of standing and sitting around and shooting the breeze at Bonneville, and you find pretty quick that you're kind of all brothers out there—even the people running in your own same class!—and that the *real* enemy is the salt and the clocks and the damn atmosphere trying to hold you back. So you make a lot of friends and do a lot of jawing and supposing and telling of stories and lies and general bench racing. And it's also a good place to chat people up, if that's what you have in mind. Which is why Cal was hovering around Ernesto Julio's ear every chance he got and casually mentioning what a swell driver he was and all the races and hillclimbs he'd won (or almost won until something bad happened) and how, if Ernesto Julio ever needed the seat cushion upholstery in one of his new Ferrari race cars kept warm, he'd be only too happy to oblige. And when he wasn't over filling Ernesto Julio's ears with honey and wildflowers, you'd see him grinding on Big Ed about letting him out for a record run in the Trashwagon. Cal figured it might help him out a little career-wise if he notched up some impressive, three-digit numbers for himself across the salt at Bonneville.

Only having Cal drive was no good on account of he didn't really have a lot more mechanical savvy than Big Ed and so he really wouldn't know what it was or what to look for afterwards if there was indeed something wrong with the steering. Besides, I wanted to see for myself, so there really wasn't any choice. I *had* to take it out on the next run. And I cannot tell you how eerie and other-worldly and stranger-than-science-fiction it is to be out there all by your lonesome on that vast, sun-bleached expanse of salt, following a painted black thread of a line that seems to unravel forever towards a those huge, vague, purplish mountains rising out of the mist on the horizon. It's like there's no end to it. Like you're not hardly even moving—trapped stock-still, almost, in spite of all the noise and wind buffeting and vibration—because those mountains never seem to get any closer and

the quicksilver water mirage shimmering off the salt between you and them is forever moving away from you but never seems to be getting any closer to the mountains. Even at well over two miles a minute. And there's no sense of acceleration
at that speed. None. Not even with the gas pedal mashed all the way to the throttle stops and the mighty roar of your engine melting into little more than a straining, plaintive wail out there in all that lonely emptiness.

It makes you feel very tiny and helpless indeed.

And then, at right around 4100 rpm with a good thousand or maybe even 1300
left to go if I really stretched it, I felt the steering start to get real light. Just like
Big Ed said, you know? And, also just like he said, it felt very scary indeed. My
first impulse was to pedal right out of it. But I had to find out—it was what I was
there for, right?—and so I kept my foot buried to the firewall and watched those
rpms slowly continue to climb and held onto that steering wheel tighter and tighter
the lighter and lighter it felt. Until it didn't feel like it was hardly connected to *anything!* And that's about when the front end started to wander left a little and I tried
a little tiny correction with the steering wheel but *NOTHING HAPPENED!*

Nothing at all....

So I steered a little more. And that didn't do anything, either! So I gave up in
half-a-heartbeat and backed out of it and of course that's when the wheels I'd
already turned came back down and bit into the salt and the next thing I knew the
Trashwagon swapped ends and swapped ends again (going through the timing
lights backwards in the process!) and then went into this horrible, teetering, up-
on-two-wheels slide one way and then the wheels bit again and it spun back the
other way and I honestly thought it was going to start rolling. Like a pencil rolls
down a blessed desk! Only the wind hit it sideways and maybe that's why it did-
n't and I had the brake jammed down so hard I'm surprised the pedal didn't snap
in two and I swear that car just spun and spun for what seemed like forever before
it whipped around one final time and came to a halt in a shower of salt out there
in the middle of that vast, dirty white desert with the horizon you couldn't even
see to all around it in every direction. I blinked a few times while the cloud of salt
and dust I'd kicked up kind of floated in over me and I heard the bigger salt peb-
bles spatter against the sheet tin and aluminum and then it was very, very quiet.
So quiet you could hear sweat drip....

Well, I knew I was damn lucky to get away with it, and Tommy Edwards and
Carroll Shelby and Chuck Day and Ernesto Julio and a bunch of the Bonneville
hot rod regulars from California came over to get a look at the size of my eyes
and kind of congratulate me for riding it out—not that I had much of a damn
choice, you understand—and it turned out Chuck had been out there by the far-
end timing lights where everything got so damn exciting and he had a few observations to share: "Car looked like it was maybe kind of motor-boating just before
you lost it."

"Motor-boating?"

"You know. Like a speedboat. Nose up in the air. Ass end just skimming the
water." He held his hand out flat with the palm raised up at about a thirty-degree angle.

"Really?"

Chuck nodded.

"Any idea what I can do about it?"

Chuck thought it over for a minute. "Well," he mused, "when a speedboat does that, what's holding the front end up like that?"

I thought it over for a moment. "The water?"

He rubbed his chin. "Nah, I don't think so. I mean, it's not even *touching* the water."

He had a point there.

"The power?" I tried again. I mean, I already knew how the Trashwagon kind of reared back onto its haunches under full-throttle acceleration in first and second gears.

He thought that one over, too. "Nah, I don't think so. That's just the car acting like a big torque arm when you goose it hard. But you're not doing much accelerating any more at the speeds you were doing."

"Well, what then?"

"I dunno. What about that speedboat? What keeps the front end floating up there over the water when it goes on plane?"

And that's when we looked at each other and Chuck realized he maybe had the answer. It was "plane." As in "airplane." He figured what was lifting the front wheels of the Trashwagon off the ground and likewise holding the front end of a speedboat up over the water was the same blessed thing I didn't really believe in that kept those big, heavy airplanes up in the sky where they didn't belong: plain old *air!*

"But air is nothing!" I protested.

"Just because you can't see it and don't notice it doesn't mean it's nothing," he argued.

And, after I thought it over a little, I realized maybe he was right. "But how do I fix it?"

Chuck thought that one over a little. "I think you gotta try something to keep all that air from packing up under the front end."

"But we never had this trouble before…."

"You were never going this fast and you never had that bellypan underneath before."

That made sense. "But what should I do?"

"You got any of that galvanized tin left?"

Well, I had about half of the Mormon Tabernacle Choir Easter Show sign left and Chuck kind of looked at it and looked at the front of the Trashwagon and then kind of looked at it some more and he decided what we really needed was some kind of cowcatcher thing on the front to keep the air from packing up underneath. Personally, it sounded all wrong to me, seeing as how the whole idea of the bellypan was so's the air would just shoot right under the car and adding that plow thing on the front would be just like putting a damn windshield up on the underside of the car. But I already knew that Chuck was probably a hell of a lot cleverer than me when it came to mechanical stuff, so I figured it couldn't hurt to give it a try. I mean, no question we couldn't keep it the way it was, and so we didn't really have anything to lose, right?

So Chuck used a couple pieces of two-by-four and the back of Big Ed's pickup as a brake and folded and tack welded us up this nifty, kind of V-shaped cowcatcher deal (which wound up with most of the *"on Temple Square in the heart of Salt Lake City"* address of the Mormon Tabernacle Choir right across the front) that came down and forward to a sort of prow front barely three inches off the salt and sloped up and back around the Jaguar grille opening a half-foot or so on either side. And then, just for the heck of it, Chuck had me pull the expanded metal large-bug-and-small-bird-straining material out of the Jag hood's grille slot and he made a solid tin plate to fit in there instead. It was the last piece of road sign we had left, and that's how the Trashwagon wound up with most of the word "Choir" in Olde English bible script kind of running sideways/vertical up where that snooty and expensive Jaguar grille once had been.

It was dark by the time we got done and so we headed into town (or what there was of it, anyway) and had dinner at a little truck stop joint on the Nevada side of the line where a lot of the racers went to eat. Not that they had much of a selection. And you could tell the owners really appreciated what the Lust For Speed had done for their business, on account of how they'd put pictures of some of the record cars that had run at Bonneville all over the place. Including a signed picture of Englishman John Cobb and the Railton streamliner he'd used to set a 394.20 mile-per-hour World Land Speed Record across the salt flats on September 16th, 1947. Nobody'd gone any quicker since. But they would. That's the one thing you knew for sure about speed records at Bonneville. They were always Big News at the time but, in the end, they were always just another line in the sand that somebody, sooner or later, was going to step over.

You could count on it.

The Healey guys were already there (including Tommy and Carroll Shelby and Donald Healey and Roger Menadue) and they were about halfway through dinner when we walked in and of course they all wanted to know how I was doing after my Big Moment out on the salt and also how things were progressing on the Trashwagon. And then who should come in right behind us but Ernesto Julio and Big Ed Baumstein. They'd just been out for a little nighttime ride in Ernesto's new Ferrari and seen the speedometer needle nudge up to the far side of 150 on a long, flat stretch of highway. But the certified timing equipment out on the salt flats wasn't quite agreeing with the big Ferrari's speedo, seeing as how the official clocks had the car at 143 and change when the speedometer needle was hovering tantalizingly close to 160. Then again, one of the main reasons you own a road car like a Ferrari is to impress people, and there is nothing on earth that impresses people like an optimistic speedometer. Still, Ernesto Julio wanted to know if his new 340 America coupe would indeed do the "150-plus!" he'd been promised by Carlo Sebastian. And maybe that's why he looked at Chuck Day kind of sideways and wondered out loud where he'd been all afternoon when he was supposed to be looking after the new Ferrari and maybe finding some way to goose a little more speed out of it. Chuck kind of flushed and started to explain but Ernesto just laughed it off—I think he just wanted to make Chuck squirm a little, you know?—and insisted we sit down and share a table with him and Big Ed.

I kind of wondered where Cal was—not that you ever really worried about a guy like Cal Carrington—while we sat down at one of the little Formica-topped tables and ordered food that I suppose really wasn't all that great (at least not compared to my mom's kitchen, anyway) but at least there was lots of it and, after a long day on the salt, it tasted absolutely wonderful. I had the chicken-fried steak special with sweet corn and dinner rolls and mashed potatoes with plenty of gravy—my mom always said it was important to eat a balanced meal—and Chuck had beef stew with plenty of green peas and carrots and potatoes in it. Big Ed and Ernesto both naturally opted for the most expensive thing on the menu—the T-bone steak—and they both allowed as how it wasn't too bad so long as you took enough time to chew it. Although, as Ernesto noted, that might easily take you all the way to breakfast. When the waitress came by to ask us how everything was, Big Ed held up a forkful of steak, looked up at her with a big, hayseed grin and said, "Everything's fine, ma'am, except this horse is still fighting for his life...."

We got a pretty good laugh off of that.

Anyhow, Chuck and me just mostly sat and listened while Ernesto and Big Ed talked about all kinds of business stuff and fast car stuff and sports stuff and great vacation places stuff and then discussed good places to eat in New York and San Francisco and Chicago and St. Louis and Savannah and Havana and even Rome. And you got the littlest tickle of a notion that they were having some kind of a contest. Friendly, you know, but a contest nonetheless. And strangely enough, the object of the whole thing seemed to be impressing Chuck Day and me. Impressing a couple of dirty-fingernail, grease-monkey mechanics, can you believe it?

But that's the way it was.

I tried calling home long-distance on the pay phone, but it was hard getting through to the operator to place the call—I mean, there was only one of her for a place the size of Wendover, and you had an extra double-the-normal-population going on when the Bonneville Speed Weeks were in town—and, when I finally did, there was no answer. So I tried again before dessert. And then again after dessert. I finally got through when the bill came and Big Ed and Ernesto Julio got into an incredibly big argument over who was going to have the pleasure of paying it. It started out nice and pleasant and friendly, but then neither of them would back down and it turned into some dumb kind of rich-guy contest again. Like two rams with gold-plated horns butting their heads together. And you could tell from the look in their eyes and the way their voices were getting louder that neither of them was about to give up. Why, they were determined to pay for each other's dinner even if they had to buy the damn restaurant and throw the other guy out by the scruff of his neck! It was actually a little embarrassing if you want the truth of it.

Which is why Chuck excused himself to go have a sit in the john and I went over to try my call again. And this time I finally got through. "Jeez, Honey, where the heck were you?" I asked innocently.

"I was at the hospital! The baby's sick!" she screamed into the receiver. There was a desperate, panicky edge in her voice that damn near cut me in half.

"My God!" I gasped. *"What's wrong?"* All of a sudden, without having done anything, I felt like I was a million miles away from where I should have been and a complete louse, jerk and heel on top of it. *"What happened? Tell me what happened!"* I was sounding pretty desperate and panicky myself, to be honest about it.

Well, it turned out little Vincenzo had started out being cranky and crying around mid-afternoon, and then he turned red and felt warm just before dinner. And then he stopped crying and just started whimpering a little and his eyes got all glazed-looking and he felt even warmer and so Julie took his temperature and it was way up to 103 degrees. So she called the doctor and he had her take him to the hospital—she had to call my dad to drive her over in his Mercury—and they gave him some medicine at the hospital and told her to bring him back if it got any worse and now he was real quiet but the fever still hadn't broken and what the hell did I think I was doing being three-quarters of the way across the blessed country when something like this was happening? She was pretty damn upset about it. And so was I.

Tommy Edwards and his bunch were just leaving, and he noticed the perturbed look on my face over by the pay phone. "What's the problem, Sport?" he asked.

So I put my hand over the mouthpiece and told him.

"Look, we're about wrapped up here tomorrow afternoon and I've got a bloody plane ticket out of Salt Lake tomorrow evening. Why don't you use it and I'll make the run back cross-country with Cal in your rig."

"You'd *do* that?"

"Why not? You've done some awfully nice things for me. It would be a privilege to return the favor. Besides, I'm not doing anything important for the next few days. It'll be nice to see a bit of the American countryside."

I couldn't believe it, you know?

So I told Julie I'd be flying home the next evening and promised I'd be calling her every chance I got in between now and then. When I hung up the phone, it suddenly occurred to me that I only had one day left to win Big Ed's bet for him. And right on cue, Cal Carrington came banging through the door with the news that he'd just run a flashlight over the time sheets posted in front of the official tent out on the salt and our friend Skippy Welcher had managed 153.69 miles-per-hour with his C-Type after a fresh set of plugs and a little engine tuning for the altitude and pumping the tires up to about 60 pounds each plus a tonneau cover snapped in place over the passenger side of the cockpit.

It wasn't looking real good for us.

"What *you* need," Chuck Day observed slyly, "is a little California Horsepower."

"What's that?"

"It comes in a jug," he said with a mysterious grin. "C'mon. I'll show you."

So we sneaked back out to the salt flats—and, by the way, the row between Big Ed and Ernesto Julio over who was going to pick up the tab and buy the other guy dinner was still going full-tilt!—and it was so damn vast and quiet out there under that huge, infinity-deep sky with enough star and moon light to make the 100 square miles of salt all around us glow the same dull, bluish silvery-white as a weak florescent bulb in an overhead bench light. And it was so quiet you could hear an ant fart. The only sound of any kind was a faint, naked whisper from the wind and the echoing click-click-click of a socket wrench ratcheting a 5/8ths nut off under a tarp awning in the paddock someplace. Chuck led me over to one of the hot rod trailers, where we found a couple guys he knew inside fussing over the multiple-pulley belt drive on a GMC-supercharged Chrysler engine. Behind them, up along the wall of the trailer, were a bunch of five, ten and twenty gallon metal cans, spouts all tightly sealed and wearing official-looking labels with lots of type and little skull-and-crossbones "POISON" logos on them.

Chuck explained to his buddies as how we weren't really looking for an official record here at Bonneville but just to settle a bet and how they could maybe help me out with something slightly special for the fuel tank.

"Well, y'gotta be a little careful with this stuff," the old-timer of the two allowed. "The methanol all by itself ain't too bad, but y'gotta hog out the jets a mite an' it kinda eats up some of the stuff in the carburetors."

"I was thinking of something with maybe a little more kick to it," Chuck explained.

"Well, then of course 'pop's' the thing."

"Pop?" I asked.

"Nitromethane. It does for an internal combustion engine what spinach does for Popeye."

"It does?"

"Sure does. Only y'gotta be *real* careful with that stuff. It'll blow the cylinder heads right off their studs if y'get a mite too frisky with it."

"Either that or poke a conrod right through the side of the block!" the other guy threw in.

"Yeah, y'gotta be careful. I always use a little benzene or something to cool the charge off a li'l when I'm puttin' 'pop' to an engine."

"And you say I've still gotta hog out the jets?"

"Oh, absolutely. Otherwise you'll run so lean it'll melt'cher pistons like plumbing solder."

I looked at Chuck Day. "Are you sure this is such a good idea?"

"You want your share of that thousand bucks?"

And so that's how we wound up staying up half the night re-doing the fuel system on the Trashwagon for a little "California Horsepower" while Chuck's buddies mixed us a special blend they figured would give us a nice little kick in the pants without the death-blow wallop you wind up with if you get a little too ambitious with 'pop.' And that's also how I wound up flying home out of Salt Lake City in a Douglas DC-6 "Cloudmaster" with a fresh five hundred bucks bulging in my pants pocket the very next evening, after Chuck's cowcatcher deal worked like a champ and kept the front wheels more or less close to the ground and we even took a chance and pulled the fanbelt off completely before pouring in two gallons of this stuff his buddies mixed that made your eyes tear and your skin break out something awful if you got any of it on you. Big Ed even told Cal to go ahead and drive it—I honestly think he was still a little spooked, you know?—and damn if Cal didn't hold it straight and true on the black line as he cruised through the lights, stable as you please, at an electronically-timed 163.343 miles-per-hour with the word "Choir" running proudly south-to-north over the grille opening in Olde English lettering!

You can look it up if you want to.

24: A Few More Lessons Learned

What with an hour stopover in Chicago I got into Idlewild around dawn and, to tell the truth, I was almost getting used to this flying stuff. Except for the takeoffs and landings, anyway. Especially the takeoffs. Even though Tommy said that the landings were really the hardest part. "Any landing you can walk away from is a good landing," he told me once. "Being able to re-use the airplane makes it a bloody *great* landing!" And when you hear that kind of stuff spilling oh-so-casually out of an experienced pilot like Tommy, it tends to make you a little nervous. Or it did me, anyway. But, like I said, I was getting used to it once the plane was up there in the sky (another thing Tommy told me was that "altitude is insurance," and the higher up you are, the further away you are from that hard bump at the bottom!), and I'd even had a little firsthand demonstration out at Bonneville of the rushing air pressure that keeps an airplane up in the sky. Hell, it damn near killed me!

What with it being so early and all and my pocket jammed chock-full of The Skipper's money, I splurged and took a cab all the way back to Passaic. From Idlewild, can you believe it? But I wanted to get home on account of I was worried sick about the baby. And I was dying to see Julie again, too. But the duplex was all dark and quiet when I got there and so I sneaked in through the back porch and tiptoed down the hall and peeked into the bedroom and there was Julie all curled up on the bed around the tiny form of little Vincenzo—both of them breathing regularly and sleeping peacefully—and I just can't describe the flood of relief that went through me. It made my knees go all wobbly, honest it did.

Julie opened one eye and gently raised a finger to her lips, and so I took my clothes off and showered up real quick and laid down next to her and curled myself up around the both of them. And that's how we stayed and slept together for the rest of the night. It was the deepest, darkest, most peaceful and bottomless kind of sleep you can imagine. I even remember thinking, *'if this is what death is like, then it must not be so bad after all.'*

The baby woke us up around eleven and it was obvious the fever had passed and little Vincenzo was just plain hungry. So we sat around the kitchen table and Julie made us some bacon and eggs—like it was a blessed Sunday morning, right?—while I aimed spoonfuls of mashed bananas with a little brown sugar and vanilla mixed up in it at Vincent's mouth. Not that he couldn't feed himself, of course. Sort of. After breakfast I actually helped Julie with the dishes (only I was only allowed to dry, on account of Julie was convinced I was too dumb and inexperienced to wash), and then we decided to load Vincent up in his stroller buggy and take a walk over by the Sinclair. Just to see what was going on. I mean, it was Saturday and we usually kept the shop open until two or three in the afternoon (at least!) and nobody was expecting me back until Tuesday. So I kind of thought it might be interesting to just drop in. And imagine my surprise when I heard a horn honking from over a block away. Whoever it was sounded pretty damn impatient, and so I excused myself and broke into a run and rounded the corner to find some guy in a creamy yellow Olds convertible with out-of-state plates on it next to the pumps leaning on his horn and an elderly couple standing by the locked office door looking very perplexed indeed and this tweedy college-professor type with a notepad in one hand and a thin-stemmed pipe clenched in his teeth walking around the Volkswagen Big Ed and me had for sale—he'd been there before—and little Danny Poindexter and his equally sawed-off and neatly-dressed and -coiffed buddy 'Fos' just pulling up to the pumps in 'Fos'' mother's Lincoln Capri and the shop all pitch-black dark inside and—*omigod!*—the smell of burnt wood and a serious electrical fire hanging in the air!

Well, I rushed past the guy at the pumps and told him to keep his pants on (in a nice way, of course) and waved *"Hi!"* to Danny and 'Fos' and yelled over my shoulder to the college professor type that I'd be right with him and gently excused myself past the elderly couple who had come by to pick up their Dodge that had needed a water pump rebuild and fumbled my key into the lock and let myself inside. Jeez, the burnt wood and electrical smell was just awful! And I could feel my feet sloshing through water on the floor, too. *My God! What the hell went on here??!!* I flicked the light switch, but nothing happened. So I felt my way along behind the register counter and found the flashlight we always keep there and headed out into the gloomy half-light of the shop with all the doors down and the lights off and just the sunlight filtering in through the windows of the overhead doors for illumination. I ran my flashlight beam down the wall and it wasn't too hard to locate the source of the problem. Somebody'd tried to *back* the blessed tow truck up into the shop, and they'd raised the damn boom up to make room and raked it right across the fat conduit tube that brought outside power in to our circuit breaker box. It must've been one hell of a mess, what with the wall all blackened and a ragged, smoldering hole burned through the roof and water all over so you knew the Fire Department had been there....

The guy in the Olds honked his horn again.

'Jesus!' I thought, *'keep your damn shirt on!'*

Well, there was no power to run the pumps—or anything else for that matter—and so I went back outside and, in a very nice way, explained to the guy in the Olds that I couldn't pump him any gas.

"But the sign says you're open," he argued with me.

"We *are* open. Only we've had a fire and I don't have any power to run the pumps."

He looked at me like I'd done it on purpose. "Do you know how long I've been waiting here?" he asked in the haughtiest, nastiest voice you would ever use to someone outside your own immediate family.

"Yes, I do," I wanted to tell him, *"I heard you honking your fucking horn from three blocks away."* But instead I said, "I'm sorry," and then had to kind of jump back to keep from getting my toes run over as he squealed away from the pumps. The bastard.

By then Julie and the stroller with little Vincenzo in it had wheeled up next to me. "My God, what happened?" she asked.

So I told her about the apparent electrical fire and of course by that time the elderly couple had ambled over to ask about their Dodge and here was Danny Poindexter right in front of me expecting—as guys like little Danny Poindexter always do—to be taken care of immediately and I could see out of the corner of my eye the college-professor type heading over, notebook pad in hand, to ask me an entire grad-school final exam about the Volkswagen we had for sale and here came one of our regulars with an MG TD pulling in with a bad sputter in his engine and right behind him our buddy Carson Flegley in his Healey Hundred.

'Welcome home,' I thought to myself. *'Welcome home.'*

Well, I managed to get Carson and the TD guy talking to Danny and his buddy 'Fos' and that gave me a little time to actually do something worthwhile and find the key and the work order for the Dodge in the darkened office and luckily I took the time for a quick, manager-style once-over under the hood and discovered there was no water or antifreeze in the radiator on account of whoever filled it had forgotten to check the petcock on the bottom first and so it had all leaked out on the pavement. Not to mention that, although the fanbelt was snug, the bolt on the tensioner arm for the generator was only finger-tight (although that was easy enough to fix, seeing as how the same idiot who let all the water and anti-freeze run out had left two of my good box-end combination wrenches of the appropriate size laying on top of the blessed battery!), and that worried me enough that I decided I'd better go over everything before I gave the car back to the nice elderly couple.

In the meantime, the college-professor type with the pipe and the notepad was buzzing around my ears like a damn mosquito on a Boy Scout overnight, asking me all about fuel mileage and air cooling and fuel mileage and traction in the snow and fuel mileage and could we service the car and fuel mileage and howcome a gas station in Passaic had a damn-near brand-spanking-new Volkswagen for sale anyway and had it maybe been in a wreck or even stolen or something and what about the fuel mileage and if it'd maybe been running around with the speedometer disconnected on account of it only had 688 miles on it and everybody and their brother knew people who sell used cars do that all the time—not that he was actually *accusing* me of anything, you understand—and what sort of fuel mileage did it *really* get and how he'd been over to the dealership in Weehawken and they were only asking a hundred-and-fifty more for a brand new one right off the lot! Now bear in mind that I dearly wanted to sell this particular Volkswagen on account of all the profit on the wholesale deal we'd made with Bob Fergus for Danny Poindexter's MG was tied up in that car. But, at the same time, there are people you are just better off not selling to. And this guy had *Pain in the Ass* written all over him. In boldface, Olde English type, in fact.

"Look," I finally told him. "We got the car in a trade deal for an MG from a dealer in Ohio, okay? You can call and ask him about it if you want. And the only miles it's got on it are driving back from Ohio and a hundred or so more he put on before we got it. And it did maybe an honest thirty miles per gallon or so on the way back from Ohio."

The college-professor type looked absolutely horrified. "Only *thirty??!!"* he gasped incredulously.

"Well, y'gotta understand that it was carrying four full-sized adults..." I glanced over at little Danny Poindexter and his pint-sized buddy 'Fos' and silently complimented myself on how quickly I was picking up this car salesman stuff, "...and that's climbing through the mountains in Pennsylvania and stuck in rush-hour traffic coming home, too." In fact, as I thought about it, thirty miles per gallon was a pretty amazing figure under those conditions. But this guy had obviously read a magazine or heard a story somewhere and you could see as how the notion of only thirty miles per gallon was really offending him.

"Are you sure there's nothing *wrong* with it?"

"Nope," I said as I put the radiator cap back on the Dodge. "That's what it got."

"Hmm," he said, sucking viciously on his pipe. "And what about the price?"

"The price is on the front window."

"But I can get one exactly like it—brand new from the dealer!—for just a hundred-and-fifty more."

"Hey, it's a free country," I told him. "If you want to pay a hundred-and-fifty more for the same exact car, that's your prerogative." I looked him right in the eye. "That's what makes America the great country it is."

And with that I turned on my heels and went over to settle the bill and deliver the keys to the nice old couple with the Dodge. And I didn't charge them for the extra slug of anti-freeze, either. Then I headed over to where Danny Poindexter and Carson and 'Fos' and the MG regular were having a discussion around Carson's Healey Hundred, and of course I started things off by telling them how Big Ed won the bet with Skippy Welcher out at Bonneville—they all seemed pretty tickled about that—and then Danny Poindexter allowed as how he really needed to talk to me about Big Ed's Arnolt-Bristol, seeing as how he liked it a lot and he thought he could get his folks to go for it since it was still only a two-liter, But he'd contacted the Arnolt people in Chicago and they told him he'd have to order one and wait for it just like Big Ed did. Not to mention that he had his somewhat bent-up TR2 to deal with and he wondered if there was maybe any easy, fast and simple way I could ease him into Big Ed's car and take the slightly-bent TR2 off his hands.

As is, of course.

"I'm pretty sure we can work something out," I told him.

And by then the college-professor type was hovering again, pestering me about the price and the fuel mileage on the Volkswagen, and I finally pointed to Danny and 'Fos' and said, "Look, these guys were in the car on the way back from Ohio. Why don't you ask them?"

Well, it turned out that Danny and 'Fos' actually knew this guy—even though he didn't recognize them—on account of they'd had him for some chemistry class in prep school that they'd both flunked. "Well, it's really hard to say about the fuel mileage," 'Fos' explained while quietly slipping a wink at Danny. "It depended a lot on the terrain."

"It sure did," Danny agreed. "Oh, it had to struggle a little on the uphills with four of us and all our luggage on board..." you could see the college professor was all ears, "...but I bet we were getting eighty or ninety miles per gallon on the downhill sections..."

A huge smile blossomed around the stem of his pipe. *That's* what he wanted to hear!

"All right then," he said like he was planting the blessed flag on Iwo Jima. "I'll give you a hundred less than you're asking for it. Right now. Cash money."

Now, a hundred less than we were asking was still a fairly good deal. But I'd learned a little something from hanging around with the likes of Colin St. John, Bob Fergus and Big Ed Baumstein. "Look," I said in the most reasonable and yet deliberately patronizing voice I could muster, "if we'd wanted a hundred less for it, that's what we would have put on the window..."

It was amazing how the resolve in his face just wilted. But now it was time to keep him on the hook. "Tell you what," I told him. "We're pretty firm on the price, but, if you like, I'll call my partner and see if he'll come down a little." I looked at the college professor guy apologetically. "It's his money, see? I just work on 'em."

So I went into the office and called my sister Mary Frances to see how she was doing, and then I came back out and offered the guy twenty-five bucks off. "My partner didn't really want to do it. I mean, it's already a hundred-and-fifty less than the dealer wants for the same damn car."

"Make it seventy-five," the college professor type said with new zeal and fervor in his eyes. And it reminded me what Big Ed and Bob Fergus had taught me about the bargaining process. You can't let the other guy take control. After all, once he's Made The Commitment, it's only a question of who's going to be picking over the other fellow's bones.

"I'm sorry," I told him earnestly, "but I can't even call him back with an offer like that. He'll just get mad at me."

"How about fifty?" he said, his voice cracking just a little.

I let out a long sigh, slowly shook my head, and went back in the office and called my mom to tell her I was home safe and to see how her Baltimore orioles were doing with their nest in the back yard and then I came back out with a grin the size of a watermelon slice plastered all over my face. "He'll go *thirty!*" I said like I'd just discovered electricity.

And the deal was made.

A little later J.R. Mitchell showed up in an electrician's truck with his bicycle loaded in back and I finally found out what had happened at the station. "It was pretty terrible," he said in a miserable, wavering voice. "It started yesterday afternoon. That Marlene that Butch used to be married to came by with a lawyer and there was a lotta yelling and stuff, and then Butch just took off after they left and told me and Raymond to close up when we were done with the cars."

"Where'd he go?"

J.R. shook his head. "No idea."

I had a pretty good idea. "Then what happened?"

"Well, I opened up right on time this morning and pumped some gas and fixed a tire with a hole in it..."

"Good for you. But what about the fire?"

J.R. swallowed hard. "Well, then Raymond showed up and he had this engine block in back for a Jaguar engine rebuild that needed cleaning, and I had the idea we could maybe use the tow truck to hook it up and haul it out to the drain by the curb so's I could clean it and..." his voice choked up and I could see his face starting to burn and tears welling up in his eyes, "...and..."

"Who was driving?"

The tears started pouring down his cheeks as he sobbed, "...It was *me*...*I* did it...I know I shouldn't've...I...I...I'm *sorry*..."

I put my arm around his shoulder. I mean, there was nothing else you could do. "That's okay," I told him. "That's okay."

He looked up at me miserably. "We *tried* t'put it out," he choked. "Me and Raymond did. Dumped two whole fire extinguishers on it. But it was up where you couldn't really get at it and burning pretty bad and then a piece of the rafters or something fell into the parts tank and it flared up and burnt Raymond's arm..."

"Bad?"

"...not too bad, but he had t'go to the hospital t'get it fixed after the guys from the Fire Department came."

"Who called the Fire Department?"

"I did."

"And then what did you do?"

"I tried cleaning up a little after they left—I squeegee'd most of the water out of the service bays—and then I locked everything up and took my bicycle to find an electrician who was open on Saturdays. I thought maybe I could have it all fixed again before you got back on Tuesday."

I looked down into his tear-stained face and gave J.R. Mitchell an approving smile. "You did good," I told him.

"I *did?*"

"Uh-huh," I nodded. "All except trying to burn the shop down in the first place."

There were more tears then, but they were the grateful kind. And I gave him a nice, warm hug to go along with them. It was the first time I'd ever hugged a young boy the way fathers and grown-ups do, and I've got to say it felt pretty damn good.

It was something I was going to have to learn how to do sooner or later anyway.

So the upshot of the whole day was that I made two highly profitable car deals and picked up a somewhat damaged but almost-new TR2 to fix up and make yet another wad of cash on plus the insurance company wound up redoing the roof and the electrics for me and I learned that you really can't leave a car shop without a captain for very long or you're going to have lots of angry customers and multiple raging disasters on your hands.

It's just the way things are.

But I could still take off for a weekend so long as J.R. and Butch were around. And Butch did show up again on Monday following a three-day binge that ended with him wheeling into the driveway of my Aunt Rosamarina's house at three-thirty ayem Sunday morning and banging on the screen door for her to let him in and then getting into an angry shouting match with her that got him so mad he tried to lunge at her and actually took two real steps out of his wheelchair! It was like a miracle, you know? And the very next afternoon she had him down at the V.A. hospital again to see about a walker. He wasn't real keen on the idea, of course, since it meant a lot more trouble and effort and therapy. But she made him.

We had a race coming up the very next weekend at Thompson, Connecticut, and of course it was all I could do to get the Trashwagon re-converted from Bonneville trim to road-course duty in time. Not to mention that we somehow had to get it painted on account of Charlie Priddle's new rule about *"no bare metal or primer"* and *"a neat and clean appearance."* Which, in the Trashwagon's case, was going to take a bit of doing. Especially with only two days left and me still with all four carburetors spread all over my workbench to clean and re-jet from our "California Horsepower" cocktail mix back to good old ethyl and the original Ford truck radiator somehow having picked up a few seam leaks in transit. And add on top of it all getting Carson's Healey and Buster Jones' Jag and my MG guys and Danny Poindexter's freshly ex-Big Ed Arnolt-Bristol ready for the race weekend. But, as always, we managed to get it done (at the very last second, natch, and after putting in back-to-back eighteen-hour days), and solved the paint problem on the Trashwagon with a few cases of silver spray paint that somehow "fell off a truck" conveniently close to Big Ed's scrapyard. Only it wasn't very *good* silver spray paint—kind of the hardware-store variety, right?—and on top of that I had all able hands busy with mechanical stuff and so I entrusted the painting duties to Tater, who did quite a bit of blind-alley experimenting trying to find the ideal nozzle-to-panel spray distance and coat-layer thickness. Plus, thanks to trying to keep up with the overspray, he wound up painting *everything!* And I do mean *everything!* Even the radiator and the wiring and the battery and the backing plates on the blessed brake drums. And about half the tires, too. The end result looked like a full-size edition of one of those gilded, blemished, tinfoil-colored Santa's Sleigh table centerpieces that fifth-grade cub scouts make for their moms at Christmastime. Or maybe it was more like fourth-graders. Plus it would rub off like crazy any time you got anywheres close to it on account of the paint didn't really bite into the metal very well.

But at least we got it done (even if it looked like hell!) and the bunch of us met at the Sinclair just before daybreak Saturday morning for the drive up to Connecticut. And damn if Big Ed hadn't taken his half of Skippy's thousand bucks and a wad of his own cash and picked up one of those brand new two-seater Ford Thunderbirds that had just come out. To be honest, Big Ed didn't have a lot of clout going for him at any of the Ford dealerships in town—he'd always been kind of a Caddy guy until he got involved with sports cars—and so he had to about buy the sales manager at the Ford store a fresh set of white leather shoes and a new diamond pinky ring in order to get the very first one in the area. But—what the hell—it was Skippy's money anyway. And I had to admit that Thunderbird was a pretty sharp-looking piece. Especially since Big Ed had to take one in lipstick red instead of his usual white with red interior on account of that was the only car available. It was an automatic, too (although, to tell the truth, Big Ed was probably better off with an auto—not that he'd ever admit to it!). Ford called their new Thunderbird "a completely new kind of sports car" and "a personal luxury car" and you could tell right away from its size and weight and all the plush doodads and power features that it was never going to scoot around corners like a Jag or a Triumph or an MG or an Austin-Healey. But that's not what it was meant for, you know? It was aimed smack-dab at rich, flashy guys like Big Ed who wanted the flamboyant, look-at-me style and stature and pizzazz of a sports car with the comfort and ease of operation of one of his Cadillacs. That '55 Thunderbird took dead aim at America's country-club set and hit a whole bunch of them right square between the eyes.

"How's it drive?" I asked Big Ed.

He took a long, deep drag on his cigar and slowly exhaled. "So smooth you don't even notice it."

Like I said, right between the eyes.

To be honest about it, I was in a little trouble with Julie back at the duplex for taking off again just after I'd gotten back home, but I explained as how there was only this race and the one two weeks later at Watkins Glen and then that was pretty much it for the season. I even asked her if she wanted to go along. "What, so I can sit in the frickin' room all by myself with nothing but spiders and mosquitoes for company while you go off jawing and getting drunk with your racing buddies and then come back at three in the morning and pee in our suitcase?"

She had a point.

But at least the Thompson weekend was close by and just a Saturday-Sunday event, so I could be home in plenty of time for the Labor Day backyard cookout my mom and dad had planned. Being a staunch union guy, Labor Day was a very big deal to my old man, and it was amazing how chummy the rest of the family had become ever since little Vincenzo was born. It was almost like they were all little kids again, and suddenly Julie and me had the toy everybody wanted to play with. Especially my mom and Sarah Jean and even more especially Mary Frances, who always got a warm, happy, but sadly faraway look in her eyes whenever she was around the baby. And she was coming with that brilliant, socially committed, and perpetually-running-around-with-a-rocket-up-his-ass Leonard Putzman guy from Greenwich Village, so it promised to be a pretty good show between him and my old man. I was even looking forward to it. Really I was.

Thompson Speedway started out as kind of a local oval track up in Connecticut that ran stock car and jalopy races on Friday and Saturday nights and Sunday afternoons (although a lot of the church-going locals were none too happy about the Sunday races and made a lot of outraged speeches about it at town meetings and such) and, at one point when they repaved the track, they added kind of an "X" in the middle so they could feature "Figure 8" demolition races, which amounted to sort of a big game of "Chicken" played by guys who didn't care if their cars got wrecked. In fact, that was the point. Especially since the track promoter offered more under the table for a really stupefying crash than he did over the table for winning. Or at least that's what I heard, anyway.

But the sportycar crowd was looking for places to run, and here was this short paved oval with some extra legs to it just sitting there waiting for them, and so they started running time trials and side-by-side match races like that one Big Ed and The Skipper got into when they were both running Jag 120s and took each other kind of mutually into the guardrail. Still, it wasn't much of a track for road racing, and so some of the deep pockets in the SCMA (and there were always plenty of those around!) prevailed on the track owner to extend the course out into the countryside just a little—you know, through the parking lot and around that little stand of trees over there and then over a small hump that you could almost call a hill and back to the oval again—and, when it was finally finished, it was barely a mile-and-a-half long and looked more like somebody's freshly-paved driveway than a real racetrack. That's how short and narrow it was. But it was far better than those SAC base circuits when it came to looking and feeling like a real country road, and yet it was all private and purpose-built so there were no hassles with the police or the local or state government about holding races on it. And that was a very big advantage indeed.

The weekend at Thompson didn't draw nearly the kind or quality of entry we'd seen at Lockbourne in Ohio a month earlier, but there was a decent crowd and crafty old Donald Healey had just sort of "casually dropped in" to show off his supercharged Healey Hundred "streamliner" that had just gone an incredible 192.6 miles-per-hour out at Bonneville. In fact, there was a big poster detailing all the records those two Healeys had broken out on the salt. Although the fine print at the bottom said "International and/or American class records," on account of it turned out that one of Herr Hitler's pet Mercedes-Benz record cars had run in the same "supercharged under 3-liter" class as the Healey streamliner and went a wee bit faster than the Healey—like by a solid fifty-five-plus miles-per-hour!—back in 1939. But that happened over in Europe (where a lot of people we still pretty miffed about some of the other things Herr Hitler was just getting into around 1939), so the Healey streamliner had to be satisfied with the "American" records. And that was just fine with Donald Healey, so long as he got the hoopla and head-lines that went along with it. Plus the 100S prototype set four new legitimate international class records (including 24 hours at an impressive 132.2 mile-per-hour average!) and the MG guys did pretty good, too, what with that EX-179 streamliner of theirs knocking off 35 new International and American speed records. But it was Donald Healey who'd come cross-country to show his cars off where he knew the sportycar people would gather, and, once again, you had to be impressed at how that guy milked every last drop of publicity and visibility out of whatever his cars could manage.

He was one sharp guy when it came to that sort of thing.

But, like I said, Thompson wasn't really one of your bigger or more impressive race meetings. The track was real tight and tiny and narrow and even a little claustrophobic and you really couldn't run a lot of cars together on it at one time because there simply wasn't enough room. Not to mention that the good, upright, church-going people of Connecticut had these Blue Laws so you couldn't fire up a race motor or run any hot laps before 2pm on the Lord's day. As a result, the SCMA officials had broken everything up into these little ten-lap, fifteen-mile races of just eight or ten cars each. And there were no big Cunninghams or anything like that on hand (although Briggs was there with that little jewel of a 1500cc OSCA of his to run in the smallbore modified class), so it was pretty much a foregone conclusion that Creighton Pendleton would breeze home to victory in the big car feature race in his hotrod Ferrari. Which he did. But this guy everybody called "Smilin' Jack" Ensley (after the comic strip, right?) did a hell of a job in the "unrestricted" race with one of those brutish Kurtis Kraft 500Ks. In fact, for my money, that was the best damn race of the day. It started with this Tippy Lipe guy grabbing the lead in a tiny and clever little hybrid featuring a supercharged Porsche engine in a dinky little Cooper chassis. Boy, was that thing ever *quick*. Especially around a tight, hemmed-in little circuit like Thompson. In fact, he looked like he had it in the bag—just running away from this Chrysler-engined Maserati single-seater and Ensley's five-and-a-half liter Kurtis and all the other big iron—but then the rubber band broke (or maybe the hamster got winded?) and he dropped out and then it was the Maserati in front looking like *he* had it sewed up but then here came Ensley driving the blessed wheels off the damn Kurtis, reeling in and passing the Maserati and going on to win. It was a damn fine job, chucking and wrestling a big truck like that around Thompson Speedway.

Our Ohio friend Bob Fergus was there with his Austin-Healey and again I was hoping Carson would give Cal a crack at him in the black one. But Carson was determined to try and get better at this racing stuff so's he could impress my sister Sarah Jean (she was home helping my mom make more kinds of salads and side dishes than there are stars in the sky or grains of sand in the desert for our big Monday cookout), and this represented a perfect opportunity to try and brush up his skills a little. Not that he had any. In any case, Bob Fergus came from the back of the pack to win the fifth race of the day ahead of eight other guys in Healey Hundreds (including our boy Carson, down towards the rear in seventh place) and one poor fish in a Sunbeam Alpine that simply didn't have a chance. I enjoyed watching Bob Fergus drive—he was so blessed *smooth,* you know?—and it was nice he got to do it in front of Donald Healey, too. No doubt he'd have the inside track on getting one of those new 100S models as soon as they became available. Hey, the reason somebody like Donald Healey built special, hopped-up, lightweight race cars was to impress the folks on the dull side of the fences and make them want to own one of the street versions. And, no matter if you were selling Ferraris like Carlo Sebastian or Jaguars and such like Colin St. John or taking deposits on the new Healey 100S, it only worked if you got a genuine 'shoe in there who knew what to do with the damn thing once he got behind the wheel. Sure, money was important. I mean, you couldn't *give* the things away. But it wasn't everything….

In any case, I went over to congratulate Bob afterwards and, while I was at it, mentioned as how I'd sold that Volkswagen me and Big Ed got from him.

"You want another one?" he asked.

"Sure," I told him without thinking. But then I thought it over. "That is," I added slyly, "depending on how much you want for it."

Bob answered with a big grin. "You're learning how it works, aren't you?"

"I guess I am." And then I thought of something else. "And how the heck are we gonna get it back from Ohio?"

"Maybe I can arrange for you to get it right off the truck. There's no reason why it has to come all the way out to Ohio just to get it back to you on the east coast."

"But that'll leave an empty space on your truck to Ohio."

Bob slipped me a sideways look. "You have anything in stock I might be interested in?" And then he added: "Wholesale, of course…."

I thought it over and of course the first thing that came to mind was Danny Poindexter's slightly rearranged TR2. But I didn't say anything. Not yet. I wanted to maybe fix it first. Or maybe not. But I sure as heck wanted to talk to Big Ed about it before I did or said anything.

Speaking of Big Ed, he was having one hell of a time with the horribly painted Trashwagon (in fact, it was so bad that some of the armband people out on the corners started calling it "The Silver Smudge") seeing as how he couldn't keep it pointed front-end-forward for much more than a lap at a time. He'd go out, take a kind of exploratory lap, step on the gas, and spin. So he'd ease off, everything would seem okay, and he'd put his foot in it again and spin. In fact, he spun it so damn many times I lost track. And of course old Charlie Priddle was having a field day watching Big Ed embarrass himself (and me!) and was already making plans to call him up before another Drivers' Committee tribunal for being such a dangerous and ham-fisted oaf behind the wheel. Especially seeing as how he was still on probation. But the magic of it was that he wasn't hitting anything—I'll take dumb luck over meager skill any day!—and I explained to the guy on the flagstand that he was having "a little trouble with the steering" and that we were "trying to sort out." So all they could do was shake the black flag at him. To tell the truth, I wanted Big Ed to let Cal give it a try, but then we split a radiator hose where somebody—and I'm not saying who!—had run it a little too close to the steering gear and so we missed the only practice session when Cal would have had a chance to take it out. In the race, Big Ed managed to loop the Trashwagon seven times in ten laps and finished dead last. If you do the math, that's one spin every 2.14 miles. We all agreed that had to be some kind of a record.

It was nice having a free day on Labor Day Monday after the Thompson weekend and, after little Vincenzo's usual pre-crack-of-dawn crying and feeding, we slept in a little and then read the leftover Sunday newspaper together with the baby between us in the bed and a nice, steaming cup of coffee on each of the bed-stands. I never figured I'd be the kind of guy to go in for that sort of thing, but it's amazing what you start finding out about yourself once your life switches over from things you *want* to do to things you *have* to do.

And, speaking of things we had to do, we got up around eleven and Julie cleaned the apartment real good while I ran the wet laundry through the wringer on the washing machine and then hung it out in the yard to dry and then ran the mower over our so-called "lawn" (it was a ten-minute job, even with a smoke break), and then we got cleaned up and assembled all the stuff you have to bring along anyplace you go if you're also bringing a seven-month-old baby along. It was such a nice day we decided to walk over to my folks' house with the stroller buggy instead of drive—hell, it was only about eight blocks—and I made sure we went by my Aunt Rosamarina's house to maybe see if Butch was there. Sure enough, he was out in the drive in his wheelchair with his shirt off, carefully painting my aunt's screen door with his good hand while holding the paint can between his knees.

"How're y'gonna get at the top?" I asked as I wandered up the drive.

"I'll wait'll this end dries, have Rosy take it off the hinges and turn it upside-down, an' I'll do the rest of it."

"Rosy?" I said incredulously. Nobody'd ever called my Aunt Rosamarina "Rosy" in her life! Or at least not since I'd been around to hear it anyway.

Butch looked up from his painting with a warm, wicked flicker in his eye. "Why not 'Rosy,' huh?"

"I dunno," I shrugged. "It just sounds, I dunno…."

Butch went back to his painting. "How was the race at Thompson?"

"Okay, I guess. Big Ed set a world record for spinning out."

"Figures."

"That's two records in two weeks," I reminded him.

"He's true World Class, isn't he?"

"Yeah. I guess." Then I thought of something else. "Say, why don't you stop by my folks' house with, umm, Aunt R…, I mean, Ro…uhh, I mean, you know, *her?"*

Butch looked up at me kind of sideways. "And why would we want to do that?"

"There's always lots of food and…"

"I don't care much about *what* I eat, but I sure as hell care who I eat *with.*"

"But you'll be with me and Julie. And Carson'll be there, too, most likely."

"It's hard for me t'contain my enthusiasm."

"It'll be fun. You'll see."

"No it won't. Don't kid yourself. And besides, me an' Rosy are plannin' t'go over to the shore an' maybe rent a rowboat…."

"Really?"

Butch scowled at me. "Y'think that's funny r'somethin?'"

"N-not at all, Butch. Not at all."

"Good," he snorted, and went back to his painting. But you couldn't miss the little half-smile hidden under his nose. And then I heard footsteps coming down the linoleum stairs and there was my Aunt Rosamarina—in blessed *Bermuda shorts,* for God's sake!—carrying a pitcher of fresh-squeezed lemonade and two glasses.

"Would you like some?" she asked through the screen door.

"T-thanks," I kind of stammered. "But I, uh, really gotta be getting' over t'my folks' house. We're late already…." I started back towards the street.

"Come by anytime," my aunt called after me.

"Yeah. Anytime," Butch added.

Boy, Butch and my Aunt Rosamarina!

'Rosy,' fr'chrissakes!

Who'd've ever thunk it?

The usual suspects gathered for the Labor Day barbeque over at my folks' house, and I must admit Little Vincenzo was the star of the show. The new baby in the family always is (especially if it's your first, and even more especially—at least in our family, anyway—if it's a boy), and it was kind of nice being around the center of attention for a change. Judging by the redness of his nose-o-meter, Tina's loudmouth wholesale paint salesman husband Roy already had a good start on a snootful going before he even rang the bell, and that would of course mean a few less whisky-and-sodas out of my old man's supply, a lot of really smutty stories whispered just loud enough that the women couldn't help hearing—that always made me real uncomfortable, you know?—followed by a lot of bass-register snoring in front of the TV set by around 4:30 or so in the afternoon. My bossy oldest sister Ann Marie showed up with her two kids—I noticed her nasty little boy had advanced from the Skinned Knee to the Black Eye stage and the little girl was making her first darling little baby-step attempts at using lipstick, rouge and heavy eyeliner makeup to give herself the glamorous look of a street-corner hooker—and of course Tina's skinny little milquetoast husband Jerry was following behind the whole bunch loaded down with a lethal, forty-pound dosage of her famous cabbage, bean and peanut butter casserole. Only this time she'd experimented with five different kinds of beans—kidney, wax, black, red and butter—plus a grated Swiss cheese topping. It went good with dill pickles. Or at least that's what she said, anyway. But, like I said, it was nice the way they all gathered around little Vincenzo and oohed and aahed and giggled and googled and made the kind of faces and noises that would get you a one-way ticket to Bellevue if you did them out in public.

Carson Flegley stopped by in the Healey to squire my sister Sarah Jean around for the afternoon, and it was nice the way they hung out real close together all the time now (although you never seemed to catch them actually *touching),* and even Big Ed Baumstein dropped by for an hour or so. I'd invited him on account of he was little Vincent's godfather, and of course he brought all kinds of stuff—some really expensive scotch and cigars for my dad, candy and flowers for my mom and an enormous, even-bigger-than-the-last new Erector Set with an electric motor in it for the baby—but I could tell he felt a little uncomfortable being around all these family members he didn't really know. Plus I knew he made my old man uncomfortable just because he was driving that shiny new Ford Thunderbird. And bright red, too! But he excused himself pretty early. Right after the appetizers, in fact. Said he had someplace else he had to go, although I don't have any idea if it was true or not. I saw him to the door and he reached up and pushed a couple folded-up twenties into my shirt pocket. "This is fer th'kid's college fund," he kind of grumbled. "Don't'cha be spendin' it on anything else."

"You don't haf'ta do that," I told him.

He looked up at me and then past me to all the family milling around in the living room. It gave him a kind of sad, faraway look in his eyes. "I do it because I want to, kid," he explained, as much to himself as anyone else, "I do it because it makes me feel *good.*"

And then he turned and walked down the steps to his brand new Thunderbird, eased himself behind the wheel, fired up a fresh dollar cigar, and tooled silently off down the street. I remember thinking how all alone he looked, and I think it must've been the first time in my life that I ever felt sorry for Big Ed Baumstein. And then I turned around and looked back into the house, back at Tina's loudmouth husband Roy telling dirty stories in already slurred sentences and Ann Marie telling Jerry in no uncertain terms where to put this side dish and what to cover with tinfoil and my mom fluttering around in her apron like one of her favorite birds over a nest full of chicks and my own Julie carrying little Vincent with Sarah Jean and Carson looking in from either side of her like some dumb bible portrait—except for Carson's glasses, anyway—and my dad going out the back kitchen door with a platter full of raw meat and Tina and Ann Marie's kids chasing each other all over the place like ricocheting chrome pinballs and, again for maybe the first time in my life, I felt awful damn glad to belong to this family.

Even if they did drive me nuts.

It being Labor Day and all and my old man having actually been on the bargaining committee that managed to get a ten-cent-an-hour pay increase, better benefits, and double-time instead of just time-and-a-half on Sundays on the new four-year union contract (not to mention getting one of the company management guys who was even meaner than my old man fired), we were celebrating with real

T-bone steaks on the grill. Not *great* T-bone steaks, mind you (my mom said you just got to enjoy the flavor longer on account of how long they took to chew), but T-bone steaks nonetheless. And that was a pretty big deal for a household like my old man's. Although he did have a few hotdogs for the kids or anybody with dental work in progress.

About halfway through the first round of steaks Mary Frances showed up with jerkoff-of-the-month Leonard Putzman in tow (only by now she was calling him "Lenny" in an exasperated and no-longer-much-impressed-at-all sort of voice), and he was even wearing a *clean* grubby Sears denim work shirt for the occasion. And it didn't take him five minutes to turn whatever the heck we were talking about into a desperate political discussion. He had a real knack for it, you know? And I guess he figured, what with my old man being a professional working stiff and all, that he'd have a little sympathy and understanding at the head of the table. Only my dad failed to see the similarities between what he and his union buddies were after and the total remanufacturing of the entire global social and political system that little Lenny had in mind. Plus he had this exceedingly irritating way of expressing his views. Like anybody who disagreed with him was some kind of idiot. Not to mention a criminal pig.

My old man didn't much care for it. "Lemme see if I understand you right," he asked Lenny, his eyes narrowed down like gunslits. "The way things're now, some of us get t'eat steak and some of us eat hamburger and the tans and slants on the other side of the world gotta get by on a bowl a'rice a day or they starve."

"That's right."

"And so you're gonna take my steak away and grind it up inta more hamburger and mix it up with that rice from the other side of the world and then split it up so everybody eats the same crap and nobody gets any more than anybody else?"

"That's the fair way to do it," Lenny explained with a gleam of benign justice in his eyes.

Without a word, my old man reached out his big barbeque fork, speared Lenny's steak right off his plate, put it back on the serving platter and flipped him a pale-looking wiener. Without a bun or anything. "Okay, Lenny, why don't we start with you?"

Well, that got a pretty good laugh. Even out of me.

But Lenny was not the kind of guy you could easily shut up and, between mouthfuls, he was constantly explaining all the stupid, horrible and unforgivable things our U.S. government was doing to The People and all the stupid, horrible and unforgivable things the Soviet government was doing to The People and all the stupid, horrible, unforgivable things the European governments were doing to The People and I figured I maybe ought to excuse myself and go to the can or offer to put more steaks on or something on account of it was obviously going to take him a long, long time to get around to Canada. Mary Frances came out while I was pushing the second helping of steaks around on the grill.

"How're y'doing?" I asked her.

"What does it look like?"

I shook my head, stopped my tongue for just a heartbeat, and then blundered right in. "Looks t'me like you've picked another real winner."

"I've got a real talent for it, don't I?" She said like she was eating something sour. She was looking pretty disgusted with herself.

"You want to know what I think?" I said carefully.

"Probably not. But tell me anyway."

"I dunno, Mary Frances. It's like you're looking for something in all these creeps that you already *got.* Better'n any of 'em, in fact."

"Got? And just what exactly *is* this thing I've already *got?"*

I shrugged. "I don't know what you call it, but I can see it in your eyes and hear it when you talk. You don't need some jerk with some phony plan or purpose in his life to put things together for you. Don'cha see? You're looking for something on the *outside* that you really gotta find *inside....*"

She stared down at the steaks sizzling on the grill. "But what if I don't like what I see when I look inside?"

Without thinking, I reached out and put my arm around her shoulder. *"Y'gotta ease up on yourself a little,"* I whispered in her ear. *"Things happen. And then they pass and they're gone and there's not one damn thing you can do about it. Unless you wanna drive yourself nuts, y'gotta let 'em go an' move on to the next thing."* I leaned in even closer. *"Y'gotta learn t'be a friend t'yourself, see?"* I gave her shoulders a little squeeze.

"Thanks, Buddy," she kind of sniffled. "You're a real pal."

That made me feel pretty good in a bittersweet kind of way. Like I somehow actually *belonged* turning the blessed Labor Day steaks on my old man's backyard grill.

Back inside, the "discussion" between my dad and Lenny Putzman had escalated two cold Knickerbockers (on my old man's side), one pale weenie (on Leonard Putzman's side) and at least ten decibels. And it kind of escaped me as to how you could possibly win the hearts and minds of people and reconfigure the whole damn world if mostly what you did was piss them off and make them want to sock you in the nose. And the Putzman family nose was quite a tempting target, if I do say so myself. In any case, the current topic was the Plight of the Working Man and how He (the Working Man) was being exploited by the Bourgeois Capitalist Pigs that ran Wall Street and Washington and even my old man's chemical plant over in Newark. And my old man—who was about as patriotic an American as you could ever find so long as he didn't have to actually dodge bullets for the privilege—had had about enough of Lenny's shit.

"LEMME SEE YER HANDS!" he demanded.

"M-my *what?"*

"Yer hands. Lemme see yer hands."

So Lenny held his hands out and my old man turned them palms-up and looked at them closely. Then he looked up at Lenny and a dangerous, crocodile smile spread across his face. "Y'ever use these things fr'anything tougher than pickin' yer damn nose?"

Lenny flushed bright red. *"I don't have to take that!"* he bleated. "We're *leaving!* Come on, Mary Frances."

Mary Frances sat right where she was.

"I said we're *leaving.*"

She didn't bat an eyelash.

"Are you coming with or aren't you?" Lenny demanded.

"I don't think I am," she said evenly.

"If you stay here now, don't bother coming back to the apartment later," he warned.

"I'll only come to get my things."

"I'll bring her," I chimed in.

Leonard's eyes swept contemptuously around the table. And it made me a little sad that we were providing him such a grand opportunity to feel even more wronged and victimized and self-righteous and sanctimonious than usual. And that was too bad, because he enjoyed it so.

All the Team Passaic regulars knew that Watkins Glen was going to be our last race of the season, and that naturally meant that everybody and his brother wanted to go and so there was an even bigger rush than usual getting ready since we had all sorts of stuff to fix and just two weeks between Thompson and The Glen. Not to mention that Charlie Priddle and his gang at the SCMA had once again proved that their resolve was cast in solid tapioca pudding since they'd sniffed the winds of membership opinion and then boldly picked up the mantle of leadership and led them wherever the hell they seemed to be going. Which, in this case, meant burying the hatchet and benignly offering SCMA sanction to the '54 Watkins Glen races seeing as how most of the members with the brass and deep pockets to go racing in the first place were planning to enter anyway. Tommy Edwards called it *'rear-view-mirror leadership'* and I guess that fit pretty well.

In fact, seeing as how it was not only the last but also looking to be about the biggest local event of the season (not that Watkins Glen is anywheres near that close to Passaic, but your whole sense of time and distance gets sort of rearranged when you start traveling all over hell-and-gone to places like Sebring and Bonneville) and moreover, since all my guys were going, I'd decided that we'd actually hang a "Gone Racin'" sign on the door and close down the repair shop for a couple days. Oh, we'd still keep the gas pumps running—Raymond and Tater would see to that—but I left strict instructions that they shouldn't do much more than change oil, fix flats and maybe screw in a few sparkplugs while we were gone. It isn't that I didn't trust them (although, to tell the truth, I had my doubts about Tater), but I knew what I figured they were capable of when left to their own devices and, very frankly, it wasn't much. But you gotta keep the pumps running for your regulars, or they'll find somebody else with pump islands and a grease rack and a big smile and maybe a penny-a-gallon cheaper gas and, next thing you know, they're buying Shell or Mobil or Texaco down the street and getting all their fan belts and carburetor rebuilds and windshield wiper blades over there and you never see them again. I don't know what it is about people and their corner gas stations, but they get used to stopping in and very much expect you to be there—like the pharmacist at the corner drug store or the dry cleaning lady who can hardly speak English or the guy across the street in the white paper hat who makes you hamburgers and heroes for lunch and pepper-and-egg sandwiches for you on Fridays—and that's something you really don't want to mess with. It's just not good business.

So it turned out just *everybody* was going to The Glen. Even my sister Mary Frances, who was set to share a room with Sarah Jean and maybe try to puzzle out just exactly what she was going to do with herself. And, because they were going and she liked my sisters, I even got Julie to agree to come and bring little seven-month-old Vincenzo to his very first race weekend (at least after I promised Julie on my mother's eyes and the souls of my dead ancestors that I'd submit to immediate castration with a rusty claw hammer if I went off and got drunk with my racing buddies again). I even called up J.R. Mitchell's parents—they seemed to be pretty nice people—and set it up so's he could come to his own very first race weekend and sleep on a roll-away cot in the cabin with Cal and Carson. Oh, Cal figured to be out raising a little hell at night over in the bar but, what with Carson and Julie and my sisters around, I was pretty sure J.R.'s eyes wouldn't get popped open too wide for an innocent teen-ager. Besides, it didn't seem to do me much harm, did it? And he could ride up with Buster Jones in his Jag or Danny Poindexter in that deep metallic maroon, ex-Big Ed Arnolt-Bristol that I almost killed Sylvester and me in or, if it was real hot or cold out, he could ride with Big Ed in his brand new Thunderbird on account of it had a cozy, removable fiberglass hardtop that made it almost into a coupe and a real American-style heater/defroster that you actually had to turn down occasionally, and even the optional air conditioning! And Big Ed had a space open since he'd kind of soured on that Nanette person he was seeing (as he put it, *"that broad should only open her mouth fer one thing, and it sure ain't talkin'"*), so he was driving up solo. Or he could even catch a lift with Danny's rich buddy 'Fos' in the brand new Porsche coupe he'd just picked up. 'Fos' was really keen on that car and how much he'd paid for it—and it was an awful lot of money for a 1500cc coupe that looked suspiciously similar to a Volkswagen if you peeked under the skin—but, like the VW, you had to be impressed with the stuff it was made out of and the way it was screwed together. And, small as it was on the outside, even Big Ed Baumstein could fit inside it (although Big Ed would never consider owning a Porsche himself on account of it was German and the tongue-clucking, head-shaking and finger-waving from his Brooklyn relatives would never end—besides which he thought it had no style and "looked like a damn gumdrop").

Like I said, it figured to be a hell of a turnout for Team Passaic at Watkins Glen, what with Cal and Carson and everybody in on the program. Plus they'd added a whole practice day on Friday (which was a heck of a good idea!), so most of us figured to get on the road Wednesday (or *real* early Thursday morning) so's we could get the cars through technical inspection at Smalley's Garage on Franklin Street and be all set and ready to go for the drivers' meeting and first practice early Friday morning. What with lots of stuff to pack and finish up around the shop, Julie and little Vincenzo and me were planning to drive up early Thursday in the second "brand new" used Volkswagen that Bob Fergus had arranged for us to get off the truck he had heading out his way (at least after we made a decent deal and I got the front end straightened out enough on that ex-Danny Poindexter TR2 that it would roll up the ramp and take the VW's place for the truck ride out to Ohio). That second Volkswagen was painted a kind of deep brick red, and again I had to marvel over just how simple and well-screwed-together it was. If a little cramped and noisy inside. But it was frankly amazing how you had to crack one of the side windows a bit before you shut the blessed door or it made your ears pop.

I figured I'd sell a lot of them on that feature alone!

But there was a lot of work to do, and right about fifth or tenth on my priority list was that we had to do *something* about how the Trashwagon looked. I mean, that splotchy, smudged and pockmarked silver paint that looked like a lazy six-year-old did it and that also came off all over you if you were so much as within ten feet of it just had to go. So I had J.R. run down to the hardware store and get some nice, shiny, gloss-black spray paint and we tried laying it down over the silver. After looking at those California hot rods and streamliners out at Bonneville,

I'd started visualizing the Trashwagon all straightened up and tidy (but still of course with the trash-can-lid Continental kit on the rear deck—I mean, that went without saying!) painted up in a gleaming, glistening, ten-foot-deep coat of flawless, shimmering black paint. With maybe even pinstripes or a discrete little flame job on the front, you know? Just to piss off Charlie Priddle's bunch. Only, once again, I was learning a little something about paint types and surface preparation and all the other, top-secret, insider Bump-and-Paint shop stuff I knew nothing whatsoever about. And, as usually happens in those situations, what I learned is what I *really* should have known before I ever even started. That's generally how you find things out in real life....

Turns out the way it works with paint is a lot like the way it works with blood types and transfusions, you know? If you've got a layer of, oh, say, "Type A" paint (or "Type B" paint or "Type AB" paint) you can paint over it just fine with some other "Type A" paint (or "Type B" paint or "Type AB" paint) but if you try to paint over "Type A" paint with either "Type B" paint or "Type AB" paint, it doesn't work worth a damn and the patient dies. And then there's that lacquer vs. enamel thing (which, can you believe it, has nothing whatever to do with what color you want!), which I guess is a lot like being Rh Positive or Rh Negative, so that—even if you get everything else right—if you get that part wrong, the patient also dies. Only this time in agony.

Which is pretty much what happened to the Trashwagon, seeing as how the nice, smooth, heavy coating of "Type A/RH Negative" gloss black paint we laid on top had a delayed but thoroughly devastating reaction with the apparently "Type B/RH Positive" splotchy silver paint underneath. So instead of drying into the foot-deep, shimmering, mirror-finish black I'd envisioned, it kind of crazed and cracked and crinkled and came up in big, ugly clumps that looked like iron ore or something.

It was worse than awful.

So I had everybody in the shop grab sheets of wood-grit sandpaper and handfuls of steel wool to take down the worst of it and then we gave it a quick-and-dirty once-over with some marginally finer-grit sandpaper and meanwhile I sent J.R. down to the hardware store to find us some "O-Type" paint you could put over damn near anything. He came back with three gallon buckets of this stuff they use on concrete garage floors and such, and that Colin Chapman guy from Lotus would have been absolutely horrified at how much those paint buckets weighed! Why, it was so thick and heavy you couldn't get it through a spray gun. No way! So we used brushes. And I'm talking *exterior* brushes, not those dinky little one- and two-inch jobs you use for windows and trim. But it worked out okay, since the guy at the hardware store told J.R. that the stuff was usually laid down with push brooms....

And I had to admit, it *did* cover pretty well. In fact, it filled in all the dimples, cracks, seams and divots less than a half-inch wide! In the end, it left the Trashwagon looking like it'd been dipped in a huge pool of muck. Not mud, mind you, but *muck!* Plus it didn't dry particularly quick, and we were kind of counting on it to finish the drying process on the long tow out to Watkins Glen behind Big Ed's pickup. During which the forward-facing nose, hood and fender panels figured to pick up a jewel-like encrustation of dead insects. Or mostly dead insects, anyway. But I managed to get everybody on the road by 10 PM or so on Wednesday night. And then I went home, had a little cold chicken and a beer or two out of the icebox, laid down for just a second before I took my shower, and next thing I knew, the damn alarm was going off.

Even though it was still dark outside.

Well, like I said, the idea was for Julie and me to get on the road early in the Volkswagen, and I was really in a good mood seeing as how this was going to be Julie's and the baby's and my first-ever road trip and race weekend together. Or it would be as soon as we got done packing all the things Julie figured we need-ed into the Volkswagen. I mean, I tried to explain to her that you really didn't have to put the entire contents of our duplex into the car for just a few simple days away at Watkins Glen. Not that it would fit anyway. But she seemed to be of a mind that what you really want to do when you travel with a baby is put a trailer hitch on the back of your car and simply hook your whole house to it. Or at least the bedroom, kitchen, and a closet or two....

"Honey," I asked her, "why does he need the snowsuit with the mittens in the sleeves?"

"It might be cold. Do you know how easy it is for a baby to catch cold?"

"And howabout the two dozen baby shirts and sweaters?"

"You know how he is when he eats. You don't want him going around with strained beets, carrots and bananas all over him, do you?"

I started to say he was going to have strained beets, carrots and bananas all over him at least three or four times a day no matter what you did, but I had the good sense to bite my tongue.

"And what about these shoes? Why are you taking five pairs of shoes for yourself?"

She fixed me with a withering stare. "Do I tell *you* what to pack?"

Well, she had me there. Then again, all I was bringing was my usual small duffel with the fake leather, zip-up toiletries kit inside—not much more than a few T-shirts and pairs of socks and underwear, a sweatshirt, an extra pair of jeans, a toothbrush, a small, sample-size tube of toothpaste, a safety razor with one extra blade, some shaving soap, a comb, a few loose Anacins and a small package of Bromo Seltzer in case I stumble into a rough morning—but Julie's damn *toiletries* bag was bigger than my whole blessed duffel! The straw that broke the camel's back was when she dragged out a whole laundry bag filled with every single dia-per we owned. "My God, Julie!" I yelled at her. "We're only going away for a couple of days!"

"Do you know how many times I have to change him every day?" she said fiercely. And then added: *"Hmpf. But you wouldn't then, would you?"*

It was, once again, an excellent time to keep my mouth shut.

Still, I had to draw the line when she wanted me to lash his crib, mattress and high chair to the roof and find space in back for little Vincent's beloved circus mobile that hung over his crib and played *"The Daring Young Man on the Flying Trapeze"* if you rewound it every thirty seconds. I'm surprised she didn't want the dining room set, too. I swear, General Eisenhower didn't pack that much stuff for the blessed invasion of Normandy!

But, like I said, I kept my mouth shut as much as I could and went along with what Julie wanted as much as I could and tried to keep from yelling at her about how blessed long it was taking for her to get her things and the baby's things together because, after all, this was going to be our first great Road Trip/Race Weekend traveling adventure together as a real family and I sure wanted to get started off on the right foot. Even if I was hopping from that foot to the other because it was already damn near eight o'clock and I'd figured we'd be on the road by six. Or maybe six-thirty. I tried to grit my teeth and bear it—even if it was threatening to screw up my dental work—on account of I really wanted this to be a great experience for us. Which just shows how much I knew about traveling with a mother and her seven-month-old baby. And especially a seven-month-old baby who has just eaten a tiny little, mashed-up taste of my married sister Tina's leftover Labor Day cabbage, bean and peanut butter casserole (the one with *five* different kinds of beans and the grated Swiss cheese topping) for breakfast. In a car built so blessed air-tight it makes your ears pop if you slam the doors without cracking a window first....

Suffice to say that traveling with tiny children—and especially heavily loaded and ready-to-explode tiny children like our own little Vincenzo was that particular day—is hardly traveling at all. Because the baby is cranky and uncomfortable and that makes the mommy cranky and uncomfortable and that makes the daddy cranky and uncomfortable and moreover worried about the dangerous, ugly, disagreeable and thoroughly unreasonable argument that is liable to erupt at any moment—over damn near *anything!* The worst part is that, even though you can see it coming like the advancing funnel cloud of a giant killer tornado, you're helpless to stop it or get out of the way. And, even if the argument *doesn't* erupt, you're still sitting on that razor's edge of tension knowing that it's in the vicinity and threatening. Not to mention that you're stopping every tenth or fifteenth mile to change diapers and let the cabin air out a little. Or that the trunk on the VW with the dirty diaper bag inside it sits directly in front of you (or, more to the point, directly in front of your nose) and it didn't take very many dirty-diaper stops at all before I quietly ditched little Vincent's diaper bag in a nearby trash can when Julie wasn't looking. But then she caught me tossing the diaper with his latest digestive accomplishments in after it.

"What are you *doing?"* Julie demanded.

"Hopefully allowing us to breathe through our noses again."

"But those cost *money!"*

I smiled at her as sweetly as I could. "It's a vacation, Honey. Let's splurge."

To tell the truth, I was also pretty damn anxious about how late it was getting and how far behind schedule we were. What with our extended Packing-To-Leave ritual and the multiple diaper stops and the fact that a heavily loaded Volkswagen is hardly the world's fastest form of conveyance—especially up steep hills—I could already see that there was no way we'd make it to Watkins Glen before tech inspection closed. And I hoped and prayed that my guys would be smart enough and organized enough to get through it without me. Hell, they *should* be able to do something as simple as that! But I knew I was supposed to *be there,* you know?

And it was making me antsy as hell that I wasn't going to make it. In fact, I started getting a little more impatient and a little more impatient every time we had to stop. Finally, Julie looked at me in that special way wives have of looking at husbands and husbands have of looking at wives when the other person needs to be gently blasted right between the eyes with the obvious:

"Look, Buddy. You're not gonna make it in time. It's just not going to happen. So why don't you just make a call to that Smalley's Garage you were talking about and make sure everything is okay. Then you can relax and enjoy the ride."

I opened my mouth to tell her—like husbands do to wives and wives do to husbands all the time—just how impossible and ridiculous and out-of-the-question that was. Only by then I'd thought it over and realized it was probably a pretty good idea. And so the next time we made a gas-station poop stop for little Vincenzo, I went to the pay phone and got the operator to get the number of Smalley's Garage on Franklin Street in Watkins Glen, New York, and made myself a little station-to-station (get it?) phone call. "Yeah," the voice on the other end yelled into the receiver—there was an awful lot of noise and hubbub in the background—"I'm pretty sure they're here someplace. Hang on."

So I waited and fed more change into the slot and waited some more and then, finally, I heard Cal's voice on the other end. "What's up?"

"We got kinda, uhh, *detained,* see?"

"So?"

"So I just wanted to make sure everybody got there okay and got through tech and…"

"Everything's under control."

"It *is?* " I was actually a little disappointed.

"Yeah. We got Danny and Buster and the MG guys through tech already and Carson's going through right now, and I got the Trashwagon lined up right behind him."

I was stunned.

"So you have a nice trip up," Cal told me, sounding just the least bit cocky and pleased with himself. "We got everything under control at this end."

"You *sure?* "

"Sure I'm sure. We'll see you later at the Seneca. You'll buy me a beer."

Of that I had no doubt.

Well, that was quite a load off my mind, and our trip settled down into a sort of pleasant rhythm by the time we passed through Port Jervis. We weren't making very good time what with all the feedings and the cleanings—I swear, sometimes little Vincenzo amounted to nothing more than a damn food-processing machine!—but it was kind of nice in between with Julie sitting beside me on the front seat of that Volkswagen and that steady, thrumming drone of the engine all around us like we were inside some metal-lined beehive and the early fall colors kind of wheeling by the windows and the Delaware River off to our left as we swept and swooped our way up that wonderful section of Route 97 I was coming to know so well from our race-weekend road trips to Watkins Glen and Callicoon. You really couldn't ask for a more scenic or dramatic stretch of road, and we were flowing along at that nice glide pace you can find sometimes more or less halfway between just puttering along and going fast enough to make your passengers grab for something to hold onto and curse at you through gritted teeth. It's an effortless, creamy, floaty kind of sensation when you hit it just right, and even little Vincent seemed to be enjoying it, his eyes big and wide as billiard balls as he watched the towns and fields and forests and cliffs and scenery passing by. And then, after a long time, you could see him getting tired and he'd fight to keep his eyes open so's he wouldn't miss anything but it was no use and eventually he'd fall asleep in Julie's arms and she'd look down at him and then over at me and smile, and it was the kind of feeling you'd like to be able to capture in a bottle or press into a pill somehow so's you could have a dose of it handy anytime the world got a little too ugly or overwhelming.

We didn't get into Watkins Glen until well after dark, and first I puttered the Volkswagen up Franklin Street to see what was going on before we headed up the hill to the Seneca Lodge. It was pretty chilly outside, but there were still all kinds of sports cars parked all over the place and prowling through town and all kinds of shops still open hawking souvenirs and books and checkered flags and toy racing cars and picture postcards and beaded Indian moccasins and little birch-bark canoes. The bars and restaurants were filled to overflowing all up and down the street and the people milling around outside in parkas and heavy winter coats and stocking caps were laughing and talking about cars and racing while they waited for tables. Chilly or not, you could still feel the old Race Weekend electricity buzzing in the air and, like I've said before, if you've got The Bug yourself—no matter how many times you've seen and felt it before—it always makes your pulse beat a little quicker and the tiny hairs in your ears frizz up in anticipation.

Julie and the baby and me checked in at the Seneca Lodge, and this time we were off in one of the small, individual cabins (which were about the approximate shape, size and appearance of an exceedingly spacious and well appointed outhouse—only slightly better-smelling), and it was hardly the most romantic sort of place, what with a naked lightbulb glaring at us out of the middle of the ceiling as soon as I flipped the light switch on and a fine, fat, powdery-gray resident moth fluttering around it. Not to mention a daddy longlegs the diameter of your average coffee saucer grinning up at us from the pillow. Or at least I figured he must be grinning, judging from the way he'd made Julie jump.

"Oh, jeez, it's *harmless!*" I scoffed.

"I don't care if it's STUFFED! Get it the hell out of here!"

So I gave her a big, Exasperated Male-type sigh, went outside, found a bucket, found a broom, thought about it for a moment, found a pair of heavy leather gloves, put on my steel-toed workboots, and came back inside to take care of the daddy longlegs. Only by then it was gone.

"Where'd it go?" I asked Julie, who was still frozen against the wall by the doorway.

"Under the bed."

So I got a flashlight and kneeled down to look under the bed and, sure enough, here were two beady black eyes staring at me. Only these seemed quite a bit larger than a daddy longlegs' eyes. And they were staring at me out of a nervous little brownish-gray fur ball with a long, naked pink tail. "He's not down here," I told Julie.

"But he's *got* to be. I saw him crawl down there...."

"Well, maybe the mouse *ate* him."

"The WHAT??!!"

I swear, you could see light under the soles of her feet for at least two or three whole seconds.

Well, needless to say I had to go on a little Local-Flora-and-Fauna search-and-destroy (or at least search, capture in the bucket and put *waaay* outside) mission all around the cabin while Julie and little Vincent waited out in the Volkswagen with the engine running and the heater on full blast. Or as full blast as the heater gets in an idling Volkswagen, anyway. To tell the truth, tough and independent as she was, Julie never much cared for large bugs or small, furry critters sharing our sleeping and bathing quarters. And that mouse made a real game out of it, jumping ship between the broom and the bucket and squirting off along the baseboard molding like a jet-propelled fur bullet and then disappearing through a crack in the woodwork no wider than a damn sparkplug gap. I always wondered how they did that. But I pretended like I'd caught it and put it outside anyway just to put Julie's mind at ease, and then I kind of draped one of little Vincent's sweaters on a bent-up wire hanger around that robot's-eyeball lightbulb dangling from the ceiling so it made the room glow kind of a deep, warm autumn orange. And also so's you'd be less likely to notice any of God's four-, six-, eight- or thousand-legged creatures sharing the accommodations with us. "There. That's better now, isn't it?" I asked Julie as I showed her back into the cabin.

"You sure you got everything?" she wanted to know, although sounding just a little bit embarrassed at how that daddy longlegs made her jump.

"Yeah," I assured her with a nice, manly swagger in my voice. "The place is clean."

She looked around uncertainly. Nothing seemed to be moving or staring back at her.

"You want to maybe get something to eat before we go to bed?"

"You mean do I want to go over to the bar and watch you get stinking drunk with all your racing friends?"

"That's not what I mean at all," I lied. And not very well, either.

"Look, little Vincent is already asleep and I need to get cleaned up before bed. If you're absolutely *sure* you got all the...the...*things* out of the cabin, you can go over and get me a hot soup or a sandwich or something and have a drink with your friends while you're waiting. *ONE drink,* understand. Not fifteen or twenty."

So I kissed her on the cheek and headed over to the Lodge, and promised myself over and over that I'd just stay there a minute or two.

Believe it or not, I was actually back in the room with Julie's soup and sandwich in no more than an hour and a half (although, to be honest, the take-out food service *was* pretty slow, and I of course had to polish off the three or four or five drinks that Carson and Big Ed and Tommy Edwards and even Cal Carrington—!!!—bought for me plus the one I grabbed off the bar to take back to the cabin when I left). But I figured that was still pretty good. For me, anyway. On a race weekend. Besides, after last time, I really wanted to get started off right with Julie. And it was important for me to set a good example for little Vincent, too. But I have to admit, as I laid there in the darkness with Julie in the bed next to me and little Vincent kind of in between us, my eyes were wide open and my ears were straining to hear the noise and jukebox music and the sports cars growling past in the parking lot with the wet gravel crunching under their tires and most especially the shouts and laughter bubbling over at the Seneca bar.

God, I wanted to be there in the thick of it....

It rained pretty hard during the night and Friday morning dawned damp, cold, misty and nasty—the kind of weather that chills you right through to the bone—and I told Julie she and little Vincent could just stay in the cabin if they wanted while I went off to get my guys through practice and qualifying. But she said "no," on account of there really wasn't anything to do in the cabin except stare at the walls and play hide-and-seek with the spiders and mice. Besides, she'd come up to go to the races with me and help me out a little if she could, and that was exactly what she was planning to do. Just as soon as she got the baby fed and cleaned and freshly diapered and bundled up like a damn Eskimo and packed up all the stuff she thought she might need at the track that day and meanwhile it was getting later and later and so I was naturally pacing and fidgeting and gently suggesting through clenched teeth that it would be ever so nice if we actually got to the track before practice started. Or ended, for that matter. Which of course launched us into our very first argument of the day. Or maybe it wasn't really an argument, seeing as how an argument actually requires two opposing opinions or points of view. So this was more of a yelling match.

I got us a couple sweet rolls and paper cups of coffee from the Lodge while Julie put more stuff than I could believe back in the Volkswagen and we headed off for the track. It was one of those dark, cold, forbidding and yet beautiful upstate New York fall mornings when the sky is gray and hard as a granite headstone and the pavements are shiny black from the overnight rain with wet leaves scattered all over them and the fields and lawns an almost luminous green under a damp, patchy mist and it mostly looks like an excellent day to be huddled inside around a fireplace with a nice mug of hot cocoa, a stadium blanket over your lap and some thick woolen socks on. Or, in other words, not the best sort of racing weather at all. And it didn't help matters any that the so-called "defroster" on the Volkswagen was marginal even in the best conditions and damn near useless before the engine got up to temperature. So I was pawing at the windshield with my sleeve as I drove (and driving pretty fast, seeing as how I figured I really needed to be where we were going about ten minutes ago!), and so of course Julie was after me for driving too fast with the baby and her in the car and also because I maybe couldn't see where we were going and of course I was snapping right back at her for making us late in the first place by taking so damn long to get ready and, to be honest, this had all the makings of a really ugly day in every respect you could think of.

Luckily the drivers' meeting was still going on when we got there, and I found our guys' spot in the paddock—right next to our friend Brooks Stevens and his Excalibur team—and damn if that kid J.R. hadn't gone and checked all the fluids and tire pressures and warmed all the cars up and even had them lined up in a neat, military-type row according to class and race group. He looked about frozen, too, seeing as how he'd been working since about dawn and only had this light little windbreaker on over his sweatshirt. I gave him the rest of my coffee and told him to go sit in the Volkswagen for awhile to warm up.

"T-that's o-okay," he said through chattering teeth. And that's when I noticed the look on his face. I'd forgotten that this was his first-ever race weekend, and he had that same giddy, star-struck, gobsmacked glitter in his eyes that I had that first race day at Bridgehampton what seemed like at least a million years before. I couldn't believe it had only been three summers. Why, everything in my life had changed. *Everything!* I'd grown up, for chrissakes. I had a wife and a son and I was running a damn business and I actually seemed to know what I was doing around a racetrack. That was the really amazing part, you know?

It was always good to see Brooks Stevens and Hal Ullrich and the rest of the Excalibur guys out of Milwaukee, even though their Henry J-based cars weren't really competitive since they had to run in the modified class on account of Brooks could never sell old Henry Kaiser on the idea of going into production and building a real, all-American sports car to maybe sneak a few two-seater sales away from the Europeans. And now Chevrolet had their Corvette and Ford (and Big Ed) had their Thunderbirds and Kaiser had decided to go with Dutch Darrin's stylish-to-a-fault—or at least that's how Brooks described it with his usual wry sparkle—Kaiser-Darrin roadster with the doors that slid forward into the front fenders and the grille that looked like Marlene Dietrich puckering up after sucking a lemon. You could tell Brooks was a little disappointed by that, since the Excalibur was more of a real sports car by far and had a genuine, all-American, Sabre Jet look to it. Still, he'd designed the Kaiser Manhattans, which were really smooth and sexy and elegant-looking cars and right up there with Raymond Loewy's Studebaker Starliner coupes as maybe the handsomest American sedans on the market. But good looks are only one small part of the overall picture in the world of automotive retailing—you've got to have solid, modern mechanicals, good reliability and resale value, a strong dealer network, and some really snappy advertising at the very least to go along with it—not to mention that John Q. Public and Fred Average are maybe looking for something a little more straight-laced, stodgy and middle-of-the-road than a four-wheeled, five-passenger equivalent of Rita Hayworth or Lana Turner parked in their driveway.

But Brooks was always upbeat and charming, even though polio had made it so's he couldn't get around real good or ever race cars himself, and you could tell he took a great deal of pleasure out of fielding his race team and hanging around at the races. Even on a cold, damp, blustery day like the one we were enduring at Watkins Glen. "The English race in weather like this all the time," he observed, blowing into his hands. "But then, they don't really have a choice over there, do they?"

Carson and Sarah Jean had tried to build us all a little campfire, but the wood was wet and so what we had was kind of a smoky pile of twigs that snapped and hissed at you and made your eyes sting like hell if the wind was blowing the wrong way but didn't have much going for it in the way of actual heat or flames. My sister Sarah Jean was crouched down on her knees next to it with a race program in either hand, trying to fan it with one of them and shield it from the wind with the other. Go figure. She looked up at me with a feeble but proud little smile.

"Having a good time?" I asked her.

The smile brightened up a few watts. "Well, the weather could be a little nicer."

"The weather could be a *lot* nicer," I corrected her. There was no more rain, but the sky was still dark and threatening and a really stiff, cold wind had come up that cut right through you.

"But it's nice to be *doing* something," she added softly.

"Yeah, it is, isn't it?"

It warmed me up a little that she understood what it was all about.

My guys came back from the drivers' meeting and damn if Cal wasn't carrying his helmet and goggles again. "Who's the sucker this weekend?" I asked him.

"Aw, I met a guy in the bar last night who wants me t'drive his TD in the all-MG race."

"He just up and *asked* you, right?"

"Well, I had to do a *little* persuading…."

Carson rolled his eyes.

Turns out some of the MG guys in the bar got into a friendly and typical little race-weekend argument about whether the snappy-looking new TF with its faired-in headlamps and raked-back grille was actually any better or faster than the old, upright-grille Mk II TD it replaced—to be absolutely honest, there wasn't all that much difference except the styling as far as I could see—but of course Colin St. John had been telling everybody and his brother (and especially the TD owners!) that the new TF was nothing less than "a great engineering advance" and "aerodynamically revolutionary" and naturally the longer the discussion in the bar went on and the more rounds of booze were ordered to fuel it, the more it started sounding like some sort of a challenge. And of course several of the MG guys had seen Cal run in his ratty old '47 TC and how well he'd done the few times he drove Carson's black TD, and so a couple of the TD faithful prevailed on a guy with a pretty nice TD who wasn't a particularly great driver to let Cal have a go in it. For the honor and glory of TD owners everywhere, you know?

And Cal was happy to oblige.

Personally, I was hoping that Big Ed would give Cal a few laps in the Trashwagon. Even just in practice. I wanted to see what a talent like Cal could do with it, right? And also if he'd have the same sort of handling problems with it that Big Ed did at Thompson. And again at Watkins Glen, for that matter. We'd entered it in the Seneca Cup race for "unrestricted" cars (which was the first race on the schedule at ten o'clock Saturday morning and therefore also first practice on Friday) on account of it was kind of a hodgepodge group with everything from George Weaver's old Grand Prix Maserati and that other Maserati open-wheeler with the monstrous Chrysler Hemi shoved under the hood and a guy named Paul Timmons in the ex-Walt Hansgen Jaguar special that won the main race at Watkins Glen the year before, plus a few too-highly-modified-to-run-in-"stock"-class Jag 120s and a few legit Jaguar C-Types—including our old friend Skippy Welcher and that slick, smooth and fast Dr. M.R.J. "Doc" Wyllie character from Pennsylvania by way of South Africa—and some other homebuilts and hybrids like our Trashwagon all the way down through Porsches and Triumphs and

Arnolt-Bristols and Austin-Healeys (like Carson's) that were either too rare or expensive or hopped-up to run in the "production" classes, plus a couple of those tiny little tin-turd Formula III Cooper open-wheelers that didn't seem to fit anywhere else. Including the one we'd seen at Thompson with a supercharged Porsche engine in the back that everybody said was going to be *really* fast if they ever got the bugs worked out of it. I mean, it didn't weigh anything, you know? Plus, just like our Trashwagon, it already had earned itself a nickname. People were calling it "the Pooper." For Porsche-Cooper, of course!

Julie came over and asked if there was anything she could do—like maybe time cars or something—but I only had two stopwatches, one for me and one for J.R., and besides, none of my guys in that first group looked exactly necessary to time. In fact, besides getting a few laps on Big Ed, I was planning to mostly keep an eye on George Weaver's Maserati, "Doc" Wyllie's C-Type and that tiny but menacing little "Pooper" thing. "Nah," I told her. "J.R. and me got it pretty well under control." I looked behind her and saw that she had little Vincent over with Sarah Jean and Mary Frances, huddled around that pathetic excuse for a campfire with my old Army blanket wrapped around them. To be honest, they looked like refugees. "Why don't you and the girls get into Big Ed's Thunderbird with little Vincent and put the heater on? I think you can all fit."

Julie gave me a sour look. "I came up here to help you," she said with an edge as cold as the weather in her voice. "I don't want to feel like the frickin' squaw with the papoose."

"But, Honey," I said absently as I watched the first group of cars fire up and pedal out onto the track, "you *are* the squaw with the papoose this weekend...."

It was maybe not exactly the right thing to say, and you could feel an actual tremor pass though the earth when she slammed the door to Big Ed's Thunderbird.

The wind had blown the track fairly dry by the time that first group started circulating, but it was still gray and damp and cold and threatening and really the kind of weather that made you wonder, someplace deep down inside yourself, just exactly why the heck you were doing this. Even if you didn't say anything. But there I was on the fences anyway—with young J.R. right beside me—watching my guys Big Ed in the Trashwagon, Carson Flegley in his hopped-up Healey and Danny Poindexter in his ex-Big Ed Arnolt-Bristol motoring around. Along with our buddy Tommy Edwards in some guy's Allard J2X with an experimental, Hilborn fuel-injected Oldsmobile Rocket 88 engine under the hood. Plus none other than S.H. "Wacky" Arnolt himself in one of the white-with-blue-racing-stripes "factory team" Arnolt-Bristols plus ex-MG racer Denny Cornett in a sister car just like it. I gotta admit, I had a real soft spot for those cars.

As you can see, I had a lot of people to keep track of in that first practice group. But it was one less almost immediately when Big Ed failed to come around on only the second lap. He showed up again about three laps later with some telltale hay and straw jammed in around the Trashwagon's rear fender, and then he was gone again a lap later, back again (this time with straw and hay kind of falling off the *other* rear fender) and I even got to see him swap ends in person on the very last lap of practice when he looped it in grand style coming out of the final corner. Fortunately, my other guys were pretty much behaving themselves. Even if they weren't going particularly fast. But then I didn't expect them to, either.

"This damn thing!" Big Ed groused as he switched the Trashwagon off in the paddock. "It feels pretty good and feels pretty good and then...*WHAM!*" —he snapped his fingers—"It just goes right around on you."

"Any idea what's causing it?"

"Hey, *you* built the damn thing. *You're* the big mechanical genius. I just hang onto the wheel and stomp on the damn pedals is all."

"But what does it *feel* like?"

"Well, t'be honest," Big Ed explained through pursed, bewildered lips, "it feels real good right up until it feels like I'm going backwards."

It wasn't the sort of feedback you could really build much engineering on. So I checked all the tires and poked around under the car and couldn't find a thing. Plus I didn't much enjoy crawling around on that cold, wet grass. I even had Big Ed fire it up one time just to get some blessed heat down there! Meanwhile Cal had gone out in that guy's TD to practice for the all-MG Collier Cup race, and he did his typically excellent Cal Carrington sort of job, taking second-quickest time by a heartbeat in a knot of four Fast Guys up head-and-shoulders above the rest. And the other three were all in TFs, too. Which, all things being absolutely equal (which they never are in racing, but that's another story), appeared to be just a wee bit sleeker and therefore likely a bit faster on the top end down that long, 1.3-mile main straightaway.

Julie came over again during lunch break and asked if there was anything she could do to help out or anything we'd like her to get us from the makeshift and thoroughly mobbed concession stand in the paddock, so I gave her a little folding money and had her go get us some hotdogs or hamburgers and coffee or tea or cocoa or something—anything the least bit warm!—but after she waited in line for half an hour with that frigid wind whipping right in her face, all they had left was your choice of cold egg salad or even colder tunafish salad and ice-cold pop to go with it. "Jeez, is this all you got?" I asked as I rooted around in the engine compartment of Buster Jones' Jaguar.

It instantly got several degrees colder, and another one of those marital tremors passed through the earth as she went back to Big Ed's Thunderbird and slammed the door behind her.

I thought it was a perfectly legitimate question....

There's always a Story of the Weekend in any racing paddock, and the big one being whispered and chatted all over the place that cold, gray, damp and windy Friday at Watkins Glen was about how this would be the last race *ever* for the Chrysler-powered Cunningham C-4Rs that I'd seen dominate so many "amateur" races here in America plus that famous outright victory at the Twelve Hours of Sebring in 1953. More importantly, those cars had carried our blue-and-white American racing colors over to Le Mans and Reims in France and done us all proud—even if the best finish they ever got over there was third. But Briggs had seen the writing on the wall that his three-year-old C-4Rs were getting a bit long in the tooth to run against the latest from Ferrari and Jaguar and Mercedes-Benz. The Chrysler-powered cars were just too damn heavy, and he'd decided to retire them and work on some brand new, top-secret All-American challenger to take on the Europeans on their home ground. In the meantime, everybody on the team agreed that Briggs' much-modified, white-with-blue-stripes 4.5 Ferrari (the one with the big, gaping holes on the front that they'd tried with water-cooled brakes at Le Mans) was now the fastest thing in the stable. And so, for Watkins Glen, they'd decided that Briggs should run the old C-4R to parade it around in its very last race and they'd put their lead driver, Phil Walters, in the Ferrari to give them the best shot at winning. And, in fact, that's how they practiced and qualified, with Walters taking fastest time a solid few ticks ahead of—you guessed it!—Creighton Pendleton the Third in *his* Ferrari.

Briggs himself was trundling around fourth- or fifth-fastest in the C-4R, almost unnoticed.

But what nobody except the team knew was that a lot of them—and Phil Walters especially, since he'd done so much of the testing and development work on those cars—wanted the old C-4R to go out with a little glory and fanfare. And so they took that particular C-4R and lightened the shit out of it by the old, time-proven and well-respected method of yanking off everything that would come loose, set it up with Weber carburetors and even tried out a hot new camshaft that they'd never even bench-tested on a dynomometer. Now this wasn't the kind of thing you'd expect out of the careful, experienced and maybe even a little bit con-servative Cunningham team. In fact, is was more the sort of thing you'd expect out of a crew like Cal and me when we were working on that derelict, piece-of-shit '47 TC of his in my Aunt Rosamarina's garage. Only the Cunningham guys maybe did it a wee bit better.

Meanwhile, over in the Team Passaic bivouac, I'd been grinding on Big Ed to give Cal a shot in the Trashwagon. And, seeing as how he'd done such a swell job in the TD and also seeing as how Big Ed was getting sick and tired of watching the scenery rotate around and furthermore seeing as how Big Ed's lips had turned a nice shade of iris blue and his teeth were chattering around his cigar and what he mostly wanted to do was shoo Julie and Mary Frances and Sarah Jean and lit-tle Vincent out of his Thunderbird (where they'd been sitting all afternoon, crammed together with the engine running and the heater dialed to a nice, toasty warm while they took turns holding the baby and talking about whatever it is that females of the species can talk about almost forever when they've got a baby to pass around) and drive himself back to the Seneca Lodge for a nice hot shower and a fistful of stiff brandies, he finally agreed to let Cal out in the Trashwagon for the final practice session of the day.

Julie came over with little Vincent all bundled up against her after Big Ed evicted the lot of them from his Thunderbird and headed off for the Seneca. "Is there anything I c-can do?" she asked, looking cold and miserable and exceed-ingly uncomfortable.

"Look," I said, "why don't you use the Volkswagen and take my sisters and little Vincent back to the lodge? I mean, I've got two more sessions with my guys and I've got to give the cars a final once-over afterwards and get everything but-toned down for the night. Why don't you just take off and I'll catch a ride with somebody else and be back in plenty of time to take you guys to dinner."

She looked at me kind of sideways. "In time for dinner, huh?"

"Sure I will," I promised. "Scout's honor."

She clutched little Vincenzo even closer and looked down at the ground. "I don't feel like I've been much help."

"Oh, you've been *plenty* of help," I told her, trying like hell to sound like I really meant it and not like I was just blowing her off.

But they always know....

So the girls left with little Vincent and Cal climbed aboard the Trashwagon and headed over to the pre-grid to line up for practice—we'd agreed he'd start at the back and kind of let everybody go so's he could feel out the Trashwagon without a lot of other solid objects flailing around—and I left J.R. in charge of the pits in case any of my other guys needed anything while I went down to Turn One so I could maybe watch and suss out what the Trashwagon was doing. Or not doing. Cal wisely took it through slow on the first lap, kind of weaving the car around a little to get the feel of it and letting a nice gap open up between him and the rest of the field. And then I just sat there through The Big Silence until the pack came around again—George Weaver's Maserati and "Doc" Wylie's C-Jag and Tommy Edwards' Allard and the Chrysler-engined Maserati and that amazing little supercharged "Pooper" hybrid already well clear of the rest—and then the big mid-group hurtled by like the damn Oklahoma Land Rush, with our boy Skippy Welcher right smack-dab in the middle of it in what should have been one of the fastest cars. And he was doing his usual awkward and untidy job of it by braking right down the middle of the track so nobody could pass him on either the inside *or* the outside and then turning his C-Type in way too early and then trying to keep from sliding right off by jamming the brakes on again in the middle of the corner and then trying to save it with a typically furious application of flying elbows—his hands a vivid blur on the steering wheel—but of course the car wouldn't steer worth a damn with the front wheels locked up, and so he more or less plowed right off. But he was going fairly slowly by then and so when he released the brakes naturally the tires bit in pretty good and he shot right back onto the track and damn near collected "Wacky" Arnolt in his Arnolt-Bristol that shouldn't even have been able to sniff the fumes off a Jaguar C-Type's exhaust pipes. The truly amazing thing was how The Skipper could be so genuinely *bad* as a racecar driver and still enjoy it. But then he was nuts, and that always explains a lot of things.

About a half minute later I saw Cal exiting the final corner, way down the pit straight from me and all by his lonesome, and I could hear the throttles on those four Strombergs flop wide open as he nailed the gas pedal to the firewall. And it was pretty damn impressive how the Trashwagon reared back on its haunches and really gobbled up that straightaway, the exhaust blasting out a little snort and the nose making a little dip each time he shifted. I felt a real glow inside at the way that big hotrod Caddy engine ate up the pavement. Cal got on the brakes pretty late and you could see the car kind of lean forward on its nose and squirm around in the back end under hard braking as he set it up for the corner. And then Cal smoothly arced it in towards the apex and it looked great for a second and then—just like Big Ed said—it suddenly jerked up all funny in the rear and swapped ends. Just like *that!* There was a peal of scorched rubber and wisps of smoke off the tires, but it fortunately spun down the middle of the roadway without hitting anything and wound up parked right in the middle of the track pointed the exact opposite way with an obviously bewildered Cal Carrington at the wheel. He looked around and noticed me over on the far side of the fences and kind of shrugged and rolled his palms up. *What can you do?* At least he'd remembered to put the clutch in and blip the engine so it didn't stall, and, after checking the gauges and getting a wave-off from the flagman, he took off again. But he was late coming around on the next lap and, when he did appear, there was a fresh dent and yet more hay on the back end. Plus he was going much more slowly, and he looked right at me and pointed his thumb back towards the paddock as he trundled by....

So I hustled back to the Team Passaic compound in the paddock and sure enough found Cal crouched down next to the Trashwagon, staring at the rear wheel with a puzzled expression on his face. "Big Ed's right," he said, scratching his chin. "You can get going pretty good in this thing, but then—if you try to push it—she just all of a sudden snaps away from you."

"What does it feel like?"

Cal looked at me and smiled. "Awful."

"That's not what I mean."

"I know. But it feels awful all the same. It's like the back end suddenly hits an oil slick or something. Just like *that!*" He snapped his fingers. Just like Big Ed did.

Well, for sure there was something wrong under there somewhere, and so I laid a canvas tarp down on the cold, wet grass and crawled underneath again and looked and poked and prodded, but I still couldn't see anything wrong. So I got some plywood to keep the floor jack from sinking into the ground and loosened the lugnuts and put it up in the air and removed the rear wheels and looked some more.

"What's that?" J.R. said from over my shoulder.

"What?"

"That!" He pointed his finger at the rear axle. And then I could see it, too. A rough little shiny spot. And so my eyes followed up from that spot and there, sure enough, was a matching little shiny spot on the frame. It was those damn lowering blocks we'd put in between the axle and the springs! They were just too fat, so when the car leaned hard into a corner, the axle was running out of travel and grounding on the damn frame. And of course when that happened, everything went Instant Solid like a blessed coaster wagon and spit the ass end around before the driver could so much as clinch his sphincter muscle. Although he'd generally catch a good grip on the seat upholstery by the middle of the first rotation.

Like most racecar problems, it was really simple and obvious once you got it figured out.

Well, I figured I could maybe fix it, but I knew it would be a hell of a lot easier on a lift in a regular shop with a vise and a workbench—and preferably a nice, *warm* regular shop with a vise and a workbench—so I put the wheels back on, made sure my guys had everything under control, loaded some tools in back and simply *drove* the Trashwagon down into town to see if I could maybe find a gas station or garage that would let me use the facilities. The cops in Watkins Glen tended to be a little lenient regarding racecars on public roads during the race weekend. Besides, most of them were up the hill directing traffic in and out and watching the practice and qualifying sessions in between like everybody else.

Sure enough, that same Atlantic station on Franklin Street where I got Big Ed's four flats fixed on race morning the first time we came to Watkins Glen was only too happy to oblige, and the kid there even knew a machinist in Montour Falls who could make damn near anything out of metal if I really needed it. And I knew I might, seeing as how one of the inborn problems with a half-breed one-off like the Trashwagon is that you tend to build it out of whatever you can get your hands on at the time and then you kind of forget exactly where all the bits and pieces and miscellaneous hardware came from. Like fr'instance I quickly realized that I couldn't just yank the lowering blocks out and bolt it all back together on account of I'd used these longer U-bolts that didn't have enough thread on them to work without the blocks. And I didn't much fancy using a two-inch stack of washers under each of the eight nuts. Not that the gas station had a ready supply of that many washers of the right size anyway. So I took one of the U-bolts with me and hitched a ride back up the hill with some guy who'd stopped to fill up his Porsche, but by then practice was over and the people left in the paddock were mostly hanging around shooting the breeze and shivering and drinking ice-cold beer. Even though it couldn't have been more than a degree or two above freezing. Can you believe it? Anyhow, I finally located Cal and Carson over by that intriguing little Porsche/Cooper thing, and we made a deal for Cal to hitch a ride back to the Lodge with somebody else while Carson and me took the Healey back down the hill to go looking for what I needed to fix the Trashwagon. And naturally it turned into one of those long, desperate, running-around-like-crazy-without-getting-much-of-anything-accomplished Race Weekend Field Repair experiences that usually start right about the time most regular folks are locking up and heading home for supper....

First we went back down to the gas station to get directions to the nearest auto parts store that might still be open—and of course they were just closing!—but they kindly opened back up for us. Unfortunately, they didn't have any U-bolts the right size and maybe only half as many washers as we needed. But I bought them anyway, just in case. And they suggested another, bigger store in Elmira, but we called and it was already closed and so we tried another one in Ithaca and he said he'd wait for us but when we got there he didn't have the right size U-bolts either. But he did have a bunch more washers and so I bought those and we back-tracked to Watkins Glen and had the guy at the gas station call his machinist friend and then went over to his shop and had him carve up the lowering blocks with a bandsaw so they were only maybe ¾ of an inch thick—I figured that would about do it—and then we went back to the Atlantic station where the kid was still waiting for us inside and Carson even helped out a little while I put the thinner lowering blocks in and wrestled the back axle into place and put the U-bolts back on with a tall, heavy and thoroughly unseemly stack of washers under each nut and it was damn near eleven by the time I had it all screwed back together. But while we were running all over the place and messing around with the car, I caught myself thinking every now and then about Carson Flegley and how I felt about him and my sister Sarah Jean hanging around together. And I must admit I was feeling pretty okay about it. I mean, he wasn't the most exciting or effervescent or attractive kind of person you might ever meet—in fact, he was dull as a lead penny in most respects—and the fact that his family ran a funeral home still gave me the creeps whenever I stumbled over mental pictures about exactly what that line of work might entail. But no question Carson Flegley was a solid, dependable, nose-to-the-grindstone type—somebody you could count on—and I found myself getting more and more comfortable with the notion that he might be a pretty decent match for Sarah Jean. Besides, the fact that he'd wanted a sports car and then wanted to try his hand at racing and then, in spite of not having a thimbleful of natural talent for it and being scared to death half the time, sticking it out and trying to get better at it said a lot for the scrawny little guy underneath that thinning hair and behind those thick eyeglasses.

I figured it actually might work out for them, you know?

Or at least I hoped it would, anyway.

After I finished tightening up the last lugnut we took the Trashwagon down off the lift and the kid at the station allowed as how, if we wanted to, we could leave it there overnight and pick it up first thing in the morning. I looked at Carson and Carson looked back at me and I told him "no," that we'd take our chances trying to run it back up the hill and back into the paddock under the cover of darkness rather than around dawn when the sound out of the dump pipes would echo from one end of Lake Seneca to the other. Then I tried to offer the kid a little something for his trouble, but he said it was okay and he was glad to help us racers out any way he could. That's the way a lot of the people are in Watkins Glen.

So Carson fired up the Healey and switched on the lights and I fired up the Trashwagon and tucked it right in behind the Healey's rear bumper—Jeez, I couldn't believe how *loud* it sounded!—and so I kept it barely off idle as we looked both ways and crept out onto Franklin Street and it should come as no surprise to anybody who knows about such things that we didn't make it three blocks before we had flashing red lights and a siren going off behind us.

Oh, shit.

Here we go again....

Well, I must admit the cop only went through the usual *"What about the license plate? What about the headlights? What about the mufflers? What about the windshield? What about the horn?"* stuff for about five minutes before he gave me a chance to explain as how this was a genuine (and, might I add, highly popular with the crowd), homegrown, all-American race car running in the big sportycar races up the hill that brought so much fame and income and worldwide notoriety to the good people of Watkins Glen and the surrounding area, and furthermore that we had just performed some Emergency Major Surgery to get it ready for tomorrow's race and were only driving it on the street at this hour so as not to have to wake up the good people of Watkins Glen and the surrounding area at some ungodly hour the following morning.

Officer.

Sir.

The cop looked at me—as cops often do—like it was the biggest load of unadulterated bullshit he'd ever heard in his life. Then, with the rotating red beam of the mars light playing across his face, he shook his head slowly, rolled his eyes up towards the heavens and sighed mightily. "You know something?" he said wearily, looking at the sky.

"What's that, Officer? Sir?"

"I'm not gonna bother to write you up."

"You're not, Officer? Sir?"

"No, I'm not." He looked down at me the way cops do. "And do you know *why* I'm not going to write you up?"

"No, I surely don't. Officer. Sir."

"Because there's not enough lead in my pencil to write all the damn citations this heap of junk deserves. You understand me, son?"

"Yes I do, Officer. Sir."

He sighed again and shook his head. "Just follow me. And keep it down, okay?"

"I surely will, Officer. Sir."

And with that he got back in his squad car and led Carson and me all the way back up to the paddock with the mars lights rotating. Just like a blessed parade.

Well, we thanked him up at the paddock gate and he just looked at us real disgustedly and headed back down the hill towards town (although I do believe I caught just the littlest flicker of a smile at the corner of his lips as he turned the squad car around) and then I followed Carson's headlights back to our spot in the pitch-black and icy-cold paddock, dropped off the Trashwagon, climbed into the Healey, and we growled off into the night, following those two dancing blobs of headlamp light down the darkened country roads of Schuyler County.

"Hey, thanks a lot," I told Carson. "Sorry about the trouble with the cop."

"It wasn't your fault. Besides, it's things like that—things *exactly* like that—that make race weekends so...so..."

"So much fun?"

His face brightened. "Yeah, that's it. But it's even more. It's like...it's like...."

"An adventure? An obstacle course?"

Carson brightened even more. "Yeah, that's it. But it's even...it's even...."

"Like going to the circus, traveling with gypsies and a top-secret commando raid into enemy territory, all at the same time!"

Carson looked at me, dumbstruck. "Y'know," he said solemnly, "someday you maybe ought to write a book about it...."

I figured I was going to catch hell from Julie for more or less ditching her and coming back so late after promising I'd meet up with her for dinner, so I talked Carson into taking a quick detour into town for one last cruise up and down Franklin Street in the Healey. Just to soak it all in and see what was going on. And there was plenty, what with people and sports cars all over the place and every bar and eatery and souvenir shop still doing a land-office business and chatter and laughter about cars and racing just about everywhere. Even with the cold and late hour and everything. To be honest, I felt like stopping in for a bite to eat and maybe a few drinks myself, but I knew I'd better get back to the Seneca and take my inevitable and well-deserved dose of shit from Julie so we could make up and get to bed sometime before three ayem. I mean, you really don't want to go to sleep angry at each other, do you? So I rotated my head around and took one more long, lingering look up Franklin Street—long enough to last me all winter, hopefully—and we turned right on 329 and headed back up the hill towards the Seneca.

It was pretty chilly in our cabin, and even chillier on account of Julie was naturally giving me the frost for coming back so late and ignoring her all day and missing dinner and leaving her and little Vincent stranded while I went to fix the Trashwagon, and besides that the baby was sniffling and coughing a little bit now and that, of course, was my fault, too. And I was giving her the iceberg treatment right back for not understanding that this was our damn livelihood and I was only doing what I *had* to do and how it was really *nice* of me to send her and the other girls back to the lodge in the Volkswagen while I took care of things in true Manly Martyr fashion on the front lines. Or at least that's the way I saw it, anyway.

"I don't know why you even want to take us with," she hissed between her teeth. "You don't pay any attention to us. You just fool around with your friends and their damn cars. It's like we're not even there."

"I just got busy is all," I groused right back at her.

"You never think about us at all on a race weekend."

"Of course I do."

"No you don't."

"Didn't I send you back here with the baby?"

"You were just trying to get rid of us."

"No I wasn't."

"Yes you were."

"I was just trying to be *nice,* that's all."

"Hmpf."

I *"Hmpf'd"* her right back.

We were glaring at each other and it was obvious this discussion was going nowhere except into ever-tightening little circles—kind of a Death Spiral, actually—and, if you've got a halfway decent marriage going, there comes a time when you start feeling like both of you are looking for some sort of ripcord or escape hatch or something.

"So," I snarled at her, "did you eat anything?"

"No!" she snarled right back. "We were waiting for *you!"*

"Well, here I am."

"At quarter to midnight."

"I couldn't help it."

"You *never* can help it, can you?"

"No, I can't."

"The baby and I could starve."

"You don't look like you've missed too many meals."

Boy, did that ever turn the ice to fire!

"And what do you mean by *that?"*

"I mean you both look real, uhh, *healthy...*"

"Healthy, huh?"

"Yeah. And hungry, too."

"We *should* look hungry. We haven't eaten any dinner."

"So, you want me to go get us something?"

"The kitchen's closed. I already tried."

"I can find us something."

"You just want to go off and get tanked with your friends!"

"Sure I do! But I'm not gonna. I'm gonna get us something to eat and be right back."

So I stomped out and went over to the lodge—as you can imagine, the place was totally up for grabs—and I asked one of the Brubaker guys behind the bar if there was maybe any way I could get my poor, shivering, starving wife and child a crust or crumb of something to eat. The Brubaker family owns the Seneca Lodge, and they're some pretty nice and friendly people. In fact, sometimes late in the evening, it's hard to tell the guys behind the bar from the customers.

Well, he said the kitchen was closed but he'd go back and have a quick look and damn if he didn't come up with some salad, a leftover slab of turkey breast with gravy and two baked potatoes that were still warm and a couple nice slices of blueberry pie for dessert. "What do I owe you?" I asked him.

"The dining room register's closed and I don't have a menu. Just take it. Everything but the pie would've wound up in the garbage anyway."

"You sure?"

"Yeah. But just this once." He leaned in closer and added, "and don't tell anybody, OK?"

"Mum's the word. Can I buy you a drink?"

"Only if you're having one, too."

So I bought us a drink—manhattans for each of us—plus one for Cal and one for Carson and one for Mary Frances and a Pink Squirrel for Sarah Jean and a white wine for Danny Poindexter and another one for 'Fos' and a beer for Buster Jones and an English stout for Tommy Edwards and a double gin-and-tonic for Big Ed Baumstein and....

It would've been cheaper to pay for dinner, you know?

But I only did the one round like a good boy—even though I could feel the warm rush off the racing chatter and clinking glasses and wanted like hell to stay—and headed back to our cabin with the tray, and damn if Julie hadn't found a couple candles and we had a nice little late candlelight supper together while little Vincent slept peacefully on the bed, surrounded by pillows, and after dinner we put the candles out and got into the other bed and snuggled together and listened to the wind that was still blowing outside and the creak of the trees and the scratching of twig fingers against the windowpanes. You could feel the winter coming, and we snuggled together even tighter against it.

It's frankly amazing how, if you know each other pretty well and begin to understand how the marriage game is played, you can be cold and hungry and tired and angry and yelling and snarling and spitting at each other at quarter-to-midnight and cuddled up all soft and warm and well-fed and doing things you never discuss with anybody—including you—by one ayem.

Race morning dawned just as cold and grim and blustery as the day before, and on the way over to the track I was kind of hoping we'd get our races out of the way without major incident and maybe even get out of there early and on our way home on account of I had a nice afterglow going with Julie and I sure as heck wanted to hang on to it. You learn pretty quick that those things are both precious and fragile. But of course then you get to the racetrack and you hear the engines warming up against the cold and see the crowd filtering in and feel the tension in the air and sip your coffee or cocoa and all of a sudden you've got that buzz again.

It's a kind of disease, actually.

And there's no known cure, either.

Big Ed and most of my guys were out in the very first race at ten ayem, and I was kind of hoping that Big Ed would let Cal drive on account of I was pretty sure we had the handling problem solved on the Trashwagon—not elegantly, mind you, but *solved*—and I thought it would be neat to once-and-for-all see what the Trashwagon could do. But Big Ed was adamant that he would drive because he really wanted to beat Skippy Welcher in his damn C-Type again—just like we had at Bonneville—only this time *mano-a-mano* instead of with timing slips. And it didn't matter to him where they finished overall. Not one bit. Why, they could be dead last and next-to-dead last, just so long as Big Ed was at the wheel and the Trashwagon finished ahead of The Skipper's C-Type.

That's how bad Big Ed wanted to beat Skippy Welcher.

But, based on qualifying times, Big Ed had to start dead last (neither he nor Cal finished a lap in anger at speed without rotating a few times) while The Skipper was mired just above mid-pack, surrounded by cars that should have been nothing more than faint specks in his mirror. They had that famous Brit racer and recent MG EX-179 streamliner record-setter at Bonneville, Captain George E.T. Eyston, on hand as Chief Steward and he led the field around on the pace lap at the wheel of that same gaudy-but-futuristic Buick Skylark showcar we'd seen at the GM Motorama at the Waldorf Astoria Hotel in New York. I was pleased to see that our friend Tommy Edwards had actually grabbed the pole in that fuel-injected, Oldsmobile-powered Allard, but he had fast guys all around him and he'd told me before the race that he was going to take it a little easy early on and try to save the brakes. A lot of the drivers were complaining about two corners where you had no place to go—except into the scenery or off into outer space!—if you arrived without brakes, and that was certainly not the kind of thing an experienced driver like Tommy wanted to do with somebody else's car....

At the drop of the green, George Weaver's Maserati and Tippy Lipe's nifty little "Pooper" blasted out of the pack like they were shot from a pair of cannons and arrived well clear of the rest at corner one. Tommy Edwards drove a nice, conservative line and "let the fast blokes and the crazies go" (as he put it later) and settled in about fifth or sixth behind that Chrysler-engined Maserati and "Doc" Wyllie's C-Jag and Paul Timmons in the ex-Walt Hansgen Jag special. It was impossible to sort out the clot of cars in the middle (although Skippy Welcher was accompanied by his usual plume of dust!), but I noticed Big Ed took a charge up the inside and picked off at least four cars by corner one. Better yet, the Trashwagon didn't spin!

Some of the drama went out of things at the end of the very first lap, when George Weaver's leading Maserati (which, by the way, he called "Poison Lil") came into the pits and retired, and then, not many laps after that, the tiny little crowd-favorite "Pooper" came in with the belt to the supercharger thrown and, although he came back out for awhile, he was well back and it was obvious that the car was no longer a threat. This left the Chrysler/Maserati in first, but he was being hounded by "Doc" Wyllie's C-Jag, and it was only a matter of time before the Jag slipped by and then the Maserati took to the escape road trying to keep up and all of a sudden he was way down in fourth. Tommy was having a nice tussle with Paul Timmons in the ex-Hansgen Jag special, but he couldn't quite keep up. He told me that fuel-injected engine worked kind of like a wall switch—you either had all fluff and bubbles or JATO-assist—and that made it not the easiest thing in the world to drive. Plus Tommy was always thoughtful of other people's cars....

But even though things had gotten pretty dull up front, my eyes were glued on Big Ed and the progress he was making through the field. Oh, he still had hams for fists and clubs for feet and drove with about as much grace as an ostrich on ice skates, but no question he was making his way through the backmarkers and closing in on Skippy Welcher. In fact, judging by the times on my stopwatch, he'd very likely catch The Skipper before the end of the race!

And then he didn't come around.

Well, I expected the worst and asked one of the marshals with a field phone what had happened, but it turned out he'd just pulled off someplace rather than plowing into anything. And that was good news indeed.

And so the race played out and "Doc" Wyllie chalked up a dull-to-watch but well-earned victory with Paul Timmons took second and Tommy Edwards third and all my guys besides Big Ed finished. But none of them did especially well and, worse yet, they all came home behind The Skipper's C-Type. So we really didn't have much to celebrate over in the Team Passaic corner of the paddock. Some days it just goes like that, you know?

And the word on the Trashwagon was that something had gone *clunk!* and then all clattery down in the general vicinity of the bellhousing and surely Big Ed would have still kept his foot in it chasing after The Skipper only then the car started slowing down all by itself as several large, ugly pieces of clutch and fly-wheel shrapnel exploded up through the front of the transmission tunnel—he was damn lucky none of it hit him, if you want the honest truth of it—and so he had no choice but to park it.

Damn!

Well, they hauled the Trashwagon in on a hook and I could see it was going to be a mess getting it on the trailer what with the driveline locked up solid, but I put that off for a little bit while we all went over to the fences to watch Cal drive that other guy's TD in the all-MG "Collier Brothers Memorial Trophy" race that came up next. And did he ever do a job! There were no less than 32 MGs entered, and every last one of them a supposedly bone-stock TC, TD or TF. Although, judging from the exhaust notes—including the one on the "well-prepared" example our boy Cal was driving!—there seemed to be some pretty creative interpretations of "bone stock" running around out there! In any case, it was nip and tuck up at the front, what with Cal in the TD and three other guys in TFs getting away from the rest—but not from each other!—and having the best damn race you ever saw! By about half-distance, one of the TFs had dropped away a little bit—he just couldn't match the pace of the other three, you know?—but you could still cover the lead trio with a blanket and not one of them could get away from the other two. From where I was watching down by the last turn, I would usually see Cal in third and dipping to the inside to out-brake one or the other of the TFs to take second, and then do the same to the other one down at turn one to retake the lead. But he could never hold it on account of the two TFs—both of which had exhaust notes every bit as crisp as Cal's, and maybe even a wee bit crisper!—would slipstream him down that long, 1.3-mile straightaway and steam past into the lead like a two-car freight train before the next corner. And then they'd likely as not go in side-by-side, trying to outbrake each other and there'd be no place for Cal to go. "You've just got to bloody wait it out in those situations," Tommy Edwards said from his spot right beside me on the fence. "Even if you're bloody well faster, you can't go if there's no hole."

I could see what he was talking about.

What was called for here was a bit of guile and patience—that's what you need when you can't just streak away from the other guys—and damn if Cal didn't figure it out! What he had to do was break up the other two guys so's he could be in second rather than third heading into the final corner. And the way to do that was to hang back a little on purpose on the second-to-last lap and stay in second spot through that last corner and even brake a little early and leave a bit of a sucker hole for the third-place car, like he could maybe get by on the inside. But Cal was watching him like a hawk in the rearview mirror and, as soon as he took the bait and dove for the opening, Cal went in deeper and swept right across his bows, slamming the door right in his face. Well, there was nothing for the poor fish in the TF to do but lock 'em up and take a quick plow towards the trackside scenery with rubbersmoke squealing off the tires. It was just a tiny little bobble—not even enough to send him off the road or anything—but it killed his exit speed out of the corner and gave Cal the four or five carlengths he needed so he could concentrate on the TF in front. Who now had what appeared to be a safe eight- or nine-carlength lead on Cal's TD. It was the biggest lead of the entire race! "It's in the bag now," Tommy whispered through a cobra's grin. "You watch. He'll eat him up now."

And sure enough he did. Cal drove his best, smoothest, fastest line ever through the next several corners, took an absolutely perfect exit onto that long, 1.3-mile straight—braking just a tad early and getting the car all gathered up so he was hard into the gas before he even clipped the apex—and this time it was *Cal* in the slipstream, reeling in the leading TF and making ground through the hole it was poking in the air. And Cal had it all figured out, too. He feinted to pull out and the guy moved to block and he showed a fender in the other mirror and the guy moved to block the other way and by then they were getting to the Last Possible Moment for applying the brakes if you wanted to make the next corner and so the guy pulled to the inside to guard his line while Cal pushed him deeper and deeper into the braking zone and *that's* when Cal made his move—he'd never lifted off the gas for an instant, keeping it flat on the floor even though it looked like he was going to eat the other guy's license plate!—but now he dropped back for a heartbeat, lined up for an absolutely perfect line through the 90-degree right hander, and swept under the leading MG at the exit while he was fighting to keep from going off the road.

Why, he had two or three whole carlengths in hand at the checker!

Wotta race!

Well, of course, the place went absolutely nuts afterward and all the TD guys—in fact, all of the MG guys, no matter what they were driving!—were shaking Cal's hand and clapping him on the back and offering him warming things to drink out of their thermos bottles (and we're not talking just coffee and tea here, either), and I must admit it was a pretty good feeling to be pals with a guy who could drive like that. Even if he wasn't exactly the most thoughtful or trustworthy person in the world. But I noticed Big Ed didn't look especially happy about it. Oh, he congratulated Cal and threw a big, meaty arm around his shoulders and even offered him one of his dollar Cuban cigars. But there was a little edge to it if you looked real close, and no doubt Big Ed Baumstein was just a tiny bit jealous of what Cal Carrington could do with a racecar.

Maybe even more than a tiny bit.

By then the wind had kicked up even more and people all over the paddock and along the fences were wearing gloves and parkas and stocking caps like it was the blessed Dartmouth Winter Carnival or something. But they were there—lots of 'em, in fact—and that should tell you a little bit about the sports car bug and what it does to otherwise ordinary human beings.

Next up was the Glen Trophy Race for production sports cars over 1250cc, and that meant mostly Jag 120s in Class C and Healey Hundreds in Class D and TR2s in Class E and Porsches in Class F. The MGs would've been in Class F, too, but, since they'd given them their own race (which was good because there were so many of them, and also because no way could even the best of them have run with the quicker Porsches) it had worked out so the owners and fans of each of the popular makes were absolutely guaranteed that they'd have some kind of first-in-class trophy to brag about around the bar that evening. In fact, you couldn't have planned it out any better if you tried.

Buster Jones was in that race and running with his usual, exemplary mediocrity, but then he somehow caught a stone right through the radiator core off somebody's tire or something, and wouldn't you know it was way down where you couldn't get at it without pulling the damn radiator and so I had a bunch more work to do before we could load up and head for home. And it was starting to threaten rain (or maybe even snow?) and not really the sort of day you wanted to be field-stripping a Jag 120. Plus we still had the locked-up Trashwagon to get loaded. And, speaking of loaded up, it was becoming very clear that, what with all the thermos cups full of hearty congratulations the MG guys had been feeding Cal Carrington, he was going to be just about useless when it came to packing up and getting ourselves back on the road. Why, a few of those TD guys would've had Cal bronzed and mounted on a marble pedestal in Rockefeller Center if they could. Not that he could have stood there for very long in his current condition.

I missed the end of the Glen Trophy race but it was—as expected on the long Glen course with that particularly long back straightaway—a Jaguar benefit, with XK 120s taking the first fourteen places. But then came some guy in a Porsche to take the F Class honors ahead of one of the slower Jags and then a TR2 taking the "E" class win just ahead of three Austin-Healey Hundreds (which finished 1-2-3 in Class D) and another Porsche, which took second in Class F. As you can imagine, there was a lot of gab and bullshit and loyalty conflicts about the battles between the Porsches and the Triumphs and the Healey Hundreds—even though they were running in different classes and everybody came away with a "win"—and you come to understand after you've been around it for awhile that the races are never really over when the checkered flag falls. Nope, it usually takes until closing time at the bar that evening. With, if it was really a closely-fought contest, possible "what if" and "if only" aftershocks at other bars and around other paddock beer kegs for months and even years to come.

Naturally 'Fos' was particularly proud of the way "his" Porsche (even though he himself wasn't exactly racing) had beaten all those British Triumphs and Healeys with bigger engines. And the fact was you had to be impressed. Only he didn't have to be so damn smug about it.

I also missed the next race, the Queen Catherine Cup for smallbore "modified" cars in classes F, G and H on account of I was crawling around under Buster Jones' Jag and trying to figure out how to get the Trashwagon loaded up, but, as expected, it was OSCAs 1-2-3-4 followed by some oddball British racing specials, mostly with hot-rodded MG engines under their generally oddly-shaped hoods, a couple handsome and petite Siatas taking 1st and 2nd in Class G, and then the inevitable 750cc tiddlers running in H Modified. Most of them were Italian—pretty little miniaturized, bargain-basement racing cars from tiny little garage-operator manufacturers like Stanguellini and Bandini—but there were also a few American homebuilts. By far the neatest of that bunch was "Candy" Poole's PBX, which was a regular on the SCMA racing scene and always held its own against the best of the "professionally-built" tiddlers from overseas. Not that a back-alley garage in Italy or England was all that much different from a back-alley garage in New York or Connecticut or even Passaic, New Jersey.

By then Hal Ullrich had come up with the bright idea of disconnecting the driveshaft so's we could get a few helpers and roll the Trashwagon onto the trailer (now why didn't *I* think of that?) and I was just finished loading everything up and lashing it all down when the big guns lined up for the final race of the day. To be honest, I was chilled right through to the bone and really looking forward to being in a nice, warm car heading for home. Only I wanted to see this race on account of the scuttlebutt that had spread like wildfire through the paddock was that Phil Walters and Briggs Cunningham had swapped rides at the last moment and so Phil was going to drive the lightened, Weber-carbureted Cunningham C-4R in its very last race. Which meant that Briggs was starting on the pole in his much-modified Ferrari—right next to Creighton Pendleton the Third's Ferrari, natch!—and Phil Walters was way back in fifth slot behind another Ferrari and the second C-4R and right next to "Smilin' Jack" Ensley in his stout-looking Kurtis. Plus there were a bunch more, slightly smaller-engined Ferraris and Walt Hansgen's C-Type Jaguar and so forth snapping at their heels, and by far the strangest car of the bunch was famous business tycoon and Gold Cup hydroplane racer Lou Fageol's twin-engined Porsche special—one engine in front driving the front wheels and one engine in back driving the back wheels—which went pretty fast but looked and sounded like something out of those old Buster Crabbe *Flash*

Gordon serials. Plus the corner crews—who had done a fantastic job all weekend under the guidance of a guy named Fred German, who really understood what racing was all about—had reported that the track surface was breaking up on some of the corners, and so chief steward Captain George Eyston called a drivers' meeting just before the Grand Prix to advise them all about it.

"You about ready to leave?" Julie asked over my shoulder.

"I'd kind of like to watch this race," I told her.

"It's going to rain."

"I've got an umbrella."

She rolled her eyes. "You never get enough, do you?"

It wasn't really a question.

So Julie went back to the Volkswagen with the engine running and little Vincent and my sister Mary Frances inside—both my sisters were really great with the baby—while I went over by the fence down at Turn One with Cal to watch. Carson had already taken off with Sarah Jean in the Healey and Big Ed had left with J.R. in the Thunderbird and so had Danny Poindexter in his Arnolt-Bristol and "Fos" in his Porsche and Buster Jones in his Jag as soon as I got finished with his radiator—light hitters, all of them—while we stood there shivering in the cold and wind as we waited for the cars to come around. Not that my buddy Cal was much feeling it, thanks to all the victory libations the MG guys had poured down his throat. Although they didn't exactly have to tie him down and force him. Which is why it was a good thing we found a spot by one of the fence posts, on account of it looked like that was about the only thing holding Cal up. To be honest, I'd never really seen Cal like that. Oh, I'd seen him after he'd had a few—even a few too many—but he always seemed to have himself sharp and together and never went into that wavering, half-empty-sack-of-corn-meal-mush posture that your garden-variety rumpots are so famous for.

"Whaddaya think?" I asked as we waited for the cars to come around on their pace lap.

"I think it'sh gonna be way too long till the nexsht racshe weekend." So that was it.

"I mean about this race."

"I shtill think it'sh gonna be way too long."

You could see he was into that fabulously maudlin, melancholy state of mind people sometimes get into during the late innings of a major-league drunk. And it wasn't like him at all. But the end of racing season and the coming of winter meant more to a guy like Cal Carrington than most people. Sure, he'd won his last race of the season in great style, but now he was going off the drug cold-turkey for at least five months—with no real prospects on the horizon even then—and you could see it was making him all cold and hollow inside.

But I knew it would all vanish once the green flag waved and the engines roared. Even on a day like this and feeling the way he did, that always gave you a hefty shot in the arm.

So the cars came around and lined up in even rows and Captain George Eyston looked them over and waved the green flag and Briggs Cunningham got just the right amount of wheelspin and a really great launch in his white-with-blue-stripes Ferrari and squirted away from the rest, but Creighton Pendleton wasn't far behind and you could see Phil Walters in the lightweight Cunningham taking a peek down the inside of the car just ahead as the field roared out of sight. And then we waited through the quiet, following the echo of the cars around the backside of the course and then it disappeared for a little while and then started to build again from the opposite direction and then they burst around that last right-hander—Creighton Pendleton's Ferrari on the point, but Walters in the light-weight Cunningham up to second and stalking, a good race between Hansgen in the C-Jag and that Dick Irish guy in somebody's Ferrari Mexico coupe, and another good race a few positions further back between Lou Fageol's odd twin-Porsche contraption and "Smilin' Jack" Ensley's Kurtis 500. They stayed pretty much like that for several laps, and I was really pulling for Phil Walters in the Cunningham to get by Creighton Pendleton's Ferrari and win the C-4R's last race. And I figured he just might do it, too. Jerk that he was, Creighton was still a heck of a driver, but you could see he was obviously a lot more comfortable on the flat, wide-open airport circuits where he'd had so much success that year (and where, incidentally, the penalty for screwing up was seldom more than collecting a few pylons or a handful of hay) and maybe just a bit spooked going fast around a true road circuit like the Glen. Phil Walters, on the other hand, had raced at Le Mans and Reims in France and excelled on the natural road circuits like the old Elkhart Lake and Watkins Glen layouts. Plus he knew how to be patient and put the old pressure on. Get a guy so he's keeping one eye glued to the rearview mirror and that's one less eye he can focus on where he needs to be going. And especially when you've got pavement breaking up here and there and some of it starting to get real slick on account of....

Rain!

Oh, it started off as just a faint, cold sprinkle. Hardly enough to worry about. But then it came down a little harder. A drizzle, you know? And that was all it took for Phil Walters to slip past Creighton Pendleton with ease and motor off into the distance. I mean, the race was really over at that point. Finished. Especially since the rain was coming down even harder and the track surface was getting so slick in places that Fred German dispatched a truck with fifty pound bags of cement mix so his workers could spread it over the worst spots. Between cars, that is. Like I said, the course workers did one hell of a job that weekend. And they were about the only people left besides Cal and me. Everybody with two- or three-digit IQs had already made for the exits. But there we stood, Cal and me—just the two of us, all by our lonesome on the fence—under an ugly, blackened sky with that damn-near useless little umbrella pointed up into the wind so it wouldn't snap inside out on us and our wet clothes wrapped and cinched around us as best we could and the wind and rain pelting in at us almost sideways and the racecars droning by one-by-one on spattering little wakes of spray with cold, empty gaps of quiet in between. But we had to stay to the end, you know? Just to see Phil Walters and that fabulous, all-American Cunningham C-4R take its final checkered flag.

It was a matter of respect.

I hate late fall. The racing season is over and another summer has leaked away, and you know you've got a whole damn winter to slog through before the skies get bright and the birds chirp and you get to hear the engines roar and the squeal of rubber against pavement again. And in between you've got winter with its gauntlet-run of holidays and family gatherings that nobody much wants to go to but everybody does anyway. Just like last year. Plus it gets so damn ugly outside when late fall rolls around, what with gray skies and chill winds and the leaves all withering up like dead skin and the nights falling earlier and earlier and the faces on the people you meet getting paler and paler from lack of sun. Of course the silver-spoon types take off for Bermuda or Palm Beach or wherever just so's they can come back every now and then to show off their tans, but, for the rest of us, it's just a long, slow slog from one year to the next.

The only real bright spot is Halloween which, even though it mostly celebrates all the darkness and foreboding of the season, manages to brighten things up with false faces and kids' pranks and the now-annual road racer's costume party over at the Flegley family funeral home in East Orange. Not that anybody except the attendees were supposed to know about it. I mean, people get pretty solemn and serious about the Dearly Departed, and the last thing they really need to know is that a bunch of sportycar types are whooping it up in the casket showroom or using poor old Uncle Sydney's coffin as a place to set drinks and ashtrays.

We made a deal to drop little Vincent off by my folks' house for a change (and you can bet Julie's mom was plenty frosty about it, but she got to see him all the time and my mom was getting those Bassett-hound eyes about not seeing him enough), and I have to admit that things were cruising along pretty decent at the shop and even at home right then. Julie really got into the spirit of things and decided to go as a gypsy fortune teller and I must admit she was looking pretty good on account of she'd gone on a diet and dropped a few pounds and she really had this glow about her, too.

I went as a cowboy seeing as how I didn't really think ahead too much and Big Ed had given little Vincent a whole Roy Rogers cowboy getup he was way too small for, including a tooled leather double-holster set with a pair of matching chrome cap pistols that I hooked up on this wide cowboy belt with a big silver buckle that I got out near Bonneville plus a little, red felt Woolworth's Five-and-Dime cowboy hat that looked absolutely ridiculous perched up on top of my head. Which, of course, is the whole idea on Halloween. Julie even found me one of those Sunday-go-to-meetin' cowboy shirts with the fancy stitching and mother-of-pearl buttons down the front. But I had to make do with the scruffy black, steel-toed workboots I had left over from my old man's union job at the chemical plant in Newark (and which I wore pretty regularly when I was working around the shop on account of every now and then you drop a sledgehammer or an acetylene bottle or an engine block on your toes). Big Ed came in his gorilla suit again and Carson was of course hosting as Count Dracula with Sarah Jean as the Lady In White with bright red lips and lots of eye liner over talcum powder-colored makeup and wearing what looked to be an awfully familiar wedding dress—I could tell by the stitched-up front—but with a white top on underneath seeing as how she could never fill out one of Julie's outfits. She had this flowing, white satin cape thing that looked like it was made out of draperies or something over her shoulders, and it was nice to see her digging in and having a little fun. Naturally all the racer types were there and they even had a rented jukebox playing downstairs—only not too loud, of course—in the casket showroom. I guess Carson rented it someplace, and it came complete with all the top hits like *Papa Loves Mambo* by Perry Como and Rosemary Clooney singing *This Old House* and her duet with Sammy Davis Junior, *Hey There,* from the Broadway show *The Pajama Game* and especially *Shake, Rattle and Roll* by Bill Haley and the Comets and of course that huge hit record *Sh-Boom* by the Crew Cuts that you could barely understand.

Danny Poindexter and his buddy 'Fos' showed up in these furry caveman outfits—I was starting to wonder just a little about those two—but the most amazing costumes had to be the rented Cleopatra and Marc Antony duds on Sally Enderle and Creighton Pendleton III. They were real Hollywood Costume Department quality, and the Cleopatra one showed an awful lot of Sally's smooth, sleek, freshly Palm Beach-tanned skin. She also had this pretty realistic-looking rubber snake, and she'd do these really dirty and suggestive things with it on the sly whenever she caught me staring at her. But I couldn't help it, you know? I mean, I couldn't even believe that I'd once been to bed with somebody who looked like that. And I even more couldn't believe she'd waste any of her attention on me. And the thing I *most* couldn't believe was that I hadn't enjoyed it one tiny bit while it was happening. What the heck was wrong with me, anyway?

But of course I knew she was just screwing around to keep me in heat and prove she could do it. And maybe do a little light-duty home-wrecking on the side. Or at least that's what one side of my brain was telling me. The other side (the one where the little devil whispers in your ear?) wasn't saying much of anything. It was just breathing very hard.

And, wouldn't you know it, I ran into her face-to-face in the narrow little hallway leading to the johns. Er, *lounges.* The light from the next parlor was behind her and it made that gauzy Cleopatra outfit go damn near transparent, and I caught myself wondering why God in his infinite wisdom would waste such an incredibly thoroughbred chassis on an individual with the interior spite, brass and conniving nature of a Sally Enderle. But mostly I just stared. She was walking right down the middle of the hallway so's I had to move to one side to try and get around her, but Sally glided slightly and gracefully over to block me. She held her rubber snake up and wiggled its head in front of my face. "Care for a little kiss, Buddy?"

"Uhh," I said with my back kind of up against the wall, "that's okay. Really."

"You know," she continued in that same whispery, teasing, singsong voice I remembered from our night together in Elkhart Lake, "you never talk to me any more...."

"I...I don't see you that often." Boy, I could see right down the front of that Cleopatra outfit!

"You ought to at least say 'hello' when you do." She rolled her eyes up at me like some famous movie vamp. "Just to be polite...."

"I...umm...I'll be sure and do that."

And then, without warning of any kind, she pressed herself up against me so I could feel all those taut curves and smooth skin and her warm, moist breath on my cheek. "I still think about that night at Elkhart Lake," she whispered directly into my ear. And then—just for an instant!—I swear she flicked the tiniest tip of her tongue inside. And then she immediately backed away, looked at the weak-kneed, shell-shocked expression on my face, smiled grandly (like she was real pleased with her work, you know?) and headed back up to the party.

I stood there alone in the vacant hallway for a while—thunderstruck—listening to the hot, urgent echo of her voice over and over like the ocean in a seashell. And then I went to take a pee.

Okay, maybe I did a little more than take a pee.

But that's really none of your business, is it?

I found Tommy Edwards later over by the tapper keg and went over to say "hi." He was wearing his dress R.A.F. suit and looking really fit and dapper and happy and just a little bit like the cat who ate the canary. "What's with you?" I asked, pouring us each a beer.

"To be frank about it, I'm feeling rather splendid this evening."

I looked at him kind of sideways. "You don't look like you've had that much to drink."

"Oh, no," he laughed. "It's not that at all. I just…well…."

"Come on," I urged him. "Spit it out."

"Well," he leaned in a little closer, keeping his voice down. "I got a call from Briggs Cunningham the day before yesterday."

"You did?"

"Bloody well right I did," Tommy nodded. "Right out of the blue."

"What did he want?"

"Well, you know John Fitch is living over in Europe these days and it seems Mercedes is planning a comeback in long-distance sports car racing next year—you know they've already blown the bloody Italian and French and English teams into the weeds on the Grand Prix circuit."

"Yeah. I follow it a little in *Autosport* and *Road and Track*. It's that Juan Manuel Fangio guy from Argentina, isn't it?"

"Quite right. And isn't he a piece of work?"

"They say he's the best there is."

"Well, I'm of course a bit partial to Stirling Moss. And Ascari's always to be reckoned with. That crazy Frenchman Behra can go as fast as anybody—any time, anywhere—and he's braver than Dick Tracy to boot. And the young Brit Mike Hawthorn looks like the business, too. The English motoring press are over the moon about him. But, if results count for anything, you've got to give the nod to Fangio. He's just bloody incredible."

"Fast?"

"Not just fast. But so smooth, too. And what patience! What pace! What bloody racecraft!"

"What makes him so good?"

Tommy thought about it for a moment. "I think it's his vision."

"He *sees* better than the other drivers?"

"Not better. Further…."

"I don't get it."

Tommy licked his lips and tried to explain. "He's got this rare knack for being able to see all the way to the checkered flag. Most drivers are lucky if they can see as far ahead as the next bloody corner." You could see the admiration—and just a little bit of envy, too—glowing in Tommy's eyes. "He's something special, all right."

"But what has Fangio got to do with you and Briggs Cunningham?"

"Oh, right. I got a bit sidetracked, didn't I?" Tommy took a quick sip of his beer. "Well, it seems that Mercedes is going back into endurance racing in a big way. Like they did with the 300SL coupes two years ago. They've got some bloody fabulous new sports car they're building and the long and short of it is that they've asked John Fitch to be on the team."

"Like he was in Mexico the year I went down with Big Ed."

"Precisely."

"But who's going to drive for Cunningham?"

"Exactly!" Tommy said with a huge grin. And then his voice went down to no more than a whisper. "Seems Briggs has ordered one of those new D-Types from Jaguar—oh, what a magnificent car!—and I understand from Phil Walters that they're building something rather special themselves down in Palm Beach."

"I've heard rumors…."

"Phil told me the new C-6R is smaller and lighter than anything they've ever built before. And the whispers I've heard about the engine are just unbelievable."

"Are they going to use a Chrysler again?"

"Too big and heavy."

I thought for a moment. And of course it occurred to me that the Cunningham team had been running that much-modified 4.5-liter Ferrari of theirs with some success. "A Ferrari V12?" I guessed.

"There was talk of it. But Briggs wanted something all-American. Show the flag and all that. Besides, you know about the business when he went to see old Enzo about that broken rocker arm at Le Mans."

"Seems I heard something about it."

"Well, old Enzo told him, *'Ferrari rocker arms do not break!'* Even after Briggs took the bloody thing out of his pocket and laid it on his desk! Wouldn't even give him a free replacement! Made him bloody well pay for it!" Tommy shook his head and laughed. "There's only one Enzo Ferrari, and for that we should all be thankful."

"But you still haven't told me what engine."

Tommy glanced quickly over both shoulders. "You know who Carl Kiekhaefer is?"

The name rang a bell, but I couldn't exactly place it.

"He's one of your American farm-boys-made-good from somewhere up in Wisconsin. A real Horatio Alger sort. Clever as the dickens. Had his first patent and was running his first business before he was twenty-one."

"So?"

"So now he owns Mercury Marine—the outboard engine people?—and it seems he bought a street Cunningham or two from Briggs. They didn't sell very many. But the bloody point is that he's always supported boat racing in a big way and next year he's going into car racing."

"What kind of car racing? Le Mans?"

"No. Mostly stock car racing with a team of those new Chrysler 300s."

I'd seen sneak preview pictures in the magazines of the new, Hemi-powered Chrysler 300. It looked like a pretty mean machine. Even if it was a little on the large size. "But what has that got to do with Briggs Cunningham?" I asked.

"You know there's talk of a three-liter limit at Le Mans?"

"I remember reading something about it."

"Well, it seems this Carl Kiekhaefer fellow thinks he can put two of his six-cylinder, two-stroke marine racing engines together in some sort of inverted vee or something and make a three-litre Vee-12 that will absolutely blow the Ferraris and Jaguars and even that new Mercedes-Benz right in the weeds."

"Wow! Have you seen it?"

"No, it's all still very much in the talking stages now. But the point is that John Fitch is going over to Mercedes and so they're moving that bastard Creighton Pendleton over to share the new car with Phil Walters and damn if Briggs didn't ring me up to see if I'd like to share the second car with him at Le Mans."

"Wow!"

"It's the opportunity of a bloody lifetime."

"But wouldn't you rather be in the new car?"

"Not on your life. A brand new car with a brand new engine at Le Mans? No thank you. But sharing a new D-Type Jaguar with a careful, steady sort like Briggs...." His eyes kind of misted over.

"Boy..." I breathed, my eyes misting over a little, too "...the Twenty-Four Hours of Le Mans."

"Here's to it!" Tommy said grandly, and we clinked our glasses together.

"Y'know," I told him, "I've always dreamed of going to Le Mans. Ever since I first heard about it that day in Colin St. John's shop."

Tommy shot me a conspiratorial wink. "We might be able to arrange something."

"Really?"

"I shouldn't be too surprised. After all, there are wrenches that need turning and wheel nuts that need to be spun off and on. You're as good at that as anyone."

"Are you *serious??!!"*

"Why not? I think we might be able to make it happen...."

Needless to say, I was pretty damn excited about the prospect of going to the biggest, best and most famous damn sports car race in the whole world! But I was careful not to say anything to anybody. Especially Julie. I mean, that was the kind of thing you needed to save for exactly the right moment. And then only after all the details and arrangements had come through. You had to be careful not to go off half-cocked, because otherwise you could wind up in an enormous screaming match for nothing. Because for sure Julie was not going to much fancy the notion of me traipsing off to France for a few weeks. Not one bit.

Naturally most of the talk at Carson's party was about racing—Julie was looking pretty bored by it all, if you want the truth of it—but, after my conversation with Tommy, I made a real point of going over by her and chatting her up a little and even suggested we maybe sneak away by ourselves for a couple minutes and go looking for that oversized, lardbucket-edition white coffin with the fancy gold trim that I'd proposed to her in precisely two years before. But the white one was gone—apparently somebody of substantial size and bank balance had passed away in the interim—and now they had a mahogany one on display. It just wasn't the same, you know? But we decided to sneak inside anyway—just for the hell of it—and I remembered the smell and the feel of it exactly, the satin lining all smooth and fresh and cool around us and the lid right there in front of our faces in the darkness where you could sense it and sniff it even though you couldn't actually see it. No matter how hard you looked.

"You know," I whispered, *"it seems like a million years ago."*

"I can't even remember what things were like before."

"They were simpler, that's for sure."

"But would you do it again?"

It didn't even catch me off guard. *"You bet I would."*

"So would I."

"Even when I piss you off?"

"You always piss me off."

"I can't help it. It's part of my charm."

"Like when I bought you a brand new suit for Christmas and you got me a goldfish and some dimestore earrings?"

"That was a dimestore goldfish, too."

"Or the time you left me in the room all by myself while you went off drinking with your racing buddies and came back and peed in our suitcase?"

"Hey, never a dull moment."

"You can say that again. It sure hasn't been dull."

"It's been kind of fun, if you think about it."

"Let's just leave it at 'it hasn't been dull.'"

"Whatever you say."

Then we just laid there in the dark together for a couple more heartbeats, listening to the muffled sounds of the party outside and the faint rustle of the satin casket lining around us.

"Buddy?"

"What?"

"I've got something to tell you."

"What?"

There was a pretty long pause. *"I'm pregnant again."*

Of course, the good thing about hearing that kind of news in a casket is that you're all set and ready to go if the shock up and kills you.

"Are you s-<u>sure</u>?"

"Of course I'm sure."

Well, that explained the glow.

"I'm pretty sure it happened in the cabin up at Watkins Glen...."

So now I was going to be a daddy for the second time sometime around about the middle of June—or the exact same time as the Twenty-Four Hours of Le Mans!—and it was amazing how that knowledge shot through me like the feeling you get if you lean too far out of a window on one of the upper floors of the Empire State Building. Not that I've ever exactly done that, but I'm pretty sure it feels the same.

Luckily it wasn't but a few days later, while I was carrying little Vincent and a fresh diaper-load of sweet potatoes from one end of the apartment to the other, that he kind of tugged at the collar of my shirt to get my head turned around, looked up at me with those wide, miraculous eyes of his, and said, *"Dada!"* just as clear and perfect as you please. And that made me feel a lot better. In fact, it made me feel better than I ever remembered feeling in my life....

Back at the shop we had plenty of work to keep us busy, and I had the Trashwagon's driveline all torn apart so Roman Szysmanski could make us up a new aluminum flywheel from scratch that would work a little better than the bolt-together job we jury-rigged together the first time. And meanwhile I sent the thing over to the Greek's shop and had them finally do a proper paintjob on it. Gloss black, natch. And then Big Ed had his truck sign painter go over and put:

THE FABULOUS TRASHWAGON

in glorious, gold-leaf, P.T. Barnum Circus Wagon lettering across the rear deck just underneath that goofy, trash-can lid Continental kit. You know, kind of like Smokey Yunick had "Fabulous Hudson Hornet" slathered all up and down the side of Herb Thomas' racecar at that NASCAR stock car vs. sportycar race at Linden, New Jersey? Plus the sign painter even put a few matching gold-leaf flames licking out along the edge of the hood. The Greek straightened everything pretty good before he painted it, too, and even if it didn't look low and sleek and svelte and handsome like that Palumbo Panther of my daydreams, it looked a thousand percent better than it ever did before. Not that a thousand percent is saying all that much.

But things never stay the same when you're running a damn business, and anytime you start feeling complacent and like everything is going along fine, something is sure to hit you right square in the back of the skull—and *always* from the blind side!—that gets you to scraping and scrambling all over again. This time it was our sawed-off hillbilly parts runner, Tater Tuttle, of all people. Seems he'd run into some waitress and her live-in bartender boyfriend at a bar and pool hall someplace and they wound up filling his head with wild notions about going into the restaurant business. As a cook, I mean.

"A'course, I'd hafta start out as a *saucier...*" he made the French word *saucier* sound very classy indeed. "...just t'learn the ropes, y'know?" You could tell he was really enthralled with the idea. "But then you become a *sou* cook—that's a 'second cook,' see?—and you learn how to do that for a couple more years and then you make it as a cook all by yourself and then maybe even as a chef. Or a master chef, even. They write their own cookbooks. And then you own your own restaurant and rake in the dough hand over fist."

It sounded too easy to pass up.

"Or I might be a bartender, too. You make great tips if you get into the right joint, and they never go to bed before three in the morning or get up before two in the afternoon!" he added, his eyes all wide and excited.

Yep, it sounded like a perfect job for him. No doubt about it.

I thought for a moment about mentioning that he wasn't really tall enough to see over your average bar—there'd be just this little bun-top of a rust-colored pompadour bobbing along in front of the liquor bottles—and also the difference between working on the serving side of a bar and receiving drinks on the consumer side, but you could see he was all excited and there was no point trying to argue him out of it.

I mean, you can't blame somebody for wanting to better themselves....

So Tater left and that had a kind of bank-shot effect on his younger brother Raymond Tuttle, who was pretty much our main backup parts-replacer-type mechanic at the Sinclair. Oh, Butch was getting around a little better on this walker thing my Aunt Rosamarina made him use most of the time instead of his wheelchair, but he still had only about a third of a set of good mechanic's hands anymore and, what with the walker and all, it was tough getting around and he couldn't really apply the kind of torque and leverage that a self-sufficient mechanic needs to call on a hundred or so times a day. And now Tater was gone and so Raymond didn't have anybody to sit and have lunch with except Tater's old hound dog, Barney. And Barney missed Tater something awful. Why, he'd get to howling at the light fixtures like they were a full moon sometimes when it really got to him. Plus I found out later that my slick and slimy buddy Colin St. John was also short-handed and had secretly approached Raymond Tuttle about maybe going to work for him at a real, live *dealership* instead of just some streetcorner gas station.

And of course that's the way it goes in this business. You put in the time to train somebody and eventually—if they're not very bright or good or ambitious—somebody else with a shop nearby needs help and hires them away from you. Or, if they do happen to be bright and good and ambitious, they take everything they've learned at your place and go open up a little back-alley, low-overhead shop of their own just a couple blocks away, go into competition with you and try their best to steal some of your best customers.

But, like I said, you can't blame somebody for wanting to better themselves.

So I was once more in desperate need of an experienced wrench-spinner, and so I decided to maybe take a run at Sylvester Jones over at Westbridge again. Under the guise of a parts run, of course. Only he wasn't there.

"'E's been gone for three bloody weeks now," Barry Spline told me while I stared at the naked bench where Sylvester's tools and equipment had been. "Started out the usual bleedin' way. He'd be off drunk instead a'workin.' No bloody surprise. But something must've been up, because he didn't come back like he always did before. I think maybe something was going off at home or something. And then he showed up drunk and angry one day and got into an awful bloody row with Colin. Screaming and bloody Lord knows what all over the shop." Barry shot me a sorry glance. "'E looked worse than I've ever bloody seen 'im, and that's the truth."

"So what happened?"

"Dunno. Oh, Colin fired 'im, of course. But that bloody well went without saying, didn't it? Only this time Sylvester picked up all 'is bloody tools and things and threw them in the trunk of that ancient Plymouth of his and just took off. Just like that. Poof!"

I mulled it over. "You have any idea what was eating him?"

"Who knows?" Barry drew in close. "You know how those people are. They live like bleedin' animals...."

I thought it over a little more. "You have an address for him?"

Barry looked at me funny. "Yer not thinkin' of going up t'bleedin' Harlem lookin' for 'im, are you?"

"Why not? It's broad daylight."

"It's still dark up there, mate. It's still bloody dark as hell up there."

So I took the address and drove north through Manhattan and on up into Harlem. It was a chilly mid-November day with an overcast sky that didn't cast any shadows, and it was amazing how things changed and all of a sudden *I* was the face that stood out in the crowd instead of the other way around once I passed over into Harlem. Oh, down the main streets nobody much seemed to notice or care, but when I turned off onto the side streets and passed by the weary, slouching old apartment buildings and the boarded-up windows and the empty lots littered with bricks and trash and empty bottles and old tires and maybe the front seat of a deceased Ford or Chevrolet sitting next to a blackened trash barrel like it was somebody's living room, all of a sudden I felt as white and bright as a 150-watt light bulb. And my first notion was to forget the whole thing and just turn left at the next major intersection and head back to where I belonged.

But I didn't.

Nope, I pulled Old Man Finzio's tow truck up in front of the old, red-brick apartment building wearing the address Barry gave me, swallowed hard, rolled up the windows, locked the doors and headed inside. And it was dark and dank and smelled like old cabbage in there, and there was a baby crying someplace and a couple young men sitting on the steps inside. They stopped talking and their sullen, upturned eyes followed me silently as I passed them and headed up the stairs. To be honest, I don't think they knew what to make of it any more than I did. Anyhow, I found the door and knocked on it—that baby was still crying something awful in one of the apartments down the hall—and then I heard the click of the latchbolt and it opened a crack with a chain lock across it. An unfamiliar eye stared down at me from a good six feet off the floor. "Who you?" the eye asked gruffly.

"Ahh, I'm Buddy. Buddy Palumbo."

"What'choo want?" The eye was obviously not interested in polite conversation.

"Ahh, I'm looking for Sylvester Jones...."

The eye didn't say a word.

"I used to work with him...."

It didn't even blink.

"I, ahh, kind of wanted to talk to him."

"He don't live here no more," the eye snorted, and went to close the door.

"But *wait...* " I said. And I think I maybe even put my foot in the doorway. At least judging by the black-and-blue marks I found on it later. Not that I felt it at the time. "I just want to *talk* to him."

The eye eased away from the door slit and obviously looked at somebody else in the room. There was some muffled conversation and then it looked back at me. "You'll find him down in th'alley out back most likely. He livin' like a dog down there. Jus' like a damn dog." And with that, the door closed.

So I stared at the painted wood for a moment and listened to the baby bawling down the hallway and there was nothing left to do but take another deep breath and head back down the stairway, past the three glum, silent young men whose eyes followed me like searchlights, out around the side of the building to the alley. And there was Sylvester. Underneath an ancient Nash with its front wheels up on cinderblocks, wrenching away on the ground with the usual butt-end of a Lucky dangling from his lips. He looked pretty terrible, if you want the truth of it.

"Hey, Sylvester," I called out.

He looked up at me, and it was like it took a while for his eyes to focus. "What th'damn hell're *you* doin' here?"

"I came up to see you."

"Ain't you got no sense a'tall?"

"I guess not."

With great effort, he weaseled his way out from under the Nash and unsteadily rose to his feet. You could tell he was pretty drunk.

"What's going on?" I asked him.

He eyeballed me up and down. Drunk as he was, you could still tell he was pretty much amazed to see me there in that alley in Harlem.

"I'm jus' workin' on cars. Same as always...."

He looked a little bit embarrassed, too. You could see it if you knew what to look for.

"Isn't it a little easier in a shop with a lift?" I asked him.

He looked down at his feet. "It don't make no differents."

"I heard you left Westbridge."

"It wuz jus' time t'move on, thass all."

"You sure?"

He looked up at me angrily. "Look, ah didn' ast you t'come nosin' aroun' here. You can jus' go back where y'damn came from far as ah care."

I wasn't sure exactly what to say.

So I said the truth.

"I need you over at the Sinclair."

He looked at me kind of sideways. "We tried that once't. It didn't take."

"Things are different now."

"How so?"

"They're just different is all. You'll see." I waited a heartbeat. "Looks like things're different for you, too."

"That ain't none a'your business!" he snapped.

"'Course it isn't. I never said it was."

"Damn straight."

"But I'm short-handed an' I got more car business than I can handle, and our buddies Colin St. John and Barry Spline went and hired Raymond away...."

"He went t'work fr'*them?*" Sylvester said incredulously.

I nodded.

"*Haw-Haw-Haw...*" he guffawed. "*...He'll* learn!"

"But the point is I need somebody—somebody like you, see, who knows the ropes—and I can maybe offer you something a littler better than your, umm, 'current' situation...Where are you living, anyway?"

"Th' Taj Mahal, what's it look like?"

"No, really."

Sylvester looked down at his feet again. "In there." He pointed his thumb over his shoulder at a garage door on the alley. "Ah gots t'stay there t'protek mah tools."

"What about the apartment upstairs? The one with your wife and kids in it?"

Sylvester shot me a piercing stare. "Do ah ast you about'cher personal business?"

"No."

"Maybe you kin do the same fr'me, all right?"

"Fair enough." I ran my eyes around and noticed pairs of eyes staring suspiciously down at us from back porches and behind tweaked windowshades and curtains on both sides of the alley. "You feel like getting something to eat?"

"Ah gots this ol'car t'fix," he protested feebly.

"It'll keep. It's not going anywhere."

So he packed his stuff up and locked it all in the trunk (and even added a chain with a padlock around the deck handle and the rear bumper) and we took the tow truck back onto one of the main streets and just enough blocks south that there were a few scattered white faces among the black and brown ones and found ourselves a sandwich shop. Sylvester didn't open up and tell it to me all at once, but it turned out his second wife and the mother of his two sets of twins had gotten herself a powerful large dose of the Lord at Sunday church and had started disapproving of Sylvester's boozing and gambling and staying out until the wee hours and coming home every now and then smelling of strange perfume. In fact, she'd gotten herself such a powerful large dose of the Lord that she'd invited one of the lay deacons of her church over for a fried chicken dinner after services one Sunday and he'd more or less decided to stay. He was a great big towering pyramid of a man named Thornton Seaberry, who worked as a bus driver in Harlem on the weekdays, took his church business very seriously indeed and surely did enjoy her fried chicken.

Like I said before, you can't blame people for wanting to better themselves.

Although I didn't exactly mention that to Sylvester.

So I listened for a while as little bits of the story came out, and then I made him an offer that was maybe a little more than too good. But I figured that was okay so long as he'd come over and live on the Jersey side and get away from all that mess and trouble he'd gotten himself into in Harlem. I told him maybe he could get straightened out enough and make enough money that he could get her back. If that's what he really wanted, anyway. Or he could just start fresh if he wanted to, you know?

Sylvester listened to all of it (and you could see as how the food had sobered him up just a bit), and then he thought it over while he picked at his teeth with a wooden toothpick. "Y'all remember when I tole you once't that you wasn't about t'save mah life an' I sure as hell wasn't about t'save yours?"

"I remember."

"Well, thass s'true now as it ever was, unnerstan?'"

"If you say so."

"But damn if I ain't gonna let a stupid-ass white boy like you try anyway."

"Then it's a deal?"

"Hey, that monster deacon a'the church man ain't about t'leave mah house, an' winter's comin' on an' it's gittin' too fuckin' cold fr' an ole man wrenchin' in that alley...."

And so Sylvester came back to work at the Sinclair the week before Thanksgiving.

I had to find a quick, temporary place for him to stay and so I of course asked my Aunt Rosamarina about the place over her garage seeing as how now Butch was established pretty much full-time in the house, and I have to admit she didn't seem real keen about it. But Butch was more to the point:

"A *nigger?*" he said disdainfully over my Aunt Rosamarina's kitchen table.

"Look, Butch, you can call him what you want. But he taught me as much about fixin' cars as you did. Maybe even more when it comes to Jaguars and MGs. We *need* him over at the Sinclair right now. I mean, you're gettin' around a little better and all, but there's still a lot of stuff you can't do..." Butch glowered at me, "...and I've only got J.R. after school this time of year. I figure it's my good luck that Sylvester's sort of, umm, 'between positions' right now...."

"But a...a..." You could see he was rolling it over in his mind. "...I mean, I ain't like I never worked side-by-side with 'em. But there was always a *line,* see. And it was a line you just didn't damn well cross." He swiveled his eyes up at me. "Not from either side."

"A-and now there's all that...that...*integration* business the Supreme Court stirred up," my aunt added with a worried look on her face. "I read they had a student march against it in Washington and near riots in the South."

I looked Butch straight in the eye and then over at my Aunt Rosamarina. Jeez, she looked about petrified. "Look, it's only temporary until we can find something, aaah, 'more appropriate,' see?" Neither of them looked exactly convinced. "Besides," I added, still looking them straight in the eyes, "he's a friend of mine...."

Well, it wasn't exactly an easy sell and I had to promise over and over that it was only for a few days and also that we could tell the neighbors if any of them asked—and you knew there'd be plenty of whispering—that Sylvester was just a handyman doing some odd jobs for them, and damn if I didn't help Sylvester move his tools into the shop at the Sinclair and his old straw suitcase of clothes into the apartment over my Aunt Rosamarina's garage the weekend before Thanksgiving. And it made me feel pretty damn good, if you want the truth of it. Even though, just like in the alley behind Sylvester's old apartment in Harlem, I felt pairs of eyes staring suspiciously down at us from back porches and peering out from behind tweaked curtains and windowshades all up and down both sides of the street. It's just the way things were.

Thanksgiving rolled around like it always does a month after Halloween and that meant the usual holiday gathering over at my folks' house—complete with all the relatives and trimmings, of course—but it was nice that little Vincenzo was still the star of everybody's show (although I knew he'd only retain that position until the next baby was born) and it was nice how my mom and Julie's mom and Sarah Jean and my married sisters all of a sudden seemed to have so much to talk about with Julie. Even though it left me pretty much on the outside. But it was a lot like all that Wedding Planning that went on before we got married. Girl stuff, you know? And, like most guys, I came 'round to considering myself lucky not to be included. In fact, it was sort of a privilege.

But neither was I too happy with the prospect of joining "the rest of the boys"—that would be my old man and my sister Tina's loudmouth husband Roy and my other sister Ann-Marie's meek and henpecked little husband Jerry—gathered around the TV set in the den with the windowshades pulled down so they could see a little better, having a pre-dinner drink or two while they watched whatever was on and listened to Roy tell a few of his famous dirty stories. So I went out on the front porch and waited for Carson to arrive and maybe even my sister Mary Frances. She was supposed to come, and I was as usual looking forward to seeing her with a combination of worry and anticipation. I liked her the best of all my sisters—I know you're not ever supposed to come out and say that—but I also worried and fretted over her the most. She just had so much spirit and spunk and smarts, but all it had ever done for her was lead her up one stupid blind alley after another.

Of course she didn't show up until well into the main course—that almost went without saying—and once again she brought a surprise guest along with her. He was kind of a pale, timid, reedy-looking guy with tortoiseshell glasses and thinning, reddish-brown hair, and I knew right away that I'd seen him before, only I couldn't quite place him. But he was very quiet and polite and, to be honest, by far the most sufferable of all the insufferable companions she'd ever brought over by my folks' house.

"He looks familiar," I whispered to Mary Frances when I passed her in the kitchen.

"You saw him at the New Year's Eve party."

"I did?" And then it hit me. The saxophone player. The guy who was cruising way out there in the stratosphere on that amazing sax solo while people in turtlenecks and jeans and even leotards on the rug in front of him swayed back and forth in the thick, smoky atmosphere and that sweet, strange smell wafted in on a cloud of giggles from the group out on the fire escape. That was one hell of a party. "Is that what he does for a living?" I asked.

Jesus, I was getting more like my father every day!

"Oh, he plays with some of the big bands when they're in town. And some jazz combos at the clubs, too. Occasional fancy weddings. He even plays classical with the symphony...." She looked up at me. "He's a heck of a musician."

"I know," I agreed patiently. "But is it, you know, *steady?*"

"Oh, he's in the union," she assured me. "He does all right."

I wasn't so sure. But, like I said, he was by far the nicest and most thoughtful of the guys she'd ever brought home. Even if he wasn't exactly much of a conversationalist. But that was more or less refreshing compared to her old novels-in-Esperanto blowhard Oliver Cromwell or that let-me-show-you-how-to-fix-the-world idiot Leonard Putzman. His name was Pauly Martino, so at least he was Italian, and I liked that he had a kind smile and even blushed and put his head down when Mary Frances bragged on him that he'd played backup behind Frank Sinatra and Rosemary Clooney.

Maybe he'd work out after all....

I sure hoped so.

To be honest, things over by my Aunt Rosamarina's house and garage apartment weren't working out as rosy as I'd hoped, and there was a lot of tension going on even though nobody was speaking to anybody else. Oh, Butch and Sylvester didn't have too much problem wrenching in adjoining bays at the station except for a few minor skirmishes and flareups—hey, they were both grouchy, independent, leave-me-alone/don't-mess-with-me kind of guys—but the living situation was no good at all for anybody, and I could see I had to help Sylvester find something in a more appropriate part of town. Or, as he put it: "Ah'd druther be a fust-class citizen inna secon'-class neighbo'hood than a secon'-class citizen in a fust-class neighbo'hood."

Not to mention that he couldn't exactly waltz into a streetcorner tavern for a little drink on the way home from work. At least not unless he wanted to get his teeth rearranged.

He found a place for himself over around Jersey City in a darker part of town and Butch and me helped him get an old Ford beater set up to make the commute every day, and you could see as how he was straightening out just a little. But even then I worried it was maybe only a temporary deal, seeing as how I could tell he felt like more or less a foreigner over on this side of the Hudson and it might only be a matter of time before he'd want to get back to the life and people he knew and the action he craved every now and then back in Harlem. It was like he told me, you know? About how you can't save people from themselves?

It's a lesson you always have a hell of a time learning....

In any case, I had him for a while and I needed him, and so that made it a good fit for both of us. Like Big Ed always said, *"that's what using's for,"* and at least the cars were getting fixed right—and getting fixed right the *first* time, which is quite an important consideration—and I've got to say that Sylvester developed a real knack and feel for those Volkswagens. We'd put three or four of them out on the street by then and we were even getting some referral business from people who'd bought from a dealer but hadn't been real happy with the service end over there. And all four of us—me, Butch, Sylvester and even young J.R.—had already gotten to the point where we could about fix anything you could think of on a Volkswagen damn near blindfolded. Only problem is that you had to be a little careful on account of you could rip your hands bloody on that damn sheet-metal engine shrouding if you weren't careful....

Meanwhile the world kept spinning around us and, like always happens in the off-season from racing, I was actually finding time to leaf through a newspaper every now and then with my morning coffee. There was a big political mess going on halfway around the world where the Chinese communists had re-elected Mao

Tse-Tung as their Chairman but we signed a mutual defense treaty with this other group called the Nationalist Chinese, who were more our sort of good, solid capitalists but, unfortunately, didn't actually live in China anymore. Lionel Barrymore the famous actor died and the Senate finally had enough lip out of "Tailgunner Joe' McCarthy and voted to censure him, 67 to 22. And about time, too. Willie Mays got voted the National League's Most Valuable Player after the Giants beat the Cleveland Indians in the World Series back in October (hey, at least it was a New York team, even if it wasn't the Yankees or the Dodgers) and a week later the good people of Jackson, Mississippi, voted 2-to-1 to continue school segregation. Television was getting better all the time, what with *The Ed Sullivan Show* starting up on CBS and NBC countering with that funny guy Steve Allen in something called *The Tonight Show. Dragnet, Topper, I Love Lucy* and *Ozzie and Harriet* were all back for another season, and *Lassie* finally had pups (although they never made it real clear who the father might have been!). But the biggest news on the small screen was the new *Disneyland* show from Walt Disney Studios and their multiple-episode Davy Crockett story that aired in December. Why within a few weeks, every school kid on the street was either wearing a coonskin cap or begging for one for Christmas and singing that damn *Davy Crockett* theme song over and over and over again until you wanted to take the furry tail of that blessed coonskin cap and shove it down their throat.

Christmas rolled around on schedule like it always does right about the time you get done digesting Thanksgiving, and this time we got a nice little tree for the duplex and Julie decorated it with ornaments and lights and stuff and put up Christmas stockings for me and her and little Vincenzo and even her mom on the wall molding that we pretended was a sort of mantelpiece. It looked really cozy when I came home from work and saw those colored lights through the windows and the big, red felt bow on the door with evergreen boughs and pine cones kind of dangled all over it. Julie had a real knack for that kind of stuff. And then I stayed home with the little guy and watched TV on a Saturday afternoon while she went out shopping and damn near bankrupted us buying presents—and way too nice presents, if you ask me—for just about everybody in creation.

"Why d'ja have to buy a damn two-foot Raggedy Andy doll for my sister's little girl?" I demanded. "And a silk tie from a fancy men's shop for that loudmouth asshole Roy? You should've got him a nickel-plated cocktail strainer over at Woolworth's!"

"You know all about Christmas shopping at Woolworth's, don't you?"

Well, she had me there.

But I really didn't see why you had to be so damn nice to people just because they were family. And especially the ones you didn't much care for.

"If you had it *your* way," Julie growled at me, "we'd give everybody tune-ups and carburetor rebuilds for Christmas. That'd be your style."

"No," I snapped right back, "it's got to be one or the other. I'm not givin' anybody a tune-up *and* a carburetor rebuild."

She opened her mouth to let me have a little more, but then she couldn't help herself and started laughing. And that made little Vincent, who was sitting in his high chair watching the whole thing back-and-forth like a damn tennis match, brighten up like a Broadway stage footlight and pound happily on the tray in front of him. Naturally sending a colorful eruption of mashed yams and strained beets flying in all directions. He seemed pretty proud of how high up the wall he could get some of the stains.

Sure, I was a little burned about the money. But I was even happier that we could more or less afford it right then—even if it meant we owed a little more and couldn't put anything away for a house of our own like we both agreed we ought to—and that there were times in our little apartment when all three of us were smiling and enjoying each other's company and the world outside was so far away it couldn't touch us at all.

Christmas day there was the usual drag-me-by-the-ear-to-morning-mass ritual, and I was happy to see that little Vincent didn't seem to like it any better than I did and made his feelings clear by screaming at the top of his lungs during all that droning Latin stuff that I'm sure must be very inspirational if you speak the language. Afterwards we had a kind of noonday gut-stuffing over at my folks' house—I mean, who needs turkey and dressing and ham and potatoes au gratin and side-dish rigatoni with gravy and three kinds of homemade pie for dessert (á la mode with vanilla ice cream and whipped cream and a cherry on top if you want it) in the middle of the day? But it was a memorable family meal on account of Carson Flegley was there and, after looking back and forth nervously with my sister Sarah Jean a few hundred times and waiting for the exact right moment (which of course never came) timidly stammered out that they were planning to get engaged. My mom's face broke into the sunniest sort of smile you ever saw, and tears started rolling down her cheeks. My dad looked at them both, shifted in his seat, and belched. That was his way of welcoming Carson into the family.

Big Ed showed up over at the duplex later that same afternoon and right behind his freshly-waxed Thunderbird was a big yellow delivery truck from that fancy F.A.O. Schwartz toy store over on Fifth Avenue in Manhattan—on Christmas day, can you believe it?—and damn if they didn't unload the most amazing blessed rocking horse you ever saw in your entire life. Why, it looked like a stuffed Shetland pony—I mean it felt like real horse fuzz all over it and everything!—standing there proudly on a pair of gold-leaf rockers with its head thrown back and a white leather saddle on its back and matching white leather bridle and stirrups, all of them sporting rows of glinting, gold-tone diamond studs. Why, it was so damn big the delivery guy had a hard time just getting it through the door!

"Jesus, Ed," I told him, "don'cha think it's maybe a little, uuh, *large?"*

"It's the best friggin' one they make," he said proudly. "The guy at the toy store said the czar over in Russia had one just like it for his kid. At least before they all got shot, anyway."

"And Merry Christmas to you, too."

The baby was on the floor over by the tree when the delivery guy finally got it through the doorway and set it more or less in the middle of the room. I mean, it wouldn't fit anyplace else. Little Vincent looked up at it—towering over him like a giant shadow about to trample him to death—and his eyes went wide and his mouth opened up into the most horrendous, terrified shriek you ever heard.

"Aw, geez," Big Ed grumbled sullenly, "I didn't mean t'scare the little guy...."

"It's okay," I assured him. "He's just gotta get used to it."

Julie came in from the kitchen to see what all the screaming was about and looked at Big Ed's present about the same as if it had been a real horse standing there in our living room. That had just taken about a twelve-pound crap on the carpet....

"How d'ya like it?" Big Ed asked eagerly.

"It's...it's..." you could tell she was searching for words as she scooped little Vincent up off the floor, "...it's just...*fantastic.*"

Big Ed absolutely beamed.

And now that he was up on her shoulders looking down at the thing, little Vincent was quieting down and looking more and more intrigued. In fact, he reached out his hand towards it. So Julie looked at me and I looked at her and she brought him over and gingerly set him down on it—kind of holding him front and back so's he couldn't topple off—and I got the message right away and gave it a little rock. The baby's eyes blew open and his mouth blossomed out into a huge, gaping smile. I rocked it a little more, and he smiled even bigger and gave us a command performance recital of all those whoogly-googly-gurgly noises babies do when they're trying to make everybody in the room feel happy.

In fact, he liked it so much that this big, dangerous-looking cloud descended over his face when Julie finally took him off and set him back down on the rug. But he didn't just plop down on the seat of his pants (er, diaper) like he usually did. Nope, little Vincent stood there for a moment—all wobbly and teetering back and forth—and damn if he didn't take one...two...three steps all on his own and grab onto the leg of that rocking horse to keep from falling like a streetcorner drunk going for a lamp post.

"DID'JA SEE <u>THAT</u>??!!" I just about screamed.

It was the most amazing Christmas present either of us ever had in our lives.

Tommy Edwards dropped by the shop in early February—a week before little Vincenzo's first birthday, in fact—just to chew the fat and bring me up to speed on the new C-6R Cunningham project and our mutual prospects for Le Mans. I hadn't exactly mentioned it to Julie or anything—I mean, it was still just a bunch of smoke-and-mirror notions, and there was no point going through the kind of bitter and lingering argument it was surely going to cause unless I was absolutely dead sure it was going to happen—but Tommy was talking like it was genuinely in the bag. Even if the C-6R wasn't coming along exactly as planned. According to Tommy, the chassis and suspension and everything were looking good—excellent, in fact—but apparently that killer, top-secret, inverted, two-stroke, siamesed-six-cylinder Mercury marine engine three-liter Vee-12 that Carl Kiekhaefer had been hinting about was still in the hot-air stages and so the Cunningham guys had decided to press a three-liter Meyer-Drake Offenhauser into service just to get the project going. And, at least on paper, it looked like a good choice. I mean, Ferrari had won the World Grand Prix Championships back-to-back in '52 and '53 with Alberto Ascari at the wheel and four-cylinder engines under the hood, and they were having lots of success with big, torquey four-bangers in their 500 Mondial and 750 Monza sports cars. Plus—again at least on paper—the Meyer-Drake Offy and the 750 Monza Ferrari engines seemed to have a lot in common. They were both three-liter four-bangers with dual overhead cams and the block and head done up in a single casting so there were no head gaskets to blow, and the Offy was moreover a rugged and proven design that had become just about the only engine to have at the Indy 500. And almost all the Offies—including the one Billy Vukovich had used to win the last two Indy 500s on the trot—were using Hilborn fuel injection, and the general consensus around most of the garages, car shops and gas stations in America was that fuel injection was the Wave of the Future and amounted to some kind of Magic Bullet advantage over ordinary, old-fashioned carburetors. And they were feeling that way in Europe, too, after the way the fuel-injected Mercedes-Benz Grand Prix cars had steamrollered all the carbureted opposition on the Grand Prix circuit in 1954. So the big, four-banger Offy looked like an obvious choice. Not to mention that it was pure, red-white-and-blue American, and that always counted for a lot with Briggs Cunningham.

"The plan is to have it out at Sebring in March," Tommy told me. "And Briggs should have his new D-Type from Jaguar by then as well."

"Are you going to get to drive?"

He made a see-saw motion with his hand. "That's still a bit up in the air. But if everything comes through on schedule, I'll probably be in the new car with Briggs. It's just a shakedown run, really. We won't be expecting much."

"Still, it sounds like a heck of an opportunity."

A big smile spread across Tommy's face. "Don't I know it!"

Speaking of big opportunities, who should ring me up that very afternoon but my old roundy-round buddy and hero Sammy Speed. Or actually it was Spud Webster's voice on the line, but Sammy was standing there right next to him. "How're things goin' fr'you?" he asked.

"Same old shit. How 'bout you?"

"This and that."

I waited a heartbeat for him to get to the point. I mean, even though racers will gladly bullshit about racing until they've driven all the sane people out of a room, they're not generally the type of people to call up and just chitchat. "So what's up?" I finally asked.

"You doin' anything particular around the end of May?"

I felt my eyes opening wider. "What've you got in mind?"

"Thought'cha might like t'stand out in the sun with us fer a few hours again at this racetrack in Indiana. You were kind of a rabbit's foot fer us last year...."

"Th-thanks," I said, the heat rising on my face.

"Les went out and bought himself a Kurtis 500 this year. Oh, it's a 500A and not a 500C like the Fast Boys're runnin,' but I figger it's mebbe a top-five car again if lightning don't strike an' we get our ducks in a row."

"I dunno," I told him. "I mean, I'd love to go, but Julie's expecting again in June."

"I can't see as it'll be much help havin' *you* around," Spud chuckled into the receiver.

"Prob'ly not," I agreed. "But there's something else, too."

"What's that?"

"Well..." I was almost afraid to say it. I hadn't told anybody yet. Not even Julie. In fact, especially not Julie. It was like I was afraid I might jinx it, you know? "T-the thing is," I said, kind of licking my lips, "I might be going to the Twenty-Four Hours of Le Mans two weeks later."

There was dead silence on the other end. And then:

"Really?"

So I told Spud all about the Cunningham deal and also about how it would mean more than a week away and also about how I had the shop to run and moreover and most importantly how there was no way on earth I'd have the balls or poor judgment to ask a heavily pregnant and therefore somewhat ornery, uncomfortable and easy-to-rile Mrs. Julie Finzio Palumbo whether it would be okay if I took off for the Indianapolis Motor Speedway for a three- or four-day weekend and then come home for just about long enough to do my laundry and take out the garbage before packing and whisking myself off to France for a week or so. Especially considering that the new baby was due no more than five to ten minutes after I got back....

"Well, we'll sure miss ya," Spud grinned at the other end of the line. "Like I said, you were kind of a lucky charm for us last year...."

"Luck didn't have anything to do with it," I assured him.

But of course luck has everything to do with it when it comes to racing.

Little Vincent's first birthday came and went—Big Ed bought him a four-foot-long, battery-powered Stutz Bearcat that he could actually sit behind the wheel of and drive once he got about three or five years older (you got the idea that Big Ed didn't really have a lot of experience buying stuff for little kids, you know?)—and we'd already moved that handsome-but-enormous, exactly-like-the-shot-to-death-czar's-also-shot-to-death-little-boy's rocking horse that Big Ed got little Vincent for Christmas out onto the back porch so a person could actually walk through our living room without hugging the walls or bumping into the furniture. "What you guys need is a bigger house," Big Ed groused.

"What we need is a house, period," Julie agreed, rolling her eyes up towards the very ceiling beyond which the bird-of-prey eyes, terrier-keen ears and disapproving, chicken-clucking tongue of her mother were never very far away. Not to mention that Little Vincent wasn't too thrilled about having his favorite play toy stuck out on the back porch. And he made his feelings felt about it in no uncertain terms.

Speaking of little Vincenzo, Julie and me were beginning to learn a little about the infamous, double-edged-sword nature of babies growing into toddlers. You're so excited when you first see them take those first wild, wobbly steps—your heart soars like it's the finale of the best damn fireworks display you ever saw!—and then you're right there with them every single day, coaxing and urging and standing them upright again every time they topple over or get lazy and start to crawl. And then it's a month later and suddenly they're into everything and *nothing* is safe unless it's bolted down or padlocked shut (or bolted down *and* padlocked shut!) and every single day is punctuated with screaming, fire-alarm runs across the room or down the hall when you notice out of the corner of your eye that the baby is trying to put his finger in a light socket or eating the top off a can of kitchen cleanser or climbing into the gas oven for a little afternoon snooze. In fact, I have this theory that they know exactly what the heck they're doing the whole time, but they've also discovered that the most fabulous toy in God's entire universe is a parent. Why, you can make them do so many exciting things….

Over at the shop we were doing a nice business replacing batteries and starters and fixing busted chokes like you always do during cold weather, and also getting a little jump-start on the racing season by offering a special on pre-spring tune-ups and valve jobs and brake adjustments for our racing customers. Although I was learning a hard lesson about not letting your sportycar people with something else to drive drop their cars off in the wintertime on account of they had a habit of just *leaving* them there. I mean until spring. Which explained why Old Man Finzio was always such a stickler about that fifty-cents-a-day Storage Charges sign he kept tacked up over the register. I always thought it was kind of crude and insulting to the customers, but damn if I didn't go looking for it again before the first of March rolled around.

Butch and Sylvester had a kind of edgy, uneasy truce going on by then—I'd put them in the two end bays with my stuff in the middle between them—but you could see out of the corners of their eyes they'd watched each other work and figure stuff out and occasionally struggle and a grudging kind of respect was simmering in their pool of deep-seeded natural animosity. J.R. helped a lot where that was concerned, since he was always ready to learn and lean in and lend a hand wherever he could, and had the good sense to play dumb when either of them would mumble or grouse about the other. There's always a lot of politics in any shop—or anyplace else you get more than two human beings together for any length of time—and it's not the kind of thing you can fix or avoid. You just have to learn to live with it.

But spring was coming—you could smell it in the morning air and see it in how, surely but imperceptibly, the days were getting longer—and so we were busy as heck getting the cars ready for the racing season ahead. And I'd gone and hired myself another parts runner. To be honest, I really enjoyed doing the parts runs myself on account of it was a great excuse to get out of the shop and away from everybody and be all by my lonesome for awhile. Which is a nice place to be when you've got people and their problems boring incessantly into your eardrums from all directions. You get to craving a little peace and quiet, you know? Not to mention that doing it myself was the only way I could be sure all the parts would be right the first time. Or damn near all of them, anyway. But the fact is you gotta *be* there if it's your shop—that's one of the rules—although the other rule is that you gotta watch your payroll, because that goes on even if the customer work doesn't (or, worse yet, when you've got a shop full-up with long-term work and comebacks, so there's no cash money coming in). Fortunately we'd developed something of a reputation for being fair, honest and reasonably competent (which should give you half a clue as to just how bad the other shops in the area must've been!), and so our biggest problem was getting to be space and keeping up with all the repair and racing work. Which was a nice sort of problem to have. Even if it meant opening at seven sharp every morning and coming home at eight or nine o'clock most nights. Hey, you do what you have to do, right?

Anyhow, it turned out that the older brother of one of J.R.'s friends was a couple summers out of high school and really wanted to be a Navy pilot, but when he went down to enlist they told him he had flat feet and couldn't see real good. So he was working the night shift at a cardboard-box plant over in Jersey City and getting off right around the time I was having my morning sit-down on the can and getting ready to go over and open the shop. His name was Steve Kibble and he was a long, lean, pleasant sort of kid with a big, engaging smile and an easy laugh and exactly the right kind of addiction to anything with wheels and an engine. Especially if it was loud and fast. Plus he needed some extra money on account of that box-plant job didn't pay very well (it wasn't a union shop, as my old man was quick to point out) and he still owed his dad a couple bucks on the slightly-used Whizzer Pacemaker he used for daily transportation. He rode that moped everywhere and all the time—day, night, rain, shine, fog, sleet or snow—but his real dream the badly-trashed, seized-up-but-supposedly-complete, war-surplus 1942 Indian 741 military motorcycle he'd bought in a collection of orange crates, cardboard boxes and coffee tins that he planned to fix up and ride some day. At least as soon as he learned a little something about mechanics, anyway....

So it was a perfect fit. Steve would ride his Whizzer over after he was done with the night shift at the box plant, then maybe have a sweet roll or even a little breakfast at the place across the street and be ready to go on his first parts run by eight ayem every morning. Which was quite a welcome change from Tater Tuttle, of course, who used to roll in sometime between ten and eleven and was never good for much of anything until after lunch. Although I must admit I missed him. And Raymond Tuttle and Barney the hound dog, too. But you can't let yourself get too sentimental about the help when you're trying to run a damn business. Even though you do.

Anyhow, the new kid was pretty sharp and well-organized and eager to learn, and he'd make parts runs and help out around the shop in the mornings—he didn't know a lot yet, but you could see he was pretty handy—and I let him bring his crates and boxes and coffee tins of old Indian parts in and set them up on the rafters and over in a corner and allowed as how he could work on his motorcycle project a little now and then when he had the time. And I'd peek in over his shoulder now and then and maybe give him a little advice when I saw him doing things the hard or impossible way, like rookie mechanics always do. To be perfectly honest, I got the impression his parents maybe didn't know about the Indian project yet. So I asked him about it and he told me it was "going to be a surprise." Right. Anyhow, he'd fiddle around with his motorcycle bits and pieces—cleaning, mostly, because there was an awful lot of cleaning to do—and then he'd take off on his Whizzer about mid-afternoon and catch a few hours' shuteye before it was time for him to be back at the box plant again a little after ten.

In any case, we had a pretty decent crew going for us at the Sinclair right then, and I was frankly amazed that Sylvester hadn't bolted back to Harlem on me. But I got the feeling he knew the only way he could ever get his wife and kids back (if that's what he really wanted, since he never said anything about it and it was definitely not the sort of thing you could ask him about) was to get himself straightened out and solidly established, and damn if that didn't seem to be what he was doing. Not that he was ever especially pleasant about it. In fact, he was exactly like Butch that way. Mean and ornery on general principles, you know?

I didn't have the time, reason or inclination to go down to Sebring that year (okay, maybe I *did* have the inclination, and what I really mean is that I didn't have a decent excuse, seeing as how none of my guys were going), but I got a blow-by-blow report afterwards from Tommy Edwards, who went down to test out that new Cunningham C-6R. It was barely finished and still unpainted when race weekend rolled around, but it was still by far the lightest, sleekest, most promising and by far most sophisticated racecar the Cunningham guys had ever built. Only there were problems. The four-cylinder Meyer-Drake Offenhauser engine that did so well at Indianapolis and everywhere else on the American roundy-round circuit was proving to be a bit of a problem child when it came to adapting it for road racing. And there were good reasons for it, too. It really made you appreciate that old "horses for courses" thing, and that there's always more to success than meets the eye. Running at Indy with fuel injection and a methanol fuel blend and just the right gearing, a well-tuned Offy produced a big, wide, meaty torque band that could send a well-driven Kurtis roadster powering down those long Indianapolis straightaways in a single, mighty rush. No shifting at all. But running up and down the scale like an engine had to in road racing didn't suit it nearly so well. Not to mention that alcohol not only produces more power but also runs a heck of a lot cooler than gasoline. Although the fuel mileage isn't nearly so good. In any case, the rules for international sports car racing said you had to run gasoline, and the Cunningham guys were discovering that the Offy engine in their new C-6R tended to run hotter than blazes on gas. Especially if you got the least bit aggressive with the compression ratio or spark advance. And of course that's how you get your power in *any* racing engine. Plus the rev range they needed for road-circuit use was running that engine through some really serious flat spots and vibration ranges that it just never had to deal with on an oval track. In fact, the team wound up switching from Hilborn fuel injection to Weber carburetors to give it a little more range and then mounting them on the blessed *frame* (can you believe it?) with flexible rubber hoses connecting them to the intake manifold on account of the shake and buzz off the engine was jiggling the fuel in the float bowls until it frothed up like a blessed drugstore-fountain soda.

And even then it was woefully shy on suds compared to the latest Ferraris and Jaguars.

In the end, the C-6R crapped out at Sebring with transmission failure after just fifty-four laps. "It's a brilliant little car," Tommy said ruefully, "but it needs better power from the engine and a bit of sorting."

Still, it was a pretty decent weekend for the Cunningham team, seeing as how Phil Walters and that much-heralded young English hotshoe with the blond hair, straight-stemmed pipe, clipped manner and trademark bowtie—Mike Hawthorn—went on to win the thing outright in Cunningham's new Jaguar D-Type. Hawthorn was on loan from Jaguar for the occasion, and the car was so new it was still British Racing Green and hadn't yet been repainted in the usual white-with-blue-racing-stripes Cunningham colors. "And there was a huge row over the scoring," Tommy added with a grin. "Phil Hill and Carroll Shelby thought that they'd won it in a Ferrari Monza because they were ahead of the Cunningham D-Type at the checker. But timing and scoring said they were the better part of a lap behind. After twelve bloody hours!"

"So what happened?"

"Oh, there was a right old traffic jam trying to get into victory circle!" Tommy continued, his eyes dancing. "And then all the stewards and officials went off in a huddle and decided that the Jaguar had won."

"It's a good thing they figured it out."

"For all anybody knows, they may have flipped a bloody coin."

The other big stories down at Sebring were how well the new 300S Maseratis ran, taking a solid third and fourth overall, and Stirling Moss and Lance Macklin doing an absolutely stunning job in the brand new, racing model Austin-Healey 100S, taking sixth overall, while two more of the new Healeys finished fifteenth and sixteenth. Unfortunately, as I've said before, the new Healey found itself in the same class as the pure-racing cars from Ferrari and Maserati, so that was only good enough for fifth, sixth and seventh in the Sports 3000 class. Still, everybody knew it was a hell of a performance for what was basically a factory hotrod version of cheap, blue-collar, thermos-and-lunchbucket kind of everyday sports car. And I was thrilled to hear that the Arnolt-Bristols I loved so much won the Sports 2000 class. "Anything else?" I asked Tommy.

"Only that those new Porsche 550s are going to be something to reckon with once they get their engines sorted out. Mark my words."

Our own first race of the season was up at Thompson Speedway again the first weekend of May, and it was the usual Thompson deal with practice and qualifying on Saturday, no engines running Sunday morning, and then a bunch of short races for small fields Sunday afternoon. At least it was getting to be kind of a routine now to get all the cars ready and everything packed and on the road at a reasonable hour. Although the trees were still pretty naked, the weather for the weekend looked nice and Julie even decided to come along with little Vincent (after I promised to be good, of course), and I was feeling cautiously optimistic that the Trashwagon would manage to stay together an entire race weekend—or at least a whole race, anyway—and that Big Ed would finally be able to beat Skippy Welcher's C-Type with it. Plus there was going to be a little race for stock Volkswagen sedans first thing Sunday afternoon and we'd decided to enter Cal in our latest new/used Volkswagen "demo" from Bob Fergus. I figured he could do pretty good with it, you know? And damn if he didn't! There were five Volkswagens entered and Cal just ran away from the rest of them. It wasn't even close.

Big Ed didn't have nearly such luck in the now sharply re-painted (but still a bit ugly shape-wise) Fabulous Trashwagon. He got off to a bad start on Saturday by taking it off the track a couple times during morning practice (once frontwards, twice backwards) and then repeated the performance a few times more in qualifying that afternoon. Only this time there was nothing wrong with it except that it was really damn fast and maybe a little more car than Big Ed could handle. Especially on a tight, claustrophobic little track like Thompson Speedway. Tommy Edwards always said that when everything seems to be happening too fast and the corners feel like they're rushing up at you, the natural thing is to brake way too hard and turn in way too early. And that puts you in a world of difficulties about six or eight heartbeats later, as all of a sudden you're either running out of road and plowing straight off or lifting off the gas to try and save it. Which gets the back end all unsettled and sends you, as he put it, "through the same bloody hole in the fence, only backwards!"

Big news in the Big Car class was that Bill Lloyd (the guy who co-drove that 1500cc Cunningham OSCA with Stirling Moss to win the Twelve Hours of Sebring in '54) had one of those new 300S Maseratis that had done so well at Sebring, and he simply blew everybody away, winning both of the races he was in and setting by far the fastest times of the weekend. You had to be impressed when you took a close look at that car, too. Not only was it handsome and sexy as could be, but the casting and machine work were about the most beautiful I'd ever seen. Better than Ferrari, even. Although the welding looked like wads of chewing gum. I guess the guys at Maserati figured welds were just something you needed here and there to tack all that marvelous casting and machine work together.

Oh, and some guy showed up with a suspiciously healthy-sounding Thunderbird with worked-over shocks and six-ply Pirelli tires and ran it against the stock Jaguar XK 120s and 140s in the C Production race. And damn if he didn't win it! He ran with the convertible top up (for better aerodynamics?) and he leaped into the lead from the front row and, even though he had the fastest Jags all over him, kept them bottled up through the tight, narrow, twisty stuff and then opened up enough daylight on the front straight so's they couldn't dive under him going into Turn One. It was amazing to see a Thunderbird outrunning a bunch of Jaguars, and it made Big Ed happier than a pig in shit, seeing as how a lot of the SCMA regulars had been looking down their noses and making rude remarks about Big Ed's T-Bird. But I need to point out that those were all pretty stock Jaguars and that this was, as I said, one *very* healthy-sounding Ford Thunderbird....

But it put Big Ed in a good frame of mind, and so I had high hopes when his race rolled around later that afternoon. He was starting a ways back from The Skipper thanks to his off-course excursions in qualifying on Saturday, but all of us patted him on the shoulder and whispered in his ear and told him to just stay cool and keep calm and everything would turn out fine. And it sure looked good early on. Big Ed powered by one or two guys before they even got to the flag-stand, and picked another one off every lap with sheer acceleration down the pit straightaway. Pretty soon he had The Skipper in his sights. But Skippy must've actually looked in his mirrors (a rare occurrence under any circumstances!), and he made sure once to hog the middle going down the straightaways and braking into the corners so there really wasn't much of anyplace to get by. Big Ed'd try on one side and try on the other, and Skippy would be ready with just enough of a feint or hip-check to make him think better of it. Personally, I would've been tempted to give him a little nudge. In fact, "tempted" is probably an understatement. Only you've got to do that sort of thing out on the backside of the circuit where the race officials at the start-finish line and the people lined up along the front straightaway can't see it.

Whether it was patience, prudence or just being too damn timid, Big Ed sat back there lap after lap, scratching for a way by, and naturally all of the Team Passaic faithful were up there on the fences screaming at the tops of our lungs. Even Julie and little Vincent. And of course the thing Big Ed had going for him—whether he knew it or not—was that nobody can drive a race in their rearview mirror. Or at least not a whole race, anyway. And, sure enough, The Skipper finally got caught looking backwards when he really needed to be look-ing forward, went a little too deep into Turn One, and skated two wheels off the outside. Leaving this big, beautiful hole for Big Ed to drive through. And it was when he had the Trashwagon about halfway through that hole that The Skipper's tires bit in and the C-Type shot back across the track like it was launched from a damn catapult and nailed the Trashwagon broadside. It wasn't a very high-speed accident or anything, but it stove in the front of the C-Type pretty good, mashed in the side of the Trashwagon, and sent the two of them pirouetting into the hay-bales just hard enough to bend the steering link on the Trashwagon so's the right front wheel was pointed in the general direction of the radiator core.

Damn.

Worse yet, our old buddy Skippy blamed the whole thing on Big Ed. Said he was "crowding" him. Only this time we had plenty of witnesses who had seen firsthand what actually happened, so there wasn't even a mention of one of Charlie Priddle's trademark "Drivers' Committee" tribunals. At least not for Big Ed, anyway. Although they let The Skipper off with a little on-site wrist slap on account of, well, who knows? In racing, as in real life, some people get away with stuff and some people don't. It's just the way things are.

But, even with DNF and the fresh damage on the Trashwagon, Big Ed was feeling pretty damn pleased with himself. For a change he'd driven a reasonably decent race—even Cal and Tommy said so—and what happened was no way his doing. And afterwards—after all the smiles and the handshaking and the "what ifs" and "if onlys" and getting everything loaded up for the trip back to Jersey—Big Ed asked Julie and me if we'd maybe like to join him for dinner at this place he knew on the way home. Just the three of us, you know? Or make that four with little Vincent. That was really sort of unusual, but I got the idea he maybe wanted to talk to us about something. At least after he got done making goofy faces and gibberish chimpanzee noises at little Vincent, which took until most of the way through dessert and coffee.

"It was really nice of you to ask us out like this," I told him as he fired up his regular after-dinner cigar and offered little Vincent one.

"Ahh, I like you guys. And *this* little customer..." he made another Fun House face at little Vincent, "...he's th'best."

"Well, it's still awfully nice of you," Julie said while attempting to shoo the cigar smoke away from her face. It was like the more he paid for his cigars, the worse they smelled.

"It's good fr'me t'get out with some *real* people fr'a change."

"*Real* people?" Julie asked.

"You know. People who aren't tryin' t'*get* something off me."

"We get a lot of stuff from you," I reminded him. "Especially little Vincent."

"Aw, that's stuff I *wanna* do. It's almost like a break when y'get a chance t'do something nice for nice people."

He was getting at something. I could feel it.

And then his eyes swiveled over at me. And then at Julie. And then back to me. "Y'ever think about what'cher gonna do with yer life?"

"I thought I was already doing it," I shrugged.

"You don't never dream of nothin' bigger?"

"Oh, sure I do," I told him. Even though I really didn't. Hell, I spent most of my time just trying to keep up with the stuff I was already doing and the promises I'd already made.

"I think about it a lot," Julie said from across the table. And the look in her eye said it was absolutely true. "I want a house of our own one day. A *nice* house, with a garden and a patio and a back yard with a swing set and trees and a picture window in front and..." she let out a sigh, "...but it'll take so long at the rate we're going...."

Big Ed's eyes went back and forth between us again. "That's what I wanted to talk to you about. A way you can maybe get there a l'il faster."

Julie was all ears. And so was I, come to think of it.

"Now, y'gotta unnerstan' that this is all just pie-in-the-sky right now, and it could all come apart at the seams...."

'*Jesus, can you get to the blessed POINT!*' I thought but didn't say.

"...but there's some guys who been comin' around from this real estate company, lookin' at the property we got over by the shore..."

I knew he was talking about the scrap machinery yard over on an unkempt bluff next to a run-down and mostly abandoned freight warehouse that lost all its business when the Turnpike came in and hadn't seen much more than a few successful insurance fires ever since.

"...an' these guys seem pretty interested in maybe buyin' us out fr'the land—us an' that freight terminal next door, anyway—and buildin' themselves some kinda fancy housing development on it." He looked around to see if we caught his drift.

"So?" I asked.

"So?" He said like he was disappointed I didn't get it. "So what's a guy like me gonna do if he finds himself all of a sudden on the loose with a fat wad a'cash in his pocket?"

I looked at Julie and Julie looked at me. "I dunno," I told him.

Big Ed shook his head. "What do I like?" he asked like everybody on earth knew the answer.

"Sports cars?"

"Right!" he nodded. "Bravo! And what else do I like?"

I was about to say trashy girls with big tits, but he'd never bring up something like that in front of Julie. Or little Vincent, for that matter. "I dunno," I shrugged. "Making deals?"

Big Ed's face lit up. "That's it! Exactly! Bingo!" He looked at me like a proud father. "And what line of work does a guy go into if he's got a wad of cash in his pocket an' likes sports cars an' likes makin' deals?"

And that's what Big Ed wanted to talk to Julie and me about. About if we'd maybe like to expand our operation into a real, live, new-car dealership if the deal on his shore property came through. His idea was that he'd run the sales part up front and I'd run the service part in back. Just like Colin St. John and Barry Spline over at Westbridge. "So whaddaya think?" he asked through a beaming smile.

I was dumbstruck. Julie was, too.

"Now now none of it's fer sure yet," he cautioned, "but I wouldn't be wastin' my time or yers if I thought it was nothin' but smoke an' mirrors."

I knew I could count on that. And then something else occurred to me. "What kind of cars would we carry?"

"I haven't really thought that far yet. Maybe Jaguar? Maybe Austin-Healey? Maybe Arnolt-Bristol? Maybe Triumph? Who knows?" Then he looked at me. "Whadda *you* think?"

"Volkswagen," I said without thinking about it.

"Volkswagen?" he asked incredulously.

"Volkswagen," I nodded. "Oh, we could do sports cars, too. But I think those Volkswagens are just gonna *take off* in this country over the next few years."

"You think so?"

I nodded.

Big Ed leaned in over the table, his eyes boring into me like twin corkscrews. "Now is that yer *heart* talkin' or yer head?"

"It's my gut," I told him.

Big Ed leaned back in his chair and blew out a smooth, perfect smoke ring. "That's good enough fer me, Buddy. Good enough fer me...."

On the way home in the Volkswagen, Julie and I talked about Big Ed's plans, and, although we tried to act real cool and detached and adult and professional about it, we were both so excited we were damn near wetting our pants. So it also seemed like a perfect time to tip my hand about that possible trip to Le Mans with Tommy Edwards and the Cunningham team. I mean, no question the new baby coming and the possible new business development at the Sinclair with Big Ed would surely make this qualify as a genuine, desperate, once-in-a-lifetime Last Chance sort of opportunity. And, as I've said before, when you've got the bug, life is made up almost exclusively out of genuine, desperate, once-in-a-lifetime Last Chance opportunities.

Needless to say, Julie's initial reaction was a wee bit on the cool side. In fact, it was more like dry ice. Especially since the only other time I went traipsing out of the country on a racecar adventure was when I went down to Mexico for *La Carrera* and damn near got myself killed going over a cliff with Javier Premal in that Ferrari Big Ed was trying to buy. But I assured Julie that I wasn't going to be riding in any racecars this time—they didn't even allow it at Le Mans—and I'd be perfectly safe there in the pits while the drivers were out on the racetrack taking all the chances. She didn't look too convinced. And besides, I told her, what with the new baby and the possible new business deal with Big Ed and all the new commitments and new responsibilities I'd have and blah, blah, blah, blah....

And that's when Julie looked over at me with one of those disgusted, exasperated, how-can-you-be-such-a-selfish-and-thoughtless-little-boy expressions that wives save up for just such occasions and said: "Okay, go ahead. See if I care." Just like that, can you believe it? And then she added, "But that's only if the doctor says the new baby'll wait until you're back."

"You *mean* it?" I asked incredulously.

"Sure. Why not? You'll just be pissing and moaning and miserable to be around the whole time if I don't let you go."

"I sure will!" I agreed enthusiastically.

"But you're gonna *owe* me for this one, Palumbo. You're gonna *owe* me...."

Of that I had no doubt.

We had the whole family over for another "if-we-don't-do-it-everyone-will-think-we're-mad-at-them-or-something" Memorial Day barbecue at the duplex, and, since there weren't any major sportycar races going on in the area, I invited Cal and Big Ed to join us. Not to mention Butch and my Aunt Rosamarina. Hell, I didn't care what her neighbors thought. And, in fact, I don't think the neighbors gave two shits, either. What she might or might not be doing behind closed doors with a crippled-up, ex-marine hard-hat diver in the privacy of her own home wasn't nearly so upsetting as the marathon, all-night yowling and meowing serenades her tomcats provided for the neighborhood whenever a female feline within fifty miles went into heat. Now *that* was something to get upset about! Of course Carson Flegley was coming seeing as how he was now a prospective relative (although I kind of wished my old man would stop reminding me how handy it was gonna be to have an undertaker in the family!). Mary Frances was coming with her saxophone-playing musician friend Paul (although you could count on them to be late, of course), and it went without saying that my two married sisters and their kids and husbands would be there because, well, they knew if they didn't come everybody would think they were mad at us or something. You know how it goes.

I'd rigged up the big RCA radio in the back kitchen window so's Cal and Carson and Butch and me could listen to the Indy 500 while we were out in the little, postage-stamp sized back yard off the alley huddled around the barbecue grill the way guys do in order to avoid the squaws and being surrounded and over-run with conversations about weddings, babies, favorite recipes, home decorating and cute outfits. Oh, sure, it's hot and the damn smoke gets in your eyes out there by the grill, but at least you can talk seriously about important things like tire pressures, cornering techniques and camshaft lift (or even baseball like my old man and my brother-in-law Roy) without somebody you're going home with rolling their eyes like it's the stupidest stuff they ever heard. Not to mention that nobody's counting how many beers you've had out there by the grill.

Fact is, it's the kind of thing that makes a man want to have a bigger yard. With a patio, even….

Anyhow, the pre-race show for the Indy 500 came on while I was setting the charcoal on fire, and you couldn't make it out real good even if I turned it up all the way. But I'd recognize the names here and there, and of course the one you heard over and over again was "Bill Vukovich," and how he came from being a poor California farm kid during the depression to a genuine racing hero with a shot at being the first man in history to win three Indy 500s in a row. Lou Meyer, Mauri Rose and Wilbur Shaw had each won three, but never three in a row. And nobody could forget that Vuky had been just a steering-link bolt away from winning the '52 race, and so this very easily could have been a shot at *four* in a row. He was sitting fifth on the grid in the middle of the second row, wheeling a brand new Kurtis chassis with a brand new blue paint scheme and driving for a brand new car owner—some multimillionaire from Atlanta named Lindsey Hopkins—but he still had Jim Travers and Frank Coon as his crew, and so you knew the car was going to be set up right and that they'd be clever and shrewd when it came to race strategy. A guy named Jerry Hoyt was on the pole in a new Stevens/Offy, and Jack McGrath was once again the fastest guy in Indiana, sitting on the outside of the front row with a new track record of 142.580 miles-per-hour. Too bad he couldn't have done it on pole day. But me and the announcers and everybody else expected Billy Vukovich to be the man to beat once the race got rolling. And I listened real close when they read down the full grid to catch Sammy Speed's name. I knew from the newspapers that he'd qualified Les Gonda's new, two-year-old Kurtis on the first weekend and so he was gridded way up in ninth with a bunch of apparently faster cars clogged up behind him. But it was great to hear his name up there in the top ten anyway. And I had my fingers crossed that he'd get another good run out of it there at the Speedway and be there when it counted at the end of the 500 miles.

I was just getting ready to put the first of the steaks and burgers on when they played the National Anthem and *"Back Home Again in Indiana,"* and I held off long enough that Cal and Carson and Big Ed and me could go up on the back porch with our ears craned towards the speaker so's we could hear *"GENTLE-MEN, START YOUR ENGINES…."* and the crowd going absolutely nuts in the background.

Naturally Julie came out while the tension was building during the parade laps—jeez, she could barely get through the back door—to ask exactly when I was planning to put the meat on, and I gave her one of those lame, mumbly *"in a minute, dear"* replies and leaned in even closer to the speaker. I mean, this was the blessed Indianapolis 500, fer chrissake!

The green waved and the announcers promptly went as crazy as the crowd, yelling into their microphones as Vukovich knifed through to take third place away from Hoyt on the first lap, and then second place away from Tony Bettenhausen on the second. Which left him right on Jack McGrath's tail with nothing but empty track ahead of them. And then it got even louder as Vukovich slipped past into the lead. And louder yet when McGrath re-passed him the very next lap. And damn near frantic when they swapped positions again. And again. And again.

Wow! Wotta race!

It went on like that for fifty miles, the two of them battling back and forth and pulling away from the rest of the field. Only then, slowly but surely, Vuky began to ease away. And then McGrath came into the pits around quarter-distance with his engine running rough and he was finished with a broken magneto. One of the announcers allowed as how Vukovich had pushed him to the breaking point. And maybe he had. But the fact was nobody could keep up with Billy Vukovich that day. Nobody at all.

Meanwhile Sammy was soldiering on in about twentieth, taking it easy and saving the car after stopping early to have a bum tire changed. Tough luck. But Indy's a long race and so you've just gotta hang in there and keep plugging. And all the while fighting the gusty winds the announcers kept talking about that were blasting across the track at the exit of Turn Two and all the way down the back-straight. Still, it all seemed to have kind of stabilized (not to mention that Julie was glaring at me from the doorway in a way that was becoming very difficult to ignore), and so I went down to the grill and put the meat on. And right about the time I was taking the first steaks off and loading them onto a platter, I heard a shout and a lot of hubbub from up on the porch. *"WHAT IS IT?"* I yelled up to Carson and Cal and the rest of them.

"THERE'S BEEN AN ACCIDENT!!" Carson yelled back down.

Well, I took the stairs three at a time to get up there, but of course it was all confusion on the microphone end and all we knew for sure was that there'd been some sort of wreck on the back stretch and that Rodger Ward, Al Keller, Sammy Speed and Billy Vukovich were involved. And that there was *fire!* A lot of fire. Cal and I looked at each other, dumbstruck. And then at the radio speaker, aching to hear more....

Something really bad had happened.

You could feel it.

Well, the news came in dribbles and bits and pieces while track cleanup went on under the yellow for the better part of a half-hour, and mostly what we knew was that Ward and Keller and Sammy Speed were apparently okay—thank goodness!—and that Billy Vukovich had left for the hospital in an ambulance. And then there was a report that his car had flipped and landed upside-down and burned, but that he'd been thrown clear and wasn't inside when it hit and burst into flame. And then came another interview with somebody in the stands who said that Vukovich had been trapped in the burning car and couldn't get out. And then they were going to have a report from the hospital. But that didn't come through and so they switched down to pit lane. The reporter was asking somebody about how his driver was. And I recognized Spud's voice immediately. He sounded confused and irritated. "We think he's okay," he told the reporter. "We think he's okay." Then there was some more confusion and commotion and then:

"And here's the latest!" the pit reporter screamed into his microphone as the field rumbled past behind the pace car. "We have a report here that driver Billy Vukovich is okay. I repeat, we have a report that driver Billy Vukovich is okay...."

And all of America breathed a huge sigh of relief.

But of course he wasn't okay.

He was dead.

It wasn't until later that night, when Spud Webster called me from Indianapolis to tell me Sammy was shaken but all right, that I got the whole story. There was no emotion at all in his voice when he told me: "It was real windy there off of Two, and Sammy was right behind Rodger Ward and Al Keller with Vuky closing in to lap them as they came out of the turn—just before that little crossover bridge—and Vuky was really flying. Nobody would've caught him. Not that day. But then Rodger's car snapped out sideways. Some people thought it was the wind, but Sammy said it looked more like his right-rear axle maybe broke. And then it dug in and flipped him over and he skidded along upside-down and Al Keller swerved to avoid him. But you just can't turn that sudden at a place like Indianapolis—not at that sort of speed—and so he went into a skid and bounced off the wall and came flying back across the track and plowed right into Sammy..." Spud paused for a moment—like he was seeing it through Sammy's eyes—and then he continued, his voice flat and heavy as frozen lead. "That sent Sammy skidding down between Rodger's overturned car and the wall—all three of them kind of moving and bouncing and rotating around together—and that's about when Vuky arrived on the scene full-tilt with no place in hell to go. He made a stab at getting around Sammy, cutting it hard right, but there just wasn't room and so he hit Sammy's rear wheel—sheared it clear off!—and that launched him up into the air damn near vertical. He flew over the wall and came down hard on the nose and then the car bounced back up and went cartwheeling through a parking lot—ricocheting off cars and pickup trucks and sending parts and shit flying in all directions. And then it whacked down one last time—upside-down—and exploded into flames." He let out a long, constricted sigh. "Sammy doesn't believe he was alive to burn to death by then..." Spud added with a faint flicker of hope, "...not that it makes any difference."

Bob Sweikert wound up winning the 500 that year—a race that would always be remembered as the one where Billy Vukovich died—and there was just no joy in it for anyone. Except for the newspapers and magazines, of course. They never pay much attention to racing at all except when something really terrible happens. And especially if they've got some nice, grisly pictures to go along with it. Like the one *Life* magazine ran the following week, with Vukovich's car all crashed upside-down in the car park with smoke and flames billowing out of it like an oil tanker on fire. You could even see his hand sticking out from underneath the wreckage.

"It's just so horrible," Julie groaned. "He left a wife and a little baby. And for *what?*"

"He was doing what he loved," I offered lamely.

And then, like an idiot, I hung out all that old philosophical laundry about how we're all gonna die sometime and would you rather go though life doing nothing that charges you up and then maybe suffer through a long, drawn out, agonizing illness and empty death like what happened to Old Man Finzio? Or would you rather stick your nose up in that rare, sweet air where your senses tingle and few have the guts to go, but maybe wind up taking the Express Route to the other side as part of the bargain?

To be honest, it makes for great cocktail-hour conversation.

But that's about as far as it goes....

28: Dreams Come True

All the racer types were pretty shell-shocked about what happened at Indianapolis. I mean, you never expected a guy—hell, a master!—like Billy Vukovich to get killed at a track he seemed to almost own. And especially while he was leading by a country mile and just stroking it home for another easy win. It was like the hard part was already over, right? Not to mention that he was about to drive right into history as the first guy to ever win three 500s in a row. And it could have so easily been four. It seemed so unfair. And, worse yet, that he got caught up in an accident he had nothing to do with. In fact, that *nobody* had anything to do with. Unless it was maybe the guy running the heat-treat process on the steel they made Rodger Ward's rear axle out of at some foundry someplace. Or the guy who maybe missed a tiny flaw when he crack-checked that axle with magnaflux or zyglo like the Indycar teams always do when they tear the car right down to the last nut and bolt and completely rebuild it the week before the race. Or it could have just broken. Just like that. And the evil, sneering, three-cornered twist-of-fate in it made you feel all creepy and uneasy inside. Like there were Forces at work, you know?

People like Julie and Mary Frances were sick and disgusted over it—why, it was all so useless and frivolous and, well, *unnecessary*—while people like Big Ed and Carson and me mumbled lamely (and a little apologetically) about how it was just some freak kind of accident like being hit by lightning or stung to death by bees and that you had to back up and take a larger view of things and see that if you judged the safety of racing by dividing up the deaths and burns and dismemberments by the millions of racing miles traveled and compared it to ordinary, everyday car, bus and truck road travel and blah, blah, blah, blah.

I told you it sounded lame.

But the interesting thing was that the *real* racers didn't say much. Guys like Sammy Speed and Tommy Edwards and Cal Carrington. Oh, you could see it in their eyes. It wasn't fear, though. More a dirty-trick contempt for the way the racing gods could tempt you and tease you and then squash you like a bug on a windowsill anytime they wanted to. Although they didn't do it very often, and you never believe it's gonna happen to you. But you need to understand that racers don't believe in luck. Because it's not the sort of thing that requires belief. Not hardly.

Racers *know* it's there....

And they develop thick skins and what appear to be cold or even uncaring attitudes. At least to people on the outside. Like when Cal summed it all up for me over morning coffee in the sandwich shop across the street the Wednesday after the race: *"Look, Buddy,"* he told me like he was asking me to pass the jam, *"there's only two ways out of this life...sick or sudden."*

What more could you say?

But eventually the shock fades and the outraged pieces in the newspapers get smaller and move backwards from the front page and the op-ed section to the sports pages and the letter-to-the-editor columns where they belong, and the whole process is like when a little kid on the beach pulls a tin pail of sand up out of the edge of the tide line. First there's this jagged, hard, empty hole the same shape and size as the pail. But then the next easy wave slithers across it and peels off the rough edges and softens it up a little. And then the next wave smoothes it out and fills it in a little more. And then the next one and then the one after that until it's just a little dimple in the muck, and by the time the tide's come in and gone out it's dissolved into history and you can't even find it anymore....

So life goes on, and there are always more cars to fix and more things to take care of at home and new world events to follow and cluck your tongue over and new hit songs to tap you fingers to on the radio. Like *"Rock Around the Clock"* by Bill Haley and the Comets, which shook the whole country when it hit number one on the *Billboard Magazine* charts the week after Indianapolis. It seemed like it was playing on every station you turned to, and a lot of people didn't like it at all. Like Butch and my old man and all my old man's union buddies, for example. But it was really kind of catchy and hard to get out of your head, and just the sort of thing I needed to zap me out of the doldrums and back to the present. After all, I had to get my things together and all my ducks in a row over at the Sinclair so I could take off for France on Monday morning. And, wouldn't you know, the Cunningham people who made all the travel arrangements had me leaving the good old U.S. of A. on Monday morning, June 6th. Which, if you have been paying any attention at all, was also Julie and my second wedding anniversary.

Like I needed that, you know?

Especially considering how I already felt guilty as hell about going over to Le Mans after what had happened at Indianapolis. And even moreso with lots of work backed up at the shop and Julie looking like she was about ready to pop any moment. Even though the doctor seemed pretty certain it wasn't gonna happen until after I got back. Truth is, I was almost looking for an excuse not to go. But I'd been waiting and wanting and wishing and hoping and praying to go to the Twenty-Four Hours of Le Mans for so long and here I finally had this golden opportunity to fly over there and spin wrenches—all expenses paid, mind you!—for the best damn American team in the business. Hell, the *only* American team in the business! And it seemed pretty ugly and ungrateful of me to simply not feel like going. But I didn't, and that's the truth of it. Still, one of the things you find out as you get older is that anticipation is really a kid's game. When you're little, anticipating Christmas or your birthday or the Ringling Brothers and Barnum & Bailey Circus coming to town is half the magic. Maybe more than half. But you lose that. As you get older and that list of stuff you *have* to do starts getting longer and demanding more attention than that list of stuff you *want* to do, you get to feeling like you're sneaking away—stealing away, even—anytime you allow yourself a few moments off to wrap your fingers around a dream.

Big Ed had agreed to chauffeur me over to Idlewild Monday morning to catch the plane to Paris with some of the other Cunningham team members, and I remember kind of looking at the carpet and creeping around the duplex on tiptoes while I was packing. Julie was making a full-time job of looking the other way, too, even though I'd brought home a big box of chocolates and a bundle of roses the night before for our anniversary. That kind of stuff never cuts much ice when you're feeling guilty. They can sense it, you know? So all I got was a cold, stone-dry peck on the cheek there in the doorway when Big Ed's T-Bird pulled up to the curb around seven. "Take care of yourself," Julie said without a single degree of heat in her voice. Fahrenheit or Centigrade. I looked past her to where little Vincent was standing, barefoot in his diaper, wearing a bib full of strained peaches and oatmeal. He looked up at me with those big, wide, glistening eyes, and damn if they didn't look pretty disappointed in me, too. Even betrayed.

Or at least that's how they looked to me, anyway....

On the way over to the airport, Big Ed went through the checklist and made sure I had my passport and the directions Tommy'd given me and that I knew who I was supposed to meet up with at the airport and where. Strangely, I didn't feel particularly nervous this time about flying. But maybe I was just plain numb.

"There's something else," Big Ed said as we passed by the row of new car dealerships on Atlantic Avenue with their *"DRIVE IT HOME TODAY!"* and *"E-Z PAYMENTS!"* and *"WE WILL NOT BE UNDERSOLD!"* signs and banners on the big, plate-glass showroom windows with all the latest models inside. Outside, on the used car lots, military rows of gleaming fenders and whitewall tires lined up underneath strings of fluttering pennants and rotating spinners, with important tidbits of information like *"LOW MILEAGE,"* *"ALMOST NEW!"* *"AUTOMATIC TRANSMISSION!"* *"$999 SPECIAL,"* and *"AIR CONDITIONING!"* hand-painted in large, rounded white lettering on every sparkling-clean windshield.

"What's that?" I asked.

"The deal on the property."

"The deal on the property?"

"Yeah. My scrapyard property. Over by the shore."

"What about it?"

"It looks like it's gonna go through...."

I met the two other guys from the Cunningham team over at the TWA ticket counter. One was a thin, balding, quiet-but-pleasant little guy with glasses and gee-whiz eyes behind them named Neil Harmon. He took care of timing and scoring and overseeing all the lap charts for the Cunningham entries. You rarely think much about that sort of stuff, but it's just as important as going fast and having good pitstops in a long endurance grind. I mean, look what happened at Sebring. In fact, some people said it was Neil's lap charts—and he kept track of the opposition as well as the Cunningham cars—that swayed the stewards' decision to give the victory to the Cunningham Jaguar instead of the Hill/Shelby Ferrari.

The other guy traveling with us was a big, Viking-bruiser type with a bushy red beard named Dennis Eade. I swear, he looked to be about eight feet tall and a yard or better wide, but with happy, prankster eyes and a big, easy laugh and the unmistakable hands of a racing mechanic. Turns out he worked for Cunningham's main guy Alfred Momo over at his New York shop, and he'd been traveling with the crew ever since that first year at Le Mans with the stock Caddy sedan and the special-bodied Cadillac streamliner that the French fans called *'Le Monstre'* back in 1950. "Yeah, I seen it all," he laughed. "And some of the bad stuff twice."

He turned out to be a great guy to travel with because he had a lot of swell stories to tell and obviously knew what racing was all about. And he knew that the main thing you needed to get by was a sense of humor. Whether things go undeservedly good or incredibly bad or when the endless grind of it makes you ache all over or when you see such colossal stupidity—oftentimes your own—that you wonder why you do it, you need that old glint-in-the-eye nudge and chuckle to keep you going. And Denny Eade was a certified master. Plus it was nice heading over there with two guys who'd been there before and knew the ropes. Although I can't really recommend sitting next to a guy the size of Denny on a transatlantic plane flight. "You ever play football in school?" I asked, looking down at the armrest between us where a forearm the size of an average human thigh overflowed both sides.

"Had to," Denny answered. "It was a little bitty farm school up in a small town in Wisconsin. You had to play."

"Oh? What position?"

"Line."

"Offensive or defensive?"

"Both."

"Center? Guard? Tackle?"

"You don't understand," Denny grinned at me. "This was a tiny little high school up in a little bitty Wisconsin farm town—The Zenda Zealots, that's who we were—and I *was* the offensive and defensive line...."

It took me a moment to realize he was giving me the needle. You could always tell, because his eyes would start to dance.

Anyhow, the Cunningham people had us booked on one of those beautiful and graceful Lockheed Super Constellations—you know, the ones with the three tail-fins?—and I have to admit I felt pretty secure inside that airplane. Or maybe I was just getting a little more used to flying. Even if I didn't much like the sensation of looking out my window and seeing nothing but ocean all the way to the horizon in every direction. "Flying make you nervous?" Denny asked.

"Ahh, maybe a little," I told him. Like an idiot.

"Well, the thing you have to understand about flying over the water is that the higher up you get, the harder that surface becomes. Think about when you were a kid, and how much harder that water seemed when you hit it off the high dive compared to just jumping in...."

I remembered that.

"Well, from this height, the impact'll kill you for sure. So you don't have to worry about drowning or getting eaten when the sharks get to you."

"Gee, thanks. That's real comforting."

"And you've got the whole way down to brace yourself for it, too."

I looked over at him. "You don't know Cal Carrington by any chance, do you?"

Later on the stewardesses served us coffee and then sandwiches and meanwhile Denny and Neil gave me all the inside dope on Cunningham's previous trips to Le Mans and also on the teams we'd be facing. "Well, Ferrari's got some new cars with big six-cylinder engines—and I mean *BIG* six-cylinder engines!—but they're still pretty green and haven't done a whole lot of finishing in the races they've run so far. The way I see it, Ferrari's spread themselves kinda thin and they're maybe concentrating a little too much on beating the Germans in Formula One. Not that they're real likely to do it. Maserati's got great cars but the same sort of problem, and they're the most disorganized bunch you ever saw. Plus they're always running out of money."

"How about the English teams?"

"Well, you've got Aston Martin with their DB3S, and it's a pretty stout car but not as fast as the Ferraris and Maseratis. Although they've got disc brakes now just like the Jags. They seem to win a lot over in England, but pretty much nowhere else. And then, of course, there's Jaguar."

I crept forward on my seat. "I've seen pictures of the D-Type, but I've never seen one in person yet."

"Oh, it's a looker all right. Absolutely gorgeous. And just *made* for Le Mans. That's why Briggs bought one. But of course you never get the exact same thing the factory boys are running. Not from anybody."

"But Ferrari beat them last year, didn't they?"

"Yeah, they did. But it was the first year for the 'D' and they had the usual new-car shit going on. Particularly on the top team cars, like the one Moss was driving. And the weather was awful, and that Argentinean Gonzalez drove like an absolute madman in the wet. Although," he added, "if you get away with it, I guess you're not so crazy after all...." Denny gave a bemused sort of shrug. "And remember that the big advantage the Jags had was their disc brakes and how they could dissipate heat and last longer without fading. Only you don't brake near so late or hard in the rain and so the brakes don't get near so hot. That kind of tilted the playing field in favor of Ferrari. Like always, they had motor on everybody. In the end, it came down to a very good and experienced British club driver trying to catch one of the fastest, most fearless wet-weather guys in the world in a driving rainstorm. And the Jag was almost good enough to do it, too."

"So you think Jaguar's the hot ticket this year?"

"Well, they're not the type to make the same mistakes twice. And they've shown before they know how to win this race. And the car is *really* good...."

"So who's going to beat them?" I asked. But of course I already knew the answer.

Mercedes-Benz.

Mercedes had burst on the Formula One scene with their handsome silver grand prix cars and blitzkrieg organization in 1954, and, typical of Mercedes' thoroughness, they'd hired everybody's consensus pick as maybe the best damn driver in the world to race it for them. And that's how 1951 World Champ Juan Manuel Fangio came to drive for Mercedes-Benz. And the car was simply astonishing. They'd gone their own way on so many things. Like fuel injection and desmodromic valve gear and inboard brakes and fully-independent rear suspension and full-body streamlining and, well, lots of little things, too. But, also typical of Mercedes, it was all very well thought out and engineered and executed. And tested until they were absolutely sure of it, too.

The Mercedes grand prix cars pretty much swept the field in 1954, easily winning Fangio his second world title, and were already well on their way to a repeat performance in 1955. Plus they'd added a three-liter sports car version to the stable—the 300SLR—to contest the big endurance races like Le Mans. And just to make sure, they'd hired Englishman Stirling Moss—the other Very Best Driver In The World—away from Jaguar by offering him a Formula One seat alongside Juan Manuel Fangio as well as the sports car ride. Jaguar couldn't match it on account of they never had a grand prix car (like I've said before, Jaguar figured there was only one race in the world worth winning, and that was Le Mans) and Moss had already done a hell of a job for Mercedes by winning the thousand-mile *Mille Miglia* road race for them in Italy. Ahead of teammate Fangio and all the local-hero Italian drivers in their Ferraris and Maseratis, too. And you can bet that didn't sit real well with the Italian fans....

I couldn't really sleep on the plane, and it was strange heading east across the ocean where you took off around 10:30 or so Monday morning, flew through the shortest midday, afternoon, evening, and night you've ever experienced (even though it seemed to go on forever!) and find yourself landing in Paris the following morning right around breakfast time. It gets your system pretty damn confused, let me tell you! Which is why the team had us arrive on Tuesday so's we could get over to the circuit, settle in, acclimate ourselves, and then get a little heavy-duty sleep in before official practice started Wednesday evening.

Tommy Edwards met us at the airport—he said he'd volunteered because there wasn't much of anything to do at the track until practice started, and it was better than hanging around and making stupid small talk. "So how was the flight?" he asked.

"Long."

"You ever flown overseas before?"

I shook my head.

"It takes a bit of getting used to."

Tommy took a little detour to show us some of the sights before we headed out into the countryside to Le Mans, but I'd have to say the Eiffel Tower, *Arc de Triomphe* and *Champs Elysees* were pretty much wasted on me that particular morning. Although I was taken by the Paris traffic with its *Traction Avant* Citroen taxis that looked like low-slung gangster cars and hordes of bicycles—some with puttering little single-cylinder Solex engines over the front wheels—and mopeds and motor scooters and tons of those tippy, slab-sided *Deux Cheveaux* Citroens that reminded me of a cross between a Volkswagen Beetle and a corrugated tin storage shed. Not to mention the Panhard sedans. Who but the French would build a two-cylinder "luxury" car? And the way they *drove* in Paris! *Ooo-la-la!*

I liked it even more when we got out in the countryside, where the nice, straight, narrow little route we were on was lined with tall, slender trees on both sides, all of them clipped and trimmed like dog-show poodle legs. It was green and beautiful and you could really feel all the age and history of the landscape. Although it was hard to believe that so many wars had been fought there. I mean, it didn't look like the kind of territory people would want to fight over. It was just too pretty and peaceful, you know?

Scrutineering was going on in this big sort-of terminal building when we arrived, and you have never seen such a hubbub. There were busy French officials scurrying around everywhere you looked—each one obviously on a mission of gravest importance—and you could read the seriousness, complexity and delicacy of the situation on the faces of all the team managers. Especially the Brits and the Germans and the Italians....

"These chaps wait all bloody year for this," Tommy whispered in my ear.

"You mean the team managers?"

"No. The French officials. It's their once-a-year turn in the bloody spotlight." It was going on all around us!

"The French rather enjoy a chance to push the English and Germans and Italians around." He leaned in even closer. "It doesn't happen very often...."

And they got to use their favorite weapon, too. Paperwork. There were reams of it everywhere! Rules and forms and documents and declarations and Lord only knows what else. All around us, serious-looking Frenchmen of every imaginable shape and size—all of them wearing official armbands and dressed like it was a show opening or a the groundbreaking for a new hospital wing or a state funeral or something—stroked their goatees and arched their spines and raised their eyebrows as they compared this paper or that paper to the configuration of the cars in front of them. It was almost comical. But you didn't dare laugh....

So I kept a pretty serious and respectful expression on my mug as I handed over the fat wad of documentation the Cunningham guys had given me. And, even then, the little Frenchman at the table in front of me gave me the hairy eyeball as if I was maybe a German spy or an escaped child molester or a waterer of fine wine or something. I'll tell you, these guys made Charlie Priddle and his SCMA cronies look like a bunch of pikers! But then, this *was* the biggest damn race in the world—you could ask any of them!—and so they had a lot grander style and a lot bigger stage to play on. And they knew it, too. Even though the best threat the French had anymore was the lone Gordini in the two-liter class and the handful of 750cc tiddler DBs and such running for the Index of Performance (and getting in all the faster cars' way while they were at it!), they had somehow managed to get a stranglehold on the FIA international sanctioning body that ran and regulated all the major grand prix and sports car races all over the world. And that was something you could puff your chest and strut around about even if you didn't have much in the way of topnotch machinery anymore.

Who should I run into as I was making a few tourist rounds of the scrutineering arena (imagine a cross between a racing car show and the Republican National Convention, only spoken mostly in French and reeking of wine, cheese and dark-tobacco cigarettes instead of scotch, steak and cigars) but my old racing scribe buddy Hank Lyons. "Hey, what the hell are you doing here?" I asked him grandly.

"This is where the action is, isn't it?"

"It sure is!"

"How about you?"

"Tommy Edwards got me a sort of fill-in job wrenching and swapping tires for the Cunningham team. And you?"

"I'm covering this race for *Road and Track*."

"No!"

"Yeah," he beamed. "Can you believe it?"

I shook my head.

"It cost me everything I could scrape together to get over here, but there's a chance I'll get to stay."

"Doing what?"

"Well, if my story's any good, they may just let me cover the European racing scene for them!" His face was lit up like there was a spotlight on it.

"*Wow!*"

"Yeah! *Wow!* Isn't it *great??!!*" But then I saw a little of the dazzle bleed off. "A'course," he added softly, "it doesn't pay all that well...."

"Hey, who needs money?"

"...and I'll probably wind up living in some old Fiat Topolino or something..."

"Just think of it as a mobile home."

"And Lord only knows what I'll do in the wintertime."

"Go down to cover that Grand Prix race in Argentina, of course!" I'd read about that one in *Autosport*. Hank looked impressed that I'd even heard of it. "So," I asked him, "as a automotive journalist professional, how do you size this one up?"

"Well," he said, mulling it over, "if the race only went from here out to the track and back, you'd have to go with the Ferraris. That new, 4.4-liter six looks to be one hell of a strong engine. They say it's got even more power than last year's V12—or at least that's what Ferrari's saying, anyway—and some of the Italian scribes claim it'll top 200 down the straightaway towards Mulsanne..."

I let out a low whistle.

"...but of course those guys think Enzo walks on water, too."

Hank went on to explain that Ferrari had some problems with their driver lineup, too, since upcoming ace Mike Hawthorn had switched to Jaguar and their top driver, twice-World Champ Alberto Ascari, had unaccountably been killed in an informal testing accident just a few weeks before. "It was the usual Ferrari deal. He keeps all his drivers at arms' length and pits them against each other to make them go faster. Ascari won two world championships for Ferrari in '52 and '53—that's when they were running to the two-liter formula—but then they got into a row and he packed up and went over to Lancia. It was a brand new team, but they had Vittorrio Jano, who designed all the great prewar Alfa Romeos, working for them, and he came up with a great V6 sports car and then a V8 grand prix single-seater. Fantastic cars! But the production-car side of the Lancia business couldn't really afford it, and so the team was running out of money."

"So what happened?"

"Well, the sports cars won a lot of important races—one, two, three at *La Carrera* in '53, the *Mille Miglia* with Ascari in '54, and they certainly should've won Sebring that year when Moss and Lloyd took it in the OSCA—but the whole team skipped Le Mans, and the grand prix car was taking a lot longer than expected to get together. It was a pretty innovative design, and there were some of the usual teething troubles. And naturally Ascari was getting impatient. But it looked scrappy as hell when it was done, and Ascari proved right away that it was fast. Why, he was chasing Moss in the Mercedes for the lead in the late stages of the race in Monaco—just three weeks ago!—and getting closer every lap! Driving *right* on the edge! And you could see Moss was slowing and that there was smoke coming out of the Mercedes. And then the Mercedes barfed its engine and Moss pulled in, and all Ascari had to do was cruise around to the start-finish line, take the lead, and motor on to the finish. Only he had no way of knowing that Moss was out, and so he was still going like hell. Only now the fans were waving wildly and cheering him on because they'd heard about Moss over the P.A. But Ascari thought they were urging him on so he pushed even harder. And that's when he went just a hair too deep into the chicane, tried to save it, and shot through the railing and did a swan dive into the Mediterranean."

"You're joking!"

Hank shook his head. "It was no joking matter, either. The car crashed into the sea and it was several seconds before his helmet bobbed back up to the surface and the frogmen pulled him out. Everybody was sure he was dead."

"Jesus, he had the race won," I mused, running it over in my mind.

"Yeah, that's the irony of it. And then he was at Monza four days later where his friend Castellotti was testing a new Ferrari sports car for some minor Italian race—Lancia had given up on their sports car team and so Ascari was already signed to drive with Ferrari again at Le Mans—and he decided to take a few laps in Castellotti's car before he went home for lunch. And that's when he got killed. During a damn test session that didn't mean anything, with nothing to win or prove and nobody around."

"How'd it happen?"

Hank shrugged. "Skid. Crash. Who knows? It happened."

"It makes no sense."

"Nothing makes any sense. Except fiction, maybe. But, deep down inside, I think that's why I'm so addicted to this stuff." He thought it over for a moment and then reeled it off for me. "There's just so much more drama and destiny and fate and irony and joy and agony and suspense, aspiration, disappointment and redemption than you ever find in real life…."

I never would've put it in those exact words, but I sure knew what he was talking about.

By that time we'd wandered over by where the red cars were going through technical inspection. "It sure looks the part though, doesn't it?" Hank observed about the new Ferraris. While we were standing there giving the new Ferrari 121LM and 118LMs the once-over, we noticed a heated discussion going on between the Ferrari team manager and one of the French officials. Or maybe it wasn't a discussion after all, since a discussion generally requires at least two participants. In this instance, the Ferrari guy was animatedly explaining or pleading or demanding something in a rush of machine-gun French (plus a few Italian hand gestures) while the French official just stood there with his face upturned and eyes serenely half-shut like he was on the back deck of a yacht anchored off the coast of Monte Carlo, savoring the gentle evening breeze wafting in off the Mediterranean.

It was hard to keep a straight face, you know?

But I was pleased as heck to see they'd put our friend Phil Hill in one of the factory Ferraris. I knew that Ernesto Julio had done a lot of lobbying on his behalf (or, more accurately, Carlo Sebastian did on Ernesto Julio's behalf after Ernesto did a little arm-twisting and mentioned once or twice how very nice the new race-cars from Jaguar and Maserati were looking…). Still, it was great to see Phil with a genuine factory ride—albeit in one of the "small" 3.7-liter 118LMs instead of the 4.4-liter 121LM reserved for the team's big guns, Eugenio Castellotti and Paolo Marzotto. Who both just happened to be Italian. But it was a pretty big break for Phil, and also nice that he got teamed up with that Maglioli guy who we'd seen run so well at *La Carrera* and elsewhere. Not only was he fast as stink—especially on open roads—but he was the kind of driver who usually found his way to the finish line, too. You can have all those "win or bust" types, as far as I'm concerned. Anyhow, Phil noticed us standing there and came over to say "hi." Which was real nice of him. "So," I asked, "howzit going?"

"Well," he offered with a thin smile, "there's times I wish I spoke a little Italian." He looked over at where the Ferrari team manager was now quarrelling angrily with two of his own mechanics while the serene little French official looked on approvingly. "And then there's other times I'm glad I don't."

"How do you like your chances?"

"Oh, a race like this, you never know. So much can happen. It's like a cross between Russian Roulette and a lottery…."

"How about the car?"

"Ask me again tomorrow night. After I've driven it."

But Hank was sure right about those Ferraris looking the part. I don't know how the heck they do it, but each new model racing Ferrari has this way of looking sleeker and meaner and more dangerous than the last one, but yet still keeps that special, carnivorous, warm-blooded animal *heat* that's so much a part of the Ferrari bloodline. Why, you could almost hear their stomachs growling as you wandered by.

By contrast, the Jaguars and Astons seemed much more reserved and military in their British Racing Green paintjobs. Not that there was any consensus whatsoever as to precisely which shade of green "British Racing" might be. The Jags were a really dark, yet creamy sort of color—almost black in certain light—while the Astons had this sharp, sort of metallic Sherwood Forest kind of shade that I really liked. Plus Aston had a special car with a Lagonda V12 engine inside and a massive eggcrate grille on the front that they had high hopes for. Although the Jags looked the better racecars. Just like Denny Eade had told me on the plane, Jaguar's new D-Types were absolutely stunning. They were just so *smooth,* you know? And it was amazing how all the lines flowed together from the small, oval, slightly-pursed-lips front radiator opening and plexiglass headlamp covers all the way back to the fighter-plane fin on the headrest. Hank leaned over and whispered in my ear, *"Somebody once said that Le Mans is an English race held on French soil, and that's the Great British Hope right there…"* I could see what he meant. You couldn't miss that there were far more English teams than anything else going through scrutineering.

"How d'ya rate their chances?" I asked.

"Well, they'll be around at the end, that's for sure. And they've got the pace and brakes for it. But they're up against some tough opposition. Especially from Ferrari and Mercedes. They haven't forgotten how they snookered themselves with the C-Types back in '52."

Barry Spline had told me about that one. About how they knew Mercedes was building the 300SL coupes—the same ones I saw win down in Mexico later that year—and that rumors about how fast and powerful they were going to be prompted Jaguar to hot up the engines and put some sleeker, more aerodynamic bodies on their factory C-Types to meet the challenge. After they'd already won the damn race with a C-Type the previous year. And then practice opened three days before the race and the new Mercedes wasn't nearly so fast or awesome as everybody expected. But they *were* durable, and went on to win in a walk after all the team Jaguars went out with overheating on account of that sleek new aerodynamic bodywork didn't allow enough air into the blessed radiators. But then, the English had a lot of reasons to be gun-shy and trigger-happy at the same time when it came to the Germans....

"How about Jag's driver lineup?"

"Solid and plenty fast. And of course they've hired-on Mike Hawthorn since Moss left for Mercedes."

"Is he as good as everybody says?"

"Moss?"

"No, Hawthorn."

"Well, no British driver could ever be as good as the British press seems to think. To read their stuff, he doesn't even cast a shadow."

"That's a lot to live up to."

"Well, that's the English way, isn't it? Heap the pressure on. Duty and country, old boy. And don't forget to be humble about it afterward." Hank looked at me kind of sideways. "Remember, he's only been racing about three years."

"Really?"

Hank nodded. "Came on the scene out of absolutely nowhere in '52—wound up driving Formula One in some outclassed, show-the-flag Cooper-Bristol—but he did amazingly well and took fourth in the World Championship. The next year he was driving for Ferrari."

"Wow. He must be *fast!"*

Hank rolled his eyes. "He's up there with the very best. The *very* best. And he's got plenty of grit and he's viciously competitive. *All* the good ones are. But he pushes really hard all the time and he's, uhh…" I could see Hank was looking for the right words, "…uuh, let's just say he's, umm, wound pretty tight."

The other heavy runners—and the ones everybody else was keeping watch on out of the corner of their eyes—were the beautiful new 300SLRs from Mercedes, done up in their usual liquid-silver paintjobs and immaculate in every detail. They were distant relatives of the 300SL coupes we saw at *La Carrera*—just like Jaguar's C-Types and D-Types were distant relatives of an XK120M—only these were the real thing. All-out racing cars with full-width bodies and powerful lights for nighttime racing and an extra seat bolted in that only got used at the Mille Miglia. Nothing really prepared you for how beautifully turned-out they were. Or how brutally handsome. But they didn't really remind you of a wild animal like the Ferraris did. No, the only thing the Mercedes reminded you of was a machine. A war machine. Oh, they didn't figure to have the power of the Ferraris or the brakes of the Jaguars and they'd certainly gone their own way technically—like the straight-eight engines with fuel injection and desmodromic valves that opened and closed without valve springs and four-wheel independent suspension with inboard drum brakes front and rear and bodywork made out of lightweight magnesium—and you had to be impressed with how they'd designed and engineered and developed every bit of it themselves. But then, they had a bunch of great technicians and tremendous discipline and organization. And that went from top to bottom on the racetrack as well as in the shop. At the head of the whole thing was that big, puffy Herr Neubauer guy Hank and me had seen for the first time at *La Carrera*. He still looked like an unmade bed, but it was obvious everybody on the team felt his eyes on their backs. They also had this handsome, silvery-haired, granite-jawed chief engineer named Rudolph Uhlenhaut, who'd been with Mercedes before and through the war (although, according to Hank, he had a German father and a British mother) and was reckoned to be a world-class driver in his own right based on what he did when he went out to test the cars. In fact, he was listed as a reserve driver right there at Le Mans for just that reason.

But the Mercedes machine didn't stop with radical yet dead-reliable racecars and a perfectly organized team that didn't tolerate panic, stupidity, emotion or indecision. They went after the top drivers, too. But the cool heads, not the hotheads and the ones out to prove something that Ferrari liked so much. And they'd pay whatever it took. Although it didn't take all that much to tempt a really topnotch driver onto the team that gave him—by far—the best chance of winning. And that's how they wound up with the team of Fangio and Moss in their lead car. The two best damn racing drivers in the whole blessed universe! And they backed them up with a second car for German ace Karl Kling—the guy who won *La Carrera* for them the year we were there—teamed up with French driver Andre Simon, plus a third 300SLR for our friend John Fitch and another French driver named Pierre Levegh. It always helped to have a few French drivers on the squad when you ran the Twenty-Four Hours of Le Mans. And especially there at scrutineering....

I wanted to say hello to my friend John Fitch, but I didn't see him around. Besides, we were already getting the hairy eyeball from one of the German mechanics for maybe being a little too interested in the technical details of the car. Or maybe he was just worried that we were souvenir hunters. In fact, that was probably it.

The other nifty German cars were the squat, compact little Porsche Spyders that Tommy Edwards had taken such notice of at Sebring. They had that typically molten-lump-of-solder Porsche look and really didn't get your Fashion Pulse pumping like the stylish big iron from Ferrari and Jaguar and Aston and Mercedes did. But they looked dangerously purposeful and without any stupid frills or pretenses, and I noticed that one of the drivers was that Zora Arkus-Duntov guy who'd once raced for Allard alongside Tommy Edwards and designed those Ardun overhead-valve cylinder-head conversions for Ford flathead V8s. It's nice when you can find a driver who actually understands what goes on inside the mechanical guts of a car. Not that it happens very often. Anyhow, those 550s made a sound like I'd never heard out of a Porsche before. Oh, it was still an air-cooled, four-cylinder motor stuck back there behind the driver. Only now it had four overhead cams operated by shaft drive and bevel gears. That amounts to an awful lot of metal whirling around in a very small space.

"There's no adjustment built into it," Hank whispered in my ear. "The valve gear on each engine's got to mesh together perfectly to get all the valves correctly timed and clearanced."

"Really?"

Hank nodded. "I heard it takes one of their technicians almost forty hours to assemble one."

That was sure a lot for what amounted to a ridiculously overdeveloped Volkswagen motor. "What's the point?" I whispered back. I mean, you don't want to be disrespectful.

"I guess so that, once you've got it right, it stays that way."

"Sounds like an awful lot of trouble."

Hank shrugged. And then he leaned in right next to my ear. "I also heard," he added with a hint of a snicker in his voice, "that when they finished the very first one, the clearances were figured to such zero-tolerance, Teutonic perfection that it wouldn't turn over...."

One of the Porsche mechanics glared at us like maybe he'd been eavesdropping.

We spent some time looking at the little two-cylinder, Panhard-powered DB sports-racers and Monopole coupes running in the 750cc class. They were all dainty, slippery, elongated little things done up in proud French blue, but it was kind of hard for me to grasp why anybody would want to expend so much time and effort on building the slowest true racing cars in the event. "The French have always been big on getting the most out of the least," Hank explained. "Besides, next to the overall, the prize everybody remembers is the Index of Performance, and the best thing for that is a very tiny engine and a small, light, really aerodynamic car that can milk a lot of top speed out of not much motor."

Their opposition in the 750 class amounted to four Fiat-based Italian cars—a Stanguellini, two pretty little Morettis and this ultra-strange, "twin-boom" contraption from Nardi, which looked more like two motorcycles strapped together than any kind of automobile you might imagine. The driver sat in a little cockpit between the right-hand wheels and the engine sat directly across from him between the left-hand wheels. I'm sure it looked just grand on paper, but, there in the flesh and metal, it was about as odd-looking a contraption as I'd ever seen. *"Y'know,"* Hank whispered in my ear, *"there's an old saying in racing that 'if it looks right, it may just be right, but if it looks wrong, it's sure as hell screwed up.'"*

Across the way from the Nardi were some of the smaller British teams. Bristol had the same three cars that had soldiered on to an amazing seventh, eighth and ninth overall and first, second and third in the "Sports 2000" two-liter class the previous year, only now with those ungainly, humpbacked coupe tops with the two strange fins down the back chopped off so they looked more like proper sports-racers. And much the better for it, too.

"They'll be around at the end, too. You can count on it," was Hank's assessment.

Triumph had three of their gutty, blue-collar TR2s fitted with single racing windscreens, tonneau covers and two big Lucas driving lights stuck in their grille openings, and MG had come over with two of their slick new EX-182s that didn't have a chance in hell against the outright-racer Porsches and OSCAs in the "1500 Sports" class, but that were widely acknowledged to be prototypes for the long-rumored new MGA that all the US dealers had been crying for to replace the old, upright, T-series cars. And those MGs looked really sharp, too, with their metal tonneau covers and a single Lucas driving light cut into the right-hand side of their grilles. Plus we were pleased to see they'd signed on expatriate

Brit/American Ken Miles as one of the drivers. Like Mercedes, they knew it was good press to have an American on the team. Especially if you planned on selling a bunch of cars over in the States. I thought the EX-182s seemed a lot lower, more slippery and less chunky that the TR2 Triumphs (although with less motor under the hood by 500cc) and already you could sense a real serious Hometown Rivalry springing up between those two.

Meanwhile, crafty old Donald Healey had been writing letters and making a lot of righteous-sounding noise in the racing press (and everywhere else he possibly could!) about how his cars—which were genuine, volume-built, go-to-market production sports roadsters that a person without an oversize bank account could actually dream of owning one day—shouldn't be expected to run in the same racing class as the full-out, purpose-built and ridiculously expensive Aston Martin DB3S, Ferrari 750 Monza, and Maserati 300S racecars that also ran in the "Sports 3000" category at Le Mans. Not to mention the much-feared, factory-run 300SLRs from Mercedes that nobody could buy at any price. And so, after making as big and visible a fuss about it as humanly possible (or possibly even more?), Donald Healey's factory team boycotted the race. And he had a good point, too. Although there *was* a "private entry" of one of the brand new 100S models in the hands of "privateers" Lance Macklin and Les Leston, who just happened to be occasional factory team drivers on the Austin-Healey squad when they did go racing. After all, whatever happened regarding Ferrari and Maserati and even Mercedes-Benz didn't change the fact that they had to keep an eye on MG and Triumph....

The other British cars that caught our attention were the little 1100cc Cooper and Lotus sports-racers powered by the new, nifty, compact and lightweight Coventry Climax engines. It was a lovely little four-cylinder job that Hank told me had been originally designed to win a government contract for a new portable fire-pump engine for the British Army. Coventry Climax was a big industrial firm that built all sorts of lift trucks and such, and one of the major military specifications for this new fire-pump engine was that it "could be carried by two marines in full battle dress." So it was quite small and used an all-alloy block and cylinder head and a single overhead camshaft to produce the most power and keep the weight down. In fact, they called it the "FW," for "Feather-Weight." Well, the British smallbore racers got one look at it and decided it was a much better deal than the hot-rodded, cast-iron Ford and MG boat anchors they were using. And so Climax—always keen to Win One for England, reap a little publicity and, not incidentally, sell a few more motors—came up with an 1100cc "FWA" ("Feather-Weight Automotive") version for automobile racing. And the cars those back-alley English racecar builders stuck it in were really something. And really different, too.

The Cooper garage in Surbiton turned out a stubby little rear-engined car with a chopped-off tail—people called it the "Bobtail"—that obviously evolved out of the tin-turd, motorcycle-engined Formula III cars that had built such a reputation for them. The driver sat right in the middle—just like in the formula cars!—with a kind of phony "passenger seat" snuck through a loophole in the rules to underneath a tonneau cover right beside him. The car looked stoutly built and the driver looked well-protected, and I liked that. In fact, the tubular space frame was all smooth, rounded curves that went right out to the edge of the bodywork and reminded you of maybe the ribcage section of a dinosaur skeleton.

Their rivals across the way were Lotus, and this was the first time I'd ever seen a Lotus car in person. It had to be about the lowest, leanest, sparest and most it-came-from-outer-space-looking racing car on the planet. Why, it made everything else in the hall look tall and fat and stodgy by comparison. And also more substantial. When they lifted the hood or if you peeked inside the drivers' compartment, all you could see were small, straight, lightweight tubes welded together in triangular sections and then backed up with thin panels of aluminum sheet to make it a little stronger. In fact, it looked to me just the least bit spindly underneath. Not that I'm some kind of engineering genius or anything. And the hammered aluminum bodywork over it all was slick as a bullet. Complete with rear fenders that turned into these two smooth, softly rounded fins to help directional stability at high speed. I guess.

A shortish, exhausted and obviously highly exasperated young Englishman was standing next to one of the cars—imagine sort of a dumpy, worn-out edition of David Niven—and having himself one hell of a discussion with another of the French officials about the driving lights on the Lotus. It seems they'd rigged up this clever system to roll them up out of the bodywork when they were needed. So they could be down out of the airstream when they weren't, right? But the official—and this time it was a big, lumbering sort of guy with droopy lips and a farmer's hands and a small, frayed military ribbon pinned to what might well have been his only jacket—was holding another fat ream of paperwork and shaking his head *"non"* no matter what the Englishman said. Hank tugged at my sleeve. "You know who that is?"

I shook my head.

"That's Colin Chapman. The guy who builds these things."

"Really?" I was pretty damn impressed. Especially after all the stuff I'd read in *Autosport* about him. "He looks like he's having a little trouble with that official."

"Well, they figure it's their job to make things as miserable as possible for the English and German invaders. I mean, there's a lot of getting-even to be done here." He leaned in close again and whispered: *"And believe me, it's not lost on these guys that the Lotus might very easily swipe the Index prize away from the French cars. Remember, that's all they have left...."*

Later on I went back by the Cunningham guys to find out about the place we were staying and set up my transportation to the track the next day. They'd made it through scrutineering pretty easily since Briggs was widely recognized as a Great American Sportsman around those parts and moreover had never shown the bad form or poor manners to actually win there at Le Mans like the British and German and Italian teams had. And after that Hank and I went outside and wandered far enough away so that all the noise and hubbub faded into the night. He led me up a cobble street, past darkened shop windows with painted signs in French hanging over them. You could hear the click of our shoes against the stones.

"You know, I can't believe I'm really here," I said in a hushed but excited voice. "It doesn't seem real, does it?"

I shook my head. "It feels so strange. So different from home. So far away…."

"You'll be okay once you get busy at the track tomorrow."

We came to a small village square with a sad, weary old church facing it. Hank brought us to a halt and we stood there for a moment, just looking at it. In the moonlight it had the look of a giant, towering old tombstone. But with darkened windows that looked like empty eyes, looking upward, pleading. "I guarantee you that church has seen more weddings, baptisms and funerals than any church in America," *Hank whispered respectfully.* "More bullets, blood and bayonets, too…." *Maybe it was because I was tired or maybe I was just homesick, but I felt like I didn't belong there at all. Almost like I was creeping through somebody's private graveyard without their permission, you know?*

29: *Le Mans at Last*

The Cunningham team had us booked into this sort-of country home/guest house near the track that was big, old, gracious and friendly and very, very clean. It was run with a big smile and an iron fist by a great, cheery whirlwind of a French lady they called *Madame Toot-Sweet* and her silent, sparrowlike little husband, who apparently had no name. She was a wonderful cook and housekeeper. I guess the team had stayed there several times before when they came to Le Mans, and it was almost like long-lost relatives coming for a visit when they showed up. The mechanics were billeted in a sort of converted barn out back where they'd put in bunks and a sort of basic wash stand—you had to go inside the house for anything much more than a splash of water on your face, if you know what I mean—and, even though they'd cleaned it very well, the place still smelled a little of hay and horses. But I slept as well and deeply as I ever had anyplace, and the next thing I knew, Denny was shaking me awake for breakfast. "You didn't go out drinkin' last night, did'ja?" That was the first time I'd ever heard Denny sound serious about anything.

"No," I told him, rubbing my eyes. "I was just tired, that's all."

"Good. Because Mr. Cunningham doesn't much go for that."

"He doesn't?"

"After the race, fine. But from now through Sunday night, we all gotta keep our eyes open and concentrate on gettin' the job done."

Anyhow, it was well past ten when we got out to the circuit—my insides were all still pretty flopped around where time was concerned, and I had to pretty much rely on clock faces and the position of the sun to straighten me out—and we had a lot of moving and unpacking and organizational stuff to do in order to get ready for the first evening's practice. Denny'd explained on the way out as how the Le Mans circuit was really made up out of ordinary French roads that went from one town to another, and so, just like Watkins Glen and Elkhart Lake and Bridgehampton, there were a lot of local and civic problems to address and people to accommodate and things to get squared away and palms to grease in order to pull the race off. Only they'd been doing it since 1923—except for the war years, anyway—and so they'd gotten it down to a pretty smooth operation. The roads were open to normal traffic during the daytime on Wednesday, Thursday and Friday, and then closed off in the late afternoon for a few hours of daylight, twilight and nighttime practice so the cars could be tested and readied, new drivers could learn the circuit and important details like nighttime pit signaling and the aiming of headlamps, driving lights and fog lamps could be adjusted.

I've got to tell you I was pretty damn astounded by what I saw when we finally got to the circuit. Why, it was only Wednesday—four full days before the race!—and there was already a huge, circus-tent city of vendors and eateries and sideshow attractions blossoming behind the paddock and the camping areas were already filling up with camper trailers and canvas tents and awnings and thousands of fans walking around everywhere looking at the cars and each other. Before first practice had even started! And you had to be impressed with the somewhat cramped but covered pit counters they'd built along the front straight—enough room for sixty teams!—and the six enormous grandstands, five of them covered against sun or rain and the middle one a double-decker, right across from the pits. The scale of it all was simply staggering.

All except the track itself, that is....

In fact, as we were first approaching the grandstands to get into the paddock area, I turned to Denny and asked: "Where's the track?"

He looked at me strangely. "You're on it."

The shock hit me like a blast of wind. The road we were on was smooth enough, but very narrow. Not any wider than some parts of Watkins Glen or Thompson Speedway, for gosh sakes. On the left there was nothing but a sort of waist-high, wattle fencing that workers were busily covering up with *DUNLOP* and *CASTROL* and *MARCHAL* banners. It was backed up by an earthen berm, and behind that there was a simple white picket fence that ran the length of the grandstand area to keep the spectators back from the racing surface. They'd also built a permanent concrete underpass tunnel right about where the pits started so people could get back and forth to the grandstands and infield attractions. "Geez," I said, "it looks kinda narrow here for a race with sixty cars in it." I mean, the runways at Sebring were downright vast compared to this. "How fast are they going right here?"

Denny shrugged. "Oh, the Jags and Ferraris and Mercedes'll be touching maybe a hundred and a half right here." He gave me a wink. "Hopefully the C-6R will, too."

While we were setting up, Denny and the guys explained that the track opened up a little past the pits, and that the long, three-plus-mile straightaway from the right-hander at Tertre Rouge to the hairpin at Mulsanne gave the cars plenty of time to sort themselves out. Even on the opening lap. Or so they said. "The real trouble comes later, when you've got the Fast Guys passing the little tiddlers going maybe sixty miles-per-hour slower. Especially early on, when there haven't been many retirements and there's a lot of traffic out there. And then later, when it gets dark. Or if it rains..." He shot me another death-house grin, "...like it usually does here."

They had me sorting and checking tires and setting out tools and equipment for a couple of hours, and then Denny pulled up to the back of our pit stall on a little putt-putt French motor scooter and asked if I'd like to sneak away for a tour around the course before they finished blocking the roads off. "Can we *do* that?" I asked him.

"Well, we sure as hell can't if we ask permission," he laughed. "Get on."

So I did.

Now, as I've explained before, Denny Eade is one of your giant, economy-sized individuals, and there wasn't much more than a postage-stamp sized section of upholstery left behind him on that motor scooter's seat. Not to mention that the two of us had the rear springs on that poor scooter pressed down just about solid. But overloading motor vehicles is kind of a national pastime in France—in fact, all over Europe—and so, somehow, they seem able to take it. Even when the fender is rubbing right down against the rear tire.

There was a very official-looking Frenchman with gold braid on his cap at the end of the pit lane—it was only separated from the actual racing surface by a yellow warning line painted on the pavement—and he stiffened and glared at us disapprovingly as we approached. But Denny just smiled and waved to him like we were late for lunch with the Prime Minister or something as we sputtered past.

"Y'gotta act like y'own the place," I heard Denny say through his shoulder. "Otherwise you spend all day gettin' told what you can't do."

I've got to admit that it wasn't the greatest view imaginable, seeing the race-track from the back of an underpowered and highly-overloaded motor scooter with Denny's massive back and neck right in front of me, but I could kind of lean up and peer out past his ear on either side or turn my head and see the edges of the track as it wheeled past. And you can bet that it wasn't wheeling past very quickly, either.

The pit straight blended into a wide, sweeping right-hander that curled under-neath the famous Dunlop pedestrian bridge that looked like a huge tire crossing the circuit, and then went past another camping area that was already starting to fill up and into a thick, woodsy section where tall, skinny trees came right up to the guardrails. It seemed dark through there. The road swung left and right through the narrow, fast but claustrophobic "Forest Curve" esses, where the ban-ner-covered trackside barriers seemed to come almost to the edge of the pavement and there was no place at all to go if something went wrong. Just beyond the bar-riers, workers were assembling tents and rides and sideshow attractions for the carnival that went on all weekend long there in the forest. I figured it must look pretty fantastic at night for both the drivers and the people up on the Ferris wheel and sky scooters and such, catching little glimpses of the passing racecars through the trees. We went under a second bridge and next came the tough, important right-hander at Tertre Rouge that leads onto the famous straightaway towards Mulsanne. Only I'd always imagined a straightaway as being more or less straight. And level. But this wasn't either. It climbed and drooped and undulated the way country roads do (you could really feel the little French scooter straining on some of the rises!) and there were thick stands of forest here and there along the sides. But the amazing thing was how it just went on and on and on, and it seemed to take us forever to reach the gentle kink to the right that came a little ways before the braking zone for the hairpin. "This spot's a booger," Denny said through his shoulder. "It's a real needle-thread in a fast car. Especially at night in the rain when you've got slower traffic to get through."

I couldn't even imagine.

And then, at the end of this monstrously long straightaway where whatever sort of car you were driving would reach its absolute top speed (and maybe then some) they had this tight, fiddly little hairpin—more than ninety degrees and low second gear for everybody!—and the important thing here was how late you could brake and how quickly and in how short a distance you could get rid of all that speed. Oh, and for how many laps, too, since running out of brakes was sort of an Occupational Hazard at Le Mans. At least there was an escape road. Another, far shorter straight followed with another stretch of woods running along it, and then the road blended gently right and into a fast, sweeping left that led into a much tighter, sweeping right at Arnage. And then it was flat to the floor again for the fast, narrow, needle-thread section through Maison Blanche and onto that narrow end of the front straight again before the pits.

I couldn't believe the length of the track. Or the width in some places, come to think of it.

But the most amazing thing was simply the scale and variety of everything and how it was spread out and scattered over more than ten square miles of French countryside. I mean, you could never get people to accept that sort of thing over on our side of the Atlantic. Not for a damn sports car race. But here in France it was like a national holiday, and you could tell not only how much the locals loved it, but also how very proud of it they were.

Turns out practice is kind of a funny deal at Le Mans. Besides the usual figuring-out-the-car and finding-your-way-around stuff that goes on at every racetrack, there's also a lot of spoofing and spying and psychological warfare going on to either hide what you've got or spook the opposition into thinking you've got more than you have. And the things that caught everybody absolutely flat-footed were the air brakes on the new 300SLRs from Mercedes-Benz. Nobody'd even noticed it in scrutineering—hey, nobody was looking for it!—and of course the Germans always did know how to keep a secret. Imagine the shock and amazement on the faces of the early fans gathered in the woods on the approach to the slow hairpin (where all the cars arrive at absolute full-tilt and then have to throw out the anchors and get the thing hauled down for that acute, thirty mile-per-hour right-hander at Mulsanne) when the whole panel behind the driver's compartment on those silver 300SLRs—headrest and all!—suddenly lifted up into the airstream on hydraulic struts like the flaps on a blessed airplane wing. And that was nothing compared to the effect it had on the following drivers....

Well, you would've thought a damn bomb went off!

News of the new gimmick spread like wildfire through the pits and paddock, and pretty soon all the major teams had rushed some of their people over to their signaling stations at Mulsanne to take a look for themselves. Almost everybody planned to have a signaling and observation station set up at Mulsanne for the race itself. Just one lone guy with a pit board and a field-telephone line to the pits. You needed somebody there because it was about the only place on the circuit where the cars were going slow enough for the drivers to read the damn pit boards! I mean, you sure didn't have much of a chance while flashing past the pits at 150 or so on that narrow stretch of road with faster and slower traffic to sort out all around you! And especially at night with all the glare off the pit lights and the grandstands. Plus, if your driver had lost track of his laps (and you could almost count on that happening at Le Mans), Mulsanne was the place to let him know he had to pit for fuel. If you let it go until the pit straight, he'd have to make another 8.384-mile lap before he could pull in for gas. And he just might not make it. Plus, if there was anyplace on the circuit where you were likely to slide off and get yourself high-centered on an earth bank without damaging the car too badly and have to dig yourself out, Mulsanne was the place. So it was nice to be able to ring the boys back in the pits and tell them that, no, the car wasn't destroyed, but they could safely go out for a crepe or a café latte or a bowl of mutton stew or something because it was going to be a while—maybe a *long* while!—before their boy dug himself out and came around again. As in everything else, the rules at Le Mans were pretty damn specific as far as what you could and couldn't do if your car got stranded out on the course. Only the driver could work on the car or dig it out or even touch it once it had left the pits and until he got it back there again. If he accepted assistance of any kind—from his crew or spectators or anybody else—the car would be disqualified. And, as I could already see, the French were real sticklers when it came to the rules. It was kind of their specialty....

But back to the Mercedes air brakes. They were such a simple idea, really. And absolutely perfect for a circuit and race like Le Mans. And, just like all the other innovative stuff on those silver cars, they *worked!* At first the Mercedes drivers only used them at the end of the long straightaway heading into Mulsanne. And, when they went up, it was like the hand of God reaching down out of the sky to slow them from top speed. Oh, the Jags could brake almost as well with their discs—maybe even just as well—but the point was that the Mercedes air brakes were taking a lot of the burden and heat buildup off those inboard drum brakes of theirs, which were figured by most of the opposition to be their Achilles' heel. Especially over 24 hours.

Well, that's obviously what the guys at Mercedes figured, too. And, typical of Mercedes, they'd done something about it. Plus the Mercedes drivers discovered there was a little side benefit in that the air brake really planted the back end of the car so it didn't get all squirrely under heavy braking, and it wasn't long before Fangio was fooling around with it through some of the fast corners to make the car handle better. And meanwhile everybody up and down pit lane was whispering and jabbering and flipping through the rulebook like crazy to see if those air brakes could possibly be legal and some of the whiners were complaining that they were unsafe because they blocked the vision of following drivers and caused buffeting that upset the cars behind and blah, blah, blah. But, after you swept all the tears and bullshit away, the simple fact was that Mercedes-Benz had caught everybody with their pants down.

Again.

Oh, the 300SLRs weren't quickest after first practice (although you got the feeling they maybe weren't trying to be?) and, typically, it was the new 4.4-liter Ferrari of Castellotti at the top of the charts, showing off the power of that raw-sounding straight six. But the big boys were all playing it pretty close to the vest, and Tommy Edwards told me he heard the Jaguar guys pedaling out of it and just cruising down that long straightaway to Mulsanne. "Makes good sense, really. Why show your hand? It's nonsense to beat on the car now, what with two more evenings of practice and then 24 bloody hours to run in anger."

It stays light pretty late around the middle of June, and so it was well past ten when we sat down for a late team supper at Madame Toot-Sweet's place. I'd called home from the circuit—it took me damn near an hour to get through—and it was hard to believe that it was just after lunchtime back in Passaic and that it'd been raining all morning. I asked Julie about the baby and her mom and my folks and how things were going at the shop and all, and then she asked me how things were going with me and I tried to come up with a few words to explain all about France and Le Mans and all the big international teams and what a staggeringly huge and foreign and overpowering and exciting and intimidating event this was in so many ways. Only it came out like this: "Oh, it's okay."

During a delicious dinner served on some really swell china, the team held a little strategy meeting and it was decided that the Offy-powered C-6R simply didn't have enough suds (not that this was really any big news to anybody) and that the D-Type, even if it wasn't up to the specifications of the latest factory cars, was surely the best weapon in the Cunningham arsenal. So it was decided that Briggs and Tommy Edwards would soldier on with the C-6R and the D-Type would be handed over to the "A-Team" of Phil Walters and Creighton Pendleton. I could see out of the corner of my eye that the news didn't go down especially well with Tommy Edwards—he'd driven the "D" that day and *really* liked it—but he was enough of a team player and a military man to know that you followed orders and did your job and shut up and kept a cheery face about it as well.

The next evening's practice was marred by on-and-off rain showers and a near-disastrous incident in the pits when Moss' Mercedes bumped into (or was cut off by, depending on whose story you believe) one of the little French DB tiddlers. With the end result that a few journalists and star French Maserati driver Jean Behra got scattered like bowling pins and had to be carted off to the hospital. Fortunately without serious injuries. But it was beginning to occur to me that the pits at Le Mans could be a pretty dangerous place. I mean, the only thing separating the pits from the racetrack was that painted yellow line, and so there was an awful lot to keep an eye on. And so many people to trust, too. And you didn't know hardly any of them....

That night, with Mr. Cunningham's approval, I invited Hank Lyons to join us for our late dinner after practice ended. And John Fitch even sneaked away after the regularly-scheduled, after-every-practice-session Mercedes team meeting to join his old friends from the Cunningham squad at Madame Toot-Sweet's place. I'm sure he asked first, and I guess Neubauer let him do it on account of he didn't figure our cars were really much of a threat and also because he knew he could trust John to keep his mouth shut about technical things and strategy and such. And of course he could. But it was great to see him again, and everybody seemed genuinely happy that he had such a fantastic car for the race. Especially Briggs and Tommy and Phil Walters. "All well and good," John allowed, "but we all know having a good car and a great team is just the first few drops in the bucket when it comes to winning at this place!"

The rain had slacked off and so after dinner a bunch of us went out to the back garden and sat around on some stone benches and wrought-iron chairs and looked up at the sky. It was still pretty overcast, and so there were no stars or moon but just a kind of dull, gray glow from where their light tried to get through. "Maybe this is a good sign," John said.

"How so?"

"You can't expect damp weather like this to hold on for three more days. I think maybe it'll clear up for the race."

"You know it's going to rain like hell during the race, John," Phil Walters laughed. "It's a tradition over here."

"Most likely from bloody midnight to six ayem," Tommy tossed in.

"And then you get the fog and mist," Creighton added.

"That must be why we love it so," John grinned.

It got quiet then, and so I asked John about his co-driver. The Frenchman.

"Oh, he's quite a story," John said enthusiastically, his eyes twinkling. "I had dinner with Pierre and his wife last night. They don't live very far from here. Wonderful people."

"I've never heard of him," I admitted.

"Well, you're not French, are you? He's quite a famous and important fellow over here." And then he told me the story of Pierre Levegh. To begin with, his real last name was Bouillon, and I guess he was quite the skater and skier and ice hockey and tennis player when he was young. He adopted the last name "Levegh" when he started racing in honor of his uncle, who had been a great French racing driver for the Mors team back around the turn of the century when cars had barely been invented yet. John said Pierre's uncle won his first race in 1898, and that one of the Mors racecars he drove featured a 10—that's right, *TEN!*—liter V4 and chain drive to the rear wheels. Or, in other words, a paltry 615-cubic-inch four-banger! Racing on dusty, rutted, hump-backed horse trails from one town to another on skinny balloon tires mounted on wooden wheels and with brakes that weren't much better than dragging your feet. Wow!

At any rate, Pierre adopted his famous uncle's name when he went racing himself, and his main goal in life had always been to win at Le Mans. I mean, it was the biggest damn race in the world and it was right there in his own back yard, right? And it would be great to win it again for France, too, seeing as how the French hadn't had much luck there since the new cars started coming out from Jaguar and Mercedes and Ferrari after the war. A father-and-son racing team named Rosier had managed to win it *pour la France* in a 4.5-liter Talbot-Lago in 1950, and Pierre Levegh showed up two years later in an almost identical car to give it another try. It was a big, powerful, lumbering thing, and looked absolutely outdated compared to the too-clever-by-half "streamlined" Jaguar C-Types and the 300SL Mercedes-Benz gullwing coupes. But it had a lot of torque and it was fast and rugged, and damn if Pierre Levegh didn't wind up leading the race. And all by himself, too, since he was afraid if he handed the car over to his co-driver something bad might happen. And so the hours droned on—through night and rain and morning mist—and still Levegh pushed on in the big, French-blue Talbot, leading the feared Mercedes team by over a lap and seemingly well on his way to the most amazing victory in Le Mans history. It was like a movie. Like a fairytale. Like Joan of Arc....

But he was exhausted. And yet still he refused to hand over the wheel. And that's probably why, during the very final hour, he missed a shift and blew the engine. And that was the end of it. He wasn't even listed as a finisher, since a car has to cross the finish line under its own power in order to be classified at Le Mans. "It was one hell of a drive," John allowed respectfully.

"I dunno," I said. "It seems kinda dumb t'me. I mean, he threw it all away...."

"Oh, the press took him apart afterwards. Called it fear. Called it foolishness. Called it vanity. Called it pride. But he so nearly made it. One lone Frenchman in an outdated car up against the might of Mercedes and the rest. Like I said, it was one hell of a drive, no matter what anybody had to say about it afterwards."

He was no spring chicken, either. Pierre Levegh was pushing fifty when Mercedes invited him to join their team and paired him up with John Fitch for this year's race some three seasons later. But they'd seen what he could do. Hell, he damn near beat the lot of them single-handed and they knew it. Not to mention that it was good politics to have a couple French drivers on the squad at Le Mans. Especially when Mercedes wanted to sell some cars there in France now that The Great Unpleasantness (as some of the British scribes wryly put it) was over with. And there were some special considerations when it came to wooing back the French public. "Did you notice that tumbled-down, empty place with the ragged wire fence around it on your way into the track?" John asked me.

"I think so."

"That was a German concentration camp during the war...."

The final night of practice before the biggest race in the world went a bit later than the others so the teams could do the final tweaking on their headlamps and driving lights and pit lights and such in genuine darkness, and it wasn't until afterwards I heard there had been an accident out on the circuit involving the lone three-liter Gordini. The car had been destroyed and one of the French drivers had gone to the hospital with severe head injuries. But nobody making pre-race preparations in the pits seemed to take much notice. "I know it sounds cold, but sometimes it's like a bloody military camp here," Tommy explained without emotion. "As long as you're hearing about terrible things happening to other people instead of seeing and experiencing them yourself, the game's still on. That's just the way it is."

I couldn't sleep at all that night. It wasn't about the driver who got hurt—that was like something that happened a million miles away, like something I'd maybe read about somewhere in a newspaper—but more like a combination of excitement and anticipation and nervousness and dread all wrapped up into this gnawing little frenzy that made my hands clench and muscles tighten up under the bedsheets. Even though it was dark and serene as liquid velvet outside. I got the feeling I wasn't the only person lying awake that night....

We were up around seven and had a good breakfast—all the old hands had warned me to have a good, solid breakfast, take a good, hefty dump and shave and wash up better than I ever had in my life because it was going to have to last me a long, long time that particular day—and we were out at the track by nine to get everything ready. The weather had turned nicely, what with the sun shining down and a comfortable breeze shooing the storm clouds away. Although the reports traveling through the paddock suggested there was rain in the forecast overnight. But what could you do about it?

I frankly couldn't believe the crowd that was gathering and the immense, tangled traffic jams spreading out all around the circuit. Why, there were people everywhere! And especially in the grandstand area across from the pits and surging through the concrete underpass into the paddock to get a look at the cars and teams before the race actually started. Why, it was like a damn anthill even well before noon, and the start wasn't even scheduled until 4:00 PM....

We made ourselves busy laying everything out—spare wheels checked and stacked over here, tools laid out on a table like a surgeon's tray over there, spare parts logically crated and stacked and stored, cooler for cold drinks, floor jack, jackstands, pitboards, air canisters, cases of oil, check and double-check the fueling rig, lights for night pitstops, clipboards and watches for Neil Harmon's timing and scoring crew, folding chairs for those long, nervous hours, barbecue gloves for handling hot exhausts or brakes or whatever…and on and on and on. No matter how much time and how many hands you have working, it never seems to be enough, and there's always a sense of frenzy and panic as the time gets closer and the crowds seething and jostling and staring or politely peering in all around you get thicker and thicker, and every time you look at the car or the stuff laid out in the pit stall you have this nagging feeling that you've forgotten something terribly important. Only you can't think what it is….

The schedule called for all the cars to be lined up in their proper grid positions and at the proper angle for the traditional Le Mans start by 2:00 PM—two full hours before the race—and there was an awful scene when the Moretti team tried to push their pretty little 750 coupes out to their spots near the very back end of the grid at two minutes after two. The head French grid official at that end of pit lane—who must have been a very important man in those parts judging by the sash of military ribbons he was wearing—pointed to his watch and explained in clipped tones that they were late and therefore couldn't start the race. Can you believe it? And the other officials backed him up, too. After all, there would always be more racers—there always were!—but the rules would endure forever. And they were there to see to it!

It actually would've been funny if it hadn't been so sad. I mean, these poor Italian guys had come all the way from Italy with two cars and four drivers and a team of maybe eight or ten crewmen and had spent God-only-knows how much time and money (including, like almost every smalltime racer everywhere, money they really didn't have) to get there and had stayed there in France for four days already and run three practice sessions on three successive evenings and had their pit stalls all full of spares and tools and tires and everything else—ready to go!—and now the officials weren't going to let them start because they showed up two stinking minutes late for their grid positions a solid hour and fifty-eight minutes before the race was even due to start. But the French officials were adamant. The rules were very clear. It could be no other way. The last thing they would ever presume would be to break their everlasting covenant with the sanctity of the rules….

"What a bunch of bullshit," Denny groaned. "Why don't those assholes just let 'em race?"

"Well, you have to understand a little something about these once-a-year officials," Tommy Edwards explained through a humorless smile. "All of a sudden they have all this power. But power doesn't feel like much of anything unless you bloody well use it. So the power they feel is always in direct proportion to the anguish they can cause for the teams and drivers."

That, sadly, sounded about right.

And meanwhile, the Moretti team manager was pleading and begging—you could see he was next to tears—while a crowd of gendarmes gathered and quietly pushed the two little Morettis away. I hate to say it, but it did cross my mind that those two little Morettis amounted to fully half of the Foreign Opposition to the hometown French teams in the 750cc class. Which was for sure the only class any French team had a hope of winning. Not that I'm a cynic or anything.

The flurry and hubbub over the Moretti tragedy slowly died down (or got moved back out of sight where you couldn't see or hear it, anyway) and now the whole of the front straightaway was choked with people meandering up and down and camera shutters clicking like a swarm of locusts and bands playing and the public address system crackling and echoing excitedly (albeit incomprehensibly) in French and low-level grunt crewmen like me keeping an eye on the cars and pit equipment just in case we had any souvenir hunters in the vicinity.

It seemed to take for damn *ever* for the race to roll around, and all the time there was this sensation of the noise and tension getting higher and tighter and tighter and higher. And then it clicked up another few notches as the big clock at the start-finish line tocked its way towards four and the gendarmes and grid officials started shooing everybody and each other out of the way and the crowds slowly dispersed off in all directions until, finally, the track running between the pits and grandstands was empty except for the cars lined up along the pit counter on one side with their noses skewed at about a 60-degree angle towards the first corner and the drivers slowly taking their positions across the way, directly in front of that sign-covered wattle barrier backed up by the earthen berm that separated the racetrack from that little white picket spectator fence and the seething, glittering, vibrating crush of spectators behind it that stretched all the way to the very top of the grandstands and as far as you could see in either direction. It occurred to me all over again that this was a terribly narrow stretch of roadway for this sort of start. Not at all like those wide-open runways at Sebring. But, after all, they'd been doing it for years....

I remember it got deathly silent—so quiet you could hear birdcalls and race programs rustling and even the buzz of honeybees—by the time a very distinguished gentleman named Count Maggi stepped out of a crowd of dignitaries, waited for the final click of the big minute hand on the clock at the start-finish line, and dropped the French tricolor to get the race underway. It seemed to almost happen in slow motion. And then all hell broke loose. The drivers scampered across and the field fired up like one huge, disjointed, 288-cylinder engine and freight-trained past us in a bellowing, whirlwind explosion of dust and grit and noise. Englishman Roy Salvadori made a blinding getaway in one of the Aston DB3S models, but so did Castellotti in the big 4.4-liter Ferrari, and it was the red car in front as the field streamed away from us and disappeared to our right under the Dunlop bridge for the very first time. There were still stragglers leaving in front of us, and the very last to go was '53 winner Tony Rolt, who had a heck of a time getting his Jaguar D-Type fired and was well behind even the slowest of the tiddlers by the time he got it rolling. "Won't mean a damn thing after 24 hours," Denny Eade assured me. "In fact, he's better off being out of all that mess." And I knew he was right.

Meanwhile the French announcers were screaming and jabbering at near heart-attack speed, and I closed my eyes and listened to their noise while I tried to imagine the tightly bunched field jostling its way side-by-side through the esses, snaking past the carnival, taking that sweeping right at Tertre Rouge and finally breaking free onto that long, long straightaway towards Mulsanne where they'd finally have a chance to sort themselves out. Driving etiquette at Le Mans demanded that slower cars keep more or less to the right so that the faster cars could overtake on the left down the straightaways, but the way a Le Mans start shakes everything up in a bag means that the first few laps are absolutely frantic. Stirling Moss was a fairly decent sprinter and practiced hard at it, so he'd become famous for making great Le Mans starts. But Hank Lyons told me it had nothing whatever to do with trying to gain an advantage in the race. "Nope, he just knows that the most likely time to have an accident is when all the cars are bunched up together like that at the start, and he knows the best place to be if there's an accident is in front of it...."

That made a lot of sense.

But Mercedes had elected to start Fangio, and so he was disappointingly far back as the field came around some four-and-a-half minutes later to complete their first lap, with Castellotti's bright-red Ferrari out front, Hawthorn's green D-Jag second, and then Maglioli running a close third in the 3.7-liter Ferrari he was sharing with Phil Hill. I was happy to see that. There was a gap after Maglioli, and then—Holy Cow!—Phil Walters in our own white-with-blue-racing-stripes D-Jaguar from the Cunningham team! We all cheered as he went by! But he had plenty of company in the form of another of the British Racing Green factory D-Types, the bright yellow Belgian D-Type, Fitch's teammate Levegh in the first of the Mercedes, two Astons and their Lagonda-powered sister car all mixed up in a bag, the first of the handsome three-liter Maseratis sounding absolutely beautiful, Kling's Mercedes, Trintignant's Ferrari and, finally, Fangio in the last of the three Mercedes. But you got the feeling he wouldn't stay there for very long.

By the end of the second lap, our boy Phil Walters was pressuring Maglioli's Ferrari for third and the old master Fangio had pulled himself up to sixth overall, and by the end of the next lap Fangio had caught "our" Jaguar and swept past at a tremendous rate to take fourth place right in front of the pits. Poor Briggs in the C-6R was already struggling well down the pack with a balky transmission that wouldn't serve up first or second gears on a regular basis, and that's a marvelous sort of thing to have happen just three stinking laps into a 24-hour race. Unbelievably, the frontrunners were already knifing through tiddler traffic at the back end of the field, and of course that's when things start to get nerve-wrackingly interesting for drivers and crews alike. One wrong move, one faulty decision, one poor guess or one half-a-heartbeat error in judgment is all it takes to wad the whole thing up in a ball. Or worse.

Then next lap Fangio's Mercedes roared past Maglioli's third-place Ferrari—again, right in front of the pits—and you got the feeling that you now had the three heaviest runners in the first three places. Hank told me it's not unusual for teams to designate a "rabbit" to run flat-out in an effort to break up the opposition. But he also said Fangio and Moss were so uncommonly smooth that they could go very fast while taking less out of the car than other drivers, so it was hard to tell if that was really Mercedes' strategy. For sure Castellotti in the big-engined Ferrari and Hawthorn in the second place Jag D-Type were, to use Tommy Edwards' words, "giving it plenty of stick!"

Usually you expect a race like this to start stringing out at the front. But not this one! At the end of a full hour of racing, Castellotti still led in the Ferrari, but Hawthorn's Jag was only a few ticks behind and Fangio's Mercedes even closer than that to the Jag. Then a gap of almost a minute to the Maglioli/Hill Ferrari, another thirty seconds to Phil Walters in our Jag running a promising fifth over-all, and then fifteen more seconds back to Kling and Levegh in the other two Mercedes. So things had pretty much stabilized everywhere but at the very front, where Castellotti, Hawthorn and Fangio were putting on one hell of a show. And the crowd was absolutely loving it!

Ten minutes into the second hour Hawthorn's Jag and Fangio's Mercedes both found a way around Castellotti's Ferrari and began drawing away. And then Fangio dove inside at the daunting entry to the fast sweeper under the Dunlop bridge and took the lead. But Hawthorn wasn't having any of it. He uncorked the motor on the Jag and re-passed Fangio down the long straightaway towards Mulsanne. And, all of a sudden, we were witnessing a Blood Duel for first between two of the toughest, keenest, fastest men in the world. One an old master who had taken the measure of everyone he had ever faced at one time or another, the other the new British "comingman" out to make a name for himself and prove his growing reputation. And you could tell it was serious just by looking at a stopwatch, since the lap record was taking a beating almost every time around as the two of them battled back and forth while carving their way through slower traffic. It was the kind of race that makes you hold your breath every time the leaders go by....

There were some minor diversions in the pits—one of the DBs caught fire slightly and had to be sprayed with an extinguisher and Castellotti came in to have a suspect wheel changed and took on fuel while he was at it—but all eyes were on the fight at the front. Even though we all knew that pitstops for fuel, which were due sometime around the two-and-a-half hour mark, would probably break them up. Then Briggs came in to have the transmission in the C-6R looked at. It was a Z-F gearbox that they'd mated to the Offy engine, and he was having all sorts of problems trying to select first and second gears. Sometimes it went in, and sometimes there was nothing. We checked what we could see, but the problem was obviously internal, so there was nothing we could do but send him back out and tell him to soldier on the best he could.

What else could you do?

I looked back over my shoulder and noticed Tommy sitting there on the pit counter with his chin in his hands, looking like a guy whose horse has just finished out of the money. "It's the only bloody German part on the car," he said sarcastically while Fangio's Mercedes flashed by again with Hawthorn hot on his heels.

About quarter-after-six the top teams started readying for pit stops, and we brought Phil Walters in about ten minutes earlier than necessary just to stay clear of the inevitable chaos and congestion in pit lane when all the other big guns started running dry. The stop went perfectly—full tank, check the fluids and tires, and handing the wheel over to Creighton—and the car was back out quick enough to almost bring a smile to Alfred Momo's face. Almost. Meanwhile, the jaw-dropping, back-and-forth battle between Fangio and Hawthorn was still going full-tilt.

You got the feeling it was a little bit for diversion and a little bit blood serious at the same time, and they'd knocked the living crap out of the outright lap record time and again. In fact, they were about to lap Levegh's sixth-place Mercedes for the second time! Incredible!

But their race had maybe been a little too involving, and I saw a pretty frantic discussion going on in the Jaguar pits as Hawthorn had apparently missed his "IN-FUEL" board down at the Mulsanne signaling station two laps in a row. Or maybe he was just ignoring it because he was in front of Fangio and making it stick and figured from the gauge on the dash that he had plenty left to get him around. The Jaguar guys were counting on it, and they had everything ready and waiting for him when he peeled off the track and pulled in.

Or that's what should have happened, anyway....

I know I was standing on the pit counter looking back towards Arnage, waiting with a stopwatch in my hand for the leaders to come around again, and here came Lance Macklin in the lone, "privateer" Austin-Healey—driving well over to the right just as all the slower cars were supposed to—and hurtling up behind him was Hawthorn in the D-Type, a very small gap, and then two silver Mercedes. You couldn't tell at that point which one was which. Hawthorn shot past Macklin's Healey, then instantly threw his arm up in the air to show he was pitting and chopped across Macklin's bows to dive for the Jaguar pits. The move caught Macklin totally by surprise—I don't think he was expecting it at all after being passed and pulled away from by faster cars for the past two-and-a-half hours, and I'm sure you get into a sort of rhythm about these things—and he instinctively cut left and jammed on the brakes to avoid what he perhaps thought was about to be a spin right in front of him. He didn't have even a heartbeat to check his mirrors first....

If he had, he would have seen the first Mercedes, Levegh's about-to-be-lapped car, rocketing up on his left. Levegh saw what was coming and threw his arm up to warn Fangio behind him as he cut left to try and squeeze through the gap between the Healey and the fencing on that disastrously narrow piece of roadway. But there was no room. And no time, either. The right-front of the 300SLR shot up over the sloping rear deck of the Healey like a launching ramp, catapulting it all cockeyed into the air. Poor Levegh was thrown out of the cockpit and smashed with sickening force and finality into the pavement—you knew right away he was dead—while the car flew through the air and crashed head-on into the concrete stanchion at the pedestrian underpass, exploding in flames and a horrifying meteor-shower of parts and debris.

And meanwhile Macklin's Healey spun around at high speed, ricocheted off the outside fence and came scything into the pit lane at a crazy angle. People were diving in all directions—I know I was!—and I heard and felt it more than saw it when Macklin's car whapped hard into the pit counter just a few stalls up from us. And then there was just a single, strange moment of silence. Like time itself was frozen. And there I was, crouched in that frozen moment down behind out pit counter, ears and toes and fingertips on alert like a terrified rabbit listening for a fox. But there was nothing. Just the sound of the cars going by. Only much more slowly now. Blindly. And then, every once in a while in the gaps between them,

I thought I could make out this faint, horrible moaning and wailing. Like you might imagine from a slaughterhouse. It didn't even sound human. And then, like a rising tide, the swelling sound of shouts and screams and people scurrying and urgent, hysterical cries for assistance. I slowly raised myself up and looked around....

Macklin's Healey had crunched to a halt against the pit counter a few stalls up from us, but I could see he was all right. If a bit shaken. But he'd left a trail of flattened gendarmes and bleeding mechanics and broken limbs behind him. It looked like a damn battlefield. People and debris were scattered everywhere!

But that was nothing compared to what was going on across the way.

What with the fence and the berm in my line of sight and all the black smoke and bluish-white oil and water mist from the accident, you couldn't really make out what was happening. But you knew it was bad. Very bad. Levegh's body was laying in a crumpled heap on the pavement with just the top of his pale blue helmet at one end to show what it was, and further down the remains of his Mercedes were crushed up against the concrete stanchion like a squashed bug, the magnesium bodywork burning furiously with a harsh, white glare. You didn't want to think about where the rest of the car had gone....

There was chaos churning everywhere. Neubauer and Tommy Edwards and some of the others quickly and bravely stepped out onto the littered racetrack and helped wave the rest of the cars through the smoke and debris and wreckage. From our side of the racetrack there was no way of knowing how bad it was on the spectator side, but you could see how frantic the activity was and hear the sound of alarm bells and more alarm bells and screams and honking horns and police whistles and muffled cries for help and it was clear this was a disaster of terrible and unprecedented proportions. Rumors flew through the pits even as fire marshals turned their extinguishers on the burning hulk of the Mercedes and a gendarme ran across the track and ripped a banner off the fence to cover the sad little heap of Levegh's body. And of course there was talk immediately of stopping the race. But others argued it would just create mass confusion and cause a horrible traffic jam that would make getting the injured to hospitals for the care they so desperately needed impossible. And there was some merit in that. Even if it seemed callous and horrible to let the race go on. The strange thing was that elsewhere around the circuit—in the campgrounds where people were making their dinners over crackling little wood fires and where the spectators lined the fences down at the Mulsanne hairpin and over at the carnival in the trees at the esses where laughing people rode the sky scooters and kissed each other at the top of the Ferris wheel—they had no idea what had happened.

And they were the luckier for it, too.

You don't so much recover from the shock as get sucked into its vacuum, and I found myself helping one fellow with a badly broken arm and blood gushing down his forehead to someplace behind the paddock where I passed him off to somebody else—everything was just swirling and seething like we were all being chewed in the mouth of some great and terrifying monster—and then I was out on the track helping clear off the debris while the smell of the burning oil and rubber and magnesium stung my eyes and bored into my nostrils. Five men with a stretcher took Levegh's body and its race banner shroud past me and disappeared with it behind the pits. I clearly saw the stiff, bloody stalk of his forearm dangling out—you could hardly recognize what it was—and the battered gold watch on its wrist with the shattered crystal and the hands frozen forever at 6:32.

I suddenly knew I had to call Julie. It hit me like a thunderbolt. So I told Denny Eade where I was going and went off in search of a phone. They had a whole bank of them set up behind the pits, but there were already long lines. I saw a grim-faced John Fitch standing in one of them and went over and stood beside him. "I'm sorry," I said, like some tiny part of it was somehow my fault. I think all of us felt that way. All the racers, I mean.

John just stared straight ahead. "I've got to call my wife," he said in a hollow voice. "She already heard once on the radio that I was killed in a racing accident."

I saw Hank Lyons coming through the crowd. He was blackened and dirty and there was a smear of blood on his shirt, and his face had that blank, unseeing stare you associate with hypnosis. *"Hank!"* I called out. *"HANK!"*

His face turned towards me, but his expression never changed. "I was on the other side," he said simply, laying the words out like bricks.

"What happened?" I couldn't help asking.

He shook his head. "The car just blew apart. All the pieces…" his mouth hung helplessly open, "…all the pieces…into the crowd…"

"Oh my God."

"The whole front axle—wheels, shafts, brakes, *everything…"* he shook his head again, like he was trying to lose the image, "…like a lawnmower. It was like a damn lawnmower…."

It took forever to get an overseas line and then even longer to make the connection but I finally got through to Julie. She sounded very far away, but she said it was a lovely June day back in Passaic and that she'd just finished feeding little Vincenzo his lunch. He'd had mashed sweet potatoes. She wondered why I'd called, since she knew the race was going on. "I, uhh, just wanted you to know I'm okay," I told her.

"Why? Is something wrong?" She could sense it. That quick, she could sense it. I looked up at the column of black smoke still twisting up into the now leaden and heavily overcast sky.

"I just wanted you to know I'm okay," I said again. "I've gotta get back to work now."

"Are you sure everything's all right?"

"I've gotta go now," I repeated. "I love you." And then I hung up the phone before I started crying.

By the time I got back to the Cunningham pits, Creighton Pendleton had brought our D-Type in with terminal ignition problems and the car was retired. Not that any of us much cared. It slowly spread through the paddock that the carnage was of unbelievable proportions. There were already at least sixty-five dead and dozens upon dozens more carted off to the hospital in serious or critical condition, so the toll was sure to rise. You wanted to be anyplace else. And meanwhile the race droned on. John Fitch went to Neubauer and Uhlenhaut and told them Mercedes ought to withdraw the other two cars out of respect. But Neubauer thought otherwise, since the organizers had decided that the race should go on and the Fangio/Moss car was leading handily. It would help nothing to withdraw.

"I know that and you know that," John told them somberly, "but imagine what the press will say: *Ruthless Germans race on to victory over the bodies of dead Frenchmen.*"

Uhlenhaut understood what John was talking about, but the decision could really only be made by the board of directors back in Stuttgart. And by now it was early Saturday evening. But they called and efforts were made to find the directors wherever they were and the word finally came back well after midnight. At 1:45 AM, Neubauer hung out a black flag and the two remaining 300SLRs were brought into the pits and retired from the race. The Fangio/Moss car was leading the Hawthorn/Bueb Jaguar by over two laps at the time, and the other car was a solid fourth.

I guess it was the right thing to do.

Who knows?

Meanwhile it had started to rain, and the rain kept up through the night and the C-6R was down to just top gear and struggling along just to finish. But then it broke for good a little ways before dawn and there was nothing left to do but pack up our stuff and cars and pit equipment while the rain kept pelting down and the sky slowly lightened to a dull, tarnished shade of pewter. I can't remember ever having felt so low and hollow and washed away to nothing in my life.

30: *The Persistence of Memory*

I don't really remember how we came to leave the track or gather up our things at Madame Toot-Sweet's place or find our way back to Paris to catch the plane back to the states. It all came and went in a dull, numb, sleepwalking sort of blur. And then, every once in awhile, my eyes would close like I wanted to drop off to sleep. But then I'd see the smoke and white-hot crackle of flame off that burning Mercedes and Levegh's body crushed into the pavement like a busted sack of meat with a little fragment of pale-blue helmet at one end and hear the sirens and alarm bells and the desperate, anguished cries of the hurt and helpless. And then my eyes would pop open and it would stop. But only until I closed them again....

The plane ride home with the Cunningham team was the longest time I have ever spent. We'd already been up for over fifty hours, but I don't think any of us were able to sleep. At least none of us who were there in the pits when it happened, anyway. I sat and paced the aisle and sat and paced the aisle some more, and it was night and overcast and we were over the ocean so there was nothing you could see and it was more like we were trapped undersea in a submarine rather than several miles over it. And yet the time dragged on and on like you could count to fifty between one heartbeat and the next. I remember thinking that this is what death might be like if there is no God—just this endless eternity you keep waiting through and waiting through and yet it never moves or changes or comes to anything or reaches an end. I saw Tommy Edwards standing by one of the doorways, staring out through the little round porthole like there actually might be something out there you could see. "How're y'doin'?" I asked, my voice kind of all withered and cracking up on me.

"I'll get by, Sport. And you?"

I gave him a quarter-inch shrug. "I dunno. I can't sleep, that's for sure." I licked my lips. "I've never...I mean...I've never been around anything like that in my life."

"Nobody has," Tommy said quietly, still looking out the window. "Nothing like that has ever happened before. Not ever." He slowly closed his eyes, but then you could tell by the twitch and shudder that he was seeing the same thing as me on the inside of his eyelids and they snapped right open again.

"You ever seen people die before?" I asked him.

"Once or twice. In the war. But usually I was way up over it. That's one of the evil little delights of being a pilot. You get to rain death down on other people, but you don't have to watch them suffer and hurt and die."

I wanted to know more. I *needed* to know more. "So you have seen...you know...*other* things like that?"

Tommy nodded. "Once or twice."

I picked my words over carefully, trying to find the right ones. "Well, how do you...I mean, do you ever...I mean...'"

"How do you get over it?"

"Yeah," I nodded. "How do you get over it?"

Tommy turned from the window and his empty, faraway eyes slowly came into focus on me. "You don't," he said simply.

"Not ever?"

Tommy shook his head.

"Do you ever get, you know, *used* to it?"

Tommy shook his head again. "Oh," he said wearily, "you'll scab over. The brain's amazingly clever at burying things like that deep down inside and then covering it over so neatly you can hardly tell it's there..." He looked back out the window. "...But it is."

"Always?"

Tommy nodded with his eyes. But then the tightness of his jawline eased ever so slightly. "Oh, you get over the worst of it pretty quickly. The initial shock finally gives in to exhaustion. You just have to bloody wait it out for that to happen. But it will..."

"And then what?"

"You wake up and it's a little bit further away, and you wake up the next day and it's a little further away yet, and more days pass and the routine of your life grinds back into gear until it's like a nightmare you can't quite remember. Or some dark, awful thing that terrified you when you were small."

"But it never goes away?"

Tommy's eyes said 'no.'

I closed my own eyes. But it was still there, waiting for me. The smoke and the screams and the smell of the burning magnesium and that stiff, bloody stalk of an arm dangling off the edge of the passing stretcher with the watch hands frozen at 6:32.

"It'll haunt you," Tommy assured me in a sad, melancholy voice. "At night, mostly. You won't think about it for the longest time. And then—in the flash of an instant in the middle of the night when you least expect it—it'll be back just as real and horrible as ever."

"So what do you do?"

Tommy shrugged. "There's nothing you can do. You can drink if you want to. Lots of us do. But mostly, you just press on...."

Julie and little Vincenzo and the new baby all but ready to burst out of her belly any moment were waiting for me back at the duplex, and I almost crushed them all when I dropped my bags and hugged them to me there in the doorway. I was so choked up I was almost crying. And Julie was crying, too. So was little Vincent. Then Julie asked me if I wanted anything to eat—she knew all about what happened at Le Mans since it'd been all over the newspapers and even on the radio and television news reports—but I only wanted to take the longest, hottest, soapiest shower of my life and then, once I had myself as clean as I would ever get again, go to bed. Julie came in with little Vincent and the two of them laid down there with me and I burrowed into her and felt little Vincent there next to us and that big round part with the new baby inside and I started to cry. I hadn't cried like that since I was a little kid. And I cried myself all the way into that simple, sweet, deep empty blackness of sleep for the very first time since Le Mans.

I have to admit I stayed pretty edgy and hard to live with for several days there at the duplex. It was like anything Julie asked me or any kind of small talk she wanted to make or anytime little Vincent wanted to play with me it was irritating. And if I did catch myself playing with him or laughing with her or even cracking a damn smile, I felt guilty as hell about it. And angry, too. Mad at myself and even madder at anybody who had the cold, thoughtless lack of sensitivity to make me feel better. They had a lot of damn nerve, you know?

But Tommy was right. You may never get over it, but you've got to let it scab over as best you can and press on. And thankfully we had the new baby coming any time and I had plenty of work lined up at the Sinclair and customer cars to get ready for an SCMA race up in Massachusetts and plans to talk over with Big Ed about his new car dealership idea for the Sinclair to keep me busy. I was kind of zombie-walking through a lot of it, but it's amazing what your body and mind can continue to do even when there doesn't seem to be anybody at the controls. And of course just everybody wanted to know about what happened at Le Mans. But once I'd described it two or three times and sent it all flooding back in on me, I started telling people I was back behind the pits having coffee at one of the cafés or down at the signaling station at Mulsanne or someplace else—hell, *any*place else—when it happened, so I really didn't know any more about it than they did.

And meanwhile all the race reports had come out and the gist of things over on the European side of the Channel was that everybody and his brother was blaming the tragedy—the death toll was up over eighty by now—on Mike Hawthorn. Except over in England, of course, where the usual, patriotic-to-a-fault-and-a-half British motoring press was defending him with long, drawn-out articles that included quotes and diagrams and whatnot trying to explain what happened. The ugly irony of the whole thing was that Mike Hawthorn and Ivor Bueb went on to win the damn race and set a new distance record in their D-Type after the Mercedes team withdrew at quarter-to-two in the morning with over half the race yet to run, and that didn't sit real well with a lot of people since Hawthorn was reckoned by so many to be the cause of the disaster. Or at the very least the catalyst. But it was John Fitch who put it all in perspective for me: "Mike Hawthorn may well have caused the accident," John said, "but he certainly didn't cause the tragedy...."

There was a lot of truth in that, too.

So the Hawthorn/Bueb D-Type romped to its hollow victory and one of the Aston Martins finished an equally-hollow second and won the 3-liter class, and Mercedes-Benz put out a terse press release about circuit safety and even hinted that they might withdraw from racing if things weren't improved. All those powerful Ferrari six-cylinder jobs retired with slipping clutches—all the power in the world's no good if you can't get it to the ground—and the only real success stories, if there were any that black year at Le Mans, were the little 550 Porsches coming right on both speed and reliability and finishing first, second and third in the 1500cc class and a stunning fourth, fifth and sixth overall! Just ahead of the three Bristols that took seventh, eighth and ninth overall right behind them and went 1-2-3 for the second year in a row in the two-liter class. Although it must've rankled them just a little that they got steamrollered by the smaller Porsches. Not that you saw it much mentioned in the Bristol advertising that followed in the next few issues of *Autosport*. And the 1100cc version of the Porsche 550 co-driven by that Zora Arkus-Duntov guy won its class as well after Colin Chapman in the new Lotus got disqualified for spinning off and rejoining the race by reversing onto the circuit before he got waved back on course by the marshals. Oh, there was a heck of a row about it, but, what with everything that had happened and the awful, bloody cleanup work still going on across from the pits, I think maybe the officials were just looking for some way to show how careful they were. Or maybe they were just looking for a scapegoat. But the Lotus was out, and that was that. The EX-182 MG "prototype" co-driven by Ken Miles in the 1500cc class took twelfth overall (although only fifth in class behind the three Porsches and an OSCA MT-4), but they were thrilled to finish ahead of the two Triumph TR2s that came home fourteenth and fifteenth overall. Although you had a feeling it was just the first minor skirmish of an MG/Triumph war that would continue for a long, long time to come. But the truth of it was that nobody much cared, and the sooner they could forget Le Mans and everything that happened there, the better. For sure nobody bragged very much or for very long about what they'd accomplished at Le Mans that year. It was the kind of thing you were better off shutting up about, and everybody knew it.

The new baby came a week later on June 22nd, and, just like the doctor told us, it was much easier for Julie the second time around. But it was just as scary and nerve-wracking for me. I think the worst feelings in the world must be waiting and helplessness, and I had a giant, economy-sized helping of both while I sat there in the hospital waiting room with Julie's mom and my mom and my sister Sarah Jean. As per usual in a hospital, there was nothing to do but watch the clock, stare at the walls, and read the morning paper from one end to the other. Twice. I remember the big news on page one was that Juan Peron was in all sorts of trouble down in Argentina, what with rioting in the streets and having to call up the military to try and quiet things down and even his buddies in the US government were saying that the whole shootin' match was about to fall in on him. I personally felt kind of bad about it, seeing as how he was a big motorsports fan and supporter (it was his money and clout that put on the races John Fitch and some other Americans went down to run in South America and also the money that sent Argentine drivers Juan Manuel Fangio and Froilan Gonzalez over to Europe to show all those European stars what they could do—and it was plenty!), but I guess being a big racing booster isn't exactly the first quality you look for in a head of state/dictator-for-life sort of position. Although I'm sure it must be high up on the list there somewhere. Oh, and there was a Big Four meeting coming up in Geneva where the U.S., England, France and Russia were going to sit down and talk about how, exactly, they planned to carve up and keep an eye on the rest of the world. And Senator "Tailgunner Joe" McCarthy was back in the news (but down at the bottom of the page this time) for introducing a bill to dictate just what President Eisenhower could and could not discuss with the Russians. It was a sign of how far he'd fallen and how thoroughly his wings had been clipped that it got defeated 14-to-zip in the senate committee and even people like J. Edgar Hoover said it was a lousy idea.

Hey, you reap what you sow.

There was still no word from the delivery room and so I read the sports—Archie Moore had a big title fight coming up that very night at Madison Square Garden—and combed through the classifieds to see if there were any neat cars for sale. I even checked out the movie and fashion pages, you know? And then—finally—the nurse came in and told us the baby had come and everything was fine. Boy, you don't know what a relief that is until it happens to you. It was a little girl this time, and I had that same shaky, thrilled and terrified feeling in my gut when I picked her up and held her for the very first time. She was just so tiny and helpless, you know? And I knew it was my job to take care of her and watch over her and I felt all over again that I hadn't the slightest idea how to do it. We named her Roberta after Julie's favorite aunt who helped take care of her when she was little after her dad died in the war. But then she got sick and died herself a couple years later, before I even met Julie or cared about girls in general. "You would've really liked her," Julie told me, and the baby seemed real happy about her new name and slept all the way home in the car. I've got to say that I noticed a difference right away between this new baby girl and little Vincent. She seemed more placid and didn't fuss or squall near so much. Or maybe we'd just been through it once before and all the thousands of little things that sent us scurrying and worrying when we brought the first baby home didn't seem near so dangerous or devastating the second time around. But I could see where having two little kids around was going to be pretty much a fulltime job for Julie—even with her mom upstairs and my mom and Sarah Jean just a few blocks away.

Back at the shop I was still trying to bury myself in a daily routine and find things to keep me occupied so I wouldn't think too much about what happened at Le Mans. And so that new-car dealership project with Big Ed absorbed a lot of my attention. We both agreed that we'd need more space in order to do it, and it was just our good fortune that creaky old Mr. Mulcahy who owned the equally-creaky frame two-flat behind the station had died about a year before and now the relatives were squabbling tooth-and-nail with the lawyers and the IRS and each other over who got what. Not to mention that nobody was taking care of things like plumbing and roof leaks and stuck windows and lost keys and blown fuses anymore now that old Mr. Mulcahy was gone, and so the good tenants who lived downstairs had moved out in disgust and the bad tenants who lived upstairs and who were always a month behind with their rent anyway were now three months behind and starting to store their overflow garbage and empty beer bottles and pork-and-beans cans and old newspapers and such on the back porch of the apartment downstairs that nobody wanted to rent until the sink and the toilet were fixed and somebody got rid of all those old bottles and cans and newspapers on the back porch. And the smell.

It being our particular section of New Jersey, you could just about sense the insurance fire coming before it even started. And it started most fortuitously in the wee hours of a Sunday morning when the piggish family from upstairs (who were now four months behind and had recently, under advice from person or persons unknown, taken out a sizeable fire and theft policy on virtually everything that they owned plus a lot of stuff they didn't) just happened to be off seeing relatives somewhere near Trenton. In any case, thanks to all those old newspapers and a strong smell of gasoline, the place went up like a damn tinderbox, and the only real problem for the local police and fire department was keeping the crowd back while they let it burn to the ground. Plus a serious oversupply of suspects for their arson investigation. They even questioned Big Ed once they found out he was nosing around about the property with the estate lawyer almost before the ashes were cold, but of course he had a perfect alibi (not that Big Ed was the type of guy to go around setting arson fires—you *hired* people to do that sort of thing) since he was off at a cemetery someplace with a distinguished elderly lady who was well-respected in the community and on the library board and everything over in Teaneck.

"How the hell do you know somebody like that?" I asked him.

"Watch your mouth," he warned. "That's my mother yer talkin' about."

"Your *mother?*" I'd never really thought about Big Ed as having a mother. Although I guess he had to, didn't he?

"Yeah. My mother. I take her to see my dad's grave every year on his *yahrtzite.* That's the anniversary of his death, see?"

"You never talk about her."

"She never talks about me," he shrugged, unwrapping a fresh cigar. "Oh, she talks about my brother plenty. The bigshot ear, nose and throat man from Scarsdale." He bit the end off his cigar. "Hell," he continued, the little rag end of the cigar dangling from his lips, "I make ten times what he does, but all she wants to talk about is him and his lovely stinking wife and his lovely stinking children and what a lovely stinking home they have..." Big Ed spit it out on the floor, "...and then she rags on and on and on about the first Mrs. Baumstein."

"Your first wife?"

Big Ed nodded. "Oh, yeah." He rolled his eyes. "She raised bloody hell about it when I wanted to marry her. The whole stinking family did. *'An Italian girl? You're gonna marry a shiksa?'* They damn near disowned me." He let out a helpless little laugh. "My grandfather said *kaddish* over me. You know what that is?"

I shook my head.

"It's the prayer for the fucking dead. That's what it is."

"So what happened?"

"Aw, I was young and she was young and I was already kind of wild and I'd dropped out of school and everything and was maybe in with some guys who knew a few fast angles. We'd started up this scrap metal and machinery business, see? Me and her first cousin. That's how we met."

"So you got married?"

"Why not?"

"What'd your family do?"

"Oh, they shit a damn brick. But they already figured I was a lost cause anyway." Big Ed sighed and took a long drag off his cigar. "But then they got to know her a little, you know?" he blew out a perfect smoke ring and watched it float upwards and dissolve. "And they got to see just what kind of a giving, caring sort of person she was." Big Ed looked at me. "There's two kinds of people in this world, Buddy," he said solemnly. "Givers and takers. And my first wife was a giver." I actually saw a tear welling up in his eye. "She couldn't help it. That's just the way she was."

I'd never seen him soften up like that. "So what happened?"

"Oh, they started to come around. Little by little. And the scrap business was doing real good…" he gave me the old insider wink, "…and so we got ourselves a nice house and a few cars and then we got an even nicer house…."

"What about kids?"

Big Ed looked down at the floor. "We were kind of having a little trouble there. Oh, we were trying. But we weren't doing any good, see…" his voice trailed off for a moment, and it was like his shoulders drooped and his whole body sort of sagged. "…and that's why we went to see the doctors. And that's when they found it."

"Found what?"

Big Ed swiveled his eyes up at me and didn't say anything. And that's when I knew.

"She died?"

Big Ed nodded. "She was just twenty-six," he said, kind of choking up on it. "That's all the years she got." Big Ed looked out through the shop window and watched the cars and trucks rolling by on Pine Street.

"I'm sorry," I whispered. "I never knew that about you."

He waved it off like it didn't mean anything. "There's a lot about me y'don't know," he said in a faraway voice, his eyes still focused on the traffic outside.

I explained to Julie as how I'd have to go to the race up in Massachusetts on the Fourth of July weekend to take care of my customers, and we had kind of a fight about it seeing as how she didn't figure I should be running off all over hell-and-gone to the races if I was actually going into the car dealership business with Big Ed Baumstein. And she was furthermore not about to be stuck back home with two little kids to take care of all by her lonesome while I went gallivanting all over the damn countryside with my racing buddies. And the funny thing was, after Le Mans and all and with Vincent and the new little baby girl at home, I actually found myself agreeing with her. "I'll get it fixed," I told her without the slightest idea how. "You'll see. I've gotta finish out this season with my guys. But it's only a few more races. I'll come up with some new way to do it next year. I promise."

"You'd *better!*" she snorted.

"I will," I promised again. And I meant it, too. After all, Julie Finzio Palumbo was not the kind of person you wanted to mess with. It just wasn't a smart thing to do.

But I had a lot of unfinished business to take care of, and right up there at the top of my list was seeing the Trashwagon have one good run before it was too late. And it was almost too late already. A few of those new Ferraris and Maseratis and D-Type Jags and such I'd seen over at Le Mans would be trickling over across the Atlantic pretty quickly, and no question they represented a whole new generation of racing cars and my Trashwagon wouldn't have a chance against any of them. So I was grinding on Big Ed every chance I got about letting Cal Carrington drive the Trashwagon sometime, and maybe even that he should think about switching over from being a half-assed race car driver himself (although I didn't use those exact words) to being a wealthy car owner like Ernesto Julio or that Les Gonda guy with the birdseed and hamster-feed fortune who owned the car Sammy

Speed ran at Indianapolis. I could tell from the gleam in Big Ed's eye that he saw the benefits of becoming a team owner instead of a driver—like he might actually have a chance of actually *winning* a race someday in that capacity—but he also dearly loved dressing up in his helmet and goggles and the way it made him feel to be sitting there on the grid or parading around on the pace lap with every eye in the cheap seats staring at him. Plus he did very truly enjoy the driving part. Even if he wasn't especially good at it. It made him feel like he was maybe doing something most people wouldn't even have the guts to try. Even if they had the damn money. And very few of them had the money, either, and that was another nice part about it. It was like being a member of a very special, insider sort of club that not very many could ever dream of belonging to. A chance to say *"naahh-naa-na-naah-naahh"* to the whole effing world! I'll tell you, envy can be a delicious sort of thing when it's aimed in your direction rather than pointing out the other way....

And then there was the little matter of Reginald "Skippy" Welcher, prince among assholes, jerkoff for the ages, sole heir to the Welcher Waxout ear swab fortune, and the one creature on earth—above all else and all others—that Big Ed Baumstein wanted to beat to the finish line in a fair-and-square fight. Even just once.

That would be enough....

Anyhow, July 4th weekend brought that SCMA race at the Beverly Airport on New England's famous and snooty North Shore, just a short drive up from Boston and directly across a scenic inlet bay from Salem, where some of the SCMA bluebloods' pilgrim ancestors proudly called each other witches and burned each other at the stake. And of course the hot topics on everybody's lips were the terrible disaster at Le Mans (like I said before, I was already sick of talking about it) and the monstrous big new "Road America" racetrack they were building up in Elkhart Lake, Wisconsin, and how everybody and their brother was going to have to be there for the inaugural race weekend on September 10th and 11th. "I heard it's a full four miles around," somebody said.

"With hills and valleys..."

"And the pavement's supposed to be smooth as a baby's ass."

"It's built just for racing, too. No fences or stone walls or telephone poles to hit."

"Old Baumstein and Welcher'll be happy to hear that!"

Haw-Haw-Haw!

It was really something when you stopped to think about it: a full-scale, purpose-built road racing circuit. Not some stitched-together collection of closed-off public highways and byways or a flat, featureless, makeshift "road circuit" laid out on a bunch of concrete airport runways without so much as a mild hill or a banked corner or a single blade of grass for shade. Nope, this new track at Road America was supposed to be just what the title promised: a perfect country road just made for sportycar racing. It was hard to believe, you know?

Anyhow, there were about 150 cars entered for the races at Beverly Airport and they had the usual charity angle working to keep the locals at bay (this time they were raising money for a new wing or something at the Beverly hospital), and I must admit it was a relief to be back to a safe, flat, wide-open American airport track where there was plenty of room to screw up and not much of any-thing to hit or collect. Oh, maybe it felt a little like a kiddy game compared to Le Mans, but that was all to the good as far as I was concerned.

Phil Hill was there driving Ernesto Julio's new, bright-yellow Ferrari 750 Monza, and you could see right from the get-go that Phil had kind of advanced to a higher plateau than the SCMA club racers he was up against. The three-liter, four-cylinder Monza he was driving didn't have the sheer horsepower of some of the other cars on hand, but it was reasonably light yet tough and rugged like all Ferraris, and he allowed as how it had a real good spread of torque coming out of the corners. But the main thing was that Phil had really come into his own after racing with and against the best in the world, and there was a quiet, calm, work-manlike confidence in how he went about it and the car just seemed to be almost gliding around the circuit underneath him. The Cunningham team was still gath-ering itself back together after Le Mans, so Creighton the Third was back in his own hotrod Ferrari, but even with 4.9 liters of howling V12 under the hood, he couldn't match Phil's pace in the smaller Ferrari Monza. Nobody else could, either.

Carson Flegley seemed as shell-shocked by Billy Vukovich's death and the disaster at Le Mans as those who had actually been there, and so he'd agreed to hand his Healey over to Cal for the Beverly airport race and watch from the side-lines with my sister Sarah Jean. And Cal did his usual fine, smooth, graceful and fast sort of job with it. Oh, he didn't have much hope of winning, since there was one of those 300SL Mercedes gullwing coupes and another guy in an Aston Martin running in the same class. But damn if he didn't split them and come home second! And not all that far behind the Mercedes, either.

Oh, and Big Ed even had me take a few practice laps in the Trashwagon. It was loading up or starving or missing or something coming out of the corners—he couldn't tell which—and so he snuck me out for a couple laps to see if I could track it down. I really hadn't been out in it since that very first weekend at the hill-climb—and never on a real racing circuit—and it came to me all over again about that special, private and deliciously isolated feeling guys like Cal and Tommy and Sammy Speed told me you find inside a racing car. Where nobody and nothing can get at you and the concentration and focus of it fill you up so completely that there's simply no room for anything else to get in. It's gotta be the best damn hid-ing place in the world....

The problem with the Trashwagon was driving me nuts, though. It ran fine if you went slow, but if you started to give it a little stick, all of a sudden it'd start cutting out. But only in right-hand corners. Noplace else! Hell, you'd charge up towards a right-hand bend, squeeze on the brakes, blip her down a gear—the Trashwagon was a pretty sweet-running, sweet-handling racecar, if I do say so myself!—bend her in with the steering wheel, and then the engine would go all kind of flat and soft and sputtery. Like it was running out of fuel, you know? Only then it'd clear itself out and run just fine again a little ways out of the corner. And if I went slow to try and catch it and figure it out, it'd go away completely and run like clockwork. Back in the pits I ripped the whole fuel system apart and looked at everything and—*damn!*—it all looked just fine. Still, it was good to have the game afoot again and be out there on the trail of a solution. And the only real clue we had was that it only happening on right-hand turns. It didn't help that damn near all the corners at Beverly were right-handers. Or maybe it wasn't fuel starvation at all, seeing as how I'd taken the carburetors and fuel pump apart maybe a half-dozen times and blew out all the lines with compressed air and still couldn't find one damn thing wrong. And so I went out on the corners and listened when Big Ed drove by. Yeah, it was skipping or sputtering or something. No question about it. And nothing I did or tried made the least bit of difference. So we struggled through the weekend without finding a solution and Big Ed finished well towards the back in the feature race on Sunday. And several places behind Skippy Welcher, who, you can be sure, came over to gloat about it afterwards.

It wasn't until a week or so later in the shop when I was just giving the Trashwagon a routine oil change that I found it. The rubber in one of the motor mounts had sheared, can you believe it? Oh, the engine still sat there nice as you please since it cradles into kind of a "V," but the bum rubber mount allowed the engine to shift over a few degrees in right-hand turns. Just enough, in fact, to squeeze the plug wires for the two back cylinders on the left bank up against the steering column. Squeezed 'em pretty hard, in fact. Hard enough to chafe through those wires and ground them out! So *that* was my "fuel starvation" problem. And it brought right back to me Butch Bohunk's very first rule of automobile mechanics. The one he told me over and over and over again when I was just starting out: *"Make sure the damn electrics are in order before you start fucking around with carburetion!"*

Speaking of shop projects, we were getting pretty close to finished with our new parts runner Steve Kibble's war-surplus Indian motorcycle that came in a collection of orange crates and coffee cans and cardboard boxes. I started taking a strange new interest in it after I got back from Le Mans. To be honest, I didn't know much of anything about motorcycles. But Steve didn't know much of anything about mechanics—at least not yet, anyway—and it was like having this strange mechanical jigsaw puzzle to fool around with that maybe had a couple of pieces missing. It was just what I needed, you know? In fact, I got a little obsessive about it, like it would somehow make me feel better if I could resurrect it and make it whole again. And it did, too. That's the magic of shop projects. And I remember the fine summer afternoon when Julie came by with the new baby in the buggy and little Vincenzo toddling proudly along beside her. He knew his way around the shop pretty well by then, and even knew not to touch certain things that were sharp or hot or jagged or had chemicals in them. Although I still had to keep an eye on him. Anyhow, he was watching me with those big, glistening eyes of his while I was in the process of torquing the big through-bolt that goes through the front hub of every motorcycle, and it was kind of cumbersome to get in the right position on it while trying to simultaneously straddle the front wheel and hold the bike up there in the middle of the shop floor (sure, I know I should have had it chucked up in some sort of stand or jig, but I was a little too impatient—I mean, hell, it was just one stinking bolt...), and I was moreover using a ½-drive ratchet wrench with a longer extension than I really needed on one side and a damn adjustable crescent wrench on the other simply because that's what happened to be in my hand. And of course that's when the crescent wrench slipped off the damn nut and sent my knuckles crashing *hard!* into the cooling fins on the engine.

"*FUCKSHITPISS!!!*" I hollered at my own stupidity.

Little Vincent's eyes brightened. "*Fuckshitpiss!*" he beamed right back at me. Oh, *this* was going to be trouble....

Anyhow, I had the Greek at the body shop paint the tank and fenders of the Indian for me as a kind of a favor—bright school-bus yellow, just the way Steve wanted it—and we spray-painted the frame and everything else black so it started looking sort of like a 700-pound bumble bee. And that's what we started calling it around the shop: *The Bumble Bee.* To be honest, it came out better than anybody could have expected, and I got a genuine charge out of it when Steve kicked it over and we heard that loping, loafing, thumping *blut-blut-blut-blut* exhaust note of the 500cc flathead V-twin for the very first time. He even asked if I wanted to be the first one to ride it—I'd ridden his Whizzer around the block once or twice, so it wasn't like I didn't know how to handle it or anything—and I gladly took him up on it. I went inside and got those mirrored aviator sunglasses Cal Carrington gleeped for me on our way to the Giants Despair Hillclimb in Wilkes-Barre, Pennsylvania, what seemed like a thousand lifetimes before, threw my leg over the saddle, and took off for a little spin on the highway out of town. And I've got to admit that was about the best I'd felt since I came back from Le Mans. A motorcycle is kind of like the distilled-down essence of a sportycar. Only with the voltage turned way up. And I mean *waaaay* up! I can't tell you how great it felt to be out there on the highway with the warm summer wind whipping all over me and the sound and feel of that big, loafing V-twin right under my butt and between my legs and a sensation tingling up through the handlebars like I had the whole damn world by the scruff of the neck.

And that's about when some old geezer in a Buick who was waiting at a side-road stop sign looked directly at me—or maybe right *through* me would be more like it!—and pulled out. *Right smack-dab in front of me!* I screamed and grabbed the brakes, but it all happened in a flash and next thing I knew there was a heavy *THUMP!* and I found myself flying through the air! The odd part is how slow-motion peaceful it suddenly seemed and how I could hear quite clearly the lope of the Indian's engine as it bounced off the Buick's fender and the sound of the glass from the headlight lens tinkling down on the pavement behind me. And then I hit. *HARD!* I guess I skidded and maybe tumbled a little bit, too, and the next thing I knew I was looking up at the sky with this collection of strange, concerned faces assembling over me and asking if I was okay....

Hey, how the heck would I know?

I mean, I just got there myself.

Well, the cops came and then an ambulance showed uo, and it turned out I'd banged my knee up pretty bad putting a dent in the Buick's fender and I had a fine old raspberry finish on my ass cheek and forearm from skidding along the pavement, plus the same sort of general bump-and-bruise collection you might assemble if you, say, took a swan dive down a three-story fire escape. But I was lucky and there were skull fractures or broken bones or anything like that. But the thing I'll always remember was the poor old guy from the Buick wailing and wringing his hands and looking absolutely petrified and muttering over and over about how sorry he was and how he just didn't see me....

Didn't see me?

Why, the old fart looked right *at* me!

And that's when I came to the blunt realization that having the right-of-way doesn't count for very much on a damn motorcycle.

Of course I promised Steve I'd get the Indian fixed up for him again (even though it wasn't really my fault, but you've got to do that sort of stuff anyway), but I'd have to say there was some good that came out of it. Despite all the damn aches and pains that came afterwards and lingered long after I was sick of having them. But the whole thing kind of shocked me awake and back to reality after Le Mans. Like in those war movies where the buck private starts going to pieces after his first real action and then the sergeant slaps him hard across the face and then the private blinks a few times and says, *"Thanks, Sarge, I needed that!"* Well, there's nothing like having something scary level its barrels at *you* to ease the burden of what you've seen happen to other people.

Naturally the crash episode on the Indian didn't sit real well with Julie. Or her mom, who hissed at me through clenched teeth that if I ever hurt myself so's I couldn't take care of Julie and the kids and her like I was supposed to, she'd make damn sure it was fatal. And she didn't look like she was kidding, either. Like it or not, she reminded me, I'd managed to amass a whole heaping, bewildering and never-ending assortment of responsibilities for myself. And I had to keep that in mind when opportunities came along to have a little harmless, motorized fun that just might get me killed.

"You gotta think about somebody besides yo'self," Julie's mom growled at me. The worst of it was, I knew she was right....

31: The Road to Elkhart Lake

I had to leave Julie and little Vincenzo and the new baby to take my guys to the Giant's Despair Hillclimb and Brynfan Tyddyn road races near Wilkes-Barre, Pee-Ay, but the Saturday races were limited to under-two-liter cars on account of the circuit was really nothing more than a long, narrow driveway around Senator Newell Woods' estate, and so the Trashwagon and Buster Jones' Jag and Carson's Healey Hundred only got to run up the hill on Friday. And I think Big Ed might have had a good shot at beating Skippy's C-Type up that hill if he ever got himself a clean run, but after he saw he was only a few tenths off The Skipper's time on their first run, I think he got a little wound up and managed to half-loop or fully loop the car on his other two runs up the hill and didn't improve his time. But he still did better than Skippy, who was obviously feeling the pressure and capped off another squeaker victory over Big Ed by stuffing the oft-straightened nose of his Jag into a mulberry bush. It didn't do too much damage, but the mulberries were in season and so it looked pretty awful. And that was good.

Carson let Cal share his Healey and Cal was easily the fastest of the Healey guys—no real surprise—but again had to give best to one of the "real" racecars in the three-liter class. This time it was a Maserati 300S, which was really a lot more car than a Healey Hundred could ever hope to be. But it was a damn good run anyway. In the races, we also got a peek at the new kid on the block in the E-Modified class as two guys showed up with these new AC "Ace" models from England, and I've got to admit they looked a lot lower and leaner and lighter than Danny Poindexter's ex-Big Ed Arnolt-Bristol. Oh, and a Porsche beat all the MGs, but that was kind of becoming the expected thing and all the MG guys were muttering about how that new, envelope-bodied MG—like the EX-182 prototype we'd seen at Le Mans—couldn't get finished and on the market any too soon as far as they were concerned.

To be honest, it was hard to get all wound up over our little stateside club races after seeing how they do it for blood and money over at Le Mans, but it was also comforting to go through a whole race weekend with nothing more than a few harmless spins for excitement. Which is exactly what you got on a tight, narrow little track like Brynfan Tyddyn. But everybody was talking about that huge, new Road America race track up at Elkhart Lake and how even the big guns would be able to stretch their legs up there.

We had more of the same up at Thompson Speedway up in Connecticut all day Saturday and Sunday afternoon before Labor Day Monday, where the turnout was light because of that upcoming race at Elkhart Lake the following weekend and all anybody could talk about was making the big, cross-country trip to sample the first real grand prix-scale, purpose-built road racing circuit in the country. It was a heck of a big deal according to everybody, believe you me! Team Passaic had a middling-good weekend at Thompson, what with the SCMA splitting the 3-liter Production cars into a Mercedes 300SL/Aston Martin class and an Austin-Healey class, and Carson let Cal drive again and he won the Healey class with ease, finishing fourth overall behind three 300SLs and well ahead of the lone Aston Martin. A guy named Gaston Andrey led a Morgan sweep of the 2-liter Production class, and it was amazing to me that anything that looked so old-fashioned could run and handle so well. For contrast, Len Bastrup simply ran away and hid from all the smallbore modified cars in his new Lotus, and you could see how the Morgan and the Lotus represented two completely opposite approaches to engineering. The Morgan went with the old Ox-Cart theory, where the suspension was stiff as a board but the chassis had all the torsional stiffness of a sheet of quarter-inch plywood. Colin Chapman's Lotus was exactly the opposite, with a rigid, three-dimensional spaceframe chassis and really soft suspension so it would kind of float and flow its tires over the pavement. The goofy thing was that both methods seemed to work. Although I did notice one thing the Morgan and the Lotus had in common: they were *light!*

And speaking of light, there were a couple of those Porsche 550 Spyders there, and Walt Hansgen was at the wheel of one of them and served notice that the OSCA's days of supremacy in the 1500cc Modified class might be coming to an end. He started in the middle of the pack, but carved his way easily to the front pretty easily and simply blew everybody away. It wasn't even close. But what *was* close was the race between Big Ed in the Trashwagon and Skippy Welcher's C-Type Jag. They were running right together again, about halfway down a fairly weak field of big-bore modifieds, and you could see how Big Ed was hunting and feinting and peeking and trying to find a way by. I actually got the feeling that if he ever found his way past, he could just leave old Skippy and his C-Type in the dust. But there really wasn't enough straightaway at Thompson to use the Trashwagon's torque advantage to get by, and The Skipper was a past master at hogging the middle of the road going into the corners so there was no room to pass. Worse yet, he never made the usually-inevitable Reginald "Skippy" Welcher signature-edition Big Mistake, and so that's how they finished, with Skippy out front by an eyelash and Big Ed right on his butt. And don't think for a moment that The Skipper didn't come over to rub a little salt in Big Ed's wounds after it was over.

"I couldn't always see that car behind me..." he told Milton Fitting in a stage whisper that could've been heard in the Bronx, "...but I could sure as heck *smell* it!"

Haw-Haw-Haw!

"It's so ugly I had to turn my mirrors around so they wouldn't break."

Haw-Haw!

"It's too bad old Baumstein can't afford himself a *real* sports car!" Skippy was really into it now, and therefore serving up the usual spit shower that always came along with the commentary whenever he got excited. "Maybe we should—*heh-heh*—take up a collection?"

I saw the color starting to rise on Big Ed's neck and figured it was an excellent time to move him somewhere out of sucker punch range from Skippy's kisser. I mean, the last thing Big Ed needed was more trouble with one of Charlie Priddle's Drivers' Committee tribunals. Although I think I could've made a killing selling ringside tickets if I'd let Big Ed take a swing at him.

To be honest, I was about ready to take a sock at old Skippy myself. Oh, I know the Trashwagon was mechanically and cosmetically a far cry from the Jagillac of my original dreams, but I'd built it with my own two hands, dammit—not to mention any other hands I could lay my hands on when I needed them—and, even if there were a million kazillion things I would've done differently (or not done at all, come to think of it) if I had it to do all over again, I was damn proud of that ugly monster and desperately wanted to show everybody, just once, what it could do in the right hands.

Which is why I started grinding on Big Ed all over again to let Cal drive it at Elkhart Lake. "Look," I told him, "I've seen the cars that'll be coming over from Europe next season, and they're just a whole blessed generation past what we've got here."

"Are you saying I'm not getting' the job done?" Big Ed said with a soft, hurt edge in his voice. I knew I had to be pretty careful about picking my words. After all, not only was Big Ed my very best customer and the godfather of my son, but he was also my future business partner and the one guy, above any other and in spite of anything else, that I knew I could count on when the chips were down.

"It's not that," I kind of half-lied. "It's just that Cal Carrington's about the best damn natural-born road racer I've ever seen. You've seen it, too...."

I saw the wheels turn grudgingly behind Big Ed's eyes.

"...And, judging from the aerial photo I saw in one of the magazines, this new track at Road America might be the perfect place for a car like the Trashwagon to show its stuff. Looks like there's a few fairly tight, 90-degree corners leading onto long, uphill straightaways. Just perfect for a car with a lot of grunt and acceleration...." I could see he was mulling it over. "...Wouldn't you like to *just once* see it going as fast as it can go?"

And that's when Big Ed curled his lip, shrugged his shoulders, and said "OK."

I couldn't believe it, you know?

Well, Cal was absolutely over the moon about it when I told him. You should've seen the predatory gleam in his eye when he thought about driving something with real suds and potential (and especially one that everybody already figured was a shitbox) on a level playing field of a new track where nobody had any seat-time advantage. It was a real opportunity for him to show his stuff against the Big Boys and try to impress people like Briggs Cunningham and Ernesto Julio and Carlo Sebastian. And he knew it.

I was all smiles about it, too, and tried my best to explain my excitement to my dad and brothers-in-law at the yet-another-family-Labor-Day-barbecue-at-my-old-man's-house-that-you-didn't-dare-miss the following day. But they just looked at me with that, *"Oh, that's real nice—would you please pass the corn relish?"* expression that racers get from non-racers all the time. I mean, unless you've got the bug, you don't—hell, you *can't!*—appreciate what all the fuss is about. It's just a bunch of noise and dust and big egos and fast cars running around in circles but not getting anywhere and, especially that particular year, people getting killed for no good reason. Like religion or your taste in music, it was not the sort of thing you could really explain to people. At least not and have them understand it, anyway.

Meanwhile all the female relatives were back in the kitchen cooing and oohing and aahing at little baby Roberta. Little Vincenzo was in there, too, kind of flitting around the edges and feeling just ever so slightly left out. Or maybe a little bit more than ever-so-slightly. But he sure got his share of attention when my mom burned her thumb on a hot Dutch apple pie tin and he showed off the nifty new words he'd learned from his daddy down at the Sinclair....

Carson was there with Sarah Jean as was becoming usual on family holidays, and I had the feeling he was getting ready to pop the question if he could just get up the nerve. Which is why I made sure to keep him well supplied with booze to maybe try and loosen him up a little. And of course my older sister Tina's loud-mouth husband Roy was having no trouble keeping himself well oiled and made a point of visiting my old man's liquor cabinet on a pretty regular basis. Not that such a thing was particularly unexpected. And Marty Frances showed up again (late, of course) with that Pauly Martino saxophone player guy from Greenwich Village. And I must admit he was really starting to grow on me. Even if he wasn't much of a car guy. In fact, he took buses and trains and such everywhere and didn't even have a driver's license. Can you believe it? But he was nice in a quiet sort of way and a member of the union so he could look anybody right in the eye and say he was a musician without flinching and he apparently worked pretty steady, too. Although the hours could be pretty rough when he played weekend and one-night-stand jazz gigs at the clubs along with the symphony stuff. But you could see he worked hard and took it seriously and wasn't one of those loose-wig, Hophead Dope Fiend types you always hear about in the music business. More importantly, he'd apparently had a few long talks with Mary Frances about what, exactly, she was going to do with herself, and that it would never be enough for her to just hang around with some creative-genius type and hold his coat or his hand or whatever while he painted or sculpted or re-organized the social order of the world or wrote novels in Esperanto. Or played saxophone, for that matter. I told her out on the back porch that she maybe needed a family to look after herself, you know? And then she told me how Pauly kept telling her the same thing. And that she needed something else, too. Something of her own. Some special thing she could do and try her best at and be proud of. "I've always been disgusted with anything I ever did, Buddy," she whispered to me. "Maybe that's why I've got such a smart mouth and snotty attitude all the time."

"So what're y'gonna *do* about it?"

"Well..." she looked at me with her eyes all softening up, "...promise you won't tell the folks, okay?"

"Sure. No problem."

"I'm going back to school. City College this time."

"What for?"

"Well, this may sound crazy, but I think I want to teach."

"That doesn't sound crazy at all. In fact, that's the least-crazy thing I've ever heard out of that wiseass mouth of yours."

"But don't tell the folks," she reminded me again. "In case it doesn't work out." She looked up at me with a cold tide of self-contempt rising in her eyes. "I haven't exactly had a great record when it comes to staying with things or sticking them out...."

"You'll do fine," I told her. And I meant it, too.

I'd also been working on Julie back at the duplex to come with me to Road America, but it was a hard sell what with a three-month old baby in tow and little Vincenzo now a very busy and inquisitive eighteen months old and into absolutely everything if you didn't keep an eye on him. And moreover gaining a great command of the language, including *"Fuckshitpiss"* and the lovely phrase *"cocksucking blue-balled bastard"* that he'd picked up from his loudmouth Uncle Roy when little Vincent accidentally toppled over his beloved half-bottle of my old man's gin at our Labor Day barbecue. Thank you so very much. But, like I said, I'd been working on Julie and telling her all about the beautiful, spring-fed lake up at Elkhart and the quaint little white-clapboard cabins and hotel buildings at Siebkens and Schwartz's and The Osthoff on Lake Street and the playlot with swings and stuff for the kids and how we could maybe even stay over an extra night and just kind of relax....

"Oh, I'll be doing a lot of relaxing with two little kids to take care of while you're off at the racetrack or out getting plastered with your racing buddies."

"I promise I'll be good," I promised her. "And you'll like it. And the kids will love it. You'll see...."

She didn't look particularly convinced.

It helped when I told her that Cal was going to tow the rig out for us and Big Ed was planning to fly out and back because he had some business stuff to take care of but wanted one of his cars out there to run around in when he got there so he'd be happy to borrow us a little something out of his stable for the ride out. I was kind of keen on his Thunderbird, but it really wasn't too practical with a couple little kids and so we'd settled on Big Ed's brand new "winter and go-to-the-city" black Caddy sedan with air conditioning and suspiciously thick, heavily-tinted window glass. It was a big, spacious Land Yacht of a car just made for long-distance travel with kids (at least if you put sheets over those nice leather seats to protect them from all the smears, spills and stains that come with small children just as surely as goo-goo smiles and belly buttons).

I also reminded Julie that the new car dealership idea with Big Ed was pretty important to our future—hell, as far as I could see, it *was* our future!—and so it would be worth our while to spend a little time with him and for Julie to get to know him a little better. And I think that's what finally swung the deal and got her to agree to go. So the four of us—Julie, me, little Vincenzo and even littler Roberta—left Butch and J.R. and Steve and even my Aunt Rosamarina in charge of the Sinclair (and you should have seen how she could pump gas, check oil and clean windshields by then!) and took off cross-country for Elkhart Lake in Big Ed's black Caddy sedan during the wee hours of Wednesday morning, September 7th, 1955. And I've got to say it was nice traveling with my whole, new, four-person family for the very first time. And especially in a car like Big Ed's Caddy. Made me feel like I should've been wearing a fine Homburg hat and maybe sucking on one of Big Ed's dollar cigars and nodding condescendingly to the peasants in their Fords and Chevys and Plymouths as we tooled by. Plus it was kind of a thrill being the experienced old trail hand who knew the quick way around Philadelphia to get to the Pennsylvania Turnpike and an even bigger thrill to watch Julie's eyes when she saw those fantastic mountains and forests and valleys and faraway, misty vistas through the Appalachians. They reminded me of my eyes when I saw it all for the very first time. Even little Vincent seemed impressed. At least for a few minutes, anyway.

By then we'd learned enough about traveling with little kids that I allowed plenty of time and didn't much mind the diaper stops and the spilled juice stops and the clean-up-the-barf stops that are all a part of it. I even tried my best to help out. Not that my best at that sort of thing is really much help. And it was really kind of special for me when Julie asked if I wanted her to take the wheel for a while when both of the kids were asleep. She didn't get to drive all that often, and I could see in her eyes as she wheeled that big, smooth Caddy down out of the mountains that, just like me, she loved the magic of the road rolling under you and the great, sprawling vacuum of America sucking you gently and endlessly into it. Like I said before, nothing can get at you when you're out there on the road. Nothing. All you gotta do is keep moving....

But of course that got tougher when the Pennsylvania Turnpike ended. Oh, the Eisenhower government was hard at work building a new set of turnpikes across Ohio and Indiana so's you could one day drive all the way from Chicago to New York City and back without so much as a single stoplight, side road or railroad crossing. In fact, Eisenhower and his pals said those new superhighways would eventually stretch and spiderweb all over the whole damn country from coast to coast and border to border. Can you believe it? But they were still finishing most of it up back in September of 1955, and I remember telling Julie how much better and easier things were going to be once you could just sail across the whole blessed country at a mile or more every minute and not have to go through all those quiet little towns with their 25 or 30mph speed limits and courthouses with quaint little parks and play lots and war memorials across from them and comfy homestyle restaurants on Main Street where they made a fresh fruit pie or two every morning and had a lunch special that included coffee and a slice of that pie every day.

"Yep," I told her proudly, "it's gonna change everything."

And then we parked on the square of one of those little towns and had dinner at one of those little storefront restaurants—our waitress was named Alice and I remember I had the beef stew special (which was really good!) and Julie got the chicken croquettes and Alice had the cook mash up some hamburger meat and parsley-boiled potatoes and peas for little Vincenzo—and then we went across into the park as early evening settled in around us and I pushed little Vincent on a swing set that looked like it had been painted over every spring since the turn of the century while Julie fed the baby. "Yep," I said again, looking around at all the quiet, tidy little storefront businesses that were already closed for the night and the porch and dining room lights coming on in the houses you could see on the next street over and the creaky old custodian in gray coveralls shuffling out to take the flag down in front of the courthouse, "it's gonna change everything...."

We'd originally planned to stop for the night someplace in Ohio—Findlay maybe, if we made it that far—but the kids dozed off to sleep after dinner and Julie was smart enough to figure that if we bunked in anytime soon, they'd be up all night. So she took the wheel for awhile and I kind of half-dozed and fooled around with the radio while it got dark and maybe around nine or so we got stuck at a railroad crossing while a slow freight train scraped and screeched and clanged its way past and of course that woke the kids up—screaming, in fact—and so I took the wheel with the idea that we'd keep running until it looked like they were ready to pack it in again. But they'd apparently slept real good after dinner, and so we made it all the way to the outskirts of Fort Wayne, Indiana, that first day and bunked in well past midnight after damn near twenty hours on the road. We were lucky to find this quiet little mom-and-pop motel where the rooms were clean and reasonable and the sheets were fresh and crisp and smelled faintly of lilac. All four of us slept clear through until dawn. Or almost dawn, anyway, on account of the dirt farmer across the road owned a rooster with a real World Class set of lungs who announced the coming of daylight so loud they knew about it in Toledo. Or maybe even Pittsburgh. If you're not a farm-type person, that sort of noise shocks you awake like a lit brick of ladyfingers tossed in through the window. Which of course meant both the kids were up and squalling and there really wasn't much point in doing anything except cleaning them up and changing diapers and getting dressed and loading the car and hitting the road again. I mean, you can forget about ever getting back to sleep again once the kids wake up. It's a basic rule of parenting. As is the necessity of keeping them awake a little when they want to snooze off during a long day of travel if you want to get any sleep yourself the following night. But of course, like a lot of things, that's something you don't learn until you haven't done it a few times. But you do….

Time was on our side, however, since we weren't supposed to pick Big Ed up at the Milwaukee airport until six that evening, and we'd gained an easy spare hour going from the Eastern to the Central time zone on our way to Chicago on US 30. It was kind of a slog through Chicago, of course, and I made it even slower on purpose by taking routes 12 and 20 up Indianapolis Boulevard and Stony Island Avenue so's we could catch US 41 that ran right along the Lake Michigan shoreline from one end of the city to the other. It was worth it, too, since I could show Julie the impressive Museum of Science and Industry building in Jackson Park that was all done up with domes and columns and statues and assorted other famous architectural doodads and looked like some monster of a Greek temple carved out of limestone. Julie read in a guidebook someplace that it was originally built as part of the Chicago World's Fair Columbian Exposition in 1893, which was quite a big deal back in the days before television. And almost right across the street was the University of Chicago, which never had much of a football team but was where a bunch of scientists with strange accents first got together to build us the atom bomb.

Further north on Lake Shore Drive we came to more of that fancy-looking Greek and Roman architecture at Soldier Field and the Field Museum and the Shedd Aquarium and the Adler Planetarium, and then we had a nice run along the lake with all these fabulous yachts and sailboats in harbors off to our right and the impressive Chicago downtown skyline spurting its concrete and steel into the sky on our left. And right in the middle of the whole stretch is Buckingham Fountain and then Navy Pier sticking out about a quarter mile out into Lake Michigan at the far end. I pointed out the Drake Hotel where I stayed myself on my way back to New Jersey with Tommy Edwards' (or, actually, Creighton Pendleton's) C-Type after that last street race in Elkhart Lake back in 1952, and the Palmolive

Building with the Lindbergh Beacon on top of it that swept over the tops of the Chicago skyscrapers every night, and we marveled at the impressive new Prudential Building that was going up on Michigan Avenue that would be the tallest building in Chicago and also at all the lovely and elegant old brownstone apartment buildings looking out over Lake Michigan where some very rich people indeed must have lived.

I had to admit that Chicago was a pretty damn handsome and interesting sort of place for a big city, and I could see in the buildings and shoreline and beaches and trees and stretches of green parkland reflecting in Julie's eyes that she was thinking the same thing, too. We were a couple hours ahead of schedule and had some time to kill, so, on a whim, I followed a sign that said "Lincoln Park Zoo," turned off Lake Shore Drive and parked Big Ed's Caddy for a spell so's we could stretch our legs and take a look around. I unfolded the baby buggy out of the trunk and loaded up a big straw bag with all the diapers and baby bottles and Kleenex and pacifiers and favorite blankies and even more favorite stuffed toys and God-only-knows-what-else you need to carry if you've got a couple little kids in tow and we went for a little stroll through the zoo they have there. It was a really love-ly place—and admission was free, too!—and what a nice treat to get out of the endless, rolling motion of the car for a while and gawk at the lions and bears and elephants and go inside the cool darkness of the slithery-reptile house that smelled awful and the fluttering-bird house that smelled even worse and see the monkeys in their cages outside screeching at each other like they were laughing while they did incredibly rude things with their private parts. Like they actually *knew* how it horrified the pasty-faced nun with the string of little Catholic school kids stand-ing right there in front of them. Next to the zoo they had beautiful flower gardens with paths and park benches and fountains that kids splashed and played in, and for lunch Julie and little Vincent and me bought Chicago-style hot dogs from a pushcart vendor. They came in poppy-seed buns, all slathered up with mustard and covered in a blessed mountain of sweet relish and diced onions and sliced tomatoes, and then another layer of pickles and cucumbers plus a little celery salt for seasoning and sport peppers if you wanted them—I swear, they made every other hot dog I'd ever eaten in my life seem absolutely naked by comparison—but of course we had to break up Vincent's into little bits for him and he didn't eat very much. Although there wasn't much left—I saw to that! For dessert we bought Good Humor bars from an old guy in a white uniform and cap who was riding a sort of three-wheeled bicycle thing with a white freezer box on the front and bells that tinkled pleasantly as he pedaled around the park. Julie even fed a little ice cream to the baby—placing just a tiny bit of it on her lips—and you could tell by the wide, gloriously surprised little smile that spread across her face and how she stretched her little hands out for more that she really liked it. But maybe the most interesting thing about Lincoln Park was all the different kinds of peo-ple you saw and even different languages you overheard. It was a hell of a neat place to be. Especially for kids.

But we had to leave after lunch and hit the road again, north on Lake Shore Drive and then Sheridan Road with the lake always right there beside us, passing Loyola University and then, further north, Northwestern University up in

Evanston (you could tell it cost quite a bundle to send your kid there!) and then past the strange and beautiful Baha'i Temple they'd just finished building across from yet another yacht-and-sailboat harbor in Wilmette. To be honest, I thought that Baha'I Temple looked like a big stone sculpture of a very large and ornate orange juice squeezer. But what do I know about architecture? And after that we passed through Wilmette and the little town of Kenilworth with all its unbeliev-ably beautiful lakefront houses and mansions and estates. Some of them were enough to make your eyes bug out, honest to God they were! But at least we fit right in thanks to Big Ed's Caddy....

Speaking of Big Ed's Caddy, it was starting to run a little low on gas and Sheridan Road was obviously not the sort of place you might expect to find a gas station. So I turned left on a street named Winnetka Avenue to try and find a sta-tion and we passed by what looked like maybe another decent-sized college or university. Only it wasn't. It was a blessed high school! New Trier High School, to be exact, which had separate athletic fields for the boys and the girls and a sep-arate, three-story music building and even a separate industrial arts building with a fully equipped car shop inside! I couldn't imagine what it might be like to go to a high school like that. But I sure hoped one day I could send little Vincenzo and even littler Roberta to a place like that!

We found not one but three gas stations all ganged up against one another at the corner of Winnetka Avenue and Green Bay Road—a Texaco, a Standard and a Sinclair—and of course I was tempted to pick the Sinclair on general principles, but I was kind of taken by the neatly-kept brick Standard station with two clean serv-ice bays and the cars waiting for work to be done or to be picked up all lined up along a nice white fence on the edge of the property with the station tow truck/snowplow and matching red Jeep runabout parked right next to them. You can always tell when somebody really cares about their station. And that's why—God help me—I bought gas for Big Ed's Caddy at the Standard. Don't tell anybody.

The guy who came out to pump our gas had a nice if weary smile and the name "Bud" embroidered on his gray shop shirt, and you could see from his hands that he'd been deep inside cars every day of his life for a very long time. But he took time out to clean our windshield and check the oil and water and the air in the tires and even made a few faces at little Vincent in the back seat. He also noticed the Jersey plates and asked where we were going—it didn't seem out of the ordinary to him at all that a young family such as ourselves might be tooling around in a brand new Cadillac, but that just tells you something about the sur-rounding neighborhood—and he suggested we could make better time heading west and picking up the new Route 41 Edens Superhighway towards Wisconsin. "I dunno," I told him. "The wife kind of wanted to look at some of those nice homes you have along the shoreline up here." I looked around to make sure Julie was still off in the ladies' room with the baby. "We're thinking we might be mov-ing here one day."

"It's a nice place to live," the guy said without batting an eye.

It made me feel pretty damn good that he took me seriously, you know?

We took a nice, leisurely ride along the lake shore almost all the way up to Milwaukee, but, thanks to that damn prize rooster living just outside Fort Wayne, were still right on time picking Big Ed up at Mitchell Field in Milwaukee.

Although it helped that his plane was an hour late, and that gave us time to read the news clippings and the captions on all the pictures they had up on the walls there, which were all about General Billy Mitchell, who was head of the Army Signal Corps and helped start up the American Expeditionary Force in World War One. Turns out he was maybe the first American to realize that an airplane might be of some military use beyond simple scouting missions, and that Navy ships, in particular, were vulnerable to air attack. He begged the top brass to let him demonstrate, and so they set a captured German ship out in a bay someplace and damn if one of Mitchell's airplanes didn't sink it! He also warned them over and over that the Japs and the Germans and everybody else in creation would be building fighters and bombers as fast as they could put them together, and what America really needed was an Air Force. But that didn't sit real well with the old guard at the Army and Navy, and he got court-martialed for insubordination for his trouble. Which I guess is sort of an occupational hazard for independent thinkers in the military. He died in 1936—right around the time World War Two was brewing and everything he envisioned came to pass—and it's too bad he wasn't around to say, *"I told you so!"* But at least he turned into a hero again, and he's got planes and airports and stuff named after him to prove it.

Big Ed's plane arrived about a quarter-to-eight, and he looked pretty happy with himself in spite of the delay and was of course thrilled to see the kids—he always was—and naturally had them all riled up and squealing within seconds. He couldn't help himself around them, you know? And it made you just a little sad that he never had kids of his own. But of course it's always easier on the grandparent/godfather end, where all you have to do is come dashing in with presents and sugar sweets and an assortment of funny faces—sort of like a P-51 Mustang coming in for a low strafing run—and then beat it for Parts Unknown once you've got the kids spoiled rotten and thoroughly overfed, overstimulated and stirred up to the fever pitch that always bleeds down into that sullen, cranky, *"I HATE IT!"* or *"I DON'T WANT IT!"* or even *"FUCKSHITPISS!"* frame of mind that only the actual parents ever see.

Fortunately it was just over two hours from Mitchell Field to Elkhart Lake, and along the way, between making faces and goobly-goobly noises at little Roberta and tickling little Vincent until he threw up, Big Ed told us that the deal had gone through for the property behind the station and he had the right connections with the zoning board (or at least he had connections with certain people who had the right connections) to get that part of it handled and that he'd just that very morning signed the deal with the Volkswagen distributor. "As of December first," he beamed, lighting up a fresh cigar, "you an' me are in the car business!"

"Really?" I gasped.

"Really?" Julie choked.

"Yes sir!" he chuckled excitedly. "Everything's signed, sealed and delivered!' He took a deep, satisfied drag off his cigar and blew out a thick cloud of smoke that turned both the kids' faces green. Julie's too, for that matter.

"That's great news," I told him.

"Oh, there's plenty t' do yet," he told us. "We gotta tear the rest of that damn building down and build us a showroom an' enlarge the shop. Oh, an' there's a bunch of papers you gotta sign, too." His eyes found mine in the rearview mirror. "I'm makin' you a full partner in this deal, Buddy. Right down the line."

I didn't know what to say.

"If I was you, I'd get your own lawyer to kind of look things over."

"Your lawyer's good enough for me," I told him.

"Buddy," he said, leaning forward from the back seat and clapping a ham-sized palm on my shoulder, "y'gotta not be so trusting of people now. You gotta watch out for yourself an' yer family. Y'gotta be *careful,* see. We're goin' inta' a business where people come in with a chip on their shoulders an' don't wanna leave until they get both ears an' the tail. Where people think yer lyin' to 'em even when yer tellin' 'em the lilywhite truth. There's people out there willin' to steal the pennies off a dead man's eyes, an' you're gonna hafta' meet an' deal with every stinking, rat-bastard one of them."

"You make it sound awful," Julie said.

"*Sure* it's awful!" Big Ed beamed. "But that's the fun of it. That's the challenge. Making *deals,* see? Every day you're *making deals!"*

He made it sound like a blessed dessert buffet.

"Uh, aren't I supposed t'be running the service part of it? The nuts and bolts?"

"*Sure* you are!" Big Ed agreed. "But y'gotta learn the other stuff, too. If it's your business, y'gotta know it from top t'bottom, see? And y'gotta watch people or they'll take advantage of you an' steal you blind...."

Julie flashed me the old *see-I-told-you-so* fish eye.

"...an' y'gotta start by havin' some legal asshole look over the papers. Somebody who works fer *you,* not *me.* Just t'make sure yer interests are covered, see?"

"O-okay," I told him uncertainly. I looked over at Julie and down at little Roberta asleep on her breast and then I found Big Ed's eyes again in the rearview mirror. "So, uhh, when it comes to all this lawyer stuff..."

"Yeah?"

"D'ya *know* anybody...."

32: Road America

We rolled into Elkhart Lake a little after nine, and it was exciting all over again to see all the sports cars parked nose-to-tail under the streetlamps on Lake Street where it curved around past Siebkens and Schwartz's and The Osthoff and the stairway down to the beach that Sally Enderle and me went down together in the lost, strange middle of a Saturday night that seemed like a whole lifetime ago. I found a place to park behind Siebkens and opened the door to unload and Julie looked at me with narrowed eyes when the little interior light came on. "You look like you're blushing," she said in a voice with danger signs hung all over it.

"Nah, it's just sunburn," I told her.

"Sunburn? From where?"

"From the park," I told her. "Lincoln Park."

"Well, wherever it came from..." she continued in that same dangerously-inquisitive tone, "it's getting redder...."

Boy, I couldn't hide anything from her!

To tell the truth, it was a little scary.

Anyhow, Big Ed got us registered and gave us the room in the second floor of the second building—furthest from the noise and hoopla at the bar—and wouldn't you know it had a swell view out over the lawn and trees to the west side of The Osthoff building and, in fact, right into the window of the very room where Sally Enderle and I wound up that other time I was in Elkhart Lake. Which meant I might be having myself a lot of those sunburn attacks during my stay there with Julie and the kids. But I could tell Julie really liked the place, what with the soft, puffy comforter and the matching flower print curtains and the antique maple headboard and dresser with the tall china flower pot on top plus the big, slowly-rotating ceiling fan to keep the cool, pleasant air off the lake circulating. Not to mention drowning out the occasional hoots and peals of laughter from the lawn and gazebo outside the bar. And, speaking of the bar, I was already itching to get over there and see all my racing friends and catch up on all the latest lies and gossip. Only I'd promised Julie I'd be good, you know? Especially with the kids along. So I made a big deal of bringing absolutely everything up from the car and folding all the clothes away in drawers and unfolding the baby buggy and setting it down at the bottom of the stairs so it was all ready for a stroll and even putting all the soap and shampoo away in the little medicine cabinet in the bathroom. And I did it all real quiet on little cat's feet while Julie fed the baby and read a story out of a Golden Book to little Vincent while his eyelids slowly lowered.

And then I just kind of stood there under that slowly-rotating ceiling fan like a damn straw scarecrow, waiting for something to happen.

"You want to go to the bar, don't you?" Julie whispered as little Vincent laid his head down on her lap.

"Just to see the guys and find out what's going on tomorrow," I told her.

"Hmpf," she snorted softly. "And maybe have a few drinks?"

"Just one," I promised like a little kid. "Honest. Just one."

She gave her head a disgusted quarter-inch shake. "And what will you do if you don't go to the bar?"

"If I don't go to the bar?"

"Will you stand there like a rocket ready to go off all night?"

I guess I was maybe looking a little anxious.

"Ahh, go ahead," she said glumly. "I don't know why I expected anything different."

"That's okay, Honey," I told her in a cheaply-rented voice, "I'll stay here with you."

She gave me the old eyeballs again. "Go on," she sighed.

"No, really," the voice lied to her.

"Buddy," she said, looking up at me, "you are an absolutely terrible liar. Now get the hell out of here."

"Are you *sure?*" the voice asked.

Her eyes rolled and I knew it was time to head for the door. And take that damn stupid voice with me. "Just don't come back drunk or I promise this will be the worst race weekend you ever had," I heard her say as the door closed behind me.

Well, everybody and his brother was drinking their fill at Siebkens' bar that night, and I right away made out Big Ed and Tommy Edwards with Ernesto Julio between them up at the bar and Cal Carrington talking with Denny Eade from the Cunningham crew over at one of the tables with a pitcher of beer between them and "Fos" and Danny Poindexter up in the little screened porch nook a few steps up and off to the side of the main barroom and the scrumptious Sally Enderle in one of her best and most revealing midriff outfits surrounded by a gaggle of admirers and an uneven line of drinks on the bar that they'd obviously bought for her. She actually seemed to notice me and gave me a little wave when I came in. I noticed Creighton Pendleton was nowhere to be seen.

It was hard to know where to start first.

So I went over and sat down with Cal and Denny Eade to make sure that the rig and the Trashwagon and all of our other guys had got there all right—they had—and Denny got me a mug and filled it up with beer and we talked a little bit about the fallout after Le Mans. John Fitch was still over there running with the Mercedes team—or at least he was until the end of the season, anyway, since Mercedes was obviously on its way to another Grand Prix championship with Fangio and they'd done well with the sports cars, too, and so there were rumors that they were going to pull out at the end of the year—and it seems Phil Walters simply decided to pack it in after what he witnessed at Le Mans. "His heart just wasn't in it anymore," Denny explained. And it was easy to understand why.

"So what're you guys running up here?" I asked him.

"Well, we've got the C-6R, of course. Briggs is planning t'run that himself. But none of us figure that project is goin' much of anywhere. It's the engine mostly. But, hell, the D-Type he bought off-the-shelf from Jaguar is a better racecar. That's all there is to it. And it cost him a hell of a lot less, to boot."

"Well, if Briggs is in the C-6R and John is off in Europe and Phil has packed it in, who's driving the D-Type up here?"

Denny rolled his eyes up towards the ceiling. "His Majesty Creighton Pendleton, of course!"

"You're *kidding!*"

Denny shook his head. "Oh, he's a good 'shoe. I'll give him that. And he's pretty decent at taking care of the car. But the way he struts around..." Denny couldn't help chuckling, "...I'm surprised he doesn't scrape his nose on the rafters!"

Well, that was bad news for Cal and the Trashwagon, and we both knew it. In even-up cars, I figured Cal could beat Creighton Pendleton nine-and-a-half times out of ten. But no question that new D-Type—and especially one looked after by the crack Cunningham crew—was going to be the car to beat here at Elkhart.

Denny went to pour me another beer, but I stopped him. Well, I stopped him after he got the glass about three-quarters full, anyway. "How're things goin' for you after Le Mans?" I asked him. I mean, that race changed everybody who was there. Plus a lot of people who weren't.

"Ahh, I dunno," Denny allowed. "I guess I've lost some taste for it. Just like everybody else. That stuff over there is just too damn serious and far away from home. You get burned out."

"You thought any about quitting and trying something else?"

"What else is there to do?" Denny shrugged. "I can't see myself going back to putting brakes and mufflers on Fords and Chevys."

And right away I could feel the old wheels turning inside my head. What with the new dealership and all, I was really gonna need somebody to look after my racers and go to the weekends with them when I couldn't. And it had to be somebody who knew the ropes and knew how to take care of things. "You any good at holding hands?" I asked him.

"Hell," he laughed, "except for tightening a few nuts and bolts, that's all I do!"

I made a note to talk to him more about it later in the weekend. I'd already learned from Big Ed that you have to be just a little bit cagey about deciding exactly what you want and exactly what you're willing to offer before you start shooting your mouth off over a few rounds of beer. Not that bars aren't great places for making deals. Hell, most all of the great racing plans and projects in the whole blessed world of motorsports get themselves sketched out first on a set of cocktail napkins. But, like I said, when it comes to a job offer, you've gotta know what you're after and what you're willing to give or it's just so much aimless conversation.

I went up to the bar to buy another pitcher for the table and say "hi" to Tommy and Big Ed and Ernesto Julio, and naturally I had not one but *three* gin-and-tonics lined up in front of me before I so much as opened my mouth. Ernesto Julio looked great as always with that mane of silvery-white hair and one of those open-front silk pirate shirts of his with plenty of tan skin and curly chest hair showing behind it. Exactly like the one I borrowed from him that other night at Elkhart Lake back in '52. "I see you've got my shirt on again," I grinned at him.

He gave me an insider sneer. "I will never lend you clothing again," he assured me through a dangerous smile. And then he turned to Big Ed and Tommy Edwards and whispered like I couldn't hear. *"He returned it full of sand. And ripped as well..."* he leaned in even closer and whispered even louder, *"...and reeking of expensive perfume...."* His eyes ran down the bar and landed smack-dab on Sally Enderle. I felt the color rising on my face and took a long draw on my first gin-and-tonic to cool it down.

"So," I asked, trying to change the subject, "what'd you bring this weekend?"

"The same old Ferrari," he said like he was talking about a Studebaker with bald tires.

"And who's driving for you? Phil Hill?"

"Phil is in Europe," Ernesto said with quiet pride. "I've managed to arrange a test for him—along with Carlo Sebastian's help, of course—for the Ferrari factory team." He cocked his head slightly. "I think he could be the first great American champion in Europe."

"He's got the talent," I agreed while looking at Cal Carrington's reflection in the mirror behind the bar. "I can think of a couple Americans who might have the talent."

Ernesto's eyes opened a little wider. "Not too many, I am sure."

"One or two," I told him. "One or two."

"Like who?"

"Oh," I hemmed and hawed for a moment, "that guy over there." Ernesto Julio's eyes followed mine to Cal Carrington. "You ever seen him drive?"

Ernesto Julio thought for a moment and then a look of recognition snapped across his face. "Of course! At Sebring!" He leaned in a little closer and whispered, "He did a magnificent job there. But has he ever driven *big* cars?"

"He will this weekend," I told him, and explained all about Cal's ride in the Trashwagon. But I was careful to make plenty of excuses for the car while I was doing it. Sure, it was mine and I wanted to see what it could do, but there was no way I could delude myself into thinking it would run heads-up with Ernesto's Ferrari Monza or Cunningham's D-Type Jag. "By the way, who's running your car if Phil Hill is over in Europe."

"I'm importing a driver," he said like he was talking about a brick of rare cheese. "I've come to admire the skills of the Frenchman Jean Behra very much, and we made a deal over the phone for him to come and run my car here at Elkhart."

"That's a heck of a choice," I told him. And I meant it. After all, I'd seen what that guy could do firsthand during his incredible drive to the front of the field on the early stages of *La Carrera* at the wheel of the lightweight little Gordini. And I knew the stories about how he'd been a middleweight prizefighter and a motorcycle champion many times over before he ever started racing automobiles. And also that Hank Lyons always said he was one of those guys who lived in that scary, skinny overlap between genius and madness when it came to what he could get away with in the cockpit of a racing car.

"Do you want another drink?" Ernesto asked me.

And that's when I noticed the three empty tumblers with nothing but ice and lime wedges in them lined up in front of me and decided I sure as hell better get back to the room!

There was no light showing under the door or sound other than the oscillating hum of the ceiling fan coming from our room, so I carefully switched off the hall light and was extra quiet with the key in the latch and swung the door open maybe an inch at a time to keep it from creaking. Julie and the kids were on the bed, sleeping soundly, and so I whispered a *"Thank you, God"* under my breath, tiptoed into the room, closed the door gently behind me, took off my clothes without so much as dropping a sock or jingling my belt buckle, and got ready to climb into bed. But that's about when my bladder advised me that I maybe ought to let a little of the beer and gin-and-tonic out before I sneaked into bed or I'd just have to get up again a few minutes later. And so I crept over to the bathroom, eased through the door, gently closed it behind me....

...and that's when I heard the damn latch click and realized I'd gone through the wrong damn door and that now I was out in the hall again! Stark naked! And with the door locked behind me! At least the blessed light was off. But then it got worse, as I heard voices coming across the patio downstairs. Jesus, they'd be coming up the staircase soon! Well, there was nothing to do but take a deep breath, square my shoulders, mutter a quick prayer to every saint whose name I could remember and rap lightly on the door.

Jesus! The voices below were getting closer and I heard the screen door slam behind them....

I rapped a little louder.

My God, they were coming up the stairs!

I banged furiously on the door and then, finally, I heard the latch click and it swung open and there was Julie, standing there in her robe, eyes half-closed, looking at me stark naked out there in the hallway like it was maybe some horribly bad dream.

"I can explain!" I told her in a voice several octaves above my own.

She looked at me from head to toe and then stared into my eyes—reading them—and finally just snorted, "Don't bother." Then she let out a long, heavy sigh and shook her head disgustedly. "Just come inside and go to bed."

Practice started bright and early on Friday morning, and I went with Cal in Big Ed's pickup and left Julie and the kids back at the hotel so's they could sleep in a little and maybe go down to the beach and relax. Not that you can do a whole lot of relaxing when you've got two little kids tugging you in four different directions at once. But it's the thought that counts, right? Anyhow, we drove south out of Elkhart on Route 67, with a railroad track running kind of parallel to us on our right and marshy ditches filled with water on both sides of the road. A signpost identified them as La Budde Creek, but it still looked like two marshy ditches filled with water to me. Then 67 took a long, sweeping, climbing curve to the left and we were headed up a steep hill with a heavy forest on our right and then, right at the top, we hit a clearing and found ourselves at the entrance gate to Road America. There was a quaint old farmhouse there that was used as the administration building and I signed in and got my credentials—Cal and the guys had already gotten the cars through tech at the County Highway Garage in Elkhart Lake the day before—and then Cal drove us out and around on an access road and across a little covered bridge into the infield. "Where's the track?" I asked him.

"It's under us right now!" he grinned.

So we stopped and got out and sure enough I could see the track carving up out of a right- hander at the bottom of a deep, wooded valley a ways downhill from us, climbing up to a sweeping left-hander under the bridge we were standing on, and then flattening out into a hard right-hander and then an incredibly steep climb up yet another hill and out of sight. And that was just one little section of it! Why, the scale of it was absolutely breathtaking! And I wasn't the only one who thought so. In fact, just about everybody who'd made the long trek to Elkhart Lake and the new, purpose-built road racing circuit at Road America quickly agreed that it was the best damn track in the country. By far. And it made you pretty damn proud that a group of enthusiasts and local bankers and businessmen and, yes, SCMA club racer types somehow managed to pull this off: a full four miles of ribbony black asphalt just made for racing, and better yet snaking across more than 500 acres of meadows and forests and steep hills and deep, wooded valleys. Four miles that went absolutely nowhere. Except straight into the hearts of all the racers who drove there.

A guy named Clif Tufte was given most of the credit for making it all happen. He pushed the project along and twisted all the arms that needed twisting and even went out poking around those 520 acres of woods and fields and steep, stony kettle moraines that ice-age glaciers had gouged into the landscape a million kazillion years ago and figured out where the blessed track ought to go. But almost as important were the locals who pledged to buy stock and the state senator from nearby Kiel who thought it was a good idea and would bring a lot of tourists and greenbacks to the region and the rich racers from the Chicago and Milwaukee regions who were always ready to help out and use their family connections and even, if absolutely necessary, turn their own pockets inside out. Not to mention the construction guys who built the wooden "pagoda" building in the paddock for the race officials or the gravel guys who ran the road graders that carved the circuit out of the landscape and especially the paving crew that covered that crushed gravel underbase with a thick, even coating of hot-mix asphalt that was smooth as a baby's bottom and yet tough enough to take the punishment of sticky tires and powerful engines tearing away at it all day long under a hot summer sun.

Cal came in from his first practice run in the Trashwagon with a huge smile plastered across his face. "This place is *incredible!*" he gushed.

"How's the car?" I asked him.

"Well, it's a little on the twitchy side and we're about out of brakes," he said like he was ordering an egg salad sandwich, "but I'd drive a damn wheelbarrow around this place!"

I took the brakes apart and put some relined shoes in and cut as many holes as I dared in the backing plates and borrowed a big drill bit and drilled as many holes as I dared in the drums and told Cal to bed the shoes in a little around the paddock and then give it another try.

And of course meanwhile I had all my other guys to look after—they were all coming in with big eyes and awed smiles hanging open under their noses and complaints about fading brakes—and you could tell Big Ed was getting itchy about taking a few laps himself. And who could blame him? But then Carson decided he maybe really didn't want to race here so much (I guess he gave himself a bit of a fright at some corner out on the backside of the course that everybody was talking about called "The Kink") and he offered Cal the drive in his Healey and so Cal said it would be fine with him if Big Ed took a few laps in the Trashwagon. Just to see what it was like, you know?

Big Ed came back in with the same glassed-over look in his eyes as everybody else. "This makes Thompson look like a damn driveway!" he gushed. "And you can really use all the power this baby has at a place like this." According to my stopwatch, Big Ed was a full ten seconds a lap slower than Cal had been in the car, and I sure hoped he wouldn't have second thoughts about letting Cal drive. I mean, I really wanted to see—just once—what my baby could do....

I was pretty busy taking care of all the cars and bleeding brakes and everything, but I did notice that Ernesto Julio's gorgeous, eye-gouge yellow Ferrari Monza was just kind of sitting there and hadn't turned a wheel all day. I saw him strolling by and asked him what was up. "Oh," he said kind of disgustedly, "it seems my driver got socked in at Orly Field and hasn't been able to get out of France."

"More likely he got socked in under a skirt someplace in Momartre," Tommy Edwards whispered to me over a beer after the Friday practice sessions were over. Tommy was driving yet another Allard for some guy out of Minneapolis, and, although he was enjoying the power of the big V8 charging up the steep hills out of the second-gear nineties, he was finding the car a bit of a handful through the sweeping, climbing and diving sections of the circuit.

"Why do you keep driving those things?" Cal asked him.

"People bloody keep offering them to me," Tommy shrugged. "It's like having a rare disease or blood type or something."

We got a pretty good laugh off of that.

"You guys want to take a walk around the track?" Cal asked.

"It'll be dark soon," Tommy cautioned.

"There's a moon."

"You'll miss dinner." The SCMA already had a bunch of grills going with bratwursts and burgers and sweet corn in its husks spread out all over them. The smell was fantastic.

"I won't starve." Cal looked at me. "Howabout you, mister Master Mechanic?"

"Sure," I said. "Why not?"

So we took off just as the sun eased down towards the treetops, walking past the pagoda building where some of the timing and scoring people were still fussing over the Friday practice times—Creighton Pendleton in Briggs Cunningham's Jaguar D-Type looked to pretty much have the legs on the rest of the "big car" field—and out onto the circuit and the long, gently rising and then falling stretch of straightaway towards Turn One. There was thick forest on both sides of us (although thankfully well back from the track) and, as the voices and shouts from the paddock dissolved behind us, it got really quiet and all we could hear was a few random bird calls and the scamper and rustle of squirrels and chipmunks in the underbrush and the sound of our own shoe leather against the pavement. As we got closer to Turn One, I could see it was a *very* fast corner. "You really come flying into here," Cal explained like he knew what I was thinking, "and the trick is to maybe not brake real late and hard and overslow the car but to kind of roll the brakes on gently just to get rid of a little speed and settle the nose and then roll right back onto the power to stabilize the car as soon as you turn the wheel and sweep into the corner. I was going down into third here in the Trashwagon, but the car's kind of bound up like that and maybe next time I'll try fourth. For sure it's top gear in the Healey. I just flick it down out of overdrive." Cal pointed over to the end of the corner. "There's a little gravel over there on the edge you can use if you need to, but it makes the car kind of unhappy...."

It was amazing to me how clearly Cal saw things and all the details he'd picked up. I think a lot of race driving is just the ability to process an awful lot of information in a short period of time. That and a magic ass that can feel what a car is doing. But if your mind's fast like that, it makes whatever's happening feel like it's happening slower. Or, as Cal always put it: *"Fast is Slow and Slow is Fast."* When I'd ask him what he meant by that, he'd explain, "if everything feels like it's happening real fast and the corners and braking zones are rushing up at you like runaway trains, you're *slow*. But if everything seems to be happening real slow and evenly and you've got all this time to see and consider things and react real smoothly—like a damn Strauss waltz, you know?— that's when you're setting lap records."

Anyhow, out of Turn One the circuit plunges downhill and curves slightly to the right into the next corner at Station Three. "This is really a straightaway here," Cal told me, "and the important thing is setting the car up for a real good launch out of three. You're braking on a downhill and kind of easing the car over to where the left-hand side of the road comes up to meet you…" I could see it in my mind, "…and the trick again is to gather the car up and be on the power real early—even before you clip the apex—to get your maximum charge onto the straight. But you have to be careful because the road kind of rises and catches you going into the corner but then flattens out at the end, so the car kind of skates. You can just listen and know who's doing it right. If you hear them lift off at the end of the corner, they came in too fast or too shallow. And that lift'll follow them like a bad smell all the way down the straightaway to Station Five."

"It will?"

"Absolutely," Cal nodded. "Going onto a long straightaway like this one, the name of the game is exit speed. That's where all your momentum comes from. You can't do it just with horsepower and a heavy right foot."

It was a long, long walk from Station Three to Station Five, across a wide-open meadow with the first part of the sunset all over it like poured brass and gold and then, almost a half mile away, into the shadow of another thick forest as the track came to yet another crest and dropped downhill to the deceptive, 90-degree left-hander at Station Five. "This ones a little fooler," Cal told me, "but mostly because you just have too damn much time to think about it. All the way down that straightaway, you're making plans about just exactly how you're going to tackle Turn Five. So it's hard to have any rhythm left when you finally get there."

"But how *do* you take it?" I asked him.

"Well, I guess you want to crest the hill a little to the right of center and then let the track come back to meet you as you brake in a straight line and get set up for the corner. It's really the same deal as the last one, only slower. You've got a steep hill up ahead and a long straightaway behind you, so you need to balance braking as late as possible so you can keep your foot in it as long as you can with getting a good charge up the hill. I guess the real key is not stuffing it in too hard and getting the power on early. And this is absolutely the best overtaking spot on the whole damn racetrack. Hell, it may be the best overtaking spot in the whole damn universe!"

"Is it a good place to watch?"

"The best," Cal assured me.

Out of Five we climbed a *very* steep hill to where the track disappeared under another one of those crossover bridges. And then almost immediately flattened out and swept through a falling-away left-hander with thick forest around the outside. "This is Six, and it's another tricky one," Cal told me, "because it pops up at you like a damn jack-in-the-box. And your gut reaction is to start turning as soon as you see it. I mean, it *startles* you...."

"But you shouldn't?"

"Nah, you got to wait for it just a little. To make a nice, clean arc out of it. You brake just before the bridge—easy, not hammering on them!—and then wait for just a heartbeat before you sweep the car in and around. Power-on again almost as soon as you turn the wheel. If you do it just right, you come out of the corner kind of already angled across towards the opposite side of the road. And that's exactly where you want to be."

Out of Six the road dropped gently and disappeared to the right around a hill. "I gotta tell you," Cal told me, "most of this track is straightforward right- and left-hand nineties, with just some nice scenery and elevation changes to make it interesting. But there are also," he stopped walking for a moment and looked me in the eye, "three or four places that separate the *real* racers from the ribbon clerks. And this is the first of them."

"What is it?"

"They call it 'Hurry Downs,' and it's nothing more than a little downhill sweeper to the right. But you enter it blind and it looks much tighter than it is. And then the road falls away just a little at the outside edge."

"And that makes it difficult?"

"That and the fact that it's blind and you're going so damn fast. All the really quick guys'll keep their right feet planted here and accelerate all the way down to the next corner. Or at least the ones in the smaller cars will."

"How about the guys in the really *fast* cars?"

"Well, let's just say that's one of those decisions you have to try and make for yourself every single lap. I could go through here flat in top in Carson's Healey and then click into top overdrive for a bit before the next corner, but I was pedaling out of it pretty much in the Trashwagon."

"Handling?"

"No. Fear."

Out of Hurry Downs the track continued dropping downhill to the sharp left-hander at Station Eight. "The braking zone's downhill, but then it flattens out at the bottom and kind of catches you. This is another one of those textbook nineties where you want to use all the road and be smooth in and out and get on the power early but not have to lift off at the end to get set up for long run through the toughest part of the track. This is probably the slowest corner on the circuit, but it's also one of the most important."

We could feel the last of the sunset on our backs as we walked away from it towards the entrance to the Road America Carousel. "This is a hell of a corner," Cal grinned. "It just goes on and on forever, falling away endlessly to the right. You can't really size it up too well from the top, but then you find yourself kind of skating down into it. There's forest right up to the edge of the pavement all the way down on the outside—with just that little row of haybales in front of it, see?—and that keeps a lot of guys out of the loud pedal." Cal shot me a sly, ever-so-slightly evil grin. "But it's really *fast* down through here! Top gear in the Healey easy, and top gear with a handful or two of brave pills in the Trashwagon."

I could hardly imagine.

"And you can *pass* people through here. Especially around the outside, since a lot of them hug the inside edge for dear life just to stay away from the damn forest!"

To be honest, it looked pretty daunting the way the road curled down and around to the right like it was drooling off the side of a mountain. Especially with that stand of forest waiting for you on the outside edge. But it was also about as beautiful and sexy a stretch of asphalt as you'd find anywhere.

"The trick is setting up for the exit down at the bottom," Cal continued. "The road flattens out again and you're really flying, and you've got to take that nice, wide, smooth sweep across the final apex there where the little divot is. And God help you and your seat upholstery if you drop a wheel off in the gravel on the outside."

"It sounds scary as hell," I told him.

"You want to see *scary,*" Cal laughed, "just look up ahead!"

It was coming on dusk now, and we were deep down in a sort of gully, running right along the bottom with a big mound of gravel and thick forest off to our left and this sort of steep valley wall with brush and scrub foliage all over it on our right. And up ahead, the road swept to the right and disappeared behind the valley wall. Which meant you were staring straight into a dense, dark forest dead ahead. And what looked like just a few feet off the pavement, too. "It looks like a pretty sharp turn, doesn't it?" Cal said with a hollow ring of respect in his voice.

"Maybe third gear?" I guessed.

He swiveled his eyes over to mine. The look in them was like cold fire. "It's damn near flat in top in the Healey."

"You're *joking!*"

Cal shook his head. "And I'm talking top overdrive, too...."

I let out a low whistle. "It's got to be like threading a damn needle at that kind of speed."

"It sure is," Cal said respectfully. "The hard part is how blind and deceptive it is. You come out of the Carousel in top in the Healey, flick it up into overdrive, come flying down to this blind kink in the road, hit the brakes, drop it down a gear..." he gave a disrespectful little grunt, "...and then discover you've got all this road left on the way out. So the next time you maybe don't brake quite as hard and leave it in top—just blip it down out of overdrive—and it scares you to death. But damn if you still haven't got some track left on the way out."

"Wow."

"So you keep working on it and working on it. And the corner tries to sucker you in, too. The faster you go here, the more tempted you are to turn in early. Just to get away from all that forest out there. But God help you if you do."

"What happens then?"

"Oh, I suppose you drop a wheel off and then you try to catch it. But it's like Indianapolis. You just can't drive on opposite lock and quick reactions at that sort of speed."

"So?"

"Oh, the wheels probably bite in while you're all catty-wumpus sideways and then you shoot across into the haybales and stuff on the inside and write the car off."

"Just like that?"

Cal nodded. "This is one of those places you gotta sort of screw yourself up for every single lap. You come charging down towards this kink and one side of your brain is saying *'I can take it flat,'* and the other side is wondering why you ever wanted to do this stuff in the first place."

"Even *you?*"

"Sure," Cal said like it was nothing. "You gotta be crazy not to be afraid. But it's standing up to that fear and not letting it rattle you that's really the best part about it." He stopped walking for a moment and looked at me. "I don't know how to describe it, but when you get it right, you just glide through here like a ballroom dancer on a marble floor. It's a pretty special sort of feeling."

I wondered what something like that might feel like. Inside, I mean. And I was pretty sure at that very instant that I'd never know. Nope, Cal was a different sort of creature from you and me. Not better or worse or more favored or less caring or just plain crazier. Only different. I had the racing bug because it was more interesting and exciting than everyday life. But for Cal, it lit him up from the inside out. It was like an addiction. And, like all addictions, it steamrollered over everything in its path make him want more....

He couldn't help it.

But it was neat the way it lit him up, and I've got to admit I was jealous of that. Not just of how good he was—and Jesus, was he ever!—but also of that strange, even scary electricity you could see in his eyes and hear in his voice when he talked about the driving.

"Anyhow," he said as we continued walking along the bottom of this deep, wooded gully with a cathedral arch of trees overhead, "what makes that kink even more special is that it links two really fast sections together..." I could see that, since the roadway through the bottom of the gully meandered gently left and then right, and was obviously flat out, "...so if you take it at the max, you carry that speed all the way down to the corner at Station Twelve. If you get it right, this is the fastest part of the track down here." Way up ahead, I could see where the road made one final, gentle bend to the right and then swept uphill in another right-hand ninety. "I was talking with Tommy, and we figure you can shave off damn near a second by taking The Kink flat out. Maybe even more."

"Really?"

Cal nodded. "Like I said, it separates the *real* racers from the ribbon clerks."

As we approached the corner at Station Twelve, Cal showed me how you started on the right and then angled over to the left so you were braking and downshifting in a straight line, and then how you kind of pitched the car and planted the gas to get a nice head of steam for the climb up the next hill. "The road kind of rises up to meet you and catches the car here. But then it sort of falls off on the very outside edge, so you have to be a little careful."

It was pretty much dark now as we climbed the hill towards the covered crossover bridge we'd taken into the paddock earlier in the day. Cal showed me how you exited 12 on the left side of the road and then kind of eased the car over to the right as the road curved left to set up for the bridge turn at Station Thirteen. "This is the other tough one I was telling you about. The road just disappears to the left underneath the bridge and you can't see where you're going. You can't even see the apex because it's hidden behind the bridge abutment."

The concrete walls supporting the bridge looked frighteningly solid to me.

"But this one's also pretty much flat out."

"It *is?*"

Cal nodded. "Or at least it is in the Healey, anyway. I gotta work on it a little more in the Trashwagon. It feels pretty skittish through here."

I imagined it would!

"The trick is you gotta sorta turn in blind and more or less aim for the bridge abutment...."

"Aim for the bridge abutment?" I asked incredulously.

"Oh, it's not so bad," Cal laughed. "You're sliding anyway and, by the time you get there, the bridge abutment is gone and here comes the apex around to meet you..." he pointed to a little divot dug into the dirt on the inside edge of the road, almost all the way out from under the bridge. "The road is still climbing and sort of catches you under the bridge, but then it flattens out again at the end and so the car wants to skate a little," Cal told me. "And you definitely don't want to get suckered in too early here, or you'll wind up off in the dirt and into the haybales over there." He pointed to a pile of haybales just past the exit of the corner where an access road that was also the escape road from Turn Five met the track surface.

We'd climbed all the way up out of the valley by now and there was another short little straightaway cutting across an open meadow to the last turn on the racetrack at Station Fourteen. "This is another textbook, late-apex ninety," Cal explained matter-of-factly. "But you can see the road drops away just a little in the braking zone. I don't think it pays to go in real deep here, because you've got the long start/finish straightaway going up the mother and father of all hills up ahead, and so what you really want to concentrate on is getting a good launch and exit speed."

"Exit speed, huh?"

Cal nodded. "You dive-bomb somebody here and you've got a pretty good chance of being re-passed going up the hill."

And he was sure right about the hill. It maybe wasn't quite as steep as the near-vertical climb from Station Five to Station Six, but it just went on and on and on. Or at least that's what it felt like to my feet and legs, anyway. Up ahead at the top the grade eased off some—but still climbing—and we could hear very faintly the sounds of all the racers and workers and track officials and hangers-on at the barbecue at the base of the wooden pagoda building on the start/ finish line. "Well," Cal said to me, "that's a lap of Road America."

I ran through it again in my mind. "It's really something, isn't it?" I couldn't believe that anything this huge and impressive and ambitious could get built just for road racing. Especially here in the United States, where most people figured a racetrack was either straight or oval or the Bonneville salt flats.

"It's fantastic," Cal agreed. "It's like the best damn country road you could ever imagine. Only with no fence posts or telephone poles or marker stones or ditches or road signs or bridges or railroad crossings or rural mailboxes to run into."

"It's not like there's nothing to hit," I reminded him.

"Yeah, but it's a hundred percent better than those old open-road tracks. Maybe two hundred percent." You should have seen the look in his eyes. "And it's a million times better than those flat, dumb airport tracks."

I had to agree with him there.

After our tour we went over and joined the other racers at the barbecue, but I knew it was getting late and that I'd better get back to Julie and the kids. Tommy Edwards agreed to give me a lift back in the Allard he was racing. "You sure?" I asked him. "I don't want to drag you away from the party…."

"No problem, Sport. It's just a quick run up the road." So I climbed into the Allard with Tommy and he fired it up—the big, rumbling V8 absolutely shattering the nighttime stillness—and we took off down the hill and across the covered bridge over the track at Station Thirteen and left out onto Higway 67 towards Elkhart Lake. And that's when I really noticed that the track was a lot like the local roads of the area, as 67 plummeted downhill and swept into a high speed right-hander that fed into a long, flat straightaway towards town. There were fireflies twinkling over the fields and a chorus of frogs croaking back and forth to each other from the twin, marshy ditches of La Budde Creek on either side.

"We took a walk around the track," I hollered to Tommy over the wind noise and the frogs and the bellow of the exhaust.

"What did you think?"

"It's pretty amazing, isn't it?"

"It is that," Tommy grinned appreciatively. "I love the bloody size and scale of it. And especially all the elevation changes."

"Cal says it's mostly a bunch of textbook, late-apex nineties."

"Sure it is," Tommy laughed. "Plus three bloody moments of abject terror every lap!"

"He said that, too…"

And right about then is when the cop car appeared out of nowhere behind us and the damn mars lights and siren came on.

"Oh, bloody hell," Tommy groaned, pulling the Allard over to the side and switching it off. I noticed it was really quiet except for the rustle of the wind through the reeds and the sound of the frogs and insects. I looked up and couldn't believe how big and clear the sky was or how many stars were out there winking down at me.

By this time the cop had climbed out of his cruiser and walked over by the Allard. He was obviously in no special hurry. "Do you know how fast you were going, sir?" the cop asked Tommy.

Tommy looked down the road and saw a 60mph speed limit sign. "I'd guess about sixty, officer," Tommy said politely.

"If you'd been going sixty, I wouldn't have pulled you over," the cop said gravely.

"I'm afraid the speedometer on this car is way over there," Tommy pointed to the speedo dial that was almost directly in front of me on the passenger side, "so it's sort of hard to read. It's a silly way to build a car, but that's the way Allard's always done it."

I could see right away that Tommy was wasting his time. I mean, one of the main reasons why the locals wanted the new racetrack was because of all the money it brought into the area. And deputies all over Sheboygan County had decided that they were going to do their level best to make sure as much of it as possible stayed behind when the racers left town.

"I clocked you at sixty-seven miles-per-hour," the cop said like he was solving the Hope Diamond case. "That's seven over." He obviously didn't think we could add or subtract, either. "I need to see your license."

Tommy pulled out his wallet and handed over his license. The cop took a flashlight off his belt and looked at it. "What the heck kind of license is this?"

"It's English," Tommy explained.

"What are you doing with an English driver's license," the cop asked suspiciously.

"I'm English," Tommy told him, now starting to sound just the least little bit annoyed.

"Hmm," the cop said, staring at the license and not knowing exactly what to do. "I think we're going to have to bring you into the station and have you post bond for this one."

"For seven bloody miles over?" Tommy asked incredulously.

The cop eyeballed him dangerously. "Have you been drinking, sir?"

I felt a quick, cold wind go through my gut. It must've passed all the way over from Tommy's side of the car, because he shut up in a hurry.

So we followed the cop back to the station house and he made Tommy do some stupid walk-the-line tests, but Tommy sailed right through them. And then he had him post a thirty-dollar cash bond—thirty damn dollars, can you believe it?—and checked out the Allard's registration and all of its road equipment before he let us go.

What a jerk!

Anyhow, it was damn near ten o'clock before we got back to Siebkens, and naturally Julie was madder than hell that I'd left her alone all that time with the kids. But she eased off just a little (and I mean *very* little) when I explained that I'd actually sort of been in jail rather than out carousing with my racing buddies. I mean, she could see I wasn't drunk. But I sure as heck was hungry. Come to think of it, I hadn't eaten anything since the sweet roll and orange juice I had for breakfast. "Did you guys eat anything?" I asked her.

"We went across and had some dinner at Schwartz's. I had to borrow the money from the front desk because you didn't leave me any...."

Oh, Jesus, this was no good.

"...I'm sure the dining room's closed by now."

"I can get myself a sandwich in the bar."

"Oh, *right!*" Julie snorted. Boy, there was a lot of frost in that room.

So I went down to the bar and ordered myself a roast beef sandwich with the idea that I'd just grab it and take it back to the room and try to make up with Julie a little. Why, I'd even bring her a slice of that swell German chocolate cake they kept by the sandwich board. And that's about when Cal came over and said: "I gotta talk to you." There was a funny look in his eyes.

"Sure. Talk away." I told him.

"Not here. Let's go outside."

"What's the big deal?" I asked as he led me through the screen door and out into the night. There were all sorts of sportycar people wandering around on the lawn and terrace and around the little gazebo, so he took me across the street and down the steps to the beach. I couldn't help that it reminded me of that night with Sally Enderle.

At the bottom of the steps he stopped, took a deep breath, and turned to face me. "I've got to tell you something," he said, his voice almost cracking on him.

"Jesus, what is it?"

He licked his lips. "I can't drive the Trashwagon for you."

It came like a shot from left field. It was the last thing I was expecting. "Whaddaya mean, you can't drive it?" I asked incredulously.

Cal's eyes dropped to the sand. "Jean Behra's not coming this weekend. He couldn't get over here or something. Ernesto Julio asked me if I wanted to drive his Ferrari...."

I instantly felt all these feelings swirling around inside me, but I was kind of numb at the same time. "Couldn't you drive for him some other time?" I asked weakly.

"I already told him I would."

Well, first off I was crushed. And then I thought about the major dose of shit I was going to take from Big Ed and I felt even worse. I mean, here I'd begged and pleaded and cajoled to get Cal this shot in the Trashwagon, and now here he was saying *'Adios'* and walking off into the sunset on account of he got a better ride someplace else. It plain and simple stunk, you know?

On the other hand, I'd done the whole thing—hell, I'd built the damn car, to be honest about it—in order to give Cal a chance to show what he had and what he could do, and no question he had a better shot at doing just that in Ernesto Julio's Ferrari. And then the last part was that I really and truly wanted to see what that car could do. I mean, I'd built it with my own two hands and we were coming to the end of its chance to do anything and I knew it. I'd really wanted and looked forward to this one opportunity to see it run to the max. And now here was my talented but addicted friend—who had just betrayed me!—standing there in front of me feeling about as lousy and miserable as a selfish, careless, thoughtless, occasionally cruel and always self-centered guy like Cal Carrington could ever feel. And the amazing thing is I felt sorry for him.

"You gotta do it," I finally told him. "You gotta take the opportunity."

I meant it, too.

And we shook on it.

So Cal went back up the stairs towards all the laughter and clinking glasses at Siebkens bar and I stood down there on the beach by myself for awhile, listening to the waves lapping in and watching the tiny pinpoint of the bow light on a little fishing boat hovering over the water way out by the weedbed where they went after walleyes at night. And I remember feeling older. Not older than anything or anybody in particular. Just older.

Later on I went back to the bar and picked up my sandwich and Julie's cake, but then I had to find Big Ed and tell him what had happened. It wasn't hard. He was right up front-and-center at the bar with Tommy Edwards and Ernesto Julio and a bunch of the other racer types. I tugged on his sleeve. "I gotta talk to you."

"Sure thing! Have a drink!" he boomed. He'd obviously had several already. "Pull up a slice of bar, Buddy." He clapped his arm around my shoulder. *"DOUG!"* he bellowed at the bartender, *"we need another drink over here!"*

"No, I really don't want one," I told him. "I gotta get back to the room."

"You don't *want* one?" he asked, kind of mock backing away from me.

I shook my head. "But I gotta tell you something." I swallowed and let him have it. "Cal's gonna drive Ernesto Julio's Ferrari."

"I know all about it," Big Ed shrugged.

Ernesto Julio leaned his silvery mane of hair over from two barstools down. "I ask Big Ed first," he said like it could never be any other way. "It could never be any other way."

"And you're not pissed?" I asked Big Ed.

"Hell, no. I'll drive the sonofabitch myself. That's what I really wanted t'do anyway."

"So it's okay?"

"Sure it's okay. In fact, it's better than okay. Here, lemme at least buy you a drink t'take back t'yer room." He bought me a double gin-and-tonic.

Back up in the room the kids were asleep and while I wolfed down my sandwich and Julie ate her German chocolate cake, I whispered the news about Cal and Big Ed and the Trashwagon and Ernesto Julio's Ferrari. I also noticed that most of the frost had more or less dissipated. Which was nice. Afterwards I took a hot shower and laid down with her in the darkness under that rotating ceiling fan and told her the rest, all about the racetrack and Tommy and my run-in with the local cops and also how pretty and peaceful it was down by the lake at night. "I took the kids down there today," she said dreamily. "You were right. This really is a beautiful place."

"I told you so."

"Somebody down there said there's a footpath all the way around the lake. I'd really love to walk it some day."

"All the way around?"

I felt her give a little shrug. "Why not. They said it's only about four miles."

It occurred to me that's exactly how far Cal and I had walked around Road America.

"Sure," I agreed. "We'll do it someday when the kids are a little bigger."

"Oh, and that's something else. Over across the street at Schwartz's they've got day camp and games for the kids. They break them up into age groups and keep them entertained so the parents can have a little time to themselves."

I could feel Julie's body next to me in the bed and I had to admit, that sounded like a very interesting proposition indeed. "Next time we come to Elkhart Lake, we can stay over there," I told her.

"It's better for families," she yawned, and nestled in a little closer. "There's more things to do."

"There's lots to do here, too."

"Yeah, sure" she snorted softly. "If you like drinking yourself stiff and talking about cars...."

It looked overcast and threatening the next morning so I left Julie and the kids at Siebkens again—only this time with a little breakfast money!—but I came back to get them at lunchtime. And naturally they weren't ready. But that goes without saying when you're talking about a mother with two little kids. So I kind of paced up and down and tried not to look overly agitated while Julie picked out the things she wanted little Vincenzo to wear and changed his diaper one more time and finished feeding the baby and had me fold the buggy up and put it in the trunk and oh, what about the umbrella and his rain hat and the suntan lotion and the bag with all the baby goodies in it? And then, when we were finally all packed into Big Ed's Cadillac—with the engine already running, fr'chrissake!—would I be a dear and run back up to the room for another pair of socks in case these got wet or dirty and his beach pail and shovel in case he wanted to play with them at the racetrack?

Sometimes it's like women have no sense of urgency at all.

In spite of everything, we managed to get back to the track in time to watch some of the afternoon races together from down at the greatest out-braking spot on the planet at Turn Five. Although it took a little explaining to get Julie to understand that "Turn Five" was really only the third corner on the track on account of they named the turns after the flag stations at Road America. "Well *that's* silly," she told me.

"It's not silly," I argued. "It's just confusing."

Anyhow, the first race for G Production (up to 1300ccs) cars was about half over when we finally got settled in, and it was pretty much a runaway for some guy with a suspiciously healthy-sounding "stock" MG being pursued at a distance by a large, strung-out herd of other MGs plus two lonely Volkswagen Beetles way at the back. But I didn't care. Big Ed and me were still going to sell a whole shitload of 'em. I was sure of it. And I was pleased to see that little Vincent actually seemed to be interested in the racecars going by for at least thirty-five or forty seconds before going on a major worm, ant and beetle hunt with his beach pail and shovel.

I had to run up into the paddock to check the fluids and tire pressures and make sure everything was okay with Carson's Healey that Cal was driving in the next race, but I got back down to Turn Five in time for the start. As per usual, Cal had all the other Healey Hundreds covered, but he just had no chance against the three fastest Mercedes 300SLs on a track with as many horsepower-sapping hills and straightaways as Road America. But it was a pretty exciting race anyway, what with the 300SL Gullwings of Paul O'Shea and Bud Seaverns dueling back and forth for the lead with yet another 300SL not too far behind and just sort of waiting for them to maybe take each other out. Compared to the "real racecar" 300SLRs I'd seen at Le Mans, the production versions looked awful heavy and clumsy and cumbersome around tight nineties like Turn Five. But you couldn't argue with their power steaming up the steep hill to Six and their drivers said they stayed nice and stable through those difficult, fast sweepers at Hurry Downs, The Kink, and the Bridge Turn where fast laps are really made at Road America. We had a moment of excitement when Paul O'Shea apparently overestimated his brakes and had to take the escape road, but he battled back to catch Seaverns and take the win by a whisker at the end. Like I said, there was no way Cal could keep up with those guys in the Healey, but he ran a strong if lonely fourth overall to take first place in the nonexistent "Healey Class" and actually finished ahead of two other 300SLs. A guy named Bob Goldich won the 2-liter production class in a Triumph TR2 after a nice drive, but he was way back in ninth overall.

The next race was for smallbore modified cars, and I really wanted to see the new two-liter Maserati that this Ted Boynton guy showed up with. Everybody in the paddock seemed to think it would run away and hide. But you could hear it was running ragged and so the race boiled down to Frank Bott and Briggs Cunningham in the *real* Maserati brothers' 1500cc OSCAs against a small squadron of Porsche 550s. There were only 16 cars in the field and that's not really enough to provide a decent show on a track the size of Road America. Oh, they battled back and forth at the start with one of the Porsches leading, but then he got passed by Bott's OSCA and then they seemed to get all strung out and the race kind of stabilized. Or got boring, depending on your point of view. Plus it was starting to spit rain and little Vincenzo was getting tired and cranky and little Roberta had maybe also been out too long and she was squalling, too. So I took one final peek at our spot in the paddock—just making sure my guys and our cars and everything were all set and ready for the big day on Sunday—and we packed it in and headed back to Siebkens before the last race even started. Can you believe it? But it was the F Production race for 1500cc cars and that meant Porsches and more Porsches, and, since 'Fos' didn't race and wasn't real interested in having Cal or somebody race his car for him, we really didn't have anybody to root for. Still, I hated to go because those cars are always real entertaining to watch. Especially when the track gets a little damp and there are Porsche People bragging rights at stake...

There was another big cookout at the track that night for the workers and entrants and officials, but we had an early dinner over in Siebkens' dining room—Just me and Julie and the kids—and it was amazingly calm and quiet in there. The food was good, too. Better than good, even. But it always seems like the air around Elkhart Lake makes you hungrier. And makes the food taste better, too. The cloud cover had passed on to the east and the rain had stopped, and so after dinner we went down to the beach and watched the last of the sunset together. You could see the sky was nice and clear over to the west with just some high, fluffy clouds all painted up orange and purple and crimson with the last of the sunlight, and for sure it was going to be a beautiful day on Sunday. I stood behind Julie with my arms around her while she was holding little Roberta and that great smell from her hair filled up my nostrils as we looked out over the lake without saying much of anything. Over by the water's edge, little Vincent poked a stick around in the sand and found himself a couple empty clamshells. Which he then tried to eat.

After it got dark and the stars started coming out we headed back to our room, and you could hear from the bar that the racers had returned from the party at the track. "It's really nice here," Julie said softly as we climbed the wooden stairway. "I'd love to come here again when there's no race going on."

Of course that had never occurred to me. You know, that people would actually come here just to enjoy the lake and the town and the peace and quiet without a race going on. It actually sounded a little suspicious to me.

We went to bed pretty early but of course I couldn't sleep with the noise of the racing crowd in the bar whispering in my ear like the little devil you see sitting on people's shoulders in cartoons, and so I finally and very quietly got up, slipped on my clothes, and headed for the door. I swear, I actually think I *heard* Julie's eye slide open. "Where do you think you're going?" she asked in a dangerously low whisper.

"Just out for, umm, some dessert," I whispered back.

"Is that the dessert with the rum sauce or the bourbon sauce?"

"No. Honest. I'll be right back."

She didn't look especially convinced.

"You want me to bring you anything back?"

I could sense her mulling it over. "A husband who doesn't stay out till all hours getting shitfaced drunk with his racing buddies would be nice...."

Ouch!

"...and maybe just a little tiny slice of that German chocolate cake if there's any left."

"You got it," I quickly agreed. And even went back over to the bed and gave her a little kiss before I headed down to the bar.

As always on a Saturday night at Siebkens when the races are in town, the place was packed to the rafters and full of the kind of noise that makes your eyes all hungry and the blood dance in your veins. I don't know what that excitement is, but you could make a million kazillion dollars if you could only figure out how to bottle it and sell it. And, speaking of bottles, I had one with Tommy and another with Denny Eade (and of course started planting a seed about him maybe coming to work for me and looking after my racers next season) and reminded Big Ed up at the bar to maybe stop knocking back the gin-and-tonics around midnight on account of he had a drivers' meeting at 8AM, morning practice and our big race the next afternoon. I guess he'd gotten into another minor skirmish with Skippy Welcher in the paddock when The Skipper backed out of a parking spot without looking and damn near ran over Big Ed's foot with his C-Type. "I'm gonna get that sonofabitch tomorrow," Big Ed snarled. "You just wait and see."

I didn't much like the look in Big Ed's eye, and so I quietly relieved him of two of the gin-and-tonics lined up on the bar in front of him. I mean, it was for his own good, you know?

And then I did the right thing and ordered two slices of cake from the sandwich bar and maybe a little nightcap to take back to the room, let my eyes take one more long, lingering sweep around the bar—geez, it was like a damn lodestone magnet trying to suck me in—and headed out the door. I was all the way across the parking area and around by the shrubbery on the side of our building when I heard somebody behind me. *"Buddy?"*

It was Sally Enderle's voice. No question about it.

I turned around.

She was standing there behind me in her stunning, midriff-baring best, and her lips seeming almost liquid in the dim, shadowy light from the low-watt bulb up on the porch.

"How're things goin'?" I asked her, just kind of making conversation. "How's Creighton?"

"How would I know?" she said like she didn't give much of a damn one way or the other. And then, without any warning at all, she pulled in real close to me. Why, she damn near crushed my chocolate cake! *"You remember that night we spent here together?"* she said all breathless and dramatic like people do in the movies.

"S-sure I remember it," I choked. "B-but that was th-then," I mumbled—Jeez, I could see right down her top! "I'm, umm, *married* now, see…."

"I know," she whispered like it didn't make any difference. *"But that doesn't mean you can't go for a little midnight swim with an old friend, does it?"*

I didn't know what to say. I mean, I knew she didn't give two shits about me—not really—and she was probably just doing this to make a little trouble and keep herself from getting too bored. I guess girls like her do stuff like that just to keep themselves amused. But gee whiz, there she was—all gorgeous and ready right in front of me!—and it didn't much matter that she was tempting me and egging me on just because she wanted to prove to herself that she could. And I've got to admit she was looking awfully good. Not to mention that Julie and me hadn't really gotten much back into the swing of things since little Roberta was born. In fact, I was even starting to question my own memory. I'd always remembered that other night with Sally as a pretty scummy experience. And yet now, looking down at her beautiful, upturned face and those other two beautiful, upturned things just below it, I wondered how that could possibly be….

"C'mon," she whispered, *"let's go for another swim."* She ran the tip of her tongue across the lobe of my ear and I felt the heat starting to rise below my belt buckle. *"Nobody has to know…."*

And that's when I realized that everybody and their brother would know. She'd see to it. This wasn't anything to do with romance. Hell, it wasn't even to do with basic humping in the sack. Nope, this was about toying with people and screwing up their lives just for the fun of it.

"I can't do it," I told her, and backed away.

"You can't *do* it?" she said incredulously. "You're turning me *down?"*

I nodded. "Even if nobody else knows, *I'll* know. And I don't want to know anything like that. It's just not worth it."

"This isn't worth it?" she said, kind of showing herself off a little. She was one gorgeous and sexy lump of poison, no question about it.

"Look," I told her, "you don't really like me. Not really. And it wasn't any good between us the other time."

"It *wasn't?"* she almost gasped.

And that's when, for the very first time, I felt the a little sorry for her. "You really don't know the difference, do you?"

"Difference between what?"

"I'm sorry, Sally," I told her, "but I promised to bring this dessert up to my wife. And that's exactly what I'm going to do." And with that I turned away and headed up the stairs. Oh, I knew that moment was going to come back and haunt me a thousand times—whenever Julie and me were fighting or weren't getting along or whenever I went back and took a little inventory of all the missed opportunities in my life—but right about then I was feeling pretty damn good about it.

Sunday dawned warm, bright and sunny—more like lazy late summer than early fall—and I had an early 6 ayem breakfast with Big Ed and the rest of my guys and rode out to the track with them while Julie and the kids slept in. We left them the Caddy so's they could come out later on whenever they felt like it. That was better than me going back and doing the Can't-You-People-Get-You-Asses-In-Gear-Any-Faster two-step while Julie got the kids together. Anyhow, it was a lovely morning out at the track and I could see in the last warmup session that Cal was starting to come to terms with Ernesto Julio's Ferrari. He was still a ways off Creighton Pendleton's pace in the Cunningham D-Type, but you could see he was short shifting and braking sort of gently and taking it easy on the car. He told me afterwards he was saving it for the race, and that was smart. It was also smart to sandbag just a wee bit and let Creighton think all he had to worry about were the other D-Types. And you could see he had them pretty much covered. And, wouldn't you know it, Big Ed and The Skipper somehow found themselves out sharing the same piece of track again—I swear, they attracted each other like those little magnetic Scottie dogs you see in the trick shops—and damn if Skippy didn't get a wee bit optimistic with his brakes attempting a dive-bomb move on the Trashwagon coming down into Turn Five. During the damn morning warmup, can you believe it! Anyhow, he nailed the left-rear fender of the Trashwagon with his right front, and then he had the nerve to tell the stewards that Big Ed had cut him off. Well, it was all I could do to keep Big Ed from giving the little creep a well-deserved sock in the nose, and then they got into one of their signature-edition snarling matches right there in front of the officials, what with Skippy claiming that he was much faster but that Big Ed was blocking him and Big Ed saying that he was driving clean and that The Skipper was full of shit and then Skippy whining that Big Ed turned into him and Big Ed saying that The Skipper ran into *him* and that they'd sure as hell see in the race if Skippy was really faster. To which Skippy screeched right back that Big Ed would never even *see* him during the race! And that's when Big Ed sneered: *"I got five hundred bucks that says I get to the finish line first!"*

The Skipper just stood there for a moment with Big Ed's challenge ringing in his ears.

"It's your five hundred smackers, too!" Big Ed added, reminding Skippy about the bet he lost to the Trashwagon at Bonneville. And that did it.

"YER ON!" The Skipper shouted back at him, and then spun on his heels and stalked off.

The races started right after lunch and Julie and the kids showed up during the first one again. It was for the C Production cars, and that meant Jaguar 120s and 140s and more Jaguar 120s and 140s, and the two fastest guys really went at it hammer-and-tongs until they kind of collided with each other and punted themselves out of the race, which promoted Ralph Miller's Jag into first and a smooth-driving local Jag driver from Milwaukee named Jim Jeffords into second. And that's pretty much how they finished. But it wasn't all Jags, since there was one guy in a no-hoper stock Thunderbird and another in the first Corvette I'd ever seen with Chevy's slick new OHV V8 under the hood. It must've made some pretty serious power, because he charged all the way up to sixth on the first lap, then dropped back to ninth as he ran shy of brakes, clawed his way back to sixth as he learned how to live with it, and ultimately came home seventh after the car dropped a cylinder on the final go 'round. I got the feeling they just might make real racecars out of those Corvettes yet. My guy Buster Jones finished all by his lonesome in eighth—a ways behind the sick Corvette and well off the pace of fastest Jaguars—and you could see he wasn't real comfortable with those fast, blind, daunting sweepers that Cal showed me. He wasn't the only one, either.

The second race was for under-1300cc G and H modifieds, and I'd have to say that little cars don't make for much of a spectacle on a track the size of Road America. Rees Makins ran way with it in his OSCA, but we had a good battle for second overall between some guy in an Italian Abarth and Ohio racer Chuck Dietrich in a Lester MG. But the real high point of the whole thing was none other than S.H. "Wacky" Arnolt tooling around near the back of the pack in a goofy-looking little Renault 4CV Sedan. What it was doing in with the modified cars was a mystery to me, but it was sure fun to watch, what with the tires squealing all the way around the corners and the car tipping up on two wheels now and then and "Wacky" Arnolt smoking a big, fat cigar behind the wheel and tootling the Renault's little pipsqueak horn at the spectators every lap as he went by. You had to love his sense of the ridiculous.

He could drive pretty good, too....

But this stuff was all just the small-fry appetizer to the 37-lap, 148-mile feature race for the big modifieds coming up to close out the weekend, and you could really feel the excitement building as the last of the tiddlers crawled up the steep hill to pit lane and turned into the paddock while the big iron started getting ready to move out to their grid positions on the front straight. Creighton Pendleton had the white-with-blue-stripes, Alf Momo-prepared Cunningham D-Type on the pole, and our boy Cal was back on the outside of the second row in Ernesto Julio's bright yellow Ferrari Monza and not looking like all that much of a threat, what with a three-liter four-banger up against the Jag's 3.8-liter six and drum brakes up against the Jaguar's discs. But I went over and talked to him while they were getting the cars lined up, and he allowed as how the Ferrari's engine had a hell of a lot of torque and maybe wasn't pushing quite so much weight around as the Jag's bigger six. "Besides," he grinned, "I still have a couple scoops of sand left in the bag that Creighton doesn't know about. The real battle is going to be about who has what left at the end of 200 miles." And by that I knew he meant brakes every bit as much as horsepower. The track layout at Road America was simply brutal on brakes. And the faster you went, the worse it got.

Up on the front row I watched Creighton cleaning his goggles in the D-Type and looking ever so slightly bored about it, and you couldn't miss Sally Enderle standing there with all that sleek, gorgeous flesh of hers showing, handing him paper towels and taking the used ones. Boy, she was still as beautiful as any Hollywood starlet you ever saw in a magazine. But that's just not enough, you know?

I walked back down the grid to see how Big Ed was doing, and along the way I passed Tommy in the Allard he was driving that weekend—he'd qualified it just into the top third of the pack, and that was about as much as you could ever expect from a design that was getting a little long in the tooth and a short of the mark in the handling and braking departments—and he gave me a big smile and a little one-finger salute off the brim of his helmet as I went by.

"Give 'em hell," I told him.

"I just want to be around at the end and pick up a few scraps," he laughed.

Four rows further back—almost to the end of the field—I found Big Ed in the Trashwagon and Skippy Welcher in his lumpy C-Type with the taped-up front fender sitting side-by-side on the grid. What else would you expect? Big Ed was wearing this massive white knit shirt with wide red stripes across it that made him look like a damn circus tent, and he had his helmet on and goggles down and one of his fat Cuban stogies clenched hard between his teeth and another fistful of cellophane-wrapped cigars in his breast pocket. Like he just might want to unwrap another one and light it up during the blessed race, you know? But I could see his cheeks were a bright crimson red underneath his goggles and he had a dangerous, unpredictable look in his eye, staring straight ahead up the rows of cars in front of him without blinking while the tip of his cigar made slow, tiny figure-8 rolls through the air. I leaned in next to his helmet. "Take it easy," I told him. "It's a long race, and the most important thing is to be around at the finish."

"The most important thing," he corrected me without looking up, "is beating that sonofabitch over there next to me!"

I glanced over my shoulder and there was the Prince of all Assholes himself, Skippy Welcher, fastening up his helmet strap while Milton Fitting fussed with the mirrors. God only knows why, since The Skipper never used them. *"Hey, Welcher!"* Big Ed hollered over at him. *"It's five hundred bucks between you and me. Remember!"*

"I'll be buying drinks at the bar for everybody with that money!" Skippy screeched right back. It was really a pretty snappy comeback, considering the source.

The starter in the black-and-white striped shirt up at the front of the field held two flags aloft, blew the whistle he had clenched in his teeth, and rotated the flags over his head—*FIRE 'EM UP!*—and I leaned in next to Big Ed's helmet one last time and hollered: *"Remember, y'gotta be there at the end!"* over the thunderous roar of all those big, angry motors bellowing to life. *"GOOD LUCK!"* I told him, and gave him a little rap on the side of the helmet with my knuckles. Jesus, he was like electrified granite!

I went back over the pit wall and watched as the field snaked off for their parade lap, and right away I got that empty, proud and yet helpless sort of feeling that I'm sure all parents get when they see their kids going off to summer camp. I mean, there's nothing you can do anymore except watch them go. And maybe pray for them a little, you know? Then I walked back through the paddock and down the hill to join Julie and the kids and the rest of Team Passaic regulars at Turn Five. Boy, everybody and their brother was there to watch, and you could really feel the tension and excitement as the pace car led the growling, snorting field up to Turn Six and then disappeared. But you could still hear them, grumbling through Hurry Downs and fading away as they went through Eight and peeled off into the Carousel. And then we waited through the long, long silence before the pace car burst into sight again across the way, shooting out from under the bridge turn at Station Thirteen with the throttle-blipping, impatient field of big iron strung out behind it. They went down the little short chute to the last right-hand ninety at Station Fourteen and then surged up that long, steep straightaway towards the start/finish line in front of the pagoda, where they'd form up on their grid positions and wait—engines revving, feet hair-trigger on their clutch pedals, eyes fixed on the starter for even the tiniest little flinch, waiting....

You could hear the *ROAR!* from anywhere in Sheboygan County as the field exploded off for Turn One, and then the sound faded and all you could do was wait and listen and strain your eyeballs towards that crest at the end of the long Moraine Sweep straightaway where the cars would pop into view again and charge downhill into the braking zone for Turn Five. You heard them before you could see them there, and on that first lap with the field still bunched together, it sounded like a runaway locomotive the size of the Queen Mary bearing down on us. And I couldn't believe it when the first car popping over the crest was bright yellow! It was Cal! But he had Creighton Pendleton right on his ass (and every-body else, for that matter!). Even so, he made his usual smooth, perfect slide through Five (okay, with maybe just a little hint of a wiggle at the end!) and still had the lead as the field blasted up the hill towards Six. I was screaming like mad and by God Julie was right there next to me, yelling her head off, too!

And then we had to wait. And wait. And the silence was almost louder than the cars as we listened and watched for where the cars would burst into view again coming out from under the bridge. Again, you heard them before you saw them—just the faint, echoing howl as they charged uphill out of Turn Twelve and then it redoubled on itself as they swept under the bridge and then, like fire-works out of a cannon, exploded into view and the sound blasted your eardrums again and it was still the yellow car in front and the white car with the blue stripes right behind it...

...and then silence.

For what seemed like too long!

I looked at Julie and Julie looked at me and just when it was starting to feel desperate and maybe like there'd been a huge accident, the next car appeared. And then the next. And then a bunch more. They were all there, all right. It's just that Cal and Creighton were going so damn fast they'd left everybody else behind! In one blessed lap! It was amazing.

Next time past us Cal was still in front and I couldn't help remembering that first race I'd ever seen, at Bridgehampton back in the spring of 1952, where Creighton was driving his Ferrari against Tommy Edwards in the Allard, and he just sat there behind Tommy, biding his time and maybe even playing a little cat and mouse with him, until the Allard ran shy of brakes and Creighton just breezed on by. But the next time by Cal had actually pulled out a little advantage. And even a little more the following lap. And you got the feeling that he could maybe keep inching away and inching away and that there was nothing Creighton could do about it....

Meanwhile Tommy had a nice race going with some guy in a brand new, three-liter Maserati 300S who by all rights should have left that lumbering Allard in the dust, and, much further back, the Big Ed and Skippy Show was providing its usual supply of silly driving and excitement and it looked like the Trashwagon was every bit a match for Skippy's C-Type here at Road America. Or at least it was so long as The Skipper was at the wheel, anyway. Oh, the Jag could brake deeper and get around corners better than the Trashwagon. But Skippy had a real talent for turning smooth into ragged, and he'd always come in too deep and have to back out of it and steer like mad to keep from dropping off the edge at the end of the corner. And Big Ed would go through nice as you please—not all that fast, but nice as you please—and come out with the gas pedal mashed to the floorboards and torque right past Skippy's C-Type on the climb up to Six. Almost every lap! And he'd beat The Skipper up there as often as not! It was a heck of a show!

But the real race was at the front, and I was just starting to relax a little on account of it looked like Cal was just going to motor off into the sunset and that there was nothing Creighton could do about it when they started to come on lapped traffic. After only six laps! And that of course meant they came up behind Big Ed and The Skipper in short order, and it all happened right in front of us at Turn Five. The corner workers were showing Big Ed and Skippy the blue *A Faster Car is Overtaking You* flag, and Big Ed was in front by a foot or so heading down into the braking zone as Cal came over the crest of the hill—going like the blessed wind—and just as he pulled out to sweep down inside both of them heading into the corner, The Skipper took a notion to try another deep, desperate dive-bomb move on the Trashwagon. He swerved out from behind Big Ed and damn near took the nose off Ernesto Julio's Ferrari, and Cal had no choice but to nail the brakes and lock up the wheels to keep from collecting him. And meanwhile The Skipper was locking some brakes of his own and getting into one of those *Whoops!Whoops!Whoops!* pendulum deals where the car is snaking this way and that and you're steering into it one way just as it snaps around to go the other way and I'm sure he would have spun it right around and collected both of them if Big Ed and the Trashwagon hadn't been there to take the hit. The C-Type banged off the Trashwagon just when it really should have spun and that knocked it straight enough so The Skipper somehow made it through the corner (although it knocked Big Ed off the pavement and spun him through the gravel). Meanwhile you could see poor Cal watching all this mayhem taking place in front of him and trying to figure out where the heck to go. He had to damn near come to a complete stop! Which of course gave Creighton Pendleton all the time he needed to come swooping down out of nowhere, take a perfect line through Five before the dust had even settled, and breeze right past Cal climbing up the hill towards Six. And poor Big Ed was off in the dirt, grinding the damn starter on that big Caddy engine until it finally fired (or maybe he kept grinding it a little even afterwards!) and he was off after Skippy in a roostertail of dust and gravel. But The Skipper's C-Type had already disappeared out of sight under the Turn Six bridge....

We all looked across to where they'd burst up out of Turn Thirteen to see what would happen. And this time it was Creighton in the D-Jag with about a six second lead on Cal in the yellow Ferrari—it seemed like forever—and the next lap he set a new lap record and it started to look like maybe he'd been laying in the weeds and just playing with Cal. And poor Big Ed was way back behind Skippy Welcher—trailing by at least thirty seconds—and it looked like Team Passaic was about to get skunked.

But on the next lap the distance between Creighton and Cal had kind of stabilized, and you could see Big Ed had maybe even picked up a little on The Skipper. And the lap after that it was Creighton's turn to get baulked in traffic and now his lead was down to only about three seconds and all of a sudden it was starting to look like a damn race again! They were even closer the next lap. And nose-to-tail the next. And now you got the feeling it was maybe Cal's turn to play a little cat and mouse, just kind of sitting in Creighton's mirrors and trying to give him a persecution complex. And by this time Big Ed had closed the gap on The Skipper enough that he could see him up ahead, and there is nothing on God's green earth that puts the bit between a driver's teeth like seeing the guy you want to beat up ahead of you and moreover seeing the distance between you shrinking every lap. To be honest, I'd never seen Big Ed drive anywhere near that fast or well before in my life. Nobody had. And I was pretty damn proud of my Trashwagon, too.

Well, the laps were ticking away and you had to start wondering where and when Cal might make his move. No question by this stage of the race the Jag had more brakes left, so there was no way anybody figured Cal could out-brake him. And with the Jag right in front of him, killing his momentum through the tight nineties, there was no way Cal could use the Ferrari's superior spurt out of the corners to pass going up the hills. As far as sheer top speed went, you maybe had to give a tiny nod to the Jaguar. All of which left only those three daunting and dangerous fast sweepers. And *nobody* tried to pass there....

It all came down to the last lap. I saw them crest the hill into Five, Cal's Ferrari hidden like a shadow behind Creighton's D-Type, and then he jinked out to try a pass. But Creighton was ready for it and left his braking as late as those Jaguar discs would allow and Cal had no choice but to tuck back in line and follow him through the corner and up the hill to Six. *"I gotta go see what happens!"* I hollered to Julie as I sprinted across the access road to be there on the outside of the Bridge Turn when they came wailing up out of Twelve. I was out of breath and panting by the time I got there. And then I just waited, counting the heartbeats until they wheeled into view. Cal had dropped back by maybe a carlength, but he took a perfect line through Twelve and closed up a bunch when Creighton bobbled just a bit and kissed the edge of the dirt on the exit. They charged up the hill towards the Bridge Turn and Creighton lifted to set up like he always did and damn if Cal didn't keep his foot planted and slice right in under him! It was a wild, dangerous, impossible move, and I saw the Ferrari snap out sideways as it slid under the Jag and kicked up dirt at both the apex and exit. But somehow he held it! Using every damn inch of the road!

But the drama wasn't over yet. There was still that last, tight ninety at Turn Fourteen. And everybody knew the Jag had better brakes. I know I would've come down the middle of the road—or maybe even the inside!—to block, but Cal lined up on the proper racing line and then he did the most idiotic thing! He left the inside wide open! Why, you could drive a damn fire truck though there! And that's when I realized he was setting Creighton up. Sure enough, Creighton took the bait and went in *deep* up the inside. And Cal let him have all the rope he needed, too. The Jag charged past but then got all loose and squirrelly coming out while Cal again took an absolutely perfect line through the corner, eased to the inside and just motored up alongside the madly-steering Creighton Pendleton as they stormed up the hill. It was one hell of a drag race and a genuine photo finish, but Cal had him by a whisker at the checker!

Wotta race!

Better yet, who should come charging up out of Twelve next (albeit several laps down) but our old asshole-buddy Skippy Welcher in his C-Type with Big Ed in the Trashwagon right up his butt. They swept through under the bridge and The Skipper did exactly what I thought Cal was going to do and moved to the middle of the track to block a pass. But Big Ed wasn't having any of it. He stayed on the line while The Skipper tried to shut the door and they banged off each other a little—but it was like you expected it from those two by then!—and no question Big Ed had the grunt and momentum going up the hill. Damn if the Trashwagon didn't beat Skippy's Jag to the checker by at least two carlengths. Big Ed shook his fist in the air as they flew across the line—nevermind that they were battling for maybe fourteenth overall out of nineteen cars still running—and whooped so loud the people on the starter's stand of the pagoda said you could hear it over the bellow of the engines. And I bet he was still whooping and hollering when The Skipper used the back end of the Trashwagon as kind of an auxiliary brake booster going into Turn Five on the cool-off lap. Not that Big Ed probably gave two shits!

As you can imagine, I ran like crazy all the way up to the pits—shouting over to Julie on the way to meet me up there—and I just made it as Cal puttered up pit lane in Ernesto Julio's bright yellow Ferrari. Sure, he had a grin on his face. But it was quiet and strangely serene. Like he was maybe replaying that last lap over and over on the inside of his eyelids. Savoring it. Enjoying it. And also enjoying the last little bit of that rare peace-of-mind and solitude guys like Cal could only find inside a racing car. Just behind him came Creighton in the D-Jag, and I've got to admit he showed a lot of class, even if he was a stuck-up jerk. As Cal pulled over to where Ernesto Julio was standing on the pit wall, Creighton burbled by and gave Cal a respectful, almost sheepish little wave. He had the look on his face of a guy at a high-stakes, no-wild-card poker table whose kings-over full house just got beat by a natural straight flush.

It was worth it just to be in the game, you know?

And Cal waved back at him, too. It was the damndest thing you ever saw. And then of course the engines switched off and there was all the whooping and hollering and everybody pumping Cal's arm and whapping him on the back—I was doing a lot of it myself—and Ernesto Julio even planted a great big kiss on his cheek. But I guess they do that kind of stuff out in California. Then we started rolling the car over to the little makeshift victory stand in front of the pagoda—boy, you could really feel the heat off of it!—and Briggs Cunningham himself came over to congratulate Cal along the way. Which was damn nice of him, it really was. And meanwhile the rest of the cars were pulling in and I was happy to see that Tommy Edwards had not only gone the distance in that Allard (albeit without much in the way of brakes for the last fifty miles or so) and managed to come home eighth overall and ahead of that Maserati he'd been dicing with that really should have left him in the dust. But then the driver still counts for something in this sport, doesn't he? And then here came our new hero Big Ed Baumstein up pit lane, still whooping and pumping his fist in the air and surely enjoying the hell out of the view out his rear view mirror, which consisted mostly of the now badly caved-in nose of Skippy's C-Type following their little coming-together on the cool off lap.

Speaking of hollering, The Skipper was doing his share, too, screeching at the top of his lungs and shaking his fist at Big Ed. And then Big Ed stopped for just an instant next to the victory stand to give Cal a congratulatory wave and damn if The Skipper didn't run right into him again. It was no big thing—like one of those minor parking lot mishaps that occasionally wind up attached to assault-and-battery or even manslaughter charges—but Big Ed seemed to kind of enjoy the notion of Skippy bashing his smooth, svelte, expensive alloy Jaguar bodywork against the junkyard-issue back end of the Trashwagon. In fact, he swiveled around in the cockpit and gave Skippy his best assortment of rude Italian and Middle European hand gestures just to see if he could get him to do it again. Especially right there in front of the officials. But The Skipper just sat there screaming at him out of a face varying between the color of a ripe raspberry and an eggplant. *"You owe me five hunnert bucks again, Welcher. An' I'll bet you every cent of it plus drinks at th' bar for everybody that I can beat you back t'Siebkins, too!"*

"You're ON!" Skippy screamed back at him, and before you could say *"Hey, guys, is this really such a good idea?"* or even the *"Whoa"* syllable of *"Whoashit!"* those two were in gear and off their clutch pedals and tearing like hell through the paddock, weaving in and out of heavy foot traffic and heading for the gate. It was crazy, really, what with people and cars everywhere and some of the spectators already heading for the exits. But they were ahead of most of the rush, and Big Ed quickly decided to take to the grass and head off cross-country around the cars lining up on the access roads and the last I saw of him is when he squeaked through between the line of cars and a chain-link fence with only a few thousandths-of-an-inch to spare and Skippy's Jag rooting along right behind him....

It wasn't thirty seconds later that we heard the crash. Or rather the thud. There was this long, agonizing screech of tires coming from the curve at the bottom of the hill on Route 67 and then this muffled sound of a heavy impact. Then silence. And then the sound of a cop siren wailing to life somewhere around the main gate and heading off down the hill.

"Jesus, something terrible's happened!" I told Julie. "I gotta *GO!*"

I could see that Cal was thinking the same thing. *"Hop in!"* he yelled at me and I jumped into Ernesto Julio's Ferrari and we took off right there from the victory stand—before he'd gotten his trophy or gulped his champagne or anything!—and Cal was smart enough to head right back out onto the racetrack instead of trying to fight his way through the paddock traffic. He had to be a little careful on account of there were pickups and station wagons and such out to pick up the corner workers and their equipment, but we were flying anyway and he must've set a record for getting us down to Turn Twelve and the escape road that took you all the way to that curve at the bottom of that hill on Route 67. The gate was closed but we vaulted over it and headed at a dead towards what was obviously the scene of a serious accident. The cop car with the mars light rotating on top was parked next to what looked like an exploded hay barn. It was hard to know what to make of it....

Apparently Skippy and Big Ed came wailing down that hill at high speed and side-by-side—heading into a damn blind corner on an ordinary, everyday, two-lane public highway, for gosh sakes!—and, as they rounded the turn, that's when they came on the farmer on his tractor with a big load of hay hitched on back kind of meandering along at maybe fifteen or sixteen miles-per-hour. I couldn't tell exactly what happened next, but you could see The Skipper and his C-Type had more or less imbedded themselves in the exploded load of hay. And you heard him screaming in his usual made-you-want-to-rip-his-larynx-out style, so you knew he was okay. But I couldn't see Big Ed or the Trashwagon anywhere....

"LOOK!" Cal gasped. And there it was. Way up on the railroad tracks on the other side of La Budde Creek. All bent up and mangled with both front wheels torn off and the back axle askew and steam and smoke rising off it. I had to turn away.

"Oh, Jesus..." I groaned.

"But he's not in it!"

I forced myself to look again. And, sure enough, Big Ed was missing. *JESUS!* I frantically scanned the line of trees and the grass along the highway and the marshy banks of La Budde Creek. And that's when I saw Big Ed's helmet, goggles still up over the visor, sitting there in the grass by the water's edge. And my eyes followed down from the helmet into the water, and there, floating face-down, was the huge, soggy, red-and-white-striped, circus-tent lump of Big Ed's torso.

"OHMYGOD!!!" I screamed, taking off full speed along the creek bank and leaping off the edge like a runaway, windmilling airplane propeller into the creek. Only it wasn't near as deep as it looked, and so my feet kind of stopped short in the muck on the bottom and the whole rest of me slammed face-first down into the slop. My mouth was open, too. I flailed and struggled to get my head above water and took a swipe at my eyes so I could see, and that's when I saw Big Ed's head kind of blow up through the surface right in front of me—like a damn walrus coming up for air!

"JESUS!" I screamed. *"YOU'RE ALIVE!!!"*

Big Ed looked at me with dazed, distracted eyes. "Of course I'm alive," he said like it should have been obvious.

"But what the hell HAPPENED??!!"

Big Ed thought about it for a second, his eyeballs kind of blinking without actually moving the lids. "We came down that hill an' came around the corner an' saw the hay rig," he said in a detached, faraway voice, "an' I tried to swerve out left but there was this truck comin' the other way." He tilted his head slightly like he was trying to get some water out of his ear. "There wasn't much t'do but keep goin' off th'road back there..." he pointed back to the railroad crossing, "...an' the car kinda took off on that hump over the tracks an' I musta got thrown out or somethin'..." He rotated his head around, still trying to get his bearings. "I guess I musta landed here in the water." And with that he got a very determined look in his eye, sucked in a deep breath, and put his head back underwater.

I grabbed at his huge shoulders with both hands and yanked him up again. *"JESUS, ED!"* I fairly screamed at him. *"What the hell are you DOING??!!"*

He regarded me with a surprised and curious expression. "Why, lookin' fer my damn cigars, a'course...." Like it should have been obvious, you know?

Well, I guess shock affects different people different ways, and for sure Big Ed figured a drag on one of his fresh dollar cigars might make him feel a little better. And they'd still be in fine shape, too, seeing as how they came wrapped airtight in cellophane. I don't believe it'd really sunk in how close a call he'd had or how all-fired lucky he'd been, and he didn't really seem to care at all about the wrecked Trashwagon sitting up there on the train tracks. Not even when we heard the whistle of the slow freight coming a few moments later....

I remember it like some unforgettable scene from a movie. The train was one of those great, groaning, slow-moving diesel jobs with about six engines latched together one-after-the-other dragging a line of freight cars that stretched most of the way back to Chicago (or at least to Milwaukee). Slow as it was going, that's still an awful lot of momentum to try to get rid of in the space of a half-mile or so. I remember it was just coming on dusk and we could see the light from the first diesel locomotive and the headlights and taillights from all the backed-up race traffic and the cop car's rotating mars light reflecting in the creek water, and then you heard the engineer lock up the brakes on all those heavy, rusty iron wheels scraping along all those heavy, rusty iron rails. It was like the sound of an old, bent nail as big as the Empire State Building being pulled out of a slab of oak the size of Central Park. Only it lasted much longer. And there in that strange, accident-scene lighting, we listened to that sound and watched in what seemed like slow-motion as the freight train—which couldn't have been going much more than eight or ten miles an hour by then—rammed into the remains of the Trashwagon and more or less pushed it and dragged it and crushed it and devoured it until it was nothing but fragments.

We couldn't even find the damn engine block the next morning....

And so that's the story of the Fabulous Trashwagon. Julie and the kids and me went back to Passaic to set up that Volkswagen dealership with Big Ed, and Ernesto Julio invited Cal to come out to California and drive for him full-time now that Phil Hill looked to be headed for that Ferrari factory drive over in Europe. And Cal was thrilled to do it, too, since it was what he'd always wanted and also because there was maybe a certain somebody he hoped he might run into out there. Who knows? And I was happy for him, too. Honest I was. Being a racer—and I mean a *real* racer—was not just the most important thing in Cal's life. It was the *only* thing in his life. The only thing in God's entire creation that ever lit him up and made him want to try. That's the way it is with guys like Cal. And on the one hand I envied him and was jealous as hell of all the glamour and gallantry and gamesmanship of it all. But on the other I looked over at Julie and little Vincenzo and even littler baby Roberta sleeping next to me on the front seat of Big Ed's Caddy as we tooled cross-country from Elkhart Lake on our way back home, and I realized that you wind up making a lot of choices in your life. And most of 'em you don't even realize you're making at the time. It's like you come to all these hidden forks in the road that you don't even see until you're looking back at them. But somehow, some way, thanks to some incomprehensible collection of reasons and whims and instincts and intuition and maybe even destiny that you'll never understand, you wind up walking, limping, plodding, marching, skipping or running full-tilt with your hair on fire down one of those paths instead of another. And anybody who thinks it happens because they've got it all planned out ahead of time knows even less about life than I do.

As far as the racing goes, I'll admit in a heartbeat that I've still got the bug as bad as ever and probably always will. It's not something you get over or get rid of. Racing remains the most exciting, demanding, challenging, rewarding, thrilling, terrifying, frustrating, fabulous, silly, serious, and alternately hilarious or heartbreaking thing I've ever come across in my life. But I've seen its darker side, too. And how it fools you and flatters you and teases you and tempts you and tickles you and taunts you and sucks the blessed life right out of you if you let it. But of course the dirty little secret all the real racers know is that you get the life sucked out of you in the end anyway, no matter what. So what's the difference, right? But for some of us there are other things under the sun, and you've got to learn to keep your habit on a short leash if you don't want it running your life and pushing everything else into the shadows. Or even further. Which is why I decided I was going to try like hell to get Denny Eade—or somebody else just like him—to run my Team Passaic guys at the racetrack while I concentrated on building a business and a future for myself and my family. So I'd only have to go to the races when I felt like it, you know? Even if I knew deep down that I'd be feeling like it damn near every weekend they went. That's just the way it is when you've got the bug. But I'd been around it long enough and seen enough of it to also understand that racing is a bottomless pit.

In fact, that's the best thing about it....